CW00666212

The Mahabl... of Palmira

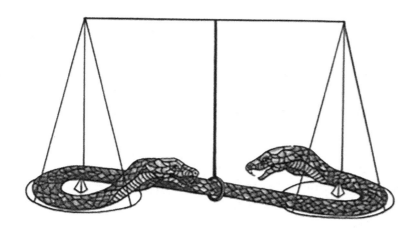

Volume One: *The Scales*

by

Daniel Ricardo Altmann

Published by Dolman Scott Ltd in 2017

'The Mahabharata of Palmira'©Daniel Ricardo Altmann 2016
Daniel Ricardo Altmann has asserted his right under the Copyright, Designs
and Patents Act, 1988, to be identified as the author of this work

Cover design by Siobhan Smith©2016

Cover illustration ©Katy Dynes 2016

Design and typesetting by Dolman Scott

All rights reserved. No part of this publication may be
copied, stored in a retrieval system, or transmitted in
any form, or by any means electronic, mechanical,
optical, or otherwise except with written permission of
the publisher. Except for review purposes only.

ISBN:
Paperback: 978-1-911412-26-7
iBook: 978-1-911412-28-1
Kindle: 978-1-911412-29-8

Dolman Scott Ltd
www.dolmanscott.co.uk

To my parents

Preface to *The Scales*

This is the first book in a two-volume retelling of the Indian epic. I first heard of the ancient work from the script of Peter Brook's play, *The Mahabharata*, published by Methuen. However, my interest was not really awakened until I came across another condensed version, which in turn led me to read several other abridgements. What struck me from these different versions, each one fine in itself, were the contradicting accounts and omissions; particularly relating to the life and exploits of one character, Karna, who is the focus of the version told here by my narrator, Palmira. My curiosity about Karna was roused, so I read a strict prose translation, in many volumes, of the Sanskrit epic poem.

The Sanskrit *Mahabharata* is thought to have become 'fixed' by about 500 CE, though the first written versions may have begun a thousand years earlier at about 500 BCE, towards the end of what is known as the later Vedic period. The first oral versions probably started towards the beginning of the later Vedic period, around 1000 BCE. I very quickly saw that the source was a completely different entity than the abridgements, in content and in texture: the condensed accounts tended to attempt to pick out just a human plot, while the original integrated human drama with conceptual drama and debate; to give a western simile, as if Homer and Plato had joined forces.

I also began to see why there was so much inconsistency of plot and characterisation in the reductions I had read. Very rarely in the original is there a definitive chronological account of a key event: in this respect the original is more of an archeological structure than a working story, with layers written by different authors, each with their own slant. A speech or event towards the end of the original epic may relate to an incident covered in much earlier verses; chronologically later events are often anticipated in much earlier passages, sometimes prophetically. This gives inevitable scope for interpretation when attempting to discern a connected plot. But in my own view there is another reason also for the different readings which occur in modern abridgments: I believe the original is much more at ease than modern storytellers with the idea of good and bad occurring in the same person, rather than being represented cleanly and separately by heroes and villains.

There is, certainly, a clear overarching story, concerning the evolution of a conflict between two sets of brothers, royal princes: the Pandavas and the Kurus (the latter sometimes referred to as the Kauravas); and concerning the role in this conflict of Karna, a person of low caste. But I don't think a single coherent version of this story can be extracted; each storyteller, taking this task on, has to forge their vision from the morass of material, and Palmira's version is no exception. I say Palmira's version, rather than my own, for the simple reason that the story would have come out quite differently had I told it directly, rather than through her. I am therefore inclined to let her take the blame for everything.

In at least two respects Palmira's version is very different from other reductions. First, it attempts to incorporate as many as possible of the key plot turns and events contained in the original epic; and in this sense to be as faithful as possible to a skeleton which can be pieced together from the bones strewn across the original. Second, it attempts to be profoundly different from the original, with entirely new tissues fleshing out this skeleton. To labour this with a different analogy: having picked out a melody from the original, I have tried to reharmonise and reorchestrate it fundamentally.

As a result, I have enjoyed little choice regarding the main plot. And it was, for me, enjoyment, since I've always found myself in difficulties if presented with too much choice. One consequent problem has been how to render plot turns in the original which seem to have been inserted deliberately to test the storyteller's improvisation, like an unexpected chord for which a melody must be found to fit. But I have willingly surrendered to these constraints, trusting that the ancient story lines can be made to work. Another challenge has been to try to absorb and maintain the interest of readers who are familiar with sketches of the ancient legends. I have certainly cheated a little by augmenting and underpinning the traditional skeleton where I felt this suited or was required by my rendition. One augmentation, for example, which will be obvious to any reader familiar with the main story line, is Charvaka, one of Palmira's central characters, whom I found mentioned in just one verse of the original epic, and who clearly represents a real person, or at least a real school of thought, active during the period in which the epic was created. Other modifications I have made to the plot may be less obvious.

In the process of navigating these challenges I have come to appreciate the instinct for drama shown by the old storytellers. Like a great tune which can cross time and place, the original has some powerful cadences which still resonate to the modern ear; and I cannot disguise the fact that these have been shamelessly used by Palmira as a vehicle to express herself, to make her own peace with the world; but my hope is that the very personal and inevitably western perspective of this version does not diminish its celebration of ancient India's immense and varied contributions to humanity.

For the benefit of her rather small audience, Palmira splits the long Sanskrit names rather crudely in two, and generally uses just the first half of a name. Palmira relates her version over twenty days; rather like the storytellers of old, who would also have spent many days on their recitals, travelling from village to village to entertain audiences far larger than Palmira's. In this first volume, after giving her own introduction, Palmira takes the action from soon after Karna's birth, on the first day of her story, up to the seventh day, with her account of the great dice game.

The description of the dice game in the Sanskrit verses is one of the earliest written accounts of gambling. There are no details there of the precise nature of the game or its rules, and readers who are not of a nerdy and obsessive disposition should feel no compunction in skimming over some of the details of the game that Palmira has contrived and recounted on her seventh day. These details are of little importance in the general scheme of things; in fact, Palmira only labours these workings for the benefit, if it can be called that, of her particular audience. As to who, when and where Palmira and her audience are, this is not the time to tell.

I finished the first draft of this book last century, in 1997. Since then it has lain dormant until a year ago, when I painfully revisited it after nearly two decades and made a number of relatively minor revisions. For help with this and with the first draft I owe an enormous debt of gratitude to Diana Syrat, whose encouragement over many years helped me to persevere with the book, and whose sensitive editorial advice helped to shape it. I am also extremely grateful to Simon Altmann, whose careful reading, thoughtful comments, understanding and encouragement have greatly sustained me. And I must thank Jane Altmann for letting me read the whole book to her, for patiently playing the dice game with me, and for her encouragement and support.

November 2016
http://mahabharataofpalmira.uk

Table of Contents

Day Zero: *Vyasa*

1 Palmira decides on a story

It seemed so long since she had heard the sound of flowing water that for a moment she imagined she was listening to the ripples of a stream. She opened her eyes. She stared in a daze at the gentle flames.

She picked up her tongs and prodded the smouldering mass. The flames flared lilac. She tapped the tongs on the grate and put them down again.

She knelt up, releasing the cushion beneath her, and then dragged it along as she sidled on her knees towards a box by the wall. The box was made of wood, colourfully decorated on its front panel. Its open lid was leaning against a sendal hanging which covered the wall. The bottom edge of this hanging was weighted down by a row of cushions, also silk, but in a heavier material and richly embroidered.

She picked out a scroll from inside the box and began to unroll it, revealing a picture of a hunting scene. Suddenly she heard a noise and turned sharply.

'Out!'

'Palmira —'

'*Out*!'

She flung her cushion at the retreating figure but missed, knocking over a crossbow by the door. Taking a deep breath she unfurled the scroll again, and gazed at it absently.

In the distance a castle crowned a hill. The castle was coloured in reds and browns. Towards the right of the picture a stream flowed down from the hill, opening out beside a grove of trees into a watercourse with preening ducks. The land was coloured green; and the blue colour of the stream became striated with the same green, as the surface of the water extended.

By the pool stood a crane, its beak pointing upwards at a descending falcon. These two birds were depicted with a most delicate attention to detail.

On the extreme right of the picture two hounds, rather less lifelike, stood watching. To the left, in the foreground, a man was seated on a throne. He was dressed in a dark green robe with a purple mantle. The mantle was fastened at his left shoulder with a brooch of amethysts and emeralds. His right hand held a lily stalk with three flowers. His left hand pointed towards a second bird of prey perched on a stool at his feet, a white gyrfalcon.

A gold crown rested on the man's head. His hair, too far receded at his brow to show there beneath the crown, fell at the sides of his neck in reddish locks curling up at the ends. Beneath the lines of his forehead his blue eyes were deep-set. The wrinkles under his eyes merged into furrows; and these in turn flowed out into the hollows of his cleanly shaven cheeks. Little spots of pink had been used to capture the force of life beneath this gaunt skin.

Palmira let go the bottom of the picture and the paper rolled itself up again. She became aware now of the two voices outside; but they were not distinct enough for her to catch the words...

'What's she doing in there? What was it?'

'I wasn't meant to see. You know she doesn't let us go in her room without permission.'

'Yes, but she was *in* there.'

'I know but I forgot to knock. And if I'd knocked, she wouldn't have let me in.'

'Yes, but you saw whatever it was, so you might as well tell me.'

'No! I just know she wouldn't want me to tell anyone else.'

'Yes, but I'm not anyone *else*! Come on, what was it you saw? Tell me...'

Palmira had now closed the lid of the wooden box. She got up, replaced the fallen crossbow, and tossed the cushion onto her bed. Her bedcover was of the same material as the hanging, and it fluttered at the force of the cushion, sending a ripple of air to ruffle the flames. Palmira glanced back at the fire. Then she heard the voices outside rise in anger. Suddenly there was silence and she hurried out.

When she saw them grappling together on the ground Palmira cleared her throat.

'What's this?' She put her weight on her stronger leg and with her weaker foot prodded first one boy and then the other. 'Henry! Eh? Henry! Come on, what's this about?'

The two combatants separated and began to dust themselves off.

'Well?' persisted Palmira. 'What will your mother say? You hardly ever argue, let alone fight. Why were you fighting?'

'You don't *have* to have a reason,' said the first Henry.

'Nonsense!' cried Palmira.

'We don't need a reason to fight,' said the second Henry. 'We're boys, remember. You're always saying boys don't seem to need a reason to fight.'

Palmira smiled, and then checked herself with a frown. 'Come on, what was it?'

'Palmira... did you actually predict *we* would be boys?'

'What do you mean?'

'You know, to our mother...'

'When she was pregnant with us...'

'Ah! No. I don't think your mother was that interested in finding out your sex. Not once I told her she was expecting twins. I think that must have put her off any further prediction.'

'But how do you do it?'

'Mother said you touched her, or listened, or something like that, and that's how you knew she was having twins. But how can you possibly tell by touching if it's going to be a boy or a girl?'

Palmira chose to ignore their questioning. 'For the last time, boys, what were you fighting about?'

'That's our secret,' said the first Henry. He had put a date in his mouth and was speaking with it lodged in his cheek. 'We'll tell you if you tell us how you do it.'

Palmira frowned. 'Let me see... You were fighting over whose turn it is at the well. Eh?'

'You've got a completely full cistern, Palmira.'

'We both pumped today.'

'Are you sure?' She looked at them sternly. 'I'd really like to have both cisterns full.'

'And why do you always have us doing work for you? We're supposed to be here for our education, not to do work for you.'

'And then when we do work you complain. You're always complaining.'

'*I'm* always complaining?'

'You are,' insisted the first Henry, sucking the last bit of sweetness from the date stone. 'If it's not the work it's our studies.'

'And if it's not our studies it's the work!' concluded the second Henry.

'That', said Palmira, 'reminds me of when the Hodja met one of his neighbours—'

'Palmira!' cried the first Henry, spitting out the date stone.

'Not another Hodja story! Please, Palmira!'

'Pick it up!' she demanded. 'Always complaining!' As she spoke Palmira set about fluffing up the cushions on the tiled floor of her yard. 'Can't you manage to keep these the right way up?' The floor side of these cushions was covered in canvas, while the top was in a much softer sarsenet which suffered from the roughness of the tiles. 'Well,' she continued, 'the Hodja had a neighbour who also was always complaining. One cold winter he was standing next to this neighbour in the market place, and they overheard a huddle of people moaning about the cold.' Palmira sat down on one of the cushions but the two boys remained standing. 'This neighbour said to him:

'"Hodja, you see how some people are never content! They're *always* complaining. If it's not the cold of winter, then they complain about the heat in summer! If it's not the heat of summer, then it's the cold of winter —"

'"Yes, yes, I see," interrupted the Hodja hastily. "But what will you have to say in the spring? I suppose you'll complain then that they're all too contented!"'

5

The boys frowned. Palmira put her hand up to feel the breeze. She took a deep breath, letting the air slowly out of her lungs. 'Now boys... I need to talk to you... By the way, which one of you came into my bedroom without knocking just now? Right, as a punishment you can go in and bring me some wine.'

'Wine? From the cask?'

'No, I filled up a bladder.'

The second Henry went inside to fetch it.

'Oh, wait!' Palmira shouted after him, noticing the bowl which now contained only stones and no dates. 'More dates, please. And there's some sour milk if you want...'

'When are you going to get those half-half dates in again?' the first Henry asked Palmira.

'Who knows? When they bring them. Now, Henry, what was your quarrelling about?'

'It wasn't anything.' Henry shook his head. 'Palmira... has anything happened lately?'

'Has anything happened? What do you mean?'

'It's just that you seem... You haven't got a new boyfriend or anything, have you?'

Palmira laughed. 'Why? Do I seem excited? Anxious? A new boyfriend! Out here? No, Henry. But it's very observant of you. No, I've got a new stock of ore coming. It's excellent quality. The best I've seen for ages. And almost as good as a new boyfriend.'

The second Henry came out slowly with a bladder of wine under one arm and two bowls balanced in his other hand. Palmira took the wine from him and he put down the dates and sour milk on the more shaded end of her table.

'I've just been telling your brother about some ore that's coming...' Palmira took a sip of wine from the bladder. 'That's what I want to discuss with you. Wait! Olives! It's your turn,' she said to the first Henry. 'Olives and honey, please — and you can take that in.'

The first Henry picked up the bowl of date stones and went inside.

'Now, Henry, what were you quarrelling about?'

'Nothing,' answered the second Henry, still standing. He picked a date from the bowl. 'When are you going to get half-half ones?'

'Who knows? With the plague about —'

'But I thought you said it was only along the coast and over the sea. Those nice dates come from even further in, don't they?'

'That's exactly why they don't want to travel nearer the coast to bring them here.'

'But... could they catch it from the things in your store house? I mean, the things the traders leave — can you catch it from things like that?'

'I don't think so, Henry. No, I don't think so. But it's probably wise of them not to travel much at the moment.'

The first Henry returned now with the olives and honey.

'On the sunny end, please,' said Palmira, 'I don't like my olives too cold.'

Henry put them down as instructed. Though the table was very low it served its purpose of keeping the food clear of the tiles. Occasionally a marauding ant would start to climb up one of the legs; but the smooth overhang of the marble top usually proved too much for these creatures.

'Sit down, boys...' Palmira dipped an olive in some honey and put it in her mouth, licking her fingers. 'Now... I need you to help me work this ore I've got coming down from the hills. I've already spoken to your parents about it —'

'Why d'you need their permission?'

'Well... It may be a little dangerous this year... Still, you two should be safe enough. Your mother isn't very happy about it, but your father managed to persuade her —'

'But aren't we going to be doing the same as last year?'

'Yes, but last year you only did it for a couple of days, didn't you? This year I'm going to need you for about fifteen days. Perhaps more if the wind holds out. I'm afraid you'll have to get here first thing each morning to clear the furnace flues —'

'When's it getting here, the ore?'

'In a few days. Till then you can get in some hemp and halfa. And there's some paper in the store that needs trimming.'

'What about Mulciber? Isn't he going to help?'

'Of course, of course. He'll come when the ore's here. But once the ore's all safely in I'm afraid I'll have to go to the coast, so I'll be leaving you on your own to work with Mulciber — don't worry, I'll only be gone for a few days. I just need to pick up a document. Of course, this year Mulciber will have to leave before dark — remember that his wife's due next month — so you'll have to do more clearing up. Now, in exchange —'

'Can we just do maths?'

'That's a good idea, Palmira, we'll work for you if you let us have a rest from the Latin and Arabic.'

'That's a fair exchange, Palmira!'

Palmira smiled. She was silent for a few moments, dipping her finger in the honey. She waved away a hornet. 'I had another idea,' she said. 'A story.'

'A story!'

'What, a *real* story?'

'What do you mean, Henry? What's a real story?'

'One that's just for fun,' explained the first Henry.

'Not for our education,' added his brother.

'I see... So you mean... one with beautiful princesses, handsome princes, lots of fighting, and a little mathematics too —'

'What?'

'Palmira, when are you going to let us read the *Abaci*?'

'When you're ready to copy it accurately, Henry, and not before. Your Latin's just not good enough yet. Besides, the *Abaci* is mainly about numbers. There's more to mathematics than just numbers, you know. But of course, if you're very impatient to start on it, perhaps we could spend the next two weeks just on Latin —'

'No! A story —'

'And a proper story, Palmira.'

'Will you really tell us a proper story?'

'Well, I don't know how proper it will be. But I expect there will be some handsome princes, some fighting, perhaps a beautiful princess even —'

'When are you going to start? Now?'

'What's it called? What's it going to be called?'

'The story?' Palmira took another sip of wine. 'I'm going to tell you the story of Karna.'

2 Palmira prepares the ground

'It's a story', continued Palmira, 'set in India a long time ago.'

'How long?'

'Well, let's see... I think it was supposed to have taken place about five hundred years before the Buddha Gautama. So that would make it a few hundred years after the Prophet Moses. So, well, you can work it out, a thousand years before the Christ of Nazareth, fifteen hundred years before the Prophet Muhammad —'

'We only asked how long ago. We do know our dates. I thought you said it was going to be just for fun.'

'Is it a true story, Palmira?'

'Well, the story I'm going to tell you is based on a story told to me a few years ago, and that in turn was based on a great and ancient story about the Bharata people of northern India. That great story may have had *some* truth in it. But Vyasa's version would have had rather less. And the story *I'm* going to tell you has definitely no truth in it whatsoever. In fact, Vyasa would probably be cross if I pretended mine was the same story at all —'

'That doesn't matter if his story wasn't true either — if his wasn't true, why should it matter if you change it? They're just both not true.'

Palmira smiled. 'I wish it were as simple as that, Henry. No one owns the truth, no one owns facts. But fiction, well, that's another matter, people get rather attached to their own... That reminds me... That reminds me of when the Hodja was once a witness called to testify in court —'

'Palmira!'

'Not another one!'

Palmira ignored their protest and continued.

'You see, a friend of the Hodja's had been accused of stealing some sacks of wheat from the village grain store: these sacks, or ones very like them, had been found at this friend's house. Well, he asked the Hodja to concoct a story in court to protect him.

'"You're not seriously asking me to lie in court, are you? Me? A respected man, a Hodja, wearing a turban, to lie in court before a judge?"

'"But that's why, Hodja. They'll believe *you*. In any case, you tell stories to young and impressionable children — surely you can leave a learned judge to make up his own mind!"

'"But my friend, don't you know that I refuse to lie even to a child! Don't you know that I always start my stories *Once upon a time there was and there wasn't...* a three-headed giant or whatever. Now you're asking me to lie in court!"'

'Unfortunately for the Hodja,' continued Palmira, 'when his friend was interrogated he actually told the court that the Hodja had been the source of the wheat. So the Hodja was summoned to explain.

'"My learned judge," began the Hodja, "I admit that it was I myself who sold the accused those sacks of barley"

'"Barley!" cried the judge. "Hodja Nasreddin," he said sternly, "we are talking here about *wheat*, not barley."

'"Yes, sir, but if one is making up a story, does it matter if one is talking about wheat or about barley?"'

'So, you see...' continued Palmira. '...Where was I?'

'How do we know where you were?' complained the first Henry.

'Palmira, will you promise not to keep interrupting with Hodja stories once you start properly?'

'Well...'

'And when you're telling it can't you try not to keep saying *well*. It's irritating, Palmira.'

'And *you see*. You're always saying that.'

'Well, I see...' Palmira narrowed her eyes slightly as she looked at them. 'Thank you, boys, it's very kind of you to point these little things out... As I was saying, the story I'm going to tell you is not true to Vyasa's. But you see — sorry — Vyasa himself in any case thought it was the sort of story you could only ever really tell your own version of. And Vyasa — do you remember him? No? Perhaps you were too young... He came from India... He had matted hair, very long —'

'Oh! *Him*! That smelly old —' The first Henry stopped in his tracks and shrank back slightly behind his brother, who looked down to avoid Palmira's glare. But when Palmira started to rise the second Henry looked up at her.

'We didn't think, Palmira, we forgot... We forgot what happened... We remember now... Sorry, Palmira...'

Palmira went inside, limping more heavily than usual.

'Why don't you think before you speak!' complained the second Henry.

'You're one to talk,' returned his brother. 'I mean *think*,' he added. 'I just forgot. Anyway, don't you remember Palmira once saying that if you *always* think before you speak, you end up never saying anything at all. And you can be sure she thought about that before she said it.'

Palmira came out again carrying a jug of water and three cups. She poured some water for herself and the two boys.

'Drink, or you'll end up with humps like camels.'

She took a few sips of the water herself and sat down on her cushion.

'Where's the wine?' she asked. The second Henry handed her the bladder, and she took a mouthful. The boys watched her in silence. They seldom saw her drinking wine. She replaced the bladder against the leg of the table, adjusted another cushion against the bare white plaster behind her, and leant back in her corner.

On the inside of the rectangular yard the plaster was exposed. But on the outside grew vines and creepers which turned in at the top to spread thinly over a wooden trellis spanning the four walls. This cast a mottled shade over the tiles; and at certain angles the sun pierced through quite easily.

The lower part of the four walls was solid; but the upper part consisted of slender white balusters supporting a plain coping on which in turn rested the trellis. Between the pillars the vines were thinned to admit the view beyond.

The marble table was at the north-west corner of the rectangle. It was against the walls of this corner that Palmira usually made herself comfortable. The twins would sit beside her against the west wall. Or sometimes facing her, leaning over the table, especially when they had books or papers to work on; from this position they could see the doorway to the house through the north-west balusters.

At the north-east corner a passage overgrown with prickly pears opened into tracks leading to the road. An opening in the middle of the north wall joined the yard to another passageway. To the left this led to the house. To the right it led to the storehouse and a workshop.

'So,' continued Palmira, 'where was I?... Yes, you see, the story of the Bharatas has been told again and again, countless times. Vyasa knew his version by heart. In Sanskrit, of course. Some of it he had composed himself, some was based on older verses. What a memory he had! He told it to me in Latin, translating from the Sanskrit as he went along — because I didn't know any Sanskrit. I can't remember how many days it took him to tell it. He called each section a *Parva*, and he told me one of these every day. He compared the story to an ancient carpet, handed down over the centuries, into which different people had woven their own threads — a carpet which one could tell must have been wonderful, enchanting, but which had become a little ragged, slightly threadbare here and there, with the occasional patch. What I am going to do for you, boys, is to try to pick out my own favourite piece, which I hope lies near the centre, the heart of the ancient carpet. And I will try to weave into it my own threads, and put my own colours in the areas I think are worn thin. So, in the end you will get Palmira's little rug.

'It's important that I tell you this,' she continued, 'because, unlike the Hodja, who changed the word *wheat* to *barley*, I will use many of the same names, the same events, the same places that are mentioned in the ancient story. But it will not be the same story. I don't even know if the places I mention exist, or ever have existed, or are where I say they are. Still, as Vyasa himself said, it is part of the very beauty of this wonderful old carpet that each person sees in it different patterns.'

'What's Sanskrit like?'

'Well, if Latin is like a mother to most of the languages round the sea, Sanskrit is like a great-grandmother. Not all of them — Arabic and Hebrew, for example, they work in a different way. Perhaps that's why you two find Arabic hard. People like Vyasa still speak Sanskrit in India today, but rather as they speak Latin round the sea.

'So... Yes, first I must tell you a bit about India at the time of the Bharatas. According to Vyasa it was a very interesting time. The Hindu religion didn't really exist yet: it was in the process of being born. They were times of change. The ending of an era, the last great flame of the kshatriya fighting caste. Yes, you'll get plenty of brave warriors, a battle or two, the occasional god, perhaps. Of course, it's mostly men in this story. Women, as usual, were given only a limited part to play. Yes... Things haven't changed very much. I suppose I can't complain for myself, of course, not now, but I've had to —'

'What exactly is this story about? It's not going to be another one about how unjustly women have been treated, is it?'

'I thought you said it was going to be fun, Palmira.'

Palmira laughed. 'Did I say that? Another thing you'll need to know about concerns the castes.'

'The castes?'

'Yes. There were four main castes. First of all there were the kshatriyas. I say first because they were the rulers. Kings and princes were almost always of this caste. Kshatriyas were trained and skilful in all forms of combat and weaponry, but particularly the bow. Not the crossbow, of course, that wasn't around in those days. The dream of every kshatriya — or so they would tell you — was to become a great chariot fighter: you see, they fought on chariots. They used their bows and other weapons while a chariot driver manoeuvred the chariot about. There were often raids for cattle and other livestock between rival kingdoms, so it was useful to have your own kshatriyas around to defend you against the kshatriyas who attacked you.'

'Were they like the old Roman chariots, these Indian chariots?'

'No, they were more like boxes. They had a rectangular floor, and sometimes quite high sides — not too high or the warrior's aim would be restricted. A right-handed warrior usually stood on the left, with his driver on the right, because it's easier to shoot towards the left if you're right-handed. The sides of the chariots were usually just wooden frameworks covered in wicker or leather — nothing too heavy, but offering reasonable protection. The weight of the actual chariot had to be kept down because of all the weapons and equipment the warriors carried with them. They even carried ropes and leather cords for repairs. All these were kept at the back of the chariot, so there had to be a sort of wooden leg under the rear of the thing. Otherwise, when the horses were unyoked — or set loose by enemy arrows — the whole chariot would have tipped backwards on its axle.'

'Oh! Did they only have two wheels, then?'

'Yes, much more manoeuvrable than four wheels. Four-wheeled ones were used for ceremonies, but not for fighting.'

'And how many horses did they have?'

'Horses? Usually four abreast. Though ceremonial chariots could have two or even more rows of them. The horses had to be specially trained because the harnesses they used were quite uncomfortable. Anyway, that's enough about chariots, boys... We were discussing castes, were we not? As I say, the warriors were usually kshatriyas. Then there were the brahmanas. These were educated in all the religious customs of the Bharatas, and studied all the branches of learning.

'Then there were the vaishyas,' continued Palmira. 'These were responsible for agriculture and commerce. Ruled, of course, by the kshatriyas. Last, and more or less least, there were the shudras. These were workers: they did most of the physical work, and were also the servants of everybody else. I believe that the four castes were supposed for ceremonies and so on to wear different coloured robes: red, the colour of blood, for the kshatriyas; white, the colour of clarity, for brahmanas; the vaishyas were supposed to wear yellow, the colour of grassland and livestock; and black, the colour of the earth, was for the shudras. But at the time of my story people would generally only signify their caste with something like a belt or sash, or a headband or headcloth in the appropriate colour.

'There were one or two other castes. Sutas, for example. These had originally been people of mixed birth, a mixture of kshatriya and brahmana, I think. But by the time of my story they were considered very low caste by both kshatriyas and brahmanas. Their colour was brown.'

'What did they do, these sutas?'

'As a matter of fact, most of the suta men were chariot drivers. That seemed to be their traditional role. Quite a skilled job, not to say dangerous. And they also had to look after the horses. But at least they were allowed to work alongside the other castes. There was a caste, the chandalas, who were not even considered to belong to a caste at all. They were outcasts.'

13

'And could anyone be a kshatriya if they wanted?' asked the second Henry.

'No!' said his brother. 'Weren't you listening? It went by birth. Isn't that right, Palmira?'

'Yes.'

'So they were a bit like knights,' remarked the second Henry. 'Like our grandfather, mother's father.'

'Exactly. There were many similarities,' agreed Palmira. 'And of course the brahmanas were rather like old Henry's clergy. In fact, kshatriyas, though they were the rulers, were usually very respectful to the brahmanas. And it was considered a terrible sin for a kshatriya to injure or kill a brahmana. Nevertheless, there was occasionally some tension between the two. And of course, as always, there were exceptions to the rule. Old Henry must have told you about bishops who could handle a sword as well as any knight. Yes? Well, similarly there were some brahmanas who became very skilled in warfare; and some kshatriyas who were peaceful and devout.'

'And what did the kshatriyas do when they weren't fighting?'

'Well... They tended to *play* at fighting. They had tournaments, contests, exhibitions. And they loved games, especially if gambling was involved. In fact they took their gambling as seriously as their fighting. If one kshatriya challenged another to a fight, or to a gambling match — particularly a game of dice — it was considered the worst of cowardice to refuse the challenge. Yes, in theory they had a very rigorous code of honour.'

'Are you ready to start, then?'

'Patience! There are still one or two things I must tell you about. And by the way — I hope you don't think I'm actually going to start the story today?'

'What!' cried both boys in unison.

'Well, look where the sun is. Besides, I have to compose myself carefully before starting it. I have to organise my mind, collect my thoughts, choose my language —'

'Oh, you're not going to tell it us in Latin, are you?'

Palmira smiled. 'I hadn't thought of that. What an interesting idea. No? How about Arabic, then?'

'Don't joke, Palmira. You know that's still hard for us.'

'All the more reason. Remember, everyone speaks Arabic along the coast. And it's your father's first tongue. Don't you speak to your father?'

'Of course we do, but not in Arabic.'

'Anyway, Palmira, you said this story was going to be fun.'

'What I meant, boys, was that I have to decide how I am going to phrase things. It's not easy jumping straight in. I must think about how I can avoid the *wells* and *you sees*. The least I can do in memory of Vyasa is to tell the story with some dignity, which will be hard enough with you two around. One day I'll tell you about Vyasa. It was he who showed me how to use the wind for the furnaces. I used to have to use bellows. Yes, he was certainly one of the most remarkable people I've met — and I've met many —'

'People! Men, you mean!'

'Admit it, Palmira, we don't get to hear of hardly any women that you've met on your travels. It's usually men you tell us about.'

'Nonsense... I suppose I may have more often met interesting men than women. But you see, that's because men seem to stop women from doing interesting things.'

'I don't think that's the only reason, Palmira, not in your case!' The boys smiled knowingly at each other.

'Well, I admit that interesting men have their attractions.'

'Surely not Vy —' The second Henry managed to stop his brother from finishing.

'As a matter of fact,' corrected Palmira, 'since you were about to ask, I was madly in love with Vyasa. The great pity is that he had taken vows of celibacy. Anyway, where was I? I do wish you wouldn't keep interrupting me. Yes... Tomorrow. Tomorrow I'll start. Tomorrow afternoon, after my siesta. *After*. I don't want to be woken up, thank you. But wait — I must tell you a little about the gods.'

'What gods?'

'The gods of the Bharatas, of course. Or, I should say, my version of them. Because I have to say that I'm not very clear about them at all. You see, Vyasa never really explained them to me properly, he just left me to work them out. Anyway, I can at least tell you about the gods which may play a part in *my* story, even if they are not really like the gods of the Bharatas.

'Well, there were the great three, Brahma, Vishnu and Shiva. Together these three seemed to be the lords of more or less everything. But it may be that Vishnu and Shiva were really parts of Brahma, or aspects or guises of Brahma. I'm not sure. At any rate, Brahma seemed hardly ever to get directly involved in human affairs, though you do occasionally hear of Vishnu and Shiva intervening. Vishnu was in fact supposed to be born into human form from time to time.

'But there were many other gods, less powerful than these three, who seemed to become involved in human affairs more often. Indeed, they sometimes used humans like pieces in a game which they played against each other —'

'Like chess?'

'Yes, except that chess was not quite invented yet. Let me see...' continued Palmira. 'In my story there are going to be three quite important lower gods. There is Indra. He was much admired by the kshatriyas because he represented strength, power, physical skill. Then there is Surya, god of the sun. In my story he represents understanding and knowledge. And Dharma. Dharma was the god of morality, of values, aims and purpose. He was much admired by the brahmanas. And there were a number of gods who will play a smaller part in my story. There's Vayu, god of the wind and weather. And the Ashwins. The Ashwins were twins, like you, though there the resemblance ends. They represented beauty and health.'

'Aren't there any goddesses?'

'Oh yes, good question. Yes. Kali. Yes, I should mention Kali. She was very important. At the time of my story, she represents... Well, she was a mysterious goddess. Some say she was the consort of Shiva. Which reminds me, there's the consort of Brahma, called Saraswati. There's a legend that she invented the Sanskrit alphabet. Now boys, once I start, I don't want any interruptions. If you don't understand something, just wait, and if it doesn't become clear in due course you'll probably forget about it anyway.'

'No interruptions at all?' asked the second Henry, looking rather worried.

'Well, if you're desperate. It's just that your interruptions are liable to break my rather frail chains of thought. I'd rather you could wait until I've finished for the day. That reminds me, talking of unwanted interruptions. Yes... I should tell you that Brahma tended to be terribly preoccupied. He was always busy concentrating. The whole world depended on him. Because if he stopped thinking about the world, even for just one brief moment, then the whole world would just cease to exist.'

'You mean, the world was all part of Brahma's imagination?'

'Yes, I suppose so.'

'But if he fell asleep, or stopped thinking about it, couldn't he just imagine it again when he woke up?'

'Oh no,' said Palmira grimly. 'You see, he was a figment of his own imagination as well. After all, he was part of the world. If everything was part of his imagination, where else could he be? So if he stopped thinking about the world, he himself would stop existing. And then he wouldn't be there to imagine it all back again, would he?'

'That doesn't make sense.'

'Isn't it impossible?'

'But Henry, where's the challenge in the merely possible? Eh? Now... all this made Brahma a little wrapped up in himself, irritable even. And when one day Indra and Surya came to him, he had no time for them. You see, Indra had aspirations to be the chief of the lower gods, on account of his great strength and power. But Surya resented this, maintaining that his own knowledge and understanding were more important than sheer power. And indeed, had Dharma not been above such self-seeking pettiness, he too would have objected to Indra's presumptions. At any rate, the other two decided that they should go and ask the great Brahma to settle the issue once and for all, and determine which was the most powerful, Indra or Surya. So they went along to see Brahma. Dharma went along as well, just in case the great god should decide that the power of Dharma's morality was more important than anything Indra or Surya had to offer.

'Brahma, as you can imagine, was rather irritated at this deputation:

'"Can't you see I'm busy! I haven't got time to deal with your petty squabbles. You'll just have to sort this out yourselves."

'"How?" they asked.

'"It's obvious," cried Brahma, rising to a temper. "Just find out which of you three has the greatest influence on the world of men!"'

Palmira took another sip of wine. 'I think that's all you need to know for the moment. We can start tomorrow afternoon. Yes? Good.'

Day One: *The River*

3 The parting

A jug of water stood shaded on the tiles beside Palmira. She drank a little from a cup on the table. The two boys were very quiet, but fidgeting.

Palmira took a long, deep breath, glanced through the creepers on the south wall, towards the grey outline of the hills beyond, and began her story.

•

It was midnight. A young woman, hardly more than a girl, crept quietly out of a tiny, broken-down hovel. She was in a little clearing, from which a single path led into the dense surrounding wood. The air was not clear enough to see the stars, but there were no clouds to disturb the moon shining alone in the black sky. The girl was walking quickly along the narrow path. She was carrying a bundle which must have been very heavy, because she had to stop every few paces to catch her breath. Her bare feet did not seem to feel the pain as they stepped on snapping twigs. They were hardened. Her big toes were long, leaning in sharply towards her other toes. She was covered in deerskins which were ragged, dirty and torn. She was crying softly as she went, snuffling between gasps for breath.

The path opened onto a river bank. She stood still for a few minutes, holding her bundle tightly, her eyes on the sparkling water, listening to the river. When her breath had steadied she looked round. She caught sight of something nearby along the bank and slowly bent her knees into a crouch, lowering her bundle and cradling it in her lap.

Then she gently placed the bundle on the ground and waded into the overgrown reeds that hid the margin of the river. She came out of the reeds carrying a large basket. It was made of wicker, in two halves fastened with leather straps. The wickerwork was tightly bound with waxed hide to keep out the water. The wax caught the moonlight as she put the basket down by her bundle. She undid the fastenings, removed the upper half, and took out a large sack and a tiny pillow. She wrapped her bundle in the sack and, straining with the weight, put it into the basket. Only the sleeping face of the baby was now visible.

Her hands moved across the sack and touched the boy's cheeks. She cradled his head, kissed it, and placed the tiny pillow beneath him to soften the hardness of the wicker. She carefully replaced the upper half of the basket and fastened it tightly.

She tried to lift the basket clear of the ground. It was too heavy so she dragged it slowly towards the water's edge. She waded in again, drawing the basket with her into the reeds. She slowly moved clear into the very centre of the river, where the water was still only waist deep. She held the basket steady in the current and whispered to her son, the two of them alone in the moonlit stream.

'Oh my child, may the gods protect you from all who dwell in water, land, in sky and heaven. May all the paths you take bring you fortune, and let no one stand against you in your chosen way. May all those whose paths cross yours find in their hearts only love, and all evil chased away. Happy is the sun who will be able to watch over you. Blessed also is the mother who will take you for her son and name you, and who will suckle you when you are hungry.'

She let go her tight grip, and the basket flew away from her in the brisk current as though it had never been still. A voiceless cry choked on her lips as she arched helplessly towards the dwindling shadow.

4 A prayer is answered

The current avoided all the little creeks and channels, and carried the basket down the Ashwa river like a horse bearing a sleeping rider; till it flowed into the turbulent Charanwati. From the Charanwati, the battling streams drove the boy into the centre of the river Yamuna, dodging all the little islands and reed beds. The Yamuna, in turn, joins the great river Ganges.

The Ganges flows from beyond the great capital city of the Bharata people, Hastinapura, all the way into the sea at the north-eastern corner of the huge triangle of India. Halfway between the point where the Yamuna joins, and the coast, is a region then called Anga. Soon after the Ganges enters this region, the river curves slowly round a town called Nagakaksha. Near Nagakaksha, on the southern bank of the great river, was a secluded shrine.

A woman was sitting on the river bank. She had been praying at the shrine; but now was just gazing blankly at the water which flowed slowly round the shallow bend, swirling with strange eddies.

A man, a little farther back from the river's edge, was still in prayer. He knelt with his face in his hands beside a huge block of stone, which was sculpted on each of its four vertical faces.

On one side of the stone the hero Rama was depicted defeating the evil demon Ravana. On a second side was shown Vishnu in the guise of a dwarf, appearing to the powerful but virtuous demon Bali. The third side was weathered in parts. It revealed a man with four arms and three eyes falling at the feet of a majestic adversary. Although the fourth side was worn almost smooth, an outline was just visible on it, of a horse, bridled and saddled, but with no rider. The shrine stood beneath a huge palm tree.

Perhaps a strange sound lifted the woman's attention from the constant bubbling of the water. Or maybe from the corner of her eye an unexpected shape joined in the river's vacant dance. For suddenly she shouted:

'Adhi! Come quick!'

Her husband looked up blearily, as from a dream, and went to the river's edge.

'Look, look at that basket. What is it? Adhi, what do you think it is?'

The basket was drifting slowly past in the shallow water. Without answering his wife, Adhi jumped into the river and quickly reached it. He undid the straps and took off the cover. He took one look inside, then turned and shouted across to his wife on the bank.

'Radha! Come and look at this!'

Radha was about to tell him to bring the basket up onto the bank, when a sound that had been pressing at the back of her mind burst through to flood her consciousness. She jumped into the water.

'Radha! Surely our prayers have been answered!'

They both stood in the water, staring in disbelief at the little face peering at them, its beautiful black eyes blinking in vain to focus in the startling light.

'Look at those ear-rings!'

'Aren't they huge! Why put such huge ear-rings on a little baby? Are they gold, Adhi?'

'They look like gold.'

'Look how tiny it is, Adhi... It must only be a few days old — and yet, see how it looks... Look at its eyes, Adhi, like lotus flowers. And it has stopped crying. See, it's looking at your eyes. And now at mine!'

The little baby did seem to be able to focus.

'I think it's a boy,' said Adhi proudly.

They brought the basket up onto the bank, and Radha tried to grasp the baby's little body through the sack. She felt something hard.

'Aaagh? What's this?'

She drew back the sack, which was bright red and lined with silk. There, gleaming in the sun, was dazzling gold. The child was wrapped in folds of what looked like chain mail, tiny rings of gold, tightly linked.

Adhi carefully picked up the chain mail with the little baby wrapped inside it, and put the bundle on the ground. The two of them gently unwrapped the mail, revealing the baby swathed in a red silk cloth. The golden mail appeared to be made to fit a large man, as armour to be worn round the chest. But they both noticed there was a small area missing from one corner.

The silk cloth around the baby was decorated with the round face of the sun, crowned with radiating flares. Radha pulled the cloth away. They discovered around the little boy's tiny chest, almost tight enough to be a second skin, the missing section of chain mail.

The boy was certainly beautiful for such a small baby. He already had quite dense hair, curling at the ends; his skin was the colour of burnished copper; even now his eyes seemed to take everything in.

Radha and Adhi looked at each other.

'Surely,' stammered Adhi, with tears in his eyes, 'surely it is the gods that have sent this wonderful, beautiful boy to us, in answer to our prayers... They have taken pity on a poor childless couple!'

5 Narada comes to town

The first thing they did when they got home was try to find a woman who would suckle the little baby, for the boy was now crying constantly.

While Radha went out to try to find a wet-nurse, Adhi stayed with the little boy. Every few minutes he would offer his little finger for the baby to suckle on, just to silence him for a few seconds. Adhi examined the golden mail. He noticed that each link was cut very precisely. And he was able to separate the linked rings without any great difficulty.

'I've been thinking,' he said to Radha when she returned, accompanied by a neighbour who had plenty of milk to spare. 'As the baby grows we will have to disconnect a row and add another one, or he won't be able to breathe. Or do you think we should take the vest off altogether?'

'No,' said Radha, 'we mustn't do that. He must have been wearing that armour for a reason. Just like the ear-rings. No, we will have to do as you suggest. Of course,' she added after a moment's thought, 'I'll have to keep adding an extra row to the bottom of the vest as well!'

And that is what they did. Rather frequently at first, because of course the little boy was growing fast. And though they were poor sutas it never once occurred to them to sell the armour, whose weight of gold they knew would have exchanged for more property than they had ever dreamt of.

They made a note of the day on which they had found the boy, and that became his birthday. Adhi called his son Vasu-shena, which means 'born with wealth'. And word got round about this little suta baby with the huge golden ear-rings. It was not unusual for older boys and girls to wear ear-rings; but not at quite so young an age, or quite so large.

Soon neighbours and friends started referring to the child as Karna-veshtakika, which means 'adorned with ear-rings'; and the name stuck. By the time he was a few months old the baby was just plain Karna.

Radha and Adhi often puzzled over the meaning of Karna's golden ornaments. It occurred to them that he might be the son, not of a mere mortal, but of a god. There were certainly legends of babies being found under similar circumstances, who had turned out to be children of gods. But they did not know whom to ask. None of the brahmanas in the region was able to help them, though they all marvelled at the boy.

Then, when Karna was just over six months old, and had added several rows of links to his armour, a very celebrated rishi passed through Nagakaksha. He was called Narada.

•

'Palmira,' interrupted the first Henry.

'I expect you want to know what is a *rishi*?'

Palmira poured a little water into her cup, took a sip, and offered it to the boys.

'A rishi is usually a brahmana, but no ordinary one. Rishis are supposed to have special powers, or to be particularly holy. Some rishis are supposed to be able to see into the future. Some, like Narada, travel around living from the gifts and charity of the people they visit. But others live in seclusion far away from villages and towns, hardly ever talking to a living soul. These are usually called *munis*. They are supposed to have conquered all — almost all — their earthly desires. Some munis are so strict they do not even look for food and drink, but die unless people place food beside them. But pilgrims will often make the journey to see them and leave food for them. Others are a little less strict, and are prepared to eat grains and nuts and fruit which they find loose on the ground. Nevertheless, they will not take the fruit actually off a tree, for example; or an ear of corn while it is still attached to the living plant; but will only gather food that is already scattered, and that no one else will want or take. And yet... Well, some rishis are *very* different... They may be very eccentric, and at times live in great luxury. Narada wasn't like this, but he was certainly very worldly, and as accustomed to the lavish company of kings as he was to the humble gifts of the poor. Now boys, try not to interrupt again until the end of the day. As I said before, if your problem doesn't keep, then it probably won't matter.'

Palmira continued her story.

•

'We must take little Karna to see Narada,' suggested Radha. 'He may be able to solve the mystery.'

'What if he takes the child away from us?' asked Adhi.

'I will not let him,' said Radha defiantly.

'What, even Narada?'

'Karna will leave us when he is ready to, and not before. The gods have made me a mother, and a mother I will be.'

So they took little Karna to see Narada. They carried with them the rest of the mail in the red sack; and also the other contents of the basket in which Karna had been found. They had also put in the sack some gifts for the rishi: some puffed rice, some flour, and some clarified butter.

The rishi had chosen to receive the townspeople in the hall of an old temple near the main square. Adhi and Radha had to wait a long time before they were even let inside the building, and by then the sun was low and reddish in the sky.

Narada's white robes made it easy to pick him out from the others in the gloom of the hall. He was standing at the far end. With Karna in her arm, Radha nervously approached the rishi. Adhi walked beside her carrying the red sack.

Without saying a word she presented the baby to the rishi, who stretched out his arms to receive him. Narada smiled, and was about to ask Radha a question when he noticed the baby's ear-rings. With his free hand he felt the rings.

'These are unusual... And certainly large enough for you to grow into,' he added with a smile, looking into the huge black eyes which stared back at him. 'So...' Narada looked at Radha. 'Why have you brought him to me? It is a boy, is it not?'

Radha nodded, but remained silent, expecting her husband to speak.

Narada tickled Karna's cheeks to make him smile.

'He very rarely smiles,' said Adhi.

Narada raised his eyebrows without looking up. 'Is that the problem?' He tried to tickle Karna's little chest.

The rishi's face stiffened all of a sudden. He looked up at Adhi and Radha. Adhi was about to say something but Radha put her hand on her husband's arm.

Narada slowly unwrapped the clothes that were swaddling the baby, and saw the golden armour. He felt it gently, passing his hand carefully over it. He allowed the swaddling clothes to fall clear as he held Karna up, naked but for his little golden vest, turning him around to examine his back.

While he was doing this Radha began to tell him how they had found the baby. When she had finished, Narada, still holding Karna, leant back against the edge of a long table nearby which was laden with gifts. He held the boy for a few moments, deep in thought. Then he put him down on the table beside the gifts, as though Karna were another one of these, picked up the swaddlings and covered him up.

There were still a few other people standing by at the fringes of the hall. With a gesture Narada ushered them out. He turned to Karna's parents.

'You say there was more of this armour. Have you got it with you?'

'Yes, sire.' Adhi reached into the red sack. First he took out the offerings for Narada, then he passed the sack to the rishi. Adhi placed the gifts on the table as Narada inspected the sack.

After examining the material of the sack itself, Narada felt inside. First he brought out the tiny pillow; then the red silk square. He looked closely at these and then passed them to Radha to hold. Finally he pulled out the chain mail. He spread it beside the baby on the table, moving aside some pots and jars to make more room. He raised a corner of the mail to his mouth and bit it. He peered at it in the gloom trying to find a bite mark.

He started to pace slowly along the length of the table and back, several times, deep in thought. Once or twice he glanced back at the armour. Karna meanwhile was gurgling peacefully on the table. His parents waited in silence, holding on to each other, not wishing to disturb the rishi's concentration.

Suddenly Narada walked quickly out of the hall. Adhi and Radha could hear him shouting for something outside. He returned wielding an unsheathed sword in his hand.

Radha screamed, dropping the pillow and square onto the floor.

Flustered by this reminder of their presence, Narada apologised to them, and reassured Radha. He put down the sword and gently held her hands.

'Don't worry, I won't touch your baby, let alone harm him. Pick him up for a moment.'

Radha did as she was told.

Narada approached the table, raised the sword high above his head, and brought it crashing down onto the spreadeagled armour. Radha, Adhi, and the table all jumped with the shock, and several pots of clarified butter rolled off and smashed onto the floor. Narada put down the sword and picked up the armour.

'I need to look at this under better light,' he said, and left the hall, taking the sword with him as well as the armour.

Adhi and Radha waited several minutes. They heard three or four more grunts and crashes from outside. Radha, without really realising what she was doing, put Karna down again on the table and began to pick up some of the larger pieces of earthenware from the floor.

Narada returned, a little breathless, and much distracted. He placed the mail in a heap by the baby and leant against the table, deep in thought.

There was just enough light creeping in for Adhi to catch the reflections from the armour. He stared at it, hardly able to contain his curiosity. Radha continued to salvage the pots.

Adhi walked nearer to the armour. The rishi ignored him. A look of distress appeared on Adhi's face.

'Radha!' he cried, holding the armour up. 'This... is not gold, Radha. It is not soft enough for gold.'

His wife got up from her pots and examined the mail with her husband. They could see that there was hardly a mark to show where the sword had smitten the metal.

'Worthless!' cried Adhi.

'What does it matter?' consoled his wife. 'We were not going to sell it, anyway.'

'But for Karna...' began Adhi.

'For Karna,' interrupted Narada, as though starting up from a dream, 'it is much more valuable than gold. Look at it. The sword has not deformed a single link by even a hair's breadth! And yet the metal is flexible enough to allow the links to be unfastened. And to allow the child to breathe as deeply as he needs.' Narada paused. 'I must think,' Narada added. 'Will you wait?'

They nodded.

Narada picked Karna up and handed him back to his mother. Again the rishi sat against the table. After a while Karna started to cry softly, and Radha rocked him gently; she let him suck at her breast to comfort him, though she had hardly any milk. Adhi picked up the pillow and the square from the floor where they still lay and put them by the armour on the table.

After a while Narada slowly raised himself and walked towards them.

'West of here, in Varanasi, lives a rishi called Charvaka. When Karna reaches the age of nine or ten, take him to see Charvaka. He is a rather strange man, but very... knowledgeable. He will advise you and your son. But take care not to let your son talk too much alone with him... Charvaka is not... not entirely good.'

Narada started to walk slowly out of the room, as though in a dream.

'Sire!' cried Radha, 'What will happen to Karna? Is he...' Her voice fell now almost to a whisper. 'Is he the son of a god?'

Narada stopped. He turned and walked back to Radha. He took Karna from her and passed the baby to her husband. The rishi grasped her firmly by the wrists.

'In the course of time, if all goes well, your son will become a great warrior. A great ratha.'

'A warrior?'

'If he chooses to become one. If he does not, he may live here in safety with you, as a suta. But if he chooses to become a ratha, let him. He will face danger. Indeed, he will face death. But if all goes well, while he has his ear-rings and his armour, no one will be able to defeat him in combat.'

'But how... What should we do?'

Narada let go Radha's hands. 'As I say, take him to see Charvaka when you think he is ready. But he must keep his armour always with him; as I see you have been doing. And most important of all, he must always wear his ear-rings.

Have you ever taken them off him?'

'No, sire,' replied Radha. 'They've been on him since the day he came to us.'

'Good. He must not remove them. They carry his destiny. They are his life... or his death.'

'But is he...' Radha's voice fell again. 'Is he the son of a god?'

'Sire, what is the meaning of the sun on the cloth?' Adhi turned his body to indicate the silk square. 'Could it be Surya?'

Narada looked at the cloth. His eyes lit up. 'Yes... That is the face of Surya... Yes... And Surya is also golden, like the mail, yet is not gold... But you must keep quiet about this... You are, after all, sutas. People will laugh at you if you tell them that your son is the child of Surya. You must tell no one.'

Narada looked again at the silk square.

'In fact... May I take this?'

Adhi looked at Radha.

'Yes, sire,' she said.

'Good...' He went to the table, picked up the cloth, folded it neatly and put it in one of the ample pockets of his cloak. Then he started to walk towards the entrance of the hall.

Adhi handed Karna back to Radha and began to collect up Karna's things into the red sack.

'By the way...' Narada called back to them. 'When is your son going to have a little brother or sister?'

Radha looked at the ground in proud embarrassment. 'In four months' time, sire.' She turned to hide her face from her husband.

Adhi was speechless.

'Are you blind?' Narada said to him, smiling. 'Don't you know your wife is expecting?'

Adhi was still a little confused as he picked up the sack to follow his wife and son out of the temple.

6 The first bow

Karna soon had a little brother, called Sangra-majit; and Radha went on to have two more boys, Pra-sena and Vrisha-sena.

Karna was very fond of them and was almost always kind and helpful to them. In fact both his parents wondered at how well-behaved Karna was. Not from sheer obedience, they observed, but because from a very early age he realised when his parents needed help, or when they were just too tired to give him attention.

Karna had grown into a quiet and serious boy. By the time he was five or six, the neighbours and friends of the family would often remark on this.

'Not a very cheerful boy, is he?'

'Doesn't play much with other children, does he?'

'Is he all right, your Karna?'

But although Adhi saw what they meant, and was a little concerned himself, he stood loyally by his son, and praised his maturity.

It has to be said that Karna, even at that age, often made grown men and women feel uncomfortable when he looked at them. There was something about his gaze which, though not quite a stare, made people avoid contact with his eyes. It was certainly not any hostility on Karna's part. It was perhaps that he seemed to see more than it was polite to see. If someone was worried about being too fat, or too thin, or too tall, or too short, Karna's eyes seemed to see their worry as clearly as their physical appearance. And so people understandably avoided seeing their own unsought reflection in his little face. Only Radha never tired of looking at him.

It is true also that Karna did not mix very much with other children. There was a time when the local children would make fun of his reserve; or laugh at his ear-rings, which certainly made a peculiar contrast with his character; or ridicule the fact that he always wore something over his chest even when it was very hot. And of course they tried provoking him physically; throwing things at him, pushing him about; or trying, usually unsuccessfully, to start a fight with him. But only much bigger children ever dared attempt to overpower him.

This taunting stopped after Karna was about four or five, mainly because the others came to accept that it was almost impossible to make him cry or show any pain. Not even when the larger boys would pin him down, sitting on his chest, and pull his hair or ears; or pull up his shirt, uncover his armour and laugh wildly at it.

'Look at this great warrior in armour!' they had taunted.

'Been in any good battles lately? Where's your bow, then?'

But Karna would not shed any tears, nor show even a grimace of pain, whatever they had tried.

Karna always covered his armour under a cotton shirt. Most male children, and most adult males as well, did not wear a shirt but just a dhoti. This was a long, usually cotton, cloth which would be wound around the hips and then round the back between the legs to tuck up in front at the waist. Children normally used quite a narrow strip of cloth, so that the garment was little more than a loincloth. But many men wore dhotis made of a wide strip coming down to the knees or below, which, with the tuck underneath, gave the appearance of baggy trousers. Even warriors sometimes appeared in just a dhoti. Though more usually, especially when fully armed, they wore light coats which came down to the knees over loose-fitting trousers. Many warriors wore armour round their chests, usually a breastplate or a corselet of metal strips. But generally they wore these over their clothes, not, like Karna, under them.

By the time he was six Karna had earned a certain grudging respect from other children. Partly because of his toughness, but mainly for the great skill with which he was learning to handle his father's horses. The horses did not strictly belong to Karna's father, since Adhi was only a driver. They belonged to a pair of kshatriyas whom Adhi regularly worked for. But Adhi looked after the horses most of the time, and Karna took great interest in them.

In spite of Karna's skill, however, the general opinion was that he was not cut out to follow in his father's footsteps.

'That boy will never make a driver,' Adhi's friends would tell him. Adhi would insist that Karna was doing all right. But privately he was worried.

'Radha, do you think it's time I took Karna to see that rishi?' Adhi asked his wife one day.

'But he's only just seven, Adhi! Remember that Narada said to wait until he was nine or ten.'

'But look how advanced he is. And he...'

But Adhi did not need to explain. Radha too felt the same doubts and concerns about her eldest son's future.

'If he is too young, the rishi will surely tell us,' said Adhi.

'Too young for what?' asked Radha.

'For... for whatever the rishi thinks we... Karna should do.'

Perhaps they would have left things for a while, were it not for Karna's growing obsession with archery.

He would watch the kshatriyas practise whenever he could. And of course, like many of the other children, he was fascinated by the tournaments and archery exhibitions which were sometimes held in Nagakaksha.

Karna had begged his father to try to get him a bow from one of the kshatriyas. Of course, Karna was much too small even to hold one of these great bows, which often stood as tall, horn to horn, as a man. So Adhi, who was surprised at the urgency of his son's pleas, promised to get him a small one which he could learn on.

Adhi was very apprehensive about this. Not because of the note of caution he remembered in Narada's words. For if Karna were able to choose to become a warrior it was inevitable that, as a warrior, he would face danger. No, Adhi was more immediately concerned by the reaction of his neighbours, on seeing a suta's son playing with a bow; and the effect this would have on his already unusual son. And also, more importantly, he did not want to build up Karna's hopes that someone could be found who would be prepared to teach him archery. Let alone that Karna might be taken on to train as a warrior. So his promise slept uneasily.

Then one day Adhi found his son practising with a little bow he must have made for himself, out of a branch, using a dozen carefully cut little canes for arrows. In his anger and shame with himself at not having delivered his promise, Adhi lost his temper. He shouted angrily at Karna.

But Karna, ignoring his father's turmoil, and smiling proudly, showed his father how well he could use his makeshift bow. Adhi watched, in silence. What impressed him was not the accuracy with which Karna shot the arrows, but the faithfulness with which his son had captured the correct kshatriya style. Most young children, given a small bow, would pull the bowstring back with the arrow half across their chest, from where they could still see all of the arrow if they looked down, and all of the target if they looked up. But Karna had noticed why the warriors all used helmets which were shaped at the sides to leave their ears exposed. He drew his little bowstring back past the side of his face, so that the end of the arrow just brushed his ear; in his vision the point of the arrow and the target were one.

Adhi left his son practising.

'Radha,' said Adhi when he got home, 'I must take Karna to that rishi, now.'

'Already?' Radha was trembling slightly, on the verge of tears.

◊

The journey to Varanasi took three days. Adhi wanted his son to be fresh and rested when they met the rishi, so he was reluctant to let Karna hold the reins.

Nevertheless, Karna managed to persuade his father to let him drive the chariot for most of the second day.

It was very easy to find Charvaka's home. The rishi was evidently quite well-known in that region. Adhi was a little nervous, rehearsing in his mind what he would say. He was clutching tightly the red sack, which on this occasion contained only Karna's things. Karna himself carried in his arms the offerings they had brought for the rishi: a large elephant tusk and some clarified butter.

'Remember to bow when you meet him,' advised Adhi. 'You should always bow when addressed by a brahmana or kshatriya.'

And when they were ushered into Charvaka's workshop, both father and son bowed low.

But when there was no response to their act of deference they both looked up. At first they could see only the clutter which filled the room. There were parts of chariots, wheels, axles, weapons, pieces of armour, agricultural implements and other devices and contraptions without name. Carefully they advanced further into the room, avoiding these obstacles. Then they caught sight of him.

They could just see the rishi's head of grey hair, nodding slowly from behind the skeleton of what perhaps had been a donkey or a small mule. The bones had been wired up to allow the skeleton to stand by itself. Through the rib cage they saw the rishi's brown cloak. He was sitting on a stool at a bench in the centre of the room. Cautiously they approached. He appeared to be writing on a dried palm leaf spread out on the untidy surface. Karna's attention was drawn immediately to an elegant weighing balance further along the bench. Beside the scales stood a little statuette, perhaps of a goddess.

Then Karna noticed an open doorway into an adjoining room. Still carrying his offerings, he moved to get a better view into this room. He saw neat piles of different types of wood, of bone, ivory, metal. And beyond them Karna caught sight of a number of beautiful bows, leaning unstrung against a wall, in all sorts of shapes and sizes.

As Adhi went to restrain Karna's curiosity, Charvaka at last noticed their presence. His two visitors immediately bowed again.

'Oh please! Please!' Charvaka waved them up. He stayed on his stool looking at them.

'I imagine you have come to see me for some reason?' he asked.

'Sire... I've brought my son to see... We have come from Anga...'

'Your son? I see... This is your son here. Very good. To see me?'

Karna came forwards now and presented the rishi with the elephant tusk and the jar of clarified butter. Charvaka bowed his head in acknowledgement and put the gifts to one side. Adhi took a deep breath, and put down the sack on the floor. He began his story.

'My name, sire, is Adhi-ratha. My son —'

'Very well, my friend, you may leave us,' interrupted Charvaka.

'But sire, do you not wish to know why I have brought him?'

'Not necessarily. The boy will answer for himself. He speaks, eh?'

'But sire, there are things he... he is too young to know...'

'Naturally. But there are things that you are too old to know. I will certainly speak with you afterwards.' Charvaka got up off his stool. 'Relax, my friend... If you could wait outside... Ah! Here we are...' Charvaka shuffled towards a shelf and picked up some rice cakes which were resting there among some similar gifts. He thrust them into Adhi's hand. 'They are quite fresh — given to me only yesterday.' He directed Adhi to the door. Adhi absently picked up the red sack and threaded his way carefully back through the clutter of the rishi's room.

'Good,' called the rishi after him. 'I will converse with your son. We will see you later.'

7 Charvaka's advice

'I wish,' said Charvaka to Karna when they were alone, 'I wish people would bring me materials which I could eat straight away, without any cooking or mixing.' He held up the jar of clarified butter as an example. 'I do quite enough cooking and mixing of inedible substances... And I am up to my ears in clarified butter. I have half a room full of it. Well, a whole room half-full. I have one pot which is twenty-five years old and still in excellent condition. It is useful for greasing arrows, and so forth, but I have more than enough for that purpose. There are many other substances I would rather be given, had I a choice. If you ever come to see me again, do mention this to your kind father. Tactfully, of course. Sugar is preferable, though I tend not to use it in comestibles. It is bad for the teeth, you know. And, unlike an elephant, I'm on my last set. Nevertheless, even sugar is preferable... Not flour, though — I usually give flour away. It doesn't last as long, you see. So if I don't give it away I have to go to the trouble of making bread out of it. And in any case, by the time I've made one piece, I'm hungry enough for two.'

'You should make two at a time, sire,' suggested Karna.

'What if I only receive enough flour for one, my boy, as is usually the case. Eh?'

'Keep it until someone has brought you some more, sire.'

'By which time I have died of hunger. Not that one actually dies of the desire, hunger, but rather through the privation of its object, food. No... Keeping oneself fed is a mysterious business... I have never quite been able to master it.'

Charvaka had put down the clarified butter and was now observing his visitor.

'Let me see you breathe, young man. Inhale! Yes. Exhale... Well, it appears to me that you are in what would commonly be described as excellent health. And your mind appears to be working.'

'Thank you, sire.'

'I'm not sure that is anything to thank anyone for, my boy, least of all me. For without the shelter of insanity, or the distractions of disease, a man is at the mercy of reality. And that is not a mercy to be thankful for. Eh?'

Charvaka paused, apparently waiting for Karna to make some reply to this point. When none came he continued.

'Well... The most useful advice I can give you, my boy, is to remember at all times to breathe. Not of course when you find yourself under water. But in almost all other circumstances you will discover that it is absolutely vital. Yes...

And much more important than eating or drinking. People will constantly be offering you food and drink, and asking you to eat up. But they will seldom offer you air or remind you to breathe. So, never forget. And do try to do it in the correct sequence, eh? In, then out. Always alternate.'

'Yes, sire.'

'Well, off you go then...'

'Is that all, sire?'

'All? All of what?'

'Your advice, sire.'

'Ah! You want more of my advice?'

'Yes, sire. Yes please, sire.'

'Very well... Since you seem such a nice and polite young man... I will give you perhaps the most profound and useful advice I know on how to deal with life's rigours. Next to breathing, of course. Naturally that has pride of place. But I can guarantee that if you follow this next piece of advice to the letter, your life will get better and better.'

'Thank you, sire.'

'My advice is simply this. Always do first what you find worst. The next thing then can't be as bad. But if you leave the worst till last, your life will go from bad to worse.'

'Thank you, sire.'

'Right, off you go then!' Charvaka took a coin out of one of the pockets of his cloak and gave it to Karna. Then he shuffled back to his stool and sat down again by his manuscripts.

'Do I have to go, sire?'

'Good heavens, are you still here? I thought I'd got rid of you... I'm usually very good at getting rid of little boys like you.' The rishi stroked his beard. 'Very well, then, since clearly you seem to have some reason for wanting to see me...' He noticed Karna studying the balance with interest. 'Have you not seen one like this before?'

'No, sire. I think I've seen something like it in the market place, at home. What's it for?'

'What's it for! Do you mean to tell me you don't know! It's for weighing, my boy. Have your parents not shown you how to use a balance?'

'No, sire.'

'You have a mother as well as a father?'

'Yes, sire.'

Charvaka shook his head. 'This, my boy,' he began, indicating the balance, 'is an instrument by which we are enabled to lift up the veil of the great Kali herself.'

'Who's Kali, sire? Is that her?' Karna pointed at the statuette.

'Well... Yes and no...' Charvaka picked up the figure. 'This is just a childish token. A silly indulgence of mine.' He put the figure on one of the pans of the balance, keeping his hand in support until the pan had fallen to rest on the bench top. Then he picked up a glistening metal weight from among several beside the scales.

'Do you know what this is, my boy?'

'No, sire.'

'Tell me, has your father got an elephant?'

'No, sire, but we've got neighbours in Nagakaksha who've got one.'

'And is it a wild elephant?'

'Oh no, sire.'

'Do you know how wild elephants are caught?'

'Yes, sire. Wild elephants are caught by tame ones.'

'Well, my boy, that is exactly what happens here.' He put the weight on the vacant pan of the balance. The scales did not tilt back. He pointed to the statuette. 'This is the wild and unknown weight.' Then he indicated the metal weight. 'And this is the familiar, trained one... I will just put another couple of trained ones on to join it — we usually need more than one trained elephant to capture a wild one. There! They are level. You see, we have used the known to capture the unknown!'

Karna stared at the floating scales.

'But sire... How did you tame your first one?'

'Ah! Indeed, my boy... Yes... Well, you see, I was given my first weight when it was at a very tender age, a mere infant. And I reared it most carefully, till it could help me train all these others...'

Karna smiled.

'Now, my boy,' continued Charvaka. 'Tell me who you are and what you want from me.'

'My name is —'

'I'm not interested in your name. Names have no significance. At least, they should have no significance, not if they are proper names, my boy. I should not be able to learn anything about a person merely from their name. A name is not and should not be a description. Unfortunately in recent times people have adopted the very regrettable and often absurd habit of using descriptions for names. Very regrettable. For one can measure the maturity of a civilisation by the insignificance of its names.'

'But sire, if names didn't mean anything, then they... they wouldn't have any meaning, sire.'

'My boy, there is more to meaning than *meaning*. I don't wish to offend, but just look, for example, at your father's name. *Adhi-ratha* — a superior ratha! Now, is that regrettable or absurd?' Charvaka looked down at Karna's brown sash. 'Isn't your father a suta?'

'Yes, sire. But sire, what is a *ratha*?'

'There you are!' Charvaka gave a little snort under his breath. 'There you are, you don't even know what your father's name means, and yet I'm sure you've been using it quite successfully all your talking life. A ratha, my boy, is a man, usually a kshatriya, sometimes a brahmana, who has shown some significant distinction in battle. Excuse my prejudice, but I doubt that this is an appropriate description of your father?'

'No, sire.'

'So, when I ask you who you are, I want an appropriate description, not a name. If you can only answer with your name, you don't really know who you are, do you, my boy?'

'Sire, I'm a young boy...'

'That's better! Exactly how young?'

'I'm seven and a quarter. Sire. And I have three little brothers.'

'And why have you come here?'

'Because my father brought me. He didn't tell me why.'

Charvaka scratched his beard. 'That's interesting. And yet you seem to want to be here?'

'Sire, I think I know why my father brought me. Though he didn't tell me.'

'You think you know?'

'Yes, sire. I'm too quiet to be a chariot driver like my father. Chariot drivers have to tell funny stories and things like that to the warriors when they're travelling on a long journey. And people say I'm too quiet for that, so I can't be a driver.'

'I see... I see. But would you like to be a driver?'

'No, sire. I want to be a warrior.'

'But you are the son of a suta. Sutas aren't generally allowed to be fighters. Fighters are usually kshatriyas, sometimes brahmanas... But never sutas.'

'Why not, sire?'

'That's the custom, my boy.'

'But that's not fair, sire.'

'Of course it's not fair, my boy! What do you think customs are for? They are just very polite ways of being unfair. Sometimes they're not even very polite.'

Karna's large black eyes looked up sadly at Charvaka.

'My boy, *life* is unfair. It always has been, and always will be. No matter what men do. That's why men look to the heavens to balance what in this life is unjust. For that by which the scales they see and touch on earth are light, they make up on the scales of hope and faith in heaven...'

Karna stood in silence, not knowing what to say or do.

'My boy, tell me, why do you want to *be* a chariot fighter?'

'I like the bow, sire.'

'But the bow is a very difficult instrument to master. I myself can hardly string a good, tall bow, let alone shoot an arrow straight! Though I can make you as good a bow as you could wish for. And any kind of arrow you care to mention. So you see, not everyone has an aptitude for the bow. What makes you think you will be able to master it?'

'I can see very well, sire. I've watched the warriors, and most of the boys my age can't see what they do. Their eyes can't follow, it's so fast. But I can, sire. And my hands are very good as well.'

'And do you boast as well as this to other people?'

'No, sire, only to you, because you asked me... I was just trying to answer your question, sire.'

'But you said how *good* your hands were, how *well* you could see.'

'I was trying to answer your question, sire.'

'I know. But remember, my boy, though your eyes may see things very *fast*, that isn't exactly the same as seeing *well*. And though your hands might be very *quick*, that isn't necessarily *good*. Is it?'

'No, sire.'

'But I think you're a little too young to understand that —'

'No, sire... My mother's always saying... If it makes people happy it's good and if it doesn't it isn't... If it makes people sad it's bad and if it doesn't it isn't...'

The rishi stroked his beard as he looked at the boy.

'I confess that I like you, my boy. I could, perhaps, get someone to teach you to use a bow. Any of the kshatriyas round here would do it if I asked them to. There, you see how unfair life is? For that matter, most of the ones in Anga know me, too. I must say, you have come a very long way just to see me. Rather shrewd of your father. I take it he supports your ambition? Yes, I could persuade someone to teach you. But my boy, even if you turned out to be very good — I mean skilled — I don't think it's likely that the kshatriyas would accept you kindly as a fellow ratha. You would have a hard time of it. You realise that? Still, when you are older, then perhaps you can decide whether you really want to go through with it. In the mean time, at least I can give you a little bow to start on.'

'Oh thank you, sire!'

'But listen... You'll have to practise in secret at first. After a while, if you become accomplished, then you can be more open about it. People will abuse you, certainly. But you will have to put up with that. By the way, you will have to stop bowing to kshatriyas and brahmanas. If you're not going to be their inferior, you must not behave as if you are. Shall we choose a bow for you, then?'

'Oh yes please, sire!'

'Very well...' Charvaka got up off his stool. 'By the way, my boy, what *is* your name? But you see how unimportant names are, eh? We've established everything we needed to without knowing your name! Nevertheless, custom and convenience demand that we refer to you by means of it, so... what is it?'

'Karna, sire.'

'*Karna*? That is indeed a strange description. What did I tell you? Regrettable or absurd? *Ear*!'

'Sire, it's short for Karna-veshtakika, sire.'

'Karna-veshta... Oh! Of course! Your ear-rings. Yes... I beg your pardon, my boy, I hadn't really noticed them. How unobservant of me. And they are rather on the large side, for a young boy, I would say. I expect that is why you are known by them.' Charvaka sat down again. 'Come here, my boy, let me have a look at you...'

Charvaka examined Karna's ears, apparently more interested in these than in the rings.

'Strange — do your earlobes often inflame like this? Are they hurting?'

'A bit, sire. It does happen sometimes. But I'm used to it.'

'You must have very sensitive skin. Gold shouldn't do this...'

The rishi drifted into silence as he examined Karna's ear-rings more carefully. Suddenly Charvaka straightened his back.

'Where did you get these from?' The playfulness with which he had been addressing the child now gave way to a note of urgency.

'I don't know, sire.'

'Does your father know?'

'I don't know, sire... but my real name is Vasu-shena—'

'Born with wealth? Because of these? You've always had them?'

'Yes, sire. And I was born with more of that gold, sire.'

'More?' Charvaka got up. 'This is not gold. What sort of more?'

'I think my father has it in the sack we brought.' Karna looked round for it, then realised his father must have taken it with him. 'But I've got some on me, sire?'

'On you?'

'Yes, sire.'

Normally Karna would never allow anyone outside his immediate family to see his armour, not if he could help it. But he felt at ease with the rishi.

He undid his brown sash and took off the little silk jerkin which covered his top.

When Charvaka saw the golden mail his jaw dropped and his eyes stared. He knelt down in front of Karna and felt the armour carefully with both hands. With great dexterity he undid some of the links, then fastened them up again. He looked carefully into Karna's eyes.

'This is not gold, either. And it is quite different metal from the ear-rings. You say there is more?'

'Yes, sire, in the red sack my father's carrying.'

'Red?' Charvaka closed his eyes for a moment.

'It was always in that sack, sire, the armour.'

'It's silk! Is the sack made of silk, like this?' Charvaka pointed to Karna's jerkin.

'Yes, sire, but red. And the armour is for a big man. My mother puts more on me as I grow.'

'Your mother... Your parents... Tell me, are they your real parents?'

Karna thought for a few moments.

'Yes, sire.'

'You have no... no doubts about that?'

'Sire, you saw my father! He's as real as you are, sire!'

'I mean... Karna, you have little brothers, have you not? Did you come out of your mother's belly as they did?'

'I don't think so, sire. She didn't have me at home like my brothers. She found me in the river in a basket. And I was already wearing my ear-rings and my armour, only the armour was very tiny then. When I grow I may be able to wear all of it one day.'

'So your mother found you in a basket!' Charvaka got up off his knees. He turned away from Karna for a moment and pulled his hand through his hair. He turned to face the boy again, looking at him carefully, as though seeing him for the first time.

'And have your parents never wondered where you came from?'

'Sire, when I was a little baby, before I could talk, they said they took me to see a rishi, another rishi, like you, sire, called Narada.'

'Narada!... I don't think the dove would like to hear you say he was like the mouse... And what did he have to say?'

'He said I probably came from Surya.'

'You mean... that Surya is your father?'

'I'm not sure, sire. I don't really know what Surya is. Is he the sun? How could I come from the sun?'

Charvaka smiled. 'Surya is the god of the sun. He must have meant that Surya was your father... I wonder why *Surya...*'

'But I've already got a father, sire.'

'Of course, yes... Karna... Perhaps there was something else found with you in the basket... Was there?'

'There was a pillow, sire. And I think there was something else with a picture of the sun on it.'

'Ah, yes... So... So if Surya is your father... did Narada venture any *maternal* connection?'

'Sire?'

'Did he say who your mother was?'

'I don't know. But I think he met my mother with my father. She said she went to see him as well.'

'What is your mother's name?'

'Radha, sire.'

'This is the mother of your little brothers, the one that found you in the basket?'

'Yes, sire.'

'Good...' Charvaka looked at Karna's face carefully again. He smiled at the boy.

'Well, well... And you are seven years old? Did you say seven?'

'Seven and a quarter, sire.'

'Well, my boy...' The rishi paused again, grasping his beard at the roots. 'Well, my boy, I think there is a chance that your dream may come true. There! You see how unfair life is? Shall we call your father in? You can put your things back on now.'

Adhi was conducted in, and stood looking ill at ease beside his son, while the rishi, grunting and snorting under his breath, examined the contents of the red sack.

'Yes... Oh yes... Now, Karna, my boy...' Charvaka put the armour back in the sack. 'Karna, why don't you go and choose yourself a bow — see, in there. You go and choose one, eh?'

Karna disappeared into the adjoining room.

'Tell me, Adhi-ratha,' began the rishi, 'was there anything else with Karna, with the baby, when you found him on the river? I presume it was the great Ganges?'

'Yes, sire, it was. Did my boy tell you all about that? Yes, there was... there was a —'

'A red square with a picture of Surya?'

'Yes, sire! How did you know that? Did *Karna* tell you?'

43

'What happened to it?'

'Narada took it. You know that we...'

'Yes, yes, he told me. I see... And I gather Narada said that Karna's father is Surya?'

'Yes... Did Karna tell you *that*? I didn't know the boy knew...'

'He doesn't know *exactly*, shall we say... But am I right in thinking that Narada mentioned nothing about a possible mother?'

'No, no. He didn't mention anything about a mother.'

'Good... Well, my friend, as I presume you know, your son wants to be a chariot fighter. I will arrange for someone near you in Anga to give him some lessons with the bow. But every year he must come and stay with me for two or three months, perhaps more, depending on his aptitudes, until he is ready to go... So that I can teach him the rudiments from which he will benefit in later life. Also, there is here in Varanasi a ratha who was taught by Kripa-charya. This man has a good action, though he has a rather indifferent accuracy of aim. Still, he will be able to correct any errors Karna acquires in Anga.'

'But sire... Ready to go... Where?'

'Not yet, my friend. No, perhaps when Karna is... thirteen. By that age, let me see, Yudhi is a little younger, he will be about eleven, Bhima will be ten, Arjuna will be nine, the twins a little younger than that, I don't recall exactly whether they were born last year or the previous... And Dur is roughly the same age as Karna. Duh a little younger. Yes, so when Karna is thirteen he will go to Hastinapura to learn with the princes under Kripa. You have heard of Kripa-charya?'

'Sire... How? I don't understand. How can little Karna learn with the princes?'

'Adhi-ratha, is not their company good enough for the son of Surya? Of course, I would like to send him to Parashu-rama, but he is very far away, and besides, I believe he is only taking brahmana pupils now. One day Karna will have to go to him. But first he will have to study the bow... It is a pity that Bhishma himself doesn't teach, but Kripa is very good. There is Drona, of course. Drona is nearly as good as Parashu, but I'm not sure where he is at the moment. I wish I did — he has some weapons of mine... So, is that agreed?'

'But... But I am a suta, sire. They will not accept him. And I have no money...'

'My friend, what is the point of naming your child Vasu-shena if you don't believe it? Don't you worry about that. I know Kripa. Leave it to me. So... I will want your son back in a few months' time. By then he should be able to string a small bow in a few seconds, let us hope.'

'Sire...' Adhi remembered Narada's mention of danger, and knew that Radha would scold him if he did not raise it with this rishi. 'Narada warned that Karna may face danger if he chooses to become a ratha.'

'That is true, my friend. There will be danger. But I will try to prepare him so that when the time comes, no one will force Karna to face it against his will. I will do my best to do my best, that I promise. Ah! Here he is, our little warrior!'

Karna appeared holding a bow which was just a little taller than him. It had beautifully carved horn tips, and was clearly not too heavy for him.

'There! You see, Adhi-ratha, your son is wise beyond his years to choose within his grasp. An excellent decision, Karna. Start with wood, later, my boy, you can go on to metal, if you take to it. You will also need a glove for your left hand. You are right-handed, eh? Naturally I don't have one in your size, but if I give you some lizard skin, perhaps you can get one made up in Anga, eh?'

'What's the glove for, sire?' asked Karna. 'I've seen them wearing them...'

'Ah! That's the difference between watching and being. You would soon understand if you were in their place. Without a guard for your bow hand, why, the skin would be quite taken off by the flapping of the bowstring — and of course by the arrow itself as it flies off. Pity, if I were still in my workshop in Hastinapura I could have made a glove for you straight off. But here, in this mess...' Charvaka waved his arms in frustration. 'So, my boy,' he continued, 'what are you going to call your first bow?'

'This isn't quite my first, sire. I made one out of a branch at home.'

'It can't have been much of a bow if you still have the skin on your hand! Well?... What are you going to call your first *real* bow?'

'But sire, why should bows have names?'

'My boy, it's an all too common human weakness these days to endow such valued objects as bows with a certain unwillingness to share. Modelled no doubt on the example of their owners. Apparently this first real bow of yours is not content merely to share that description, which could equally well have fallen on any other of the bows you might have chosen in its stead. No, apparently objects don't properly signify in the scheme of things unless they are dignified with their very own proper name. Even worse, people seem to think that names don't properly signify unless they have their very own object to designate. So, why not join your fellows and partake in these follies. Eh?'

'No, sire, I won't give it a name.'

'Are you sure, my boy? It's often wiser to share in the foolishness around you than to work up your own.'

Karna thought for a moment before replying.

'I think I'd rather do my own foolishness, sire.'

'Excellent!' Charvaka beamed at Adhi-ratha. 'You have here a boy after my own heart. Well, I look forward to working with you again, Karna, eh? In a few months' time... Let's say six months, then I can get ready and tidy my bench. Be sure to bring him back, Adhi-ratha... Before you go, my friend, let me give you some lizard skin. And a pair of rather superior bows to take to a kshatriya I know in Anga. It will give you an introduction. I think he will be more than willing to teach your boy in exchange for them, eh?'

◊

On the ride back Karna was not so keen on driving the horses. He would not let go of his new bow. But though his son was happy, Adhi was concerned about what Narada had hinted regarding Charvaka.

'Karna, listen carefully. Narada warned me that Charvaka, although he was very knowledgeable... was not entirely good.'

'Not good? I like him, father?'

'But... Narada did say to be careful. I'm not sure if we can trust this man...'

'I trust him, father.'

Adhi was much relieved. He had great confidence in his son's judgement, in spite of Karna's lack of years.

'But you will tell me if he is in any way... bad. Won't you, Karna?'

'Yes, father. I like him. He's not like other people. And he likes me, father. He would not try to harm me.' After a pause he asked, 'Father, why do you trust Narada and not Charvaka?'

Adhi did not reply.

'Next time, father, he doesn't want more clarified butter. He wants something he can eat straight away.'

8 Karna leaves home

The kshatriya in Anga whom Charvaka had in mind to teach the young Karna was a little hesitant at first. But after a few lessons Karna's aptitude made it easy for the warrior to forget about other considerations, and concentrate instead on the art of the bow.

However, during his very first stay in Varanasi with Charvaka, Karna decided thenceforth to take lessons only from the ratha there, whose technique was superior to the Angan fighter.

Over the next few years Karna went to stay with Charvaka as often as he could. And with the rishi he learnt not only to read and write, but all that he could assimilate about the construction of bows, the different types of arrow, the seasoning of wood, the preparation of bowstrings, the various materials and metals which Charvaka used, and a dozen other skills. Indeed, by the time Karna was twelve he knew as much about these things as any of the kshatriyas in Anga. There were even some matters, particularly anatomy and the treatment of wounds, about which he was already much more of an expert than these local warriors. Charvaka had taught him not only all the vital points to aim for on the torso, but also points where an arrow might pass through the body without damage, or where he could temporarily disable an opponent without lasting injury.

As regards his actual skill with the bow, his progress was exceptional. There were one or two experienced rathas in Anga who were as fast as he was. His small hands could not yet handle as many arrows as could a grown man. But none had his accuracy of aim. Already from the age of nine he had been winning all the competitions in Anga.

Although he remained a quiet boy, he was now able to relax more with other people. Or rather, for it was really the other way round, people were no longer so uncomfortable in his presence. It is true, the kshatriyas and brahmanas were not very enthusiastic about his activities. But since he was only a young boy, they did not need to take him too seriously. They tended to regard him as a passing oddity, a transient phenomenon who would gradually merge into the humbler rank of the suta as he grew older. For the same reason they tolerated his lack of deferential respect. For he had followed Charvaka's advice, and resolutely refused to bow to those who considered themselves his superiors.

There was one thing about which the local brahmanas would take issue with Karna: Charvaka. They would try to question why Karna went to see him.

Some believed outright that it was wrong for Karna to be taught by Charvaka. They even warned Adhi and Radha.

But when Karna tried to get the brahmanas to explain what was wrong with Charvaka, all they would say was that he was evil. He had after all, they told him, been banished from Hastinapura.

'For your own good we tell you this, Karna: be wary of Charvaka. He was known in Hastinapura as an evil man. Some say that it was only the fact that he was a great friend of Bhishma's which saved his life. It is said that he worships a strange goddess, Kali.'

The lower castes, on the other hand, appeared to have no objection to Karna's training under Charvaka. If anything, they were grateful to the rishi. For they were proud of Karna's achievements, despite his solitary and undemonstrative nature. They even had become openly warm and affectionate to the boy.

Now that he was growing physically, his ear-rings no longer stood out as much. And people seemed to have forgotten about his second skin. He certainly did his best never to reveal it. His mother had taught him how to add the extra links himself, so that he could continue enlarging his golden corselet while he was away.

In Varanasi, when he stayed with Charvaka, he was accepted more easily than he had been in Anga, as a strange but interesting visitor. He did not himself make friends readily with the other children there. But when he was ten, or thereabouts, he had started taking his little brother Vrisha with him to see the rishi. Vrisha, who was five years younger than Karna, had been keen to learn to read and write like his elder brother. And it was through Vrisha that Karna had begun to mix more with the children of Varanasi. For Vrisha, though the youngest, was the most talkative and inquisitive of the family.

◊

'What impresses me most of all is that he doesn't seem to need to impress...'

'It's still your throw, Charvaka...'

'When he releases the arrow he really does aim it at the target. Not at us, not at the hearts of the spectators, nor at his teachers, nor at his rivals... And yet —'

'You didn't tap!'

'What? Oh... I'm sorry, Shakuni —'

'Charvaka! Please! I thought it was a bit strange aiming for a common on a tiger. And I know your paddock is a little insecure, but if the dice rolls out of it you must throw it again.'

'I'm sorry... Yes... And yet he knows what impression he's making. He has a quite remarkable ability to concentrate, to narrow down on what he's doing, while retaining complete awareness of what's going on around him. I haven't come across it before, not to this extent...'

'Yes, my dear, certainly not in yourself at the moment — what exactly are you thinking of? Is that a blocking bet or are you laying eggs? And could you kindly not fiddle with the dice when I'm throwing! Go on, put it back in the dice bowl...'

'Sorry, Shakuni... But you know, his vision really is remarkable. The mongoose doesn't have it. Certainly not Drona. Nor Satyaki or Bhuri. With the boar it's rather difficult to tell... Of course, I never saw Parashu when he was this boy's age, but I definitely think Karna is as good if not better than Bhishma when I first saw him — and I think Bhishma must have been a couple of years older.'

'You really think he will be better than Bhishma? Why? What is Bhishma good at?'

'Shakuni! Aagh! You distracted me on purpose!'

'I'm sorry, Charvaka, but I touched down first. In any case, your bet's in the wrong column! Excellent, another thirty-two for striking the limit...'

'I don't think I like playing dice with you, Shakuni... Where did I go wrong?'

'My dear, it's better to lose the lion than leave the tiger. And just what do you think it's like for me? My sister has four, five boys now? I've lost count. But she still gives me a good game and manages to do so without mentioning her offspring once! Let alone boasting about them. Not that she has very much scope there, poor thing. Though Dur is an interesting boy... I came to Varanasi to get away from my own unpleasant child and nephews, and what do I get? Barely interrupted drivel about this Karna of yours. It really is quite unlike you, Charvaka. And by the way, one of the Pandava boys is supposed to be the best thing since his father Indra, so I expect your boy will meet his match there. Yes, Pritha's youngest... Arjuna... Really, Charvaka, the least you can do in exchange for my having to endure your effusions is to enlighten me with a little divine gossip. Is this Karna's mother a goddess as well?'

'Shakuni... You know I'm not going to tell you. Get on with the game.'

'What game? You call this...'

'Ah! Here we are! That is Karna, the bigger one. The little one is Vrisha. My boys, this is Shakuni, a friend of mine from Gandhara.'

Karna nodded his head and Vrisha bowed with considerable zest.

'Sire,' started Vrisha, as soon as he was upright again, 'is it wrong to kill a mouse?'

'Not now, Vrisha —'

'No, Charvaka, answer him,' urged Shakuni. 'It's an excellent question, my dear,' he said to Vrisha. 'I only wish my own son would ask me something. All he ever asks is *for* something. Well, Charvaka? Enlighten the boy!'

'Vrisha, I'm not sure your question has an answer.'

'Typical!' interjected Shakuni. 'Don't stand for it, Vrisha!'

'That is precisely the problem,' rejoined Charvaka. 'You see, Vrisha, standing in one place, your question does indeed have an answer, and an answer which is very easy to find out. But standing in another place, your question has no answer at all. In any case, my boy, even if I knew whether it was wrong to kill a mouse, I'm not sure it wouldn't be wrong of me to *tell* you.'

'But sire,' persisted Vrisha, 'all the other boys know.'

'Do they? Well, what do they say, then?'

'Some say yes and some say no, sire.'

'Really? And how do they obtain these excellent answers?'

'They asked their parents, sire. Their parents told them. But I can't go back to Anga just to find out, so you'll have to tell me, sire.'

'No, my boy... I suggest you pick one of your little friends and then go and ask his parents. After all, if they're good enough for your friend, they're good enough for you. There, you see, it's really quite an easy question to answer if you stand in the right place.'

'But sire, how do the parents know the answer if you don't,' objected Vrisha. 'You're the rishi. You're supposed to know more than they do. How do they know?'

'That is quite another question,' returned Charvaka. 'It may also be answered, of course, but in a different way. One way is not fit for all. So please, Vrisha, one question at a time. If you try to ask everything in one voice, you will only babble. Now, off you go...'

The next day Charvaka obliged his friend by trying to concentrate on the game. They were again interrupted by Vrisha and Karna; but by this time Shakuni had beaten Charvaka so often, in spite of the rishi's efforts, that they were both glad of the diversion.

Again Vrisha bowed low to Shakuni, who nodded in acknowledgement. 'Have you another good question for this bad rishi?'

'Yes, sire.' Vrisha turned to Charvaka. 'Sire, what is the meaning of life?'

'Vrisha! What sort of question is that!'

'They told me it's the sort you're supposed to ask a rishi, sire. They said the question about the mouse was probably too easy for you, sire. But Karna thinks this new question can't be answered, even by a rishi.'

'Oh, does he?' Charvaka looked at Karna. 'Again, boys, it depends where you are standing when you ask it.'

'I can't imagine it having an answer,' said Karna.

'Perhaps not if *you* were to ask it,' said Charvaka. 'But I think I can imagine circumstances where it may be both asked and satisfied. Yes... Suppose a glorious being descends from the sky, speaks to you, explains to you that he is the Emperor of the Moon, and that he made this world of ours from dust for his own amusement. Eh? He then proceeds to explain everything you ask him about this world and your life within it. And you are satisfied. Well, your question would be answered.'

'But what would be the meaning of the Emperor's life?' asked Karna.

'Ah, now that is another question. And that too may be answerable. But, in my view, you cannot ask a question that hopes to answer *everything* — and still make sense. One net, after all, will not catch all fish. You have to size the mesh for the catch you seek. But, if you can sensibly describe the fish, then you can sensibly describe the net to catch it with. On the other hand, if you don't even know what sort of fish you're after, well... As I say, one net will not catch all fish.' Charvaka turned to Vrisha. 'There, my boy. Is that the sort of answer you were expecting from your rishi?'

'I think his excellent question deserved a much better answer,' exclaimed Shakuni. 'Ah! If only my son were interested in questions rather than things! Tell me, Vrisha, if this Emperor of the Moon really did descend from the sky, and offered you one wish, absolutely anything you wanted, what would you ask for?'

'Could I really ask for anything at all?'

'Of course. He's the Emperor of the Moon. One wish, but anything at all, any thing or any answer. What would you ask for?'

Vrisha looked up at the ceiling as if imagining the event.

'I'd ask for two wishes.'

'Oh!' Shakuni slapped his thigh. 'Excellent! Excellent, my dear!'

◊

The time came, just after the thirteenth anniversary of Adhi and Radha's discovery of the baby Karna, when Charvaka advised them that the boy was now ready to go to Hastinapura.

A crowd of people, mostly sutas and shudras, gathered to send him off on the day he was due to leave. Radha and Adhi were both anxious, but Karna's brothers were very excited. Vrisha had managed to convince everyone that he had to keep his father company on the lonely journey back. The other two, Sangra and Pra, looked forward to making the trip themselves to visit Karna once he had settled in.

Since Varanasi was on the way, the travellers had arranged to stop off for a day at Charvaka's. This would also enable the rishi to give Karna some details to prepare him for his arrival in Hastinapura.

'I have sent a message to Kripa saying that you are a suta seeking employment as a chariot driver to the princes.'

Charvaka and his pupil were taking a leisurely walk, partly so that they could be alone; partly so that the rishi could show off a new plough he had designed, which was being put to work in a field nearby.

In one of these respects they failed immediately. For Vrisha was following behind them, not so close, he felt, as to be actually with them; yet not so far as to be unable to catch their conversation.

'I didn't tell him anything about you,' continued Charvaka. 'All I said was that you were modest. Kripa values modesty. Now, my boy, when Kripa interviews you, make sure you are alone with him. If not, make some excuse to speak to him alone. Then, when you are sure there's no one else around, just take your jerkin off.'

'What, just like that? Without any... Should I crouch down and bite his knees as well?'

'You then tell him,' went on Charvaka, ignoring Karna's remark, 'that Charvaka thinks you should train with the princes, under Kripa himself, to become a warrior. The owl will tu-whit and the owl will tu-whoo. He will run his left hand through his hair, and then his right. Then he will accept you. It's as simple as that, my boy.'

'Won't he want to ask me any questions?'

'He might. But you must understand, Karna, that though Kripa is, shall we say, suspicious of me, he, unlike some of the other brahmanas there, does have some respect for me.'

'Is Kripa a brahmana?'

'Oh yes.'

'And he is in charge of training the princes in the art of combat? Can he use the bow?'

'The owl can most certainly use the bow! He is not so good in attack. But his defence is impeccable. Mind you, he is ageing. Not like the boar. Bhishma is amazing for his age. You would just not believe, if you saw him, that he is my age! Karna, you rather surprise me with your prejudice about brahmanas.'

'It's just that the brahmanas I've met, round home, well...'

'My boy, there are as many kinds of brahmana as there are kinds of people. Even more, perhaps.'

'How's that possible?' came Vrisha's voice from behind.

'Well...' Charvaka answered without turning round or slowing his pace. 'You see, there are some brahmanas who are hardly people at all... And may I remind you, Karna, I am, after all, a brahmana.'

'Yes but I don't think of you as one...' With resignation in his voice Karna added, 'I know, sire, nor should I think of anyone but as the one that they are... What should I say if Kripa asks me about my origins?'

'As I say, I think you will find that Kripa will readily accept you. But if he enquires about your true parentage, if and only if he asks you, you may tell him about Surya. But to no one else, absolutely no one else. Do you understand me?'

'Yes, sire.'

'They would laugh at you, at best. Also, take care never to reveal your armour to anyone else. If by chance you have to, try to make nothing of it. You are probably expert enough at that by now. No, my boy, you must be the son of a suta. And why not? It is nothing to be ashamed of.'

'Even when I train with the princes?'

'Especially when you train with the princes. Let the princes worry about it. Don't bow to them, or anything like that. But don't try to conceal the fact that you're a suta. Wear your sash. In any case, they're still young. The Pandava twins may not even have started yet — they must be about Vrisha's age.'

'And what about that other person you mentioned, Bhishma. Who exactly is he?'

'Bhishma! That old boar and I have known each other since... Since we were hardly older than you. Though we did not really become friends until later. As I said, he hardly seems to have aged. It's remarkable. And yet he's the oldest living member of the Bharata royal family. Now that his uncle Balhika has died. Bhishma is the eldest son of the great King Shantanu. Balhika was Shantanu's younger brother. Shantanu also had another brother, Devapi, a year or two older. But I'm not sure what became of him.'

'Is Bhishma the king, then?'

'No, most definitely not. That's a long story, my boy. He could have been king. But no, he is not. If he were to wish to, he could still be the most powerful Bharata alive. But he does not wish it... As a matter of fact, it is Bhishma who is officially in charge of the education of the Bharata princes, since he is ultimately in charge of all the military affairs of the kingdom. But I doubt you will see him much... If you do see him, my boy, just keep well out of his way, eh?'

'Why?'

'Well... For one thing, I'm not at all sure what he would be like with juveniles. I suppose he may have had more experience of them now, with all these royal princes... But just do as I say. Avoid him... And, whatever you do, make sure you never have to fight against him!'

'Why?'

'Why? Because, like the fish who never returned to tell tale of the heron, you would not live two seconds. Bhishma is the greatest ratha in the land.'

'What does that mean?' chirped the voice of Vrisha.

'What it says,' replied Charvaka without looking round.

'Is he the biggest?'

'No, the greatest.'

'But what's that *mean*?' persisted Vrisha.

'It means, my boy, that if anyone were foolish enough to engage Bhishma in single combat with the bow, Bhishma would defeat them. Is that sufficiently clear for you, or do you want me to elaborate on the nature of defeat?'

'But I've got a friend whose father says that elephants are the greatest animals in the world. I know they can't be the biggest, 'cos you've told me that whales are even bigger. Does that mean that if an elephant fought a whale the elephant would win?'

'No, Vrisha,' said Charvaka patiently, though still without looking round. 'What your friend's father probably meant was that of all the animals in the world, the elephant impresses him the most.'

'Why didn't he just say *that*, then?'

'Because he was so impressed,' explained Charvaka, 'that he wished to dress the shapeless body of the subjective in the tailored clothes of the objective. Or in plainer words, Vrisha, he wished to draw a purple robe over a pig.'

'But what about Parashu-rama?' interrupted Karna. 'I thought you said once that *he* was the greatest?'

'Did I? Parashu is certainly the greatest teacher, which Bhishma is most certainly not, even if he were so inclined. And Parashu knows more; he is better all round with the bow. But when it comes to combat... It's true that when they did fight each other they ended up defeating each other... But you see, Parashu had been Bhishma's teacher. Bhishma was not out to kill him.'

'Parashu is still alive, isn't he?'

'Oh yes.'

'But he must be even older than Bhishma.'

'Only by a few years.'

'And were they young when they fought each other?'

'No... Not what you would call young. It was about a year before you were born, Karna... But you're right. If anyone could ever stand up to Bhishma, it was Parashu, the old mongoose. No, it will be some years before you should dare to engage the likes of them, even in practice. All in good time. Meanwhile, Karna, do try to be... shall we say, discreet about your own talent. With the princes, I mean. There is no need to antagonise them. Though I hear that young Arjuna is very promising. Do you understand me?'

'Yes, sire. Charvaka... Why exactly can't you go back to Hastinapura?'

'You know I'm banished.'

'Yes, but why? What are you guilty of?'

'My boy, I cannot easily explain it to you. Not now. When you are older, perhaps... You see, according to them I am not only guilty of wrongdoing, I also double my guilt by trying to justify it, thereby inducing others to repeat it. Others, such as you.'

'Tell me, sire... Vrisha!' Karna looked round. 'Try and walk more slowly... Go on, sire.'

'Very well. In any case, I think it's probably too late with you. Either I have already influenced you, or you yourself are naturally guilty... But it is not easy for me to explain how they see me... I think it's this... You see, if the great Brahma himself were to come out of the ground and speak to me, I would take his words at their own merit, no more, no less. I cannot conceive a sentence whose authority is determined by the colour of its ink rather than the import of its meaning.

'But the result', continued Charvaka, 'is these brahmanas think that because they can see no *thing* which I hold sacred, I indeed hold nothing sacred. And therefore, that I have no morality. They think that because I constantly raise objections to their views, I only wish to destroy, and have nothing to construct. What they don't realise is that nothing lasting can be put up without first attempting to pull it down in the imagination. Otherwise, if like them you only seek to find support, you build a flesh of wishful evidence without the bones to stand the touch and test of exercise.'

'But you do hold something sacred, sire. You hold your judgement sacred.'

'Ah! But that is what they don't like. I should at least hold sacred the judgement of my betters.'

'But how can you judge who is your better without trusting your own judgement?'

'My boy, I think for them judgement of any sort is too cold and fastidious a means of directing the passion of one's reverence.'

'But sire, how can anyone avoid it? Even if you accept something only because you trust and respect the person, it must be because at some point you've passed judgement on that person. Or at least you've passed judgement on whoever it was who told you to listen to that person. Isn't it in the end only your own judgement that stops you just accepting *anything*? So in the end you've got to hold your own judgement sacred above all else. You must hold your own dharma sacred, above all.'

'Is that not arrogance, my boy?'

'Only if you shake your head, sire. They don't call it arrogance when you nod humbly in agreement, do they? What's the nod for if it's not for passing judgement? It would be even worse to nod without passing judgement. Wouldn't *that* be leaving dharma?'

'Ah, Karna, I wish it were as simple as that...'

'But were you banished for *this*?'

'Well, this sort of thing. It's not easy to explain a view which one cannot oneself see.'

'They tortured you, sire, didn't they?'

'Well, they tied me down in the snow, up in the mountains. Yes, they put me out naked with no food, waiting for me to recant... But it was more uncomfortable for them than for me. They had to keep climbing up to see if I was ready to submit...'

They walked on in silence for a while. Then the rishi stopped.

'Karna, you know that I have always preferred to give you knowledge, rather than what some call wisdom... I have always preferred to show you how you can satisfy your desires, your ambitions; rather than to tell you which of those desires to satisfy. I did not want to turn you, but to help you on...'

'You have sometimes told me which desires it would be *wise* for me to satisfy.'

'Yes, that's true. But I hope never which desires it would be *right* for you to satisfy. If there is such a wisdom which can tell you this, I certainly don't have it. To that extent, what little wisdom I do have admits of its own folly. Well, my boy, I'm sad... I don't want to go on and look at this plough. Let's go back.'

They walked back in silence.

The next morning they got up early so that Charvaka's visitors could continue their journey to the big city. As they were making ready to leave, Charvaka presented Karna with two fine wooden bows. One was a little on the large side, for him to grow into. The rishi also gave Karna a pair of quivers containing an assortment of arrows.

'These ones here...' he said, picking out some slim metal arrows with extremely sharp points and no flight feathers, 'these can pass through almost any armour, and would go straight through a man if you were to hit the right spot. Always keep them greased, or the metal will corrode.'

'Charvaka, why won't you ever explain to me about *my* armour? And my ear-rings. When are you going to tell me about those?'

'When you're older, my boy, when you're older...' Charvaka replaced the metal arrows in one of the quivers. 'There are some other weapons I would like you to have had, but I think Drona has them. Though I'm not sure he knows I made them. Unfortunately I haven't the materials at the moment to reconstruct them — I would have to go to Hastinapura.'

'Who exactly is Drona?'

'Drona... He is another brahmana. Yes, another brahmana who can shoot with the bow. Rather more gifted than Kripa, especially in attack. But I don't know what's become of him. The last I heard, a few years ago, he was living in the woods near Hastinapura. Plotting revenge against King Drupada, I think.'

'Revenge?'

'Yes. You see, Drona's father was a most learned and austere rishi called Bharadwaja —'

'I thought rishis weren't supposed to...'

'Generally speaking, my boy, that is correct. Rishis are supposed to be able to control their sensual appetites. They are supposed to learn not to experience the presence of physical desire as uncomfortable, but as just another item of consciousness, from which the inner gaze may be averted. However, Drona's mother, Ghritachi, combined an especial liking for rishis with the most articulate charms. With which she delighted to transform, I can hardly say reduce, the most austere ascetic into a trembling fountain of desire. Yes, most uncomfortable... Indeed, I think the only other woman I have met who was quite so difficult to ignore was Pritha, wife to the good King Pandu. How Pandu managed, no one will ever know... Where was I... Oh yes, Drona... Yes, Ghritachi bore Bharadwaja two children — you see, in any case, what the world perceives as abstinence need only be one stage in the life of a rishi. He may go on to become a married householder like other people. Well, Ghritachi's children by Bharadwaja were Drona and his sister Sruta-vati.

'Now,' continued Charvaka, 'among the children whom Bharadwaja taught, in his capacity as rishi, and alongside his own two children, was Drupada, son of the king of Panchala. Drupada became very friendly with his fellow pupil Drona, and used to tell him, so Drona claims at any rate, that when he became king of Panchala he would give Drona half his kingdom.

'One imagines that Drona did not take Drupada's youthful promise too seriously. Nevertheless, he evidently allowed himself to hope for some generosity from Drupada. A position as tutor, for example. But when Drupada did become king, and Drona approached him in the midst of his court, he was sent away. Drupada did not want to be associated with a poor brahmana, a beggar in rags. Friendship is only possible between equals, Drupada is supposed to have told him. This is how Drona likes to describe it, anyway. I suspect there may be another side. As I say, I know that Drona swore vengeance on Drupada. But I'm not sure what he did to pursue it after that.'

'Where did Drona learn his archery?'

'Mainly from the mongoose, from Parashu. Yes, yet another student of his. And Parashu has the annoying habit of lending to his most promising students some of his finest weapons. But listen, my boy, another time — look at the sun — I mustn't detain you. You have a long journey ahead. Take care, my boy. Go on, up you get, I'll pass you these... Remember your exercises. And your target practice. Don't stop doing them just because you have a new teacher who gives you something else... And remember, you'll be entirely on your own. Look before you trust. Question any claim under which people can shelter for their own advantage. Watch for what men are, not for what they say they are... You know, sometimes I think it's only the deaf who see people as they really are... Give my regards to Kripa!'

•

'Palmira...'

'Yes, Henry?'

'You know this business about Charvaka staying out in the snow?'

'I do.'

'Didn't Socrates do something like that?'

'Yes he did, though he wasn't forced to, like Charvaka.'

'Palmira...' began the other Henry.

'Yes, Henry?'

'You know this business about Charvaka's... Charvaka's wisdom admitting it was folly?'

'I do.'

'Didn't Socrates say something like that... that his wisdom was that he knew he was a fool?'

'Yes, I believe he did say something like that.'

'Palmira!' Henry looked at his brother. 'I bet that's the reason she put the bit about the snow near the bit about wisdom.'

'To see if we'd notice! Admit it, Palmira!'

'Naturally. But only so that I could punish your interruption by telling you the story of when the Hodja himself spent a night out in the snow.'

The boys opened their mouths in disbelief. Palmira smiled innocently at them as she readjusted the cushion behind her.

'And now that you so kindly fell for it,' she continued, 'I'll tell it to you.

'The interesting thing,' she began, 'is that whilst Socrates stood out in the snow barefoot all night for no other reward than the satisfaction of self-mastery; and whilst poor Charvaka experienced it with no other satisfaction than the denial to others of mastery over himself — the Hodja did it just for *money*!

'You see, some of the Hodja's friends had proposed a bet to the Hodja, one very cold winter:

'"If you can stand all night in the snow in the village square, without moving out of a small circle, and you do not warm yourself with any sort of heating device external to your body, then, if you succeed, we will cook you the most delicious dinner, with the very finest ingredients. But if you fail, you'll have to provide us with the dinner."

"'Fine, it's a bet," said the Hodja. He thought how much money he would save on not having to make his own dinner.

'Well, that night the Hodja stood out there, like Socrates himself. Mind you, he had boots on, which Socrates had discarded. And of course, Socrates didn't have a turban to keep his head warm. The Hodja shuffled from foot to foot, but he did try to remain at all times within the small circle.

'To make sure that he didn't cheat, the Hodja's friends had arranged a shift where each of them took turns to sit at a window overlooking the square. From there they could see the Hodja. And all that night the Hodja could see someone watching him from that window.

'However, when morning came he had indeed managed to remain within the small circle. So he triumphantly claimed his dinner.

"'But Hodja," they cried, laughing, "you've lost your bet! Didn't you notice us all night at the window?"

"'Of course I did! You saw I didn't move from the circle!"

"'True, but how is it that you could see us in the dark?"

"'You kept a candle burning at the window all night. I saw it."

"'There you are then, you've lost your bet. You warmed yourself with the heat of that candle! And the conditions of the bet said very clearly that you were not allowed to use the heat of any external device!"

'Well, you can imagine how infuriated the Hodja was. However, he was clearly obliged under the terms of the bet to cook them a grand dinner.

'All his friends arrived in very good spirits that night, because the Hodja was a very fine cook. They sat around, laughing and joking. "No hard feelings, eh?" and all that sort of thing. And they waited for the dinner to be served. And they waited. Dinner was taking a very long time.

"'Don't worry, boys, it's cooking, it's cooking," said the Hodja every few minutes, going into the kitchen every so often to see how it was progressing.

'After several hours of this, they'd all had enough. They marched into the kitchen. And what did they see? A huge cooking pot, filled with the most delicious-looking stew, hanging over one rather small candle.

"'Hodja! What's the meaning of this?"

"'You should know. If it was possible for me to keep warm with the flame of a candle at fifty paces, surely this cauldron, with a flame actually in contact with it, will heat up in no time at all!"

'Well boys,' continued Palmira, 'I expect *you* must have dinners waiting for you at home. Shall we start up again tomorrow, after my siesta?'

'Yes, all right.'

'You don't have to — I don't want to force you to listen to my story. If you've had enough of it already —'

'No, it's all right, we'll listen tomorrow.'

'Oh Palmira,' said the first Henry, as an afterthought. 'You know that bit about leaving Dharma... You did say he was a god, didn't you?'

'Ah, yes, you see there are two words. One is Dharma the god. And the other is what he was the god of, dharma, which is moral judgement, conscience, the ability to tell right from wrong, that sort of thing.'

'Oh, that reminds me, Palmira. If Karna's right, how can we ever be *taught* to tell right from wrong? I mean, if we know it *already*, then we're not being taught it. But if we don't know it already, how do we know that what we're being taught is *right*?'

'We might be getting taught any old thing, Palmira, and never realise that it's any old thing, since we don't know yet how to tell right from wrong.'

'Boys, you better go and have your dinner now, before I give you any old answer. Off you go!'

•

Day Two: *The Academy*

9 The reception

'Modesty carries very little weight in one who can boast no other recommendation.'

Kripa was walking along a grand corridor towards his quarters at the royal palace of King Dhrita-rashtra. With him was Sanjaya, the king's ceremonial chariot driver.

'Nevertheless,' continued Kripa, 'Charvaka would not have sent this boy to us without some reason. I should therefore be obliged if you would put him through his paces. But really I cannot imagine why Charvaka has gone to such trouble to introduce a young suta to our establishment. We have never been short of good drivers. The boy will need to prove exceptional or we shall simply have to return him to Anga.'

Kripa and Sanjaya turned into Kripa's ante-room. Waiting for them there was the young suta he had been talking about.

'Young man,' said Kripa, 'your name is Karna, I believe.'

'Yes, sire,' answered Karna, coming forward from between two pillars at the centre of the chamber.

'I am told only that you are modest. Have you nothing else to boast of?'

Karna thought for a second.

'I have, sire, but I've been brought up to hide it.'

'To hide it?' Kripa turned to Sanjaya. 'He hides his talent beneath a show of modesty. Well, young man,' hecontinued, returning to Karna, 'show us what you have to hide.'

'Sire, may I speak with you alone?'

The brahmana was slightly taken aback. For a moment he hesitated, glancing at the chariot driver. Something about the boy's face decided him, and he motioned to Sanjaya to leave the room.

'Now,' said Kripa when they were alone, 'what have you to tell me, young man?'

Without saying a word Karna took off his sash and shirt. Before Kripa had time properly to take it in Karna stood there naked from the waist up, save for his golden second skin.

Kripa steadied himself against one of the pillars. Then he approached Karna. After looking at the armour, he examined the boy's ear-rings.

'Do you know who your father is?'

'I am the son of the suta Adhi-ratha of Nagakaksha, sire.'

'Do you know who is your real father?'

'I have been told that my father is Surya, sire.'

'Who told you that?'

'The rishi Narada, sire. He told my parents — my suta parents, sire.'

'Narada... And... did Charvaka have anything to say about that?'

'No, sire.'

'But... But you know that you are amnigenous... Did they not mention that?'

'Sire? What do you mean?'

Kripa hesitated. 'It doesn't matter...' He took a deep breath. Again he leant on one of the pillars. His eyes now fixed on Karna's armour. Slowly he took another deep breath.

'Karna...' He indicated the boy's clothes. 'Put your things back on, now...'

Kripa waited until Karna was dressed before continuing.

'What exactly do you want? What do you want me to do?'

'Sire, I wish you to train me with the Bharata princes to become a warrior.'

Kripa stared at Karna. He ran his hands through his hair.

'I do not train the princes any longer. Their teacher is now Drona-charya.' Kripa leant against a pillar. 'There will be problems... I shall ask Drona, but he may refuse. And you must understand this, Karna: you must show your armour to no one. Even more importantly, do not mention to anyone about... Surya. You are a suta, do you understand?'

'Yes, sire.'

'Drona may well refuse to admit a suta to his Academy. But I will ask him. You may go now. Remember what I have advised. One further thing — have you already received any training in archery?'

'I have won all the competitions in Anga, sire.'

'You have? Already? I see... Well... you shall find the competition here a little more vigorous...'

◊

Drona, as Kripa had feared, did not want to admit Karna to his Academy.

'In any case, I have more than enough pupils already. And will have into the foreseeable future, judging by the number of new Kuru princes that our king is producing. But this boy is a suta. Even worse, he has been a pupil of Charvaka.'

This placed Kripa in a very difficult position. For he had no official authority over Drona. After much thought, he decided to consult Bhishma himself.

'Bhishma, your friend Charvaka has sent us a young man of thirteen. Having evidently recognised the boy's early promise, and arranged for him accordingly a rigorous regime of training and education, Charvaka's hopes have been now so much rewarded, through the supremacy of the young boy in the province of

Anga, that his expectations have risen quite beyond any local means. Clearly aware of the unrivalled standards we demand and obtain from the young princes here in Hastinapura, and obviously eager that his young charge should reach his full potential, Charvaka is soliciting us to accept the boy to be trained with the princes.'

'And why not — won't Drona have him?'

'No. He was not agreeable to the suggestion; being, he implied, quite sufficiently provided with pupils in respect of both quality and quantity.'

'That's what he says,' muttered Bhishma with a chuckle. 'What he means is that he won't have anything to do with a pupil of Charvaka's! Drona certainly does not like the mouse. Well, if Drona doesn't want to take him, then why should he? What can we do?'

'Your friend Charvaka clearly believes this is an exceptional child. Even though you have had much more contact with the rishi than I ever have, I should be very surprised indeed if you could recall an occasion when this rishi has requested any favour from us whatsoever. Bhishma, would *you* care to return the child to him?'

'Mmm... It's true... he wouldn't have sent us the boy unless he was exceptional. In any case, you're right, I would find it very hard to turn down a request like this from the mouse. I'm surprised, to be honest, that even Drona has the nerve to refuse him. How many items of that rishi's manufacture would you expect to find on Drona's chariot! Would you like me to have a word with Drona? You know of course that I'm leaving tomorrow, so I haven't much time, but... That's an idea! Kripa, wait till I've gone. Then go on *my* authority to Drona and tell him — *tell* him — to accept the child. At least until I return... Yes, I think that should work. Why not? Yes, that'll do for the moment.'

Bhishma was often away from Hastinapura for quite long periods. Sometimes he would spend time on his own living as a hermit in the woods. Indeed, Bhishma's ability to tolerate hunger and discomfort was legendary, and put most brahmanas to shame. At other times he was called away on military expeditions, usually to assist an ally under attack.

On this occasion, however, Bhishma was to represent the Bharatas at the great Festival of Shiva to be held that year in Kampilya, the capital city of Panchala. This festival in its entirety lasted several months, and was held only once every eleven years, each time at a different city along the Ganges or Yamuna rivers.

When Bhishma went away he invariably left Kripa in charge of military affairs at Hastinapura. This itself was a demanding responsibility. Bhishma would jokingly advise Kripa to keep the gates on the main bridge into the city closed during his absence. Even though of late the Bharatas had been generally peaceable, there was always the possibility of an attack by a hostile king; and against this possibility Bhishma would always keep several chariots absolutely ready at all times, on which he and a few other select warriors, including Drona and Kripa, could lead out the royal guard at a moment's notice. While Bhishma was away it fell to Kripa to take command over such duties.

It had occurred to Bhishma, as he quickly thought over the problem of Charvaka's pupil, that it might do Kripa good to re-exert some authority over Drona. There was no real animosity between Drona and Kripa. On the contrary, Drona had married Kripa's sister, and had already given Kripa a little nephew called Ashwa-tthaman. But although Kripa had stood down graciously as tutor to the princes in favour of his much younger brother-in-law, Bhishma observed that Kripa had begun to feel increasingly threatened in his role as Bhishma's deputy.

As Bhishma had suggested, Kripa waited until he could use his authority as deputy before asking Drona again to accept Karna.

'I'll complain to Bhishma when he returns,' protested Drona. 'I'm not at all happy about this.'

Happy or not, Drona agreed to admit Karna into his Academy.

Kripa had a long talk with Karna before introducing the boy to Drona. He reminded Karna about the need to keep quiet about his origins, explaining that there was enough tension as it was among the Bharata princes themselves. Indeed, he took it upon himself to tell Karna a little about these princes and the royal family they came from.

'Karna, you must understand who these princes are. It is clear to me that Charvaka has told you next to nothing of the history of the Bharatas. Why, I do not understand, since you are obviously well educated with regard to other matters.

'I will start at the beginning,' he commenced, 'with the great King Shantanu, Bhishma's father.'

10 Kripa's history of the Bharatas

'Ganga, the goddess of the Ganges,' recounted Kripa, 'was King Shantanu's first wife. She it was who abandoned her divine nature in order to give birth to Bhishma. Later she abandoned also her husband, and for some years the king withdrew in grief from the company of women.

'Then one day Shantanu met the beautiful Satyavati, and they fell passionately in love. Like Shantanu she already had a son, Vyasa, just a little younger than Shantanu's Bhishma. Vyasa was the offspring of her earlier alliance with the rishi Parashara, and in later life was to develop into a singularly apanthropic individual. Indeed, no one seems to know quite where he is presently living.

'Shantanu was eager to marry Satyavati, but her father, by origin a fisherman, by study highly skilled in the arts of healing, was much concerned that his possible future grandchildren by this projected marriage, and indeed his existing grandson Vyasa, would be cast aside without inheritance in the event that Bhishma should assume the Bharata throne on Shantanu's decease.

'So much concerned was Satyavati's father that he put a strict and heavy condition on the marriage: that neither Bhishma nor any of Bhishma's descendants should ever claim the throne of the Bharatas; which would therefore pass entirely to Satyavati's children.

'Shantanu was in anguish: Bhishma was his pride and joy, and though still only fifteen had already won the respect, admiration and love of the Bharata people. Shantanu was not prepared to sacrifice his son's prospects, and had resolved, however mortifying it would prove, to give up Satyavati.

'But seeing his father's predicament, to which was suddenly added the burden of a life-consuming illness, and, moreover, without telling Shantanu, Bhishma went to speak to the fisherman physician, who of all in the land was best equipped to pluck his father from the river of death. Bhishma gladly and generously offered to renounce all claim to the Bharata throne. But this did not satisfy Satyavati's father: "What if your children, or your children's children, rise up after you to claim the throne as theirs, and then attack my daughter's children, plunging the Bharatas into bloody war?"

'Still without his father's knowledge Bhishma then convened a special court of brahmanas and rishis to witness, in the presence also of Satyavati's father, a most terrible and sacred vow on pain of death: to renounce all claim to the Bharata throne; never to father any children; therefore to remain his whole life celibate. Thus was Satyavati's line made royal and prosperous, while Ganga's stream sank dammed and drained from Bhishma's chastened loins.

'Once made this vow could not be unmade. Poor Shantanu, when he heard of it, would have gladly died of grief; save that for his son's sake now he was obliged to be made well, to enjoy the fruit of such noble sacrifice, rather than spurn it in austerity. So, after marrying his bride he had two sons by her, Chitrangada and Vichitravirya, both of whom died young, not long after their father, and without issue to increase his stock. Vichitravirya did, however, leave two wives, the sisters Ambika and Ambalika, who had been generously won for him by Bhishma at their swayamwara, their future husband being too sickly to take up arms himself.'

'Sire,' interrupted Karna, 'what is a swayamwara?'

'A swayamwara is a ceremony, a tournament, at which a princess chooses her husband. Swayamwara means self-choice. The candidates compete for her favours usually by demonstrating their martial prowess, sometimes even against the resisting force of their own future father-in-law; and she is the victor's prize. These beautiful sisters, Ambika and Ambalika, were thus gained by Bhishma, who was by this time an incomparable ratha. On the death of their husband, Vichitravirya, and mindful of his vow, Bhishma sought out Vyasa, who was now the only surviving son of Satyavati. You must understand, moreover, that it is not unusual in such circumstances for a childless widow to turn, if possible, to her dead husband's brother to provide issue.

'Vyasa, though now thoroughly disinclined to the royal life himself, was persuaded by Bhishma to generate descendants for Satyavati by means of congress with Ambika and Ambalika, this latter pair having to surmount a reluctant apprehension of their own fulfilment, since Vyasa was of an extremely unkempt disposition.'

Kripa stopped the constant pacing with which he had been accompanying his account, and addressed Karna severely.

'You are attending to me?'

'Yes, sire.'

'However, the two offspring of these unions were both deemed inspiring of insufficient confidence to guarantee a secure base for Satyavati's lasting hopes, the first born being blind, the second a rather delicate albino. So, in case neither of these two proved able happily to undertake royal command, and since the princesses were little disposed to repeat their experiences, a shudra woman was discovered who was agreeable to produce with Vyasa a third possible heir to the Bharata kingdom, in the last resort. So it came about that the two boys, the blind Dhrita-rashtra and the pale Pandu, were joined by a third brother, Vidura.

'Disqualification on the grounds of infirmity was a precedent bar to kingship established in the case of Shantanu's leprous brother Devapi, who was successfully encouraged to exchange his royal aspirations for those of a reclusive ascetic.

'It was therefore considered that, of the two Pandu's condition being the lesser handicap for royal duty, the prior right of Dhrita, as first born, could be waived without successional controversy.

'Pandu went on to become a universally loved and respected monarch, neither whose milky complexion nor whose indifference to military affairs deterred either the Princess Pritha, at her swayamwara, or the Princess Madri at hers, from choosing him as husband.

'But sadly, just a few days before substantiating his nuptials, King Pandu was disqualified from siring children following a hunting accident. While on the chase he hastily shot some arrows at what he took to be cavorting deer; but in fact interrupted a brahmana couple, whose prospects were evidently so fatally cut short that mindful more of his precipitate disregard for animal pleasure than of the special iniquity of brahmanacide, which clearly was not here intentional, they felt obliged to devote their expirations to invoke against the person of the king an ingenious curse; with the effect that Pandu was unable even to attempt the siring of progeny upon either of his two wives without the consequence of instantaneous death. You are with me?' asked Kripa, sternly.

'More or less, sire.'

'Fortunately for the endurance of the royal line,' continued Kripa, resuming his aimless pacing, 'Pritha had been the recipient of a boon from the rishi Durvasa. This boon entitled her to summon for her bidding, on up to five separate occasions, any divine agent whom she chose. With the sympathetic encouragement of her husband she used her boon three times to procure the visitations first of Dharma, then of Vayu, and then of Indra himself. Then she generously employed the last two entitlements for the benefit of her co-wife Madri, who was thus able to entertain the Ashwins. Pritha's first child, son of the god Dharma, is Prince Yudhi-sthira. Her second son, by Vayu, god of the winds, is Bhima-sena. And her third son, by Lord Indra, is Arjuna. Madri's sons by the Ashwins are the twins Nakula and Saha-deva.

'Soon after the birth of Prince Bhima, the good King Pandu, sensible of the unfortunate annulment of his elder brother's claim to the throne, and in spite of having been properly and righteously crowned sovereign ruler by the Bharata assembly, resolved to retire to the woods with his family, to live in humility. But before he left he officially installed his brother Dhrita as sovereign, having persuaded the assembly that with the great Bhishma as overseer of military affairs, and the wise Vidura supervisor of internal administration, Dhrita's blindness would prove no impediment to the exercise of royal power.

'Unfortunately, following Pandu's retirement from the affairs of state to those of nature, he succumbed to the curse which he had striven to resist, against his nature, so long and hard. And soon after this experience, surely more amarous than amorous, Madri, his hapless companion in capitulation, joined herself to him also in death. Now Pandu's still recent demise has sown the seeds of discord in the court.

'For the question arises: are the Pandava princes, that's to say, the sons of Pandu — of Pritha and Madri — are they the natural heirs to the throne presently held by King Dhrita, upon the generosity of his deceased brother? Or are the sons of King Dhrita, namely the princes Dur-yodhana, Duh-shasana and their brothers, are *these* boys, the Kuru princes, the next in line? You understand me?'

'Yes, sire.'

'You must also understand that after the good Pandu's death his family returned to Hastinapura. And that now the five Pandava princes, with some of the older Kuru princes, are being trained together at our Academy. And, sadly, there appears to be some antipathy between these two young parties; due more, I must add, to differences of character and temperament than to competing royal ambitions.

'It is into this uneasy setting that you will be introduced. Do you understand me?'

'Yes, sire. How old are the princes, sire?'

'Yudhi is eleven. He is a very perceptive boy, sensitive, studious, and conscientious almost to a fault, as one might expect from the son of Dharma. In fact, he appears to be hardly capable of uttering a single falsehood, of committing a single indiscretion. Bhima is ten, and... very large for his age. Arjuna is nine, but already reflecting the glory of Indra in his prodigious skill with the bow. The twins are eight. Their beauty and intelligence cannot pass unremarked.'

'And the Kuru princes, sire?'

'Dur is twelve, and nearly as large as Bhima. He is a somewhat troublesome child. Duh seems to be a smaller and duller reflection of him. You will also meet more of his brothers there — he has so many. I'm not quite sure which ones attend the Academy at present. Have you any further questions, Karna?'

•

'I have, Palmira,' said the first Henry.

'We didn't understand all of that, you know,' explained the second Henry.

'I shouldn't worry,' replied Palmira. 'Neither did Karna.'

'This Vyasa... Is it just coincidence he's also called Vyasa?'

'I don't know,' said Palmira, 'you would have had to ask my Vyasa's mother.'

'Thank you Palmira, you're being very helpful today.'

'Is that all, boys?'

'Oh, there was one thing... This Pandu, was he as pale as our grandfather?'

'Possibly, though probably not as red and pink as old Henry. Anything else? I must press on, you know, this is already taking longer than I thought it would...'

•

11 Drona

Kripa had arranged for Karna to stay with Sanjaya and his family. Because of the king's blindness, Sanjaya was much more than just Dhrita's official chariot driver. Sanjaya was in this respect more fortunate than other sutas, and enjoyed enough luxury for his household to afford Karna a room of his own.

Sanjaya found Karna more suitable clothes for his new training: some baggy trousers for him to wear instead of his dhoti, which would have tended to come undone during many of Karna's activities at the Academy; and also a little coat. But Karna continued to wear a brown sash round his waist, and a suta's headcloth.

Karna was very comfortable at Sanjaya's, and though the suta family did not find their guest very talkative, they soon became fond of him; even the children, for whom Karna's politeness was regularly held up by their parents as an example to follow.

At first the family tried to find out from him how things were going at the Academy. And they were all naturally intrigued that a suta was privileged to attend it. But they soon saw that Karna was more intent on thinking over the lessons of the day than talking about them. But the children, at least, were compensated for Karna's reluctance to gossip by being allowed to watch his exercises. This they did most evenings, spellbound, till their father finally called them to bed.

Karna devoted two hours each evening to practice and exercise in his room. Charvaka had given him stretches to keep his back supple; for the asymmetry of the bow action tended to cause back problems after some years in warriors who neglected this. Karna also worked to increase his speed. He knew that he was faster than the other boys; but he knew also that he could improve his own technique. Last, and not least, Karna did not forget the breathing exercises Charvaka had taught him.

Although onlookers were not normally allowed inside the Academy, pupils regularly were given the opportunity to display their abilities at exhibitions. Sanjaya had already seen Arjuna perform, and was particularly interested to hear what Karna thought of him. Occasionally Sanjaya's persistence succeeded in drawing a few observations from Karna.

'Don't you think it's like watching a dance?' said Sanjaya to him one meal time. 'When you see little Arjuna working with the bow... His movements are so smooth.'

'Yes, he's very good to watch,' agreed Karna.

'Don't you think he's got Drona's style off exactly? That elegance?'

'Yes. And I prefer watching Arjuna. I think he looks even better than Drona.'

'What about the other princes? How d'you think they're shaping up?'

'They're good compared to what I saw back home in Anga, or in Varanasi,' said Karna. 'But none of them can compare with Arjuna. Not with the bow. Yudhi's quite good with the sword. And he rides well.'

'What about the twins? Don't you think they're impressive? They're even younger than Arjuna, and I don't think they're far behind him, do you? They're very bright, you know, very talented, those two.'

'Yes. I was surprised because I thought they'd be mirror twins, but they're not exactly alike. But they'll probably both be very good warriors.'

'And what do you think of Bhima? D'you know that Dur calls him wolf belly! Have you seen him eat?'

'He's very strong,' said Karna. 'He's incredibly strong. He's the strongest of all of us. Though Dur's strong as well. Bhima's very good with the mace. Though I think Dur's going to be even better.'

'But if you ask me, the Kuru princes aren't in the same class as the Pandava boys.'

'Not with the bow, I suppose. Though I think Dur is just as good as Yudhi or Bhima.'

'Which of the Kurus are there at the moment, apart from Dur and Duh?'

'Vikarna, Chitra-sena and Yuyutsu,' answered Karna. 'And Vivitsu's starting soon, I think.'

There were still more sons of Gandhari, Dhrita's consort, but too young to attend the Academy.

'Sanjaya, why do the other Kuru princes not like Yuyutsu.'

'Don't they like him?'

'I don't know. They don't treat him the same. They treat him more like they treat me.'

'That's probably because Gandhari isn't his mother. He's Dhrita's son, but by a servant. That's probably why...'

Karna himself was used to being an outsider with kshatriyas, so the fact that he was regarded as something of an oddity did not bother him unduly. Of his fellow pupils he got on best with Yudhi, who was always courteous to him, and Dur, who was not, but at least paid him the compliment of acknowledging his existence.

The only other people at the Academy who seemed to take an interest in Karna were little Ashwa, Drona's son, who was usually around watching with great interest, though he was much too young to join in; and a shudra boy of about Karna's age, called Vaitanika. He was a servant of Drona's who helped with the setting up of equipment.

As for Drona himself, his attitude to Karna was quite clear. The day Kripa had introduced Karna to him, Drona took the boy to one side so that Kripa would not hear.

'Bhishma will return in a few months. When he returns, I'm afraid you will no longer be able to stay in the Academy with the princes. Till then, you will be privileged to watch and train with them. You know, I presume, that all five of the Pandava princes are sons of gods? They are already remarkable young warriors, so take care you do not offend them. And the youngest of the three sons of Pritha, Prince Arjuna, he is going to be the greatest ratha of his generation, perhaps the greatest chariot fighter the Bharatas have ever seen. Greater even than Bhishma or Parashu-rama. At his birth the great rishi Narada prophesied that he would conquer all others. So, be attentive to your privilege.'

Drona said very little to Karna over the next few weeks, though Karna did participate with the others. Because of an instinctive unease about Drona's possible reaction, Karna had no difficulty in following Charvaka's advice not to draw attention to himself by revealing his talents. He performed adequately; but was deliberately slow and inaccurate.

There was only one moment in the first few weeks when Karna was forced to stretch himself. He was drawn against Bhima in a practice bout with clubs. Bhima was already much more powerful than Karna, and could easily have injured him badly with a single blow. Since the children normally practised without helmets or armour, they were naturally not supposed to land heavy blows, but only to shape the different striking and blocking moves they were being taught. Unfortunately Bhima lost his temper after a few minutes during which Karna had successfully blocked all his attacks. Karna saw Bhima's eyes flash their anger, and dodged the huge lunge that followed. But Bhima caught hold of his escaping opponent and raised his club to swat Karna's head. Before Drona had time to intervene, Karna trapped Bhima's hand and disarmed him.

The Kuru princes laughed, especially Dur, who hated Bhima; while the other Pandavas, particularly Yudhi, hung their heads in shame.

Drona was very severe with Bhima. But he took the opportunity to speak to them all.

'You must always keep control, not just of your anger, but of all other desires and emotions which can distract your concentration. You must not let pain, jealousy, envy, the desire for revenge or any other motive colour your judgement during a fight. For when you are angry, or under the influence of any strong desire, you will be reckless, you will be blinded, you will launch into actions — as Bhima has just done — which have little probability of success.

Caught in the grip of anger, you will either not care if you fail, or you will persuade yourselves that you will succeed, often in circumstances where more balanced judgement would tell you otherwise. When you are driven by too strong a feeling — whether it is hatred of your opponent or just the terror of pain — you will be seduced by the end into adopting unlikely and untimely means. You must learn always to watch yourselves, not from the midst of your hearts, caught in the turmoil of pain and emotion, but from outside yourselves, as though you were calm spectators, strangers to the struggle within. We brahmanas have learnt to control our emotions. A fighting kshatriya must learn to do this as well as any brahmana.'

Yudhi noticed that Drona's speech only had the effect of making Bhima even more incensed with Karna. So later he also had a long talk with Bhima. For Yudhi, though the least talented of the Pandavas as a warrior, commanded a profound respect and loyalty from his younger brothers. Yudhi also apologised to Karna, offering Karna his hand, which Karna accepted gladly.

'I'm sorry too, Yudhi,' Karna apologised, 'but I'm not as strong as your brother, and I couldn't find a quieter way of defending myself at the time.'

After that incident Yudhi began to take much more notice of Karna. Karna often caught him watching his technique, as though Yudhi were searching to find something he could not quite see.

Fortunately there turned out to be no trouble from Karna's ear-rings or, at least initially, from his armour. Many young men in Hastinapura wore ear-rings, though they were usually in a style which allowed the rings to lie flat along the side of the neck. Karna's tended to stick out, almost at right angles. But the rings themselves were otherwise not too unusual in appearance, and did not attract much attention; though perhaps it was a little unusual for a suta to wear them.

As for Karna's armour, which was always hidden under his shirt, its protective qualities were not much needed in the early weeks at the Academy. The boys used light unpointed wooden practice arrows when they fought each other with bows. For these sessions they wore face guards made of wicker with narrow eye slits. If a practice arrow did hit a boy's body, it would just fall harmlessly to the ground, at worst leaving a bruise.

The fighting technique which the boys were being taught with the bow involved letting fly as many arrows in as short a time as possible. Drona, as an example, could grasp four arrows from his quiver and release them simultaneously from his bow to hit four regularly spaced targets of moderate size, and all in a twinkling.

Though there were many different types of arrow used in combat, there were essentially two broad functions which these arrows served: attack and defence.

For when two combatants were at or near the limit of their bow range, they could each see their opponent's arrows approaching in time to parry them with arrows of their own. In order to baffle their opponents' missiles in this way, fighters would generally use specialised arrows with large, angled feathers. These could deflect oncoming arrows quite easily, especially if sent spinning.

When practising this form of combat, Karna allowed his opponents to strike him frequently on the body. He therefore appeared a good but unobtrusive student. But he realised that performing below his true ability all the time was going to be very bad for his technique. So he began to go out alone to the woods every few days for serious practice, when he could stretch himself without inhibition. He took good care not to be seen by anyone. Generally he chose the rest days at the Academy. But if occasionally he was absent during the day, no one seemed perturbed by his excuses, least of all Drona. And all the while at Sanjaya's he continued his evening routine.

At first he was able to shoot with perfect accuracy only two arrows simultaneously, and even then only at targets which were set at the same height and less than a pace apart. After a few weeks in the woods he was able to hold four arrows comfortably in his hand. Though with four arrows his accuracy was much more variable. But he had noticed that even Drona could only shoot four arrows accurately when the targets where placed at regular intervals and at the same height. He continued to persevere. Slowly, alone in the woods, Karna made progress.

Karna did come up against a problem with his armour when Drona put his students to work on wrestling technique. There was nothing he could do but lock with his opponents in a clinch. His first partner, Dur, immediately noticed the hard scaly texture under his shirt. Why did he wear armour for wrestling? And why did he wear it underneath his shirt, instead of over his clothing, like kshatriyas? But Karna had prepared his explanation.

'Oh... Don't you know that it's the custom for sutas always to wear armour next to the skin?' And Karna was happy to elaborate.

'If you're a chariot driver for a kshatriya, it's very dangerous because you might get hit by the opponent's arrows by mistake, even though they're not supposed to aim for drivers. So we still need to wear armour. But you don't want to risk being mistaken for your ratha by showing your armour. So we wear it next to the skin, underneath our clothes.'

Karna had prepared further embroidery to try to justify his wearing the armour for wrestling. But the little kshatriya princes seemed satisfied with the fundamental fact that he was different from them. And Karna was able to give similar excuses to explain why he never went swimming with the princes. 'It is a custom among the sutas where I come from. We only bathe alone, in private.'

'What's it like, being a suta?' asked Yudhi.

'I'm not sure what you mean.' replied Karna.

'Well, you have all these different customs...'

'Yes... But that doesn't make me know what it's like to be a suta.'

'Why not?'

'Because I'm only one suta. Just because you see that I have things in common with other sutas doesn't mean I feel them the same. Do you know what it's like to be a kshatriya?'

'No... I suppose not... But I do know that I don't get treated like the sutas.'

'I know how sutas get treated. I can see that, just as you can. But I can't see what it feels like for other sutas, any more than you can.'

'Yes, but you talk to them, you listen to them...' Yudhi saw the traces of a smile appearing on Karna's face. Guessing that Karna was not willing to continue on this topic, but still curious himself, Yudhi changed direction slightly.

'But Drona doesn't like you... He doesn't want to teach you because you are a suta... That must be hard for you...'

'Yes, it is hard for me. I think at the beginning it was true, he didn't like me training with you because I was a suta. But to be fair to Drona, I think it's *me* he doesn't like now. I don't think Drona would like me even if I was a kshatriya or a brahmana.'

Yudhi smiled.

'What was Kripa like?' asked Karna, trying to move the subject away from himself. 'He taught you before Drona, didn't he?'

'Yes, and I think he was a bit upset when Drona arrived and took over.'

'How did that happen?'

'Drona turned up one day... We'd just finished work and were playing outside before dinner, when this man called over to us. He was thin and dressed like a beggar. He was very black then, from having spent so much time wandering around in the open.

'He asked which of us was Yudhi-sthira, and I said I was, and he asked for my ring, just to look at it, he said. I didn't trust him at first. He said he was a brahmana, but he had a huge bow and a quiver full of arrows. Most brahmanas we knew didn't carry a bow. Except for Kripa. But he pointed to his white belt and said he was a brahmana, and said we could hold his bow and quiver while he looked at my ring. Well, I could have shot him with his bow, even though it was too big for me, so I let him examine my ring while I held his weapons. Then he asked for just one arrow, he said he wanted to know if his arrow could fit through the ring. So he tried, well, a couple of arrows, until one just fitted through the ring. Then he gave me back the arrows, and started looking around.

'Nearby was a well. It was dry that time of year, you could see the bottom. And he looked down the well, and then he dropped my ring down it!

'I was very cross, and Bhima wanted to kill him straight away. But the man was very calm, just smiling... Can't you get the ring out, he said... You call yourselves kshatriya princes!... I'll show you how to get the ring out. We couldn't see how it was possible, because the well was very narrow. We couldn't climb down it. All we could see was the ring glinting at the bottom. Drona said if we gave him his bow back, he would show us how to get it out, all he wanted was the bow and one arrow at a time, we could hold on to the rest of the quiver. I gave him back his bow, and he asked for the arrow that had gone through the ring. He went over to the well, climbed onto the rim, and shot the arrow down into the well. We had a look, and the arrow was stuck in the ground at the bottom. But he'd shot it right through the ring! What good is that, we said. And he asked for another arrow from us, shot it down the well, and it split the other arrow! It just stood there, stuck on the first arrow. And then he shot another one, and then another one, until there were maybe six or seven in a chain, and he could just reach the top one, and then he lifted the chain of arrows out carefully, and the ring was tight round the bottom arrow, because that first arrow was split! We were amazed. Anyway, after I got my ring back he asked me if I'd tell the Grandsire that a pupil of Parashu-rama had come to see him.

'Is that Bhishma? The Grandsire?'

'Yes — you haven't met him yet, have you? The Grandsire at first thought that Drona wanted to fight him, on account of some sort of quarrel between him and Parashu-rama. But no, Drona just wanted to teach us. I think the Grandsire remembered my father King Pandu speaking well of Drona. And Drona told me that he'd met us once before in the woods, me and Bhima, because Arjuna wasn't even born yet. But we must have been too young to remember. Anyway, Kripa wasn't very pleased, because Drona wanted to take over as our tutor. But Kripa agreed. And he didn't seem to mind too much when Drona married his sister.

'But a funny thing happened before our first lesson. Drona made us make a promise. He made us touch his feet and said he had a particular purpose in teaching us, and that we had to promise that once he'd made us into skilled warriors, we'd carry out this task for him.'

'Did he say what it was?' asked Karna.

'No, he just said he'd tell us when we were ready.'

'What did you do? Did you make the promise?'

'We were all silent at first, we didn't know whether to say yes. But little Arjuna suddenly stepped up and said he would vow to do whatever he commanded. And after that, we all did. I wonder why Drona hasn't asked you to promise? Maybe because he doesn't think you'll be with us after the Grandsire gets back. I can't wait for him to get back — sorry I didn't mean — you know what I mean, we all like him a lot.'

'I might have to go back to Anga, then. Or leave the Academy, anyway. I'm sure Drona will ask him not to have me any more in the Academy.'

'Do you want me to put in a good word for you?'

'No, thanks, Yudhi. It would only annoy Drona even more if he found out. And it might make him suspicious of you. No, I don't know what'll happen. What's Bhishma like?'

'He's like a grandfather to us. After our father died, he looked after us. He can be a bit... frightening, if you don't know him. You know that all the warriors are much more frightened of the Grandsire than of Drona. It's strange, because he doesn't *seem* as good with the bow as Drona.'

'What, have you seen Bhishma shoot?'

'Oh, yes. You know, I think my brother Arjuna looks better than the Grandsire. But Drona says he wouldn't like to fight the Grandsire. He told us that Parashu-rama did once ask him if he'd fight the Grandsire for him, because of this quarrel between them. And Drona asked Parashu what he thought his chances were against Bhishma. Not great, said Parashu, so Drona decided against it! Some people say that it's because of a reward to the Grandsire from the gods, for making his vow about not ever marrying or having children.'

'What's the reward?'

'They think that Bhishma can actually choose the moment of his own death.'

◊

Over the next few months Karna grew quite fond of Yudhi. And also of Dur, who was becoming more friendly, and beginning to confide in Karna all his complaints against the four younger Pandavas, especially Bhima. It is true, Dur did have a lot to complain about. For one thing, they teased him constantly, mainly about his appearance. For whereas at that age Bhima was already very solidly built, a quite visible proportion of Dur's bulk lay as fat. Also the fact that Drona didn't like Dur was frequently used by the other boys to Dur's further disadvantage. For Drona tended to turn a blind eye to these activities.

Sometimes Bhima would go too far. He had a habit, which Dur was always complaining about to Karna, of pretending to drown Dur when they were out swimming in the river. Bhima would hold Dur's head under, and only release him at the last minute. In fact Bhima enjoyed doing this to all the Kuru boys, with the result that they were very reluctant to go out swimming together. Then of course they were mocked for being cowards.

But all the boys, even Bhima, gradually began to respect Karna, if not to like him. When Karna was fighting or practising with them, there were things he was able to hide from Drona which he could not so easily hide from his opponents. They began to be able to tell when he was holding himself back.

◊

One day, during target practice with single arrows, Drona took the boys to a very tall and leafy tree which stood in the grounds of the Academy. Near the top of the tree he had had placed a cloth figure in the shape of a bird, a swan. Quite apart from the difficulty involved in seeing the cloth bird through the foliage, the boys would find that holding aim was very tiring on their arms, for they had to point their bows right up into the tree.

Drona asked each of them in turn to aim at the head of the swan. But he asked them not to release their arrow until he had given them permission.

As each boy took aim, trying to hold the bow still, Drona would ask him:

'What do you see? Describe all that you can see.'

And the boys would describe what they saw. Finally, when their arms were trembling, Drona would allow them to release their arrow. One by one they missed, to the entertainment of little Ashwa, who was sitting watching the proceedings next to Vaitanika, the shudra boy. Some of the arrows flew out of the tree empty-handed, to be retrieved by the shudra, others became stuck in some part of the tree. But the swan remained intact.

When it came to Bhima's turn, he said he saw the branches and the leaves, but he could not make out the actual bird, let alone the bird's head. So Drona did not allow him to shoot.

When it was Yudhi's turn, he was able to pick out both the bird and its head.

'I can see all of the swan, sire.'

'Are you aiming at the bird's head?'

'Yes, sire.'

'And you can still see the whole bird?' asked Drona.

'Yes, sire.'

'How big is it?'

'The length of an arrow.'

'Is there anything else you can describe for me in your field of vision?'

'Yes, sire. I can see the leaves, and some of the branches as well.'

'Very well, you may shoot.'

But Yudhi's arrow embedded itself in a branch close to the swan.

At last it was Arjuna's turn.

'What do you see, Arjuna?'

'I see the head of the bird.'

'Can you describe the rest of the bird to me?'

'No sire, I cannot see the whole bird. I can only see the head which I'm aiming at.'

'Can you not see the leaves, the branches? Can you not see the rest of the tree?'

'No sire, only the head of the bird.'

'Can you not even tell me what sort of bird it is?'

'It has the head of a swan, sire.'

'But the swan is a noble and virtuous bird, Arjuna. In your mind let your target be a vulture or a crow. Arjuna, what do you see now?'

'The head of a crow, sire.'

'Good. You may shoot.'

Arjuna's arrow flew out of the top of the tree with the cloth head impaled upon it. The body of the bird dropped to the ground at the foot of the tree. All the boys applauded.

'You see what you must learn,' said Drona to the other boys. 'You must learn to concentrate, to focus only on your target, so that nothing else enters your vision to distract you. And once he is your target, even if it is your best friend, the swan, you must make him your worst enemy, the crow.'

Vaitanika nudged little Ashwa and pointed discreetly at Karna, who had been standing at the back of the group of boys. Ashwa cried out to his father.

'What about Karna, father, Karna hasn't had his turn!'

'Oh dear,' said Drona, 'we must have forgotten about Karna. We had better put the bird back in the tree.' Drona instructed his servant, who retrieved the head, fixed it to the body, and clambered up the tree. Having positioned it, he started climbing down again.

'Sire,' said Karna, 'the bird is lower than it was.'

'Oh, so you want it as high as Arjuna, do you? You think you are as good as Arjuna? Listen, Karna, you will never set eyes on his equal, never. So do not presume to compare yourself with him.'

The boys all became very quiet.

'But, just to convince you,' added Drona, 'let's put the bird back exactly where it was.'

Vaitanika climbed up again and repositioned the bird exactly where it had been for Arjuna.

Karna took aim.

'Tell me what you see.'

'I see the head of the swan, sire.'

'Anything else?'

'I see the body of the swan.'

'Oh, you do? But you are aiming at the head?'

'Yes, sire.'

'What else can you see?'

'The leaves of the tree, sire.'

'Anything else? You must tell me everything that you can see.'

'I can see the trunk of the tree.'

'And you are still aiming at the head of the bird? Well, carry on, tell us what else you can see, since you are able to see so much!'

There was a moment's pause before Karna's reply. The boys were so quiet they could have heard a butterfly approaching.

'I can see some boys, sire, towards the edge of my vision, near the ground. They are Bharata princes. I can see a small boy who is the son of the tutor, next to another boy, who is the tutor's servant. The princes are of two kinds, Pandavas and Kurus. I can see that they do not like each other... I can see the tutor... I can see that the tutor wants to train the princes so that when they are ready they will be able to attack King Drupada of Panchala...'

Karna knew that soon his arms would begin to tremble; but he did not hear any command to release the arrow. Instead he felt now Drona's grasp, and the bow being taken out of his hand.

Drona's grip was gentle, and his quiet voice free of emotion:

'Karna, do not let me see you in this Academy again. You may go.'

◊

Later that day the Pandava princes were arguing over whether or not Karna would have equalled Arjuna's feat.

'He only went on like that because he knew he wouldn't be able to hit the bird's head,' suggested Bhima. 'It was just a trick so that he wouldn't have to shoot, so that he wouldn't be shown up.'

'And anyway,' said Arjuna, 'when he'd said that bit about Drona and King Drupada, he knew Drona would be cross. So he didn't have anything to lose. He could have shot the arrow then, just to show he could do it — if he could have done it. But he was afraid of missing.'

'Arjuna's right,' agreed Saha. 'What did he have to lose? Why didn't he just shoot the arrow then, instead of waiting for Drona to come and stop him?'

'That would have been showing off,' said Yudhi. 'Don't you know Karna by now? He would think it was a weakness even to need to show off his strength. I think he would have succeeded in hitting the target. But he'd have failed to keep his dharma.'

12 Bhishma

Just two days after Karna had been banished from the Academy, and before his expulsion had reached the ears of Kripa, Bhishma returned from his festival in Panchala.

'How's that little friend of Charvaka's getting on?' Bhishma asked Kripa, reminded of the affair when Drona's name came up in conversation. 'What's the boy called?'

'Drona still does not want him, I believe. He is going to ask you to remove him... His name is Karna.'

'Karna?'

'Yes, he wears ear-rings... It's short for Karna-veshtakika, apparently.'

'Well, I must go and see him. If Drona really is adamant, I suppose I'll just have to send the boy back. But I'll see how he is coming along.'

Bhishma was fond of the Pandava princes, so he was glad of an excuse to visit the Academy to see them after such a long absence. Kripa and King Dhrita's brother Vidura went along with him, and on the way they were joined by several kshatriyas who had stopped to greet Bhishma.

'It's some time since I saw my favourite nephew,' said Vidura.

'Oh, which one is that?' asked Bhishma.

'Why, Yudhi, of course,' replied Vidura. 'As far as I can gather, he is the only one of them with a healthy distaste for combat and the affairs of war. It's a wonder how bravely he endures Drona's training.'

'Well, we shall see how this boy Karna has been enduring it. Quite a change from Charvaka, I dare say.'

'You know what I think of that rishi, Bhishma,' remarked Vidura. 'Like most things that come from Charvaka, this great prodigy of his may turn out to be nothing but a jackal in a war drum.'

'Vidura, since when have you been able to tell the difference between a jackal and a lion?'

When they arrived at the Academy, all the princes, Pandavas and Kurus alike, were excited to see Bhishma.

'So, where is that boy?' Bhishma asked Drona, in front of all the little princes. Their chattering ceased.

'Where is this Karna?'

'I have expelled him from the Academy. Just the other day, in fact.'

'Why? What did he do?'

'He... He is just not good enough. He is also rather a strange boy... And extremely arrogant.'

'I thought he was nice!' cried out the little Ashwa, to his father's visible annoyance. The other boys were uneasy. Even Bhima felt a little sorry for Karna's dismissal.

'Drona, did you examine him properly? Charvaka is no fighter himself. But in my experience he does know what he chooses to talk about. Do you mind if I examine the boy myself?'

As much as anything Bhishma was intrigued to meet the boy before he dismissed him; as he surely would have to do, given Drona's evidently clear opinion on the matter.

'No, go ahead, by all means,' replied Drona.

Karna was summoned: Drona's servant ran all the way to Sanjaya's house. Karna was just about to set off to practise in the woods.

'Bhishma wants to examine you!'

Karna put on his little warrior's coat over his shirt and baggy trousers, and tied his sash tightly round his waist. He also took along his favourite bow, a glove for his left hand, and the two quivers Charvaka had given him.

By the time Karna arrived with his equipment, a little breathless, there was an air of excitement among the princes. The kshatriyas were idly chatting away, waiting for Bhishma to finish his examination so that they could all leave the Academy and resume more important matters.

'Come here, young man!' Bhishma boomed across to Karna.

Karna approached him.

'I am told, young man, that you are not good enough. What have you to say for yourself?'

'Please examine me, sire.'

Bhishma had a good look at the boy.

'You...' He suddenly turned to Kripa, beckoning him. 'This boy's a suta,' he whispered. 'You did not tell me Charvaka's boy was a *suta*.'

'No, Bhishma... Would that have made any difference with you?'

Bhishma stared at Kripa, and then waved him away.

'You wish to be examined before all these people?' he asked Karna, waving his arm in an arc to demonstrate the full extent of the audience.

'I don't mind, sire.'

'Very well.' Bhishma's voice now began to increase in volume. 'Put your practice arrows in one of your quivers. I will need some arrows... Drona, if you have some, please... It's some years since I've used practice arrows, young man, you may find me a little out of practice with them!'

The princes laughed and the kshatriyas chuckled.

Karna and Bhishma moved apart so that their line of fire would not include the spectators. The princes were now very noisy with excitement. They were relieved that they were not in Karna's sandals. Indeed, most of them felt a little sorry for Karna. Except for Yudhi, who was sure that Karna would pass his test. He was wondering how Drona could readmit him without losing face.

Karna strapped on his face guard. Bhishma declined Drona's offer of a guard.

'You may release the first arrow,' said Bhishma.

Karna gathered four arrows in his right fist from the single quiver strapped to his right side, and drew them onto his bow; he took aim, looking to his left, with his body sideways on to his opponent, and waited. The princes were amazed, for they had never seen Karna use more than two arrows at a time.

Bhishma stood patiently in a similar posture, his left hand holding his bow in position, his right hand hanging loosely at his side, ready to cross to the quiver strapped on his left.

Some distance directly behind Bhishma was a large tree. From where Karna stood Bhishma's powerful frame seemed to take the place of the tree's hidden trunk. The branches seemed to grow out of Bhishma's body.

Karna was puzzled as to why Bhishma strapped his quiver on the opposite side. He had always been taught to place the quiver on the same side as his drawing hand; otherwise one would tend to turn square to one's opponent when crossing to gather arrows from the quiver; and Karna had learnt always to present the smallest possible target. Certainly all the princes, and Drona, and indeed all the warriors Karna had ever seen, strapped their quiver on the same side as their drawing hand.

Drona, who was to act as referee, approached to signal when Karna could release his arrows. The usual rule in the princes' practice bouts was that the first one to be hit on the body by an arrow was the loser. The referee, who counted out the seconds in order to time the duration of the bout, would also shout when a hit to the body occurred.

'Go!' shouted Drona.

Before Karna's four arrows were halfway to Bhishma, the old warrior had drawn and released two spinning baffler arrows; these deflected three of the oncoming four. Bhishma waved the last arrow casually aside with his bow and fetched two more bafflers onto his string. Karna paused, surprised. He had been expecting Bhishma to shoot at him. He could hear Drona counting the seconds in the background. Karna drew another four arrows, waiting for a moment in case Bhishma were to release his arrows... But no, Bhishma was also waiting. So Karna released his second volley. Drona had by now reached a count of seven.

This time Bhishma's two bafflers deflected all four of Karna's arrows. Karna again waited to see what Bhishma would do. The warrior lowered his bow at the count of ten, and beckoned Karna to approach him.

'What are you playing at, young man?' he asked in a loud voice, and with more than a trace of annoyance.

'Sire?'

'You're not trying! Why aren't you shooting at me?'

'Sire, I was expecting you to attack me, sire... I was waiting for you to shoot at me, sire.'

'And young man, do you also wait for your targets to shoot at you? Do you wait for your straw markers to attack you? Do you wait for trees and branches to assault you before you shoot at them?'

The princes laughed and the kshatriyas murmured.

'What will you be like in battle, young man? Will you stand there waiting for someone to try to kill you? By then you will be dead. What do you think this is, boy, a game? *You* are trying to kill *me*. It is not *I* who is being tested. It is not *I* who has to demonstrate his skill, but *you*.'

The spectators were silent.

'I believe,' continued Bhishma, 'that my reputation is already sufficient to admit me to this Academy.'

The kshatriyas muttered with amusement.

'Karna-veshtakika, that is your name, is it not?'

'Yes, sire.'

'Well Karna, if you wish to fight like a kshatriya you must learn that this is not a game with toys. Have you ever used real arrows to fight with, like a ratha?'

'No sire. I've only used them on targets, sire.'

'If you want to fight like a ratha, you must learn to kill. It is not enough merely to shoot well at a target. I want to face death from you, Karna. Do you understand me? I want to feel the message of death in your arrows. And, young man, I think it is time *you* learnt to face death. If you don't learn to fight today as though you'll die tomorrow, your arrows won't tomorrow come suddenly alive to save you.'

Not a murmur came from the audience.

'Karna-veshtakika, fill your quiver this time with real arrows, with arrows of death. You have some in your quivers?'

Karna nodded. He took a very deep breath, and sorted his arrows again, while Bhishma went to get some more from Drona. A mixture of excitement and fear was on the faces of all the young princes; except Yudhi, who was almost in tears.

As Karna arranged his arrows and checked his bowstring, his mind ran through the problem facing him.

His first thoughts concerned his armour. He could not possibly let any of Bhishma's arrows strike him in the chest, or everyone would discover the nature of his second skin.

'What use is armour that has to be protected?' he thought, despairingly. 'If only Bhishma would offer me armour, I could put it on top, and then risk being hit in the chest.' But Bhishma was not offering any armour, nor putting any on himself. No, he was sorting through Drona's arrows and restringing his bow.

Then Karna thought, surely, he will not try to kill me. Bhishma surely would not aim for his chest. He would probably disarm him instead. Yes... Of course he would not injure him! To harm him would be for Bhishma to fail.

Karna breathed a little more easily now. He decided on a strategy, and visibly relaxed, taking another deep breath. He sorted through his quiver carefully, selecting the arrows he would use.

Bhishma was nearly ready. He was also choosing his arrows with great care, having asked Drona for a wider selection than he had at first been shown. Karna stood ready now, legs slightly apart, his long, angled big toes gripping the soles of his sandals.

'Karna,' said Bhishma, 'put your face guard on.'

'Yes sire.'

Karna put down his bow and began to strap up.

'Karna,' said Bhishma again, in a louder voice for all to hear, 'if it takes me more than three seconds to beat you then you may stay in the Academy. If you are still alive, of course!'

The kshatriyas chuckled.

'If it takes me less than three seconds, you're out, whether or not you're still alive. Do you understand?'

'Yes, sire.'

Drona smiled to himself, and also understood. He could count on one hand the number of kshatriyas who could last three seconds against Bhishma at this close range.

'You may shoot first,' said Bhishma.

Karna this time grasped only two arrows, and drew them onto his bowstring.

'Karna!' Bhishma bellowed.

'Yes, sire?' came the muffled reply from under the face guard.

'Please do not play with me!'

The kshatriyas laughed.

'And don't be afraid to kill me. My death is long overdue!'

Karna's attempt to reply merged with the mutterings of the kshatriyas, who were thinking of the warriors to whom Bhishma had shouted that very taunt in the midst of battle.

As before Bhishma waited with his right arm hanging loose by his side. The audience were now completely silent.

'Go!' shouted Drona.

Karna's first two arrows were parried by two from Bhishma's first volley of four; and the two remaining arrows in this volley of Bhishma's were blocked by Karna's second pair, which the boy had drawn and released with impressive speed. Karna now had just enough time to draw and shoot another pair before he heard Drona's count of one. Then Bhishma's second volley of four arrived, tearing off Karna's face guard and shattering his favourite bow. Bhishma's third and final volley consisted of a pair of brightly feathered arrows, released with hardly any force in a slow, looping arc directed towards Karna's head. Karna watched this pair helplessly, but without flinching. Just after the count of two they gently brushed his cheeks to be caught in his ear-rings, now completely obscured by the bright feathers.

'There you have Karna-*veshtakika!*' boomed Bhishma, looking round with a broad smile.

There was a roar of laughter from the kshatriyas. The princes burst into applause, their eyes popping out of their heads. All but Yudhi. He was not clapping, and looked utterly confused. Kripa, too, was shaking his head in disbelief.

The kshatriyas began to leave, expecting Bhishma to follow them out. The boys breathed a sigh of relief. They had been afraid that Bhishma was going to kill Karna. They couldn't help thinking it had been rather unfair for Karna, who was still standing there like a statue, with the remains of his bow held tightly in his left hand, and the arrows still dangling from his ears.

Bhishma walked briskly back to return his quiver. Drona was beaming with satisfaction at the turn of events. Just before Bhishma reached Drona, he stopped for a moment, as if to brush a fly from his neck. He turned round to look again at Karna. Only now did Karna begin to unthread the arrows from his ear-rings.

The expression on Bhishma's face was indecipherable as he unstrapped his quiver and whispered to Drona.

'The boy stays.'

Drona's jaw dropped. 'But you beat him in less than three seconds,' he gasped. 'You disarmed him completely before the count of two!'

'The boy stays.'

'But... What reason shall I give?'

'What reason? What were you looking at, Drona? Are you as blind as those babbling kshatriyas? Can you see no further than your giggling princes?' Bhishma was almost hissing between clenched teeth. '*The boy stays.*'

'Yes, Bhishma.'

Bhishma departed without taking his leave of the princes.

◊

Later that night, after his brothers had gone to sleep, Yudhi got up and stole out of the palace. He rushed through the streets of Hastinapura to the Academy. He knocked at the gate. After a while Drona's servant opened up, obviously surprised to see the young prince. Yudhi spoke urgently to him, and they both went quickly into the grounds, towards the place where Bhishma and Karna had fought.

Yudhi ran to the tree which had stood behind Bhishma. He pointed up into it. There was enough moonlight for them to make out what they were looking for. The tree was too broad for Vaitanika's arms to encircle, but he managed to shin a little way up the trunk, far enough to reach the two arrows embedded there. He could not let go of the trunk with either hand, so he used his jaws to pull the arrows out, dropping them to Yudhi. Then he jumped down.

'You see!' said Yudhi, breathless with excitement. He held the thin, metal shafts up to the moonlight. 'They are hardly stained at all... but that is the Grandsire's blood!'

'How is it possible?' asked Vaitanika.

'You remember Karna's last volley? I'm not sure, but I think he waited until the Grandsire's second volley had left his bow. I think the Grandsire was fetching his third volley when Karna let these go. They must have already gone through the Grandsire when he sent his last arrows off, the pair that got Karna's ear-rings!'

'But —'

'Didn't you see the cloth of Bhishma's coat, on his shoulders, near his neck? There were two small spots of blood. I don't think even Drona noticed. These two arrows went clean through him!' Yudhi handed the arrows to Vaitanika, and then squeezed the shoulder muscles on either side of Vaitanika's neck between each thumb and forefinger. 'There!'

◊

Next day Karna was back in the Academy as though nothing had happened. The other princes were very surprised. But when they mentioned it to Drona, he refused to talk about it.

Yudhi decided not to tell the others about his discovery. But he later showed Karna the two arrows he had found.

'May I keep these, Karna. The arrows that beat the *Grandsire!*'

Karna looked at the arrows thoughtfully.

'Does anyone else know?'

'Yes, Vaitanika, he helped me get them down.'

'Oh... Well, perhaps you should offer one to Vaitanika, if he wants one. But yes, keep them if you want.'

'Did you know the arrows would go through him like that?'

'Yes... At least, that's what I'd been taught. I've never done it before to a live man!'

Yudhi could see that Karna was reluctant to talk about it, but he could not contain his curiosity.

'But how did you get them through when he was sideways on to you? Karna, tell me!'

'The arrows had to arrive just as he was reaching across to his quiver. That was the only moment he opened his chest to me. The rest of the time he was sideways on like you're supposed to be... But I didn't really beat him, you know.'

'What do you mean?... Karna, what do you mean?'

'It was only because I knew he wouldn't be cruel enough to kill me... So I could ignore his second volley. Well, when I say ignore... I thought he'd just break my bow — I've heard of people doing that, but I didn't expect him to go for my face guard as well. Yudhi, those four arrows, you know, his second volley, did you see them? They came at two different heights, one pair for my face guard, the other pair just a bit off-centre to my left to get my bow, but without even touching my arm!' Karna raised up his left arm into bow position as he relived the moment. He shook his head. 'I don't think I'll ever be able to shoot like that! No, if he'd wanted to kill me, I'd have been killed by that volley. It was only because he wanted to make fun of my ear-rings that my two arrows got through. I could see his hand hesitating just for a fraction in his quiver to make sure he'd caught hold of the right pair of arrows, you know, with the coloured feathers!'

Karna asked Yudhi to keep quiet about what had happened, and Yudhi agreed not to tell anyone. He had also been wanting to ask Karna what he had meant about Drona and King Drupada. For he had not had any chance to speak to Karna since Drona had expelled him. But Yudhi decided to leave that for another time.

13 The mantras

About two weeks after Bhishma's first encounter with Karna, he visited the boy at the Academy. He drew Karna apart from the others and sat down with him. He put his hand on the boy's shoulder, and looked at him severely. For almost the first time in his life Karna felt the need to avert his eyes.

'Was it Charvaka who gave you those arrows?' Bhishma asked him. 'The ones that went through me?'

'Yes, sire.'

'And was it Charvaka who taught you where to aim for?'

'Yes, sire.'

Bhishma looked at him in silence. Karna began to feel uncomfortable under Bhishma's glare. Rather than look him in the eye, Karna's gaze passed over the battle scars on the old warrior's face. Then Bhishma's expression softened.

'It's such a while since I last saw the mouse... I wonder when I'll see him again...'

'You mean Charvaka, sire?'

'Yes. Doesn't he call me the boar?'

'Yes, sire. Why is that?'

'Why? Why indeed... Probably because I blunder in like a pig... You taught this pig a lesson, Karna.'

'You taught me several, sire —'

'Yes, yes... The teacher usually learns more than the pupil.'

'That must be why I seem to learn most when I teach myself, sire!'

Bhishma smiled. 'You sound just like the mouse! You're not his son by any chance, are you?'

'No, sire!... Are your wounds healing well, sire?' Karna quickly added to change the subject.

'Oh yes, thank you for asking. Your arrows must have been very well greased. But I always heal fast. Even the wounds in my mind heal quickly, and that was where you hurt me most! I'm lucky you didn't miss!' Bhishma let out a deep guffaw. 'Imagine, the great Bhishma killed by a young boy!'

'But sire, I have been told that you have the power to choose the moment of your own death.'

Another deep laugh rumbled out of Bhishma's chest. 'Hah! But that's why I would have chosen that moment to die, Karna, there and then! By a young boy! I would have had to die — how could I have ever lived it down!'

During the next few months Karna continued to keep as much as possible in the background at the Academy. Apart from Yudhi, only Dur ever talked to Karna about the episode with Bhishma. Dur was rather critical of the way Bhishma had humiliated Karna for their entertainment, and was all the more admiring of Karna for coping as he had with the embarrassment. Like most of the other princes, Dur assumed that Bhishma had simply taken pity on his victim, and relented to permit Karna to continue at the Academy.

While he remained in Hastinapura, Bhishma would often visit the princes at the Academy. On these occasions he was always very friendly to Karna, always asking how the 'little suta' was coming on. But he never again mentioned their first encounter. Not until many years later, when Bhishma finally decided it was time to take to his deathbed.

◊

Every few months Karna would return to Anga to see his family. On one occasion the whole family did make the journey to visit him in Hastinapura. But only his brothers came regularly to see him there. Indeed, they would often act as Karna's own drivers, going to Hastinapura to fetch him, and then delivering him back; all as a pretext to enjoy the excitement of the big city.

During the journey Karna would usually stop by in Varanasi to see Charvaka; and also to see Vrisha, for his little brother was spending an increasing amount of time with the rishi: on the rare occasions when he had not travelled up on the chariot to Hastinapura, Vrisha would more likely be at Charvaka's than at home in Anga. And in Hastinapura Vrisha had become very friendly with Vaitanika. He managed once to persuade the older boy to let him in to the Academy to watch the princes and his brother practising. But Vrisha was summarily ejected by Drona.

Charvaka had been rather disturbed though not altogether surprised to discover that Drona had taken over from Kripa at the Academy. The rishi warned Karna to be particularly careful with Drona.

'He is a man of great powers, my boy. Do not underestimate his intelligence just because his desires sometimes cloud his vision.'

It was not long before Charvaka felt obliged to repeat his warning to Karna on a subsequent visit.

'Vrisha told me all about it,' said Charvaka. 'Didn't I warn you about Drona?'

Karna had again managed to offend Drona, and seriously enough for the young princes to wonder why Drona did not pursue another attempt to expel Karna from the Academy.

'Why were you doing it in the grounds of the Academy?' chided Charvaka. 'You could have used the woods. You're still working on your own in the woods, aren't you?'

'Yes, Charvaka,' replied Karna. 'But I don't like Drona. Why should he get away with what he does?'

The trouble had started after Karna had asked to borrow some paintings that were hanging on the wall of his room at Sanjaya's.

'Use the paintings? What for?' asked Sanjaya.

'I need them for my practice. I'm afraid it'll ruin them. If you want to keep them I won't...'

'Well...' Sanjaya extended his lower jaw past his upper teeth, as he sometimes did when mulling things over. 'Well, you know best, Karna... Take the one of Krishna, I can easily replace that. One day you should go and see the real picture it's copied from. Have you heard of it? It's on the wall by the gate of the city where Krishna lives. A huge picture. My little copy only shows his face, but there on the walls it shows him feeding a porcupine with sugar cane. You should go and see it. It's the biggest picture I've ever set eyes on... What are the other ones in there? Ah yes, take Drona —'

'Is that other man Drona?'

'Yes, it's not a very good likeness, is it? But leave me the one of Madri. Now that she's gone it would be impossible for me to get another one of her. But you can take the other two.'

'Is that Madri who was the mother of the twins?'

'Oh yes. Don't you think she was beautiful? Is the one of Pritha there as well?'

'No, just those three.'

'Do you need any more? I've got one of the Grandsire somewhere...'

'No, the two will do for the moment, thanks, Sanjaya. I prefer those two anyway because they have such dark skin, and it shows up their eyes.'

Karna left Sanjaya puzzling, and took the pictures with him to the Academy. And the following day Drona himself discovered Karna using them as targets. Karna had just released four arrows at the two faces, one of which he had mounted above the other. Each of the four eyes was transfixed by an arrow.

Drona was almost speechless.

'I can understand perhaps why you wish to shoot at *me*,' he hissed at Karna. 'But... Do you know who the other one is?'

'Yes, sire. I believe it's Krishna.'

Drona was visibly struggling to contain his fury.

'And what have you got against the great Lord Krishna?'

'Nothing, sire.'

'Can you give me no explanation for this barbarity?'

'I'm not shooting at the faces, at the people, sire. I'm only shooting at the targets... Surely, sire, if it's possible to turn a noble swan into a crow worthy to be shot at, isn't it an even better test to make targets of yourself and Krishna?'

Karna saw Drona tremble slightly for a second before regaining control.

'One day, Karna, I will turn *you* into a target. A punishment more worthy of you than our present circumstances here permit.' He pointed at the paintings. 'Get them out of here.'

Vaitanika had witnessed the scene. He had then told Vrisha, when he next saw him in the city. And Vrisha had told Charvaka.

'Your brother has a most contrary streak,' said Charvaka to Vrisha, who was just entering the rishi's workshop. 'A most contrary streak,' he repeated, turning to Karna, 'which he indulges at his peril.'

'Why didn't you *explain* to Drona?' Vrisha asked his brother.

'I gave him a perfectly good explanation,' answered Karna. 'At least it was one he should have been able to understand.'

'Anyway,' suggested Vrisha, 'you weren't even aiming at the *targets*. You should've told him that.'

'How is that?'

'You weren't actually seeing the target at all. What you saw... It was just in your mind, wasn't it?'

'You mean a sensation of it?' suggested Charvaka. 'The image of the target?'

'Yes, sire. No one actually *sees* what they're aiming at... You're just aiming at this image in your mind.' Seeing the expression on Karna's face, Vrisha turned to Charvaka for support. 'Isn't that right, sire?'

'That's ridiculous talk, Vrisha!' exclaimed Charvaka. 'You couldn't possibly tell us that Karna's arrow strikes his own image, the visual image in his mind. Could you? Yes, I know, he *has* them, visual images, images of what we call *the target* and *the arrow*. But it's the arrow that he releases, not the image of the arrow. And it's the target that he hits, not the image of the target.'

Now Vrisha turned to his brother for support. But Karna just smiled at him.

'The language of aiming and hitting,' continued Charvaka, scratching his beard, 'forces us to talk only of that about which it can and has to talk. Yes, your brother does have these sensations, and they permit the whole process to occur. In Karna's case usually with some success. You'll be telling us next that the colour of your image of my cloak is brown! Yes, my cloak is brown, but your sensation of it is no such thing. Yes, our sensations permit the whole process to happen — including the talk. But it is not these about which we talk, when we are talking normally. After all, Vrisha, you don't say, when you walk normally, that you are walking on your *knees*, just because your knees are indeed under you, supporting you? Yes, there is such a thing as walking on your knees. But that's a rather exceptional activity. Useful for certain special purposes, yes; but not for covering the daily round. Eh?'

Vrisha looked down at his legs.

'You're evidently too young yet', added Charvaka, 'to understand what it is you talk about or what you walk upon.'

Vrisha appealed to Karna. 'Do you understand what he means?'

'Yes, I think so. But I can't explain it to you in words. So don't expect me to.'

'But... How can you understand something and not be able to explain it in words?' objected Vrisha. 'You must be able to explain it if you can understand it!'

'Oh yes?' challenged Karna. 'Try explaining to me what meaning is, then. Or knowledge. You'll be wasting your time, unless you like chasing your tail.'

'I'm afraid he's right, my boy,' said Charvaka to the frustrated Vrisha. 'People do seem to think that just because you need to understand something in order to be able to explain it in words, you also need to be able to explain it in words to understand it. The latter is simply not the case. What you cannot even begin, neither can you ever end. So when it's futile even to *start* to explain something unless your hearer already understands it, then neither can you ever hope to *finish* the explanation.'

'Well!' Vrisha raised his eyes to the ceiling and made as if to scratch a non-existent beard. Then he looked at his brother. 'It's a good thing you didn't try and explain all that to Drona!'

◊

Karna's friendship with Dur grew stronger during a period when Dur was finding the demands of training particularly hard.

Since every warrior was obliged to expect and endure injury, Drona had started building up his pupils' resistance to pain, developing in them a stricter control over their reactions.

Dur found it very difficult to control his responses, not just to physical distress, but also to the affliction of any emotion. Karna, who in contrast was by nature able to observe himself with detachment, rather admired Dur's own kind of courage. The Kuru prince was able to talk more openly than the others about his feelings; with less shame about his fears, his envies, his anxieties. But though he could be frank with his friends, Dur did learn to hide his troubles from the Pandavas, who tended to use his admissions to provoke him further.

Karna's association with both Yudhi and Dur made life at times rather delicate for him, particularly after King Dhrita, out of respect for his dead brother, decided officially to nominate the Pandava princes as heirs to his throne. It was not just Dur's resentment which polarised the princes. For the reaction of the Pandavas, particularly of Bhima and the twins, was calculated to make the most of Dur's resentment. Dur would generally take his grievances to Karna.

Yudhi, on the other hand, felt too ashamed to try to draw Karna's sympathies towards the Pandavas; he was well aware that his brothers were unwilling or unable to allow their inward respect for the suta to affect their public treatment of him. It was thus that Karna found himself more and more called upon to support the Kuru side.

'It's just not fair...' Dur would complain to Karna. 'My father is always fussing over Bhima and Arjuna, as though they were his own children and I wasn't! And Vidura hates me! He's always talking to Yudhi. He never talks to me, but he's just as much *my* uncle.'

There was some truth to this. Bhima was certainly a favourite of King Dhrita's, and Vidura apparently held no liking for Dur. Although his father was in good health, and would probably remain king for many years to come, Dur was already beginning to fear the prospect of Yudhi ascending to the throne; when royal elevation might license the prowess of the Pandava princes to even keener persecution of the Kurus. With Bhima's strength and Arjuna's unrivalled skill the Pandavas would be unstoppable; a fact which they took every opportunity to remind Dur of, teasing his fears into a frenzy.

Yudhi did try to keep his brothers in check. They always listened respectfully to him, and for a while tried to behave as he requested. But their natural exuberance would soon get the better of them, and of Dur.

On one occasion Yudhi felt so angry with Arjuna's open disdain of the Kurus and, more specifically, of "the suta", that he warned him about Karna.

'Listen to what I am going to tell you, brother. If Karna ever turns against us, things could become very difficult.'

'Karna? What has the suta got to do with it?'

'Make sure you don't ever underestimate him. Listen to me!... I would not bet on you against him in single combat.'

'Since when was your betting any good, Yudhi! Anyway, when has he ever beaten me in practice? I know he sometimes doesn't seem to try. But that's because he's afraid to find out he'd still be beaten! It's only the Grandsire's soft heart that has kept him at the Academy.'

Yudhi sighed. 'Don't you ever see anything beyond what you are aiming at? Listen... If you want to get yourself killed, by all means... But don't say I didn't warn you. Always treat Karna with respect. You do not want to make an enemy of him.'

If anything, the effect of Yudhi's words went against his good intentions. Arjuna was aroused into a new and suspicious rivalry with Karna. Karna himself soon noticed it. Arjuna had begun to watch his actions more, to scrutinise his behaviour, trying perhaps to find some trace of the powers his brother had hinted at. Moreover, Arjuna began to take a special delight in beating Karna in their practice bouts, in outscoring him at target shooting; after which the invariably victorious prince would look at Yudhi as if to demonstrate his brother's misappraisal.

Yudhi could only admire, with increasing wonder, Karna's own restraint, and the skill with which he contrived always to lose in such a well-executed manner.

◊

One afternoon Karna arrived at the gate of the Academy to find the mothers of the royal princes leaving in some distress. Gandhari had her arm consolingly round Pritha. From the look on the two women's faces Karna guessed that their sons had been at war.

It turned out that the previous day Bhima had gone a little too far pretending to drown Dur when they were swimming. Dur had resolved this time to get his own back. He had obtained an infusion containing a powerful potion, with which he intended to render Bhima unconscious. Next day, while the Pandavas were in the water, he had managed to mix it in with Bhima's soup. Bhima's appetite was such that almost any exertion on his part had to be requited with some form of food. Sure enough, Bhima fell asleep soon after drinking up his soup. The other Pandavas left, expecting their brother to follow later. Dur and two of his brothers had then dragged Bhima into the water, leaving him there to his fate.

None of them had realised, however, that a poisonous water snake was lurking in the water. When the serpent encountered Bhima's inert mass, it sank its fangs into his flesh. Almost immediately Bhima was roused from his stupor. Evidently the effect of the venom on his huge frame had served merely to shock him into consciousness. In some pain, but otherwise undamaged, he clambered out to safety.

Pritha and Gandhari had managed, with much effort, to piece the story together. After the lecture the princes received from these two, and after Yudhi extracted from his brothers an oath not to retaliate, much of the teasing and baiting between the princes ceased. From that moment on, the violence between the princes did seem to be successfully confined to their permitted sparring. But it was clear that, underneath the cold exchanges, the episode was far from forgotten.

Karna tried to stay out of it, and was therefore more reserved than usual with both Dur and Yudhi. But while Yudhi understood, and respected Karna's privacy, Dur, clearly ashamed of what he had done, tried repeatedly to explain and justify it to Karna.

All these tensions were made worse by Drona's response to the episode. He appeared to use it as an excuse to concentrate his attentions on his favourite, Arjuna. From then on Drona devoted progressively less time to the Kuru princes, while giving the Pandavas, and especially Arjuna, preferential treatment.

When Ashwa had reached an age when he could start training, Drona began to spend many hours just with his son and Arjuna, sometimes forbidding even the other Pandavas to so much as watch; teaching his two favoured students skills which he did not think the others capable or worthy of. He trained these two to shoot in the dark, using sound alone. He showed Arjuna how to use unusual weapons and special arrows, which he would not even show to the others.

When Drona did involve his other students in these training sessions, it was often for the benefit entirely of Arjuna. He gave Arjuna practice against three or four simultaneous opponents spread in an arc around him. Arjuna was ambidextrous, and was therefore able to switch the bow rapidly from hand to hand as required, wearing two quivers so that he could fetch his arrows easily either way. This technique gave him an advantage when he had to shoot rapidly at targets either side of him, for he hardly needed to move his feet. A right-handed fighter needed to turn on his feet in order to switch his aim from far left to far right. Predictably, the elegance with which Arjuna was able to fend off his opponents, to which role Drona tended to assign the Kurus, would just pour fat on the fire of their resentment.

Arjuna and the other Pandavas were also taught to fight on horseback and on elephants. Here Arjuna's ambidexterity again gave him a natural advantage over the others. A right-handed fighter holding the bow in his left hand would tend to experience difficulty aiming at targets to the right of the animal, be it horse or elephant. Nor would he be able to turn the animal around quickly enough to reverse the position. Arjuna, of course, just switched hands in a flash. Not that he required this advantage against the Kurus. For when they asked Drona if they could also train on horseback, Drona refused. In a year or two, perhaps, he said, but not now.

Karna did not even bother to ask Drona. Instead, he tried to teach himself.

He began practising after dark in the woods, often with the assistance of Vaitanika, who would bravely contrive to make a sound next to Karna's target: by throwing a stone at a gong, or by pulling a string tied to a rattle.

Vaitanika also told him as much as he himself was allowed to see of Arjuna's private training. And he described the types of exercises Drona took his privileged students through. Karna then devised what he should do as best he could. With Vaitanika's help, he made some dummies to shoot around a circle in a clearing in the woods. He even borrowed a horse to practise on, though he was unable to obtain an elephant for this purpose.

'Karna,' Vaitanika called to him one day, 'did you know that Drona is teaching Arjuna about Brahma weapons?'

'What are they?'

'It seems to be mantras, mainly —'

'Mantras?'

'Don't you know what a mantra is? Surely Charvaka must use them... He hasn't told you about them? It's... A mantra's like a phrase, or a sound, which can cast a spell. You can use it when you're shooting an arrow, for example, and then that arrow is bound to find its target.'

'I thought that was called aiming?'

'No! Some mantras can paralyse your opponent. I heard him mention several... There's a mantra called Suka, which makes horses and elephants unable to walk!'

'What? You say *Suka*, and they just stop walking?'

'No! Suka is the *name* of the mantra. It's not the mantra itself. I didn't hear any of the actual mantras Drona used... I put my fingers in my ears as he said them... Well, I didn't want to be paralysed, did I? There's a mantra called Naka which forces your opponents to look up at the sky...'

'That sounds useful.'

'Don't make light of them, Karna! There's one called Nartana, which makes you dance about in a frenzy when you hear it... and there's one called Asyamodaka — it makes you kill yourself as soon as you hear it.'

'I wonder why Drona bothers to use a bow?'

'No, Karna, you don't understand, you usually need to say these *as* you're shooting an arrow...'

'No, thanks, Vaitanika. I'm slow enough as it is without having to say a mantra as well.'

But Karna was curious to know what Drona's response would be if he raised the possibility of acquiring these techniques of combat. Drona's reply was unequivocal.

'No one should become acquainted with such knowledge unless he is either a brahmana who has properly followed the full course of his studies, or a kshatriya who is undergoing severe austerities and rigorous instruction. In any case, the person privileged with this knowledge should be able to practise strict control over his desires. You, Karna, are neither a brahmana, nor a kshatriya, nor are you able to master your selfish desires. For I have long known that you are envious of Arjuna's great skill, and wish to rival his achievements for your own glorification. It is this desire which brings you here now asking for instruction. Therefore, I cannot teach you the use of the brahmastras.'

◊

'But what *is* a mantra, Charvaka?'

When Vrisha and Sangra had gone to fetch Karna from Hastinapura, Vaitanika had regaled them with stories of Drona's mantras. But on the journey to Varanasi Karna had refused to talk about them. Now, while Karna was carefully shaving off the horn of a new bow, listening to their conversation with one ear, the rishi was bearing the full brunt of Vrisha's curiosity.

'That is precisely the problem, my boy. I'm not sure what a mantra *is*.'

Charvaka was sitting on a stool by his bench, copying some numbers neatly into a table as he spoke.

'I can only tell you what mantras are for. Supposedly. But their intended function does seem to be clear: as far as I am able to tell with any precision, a mantra is a device through which one can hope to achieve the impossible. And, from what I can gather, an extremely inefficient device.'

'What do you mean, inefficient?'

'Well, consider your... What did you call that one that made your opponents dance in a frenzy?'

'Nartana, I think Vaitanika said. Is that right, Karna?'

Karna nodded with a smile.

'Well, consider it,' continued the rishi. 'One can only presume that while your opponents are thus engaged, you can shoot them more easily, eh? Well, that sounds fine, it sounds wonderful to be able to impart such motion to so much material at such a distance. But if your object is merely to contrive the death of your opponents, consider how much less motion you have to impart to how much less material in order to contrive a hole in a blood vessel in your opponent's brain. Oh yes, Vrisha, even a small bleed in the brain may cause death. I have examined brains, my boy. Well, wouldn't that be a much more efficient method than distracting them into a frenzy, or whatever these things are supposed to do?'

'Yes, I s'pose so. Could you design a mantra that would do that, sire?'

'Of course not.'

'Why not? If it's so efficient. It can't use up much effort, if you only have to make a tiny hole...'

'I just don't think such mantras are possible, my boy.'

'But I've heard you say that only a contradiction is impossible. *You're* full of contradiction, sire! Don't you remember? You told me once that there was no reason why a hawk couldn't catch an elephant. If that's possible, then surely a simple hole in the head's possible?'

'I meant that we could not exclude that possibility by the use of reason alone, without appeal to experience. I certainly do not like to say that it is *possible* for a hawk to catch an elephant. I prefer instead to say just that it's conceivable, imaginable: that it could happen in some imaginary world, in some other world than ours. For in our world some things just are not possible.' Charvaka took out a coin from his pocket. 'Isn't it perfectly clear, and true, that it's not possible for this coin to float in the air after I release it? Yet we can conceive that in some other world such a thing does happen.'

'But sire, I would never have thought that in *this* world it was possible for a coin like that to disappear inside a liquid, like salt does. But I've seen you do it! I'd never have thought it possible that a powder could catch fire just by hitting it. But I've seen you do that — I've seen you do a liquid that catches fire just when you let the air at it! I would never have believed you had mantras that could do things like that! So who's to say something can't happen? If I accept that your mantras are possible, why not Drona's? You've always told me I should keep an open mind!'

'Have I? That is very irresponsible of me, my boy, forgive me. I most certainly do not keep an open mind, and I should strongly advise you against it.'

Vrisha looked over at Karna in astonishment. But Karna just smiled without even looking up from his work.

'As I say, I like to keep a closed mind,' continued Charvaka. 'Not locked, mind you, just closed. I am certainly prepared to open it on occasion, to admit something new, to alter something already there... But only at certain times. When I'm making an observation, for example... After all, my boy, I don't let just anybody and anything come in here into my workshop. I know it looks like it, from this mess... No, you see, the great danger in leaving your mind open is that you allow in just anything. Even worse, that you allow in only that which gives you pleasure, or hope, or excitement, or a morbid alarm which once admitted cannot be expelled. Yes... There's a lot to be said for a closed mind. Not locked. Closed.'

'Yes, well, but you haven't answered me, sire. Isn't there a danger in turning away things that can happen, just because your mind is closed? Who's to say something can't happen?'

'It's obvious, my boy: the pattern of our experience. A hawk may catch a mouse or a monkey. Eh? Neither of these eventualities disturbs our understanding of the world. But for a hawk to fly off with a piece of iron? That does contradict — not itself — but the pattern of experience. Nevertheless — yes, I know what you're going to say — nevertheless, it's not *too* disturbing. If we discovered that hawks did do this, it need not upset our understanding very much. So, yes, perhaps a hawk *might* fly off with a piece of iron. But for a hawk to fly off with an elephant in its talons? That disturbs too general and too profound a pattern of this world for us readily to entertain its possibility. In another world, perhaps. Where elephants were very light, or hawks very strong, or where, indeed, force was not needed to move objects in the way we're familiar with. But in this world, no. Of course, a contradiction, a self-contradiction, that is another matter, for we cannot conceive it to find refuge in any world whatsoever. We cannot conceive a world in which it was true both that hawks caught only monkeys, and yet that some hawks caught mice. Eh?'

'But sire, what's wrong with having this pattern of experience, or whatever you call it, what's wrong with having it disturbed or upset? You're always saying that the truth is often too disturbing to face! Why shouldn't you admit something's possible, even if it is upsetting?'

'My boy, there is nothing wrong with upsetting our understanding of the world. Indeed, that is how we learn to understand it. But it must be upset properly. In the right order. The least profound patterns first; the most general ones only as a last resort. Why? One, because it works, my boy; two, because if you don't discipline yourself to the order that experience herself prescribes, you end up upsetting things in the order that most captures your imagination; and then you lose touch with the sacred line between the possible and the impossible. It is only by accurately tracing that line that you can ever move it, and appear thus to achieve the impossible.'

'But sire —'

'Yes, Vrisha...' Charvaka held his hands up and turned to Karna. 'The strange thing is that he's only like this when you're around. He's not *quite* as bad when we're alone. Are you, Vrisha? Go on... You were saying?'

'Yes, sire, but if it's just a pattern of experience that tells you what's possible and what isn't, well... How can anything contradict a *pattern*? It might not be the pattern you're expecting, but what's impossible about that? What's to stop the pattern being something else? It's not as though there's anything *making* the pattern happen. I mean, I can understand a contradiction *making* something impossible. That's a real law, which can't be broken. But just a pattern? Things could fit it, or not.'

Charvaka scratched his beard.

'In the first place, my boy, your law of contradiction has sovereignty over a world which is neither here nor there. A world peopled by the ideas of your imagination, a world no more real than the world of a story. Your law of contradiction neither rules nor even touches this world. How can it? In the second place, there *is*, in my opinion, something which is preserving the patterns that we see and discover, which is making them all happen. Kali. And this world is as it is, I believe, because of Kali's laws. But I will grant you this: in a world in which events were obliged to happen, according to law, this obligation would be observable only through patterns of experience. If we lived in such a world, under such laws — and I believe we do — then when we observed the world around us, we could only ever see the pattern, not the force, of law. But does that mean that the law has no bite, just because we only see the teeth close, and no blood? Does it mean that the law does not *compel* its subjects to move, just because we only ever see them dance in their familiar patterns of attendance?'

'I don't follow, sire...'

'Vrisha,' interrupted Karna, 'if a hawk can catch an elephant, surely you can catch a simple argument? Where's this open mind of yours?'

'Karna!' protested Charvaka. 'That's not fair on the poor boy. He's still young!'

'That reminds me, Charvaka.' Karna had put down his bow. 'I suppose you still won't teach me to use *your* mantras?'

Charvaka furrowed his brow and shook his head.

'No, Karna, I will not let you use them, not yet. When you are older, perhaps. They are no substitute for skill with the bow, which even you still have room to perfect. And besides... They are most dangerous. I myself know of someone who had the phial of liquid I had given him explode in his face, when it was hit by his opponent's arrow... I have since made the materials a little less labile. But not until you're older, my boy.'

'I see. I'm still too young to learn yours, and too much of a suta for Drona to show me his...'

14 Preparations

'What are they *for*? Why do I have to keep wearing them?'

As the years went by Karna would every so often raise the question of his ear-rings and mail with Charvaka.

'When you're older, my boy,' was the rishi's usual reply.

But then on one of his visits to Varanasi, soon after his nineteenth birthday, Karna met with a different reaction. This time Charvaka's first response was to send Vrisha out of the workshop.

'The mail...' began the rishi, 'the mail is not so important. Not now. If I were you I would still wear it, at least until you go to Parashu. How many more of the links have you got left to put on?'

'Not many. It's slowed down now. Perhaps in a couple of years I'll be wearing them all.'

'When was the last time you took it off?'

'Years ago, sire. I don't need to take it off to add the new links. It seems to stick to my back now...'

'Yes... When you do come to take it off, my boy, it'll hurt. Soak your back in brine... But the mail is not as important as the ear-rings... Everything hangs on them. One of them means your life, the other means your death...'

'How?'

'There is no need for you to know yet the precise details, Karna. When you go to Parashu, he will show you.'

'But which one is which? It would be quite useful to know! For me, at any rate. Which one means death, sire, left or right?... You don't know!'

'No, I don't know, my boy.'

'Is there no way to tell them apart? They look exactly the same to me, there doesn't seem to be any asymmetry.'

'They *look* exactly the same, yes. They have the same shape, the same volume —'

'And the same weight. At least, I think so, though I suppose they would by now feel the same to me even if they didn't.'

'Yes, they are exactly the same weight. I don't know of a balance that could tell them apart.'

'And yet they're different?'

'Oh yes. I know how to tell them apart. I would have to take them off you to examine them, but, yes.'

'And yet you don't know which does which? You mean, you can tell one twin from the other, but not say which is the good and which is the bad.'

'Exactly. It would be of no help if I did examine them. As you say, I would know which is which, but not which does which.'

'So only Parashu knows... What? Even Parashu doesn't know?'

'No, my boy. The mongoose doesn't know.'

'I see... Well, no, I don't see — my life and death are somehow hanging on these... dice of mine... and all you rishis can do is place your bets?'

'There is more at stake than just your life or death, Karna.'

'That's a great consolation to me, sire. So... if I can just get this clear while I've got you in the mood to speak... Is there no one who knows?'

'There is one man who knows which is which and which does which. He put them on you after you were born —'

'You mean I didn't come down with them already in place?'

'Karna!' The rishi frowned at him. 'He is the only one that could give you your life, or your death. But it would be no use asking him... Even with your ear-rings on he wouldn't *speak*...'

Karna looked at Charvaka in silence.

'You must of course never remove them,' added Charvaka, gravely. 'I'm afraid that unless you're wearing them, we're really not supposed to speak to you about it at all...'

A bitter smile spread across Karna's face.

'I wouldn't say you've been very informative while I've had them on, Charvaka... You know, what I find hardest to understand...' Karna's expression darkened as he slowly shook his head. 'How could *you* of all people get involved in such a nonsense?'

He glanced away distractedly as Vrisha reappeared. The boy removed his dripping headcloth discreetly, in silence. Karna turned back to Charvaka.

'Well,' Karna sighed, 'if I hadn't had these ear-rings, my life would certainly have been different.'

'True, my boy, but don't lose heart —'

'What do you mean *true*?' interrupted Vrisha, unable to restrain himself.

'What are you doing here, Vrisha?'

'It's raining, sire! And you're full of contradictions. How can what Karna said be true? According to you it's nonsense.'

'I'm sorry, my boy, we're in the middle of a conversation —'

'In the middle of talking nonsense!'

'What in the world are you talking about?'

'How could you ever tell if it was true or false that Karna's life would have been different if he hadn't had his ear-rings? I've heard you say lots of times, sire... If you can't possibly determine whether something's true or false, then it's nonsense!'

'That's not quite what I said —'

'Perhaps not quite, but near enough. And since he's *got* his ear-rings, how could we ever know what his life would have been like without them? Even if it's not nonsense, how can what he said be true?'

'Vrisha, you know I'm not interested in discussing language. As far as I'm concerned, it's a means to an end. Particularly so at the moment, when until you came in it was a means to an end which your brother and I were privately considering. Can't you go somewhere?'

'Vrisha,' interposed Karna, 'all I meant was this: that my ear-rings, and mail, have had a most decisive influence on my life. What's wrong with that? It's fairly sensible. It's even possible to determine whether or not having these pieces of metal about me did or did not change my life. Now, will that do? Off you go...'

Vrisha frowned.

'All right, what about this, then? What about if you said to me that if Drona hadn't stopped you shooting that arrow at that cloth swan, you would have hit it straight through the head? What about that, then? Try and twist your way out of that one!'

'How did you find out?'

'Vaitanika, of course. Well?' Vrisha turned to Charvaka. 'Isn't that nonsense? How could you possibly determine whether that was true or false? Not possibly. So it's nonsense.'

'Vrisha...' Charvaka scratched his beard. 'What I meant was this... Suppose I were to tell you that in this very room, at the moment, there was a grey *asphuta*. Eh? In such a case you and Karna wouldn't know what it would be like even to begin to investigate the truth of that assertion. You couldn't start, let alone finish. Why? Because you don't know the meaning of *asphuta*. And thus there is no claim about an asphuta, grey or otherwise, which would make sense to you, which you could begin to investigate. Of course, even then, it may be going too far to conclude that such a term can have absolutely no meaning: after all, if you begin to notice that I'm always happy and smiling when I tell you there's an asphuta in the room, then the term can begin to do a little work, eh?'

'Yes, sire, I know,' grumbled Vrisha. 'There's more to meaning than meaning.'

'Exactly. And in any case, let me remind you that just because truth and falsehood may be impossible to determine, this does not make something nonsense: questions, commands, expressions of preference, all these may make perfect sense without possibly being true or false. There may be insincerity attached to them, true, for there is more to falsehood than just falsehood —'

'Charvaka, please...' interrupted Karna. 'Can I remind *you* that we haven't finished our conversation?'

'Yes, my boy, I'm sorry — let me just deal with your brother... Where was I? Yes... Be this as it may, truth and falsehood can of course provide a useful test of nonsense. And indeed, you have tried to draw attention to another type of nonsense, in which no single term, such as *asphuta*, obstructs the determination of the truth of an assertion; and yet the assertion as a whole, you maintain, is such as to obstruct its investigation. Thus, if I were to claim that there was in this room at this very time a large and grey elephant, but of a breed whose presence is not detectable by any of our senses, well, again, you wouldn't know how to begin to test my claim. Eh? And, in this case too I am quite happy to consider that claim to be nonsense, even though we know the meaning of each constituent term. But now suppose that I asserted that on the uppermost branch of Karna's tree, the one that accommodated the cloth target, a tree standing at present, I believe, in the grounds of the Academy at Hastinapura... Suppose I asserted that on the uppermost branch of that tree, far above where any of us could climb, on that branch there were exactly twelve leaves. Well, in this case you do know what you need to do to test my claim. But you don't know, and will never know, whether it is true or false. It is not nonsense, because you know what steps you would need to take to verify it. Unfortunately, as a matter of fact, you will never be able to put such a procedure into effect: you will not be able to gain permission to cut the tree down; nor, as a matter of fact, will you be able to grab a ride from a passing hawk and hover beside the uppermost branch, eh?'

'But that's the whole point, sire. We do know in principle how to verify that one. But I can't even conceive how we could determine what would have happened if Karna had released that arrow!'

'Well, my boy, we are able to conceive much more than we give ourselves credit for. When it suits us. For just consider that assertion. If Karna had released the arrow, it would have struck the bird. It is by no means nonsense. As in my previous example, I concede, we cannot proceed to test its truth. But, only as a matter of fact, just as in that previous case. It is not nonsense because I can describe to you exactly what would be the procedure to test it: I simply wind the rest of the world back to the moment just before Drona prevented Karna from releasing the arrow. I then persuade Drona to give Karna the command to shoot. Karna does so. Then I examine the target. You see, my boy, I have been able to tell you how you should go about testing that statement. Sadly, we are prevented from starting the investigation, not because we don't know what needs to be done, but because, as a matter of mundane fact, the laws of this world, such as we know them, do not appear to permit such an experiment. We are not able to wind the world back. And even if we did, we may not be able to influence Drona, for he is a very brittle man. Eh?'

Vrisha frowned. 'That's easier said than thought, sire. Just because you can say it doesn't mean you can imagine it. You of all people should know better! If we were to wind back the world as you describe, and we're still in it, we would have wound ourselves back as well, and would have forgotten the future from which we started. For your experiment we'd have to wind back the world from somewhere outside it, which is a bit harder to imagine!'

'Very interesting,' declared Karna. 'But Vrisha, I just don't see your problem. Surely you must know by now that if Drona *had* let me release that arrow, it would have gone straight through the swan's head. Now, could you leave us?'

'I take my orders from the rishi, not from you.'

'Is that so? May I remind you that you wouldn't even be here if it wasn't for me.'

'So?'

'You agree?'

'Yes, there's no need to rub it in. A suta without fancy ear-rings and mail doesn't get very far...'

'Is that so? I thought you said you couldn't even understand, let alone agree, with that? You agree then that if it hadn't been for my ear-rings and my mail, you wouldn't be here now? Charvaka, could you kindly give him his orders?'

'Yes, Vrisha, please! We'd like to be alone, so go out and get wet!'

'Is that an argument?' queried Vrisha. 'Don't tell me, sire, there's more to argument than argument...'

Reluctantly Vrisha left them alone once again.

'You said life or death, Charvaka. Death, I understand, but life? I already have it. Why should I go to Parashu to gain what I already have at the risk of losing it?'

'It is true, you would risk your life. But you will also have something to gain. I will let the mongoose explain. Of course, you may decide you do not want it. In which case you do not need to take the risk. But it will not surprise me if you do.'

'When should I go?'

'I would ask you not to go... just yet.'

'Why not?'

'Because you may never come back, my boy. Your life deserves more... There is no need to go quite yet. What kind of life have you had? Hiding yourself away from the sun.'

'I'm used to it, sire.'

'I think you should allow yourself to shine before you face the dark... Drona is planning an exhibition, isn't he? A couple of years, is it?'

'More like three, sire. Yes, it's a tournament. I think it'll coincide with Arjuna's eighteenth birthday.'

'How is Arjuna coming on?'

'Very well... He's a brilliant warrior. Oh yes, they'll love him at the tournament. He's wonderful to watch.'

'Why don't you wait until then, my boy? Wait until after the tournament to go to Parashu. I know your parents will want to see you.'

'At the tournament? But even if Drona lets me participate —'

'He will not stop you. If necessary, Kripa will see to that.'

'Yes, but even so... It's just a show, sire. It means nothing. I don't want to take part, I don't need to take part, and even if I did, it wouldn't be *me*. It would just be a shadow of myself, which I've learnt to cast...'

'Well, why not take the chance to cast aside that shadow, eh? Do you always want to live in the shade? Wouldn't you like now to reveal what you can do? As you used to in Anga, before you left?'

'I don't know, sire.'

'What do you mean, you don't know!... What is it the mongoose says?... I can never remember his exact words... Listen to the fires that quietly smoulder in your heart, with neither smoke nor glaring heat... arguing amongst themselves in the shadow of your thoughts, till finally they spark and flare in action... Bah! That can't be right, I'm sure there's a rhyme there... Listen well to those blind flames. Are they the fires of fear? Of self-pity? Do they burn for fame? For attention? For love, for admiration? Which flame should you let rein to quench the others? Which flame will let you?'

Karna stared at the rishi in silence.

'Well, my boy?'

'Yes. I would like to cast the shadow aside, sire. I would *like* to. But I don't need to. More than that... It's a desire I'd find greater pride of achievement in suppressing than indulging.'

Charvaka scratched his beard.

'Let me tell you something...' he said. 'A little story... about your father. Your *real* father, Surya. Of course, I don't *know* if he is your real father, or if this story is *absolutely* true, but this is what people say. You have probably guessed by now,' he continued, with a smile, 'that your father was not married to your mother? No, your father was married to a most divine female called Sanjna, daughter to the blacksmith of the gods, Vishwa-karma. But Sanjna was so dazzled by the sheer radiance of your father that after a while she left him.

'Surya was heartbroken,' continued the rishi, 'and decided to go to his father-in-law for advice. For Vishwa-karma was a very practical god.

'"Have I done something wrong, Vishwa? How can I persuade your daughter to return to me?"

'"Surya, don't you realise that you're just too bright to countenance? Your good wife, my daughter, is exhausted by your constant brilliance."

'"Oh dear, I didn't notice."

'"Of course not, my dear. Too much light is as blinding as too little."

'"But Vishwa, there must be something I can do. Surely there is *something*?"

'"The trouble with you, my dear, is you are such a *perfect* sphere. You are too good, too roundly made, you put great Dharma in the shade. Let yourself go, just here, just there, till you are out of shape one hair. Then your brilliance should soon fade, just by a fraction, by a jade. I'd recommend an eighth or so. Reduce by that amount your glow and your good wife should quickly show. I think that if you really try you then can both see eye to eye!"

'So Surya made the great sacrifice, lost an eighth of his perfection, and regained the affections of his wife. He is still, as you see, sufficiently dazzling to deter mere mortals from his direct gaze.'

Karna smiled.

'And you think I should take a beam from my father's light?'

'Not necessarily, my boy. But you might care to reflect that imperfection has its own radiance. It has the charm of the attainable. Remember, my boy, it's not wise to be wise all the time.'

◊

Whatever Karna may have decided about taking part in Drona's tournament, this prospect dwindled following a rather unpleasant incident which took place soon after Karna's twentieth birthday.

Drona and the Academy naturally had a considerable reputation. Drona would often receive applications from pupils, if not to join the Academy, at least to receive private tuition from him.

One such pupil was a young man from Nishada, called Ekalavya. He was already extremely adept as an archer. But although he was both fast and accurate, he did not have the particular techniques of combat which he had seen Drona display, years before, in Nishada.

The people of Nishada, however, were considered by the Bharatas generally to be lower even than sutas. Drona refused to give him tuition. But Ekalavya camped out in the woods outside the city, and practised there alone. So strong was his memory of Drona leading King Pandu's forces in Nishada, so great his admiration, that he harboured no ill-feeling for him. He even went so far as to carve an image of Drona's head in clay, before which he knelt each morning in the little clearing where he had taken shelter.

One night Drona had taken the princes out into the woods to practise shooting in the dark. On this occasion he had let the Kuru princes and Karna accompany the Pandavas, less to instruct the former than to impress them with the feats his favourites had now mastered.

With the party went a huge, fierce dog belonging to Bhima. While they were practising in pitch-darkness, the dog suddenly caught a scent, for it scampered off, barking savagely. The princes heard a familiar growl. The dog was evidently about to leap upon some unfortunate creature. Then there was silence.

The princes lit a torch. A few seconds later the dog reappeared, emitting smothered yelps when it saw them. They counted seven thin wooden arrows harmlessly lodged between its teeth. The animal could not close its mouth. Amazed by this, they extracted the arrows, put the dog on a leash, and followed it. By that time Ekalavya, whom the dog had been about to attack, had himself lit a torch, and was waiting with bow drawn for the commotion to arrive.

As soon as he saw Drona, Ekalavya put aside his weapons and knelt down before him, kissing his feet. Drona caught sight of the clay head, and asked Ekalavya what it was for.

'Master, even your image gives me inspiration. You see, whether you know it or not, I am your pupil. When I practise I model myself on you, master.'

Arjuna drew Drona to one side.

'Sire, you saw what he did, in the dark? He is superior to me, and you haven't even instructed him! What would he be capable of if he actually were your pupil?'

Drona turned to Ekalavya.

'If I have indeed been an inspiration to you, Ekalavya, then you are already my pupil.'

'I am, sire. I can never forget what you did on that battlefield.'

'If you are my pupil,' said Drona, 'then where is my fee? All my pupils have promised me a favour in exchange for my inspiration.'

'Master, I have no possessions to speak of. But if there is anything in my power to give to you, or to do for you, command me, and I shall obey you gladly.'

'Anything?'

'Anything, master.'

'Whatever the cost?'

'Master, if it is possible for me to obey you, it will be an honour. Just to have seen you in action is something few mortals can have experienced. No price is too high for such perfection.'

'In that case, Ekalavya, for my fee I merely require the thumb of your right hand.'

Before the situation had fully registered in the minds of the watching pupils, Ekalavya had drawn his dagger, passed it into his left hand, and without any emotion had severed his right thumb.

While Ekalavya staunched the bleeding, and the princes all covered their faces in dismay, Drona and Karna stood staring at each other in the torchlight.

The following day Karna did not attend the Academy. Nor did he ever again ask or receive instruction from Drona.

◊

'You can always stay with us, Karna, you know that?'

'I know... Thank you, Sanjaya...'

'But why have you decided to leave? So suddenly? Drona hasn't tried to expel you again, has he?'

'No, no... Sanjaya, I don't know how, or when, I will be able to repay you—'

'For what? Don't be an idiot! Anyway, the rishi has paid quite generously for the food and clothing you've consumed over the years. How many years is it, my word? But you owe him, not us. And your parents. They've also paid us, you know.'

'Yes, but now that I will not be studying at the Academy I can't go on taking Charvaka's charity.'

'Suit yourself. But you know that our door is always open to you. Where are you going to live?'

'I'll stay in the woods.'

'Whereabouts? In case I need to get in touch with you?'

'There's some dense forest south of the city. I'll go there. I'm going to tell Vaitanika the exact spot, once I've settled... So, you can ask him if you need me. And if there is anything I can do for you... One thing... I'm not going to tell my parents. They would worry. I'll send word to Charvaka. My brothers will keep quiet for me... I don't want my parents to know. If they send you anything, any money, keep it, Sanjaya.'

'I see. So as far as your parents are concerned, what, you're still at the Academy?'

'Yes.'

Apart from Vaitanika, no one knew exactly where Karna lived or what he did over the next two years. Occasionally someone would say they had seen the suta on the outskirts of the forest, south of Hastinapura. And a few times, when he needed supplies for his weapons, Karna did come right into Hastinapura, bringing with him tiger skins or bear hides to trade. On those occasions he would stay with Vaitanika.

Sanjaya, Kripa and even Bhishma tried to enquire after him from Vaitanika and his shudra friends; but with very little definite information in reply. Drona himself was not surprised and not a little pleased by Karna's disappearance; he made no direct attempt to ask Vaitanika what had happened, but he was soon aware of the rumours that the suta had left the city.

Of the princes, both Dur and Yudhi did try once or twice to contact Karna through Vaitanika, but with no success. Only Bhima and the twins were gladdened by his absence. Arjuna, in truth, was sorry to miss Karna's competition; for Karna always made him work hard for his victories.

About a year after Karna left, Arjuna began to practise away from the Academy, in the grounds of one of King Dhrita's palaces near the outskirts of the city. Usually he worked just with the assistance of Vaitanika, but occasionally he took along one or two of his brothers.

There were several reasons for this move. One was that Drona was now obliged to devote more time to the twins and some of the younger Kuru princes; so it was generally not appropriate for Arjuna to join in. But the main reason was that Arjuna had begun to prepare for the tournament, which was to be held the following year. This occasion was in effect to be a graduation for all the princes. But, on the pretext of Arjuna's eighteenth birthday, he was to be the main attraction: Drona planned to close the exhibition with a section showing off Arjuna's skills with the bow. Arjuna wanted to keep his programme for this section a secret. And in this respect his new arrangements for practice were far more suitable.

As the great event drew nearer, Arjuna and the princes spent more and more time in preparation. During the weeks leading up to it a team of shudras, organised under Vaitanika, began getting the equipment ready and the tournament site cleared.

In the atmosphere of mounting excitement there was little thought spared for the absent Karna. Nevertheless, once or twice it was rumoured that the strange suta had been seen helping the shudras at work in the arena.

15 The tournament

The vast rectangular arena had been carefully levelled. The two long sides of the rectangle, north and south, were encrusted with a large number of tents, all of different shapes, sizes and colours. On the south side, in the centre, was a raised platform on which the royal pavilion was being constructed. There were tents also along the shorter west and east sides, but a wide gap had been left in the centre of both of these. On the west side, surmounting the gap, was a splendid arch which was almost finished. Through this the participants were to come and go. On the east side the gap had no such arch, but it was to remain without spectators: for although such arenas were very large, and the display of arms usually very accurate, there would always be some anxiety among spectators that stray arrows might reach them; and since the main line of fire was to be along the length of the arena, the gaps at either end lessened the risk to the crowd.

On either side of the platform for the royal pavilion were areas reserved for musicians. Musicians would also flank the entrance arch, to announce and comment on the performances with all manner of string instruments, plucked and bowed, and a multitude of drums, trumpets and conches. Spread around the arena itself were a number of colourful targets, banners and contraptions to provoke the imagination.

As the day approached all Hastinapura began to bubble with excitement as people speculated about the forthcoming exhibition. A favourite topic of conversation was the talent of the legendary Prince Arjuna.

And on the afternoon itself the crowds assembled. The kshatriyas and brahmanas occupied the tents with their servants; the vaishyas and unattached shudras spread around wherever they could find a space. With a fanfare of drums and trumpets the royal family appeared with their guests from afar: four kinsmen, all great kings, accompanied by members of their families. They proceeded grandly to the dazzling pavilion; it was flying pennants interwoven with gold, inlaid with jewels and ivory.

First to take his seat was the blind King Dhrita, a huge figure, dwarfing Sanjaya beside him. It was always Sanjaya who was at hand as a guide whenever the king needed a pair of eyes. Dhrita was followed by his wife Gandhari and their youngest sons, who would not be performing.

Then came Bhishma and Vidura, and Pritha, the proud mother of the Pandavas; for since Madri's death Pritha felt as responsible for the twins as for her own three sons.

By Pritha's side was the first of the four kings, her elder brother Vasu-deva, king of the Yadavas. With him was his son Krishna, who was looking forward to seeing his younger cousins. Though not yet thirty Krishna was already a legendary and striking figure. A wave of silence rippled through the crowd when they saw him enter. On this occasion he was dressed in black, save for the red of his sash and headband. But it was not these colours that gave him away from afar. Below his sash, riding loosely on his hips, was a black belt. Strapped to this was a large wallet, also in black leather, with a clasp of glinting gold. In this wallet Krishna always carried his deadly discus.

In this branch of the family the Pandava princes had two other cousins whom they had heard much of but never met. Krishna had an elder brother, Bala-rama, and a much younger sister, Subhadra. But to the great disappointment of the Pandavas these two had been unable to attend. Bhima in particular had been most upset, for Bala was a renowned exponent of the mace. The prince had been hoping to receive some tuition from him before the tournament, to help him beat Dur, his great rival with that weapon.

Taking a seat just behind Bhishma was the second visiting king, the great Soma-datta, king of the Balhikas. He was Bhishma's cousin, being a son of Balhika, Shantanu's younger brother. Soma with his son Bhuri-sravas had come all the way from the north-west foothills of the Himalayan mountains. Bhuri, who was then in his thirties, was thought by many to be an even greater warrior than his father, and could spar with Bhishma himself without discredit.

To one side of Queen Gandhari was the third visitor, her own brother and Dur's favourite uncle, King Shakuni of the Gandharas. He was renowned not for his mastery of the bow, but for his prowess in mathematics, which he was able to apply with lethal vision at the dice table.

The fourth king was from the south, a great warrior, Shalya, king of the Madrakas. He was seated near Pritha. His sister had been poor Madri, and this was the first time he was to set eyes on his nephews, Nakula and Saha.

Kripa, Drona and Ashwa were down in the arena just in front of the royal pavilion, supervising arrangements for the afternoon. Vaitanika and his team of shudras were busy putting the finishing touches to the targets and equipment around the arena. In fact, at that precise moment, ten shudras were lifting a huge, hollow iron boar, about twice the size of a real animal. They were slowly carrying it towards a thick iron post, half the height of a man, which was set in an extensive circular mounting, also made of iron. The post, though solid, had three or four horizontal holes cut through it in a vertical row; and the top of it was shining with grease. When they reached the post the shudras heaved up the boar, which had a hole cut for the purpose in its iron belly, and impaled it through this hole onto the post. The animal balanced perfectly, swaying very slightly, its four legs just clearing the circular iron base. The boar had two eye-holes and a gaping mouth armed with impressive tusks. It did not take much imagination on the part of the crowd to presume that these orifices were to serve as targets.

When the boar was quite still and everything else was ready, the musicians, who had been silent since the fanfare for the royal visitors, began gradually to build up a rhythm. Most of the team of shudras retired to the edges of the arena, but some were bravely stationed near targets which they would have to attend to during the proceedings.

Almost opposite the royal pavilion, on the north side, in a little space between two sumptuous tents, was Karna's family. Adhi, Radha, and Karna's three brothers. Radha was calm, but the others were all anxious: Adhi, on Karna's behalf, hoping that his son would do himself justice; the three young men dreading their parent's discovery of Karna's absence.

Those fortunate enough to be seated in the royal pavilion could see, to their far right, towards the east edge of the arena where only the brave or desperate chose to watch, a large perfectly circular pool of water. The pool must have been over fifty paces in diameter. At its very centre a hollow cylindrical structure stood up out of the water. This was slightly taller and somewhat wider than a man, and made up to represent a turret: it was painted at its top as a castellated wall. On the left side of the turret, facing west into the centre of the arena, was depicted a monstrous demon with ten ferocious heads. Its more peripheral heads were painted round towards the back of the turret, out of sight of the royal pavilion. The demon also had ten pairs of arms. At the centre of the demon's chest, halfway up the west side of the turret, was a round hole, maybe three or four fingers in width. The outline of the hole was painted bright red, and it had been stopped up with a plug made of rolled bark.

Around the base of the turret, just above the surface of the water, was a circular ledge. Piled up on this ledge, circling the turret and almost hiding the demon's single pair of feet, was a heap of thin logs and dry grass. Again, it did not take much to guess that this would be set alight at some stage in the proceedings. The pile of combustible material left just enough room to walk around the ledge.

Then under the surface of the water, to the west of the turret and placed symmetrically on either side as though guarding the demon, were two golden snakes, their images shifting slowly beneath the ripples.

Connecting the far side of the turret to the further, east edge of the pool was a bridge. It was formed by two narrow wooden planks meeting each other end to end halfway between the turret and the edge. The planks were covered in a fabric which had been pinned to the wood. At this halfway point the planks rested on a stone support rising up from the water. Falling in coils to the bottom of the pool were two pairs of golden chains, each pair fixed to the end of their plank resting at the halfway support. At the central ledge, and at the east edge of the pool, the other ends of the two planks were mounted on hinges. These would allow each half of the bridge to be drawn up.

Beside the stone support at the middle of the bridge a tall, sturdy pole rose up from the water. From a spur at the top of this pole hung a heavy rope; and to the bottom end of the rope, just clear of the water's surface, was attached a cow's horn. The rope was swaying very slightly in the breeze.

A little to the west of the royal pavilion, but on the central west-east axis of the arena, grew a banyan tree which had been left standing when the rest of the arena had been levelled. It stood about seventy or eighty paces across from the turret. Quite high up in the branches of this tree a brightly decorated cloth vulture had been set. On a branch next to it was fixed a horizontal metal hoop, just large enough to fit over a person's head.

In the shade of the banyan tree was the huge iron boar.

Although there were a number of other devices around the arena, and countless banners and flags, nothing caught the eye so much as the pool, the tree and the boar.

◊

All the princes performed magnificently as the first part of the afternoon's events unfolded without a single slip.

The very first item was a display of archery on horseback. Each prince galloped in turn around a circuit of targets. Their accuracy at high speed was breathtaking, and even the Kuru princes were impressive. The shudras bravely and efficiently collected the spent arrows where necessary in the few seconds' respite between participants.

After this came a display of chariot fighting in which the princes, whose chariots entered the arena two at a time, struck not only stationary targets but also banners flown from the rear of their partner's chariot. Besides using their bows the young warriors demonstrated their command of javelins. And in the case of four of the Pandavas, even threw their swords at targets. Bhima delighted the crowd by hurling maces and clubs from his chariot. He had lately taken to wearing his hair in a topknot, and for this occasion he had fixed a tiger's tooth through it to add to his fearsome aspect. Most of his missiles completely demolished their intended goal, and the shudras had to work particularly hard to clear up after his tour of the arena.

During all of this, the pool, the tree and the boar remained unscathed, adding to the crowd's anticipation.

For their demonstration of hand-to-hand fighting with swords and shields the princes wore heavy breastplates: the winner in each bout being the first to score a hit on his opponent's armour. A brief interval enabled the crowd to catch its breath, and then came a demonstration of fighting with maces. For these bouts the princes discarded their shields, though keeping their breastplates and adding the protection of helmets: one hit on the head or two on the chest were required for victory. In the last of these bouts Dur and Bhima, the two mace specialists, were drawn against each other.

This contest lasted some time, during which it became rather more than a spectacle.

Bhima and Dur were both very large young men, and very evenly matched. Bhima was slightly the larger and very much the more powerful of the two, but Dur was quick for his size and very skilful. After a while the spectators became so involved with the fight that they began cheering on their favourite. This added to the hostility between the two princes to transform the fight into a real confrontation. And of course the crowd went wild when they sensed this. Some of the crowd, as well as championing their man, began to shout insults at his opponent. One voice in particular was heard distinctly above the crowd, calling Bhima *beardless*. Bhima indeed had no promise of hair about his face or chin. The Pandava prince stopped suddenly and roared in the direction of this voice, swearing to kill anyone who ever again called him beardless. To a strange mixture of thunderous applause, laughter and silence, he dared anyone to put his oath to the test. Of course no one did, not even Dur, and with renewed aggression Bhima returned his attentions to his opponent.

Sensing that the combatants might lose control, Drona and Ashwa bravely stepped in to separate them. The princes received loud and prolonged applause, and many appealed for the fight to be allowed to continue. Drona became uneasy about the mood of the crowd, and decided to skip the penultimate item in the programme and go straight to the climax of the afternoon. The sun in any case was now quite low; if he waited much longer Arjuna might have difficulty with the fading light.

Drona tried to silence the crowd, but they were still too excited. He signalled to the shudras, and they went over to the boar. Putting their backs to it, they slowly set it spinning on its post. The noise from the crowd broke up as the excitement of anticipation took over the spectators.

Drona stepped into the middle of the arena near the boar, which had now been deserted by the shudras to spin on its own momentum. He invited the crowd to prepare for a display by the master warrior, Prince Arjuna, son of Indra. The crowd burst into rapturous applause. Arjuna had of course struck all his targets and won all his bouts; moreover the crowd could appreciate that he was in a different class from the others, and they were eager to see more of him.

A hush descended, allowing the low drone from the spinning boar to fill the arena. Drona, still in the centre, took the opportunity to announce that for this final event of the exhibition the Pandava prince would enact the legend of Rama and Ravana.

By this time all the other princes had come into the arena and had taken their seats in the royal pavilion, as keen as the crowd to watch Arjuna.

Drona signalled to Vaitanika and quickly withdrew towards the royal box. On the north side opposite Drona the tense faces of Karna's family stood out against the smiling crowd.

Vaitanika was now running towards the banyan tree with an intriguing object: a large ball made of leather tightly stretched on what was probably a wicker frame. On the leather was painted the face of a beautiful young woman. At regular intervals on the surface of the ball were fastened golden anklet rings. Vaitanika climbed with the ball right up into the tree, and placed it so that it was resting freely on the metal hoop by the vulture.

The crowd suddenly understood. The young girl painted on the ball was none other than Sita, the wife of Rama. She and Rama had been exiled to a forest far from their city. The vulture next to her was Jayatu, who had been entrusted with guarding her from the dangers of the forest while Rama was away hunting. In another flash of recognition, which was almost perceptible as the crowd caught its breath, the creature on the turret was identified as the evil archdemon Ravana, and the turret itself as his castle on the island kingdom of Lanka.

The boar was still spinning round, humming with a low groan, when a strange figure danced through the arch into the arena. It was Arjuna, dressed in deerskins, as Rama.

Rama-Arjuna, exaggerating all his movements to the delight of the crowd, stalked the spinning boar like a hungry tiger. Suddenly, with two rapid volleys, he had shot five arrows at the boar: three in one eye, two in the other. The sound of the arrows hitting the iron echoed round the arena before the noise of the crowd swamped it. Rama continued to creep around the spinning boar. He drew a large metal arrow onto his bow, and shot this into the boar's gaping mouth. It must have set off a mechanism, inside the iron beast, which locked the rotating mass into the post: suddenly the momentum of the boar tore the post and its heavy base off the ground, and the animal went head over hoof, crashing into the dust with a resounding boom. The crowd went wild.

Behind Rama a chariot now entered the arena. Along one of its sides was a banner depicting a fabulous deer. It had jet black hooves, a tail of all the colours in the rainbow, blue ears, and a back speckled with gold and silver. The crowd instantly knew the deer to be Maricha. In the legend this was a demon, in the guise of a deer, employed to distract Rama so that its wicked master, Ravana, could steal off with the lovely Sita.

Rama, seeing the chariot flying past him, released two arrows. Instead of points these had sharp, broad cutting edges in the shape of crescent moons. These cut two thongs holding the banner of the deer against the side of the chariot. As the chariot turned, the banner peeled off to reveal another behind it: this time showing Maricha in its real guise, as a horrible demon, but not with quite as many heads and arms as its master.

The chariot completed its turn and left the arena through the arch with Rama in hot pursuit. More applause from the crowd, then a hush, with all heads craning towards the entrance.

Out of the silence the musicians uncoiled a sinister and irregular rhythm, gradually increasing in volume. When the noise could go no louder, the trumpets joined in. The music suddenly stopped. From the other end of the arena an explosion startled the crowd. As the smoke began to clear they saw the horrible features of Ravana emerge from the turret like a giant snail from its shell. Arjuna was this time wearing a mask over his face; the remaining heads and arms were depicted on a huge silk cloak he was now wearing.

Ravana-Arjuna crept along the bridge past the hanging rope and cow's horn, across to dry land at the east edge of the pool. There he armed himself with four quivers which he strapped under his billowing cloak. Three of the quivers contained wooden arrows with blunt striking ends. The fourth quiver contained an assortment. He picked up a bow which had been lying with the quivers, and aimed at the banyan tree, nearly a hundred paces away. Poor Jayatu, the vulture, fell to the ground, pierced by three arrows.

The demon now leapt and danced with wicked joy, and approached the tree stealthily, to the accompaniment of the musicians. When he was right beneath it, by the upturned boar, Ravana exposed three of his quivers, and folded his cloak well out of the way. Taking four of the wooden arrows in his right hand, he aimed at Sita, high up on the hoop in the tree. The ball leapt out of the tree, but before it had time to fall much below its original height, it was buoyed up by the next volley of arrows. In this manner, showering arrows at the ball, Ravana returned towards the pool bearing aloft the captive Sita. The crowd thundered their approval: for Ravana in the story had indeed escaped from the forest with his booty in a chariot which could fly through the air.

As Ravana floated Sita across to the pool, the golden rings were torn off the ball one by one, and left a scattered trail in the dust. Sita in the legend had dropped her rings and jewellery from Ravana's flying chariot, and this trail had enabled the monkey god Hanuman to find her and report back to Rama her place of captivity.

Ravana finally reached the bridge at the far side of the pool, still floating Sita above him with his arrows. Then he quickly scampered across the planks, suspended the ball directly above the turret, and stopped shooting. Sita fell into the turret with a crash of drums and cymbals. Water splashed out from the top of the turret: the shudras must have gone unnoticed across the bridge to fill the turret with water.

Ravana now took out the bark plug which was stopping the red hole in the side of the turret. There was another explosion which hid Ravana in dense smoke. This time, when the smoke began to clear, Ravana was gone. But a thin stream of water was spouting from the hole. The crowd realised that Rama now had to rescue Sita before the water finished pouring out: for Ravana had threatened to take Sita's life if she did not submit to his embraces within his deadline.

Before the smoke had completely lifted, two shudras leapt into the pool. They grabbed the chains fixed to the outer plank and threw them to two colleagues waiting on the east edge. These shudras on dry land began to drag the chains eastwards, drawing up the outer half of the bridge. When their plank was vertical they fixed the chains taut around two posts close to the eastern border of the arena. Meanwhile the shudras in the water had been dragging their chains in the opposite direction, drawing up the inner plank of the bridge. When this was vertical they fastened their taut chains to the mouths of the two golden snakes, beneath the water near the west edge of the pool.

The tall inner plank now dwarfed the turret, and the chains leading down from it into the water seemed like two long arms, ready to embrace the painted demon from behind.

Scarcely had the shudras retired when a horse came galloping in from the other end of the arena carrying Arjuna, with tail and mask, as the monkey god Hanuman. As he galloped towards the pool he shot arrows through each of the anklet rings which had fallen from Sita. Each arrow had instead of feathers a little red flag with Hanuman's face. When Arjuna-Hanuman reached the pool he started galloping around it. Each time round he shot arrows into the cow's horn at the bottom of the hanging rope, causing the rope to swing like a pendulum. When the pendulum had acquired enough momentum, Hanuman leapt from his horse, catching the rope as he fell, and swung over the water towards the turret, landing gracefully on the ledge with only his tail trailing in the water. From under his robe he took out a small flag and placed it in the top of the turret. Water was still streaming out from the painted demon's chest, the pendulum was still swaying, and the horse was still dutifully galloping round the pool.

With a well-timed leap back onto the rope, Hanuman came out of his swing to land comfortably on his horse.

As he galloped back he sparked a flint in his hand, setting fire to an arrow soaked in oil. With his horse still galloping away towards the west, he turned in the saddle to shoot this arrow back towards the base of the turret in a high, slow arc. The pile of grass and wood caught fire. With another arrow he severed the swinging rope. The horn dropped into the pool. Now Ravana was trapped on his island. Hanuman galloped out of the arena through the arch.

On the flag Hanuman had placed at the top of the turret was depicted Rama's signet ring, with which Hanuman in the legend had convinced Sita that he was genuinely in Rama's service. Also shown was a precious stone she had given to the monkey god, which Rama would recognise in turn as a token from his wife. Hanuman was supposed to have set fire to the whole island of Lanka as he escaped to return to Rama.

Just as the crowd had begun to take in what they had seen, Arjuna, now back as Rama, galloped in through the arch. In addition to his bow, perched over his left shoulder, he was wielding a sword. As he galloped past each arrow in Hanuman's trail, he cut off its red flag with one stroke of the sword. When he reached the pool he dismounted.

Casting aside his sword, Rama selected a dozen arrows with heads shaped like duck bills. He shot them at the surface of the water, and the spray put out the fire on Lanka. The golden snakes under the water represented Nagas, snake gods, at which Rama was supposed to have shot in desperation to wake up the god of the sea; for now he needed a way of getting across to Lanka. Eventually the god had emerged from the sea, advising Rama to enlist the help of Nila to make a bridge to span the sea. Nila was the son of Vishwa-karma, and had inherited some of his father's practical talents.

Rama shot four arrows, one pair towards the top of each of the two vertical planks. The fabric which covered them dropped away to expose the beautifully painted wood beneath. He shot four more arrows. Two of these broke the fastenings at each golden snake; the other two shot away the chains holding up the other plank. The two halves of the bridge fell down into position. The paintings on the wood showed scenes of Nila helping Rama build the bridge to Lanka.

Rama strapped on three new quivers, ran across the bridge, and plucked out Sita from the turret. Water was still trickling out of the red hole at the side. He tossed the ball into the air, and using his earlier technique, kept her aloft as he returned across the bridge. He conveyed her back to the banyan tree and with great precision floated her onto the hoop. The crowd was on its feet.

Rama then selected an arrow which had a plug of rolled bark tightly bound to its tail. He turned to face the turret, aimed carefully, and released the arrow.

The trickle of water stopped as the hole was plugged once more. Ravana had been shot through the heart.

In the royal pavilion Pritha wept with pride for her son.

After a few minutes of constant applause, the crowd began to cry for more. Arjuna's display had happened so fast that the crowd had hardly had time to appreciate his exquisite skills. To Drona's amazement the shudras, of their own accord, began to set everything up again: the boar, the turret, the bridge... even the wood and dry grass around the turret. The roars of the crowd subsided.

The boar was now humming again as it spun round. All eyes turned expectantly to the arch to see if Rama would reappear.

The patience of the crowd was rewarded by the appearance of a figure clad in deerskins. But this figure took no notice of the revolving boar, and approached the royal pavilion where Drona was standing apparently powerless to control the shudras. For they had been ignoring his frantic gestures. Suddenly it began to dawn on the crowd that the person they were seeing this time was not Arjuna. The man wore a mask to hide his face. But whereas Arjuna's skin was very dark, this man's skin was the colour of burnished copper. The crowd struggled to make out who it was.

The man bowed to the royal pavilion and addressed the crowd.

'With your permission,' he cried, 'and the permission of Drona-charya, tutor to the princes, I would like to repeat for you Arjuna's performance.'

The crowd roared their approval. The royal pavilion was humming with murmurs. Dur and his brothers were very excited at this stranger who dared to attempt the deeds of Arjuna. Yudhi recognised Karna as soon as he was close enough to see his feet; but he was too apprehensive to tell anyone. Across on the other side of the arena Radha also had recognised her son. And, of course, Vaitanika and his team all knew. But the rest of the crowd saw only a masked figure clad in deerskins, and as they roared the stranger on, Drona stood frozen to the spot.

Arjuna had now made his way round the back into the royal pavilion. He shouted down to find out from Drona what was going on, but Drona did not respond.

The boar was given a little extra speed by a brave shudra who had timed his push with great care, and Karna was off.

As he repeated each move of Arjuna's, the crowd went wild again. They could not believe their eyes. And when he came out of the turret as Ravana, he reduced the arena to complete silence. For instead of taking up a bow to shoot Jayatu down from the tree, the demon picked up a javelin. Brandishing it menacingly Ravana turned towards the spectators nearest to him.

Suddenly the demon whipped its body round and hurled the javelin across towards the centre of the arena; Jayatu flew out of the tree, to the other end of the stadium, transfixed by the javelin. Then, as the arena erupted with rhythmic chants of applause, the demon snaked towards the banyan tree, wiggling its trailing cloak. As it passed within fifteen paces of Drona it paused to turn all its eyes and arms towards the paralysed brahmana, frisking its cloak like a cat's tail, before proceeding to the tree to float Sita to the turret.

Again Karna matched Arjuna move for move, driving the crowd to a frenzy. Until, right at the very end, when as Rama, he had retrieved Sita and was floating her back to the tree with his constant stream of arrows: he delicately manoeuvred the ball in the air under the canopy of the great tree, and, just before setting her down on the hoop, turned back momentarily towards the turret. In between two volleys which kept Sita aloft hovering by the hoop, and much too fast for the eye to follow, he drew the arrow with the bark plug, releasing it in a flash towards the turret. As he set Sita back on her hoop, the arrow pierced Ravana's chest, plugging the red hole.

As the crowd rose to its feet, Dur and his brothers in the royal pavilion also stood up, and joined in the ovation to this stranger wearing the mask of Rama. Karna's brothers were hugging each other across on the other side of the stadium, while his parents wept. Vaitanika ran into the centre of the arena and embraced him.

Karna waved the crowd to silence.

'With your permission,' he shouted, 'I should like to challenge Prince Arjuna to single combat.'

Immediately Arjuna jumped down from the royal pavilion into the arena.

'You have appeared here as an uninvited intruder,' he cried angrily. 'I will kill you, whoever you are, now, in single combat, on foot, or on chariot!'

Before Arjuna had finished speaking Karna had unwrapped and cast aside the hide which covered his chest. He removed his mask, and stood there with a deerskin covering only his loins. His golden armour was revealed. In the red light of the setting sun the links sparkled like embers.

Around the arena the crowd gasped and sputtered. From behind Karna there came a half-stifled scream. It was Adhi. He would have fallen to the ground had Radha not held on to him. And in the royal pavilion Arjuna's mother had also fainted; Vidura was supporting her, trying to revive her.

The crowd was now silent. Karna spoke firmly but did not need to shout.

'Prince Arjuna, this arena is meant for all, not for you alone. If you wish to speak to me, speak with your arrows.'

Kripa, with considerable presence of mind, stepped forward into the arena and put his arm on Arjuna's shoulder. He fixed Karna with a look of blazing anger, and then addressed the crowd.

'This prince,' cried Kripa, raising Arjuna's arm, 'is the youngest son of Queen Pritha. You must tell us,' he continued, addressing Karna, 'the names of your parents and your royal lineage. Then and only then may Prince Arjuna fight with you. For royal sons never fight with men of lesser birth.'

Karna did not reply, but allowed a bitter smile to play on his lips as he gazed at the occupants of the royal pavilion.

Kripa repeated his request. 'Which king or prince is your father? Which queen or princess is your mother?'

Karna still made no reply.

Dur, in the meantime, having jumped down into the arena, ran across to join Karna. The Kuru prince now addressed the crowd.

'This warrior is Karna, from Anga. If Arjuna is unwilling to fight with one who is not a prince, then, if it pleases you, and with the permission of my father King Dhrita-rashtra, lord of all the Bharatas, I will make this man here and now... King Karna of Anga!'

There was a roar of approval, mainly from the shudras and vaishyas in the crowd. But many of the kshatriyas and brahmanas present had heard of or seen the suta warrior from Anga, and they remained silent.

King Dhrita, to whom Sanjaya had been dutifully describing the afternoon's events, nodded his head in assent.

To a great cheer from the crowd, a bowl was quickly found and filled with water from the pool. As Karna knelt down, Dur sprinkled the water over Karna's head, and pronounced him King of Anga.

As the noise of the crowd abated, Karna spoke quietly to his benefactor.

'Prince Dur-yodhana, I have not come here to ask favours, nor to give them. What do you want in return for your gift of this kingdom?'

'Karna, I desire from you only your friendship.'

'So be it,' replied Karna, and he embraced the Kuru prince.

During this brief ceremony, Adhi-ratha had slowly made his way across the arena to join his son.

As soon as he saw his father, Karna bowed down to him, kissing his feet. Bhima, guessing from his suta sash that this was Karna's father, jumped down from the pavilion and shouted in rage.

'Look, you see, this *king* is the son of a suta!' Bhima turned menacingly on Karna. 'You, son of a suta, do not deserve the glory of death at the hands of the noble Prince Arjuna. Why do you not go and rule your kingdom with your whip, as befits the son of a charioteer! You are no more worthy of your kingdom than a dog is of sacred butter!'

In the royal pavilion there was rising tension. Now Krishna got out of his seat, as Dur defended Karna.

'For his skill alone,' proclaimed Dur, replying to Bhima in a thunderous voice, 'Karna would deserve sovereignty of the world, not just of Anga. The circumstances of his birth cannot cloud his person...'

Krishna was now speaking urgently to Drona at the edge of the arena.

'...If anyone here,' continued Dur, 'does not like what I have given to Karna, then let him first challenge and destroy him!'

A cheer came from certain sections of the crowd. But the kshatriyas and brahmanas had grown anxious. Arjuna and Bhima were now arguing with Kripa as he tried to calm them.

Drona, awakened into action by Krishna, proceeded quickly to the centre of the arena. Krishna signalled to Kripa to send for two chariots; then he went to the side of the royal pavilion and caught the attention of the musicians there.

'The suta's son,' cried Drona to the crowd, 'will have to leave his challenge till another day... For our great sun' — he pointed to the lightest part of the evening sky — 'has set, at last, on this great tournament. I hope, with all my heart, that you have all been satisfied by the display from these great Bharata princes, from the son of Indra, Prince Arjuna... and from... the new king of Anga!'

To the applause of the crowd Drona led Bhima and Arjuna to the first chariot, which had reached the centre of the arena, and then he invited Dur and Karna to ascend the second chariot. The two chariots, with their occupants waving to the crowd, made a slow lap of honour to a triumphant fanfare. The spectators, sensing that it was now time to prepare for dark, began to light up their torches, heralding the night of eating and drinking which was to follow. Karna's golden mail caught the flickering light of the torches as his chariot left the arena.

•

'Palmira...' said the first Henry, seeing that she had come to a pause. 'Am I right in thinking that this Nila, who helped Rama build the bridge, must have been a sort of stepcousin of Karna's?'

'He must have been the brother of Karna's real father's wife,' explained the second Henry. 'Sanjna, she was called, I think.'

'Palmira, why do you use a crossbow instead of an upright bow? You'd be able to shoot lots of arrows quickly, like Karna or Arjuna.'

'She only needs one arrow. When was the last time you saw her miss?'

As the boys were speaking, an ant had managed to attain the marble top of Palmira's table; it was crawling into the shade of a bowl of sour milk. Palmira gently flicked it away.

'It's very kind of you to exaggerate on my behalf, Henry. But, you know, the upright bow isn't the easiest instrument for a woman. My breasts seem to get in the way. Also, of course, the crossbow gives me a far greater range. I am not particularly strong, you see, I would not be able to draw a tight upright bow to full stretch. Whereas I can wind up my crossbow...'

'Palmira, why do you always spit on your bows before you use them?'

'You do it on your swords as well, Palmira — does it make them work better?'

'Haven't I ever told you? Well... You've seen me kiss bread when I have to throw it away, haven't you? I hate to throw bread away, because it is the stuff of life... so I kiss it. I hate to pick up my weapons, because they are the stuff of death. So I spit on them. It's just a silly habit which helps me through a painful need. Well, I don't know about you boys, but I'm a bit tired. Same time tomorrow, yes?'

•

Day Three: *The Scales of Destiny*

16 The king of Anga

'Dur... what exactly does it mean to be king of Anga?'

Dur and Karna had left the tournament arena behind the chariot carrying Bhima and Arjuna. They were on their way to feast at the royal palace, where Dur had just invited Karna to stay as his guest.

'Anga now belongs to *you*, Karna!'

'And it used to belong to you?'

'To my father. It is a subject region of the Bharata kingdom.'

'What does it mean, it *belongs* to me?'

'What it really means,' said Dur, smiling at Karna's apparent ignorance, 'is that you get the taxes.'

'Taxes... You mean the people of Anga have been paying you taxes? What for? What do they get in exchange?'

'Security.'

'Security? You mean, if they pay you taxes they get security from your attacks?'

Dur laughed. 'I suppose so. But not just from our attacks. There are others around who might attack them. Then we would defend them.'

'Yes, I can see you would... And now do *I* have to defend them? Single-handed? And what if they don't want to pay me? I can't raise an army, as you can...'

Dur laughed. He glanced at Karna, unable to tell if Karna's innocence was genuine.

'Yes you can — now. What do you think all the kshatriyas in Anga are for?'

'Why should they attack their own people just so I can get the taxes?... I see, because I pay them out of the taxes. Yes. But why should the kshatriyas hand over anything to me?'

'Because if they don't, you call upon your ally, Prince Dur-yodhana. He will come to your assistance with his own kshatriyas. You see how it works?'

'I do. But then these warriors, these great kshatriyas of Anga... They are little more than tax collectors?'

'Not exactly. They pay vaishyas to collect the taxes for them. The kshatriyas then take their share, usually rather more than their share, and pass the rest on to you. Remember, the kshatriya's karma is the virtuous pursuit of wealth and pleasure. Though my uncle Vidura wouldn't agree with that. He disagrees with fighting, and doesn't want to have anything to do with violence. He's always telling me, "Kshatriyas are only men, and man is pre-eminently an agricultural animal."'

'He seems to be absolutely right, Dur. The shudras are the cattle whose produce you farm, the vaishyas are the horses that keep the cattle in order; and the kshatriyas ride the horses for you. Yes, Vidura's quite right. For if a man is not lucky enough to be a farmer, then at least he's a farm animal. I suppose my father Adhi-ratha is more or less a farm dog. By the way, Dur, as soon as this chariot stops I must go to see my parents. I haven't seen them for two years.'

'When we get to the palace we'll send a messenger to bring them. You know where they're staying?'

'Probably.'

'Good. I hope they'll stay with you as my guests in the palace while they remain in the city.'

'Thank you, Dur...'

'You don't need to thank me. I meant what I said, Karna. If I ever ask you for any favours, I'd rather you refused them than just did them out of gratitude. You've already repaid your kingdom twice over with the look on Bhima and Arjuna's faces this evening. I won't forget that. And they won't, either! But Karna... Your armour... How did you get it?'

'I wish I knew. And even if I did, I don't think I could tell you.'

With a great effort Dur managed to restrain his curiosity; and he resolved never again to question his new friend on this subject.

◊

At Dur's invitation Karna decided to stay on at the palace for a few months before visiting Anga. Moreover, Dur persuaded King Dhrita to have a room at the palace made out permanently at Karna's disposal.

The palace grounds were extensive, and its inhabitants many and various; Karna was left very much to his own devices. He would see Dur quite regularly; but the younger Kuru princes were too much in awe of this hero of the tournament to approach him. As for the Pandavas and the elders of the royal household who already knew him, Karna would occasionally cross paths with them: the five princes, Kripa, Bhishma, Vidura, Drona. But of these only Yudhi would give him the courtesy of recognition. For one reason or another, the rest were too troubled or outraged by his behaviour at the tournament to speak to him. The reaction of the princes and of Drona he could understand. Nor was Karna surprised that Kripa and Bhishma had been offended by the circumstances of his display. But he had expected at least some approach from these two, if only to chastise him.

Karna saw Sanjaya quite often; indeed, he would occasionally eat at his former home with the family. And it was Sanjaya who confirmed Karna's suspicions that Vaitanika did not now want to see him. For his friend had disappeared immediately after the tournament, and Karna had been quite unable to trace him. The few shudras who knew where he was refused to talk.

It was not long before Vrisha was back in Hastinapura to visit his brother. He assured Karna that he had given Charvaka a full account of the events at the tournament. And he promised that on his return to Varanasi he would tell the rishi not to expect Karna for a while; not indeed until Karna's first visit, as king, to Anga.

During his brother's stay Karna did ask him to try to glean any information he could from the shudras about Vaitanika. But they would not talk to Vrisha either.

◊

'Why shouldn't I challenge him to single combat? Even though he's not a kshatriya, surely he would be bound to accept the challenge rather than be disgraced as a coward?'

'Now is not the time, Arjuna...'

Arjuna's anger with Karna after the tournament had slowly transformed itself into a quiet but persistent grievance against him; and it was more because of the unpunished rudeness of Karna's uninvited intrusion, than out of jealousy for an usurping rival. Indeed, his own self-confidence remained so little tarnished by the experience that he could not understand Drona's discouragement.

'Sire, I know that I can kill him or defeat him in single combat. How many times have you told me there's more to fighting than just hitting targets?'

'Yes, Arjuna, of course... The problem is... Karna's armour... I have heard tell of the existence of such mail. It has divine properties. My son, you just do not possess arrows that can pierce it —'

'But my mantras, sire? What about my mantras?'

'Karna is protected from these also... by his ear-rings. I have consulted Kripa. It is a mystery which even Kripa-charya is unwilling to talk about. But it appears that the suta's armour and ear-rings are gifts from the gods. His ear-rings protect him from the effects of mantras. For it is well known that mantras, whether voiced or not, always enter the body through the ears.'

'What can I do, then? What's the use of my skill?'

'Don't worry, my son, do not fear. One day you will fight Karna. Surely you are destined to fight him. And remember Narada's prophecy. Therefore you are destined to kill him, and avenge the arrogance of his display. In the mean time, let us take heart from Narada's prophecy, that you will conquer all. But you must wait upon the voice of Destiny before she will speak to you. Time, my son, must be propitiated.'

'But how can I ever defeat him if he is protected by his armour and ear-rings?'

'Pray to your father, my son. Pray to Indra. Pray that Indra himself should take back the gifts the gods gave Karna. And keep hope, for do they not say that what the gods give, the gods can take back.'

◊

Krishna, who had left Hastinapura the day after the tournament, returned a few weeks later with his brother, Bala-rama. Krishna had kept his promise to Bhima: to persuade Bala to teach the prince some of the subtleties of combat with the mace.

The two sons of Vasu-deva were very different from each other. To the royal princes Bala appeared quiet and contemplative, whereas Krishna seemed always to be thinking and talking on his feet. Several meals were held at the palace in honour of these guests; and while Krishna would often interrupt his eating to play and dance with the musicians in attendance, Bala would barely exchange a word.

Karna was usually present on these occasions, and the courtesy which both Krishna and Bala extended to him was a source of frustration for Bhima and Arjuna. It was even more frustrating for Bhima, who had hoped to benefit privately from Bala's tuition, when he discovered that Bala intended to include in his classes not only the Kuru brothers, but also Karna.

During one session with the mace, Bhima was drawn in a bout against Karna. Bhima immediately complained to his tutor.

'I can't fight that cowardly king in a suta's sash! He wears armour beneath his shirt, rama. It stops him feeling pain or receiving injury. It's an unfair advantage, rama!'

'Prince Bhima-sena,' replied Bala, 'I infer from what you say that you consider yourself no coward. You consider yourself courageous, am I right?'

'Yes, rama.'

'Would you be prepared to put your courage to the test?'

'Certainly, rama.'

'Even if what I ask of you requires the utmost fortitude?'

Bhima looked nervously at the others.

'Yes, rama... Ask... Ask anything of me... If I can possibly do it, I will... I'll certainly try... if I can.'

'But why should you do anything that I ask of you?'

'Rama... Because... Because you are the greatest exponent of the mace in the land!'

'Isn't the rishi Charvaka the greatest maker of bows and helmets in the land? Would you do anything he asked of you?'

'No, rama... But you I respect... I trust that what you ask of me is for my own good... Though I would try to do it also if it was for your own good, sire, whichever... I trust you, rama.'

'Very well. Now, unfortunately, the advantage which Karna enjoys from his *armour* is not one which can be transferred readily to you, Prince Bhima. For I fear that your own great advantage in size precludes the possibility of your borrowing it. However, you mentioned also the suta's sash. I see no reason why you should not enjoy the benefits of that... If Karna should be so kind as to give permission for us to borrow his sash for a while, could you wear it today and tomorrow around the court? When you fight tomorrow, we will then be able to see what improvements the garment has conferred on you.'

Bhima gulped and sweated.

'Surely, Prince Bhima, if the cowardly Karna is brave enough to wear it, you can at least be his equal?'

'All right... I'll wear it,' spluttered Bhima.

'Very good. Now, Karna, do you give Prince Bhima permission to borrow your sash?'

'Certainly not,' declared Karna, with a slight trace of irritation in his voice.

Amid the laughter of the others, Bhima himself, for perhaps the first time in his life, gave Karna a smile of the purest warmth.

◊

During this period Karna had begun to take advantage of the fact that he could now bathe without the worry of revealing his armour. At noon every day he would go to his favourite part of the river; there, after his swim, he would sit on the bank, emptying his mind of thought.

Word of this soon got round the city. In no time at all people would be already gathered there, waiting for him. They would endure the heat of the midday sun and stare at his armour as he sat drying himself. Little children would sometimes dare each other to go up to him and actually run their hands in awe over the scaly metal skin. They would wait until he roused himself from his yoga, and then the people slowly dispersed, discussing a dozen different rumours about his magical golden mail.

After a while the novelty wore off, and then Karna's audience would tend to comprise only those who sought his charity. Initially Karna had nothing to give them. But when Dur started transferring to him the taxes from Anga, Karna would always take something with him on his midday swim.

Karna first tried to share what he had brought among those who remained after his swim. But this became impractical as his audience grew again, beyond the divisibility of his gifts. Karna then tried a different strategy.

There was a stone near where he sat, small enough to accommodate just one person. When Karna had roused himself he would go and listen only to whomever was sitting on that stone. Thus it was that soon his midday audience had dwindled to one: the first to get to the stone. Latecomers would simply go away and try their luck another day.

And he would try, if he could, to give them whatever they asked for. If they wanted money, he would tell them to come to the palace gates in the evening, where he would give them money or jewels. If it was some other favour, or advice, he would also try to comply with their requests. If Karna found a request unreasonable or exorbitant, he would argue with his supplicants. But if in spite of this he was unable to dissuade them from making their request, he would try to fulfil it. So far he had not had to refuse a single petition.

One afternoon, as Karna turned away from the river at the end of his yoga, his eyes alighted on a familiar face, now overgrown with a beard and straggling hair. It was Vaitanika that day who was sitting on the stone.

Karna's smile of greeting was not returned.

'Have you been in the forest?' he asked.

'Yes,' replied Vaitanika, curtly. 'I had to hide. Drona was after me. He still is. Why are you wearing your sash? You are no longer a suta.'

'What am I, then?'

'You're a king. How can you wear that gold armour with the sash of a suta?'

'Why should I change my habits, Vai? Am I no longer Karna, friend of Vaitanika?'

'You're the king of the Angas, and a friend to Prince Dur-yodhana.'

Karna did not reply.

'It's true then?' continued Vaitanika. 'So you admit you always had that gold under your shirt? I couldn't believe it when I heard. You never were a suta.'

'No?'

'No. Do you think a suta can dream of the moment when he can at last reveal his hidden wealth?'

'I see. We are what we dream.'

'You just don't know what it feels like to be a suta.'

'I have never claimed otherwise, Vai. Nor would I have done so even if I'd never had this armour. So... Is that why you're angry with me? Because I didn't feel like a suta? Or because I didn't show you my mail? You think I deceived you?'

'You used us, Karna. You used me. The friendship you showed was just a means to an end.'

Karna looked at him for a moment.

'Even if you believed that, Vai — which you don't — I wouldn't argue with you. And it's only because you don't believe it that you're prepared to waste time arguing with me. If you want to talk, talk about something other than my friendship.'

Vaitanika was silent for a while. He knew Karna well enough not to pursue this. Karna got up and took a few paces along the river bank to stretch his legs. But Vaitanika remained resolutely sitting on the stone.

'Karna... How could you accept a *kingdom*?'

'Probably the thought of all those taxes. How do you think I can afford to be so charitable? Tell me, Vai, would you like them? Ask and I'll give you them, all of them.'

'Don't be ridiculous. In accepting a kingdom you've become a kshatriya. You've betrayed us. You've accepted the ownership of all the shudras and sutas of Anga. You've betrayed your people.'

'What people? Are you telling me that all the lower castes in Anga wear golden mail under their shirts? According to you I can betray no one. Or have you gone back to the idea that my people really are the sutas? Just who are the *us* and who are the *them*? I have never tried to draw that untraceable line by the colour of my sash!'

'The truth is, Karna, that whether they are your people or not, I expected better from you. I believed that you understood the injustice...'

'So? What would you have had me do?'

'You didn't need to sell yourself to Dur like that.'

'You're right. I didn't need to. Nor did I. Whatever I was doing, I was not selling myself. On the contrary. Did I cry out for a buyer? No. Did I offer anything in exchange? No. Perhaps you think I shouldn't have displayed myself in such a vulgar fashion before so many people. Perhaps you wish my bright armour hadn't dulled false hopes: among all those shudras who might have dreamed that their reflection shone from my drab deerskins and dark sash... No? Perhaps you're just jealous of my friendship with Dur?'

'How could I be? Friendship can't be bought, and friendship isn't what Dur purchased. He's only friendly with you because he hopes to use you against the Pandavas.'

'He may have that hope. Yes, he does have that hope. But that's not the only reason for his friendship.'

'Whatever... You let the flattery of his regard turn you away from us.'

'I see. It's just plain wrong for a suta — even a false suta like me — to befriend a kshatriya. A prince. Listen, Vai, if you want a suta to be a man, don't ask the man to be a suta. Don't give me special suta scales on which to weigh the balance of my rights and wrongs, my friends and enemies. *You* see my friendship with Dur on one pan, and my loyalty to the shudras on the other. Even if they were on opposing pans, it's not for you to say how a suta ought to feel their weight, nor indeed how *I* should. You see the colour on the two pans, and having eyes only for that, you prefer the brown to the red. Even if they were both on my scales — which they're not — what do I care about the colour? It's the weight which *I* feel. It's my dharma, and not yours.'

Vaitanika did not reply.

'You should be pleased,' continued Karna, 'and not just for me. But instead you're expelling me!' Karna chuckled. 'Is it wise for a pack of toothless dogs, seeing one of their number given teeth, to expel him?'

'Oh? We're toothless dogs, are we? And where would you be without us toothless dogs?'

'Just because you're strong and large in number, that doesn't mean that you can bite your masters. If strength and strength of numbers were enough to win freedom, cattle would be their own masters.'

'And now we're cattle, are we? Too stupid to undo the gates of our own pens!'

'No, you're not too stupid, though you seem to be trying hard to be.'

'Karna, I think I'd rather be stupid and remain inside the field with my friends, than leap the fence and at the sight of freedom turn my back on them.'

'Good, because it's just as short-sighted to jump the pen only to prance in the paddock.'

'Isn't that exactly what you've done?'

'Not exactly. I didn't jump, and I'm not prancing. The gate was opened, and I saw no point to staying inside.'

Vaitanika shook his head in disgust. 'No point!'

'You've seen a pot of water boil, haven't you? A thousand bubbles froth into the air, losing all their force.'

'Oh, I see! You've quickly tired of toothless dogs and mindless cattle — now we shudras are just empty bubbles?'

'Bubbles, but not empty... If you seal a lid over the pot, the bubbles unite with enough force to blow the cover off. Channelled in one direction, your airy bubbles can move iron. But such a thing only seems to happen when your hopes are confined along with your livelihood. Leave just a little opening, and each will to their own lot, preferring the chance of a high stake to the certainty of a low one; so the liquid boils away with much froth and little consequence. Vai, don't you see? You want to shoot arrows through the lid, when what you really need is to put out the fire.'

'Karna,' retorted Vaitanika mockingly, 'haven't you seen a pot of water boil over? It can put out the fire quite well enough!'

'And you think they're such fools as to leave the pot unattended? As soon as they hear the gush of your foam, they'll just nudge the lid.'

Again Vaitanika shook his head. 'So we just sit tight and do nothing?'

'Now's not the time for action, let alone for the show of it.'

'It's so easy for you to say that! Now that you've got what you want!'

Karna laughed quietly. 'Vai, even cattle attend to their seasons before moving. If you're more interested in the journey than the destination, then go off now and wait for it to rain in the desert. I'm not going to follow you just because you make me look a spineless coward. A man who is rushed into the fight is afraid more of his friends than of his enemies.'

'And if we wait for you, Karna, the season will be winter, and the earth all spent. I'd rather die in a struggle doomed to fail, than be trodden in the earth to rot so I can feed *their* spring.'

'Well, that's the difference between us, Vai. More than just a skin of gold. For I'd rather stay and rot with the truth than fight on a lie to keep myself so busily deceived!'

Vaitanika snorted in disgust.

'Karna, I might just be able to believe that, if the truth weren't so conveniently close to where you lie! To where you lie in comfort! If we'd known all this... you think we'd have helped you to your freedom? Which you abused the moment you got it, to choose our enemy for your friend.'

Karna smiled. 'Well, unlike yours, at least Dur's friendship comes without conditions. But as soon as you've helped this suta to his freedom, you want to put him back in chains, this time of your own. Is this really going to help you break the chain that binds all sutas? You want to fight the injustice which forces all sutas to be the same, by denying me leave to differ? If a suta ignores his sash and tries to write his own freedom, then he is condemned for betraying his fellows and their cause. While if instead he burns his cloth in a great cloud of suta smoke, he is congratulated? For doing nothing except assert his fellowship? If that's what fellowship means to you, Vai, I don't want it. Friendship is an end, not a means. Isn't that what you said?'

'And I'd hoped that while we all remained in bondage, you'd see your freedom as a means, not an end. If your friendship is such that you can really be free while we're not, then I don't want it either. Nor do we need it. We shall overturn the kshatriyas without your help.'

'Perhaps you will... Perhaps you will. But if you do, take care you don't overturn by a full circle. For when you become the new kshatriyas, you'll see only the change and not the similarity.'

'And why should we become the new kshatriyas? Just because we'd have to use force?'

'Vai, I know that you want to fight fire with fire...'

'Can you compare the fire that turns the wheel with the force that keeps it stuck in servitude?'

'You think you'll be able to stop the wheel revolving at just the right point? Why? Because *you're* different from *them*? Remember that in slavery a man's vices are chained up along with his better parts. Nothing masks the bad more surely than the shadow of the rotten. Who will see a streak of evil beside the mark of a whip? Take care, Vai, for if your wheel should find the force to turn, it may unmask itself to turn in turn again... Or do you really think you're a breed apart from the kshatriya? That's an error that comes in both directions. The fact is... the strange fact is, Vai, we are all men... Haven't you heard the story of the soldier ants and the worker ants? The soldier ants took all the best food from the worker ants and fed themselves on it. The soldiers were twice as big, greedy, domineering, with huge jaws for fighting. One day the worker ants laid a trap for the soldier ants, and drowned them all. There were no soldier ants left in the nest. So the worker ants could now eat the choicest foods. They doubled in size, and...'

'Yes, Karna, so does that argument justify locking the wheel where it is, to fix our slavery?'

'No. You must break the wheel, not turn it.'

'Oh, and how do we do that?'

'I don't know. I wish I did... Vai, listen...' Karna's voice softened. 'You're in danger, here in Hastinapura. Why don't you come to Anga with me. In a few days I'll be visiting my kingdom.'

'You expect me to go there with you? You think I want to be the farmer's dog, watching over his obedient herd?'

Karna laughed. 'If you want, Vaitanika, I will treat you like shudra dirt. If that makes you happier. Yes, perhaps you can drive for me — it's a long way. I could even give you the occasional touch of the whip, to ease the poison of my company?'

Vaitanika was silent.

'So,' continued Karna, 'how much more time are you going to waste? When are you going to be honest, and ask for what you really want? None of my other supplicants have been so ashamed or devious. Or prepared to drive me to such barren rhetoric. Did you think that making me feel guilty was more likely to get you what you want? I'm afraid you can heat water all you like, it'll still say no to fire. As I say, I know you want to fight fire with fire.'

Karna took a few paces towards the bank, and then turned to face Vaitanika again.

'I know you've always hoped I'd teach you shudras how to fight... And I think you've always known I would refuse to. I can't really explain why... I know from where you stand it must seem unfair... that I've been able to take advantage of what I've been taught. And yet I'm unwilling to give you the same opportunity. Don't think I haven't weighed it carefully in the balance, whether to teach you, or not... It is too finely balanced...'

'No, Karna. You can never have action and inaction equally balanced on the pans. One can never pass through a point where the balance of action and inaction floats too equal to resolve in action...'

Karna smiled. 'You're right... of course... Yes, Charvaka will like that one. When we stop by at Varanasi you can demonstrate it on one of his scales... Vai... Don't think I'm not grateful that you never asked me... You're not going to ask me now, are you? Because if you are, get off that stone first. I don't want to spoil my charitable reputation...'

A smile slowly broke through Vaitanika's straggling beard.

'No... No, Karna, I won't ask you...'

◊

A few days later Karna and Vaitanika were in Varanasi. News of Karna's triumph at the tournament was already well established there, and Charvaka and Vrisha had to drive away the crowd that had gathered in welcome around their chariot.

'This is Vaitanika, sire.'

'Ah yes. I'm pleased to meet you, my boy. Vrisha told me how much you helped Karna at the tournament. By the way, I presume that it was Drona himself who supplied you with the means to conjure up the thunder and smoke which Vrisha found so stirring? Yes, well, I can guess where the wretched man obtained it... So that's the use he makes of my powdered air — to impress Arjuna's admirers. Fortunately he does not appear to have discovered the secret of its manufacture... Karna, you realise that Ravana was doubly blessed by finding death at the hands of two such exalted warriors?'

'Doubly blessed?' questioned Karna. 'Was he blessed at all?'

'Don't you know why Ravana stole Rama's wife? Ah, well, according to legend there was a god once who gravely offended Vishnu. This miscreant was given a choice of punishments: to undergo either seven successive good avatars, or three successive evil ones. The offending god chose the latter, on the grounds that since he would only have three mortal incarnations before being purged of his sin, he would achieve eternal redemption more quickly and directly than if he had to experience seven lifetimes as a good person. In each of the three evil incarnations, however, the avatar was obliged to procure his own death at the hands of Vishnu: only the dutiful accomplishment of this would bring him salvation.

'Well, the first evil avatar of this transgressing god was Bali, who you know was killed by Vishnu in the guise of a dwarf brahmana. The second avatar was your very own Ravana. And legend has it that Rama was an avatar of Vishnu: thus by contriving his death at the hands of Rama, the fallen god took his second step towards salvation...'

'Who was the third avatar?' asked Vrisha.

'No one knows,' replied the rishi. 'However... You know that there are people who believe that Krishna of Dwaraka is actually another incarnation of Vishnu, in our time, just as Rama was in his... So,' continued Charvaka with a wicked smile, 'look out to see whom Krishna kills, and your question may be answered!'

'I thought Krishna was from Yadava?' said Vrisha.

'He was, he was... The Yadava people had to leave their province and their capital city, Mathura, in order to escape from Jara-sandha... You have not heard of him? He is a rather wicked but very powerful king. So, the Yadavas all migrated to Dwaraka...'

Later, while Vaitanika was unloading the chariot with Vrisha, Charvaka spoke more urgently with Karna.

'So, you've been made king of the Angas... How are they taking it?'

'Who? The Kurus loved it, of course. But the Pandavas, they haven't taken it well... Even Yudhi, though he seems to understand more than the others, he hasn't talked to me since. He is prepared to acknowledge me, which the others aren't, but that's all. And as for your friends, Charvaka, they also seem to be sulking. Kripa and Bhishma aren't talking to me now. Kripa seems especially angry about it. I don't know whether it's the fact that I appeared at all at the tournament, or perhaps it's that I revealed the armour. I don't know which — they're not talking to me.'

Charvaka sighed and shook his head. 'Perhaps it wasn't wise to reveal the mail... You remember I warned you... And Kripa himself had asked you not to reveal it... Perhaps it wasn't wise.'

'Perhaps not, but it's not wise to be wise all the time. Especially when those urging wisdom don't seem prepared to impart knowledge. In all these years

Kripa hasn't once talked to me about it, not since the first day I met him. If he'd made any attempt to keep my promise alive, I might have kept it... You're not much better, sire...'

'Yes, well... My boy, what about the mongoose, now? What have you thought about going to see Parashu?'

'I've thought about it, sire. Whether to go, or not to go. I can't decide. Oh, that reminds me — I must get Vaitanika to show you something — you and Vrisha will like it. But no, sire, I certainly can't go to Parashu at the moment, not with everything to do in Anga.'

'You've made plans for Anga?'

'Yes... I'll tell you when Vai's back, it may interest him...'

'Well, don't leave it too long, my boy. To go to Parashu, I mean. Now that you've revealed your... your armour, it's not so safe for you.'

'Why not? What's the danger?'

'Well... I don't know which way Parashu's mind is made up at the moment. It's a long time since I spoke to him... But news travels... If you are going to take the snake, it would be better that you did it sooner rather than later... It's not impossible that Parashu himself might try to force your hand, or even try to kill you.'

'But why? And what's this snake?'

'The snake is an arrow. I have seen one in Maya like Parashu's. It is shaped in the form of a snake, but with two heads and no tail... If you decide to... to throw your dice, my boy, you will do it with this arrow... The mongoose is the guardian of the snake, you see. He will teach you what to do...'

'But if he wants me dead?'

'I'm not saying that he does, Karna. Though there was a time when I know he did. Even Narada took some persuading...'

'Why?'

'We are rishis, my boy. Rishis have certain obligations.'

'And what gives you the right? What gives the rishis the power of life or death?'

'A rishi is bound by his sacred word. That's what gives us power; that is also what we must obey. In our daily round we may lie and deceive as much as anyone. But we do not lie or deceive when we contract our word. There has to be someone or something that is trusted absolutely. That's what we rishis are for.'

'Only a fool trusts absolutely. You yourself say as much.'

'I agree. But if you want law, we are all forced into folly: whether you think it wise or not, if you want law, you need to trust. In the end, it's not the ritual, not the ceremony, nor the writing, nor the seal... In the end, all the weight must be borne by the word of a few men. And while we are entrusted with this burden, we are the last refuge of the law. If it was a choice between my word and your life, my boy, you would be dead. For once the word goes up in smoke, everything else begins also to catch that fire.'

'Then why am I in danger from Parashu and not from you?'

'Ah! That's because life never fits smoothly even into the pocket of a rishi's cloak. Concerning you, Karna... I never agreed with the mongoose. A rishi has to accept the meaning of the word before he acts on it. In the end three of us reached some agreement. But Parashu would not accept our line...'

The entrance of Vrisha and Vaitanika interrupted the rishi.

'Now, Karna,' continued Charvaka, 'tell us what you're going to do in Anga.'

'In Anga? Oh yes...' Karna frowned at Charvaka, and took a deep breath.

'Yes,' he continued, with a sigh. 'My plan is this... In Anga, as everywhere, the shudras do most of the physical work. But at the moment they have to give all but their subsistence to the vaishyas, who in turn have to give most of it to the kshatriyas. The kshatriyas give what they think fit to the brahmanas, keep quite a bit for themselves, and send the rest to Hastinapura — to me.

'My plan is that the shudras should instead keep all that they produce. All that they can afford to, at any rate. For, if they need vaishyas to direct them, or if they need to employ help or advice with the care of the livestock, the crops, whatever, they will have to pay the vaishyas for the work the vaishyas do. Likewise, if they need brahmanas to administer their rites and ceremonies, they will have to pay them. And if they need the kshatriyas to protect their land, the kshatriyas will be paid for that service, too —'

'They'll like that,' interrupted Charvaka. 'The kshatriyas will like that. They'll ask you why they, of noble birth, should be subject to the whims of their former servants.'

'If they don't want to work for the shudras, then they don't need to. But they won't in that case receive payment. I will remind them that it's no more a shudra's fault that he is a shudra than it is a kshatriya's merit to be born a kshatriya. It's unjust to make a man suffer from an accident of chance; and it's unjust to reward a man for a mere accident of chance. Let them work for their reward, like everyone else.'

'They will argue, my boy, as it suits them, that everything and nothing is an accident. Since everything is an accident, there can be no justice, and a man might as well accept the gamble of his birth as any other fall of chance. Or, contrarily, since nothing is an accident, every man's hardship and reward in this life is the result of some evil or good they have committed in a previous life; so the shudra's slavery and the kshatriya's pleasure are nothing but the execution of justice.'

'If that's how they argue,' said Karna, 'I will reply that since everything is an accident, and there is no justice, then neither is there justice in my sovereignty or in my ruling, which they'll have to accept like the fall of the dice. On the other hand, if nothing is an accident, their presently reduced circumstances are nothing but a punishment they were predestined to endure; no doubt as the result of some previous misdemeanour. However, they will be able in this case to look forward perhaps to a more comfortable existence in some future life.'

'But then there are the vaishyas,' persisted Charvaka. 'The vaishyas will complain that justice demands they and not the shudras should control the wealth of the land; since it is their skill which keeps the animals healthy and the land fertile.'

'Is it just, then, that they be paid twice over? First, nature has endowed them with skill; now they want to be rewarded a second time for that piece of good fortune.'

'They will say that they have worked hard to acquire that skill, and thus that they deserve a greater share.'

'In that case, why should they deserve a greater share for the good fortune to have been blessed with the ability, and determination, to acquire their skill?'

'It's not luck, they'll say, but sheer application.'

'Where did they get the will and means for it? Where did they get their application, except through the fortune of their circumstances?'

'It's not their circumstances, they'll say: it is their own determination, which would have triumphed even over different circumstances.'

'Then they should be grateful for having been endowed with that determination.'

'They'll tell you that no one else endowed them, my boy. They will insist that they made themselves.'

'Then they are lucky to have been given the talent and the will to make themselves so well. Do they now want these gifts to be recompensed with yet another gift?'

'They will say that it is not a question of being unfairly recompensed for gifts that nature and their circumstances have provided: they will say that it is in *fair* exchange that they should receive the material reward their skills obtain.'

'Precisely. They will be paid.'

Charvaka scratched his beard.

'Karna,' asked Vaitanika, 'how will the shudras decide how much to pay the vaishyas they employ?'

'As much as they wish or as little as they can get away with. The same with brahmanas or kshatriyas. A good kshatriya will be in greater demand than a bad one, and the shudras will then be prepared to pay him more.'

'And what if a shudra no longer wants to work the land?' continued Vaitanika.

'If a shudra can do some other work, let him. His caste will not forbid him to do what his ability permits, not while I am king of Anga. If he wishes to learn how to look after animals, or... or how to use weapons, then he will have the means to pay a vaishya or a kshatriya to teach him. And if a vaishya has not the ability to do the vaishya's job, then he will have to work the land himself. But then he'll also have the shudra's rights and the shudra's wealth.'

'And all this wealth that the shudras will have,' asked Vaitanika, 'how will they administer it?'

'They'll have to decide that for themselves.'

'And what about you?' continued Vaitanika. 'What about the king?'

'The shudras will have to decide what they are willing to pay me. I will accept their decision. Even if they give me nothing.'

'And when did you decide all this?' asked Vaitanika.

'As I was jumping off Dur's chariot after the tournament.'

'My boy,' interposed Charvaka, 'are you intending to announce these plans in Anga on this visit? Yes, well, if you want my advice —'

'No, sire, I don't. I would like to learn from my own mistakes for a while.'

'Yes, my boy, wouldn't we all! The trouble is — as history itself teaches us — that men would rather be taught by the engrossing appeal of success than the disheartening digestion of failure. Yes, I myself was under the illusion that men did actually learn from their own past errors. But experience has since taught me that in their haste for achievement they're much more ready to excuse their mistakes than to learn from them. They use the past not to guide their attainments, but to justify their ambitions.'

Karna smiled. 'So you don't think my scheme has the charm of the attainable?'

'It has charm, my boy... But since you don't want my advice... What are you going to do, stay in Anga? Or will you be returning soon to Hastinapura?'

'I'll get back to Hastinapura as soon as the shudras have got things organised.'

'Well, if you're not going to be staying on in Anga, then you'd better leave your sandals there at least — sorry, that's advice... Eh? You remember about the sandals of Rama?'

Karna glanced at Vaitanika. 'I was hoping, sire, that Vaitanika might undertake to be my sandals. If that's not too undignified a situation for a shudra...'

◊

When Karna and Vaitanika arrived in Anga —

•

'Palmira, these sandals of Rama, what are they?'

'Another time, boys, another time.'

'Palmira, these sandals of Rama, what are they?'

Palmira smiled weakly. 'Oh... Well... There was a time when Rama didn't want to reign as king, and he left for the forest. But his brother Bharata found him in the forest, and begged him to return, to rule over his people. Anyway, as a compromise, Rama gave Bharata his golden sandals to take back, to sit on the throne instead of him. Which Bharata duly did: and he governed as minister on behalf of these sandals.'

'That's all?'

'What d'you mean, that's all?'

'You mean there isn't a story about the Hodja's sandals, or anything like that?'

'Didn't you want us to interrupt?'

Palmira smiled again. Then she saw a shadow dart across her tiles; a small bird had alighted on the trellis above them. It started to peck at the vines. Palmira glanced down at the table, and decided it was not directly beneath her visitor.

'Perhaps you could make me a little scarecrow, boys... Still, at least it means the wind is right...'

The boys waved their arms and the bird flew off.

'As a matter of fact,' said Palmira, 'there is a story about the Hodja's sandals. But it's not very good, so I'll spare you...'

'Palmira, are you all right?'

'Well... To be honest, boys, I'm getting on my nerves a bit... I'm getting bored with this... Perhaps I should tell you a different story... Aren't you getting a little fed up with it?'

'No, Palmira!' The first Henry looked at his brother in alarm.

'No, sire!' echoed the second Henry.

'I don't know...' Palmira went on. 'I'm feeling a bit... low. I've lost my enthusiasm for the story. Yes, perhaps we should stop — it's not such a good story after all... Maybe it's the wind? The wind from the desert gets me down sometimes...'

'You can't just stop in the middle!'

'I wish it *was* the middle, Henry. It's nowhere near the middle! We've already been at it... three days, is it? I've lost track. They'll be bringing the ore down soon. I'll have to get the furnaces ready, the charcoal, everything... I just can't be bothered any more. I really don't feel like doing it this year...'

'Come on, Palmira — you know no one else makes steel as good as yours—'

'And anyway, it might be dangerous if you stopped now... They probably only put up with you because of your steel.'

'I expect you're right, Henry. Though I've still got Vyasa's secret. Even if I stop making it, they'll still need me to tell them how to make it.'

'You said you'd tell us, one day.'

'Don't even mention that. In good time, perhaps. Not now. Think of the danger if people thought you had the secret of Indian steel! That's why I'm worried about you even helping me. Remember, you're just giving me some menial help, you're dirty shudras, and know nothing at all about what's going on, eh?'

'Yes, sire.'

'You were saying, Palmira, about when they arrived in Anga...'

'What was I saying?'

'Just that they arrived...'

'Who?'

'Palmira!'

'Look, boys, do you mind terribly if I skip the next bit?'

'You can't *skip* bits!'

'How do you know I haven't already?'

'Palmira! What happened in Anga?'

'Well, Vaitanika did stay, and... what Karna proposed was liked by some of the people, and disliked by others, and... Well, after a few months there Karna returned to Hastinapura. There! That's all! Really! I promise you, nothing at all exciting happened down there in Anga. We might as well skip straight to when he gets back to Hastinapura.'

'Are you sure?'

'Are you sure nothing important happened there, that we'd miss?'

'Absolutely. It's an out-of-the-way place, with nobody of any significance, no princes or kings or princesses or anything. Absolutely nothing. So, is that agreed, we can get back to Hastinapura?'

'All right, then.'

'Oh, Palmira, there was one thing... What's *yoga*?'

'It's a Sanskrit word... I think our word 'yoke' comes from it. Although I'm not really sure. I don't know enough about Sanskrit to know if 'yoke' comes from *yoga* or *yuga*... I think *yoga* originally meant a union, and *yuga* a pair, a couple, an even number...'

'Yes, but what does *yoga* mean? In your story?'

'*I* don't know... How should I know? Why don't you just listen carefully to how I use it, and then perhaps you'll understand what I mean by it — if anything.'

'I bet you she doesn't use it again, now,' complained the first Henry to his brother.

'I will, boys, I will. I promise. Now, where was I?...'

•

17 The scales released

Not for the first time in his life Karna noticed that when his routine of practice with the bow was disrupted, as it had been during his stay in Anga, his sleep became troubled.

Now that he was back in Hastinapura and able to practice every day, his sleep became more settled. He returned also to his daily routine at the river.

Karna's absence had done nothing to lessen his reputation among those in need. On the contrary, a rumour had spread that he had vowed never to refuse a request to the person he found on his stone after his swim and yoga. But now that he no longer had the wealth of Anga to disburse, he found that he would often have to send his supplicant away disappointed, if not empty-handed.

Though there now seemed less demand for his material charity among the very needy, Karna noticed that his stone was more often occupied by those who were interested in his advice, or in other favours not dependent upon wealth. Even brahmanas and kshatriyas, who might have avoided his company in other contexts, trusted his discretion, and his power. For the threat of sitting on Karna's stone was sometimes quite enough to dissolve a dispute between neighbours.

But there was no sign of any softening from the Pandavas, or the elders of the palace. And Karna's return had again deepened the wedge between the royal princes.

◊

A few months after his return to Hastinapura, and despite the regularity of his routine, Karna's sleep again became disturbed; culminating, one night, in a vivid dream.

He was in the tournament arena. But the place was deserted. He was dressed just in his loincloth and mail. He was holding his bow, aiming at something. It was a weighing balance. He saw that each of the pans held one of his ear-rings. But he could still feel them on his ears. There was a single arrow drawn back on his bowstring. He was aiming at the balance, but he could not tell which part he wished to hit. He looked again at the pans, and now the ear-rings had changed into snakes. The pans began to sway as the two snakes jockeyed aggressively for position, preparing to strike at each other. The left pan began to fall, and Karna directed his aim at the head of the snake coiled upon it. Then the other pan started to fall, as the right-hand snake drew some of the left-hand coil onto its pan. Karna saw that the two snakes had one body. He wavered for a moment, his bowstring taut.

He felt someone's grasp, and the bow being taken out of his hand. The grip was gentle, and the voice he heard now was quiet and free of emotion.

'Your armour makes you invincible, my son. Indra is going to try to take it away from you.'

The face that spoke to him was wearing a mask. A circular mask, of gold, the eyes behind it hidden by a blazing light which was forcing Karna's gaze away. Suspended in shadow against the flares of light radiating from behind the circle, Karna saw two huge ear-rings. Over the torso below the mask a golden mail stretched glistening.

'Do not give Indra what he asks, my son. Your generosity is known now far and wide. Indra will try to take advantage of it. Give him neither your armour nor your ear-rings. For while you have these, you can never be killed in battle.'

Karna found himself replying, though it seemed more as though someone else was speaking through his lips.

'Surya, what virtue is there in generosity if one gives only that which one does not hold dear? Needs differ according to appetite, as well as want. Who am I to judge whether he who asks has not a greater need for what I have to give? You cannot ask me to protect my life but lose my dharma?'

'What use is your dharma when you are no more? The glorious name of one who has died nobly is like a garland of flowers around the neck of a corpse. I ask you again, Karna, for there is a deep mystery ordained by Destiny, a secret which even the gods can hardly discern. I cannot reveal it to you. In time you may come to understand it. But listen to me again: when Indra asks you for your ear-rings, refuse him. While you have them still, Arjuna will never be able to defeat you in battle, even if Indra himself were to share his chariot.'

Again Karna heard a reply issue from his lips.

'Surya, I thank you for your regard. But if you wish to change my answer, give me light. While Surya keeps me in darkness, I can only follow Dharma in the dark. So you must forgive me if I repeat, that I would rather lose my ear-rings than my dharma.'

'How is it that you are willing to extend your charity to Indra, but not to your own father? Does my request not weigh as heavily as his?'

'No, because you asked in my behalf, not yours; and my need is less. I do not require the ear-rings or the armour to protect myself in battle.'

As Karna waited for Surya to reply, he began to suspect that the dream had ended. He looked around the darkness of his room in vain for a trace of light from Surya; then he finally awoke.

It took several days for the lingering presence of this dream to wear off. And then it recurred, over several weeks. Each time Karna would wake up at the same point.

◊

One afternoon a rather unusual figure had come to seek alms from Karna. It was sitting cross-legged on Karna's stone. It appeared to be a man, wearing a brahmana's white cloak, but with its head covered in a white hood.

His eyes were hidden by the overhanging cloth of the hood. Using his left hand he covered the lower part of his face with the side of the hood, like a woman pressing a veil to her cheek.

He seemed to be resting some of his weight on his right arm, for the palm of his right hand was flat upon the ground, the fingers spread delicately to point behind him. And yet his trunk appeared upright and perfectly balanced.

For some time, while Karna watched him, his visitor did not speak or make any sound. Indeed, Karna wondered whether he was breathing at all. Occasionally a gust of wind would play with his cloak. On the ground the leaves and blossoms rustled in the breeze.

Then, suddenly, the folds of the hood trembled slightly.

'My Lord of Anga, I have come to beg something of you.'

The muffled voice sent a ripple through Karna's heart.

'Sire, what can I give you?'

'I wish to possess the golden rings which wrap around your chest. And the two large rings which adorn your ears.'

'My armour, sire, is like a second skin to me. It has become a part of me. I cannot give you my skin. What land I have, cattle, horses... all these I will give you, if you wish. But do not ask me for my armour.'

'What hollow charity is it that gives only what is not desired? What will people say when they hear that the king of Anga's generosity is such a shallow exhibition?'

'If I gave you my mail in order to set people to hum praise for me, I would not be giving at all, merely exchanging. I would rather be spoken of as mean and false than as one who would buy fame with charity.'

'My Lord Karna, if that is why you withhold from me your charity, then in truth you should be spoken of as mean and false, and desirous of celebrity; for it seems then that you wish to become known as one who desires fame so little, that he will refuse to buy it. And you are ready to purchase that opinion by denying my request.'

Karna smiled. 'Just because all manner of opinion is sure to follow from my action, it does not follow that my action pursues *any* manner of opinion.'

'Good. And that is indeed the opinion I have heard most often regarding your character. As everyone knows, arrogance cares very little for the opinion of others.'

Again Karna smiled, but this time he did not reply. His visitor continued.

'I presume, then, my Lord Karna, that you give in order to help those who ask of you?'

Karna bowed his head in assent.

'Then help me, Karna. Give me your armour and your ear-rings.'

'Why should it help you to have these things?'

'My Lord Karna, do you usually humiliate those who beg of you by demanding the reasons for their poverty?'

'Not usually, no. That's because usually I understand the need which brings people here to ask of me. If you were a lowly ratha, too slow or feeble to defend yourself against your opponents' arms, I could understand why you might need my armour. But if Indra comes to me, why should he want my mail or my ear-rings?'

There was a pause before his visitor replied.

'The gods have their own kinds of poverty.'

'The brahmanas teach that poverty exists only as the privation of some desire. I thought gods were supposed not to have desires? I thought they were above that sort of thing.'

'Lord Karna, when gods appear, as men, to men, gods must appear as men appear to men.'

Karna smiled again. A sudden breeze toyed with his visitor's cloak; and departed, leaving the air quite still.

'Well,' replied Karna, 'if you were Lord Indra, to me you would appear as a father selfishly pursuing the interests of his son, Arjuna.'

'That is how he must appear to you, Lord Karna. For Lord Indra must play the mirror and reflect the selfishness that drives you to refuse him.'

Karna did not reply.

'Or do you think your interests are more deserving than Prince Arjuna's? Suppose that you are right, and that you are the more deserving; then all the more reason for Arjuna through my intercession to benefit from your sacrifice. For in this case, since you would be the richer in merit, justice would entitle Arjuna, being the poorer, to your charity.'

'And if I am *less* deserving than he is?' Karna chuckled. 'I suppose in that case justice would naturally favour the *more* deserving party — Arjuna, no doubt.' Karna laughed. 'Lord Indra — if I may address you thus — while you face me with a bow in both hands, you cannot shoot at all!'

'You misunderstand me: Arjuna has no chance against you while you wear your armour. So where is the merit in beating a man who is already beaten? How can you take pride in your own skill, when you are invulnerable to the skill of others? While you still have your armour, you will never be able to feel what it is like to succeed in the face of death through skill alone. By giving Arjuna a chance against you, you are giving your own skill the chance to defeat him, on merit. By taking away your armour, I will be giving you the chance of real victory.'

Karna sat silently in thought.

Suddenly he stood up. He began to unclasp the links covering his navel, at the lower edge of his armour. He worked his way upwards as though peeling a strip of bark from a tree trunk. When the mail was unfastened, from navel to sternum, he turned his back on his visitor.

'You must pull it off me now.'

The cloaked figure slowly got up, went over to Karna, and peeled the golden links off his back. They came away like the moulting scales of a serpent. Karna's back was sore and bleeding.

When he was free of the armour Karna took a huge breath, and sat down again. His visitor took out a bleached canvas bag from a fold in his cloak. He slipped the mail into it, and sat down again upon the stone.

'My Lord Karna, I also need your ear-rings.'

'Wait a moment, Lord Indra. Now that you have my mail, what are you going to give to me?'

'Since when does charity require compensation? In any case, I have already recompensed you, as I made clear: I have given you the gift of vulnerability.'

'I conferred that gift upon myself, Lord Indra. I could have done it without you, and I did do it without you. For it was my decision, not yours. And I could have gained it just as well by throwing my armour in the river. You have gained two things: you have gained Arjuna a chance to kill me; and you have gained the armour. Only the first of these was my act of charity. I require compensation for the second.'

His supplicant remained silent.

'Tell me, Lord Indra... I have heard a story... Perhaps you can tell me if it's true... Many centuries ago, Indra is supposed to have killed a brahmana called Trisiras, the son of Twashtri. The goodness of Trisiras was of such a degree that Indra became envious of the regard with which this brahmana was held — by both men and gods. He plotted to corrupt this man with all manner of temptations. But Trisiras resisted them all, and was held in greater favour even than before. In the end Indra could stand it no longer, and killed him with his thunderbolt. So the story goes... Is it true? Did Indra really kill a defenceless brahmana?'

'Yes, it is true. Indra did commit brahmanacide. But the gods inflicted a great punishment on him for his sin.'

'Will you not be punished again by the gods for the sin you are committing now?'

'What sin is that?'

'Taking my armour to satisfy a selfish desire in favour of your son. I may only be a suta, and not a brahmana... but are you not killing me? Everybody knows that without my armour I would stand no chance against Prince Arjuna, for is he not the greatest chariot fighter the Bharatas have ever seen?'

'I have not taken your armour, Karna. Indra has the power to take your armour and ear-rings from you by force. Had I done so, that would indeed have been sinful. But have you felt any force? No. Have you felt the might of Indra? No. You *gave* me your armour. As you yourself admitted, Karna, it was your own decision. Where is the sin, Karna? What violence have I done you?'

'Oh, but you *persuaded* me. How could I, a mere mortal, resist the power of your celestial argument? Is it right that a god should ensnare the mind of a weak mortal in this way? It is as if you had picked me up in your hand and peeled me. What difference is there between your arm and your tongue? They are both imbued with divine power. The effect is just the same. My will is powerless to resist, and yields as readily as would my body to your crushing strength. What difference is there between beating the unwilling tiger out of the undergrowth, and enticing it with bait to choose its own destruction? Your power is such to have caused my armour to drop off my body, had you chosen, without violence, without movement, without touching me. Instead, your power has caused my mind to surrender my armour to you. What is the difference?'

'There is all the difference in the world between argument and force. If I had forcibly robbed you, it would have been without your consent. If my argument caused you to surrender your armour, it was with your consent.'

'Surely not, Lord Indra. For the power of your mind forces me to consent. It is only your divine skill, by making me agree with you, which creates the appearance that nothing has been done against my will. You have changed my very will, so that even to me it appears that nothing has been done to me!'

'My arguments have only shown you what is fair and right. I have merely shown you what is right for you to do. I do not force you to carry out the conclusion against your will.'

'But if you skilfully make me believe that it is right to surrender to you my armour, surely my will is deprived of the power to resist you? You can subdue an elephant with force, or with kindness. The result is the same. It will support you on its neck.'

'Lord Karna, do you not remember saying that you yourself chose to free yourself from the chains you wore. If I did not make your decision for you, how could I have forced you? What sin did I then commit? On the other hand, suppose I did affect your decision, which you denied — in that case it was I who conferred the gift, so again, what sin did I commit?'

A sudden gust of wind from the river swirled up the leaves and petals which were scattered on the ground.

'You see, Lord Indra? Again my mind is trapped. You leave me no room to escape, like an elephant caught in the stockade. You see how you are taking advantage of my weak and mortal mind? Your reason has ensnared me! You have fenced off both sides to my argument. By the dreadful power of your persuasion, I am now almost convinced that you are right and I am wrong!'

From the mouth of the hood came a hiss, lost in a sweet-smelling breath of wind which brushed Karna's face with blossoms. Karna waited till the air was still.

'Lord Indra, would you not like to hear what it is that I ask as a boon from you, in compensation for toying with my mind? People say that Indra's most powerful weapon is his thunderbolt... But I have also heard say that Indra has other weapons of great power, whose use requires great skill, and against which there is hardly a defence. I ask for one such a weapon...'

The hood of the cloak trembled.

'I have heard say, Lord Indra, that you have a javelin. It has two parts, both duller than silver, but twice as hard. When the two parts are joined into one, there is no living thing which can withstand this javelin. Is this not so?'

'Who told you that I have such a weapon?'

'Are you forgetting that I am the son of Surya... Or did you not know? You cannot hide from the light of Surya. I want this weapon. If it is yours rightfully to give, of course... If it is, I ask you for it.'

For a moment there was only the sound of the river. Then his visitor replied.

'Very well, Karna, you may have that javelin... It is a divine astra... Providing you have joined it and aimed it well, there is no being, male, female, god or beast who can withstand it... Vishnu himself could not survive its impact. But it can be used only once.'

'Thank you, Lord Indra. When shall I receive this brahmastra?'

'You will find it on this spot tomorrow... Now, Karna, may I have your ear-rings?'

'My ear-rings? Lord Indra, you know as well as I do that if I give you my ear-rings the javelin you have promised me will become useless to me. It will weigh as nothing if Destiny is holding the scale fixed. I might as well throw the javelin in the river. For you must know that my ear-rings carry my destiny. If I part with them, I stand as little chance against Arjuna as he stood against my second skin. There can be little value in charity which exchanges one beggar for another.'

Karna received no reply.

'If, on the other hand,' he continued, 'you were to have in your possession a weapon or device powerful enough to catch the ears of Destiny herself... Well, then I might consider giving you my ear-rings in exchange.'

Still there was no reply, so Karna continued.

'Some say that Destiny is fixed. Or that she is deaf and blind, and will not listen to the prayers of men. Others say that it is not so. If Destiny has already written my story, then what difference does it make if you have my ear-rings or I have them? It will benefit you no more than it will disadvantage me. If, on the other hand, Destiny can hang a man's life in the balance, perhaps there is a way to reach her ears? Do I reach your ears, Lord Indra? Perhaps you have some other weapons for which, as for your javelin, you have no pressing need?'

'There is one... There is one which is said to have the power to conquer Destiny. You would have to learn to use it... Again, you can only use it once, and then only when you are in mortal danger. It is said that with the right mantra, and when it is released with neither hatred nor anger, there is no curse, no bane, no imprecation, no fate, no prediction, no promise, human or divine, which it is unable to transcend. Should you choose to use this power, it could overturn a decree made by Brahma himself... Lord Karna, it is known to the gods that one day you will fight Arjuna to the death. It is your destiny to fight him. But if you learn to use this weapon, and master its mantra, then your story becomes blurred even to the gods; and no one will be able to finish it but you...'

'If I can use this device only once, how is it that I can ever learn to use it?'

'You can use it many times without the mantra. But only once with it.'

'And who can teach me?'

'Tomorrow, when you finish your bathing, you will find the javelin on this spot. Next to it will be a leather case. It will contain an arrow, in the form of a snake. There is only one person who can teach you how to shoot that arrow. He is a brahmana. Parashu-rama is his name. He lives on the mountain of Mahendra. He will be able to teach you. But even he does not know the real power of the mantra. No mortal may be allowed to know its secret, save he who uses it. Alone among men you have this gift. Karna, you must tell no one, not even Parashu, of the great power you will acquire.'

They were both silent for a while. Another gust of wind caressed Karna's cheeks, leaving petals in his hair. Karna remained seated as he took out his ear-rings, and laid them out on the ground before him. He put his hands to his ears. He had never before felt their nakedness.

◊

Karna remained that afternoon on the bank, motionless, until the sun had completely disappeared. His visitor had long since departed with the armour and ear-rings. Without putting his shirt back on Karna returned, unseen, to the palace. There he soaked in a bath of warm brine to ease his skin.

The following day, now wearing a shirt to protect his back from the sun, Karna returned to the river. He did not swim that afternoon, but remained on the bank. When eventually he rose from yoga and turned towards the stone, there was no one there; but he saw three objects lying by the stone: the javelin, its two parts joined; a small pouch beside it; and a large leather sheath.

First of all he opened the pouch. It was empty, but he noticed some powder, which it evidently had contained, clinging to its sides. He smelt it. Then he examined the leather sheath.

It was flat and oblong, about the length of his forearm and the width of his hand. In the centre of the oblong the leather was slightly raised. He gently removed the arrow inside, together with the fine blue cloth which protected it from the leather.

It was made of a strange metal, light in colour and also light in weight. The arrow was not straight, but in the form of a snake coiled into two opposing arcs. One tiny metal head, its jaws open, was doubled back over its body, about to strike what would have been its tail. But instead of the tail there was another head, exactly mirroring the position of its partner. The two opposed heads were thus at the centre of the weapon, rising slightly above the plane of the two loops.

Karna felt the outside of the loops. The metal tapered to a sharp edge. On the inside of the loops the metal broadened out in strange billowing contours, to about the thickness of one finger. He returned the snake and its cloth into the sheath.

Karna had brought the red sack which had been with him when he was found as a baby, and which had served to hold the unused links of armour when he was younger. Even now it still contained his little pillow. He placed his new weapons inside. Then he returned to the palace.

Next day he swam in the river as usual. That afternoon his supplicant, an elderly woman, was too astonished by his raw and naked torso to ask for charity. She enquired instead what had happened to Karna's mail, and his ear-rings. Karna replied that he had given them away to a brahmana who had begged for them; and later that day he sent a message to Varanasi telling Charvaka much the same thing.

18 The raid on Kampilya

The news that Karna was no longer wearing his armour excited the Pandava princes as much as it worried the Kurus. But why was he not wearing it? Was the rumour true? Was he only going to wear it on special occasions? Had it been stolen?

Dur was the first to question Karna, who replied quite simply that he had given it away as alms to a brahmana. But Karna asked the prince not to talk about it to the others, and refused to discuss the matter further.

Though the Pandava princes could hardly restrain their curiosity, none of them felt comfortable about broaching the subject with Karna. However, they did not have to wait long for confirmation of their hopes. The news of Karna's alleged loss soon reached the elders of the palace. When Kripa and Bhishma heard of it they went immediately to see Karna.

'What have you done with the armour?' demanded Kripa.

'I gave it to a brahmana, by the river. I think he wanted it as a present for his son, so naturally I let him take it—'

'You *gave* away your armour? And your ear-rings!...' Kripa raised his arms in frustration. 'I just do not understand you...' He turned to Bhishma. 'What's the mongoose going to do with him now? Will he try to pursue the kshatriya death?'

'I don't know...' sighed Bhishma. 'Karna, does Charvaka know?'

'Not yet. But I've sent word to him.'

'And didn't you think to inform us?' cried Kripa.

'If I had thought it concerned you, sire, I would have.'

This was the first time since the tournament that either Kripa or Bhishma had actually spoken to Karna; but the conversation ended there.

When Arjuna learnt that Kripa and Bhishma had settled the rumour, he was all for challenging Karna immediately.

'Don't be absurd, brother!' cried Yudhi in response to Arjuna's suggestion. 'Do you think that he cannot *shoot* now that he has lost his armour? And if he can't... well, however inconsiderate he was, to put him through single combat just now would be beneath you, Arjuna.'

But Arjuna later raised the subject with Drona.

'We just don't know how good a fighter Karna is, with or without his armour. We should wait,' advised Drona. 'And... I rather agree with your brother Yudhi that it would be a little... unsubtle to challenge him at the moment.'

'*Unsubtle*? Was he subtle with me? Can you imagine what it was like being insulted like that at the tournament?'

'Yes, it was unforgivable... In fact, it was all very strange... And partly my fault. I did not realise that he was so dangerous. Or Vaitanika, for that matter. My son, have you spoken to him?'

'Spoken to him? What for? I have nothing to say to him...'

While Arjuna carried on speaking, venting his anger, Drona stopped listening to what he was actually saying, and for a while lapsed deep in thought. Then he interrupted his pupil.

'Arjuna... Listen... I have an idea. You know that soon you princes must try to capture King Drupada? That will give us an opportunity to see how Karna can fight. It will be your first real battle, too.'

'What makes you think Karna will want to go and fight Drupada?'

'The suta attended my Academy, did he not?'

'But you never made him promise to repay his debt to you. Why should he?'

'Oh, I think he will. I did teach him something, after all. Though I regret it now. And however much he detests me, he has a strange sense of obligation. What's more important, though — he is probably as curious as we are to find out what he is like in real combat. Do you think he is likely just to watch while *you* become full rathas?'

'Does that mean we'll have to fight together?'

'Not necessarily, my son... This is what I have in mind... The capital city of Panchala is called Kampilya. Drupada will almost certainly be there at this time of year. The country around the city is heavily wooded. We can conceal our force just outside the city walls, even the chariots, provided we are not too many. You and I and the Pandava princes will wait there in our chariots, along with a small force of horsemen — any more chariot fighters and we would give ourselves away.

'While we stay hidden, the Kuru princes, also with some horsemen in support, will go in their chariots through the gates of the city. Now, if we can persuade Karna to fight, he will of course go with them. As soon as they breach the city gates — they'll probably be open, in any case — the alarm will be raised. The palace guard will begin to gather their weapons. The Kurus, encountering little resistance along the way, will proceed to the main square in front of Drupada's palace. By that time the king will certainly have been alerted. Drupada, who is a very confident warrior, will lead out the royal guard, emerging through the palace gates, which open onto the square. I should think he'll probably have elephants leading the charge.

'The Kurus will have no chance of taking Drupada in the main square, since the windows onto the square will quickly fill with archers. The Kurus, with Karna, will be driven back — they will have to retreat.

'Now, by the time they reach the city gates, with Drupada on their tail, they will be travelling at some speed. As soon as Drupada's force has been lured in this way outside the city walls, that is when we appear — you and your brothers with the rest of the horsemen. Let the Kurus fly past... Then you will converge on Drupada. You should be able to drive him right back, probably all the way to the palace gates. By then the guards will have all come down from the galleries around the square, and be relatively easy picking. You, my son, will have to disarm Drupada. I want him alive, you understand?'

'What if Karna takes the king at the palace gates? He'll get the glory, and I won't get any fighting experience! Shouldn't I go in first and capture Drupada?'

'To take Drupada in the city will be very difficult, even for you, Arjuna. No, we must gamble. You are a kshatriya — you must learn to gamble... And the stakes are in our favour. It's true that if we swap the position and send you in first, then if you were to capture King Drupada you would certainly get the glory. But we would learn nothing of Karna's fighting ability. Of course, if you go in first and *fail* to take Drupada, not only will you hand the credit to Karna and the Kurus, who will be going in second, but again we will learn very little about Karna, since Drupada by then will be much easier picking... No, my son. Take the gamble and do as I suggest. We'll send in Karna first. He will almost certainly be forced into retreat. But whatever happens, we will gain some measure of the suta.'

◊

'But Karna, King Drupada is a friend of the Bharatas! The Panchalas are at peace with us. Why should we attack him just so that Drona can get his personal revenge?'

'Because you made Drona a promise. Whatever you think of it, Dur, you have do it. After all, if you feel strongly about it you can always explain to the Panchalas, as you are killing them, that you yourself have nothing against them.'

'Oh yes, Karna, thank you... By the way, why are you so keen to come along?'

'I wouldn't say I was keen.'

'You didn't refuse. And you never promised Drona anything. So why should you have to do his dirty work? Let Arjuna. By the way, did you notice how polite and respectful Drona was?... So, why are you coming along?'

'I need the practice.'

Dur roared with laughter. 'You spent two years killing tigers!'

'Tigers don't shoot arrows at you.'

'Oh, so you were never attacked by bandits in the forest? You never ran into any trouble — only peaceful hermits? Listen, Karna, you need the practice like I need my cousins.'

'This is different. Drupada is a very distinguished warrior, and he will have a guard of experienced kshatriyas. Remember, Dur, he was taught by Drona's father.'

'So? So he was given a thorough grounding in all the great religious texts. But I don't think Bharadwaja encouraged his students to use his sacred manuscripts to fight with.'

'He won't be easy to defeat. Not at all.'

'I can't understand it, sending us in first. If you do bring back Drupada it'll be another humiliation for Arjuna. Why should the wonderful son of Indra risk letting the suta get the glory? Again! Especially since he was the first to promise, remember — no, you hadn't joined us yet. He was the first of us to promise to repay Drona. Now he won't be able to!'

'He will if we fail to capture Drupada.'

'Oh yes!'

'Dur, have you ever been in a battle?'

'No, Karna, I defer to your extensive experience —'

'We could easily get killed. Especially in an unfamiliar and confined space.'

'Especially now you've decided your armour gave you an unfair advantage! You are going to wear *some* armour, I hope?'

'Seriously, Dur, we won't be able to capture Drupada inside the city — not without massacring the Panchalas.'

'Well, then it's obvious that Drona wants us to soften Drupada up so that Arjuna can take him easily. If we have to retreat out of the city, as Drona wants us to, they'll capture Drupada with no trouble at all. By capturing him where you failed, it will appear that Arjuna has beaten you. So Arjuna — and Drona — will have their revenge! If that's what you think, are you really going to go along with it?'

'Yes. I need the practice.'

'Karna, don't you *mind* that you'll make Arjuna come out the big hero?'

'Dur, it's the least I can do. After what I did at the tournament.'

Dur slapped his thigh in frustration. 'Karna, I don't understand you!'

'One thing, Dur... I'd rather you and your brothers didn't... Well, whatever does happen when we do attack Drupada — when we're out of sight of the Pandavas and Drona — I'd rather that the Pandavas didn't get to know... If we're good it'll only make Arjuna more jealous, and if we're bad it'll make them even more belligerent. Either way it'll heat up their blood. If we keep them guessing, their blood will not be able to boil over... We will just retreat calmly, chased by Drupada. Let the Pandavas go in after us and massacre the Panchalas if they want to.'

◊

Drona and his little force hid outside Kampilya, according to plan. Karna and the Kuru princes were able to surprise the guards at the main gate to the city, and stormed through. As directed by Drona, who had sketched out the plan of the city, they made their way towards the main square.

Kampilya was further down the Ganges from Hastinapura, just south of the route Karna would normally take to Varanasi. Karna now regretted that he had never taken the detour to cross the river and visit the city.

The advance party had to enter the main square under an arch which was cut through a building. As soon as he saw this Karna became uneasy. Once in the square he turned and saw above the archway several rows of ornate balconies. These were repeated on the other two sides of the square. As the chariots approached the palace gates at the far end, with the horsemen now flanking them, Karna shouted urgently to Dur and Duh.

'When Drupada comes out, I'll engage him. Cover me as we retreat. But watch the galleries, especially at the back of the square — we may become trapped!'

Drona had warned them that the Panchala guard always had at least two elephants dressed and ready for battle at all times. As he had predicted, when the huge palace gates opened the elephants came first. They were two huge old bulls, nearly sixty years old, menacingly calm, wearing all the decorations of war: bells, neck-ropes, leather girths, and the banners of Panchala. Each animal was draped the full length of its back with a rug of many colours, beneath seven warriors. Two archers were in front, then two swordsmen, followed by two warriors with pikes; the warrior at the back was armed with javelins, and held the banner.

As they retreated Karna and the Kurus parried with their arrows the missiles directed at them. But when Karna looked back at the exit to the square, he saw archers gathering on the balconies above the way out, and the way out already blocked by a row of archers on the ground. Yet another row was forming on the ground behind the first, as more archers appeared from the little alleys that fed the square.

'We're trapped! We're trapped!' shouted Dur.

The Kurus were close to panic, ducking low beneath the sides of their chariots as the elephants drove them back towards the wall of archers behind. Their horsemen were beginning to fall.

Karna quickly threw aside the quivers he had been using, full of bafflers, and asked his driver to stack up his strike arrows. First he put a heavy arrow into the temple of each elephant; then, as both beasts started to crumple, he scattered the clinging warriors with a flight of lighter arrows. Four chariots came round from behind the fallen elephants. In the leading chariot was King Drupada.

Hardly had Drupada started shooting, when his bow was broken, and the stays harnessing his horses severed, releasing them to gallop away. Karna sent another shower of arrows at the other chariots. Then he turned to help the Kurus who were bravely defending the rear.

He directed three waves of arrows at the galleries along the back wall of the square, and the archers there melted away. The ones on the ground behind them also turned to flee. But now more archers were appearing on the side balconies. And Drupada and his warriors had rearmed, and were advancing again in the two chariots which had survived Karna's first onslaught: the king and a kshatriya from another stricken chariot had both scrambled up onto one of those still moving. As Duh and Yuyutsu took them on, leaving Vikarna to tackle the second chariot, Karna spun three times around, sending a continuous stream of arrows which radiated out to the galleries around the square.

Drupada and the two kshatriyas at his side had wounded Yuyutsu. Duh was also in difficulties. Again Karna directed his attention to the king. He managed to penetrate Drupada's defence, injuring him in the arm. Drupada could now hardly hold on to his bow. Karna also pierced the shoulder of one of the two other warriors fighting beside the king. He was about to engage the second of these when he noticed Duh and Yuyutsu apparently transfixed, staring up at a low balcony on the side of the square nearest to them. Karna followed their gape, and found himself looking into the eyes of a young woman. He watched as her face formed into a scream, but the sound must have been drowned by the cries of the warriors around him. Karna hardly noticed the hail of arrows which were now raining down on him.

A piercing cry from Duh brought Karna's attention briefly back to the scene around him; then he lost consciousness. Karna's driver, answering Dur's cry to retreat, joined the others in a rush to the back of the square. Duh and Dur had been badly wounded by the kshatriya still shooting at Drupada's side. But the way out, fortunately for them, was now clear.

As their chariots rolled under the arch, chased by Drupada, Karna revived. Pulling out from his flesh those arrows that hampered his movement, he took up his bow again to parry the pursuing onslaught. He could see that Duh and Yuyutsu were weak from loss of blood, and that Dur was in pain. Few of the horsemen had survived. But the younger Kuru brothers who had held the rear were, miraculously, hardly hurt.

They gathered pace as they rushed out of the city gates, only just managing to avoid the advancing Pandavas. For Drona had evidently decided it was time to send them in.

While the Kurus tended their wounds outside the city walls, the Pandavas, led by Arjuna, drove Drupada back into the main square, now almost deserted. Hardly had Arjuna crossed arrows with Drupada's chariot, when the king raised up his wounded arm and with his other hand restrained the warrior beside him. Arjuna lowered his bow.

Drupada now offered to give himself up to Arjuna if the prince would let the other two Panchala warriors on the chariot go free. Arjuna agreed, and after letting these two climb down from the chariot, he boarded it himself. Then he gave the signal to his brothers to leave the city. Arjuna himself held the reins of his captive's chariot as he set the horses on.

When the chariot started to move, a cry came from one of the balconies. It was Drupada's daughter, calling out to her father. As the warriors in the square stared up at her, Drupada shouted to her to hide, fearing perhaps that his captors might also try to take her prisoner. But she lingered for a moment, and looked pleadingly at Arjuna. He returned her gaze with a friendly smile, and then she disappeared from sight.

A crashing sound brought the attention of Arjuna and the others to the ground. It was Bhima, who it seems had been so inspired by this glimpse of Drupada's daughter that he had begun to apply his mace to anything that moved. It was only with great difficulty that Yudhi was able to restrain his brother from going after a screaming elephant which had strayed into the square. When Bhima had regained his composure, Arjuna shouted in a mighty voice, echoing round the square for the hiding Panchalas to hear:

'I am the Bharata Prince Arjuna, son of Pandu... King Drupada is an ally and a friend of the Bharatas... We have no quarrel with him or with the Panchala people. We have been instructed to capture him, and him only, by the great Drona-charya. Your king will be returned to this city unharmed.'

◊

'King Drupada, I am glad that you were able to come to greet your old friend. You have not forgotten me entirely, have you?'

'No, Drona. What do you want with me?'

'Your friendship. What else? It is a while since we last saw each other. Is it not natural that good friends should keep in touch and see each other from time to time?'

King Drupada looked at his captors without emotion.

'However,' continued Drona, 'since you believe that friendship is possible only between equals, I propose to share the Panchala kingdom equally with you. Thus we can be true friends...'

Drupada did not reply.

'You may keep South Panchala, south of the Ganges,' continued Drona. 'I will be king of North Panchala, north of the river. Does that suit you, King Drupada?'

Drupada looked around at the faces of his captors. 'It does not suit me, but I see that it suits the circumstances, King Drona-charya. You shall indeed have an equal portion of the Panchala kingdom, if that is what you desire. But as to being my equal, I am afraid that while you have desires, you shall never be my equal. Only when our desires have been equally extinguished in death, only then will you be my equal.'

The princes held their breath. Drona stared fiercely for a moment at his captive; then he broke into a smile.

'You haven't changed much, have you? Not that I'd still want you as a friend if you had... Go on, go — you are free. Return to your half of the Panchalas. And please forgive your honourable captor, Prince Arjuna. For he was acting entirely on my own instructions, in payment of my tutor's fee.'

And so Drona set Drupada back on the chariot, to return to Kampilya.

'King Drupada!' cried Arjuna as the king was about to depart. 'Please accept my apologies for any trouble I have caused you... And, if it is not impertinent, please convey my respects to your daughter.'

Drupada smiled.

'My daughter? Which one?'

'The one I saw... I only saw one of your daughters, sire.'

'On the contrary, you saw both my daughters, Prince Arjuna. But you looked only on one. I think you want me to convey your regards to the one upon whom you looked; though your respects are owed much more to the one you overlooked.'

Before Arjuna could ask the king what he meant, Drupada was gone.

The Bharata troop gathered itself and made a weary start back towards Hastinapura. At the last turn in the road before Kampilya disappeared from view, many of the tired young men looked back; they strained their eyes into the distance, as in their minds they entered once more through those city gates.

19 The house of lac

'Yes, it is... But put it away... Careful, my boy. The snake is extremely delicate. Don't take it out into the air again, unless Parashu instructs you.'

'So you think it's Parashu's?'

'It's a snake arrow, certainly. But I doubt it's Parashu's. It's possible, but I don't think so. I have never seen his snake. But from all accounts it is very like this one, even if this is not the one. I have only ever seen one other like this... in Maya... I think the mongoose most likely still has his snake. He guards it with his life. And he would surely have sent word to the other rishis if it had been stolen. Especially if it had got into the hands of our Lord Indra! No.. I don't know what to make of this...'

'Do you know how they are made?'

'Yes... I have assisted in the manufacture of one, the one in Maya. But I couldn't make one just by myself. I doubt any one person could unaided. But this... It's most strange... You'll have to show it to Parashu.'

'Why should I go to Parashu now? I haven't got my ear-rings any longer. What do I need with Parashu? I've made my decision. It's not that I fear death, sire. I think you know that. It's just that I can think of better ways to risk it.'

Charvaka sighed and shook his head slowly.

'How do you know, Karna? If you'd only kept them, at least Parashu could have explained everything, and you would have known what was at stake...'

'I'm not interested in gambling, sire, not unless I'm forced to. So why should I gamble? As I say, I've thrown away the dice.'

'I wish it were as simple as that... Even as far as the other rishis are concerned, it's a delicate matter. At least we will not interfere. But as far as Parashu is concerned... Karna, you will still have to go to him. And, remember, he may even be able to teach you something with the bow, my boy... If he doesn't try to kill you.'

'Well, if he does try to kill me, I'm sure it'll be an educational experience, if his reputation is good for anything. Charvaka, what exactly is kshatriya death?'

'Where did you hear that?'

'I heard Kripa use the phrase.'

'The owl should know better. It's... It's the cloud you are under.'

'But I'm a suta, not a kshatriya... You mean I have the best of both worlds?'

Charvaka smiled. 'I'm sorry, my boy. I can't talk to you about it. Even if you still had your ear-rings, I wouldn't...' He sighed again. 'Why did you have to go and get rid of them? I warned you enough times. It makes things so much more difficult... Anyway, it's something you must settle with the mongoose. Even though you can't now throw your dice, you still have to sort things out with that rishi... The armour, yes... But the ear-rings!'

'I could have used the armour in Kampilya. I lost quite a bit of blood. For me, anyway.'

'You lost blood? The son of Surya?'

'I was distracted, sire. I didn't realise I was bleeding. I've never fainted before.'

'No...' The rishi shook his head. 'Still, you're healing very nicely. You're remembering to breathe, my boy, aren't you?'

'Oh yes, sire. As I say, I was distracted. But it's a good thing, really. At least Drona and Arjuna are pleased with themselves. That'll keep them off my back. I don't think Arjuna's going to bother to challenge me to single combat now he knows how frail I am.'

'Yes... Vrisha says they're already talking about it in Anga. He says the story there is that Arjuna captured Kampilya single-handed after you were defeated!'

'Sire, have you heard how Vai's getting on?'

'No, Vrisha hardly mentioned anything of importance last time he was here! But when you get there tell your brother if he doesn't come here soon, I'll have to look for another assistant. He can't devote all his time to the sandals of Rama!'

◊

The news of Drupada's defeat at the hands of Arjuna and the Pandavas, following the failure of Karna and the Kurus, had indeed been trumpeted all over Hastinapura, and quickly spread about the country. As a reward for his exploit Drona presented Arjuna with a helmet which, it was rumoured, had belonged to Indra himself, and which no arrow could pierce.

Arjuna, Bhima and the twins, inspired by their success in Panchala, organised over the next few months several successful raiding parties against neighbouring kingdoms. They were thus able to confirm in deed the substance of their spreading reputations. And as their fame grew, so did the treasury of the Bharata kingdom, which filled with the booty and taxes that the princes obtained.

But Yudhi, who did not join in these raids, was not at all happy with Arjuna's constant warring.

'This is not the time, brother.'

'Not the time? It's exactly the time, Yudhi! Don't you know that people are already clamouring for you to be installed now as sovereign? After years of King Dhrita, who's gained very little for the kingdom, they see the grain stores getting full, the treasury chests sparkling. They want to restore the Bharata kingdom to its former glory. Now that we are establishing ourselves in our own right, the Pandavas can rightfully ascend to the throne!'

'Not everybody thinks that it is right to enrich yourself and the kingdom by force of arms. You should learn to control your ambitious desires.'

'But we are kshatriyas! Anyway, I do control my desires, every kshatriya does: I restrain those desires which only bring temporary happiness at the expense of future contentment. But remember, Yudhi, we're also encouraged to procure our long-term happiness and security. That's just what I'm doing.'

'That is what you *think* you are doing, brother. Do you know that Dur thinks we plotted with Drona to have him trapped and killed in Kampilya?'

'Did he accuse you?'

'No... Not exactly. He sent Karna to speak to me... Just before he left for Anga, he came to speak to me...'

'He spoke to you? What did he say? Were his wounds healed?'

'Not completely, but they were much better. He told me that Dur thought that Drona had conspired with all of us to get the Kurus killed, and I have to say — let me finish, brother — I have to say that it certainly looks as though they were... as though they were meant to become trapped. I told Karna of course that I and you — that none of us knew anything about such a thing. But quite honestly, Arjuna, it looks to me as though Drona must have known they would become trapped.'

'I'm not sure, Yudhi. *I* certainly had no idea. Drona described the plan to me as though it would be quite simple for them to retreat. And however much I have against them, I certainly wouldn't have gone along with it if I didn't think they were going to be able to retreat safely. Honestly, brother! I even tried to persuade Drona to let me go in first.'

'I believe you. And Karna believed me, I'm sure of that. But he wasn't so sure that *Dur* would believe we were innocent... Don't you see, Arjuna, what you're suggesting now? It could hardly be more insensitive. It looks to Dur now that, having failed to kill him and his brothers — and Karna — we are planning to take over his father's kingdom.'

'But we are the rightful heirs!'

'That does not give us the right to the kingdom *now*. Even if it does pass to us when Dhrita dies.'

'Or if he willingly surrenders the throne! Surely he would willingly surrender it to us now, if he saw how popular we are, how strong we can make his kingdom.'

'*His* kingdom? Do you expect Dhrita to see it that way when he thinks you've just tried to murder his sons?'

'He doesn't think that, surely?'

'Arjuna! Of course he does! Do you not imagine that Dur has been complaining to him constantly about Drona and us? Did you notice, by the way, how unimpressed the Grandsire was with the whole business of Drupada? I think the Grandsire was more angry than he let on. Angry with Drona for not consulting him. And he doesn't think Drupada will let it rest there. We can hardly be surprised if Drupada now tries somehow to get his revenge on Drona.'

'Let him try!'

'Arjuna, you really amaze me sometimes! And considering how you go on about his daughter... You know, I sometimes wonder whether you ever see more than a bird's head at any one time!'

'I'm sorry, I'm sorry... I know I should think more carefully... Yudhi, why is the Grandsire so quiet these days? He seems troubled.'

'Of course he's troubled! Can't you see his loyalties are being divided by us? Remember, he is in charge of the military affairs of the kingdom. And yet you don't even tell him of your raids. If he didn't think of us as his grandchildren I'm sure you'd feel the sharp end of his anger... Anyway, we may have to do a lot of thinking soon. Vidura tells me that Dur might be plotting something. He doesn't know what yet. But we ought to be careful. And have you noticed that Shakuni is practically living here now? You know how friendly he is with Dur, and how cunning he is. King Shakuni is a strange man.'

'What if Dur is plotting against us? To do what? To challenge me to single combat?'

'It's not funny, Arjuna. Especially at the moment, with Karna away.'

'I should have thought that would make it safer for us, if anything... Not that I consider Karna a threat.'

'I noticed you seemed less impatient to challenge him since his failure at Kampilya... But while Karna is away, Dur feels more insecure. And all the more reason for him to cause trouble for us... Also, whatever you say, and whatever you think, which I'm afraid does not seem to be very much these days, Karna is a good influence on Dur. I honestly can't see Karna encouraging Dur to murder us in our sleep.'

'So what should we do?'

'Well, you could be more restrained in your military activities. For a while at least, till this has blown over... And be a little more tactful. Above all, we must not go around as though we are already the kings of Bharata. We must accept whatever Dhrita says. Yes, brother! Even though, as you're thinking, even though what he says sometimes originates in the mind of his son.'

'So that means I must do whatever *Dur* tells me to!'

'*Arjuna*! You don't seem to be taking this seriously! It's true that as Dur gets older his father will probably feel increasingly obliged to support him. That's perfectly natural. But we must try not to give Dhrita grounds to convert his support for Dur into a hatred against us. Think, brother, think!'

'Sorry, Yudhi. I'll try.'

◊

But it was too late, for Dur already had hatched a scheme which would confirm Yudhi's fears, and show how vulnerable the Pandavas really were.

The great Shiva festival was due to be held that year in Varanasi. At the previous one, eleven years earlier in Kampilya, Bhishma had been the chief representative of the Bharata people. Dur now asked his father if this time he would send the Pandavas to represent them. After all, argued Dur, the Pandavas were now so well known through their conquering raids that it would be quite appropriate for them to be given this honour. Dhrita agreed. It would mean the Pandavas being away for several months; and their absence from the capital would defuse tensions which had grown almost to breaking point after the raid on Drupada.

What Dhrita did not know was that Dur had already commissioned the building of an elegant house in Varanasi to accommodate the Pandavas during their stay. This itself, though surprisingly attentive, was not unduly suspicious. However, the same could not be said for the materials out of which the house was to be built. These appeared to have been chosen not so much for their structural properties as for their propensity to burn. In particular, the surfaces of the building were to be finished, wherever possible, in lac. One spark, and the whole house would be aflame within seconds, ashes within minutes.

These details had not escaped the notice of Vidura, who had taken the precaution of talking to the artisans and studying the plans.

The Pandavas, in obedience to King Dhrita, dutifully travelled to Varanasi with their mother Pritha. But Yudhi had been warned by his uncle of the danger. Vidura had advised the Pandavas not to disclose their suspicions, but to go along for the moment uncomplainingly with whatever was demanded of them. Vidura was genuinely concerned that if they were to reveal their fears, Dur might try something even more desperate. Vidura also took the opportunity to stress to Yudhi how powerful Dur was becoming in the Bharata court. Two things, in Vidura's view, had contributed to this rise, neither of which came as a surprise to Yudhi: the recent arrival of Dur's uncle Shakuni; and the fact that Bhishma had been unusually withdrawn, taking little interest in the affairs of court.

◊

The house of lac was surrounded by a moat. There was only one way in and out, through a little gatehouse in which Dur had installed a servant of his, called Purochanna. This man had been instructed by Dur, after a discreet period, to set fire to the house while the Pandavas were asleep within.

There was indeed a fire after a few weeks, in the dead of night. But things could not have happened exactly according to plan. For as well as the remains of six bodies in the scorched site of the main building itself, Purochanna's charred body was also recovered from what was left of the gatehouse.

The people of Varanasi concluded with horror that the bodies in the house of lac were those of the five princes and Pritha: there had been a feast there that very night, attended by several local people, all of whom attested to the fact that the Pandavas must have spent the night there; the last guests and servants to leave saw the gate being shut by Purochanna behind them; it was still securely shut in the morning after the fire had taken its toll; it could not be opened without Purochanna; there was no other way out.

The news quickly reached Hastinapura, and plunged the whole city into mourning. Though, surprisingly, the elders of the palace seemed to be the least affected by the information. Indeed, soon after the first reports arrived, Vidura, Bhishma and Kripa left on a visit to Panchala which they had been planning for some time.

They had been anxious to make friendly contact again with King Drupada, after Drona's excursion. And it seems that their purpose was fulfilled, for in Kampilya they were treated to Drupada's most congenial hospitality; during which all three visitors received enquiries from the king's daughter Draupadi, about the impressive young men who had captured her father.

When the three elders returned to Hastinapura, they were surprised to find that Dur and his brothers were still in mourning for their Pandava cousins.

In private the Kuru princes did not allow themselves to hope that the Pandavas had successfully been destroyed; the circumstances of the fire had been too puzzling for that. So Dur decided he should make some enquiries of his own, to establish whether there was any possibility that the Pandavas had somehow escaped.

Shakuni offered to investigate in Varanasi, mainly as an excuse to see his friend Charvaka; and he duly spent some weeks there, during which he spent most of his time chatting to Charvaka over the dice table. Such enquires as he did make, however, drew a blank. And so on his return the Kurus began to accept that they had indeed succeeded in getting rid of their cousins. But they did not dare express their satisfaction in public, in spite of the fact that they were now well established as the most powerful voice in the Bharata court. For, as Vidura had warned Yudhi, Dur was now more than the mere mouthpiece of the king. He had learnt the trick of sowing thoughts into his father's head which he could later harvest and present to the Bharata assembly as King Dhrita's considered wish.

•

'Palmira, what is *lac*?'

'Lac, Henry, is a sticky wax secreted by a tiny insect which lives on certain trees in India. I think it particularly likes fig trees. As well as using the wax, you can make a nice red dye out of it. As a matter of fact, there is a Sanskrit word *lak* meaning red. Though I remember Vyasa wondering whether lac was called lac because these insects were so tiny and numerous — you see, in Sanskrit, *laksham* means a hundred thousand —'

'Laksham?... What are the numbers like in Sanskrit, Palmira?'

'Eka, dwi, tri, katur, pancha, shash, sapta, ashta, nava, dasha! How old are you in Sanskrit?'

'Er... Ka... katur—'

'—dasha?'

'There you are, boys, a few thousand miles, and nearly as many years, and you get the Latin, *quattordecim*. Numbers are the beginning and the end of everything...'

•

20 Draupadi's swayamwara

Not long after the people of Hastinapura had got over the news about Pritha and the Pandavas, more tidings arrived which set the court alive with speculation. Draupadi, the younger of King Drupada's two daughters, was soon to have her swayamwara.

This caused much gossip. The rumour was circulating that the princess had expressed some interest in the Pandava princes, Arjuna in particular; and her choice had been expected to lie in that direction. But another topic of speculation concerned what was to happen at the swayamwara itself: for it seems that Drupada, in order to test the worthiness of his daughter's suitors, had borrowed an idea of King Janaka's.

Janaka, the father of Sita, had come by a remarkable bow which no one was able to string. Generally speaking, the stronger a bow is, and the longer the effective range of the weapon, the more difficult it is to bend; and since the bowstring needs to be very tight, some of the more powerful bows require immense strength and skill just to join the bowstring from tip to tip. King Janaka's had evidently been just such a bow; and the competition for his daughter's hand required each suitor to attempt to string this mighty bow. Nevertheless, an acceptable husband was found for Princess Sita, a suitor who was able to string the bow: his name, of course, was Rama.

It was said, however, that King Drupada's test was going to be even harder, requiring in addition to strength some remarkable archery. Many people wondered whether Drupada had been informed about the fire in the Pandavas' house. For the task facing the suitors was so difficult that it looked as though Drupada was trying to make sure that only Arjuna could accomplish it.

Drupada had originally planned to stage the festival in the beautiful square in front of his palace, the scene of his own capture. But when he heard how many warriors would be seeking his daughter's hand in marriage, he realised that he would have to accommodate them, and hold the festivities, outside the city walls. Drupada had been rather taken aback by the response to his announcement. Great kings and princes from far and wide had indicated their intention to attend. So Drupada had some trees felled and an amphitheatre constructed just outside the city, with pavilions and tents where his guests could stay.

As was the custom with these things, the festival was planned to spread over a number of days, in this case sixteen. And on the sixteenth day, under the blazing midday sun, the actual competition for Draupadi would take place.

◊

There were a few warriors who had entered the lists light-heartedly, without any desires or expectations other than those involved in the mere entertainment of competing. Nevertheless, when the sixteenth day arrived, a sombre cloud descended over all the assembled contestants.

In some cases, where hostilities had been put to one side out of respect for the occasion, the carousing of these men during their stay outside the city had been forced and tense. But now even friends were overcome by the rivalry hanging in the air.

All the Kuru princes were there: Dur, Duh, Vikarna, Chitra, Yuyutsu, Virimsa, Vivitsu, Kratha and Upanada. The last two, the youngest, were not competing. But the others had all, in some degree or other, dreamed of Draupadi.

Dur was sitting apart from the other Kurus, next to Bala and Krishna. As usual the dress of these two brothers, who were not participating, and therefore not in martial costume, contrasted greatly: Bala wore a plain grey cloak, and Krishna a purple coat and headcloth; as ever, the wallet containing his discus was strapped to his belt.

On the other side of Krishna sat three more spectators: Vrisha, Sangra and Pra. Karna's brothers had travelled up from Anga the previous day. Although Karna was sitting with them, he showed no desire for conversation; and they instead were listening attentively to Krishna.

Vrisha was curious about Krishna's wallet.

'Is that where you carry your discus? I've heard you never go anywhere without it.'

'I have two of them in here, Vrisha.'

'Two?'

'Of course. In case my enemy has a friend.'

'But what if your enemy's friend has another friend?'

As he replied, Krishna placed one hand gently on Vrisha's arm.

'By the time his first two friends have completed their karma in this world, the third will no longer be an enemy to Krishna!'

'Will you show me one?' asked Vrisha, looking at the wallet.

'I don't like taking them out except to use them. But I believe you know the person who made them for me.'

'Not Charvaka?'

'Indeed Charvaka. Ask him to show you one. He usually had one or two in his workshop in Hastinapura, before he was banished. Perhaps he finds it difficult to get the materials in Varanasi... You should have seen his place in Hastinapura! He showed me round it with my father when I was a young boy.'

'When is Princess Draupadi going to appear?' asked Sangra.

'Oh, quite soon,' replied Krishna, showing a gold-capped tooth as he smiled. 'But first they will have to light the ceremonial fire, and formally announce the challenge.'

'Why are all the women here veiled?' asked Vrisha.

Krishna removed his hand from Vrisha's arm and opened out the other, revealing the jewelled rings on each of his fingers.

'So as not to distract us from the beauty of Princess Draupadi. Though I doubt there would be danger of such distraction, even if all the other... Ah! See, there is Prince Drishta-dyumna. In a little while he is going to announce the challenge for his sister!'

'Krishna, how can you throw the discus with all those rings?' enquired Vrisha, returning to his earlier theme.

'Why, they positively aid my grip! Of course, they would be a nuisance with the bow. I remember Kripa-charya telling me I would never make an archer, for that reason.'

'Why aren't they here?' asked Sangra. 'The other Bharatas?'

'Yes... It is interesting that neither Kripa nor Lord Bhishma are here. Drona's absence one may understand! But the others... Perhaps they are still mourning? Yes, one would expect King Dhrita, even though he is blind, to attend an occasion like this. Perhaps they are too embarrassed by Drona's raid? Though I rather think Drupada has come out of it a winning captive that has gained in loss.'

'How is that?' asked Vrisha.

'Because I doubt whether word of Draupadi's beauty would have spread so far and fast had it not been for the praise of my poor cousins.'

'Oh yes,' agreed Vrisha. 'Karna said it was the only time he saw her, at the raid... Krishna, who do you think will win Draupadi?'

'I am much too wise to make a prediction, Vrisha. But, if you're curious,' Krishna added with a playful smile, 'just look around you at these mighty warriors! Who do *you* think is going to win? Ah... Perhaps you don't know many of them?'

'I've only seen a few of them before,' confirmed Vrisha. 'I remember some from the tournament — I remember you there, in the royal pavilion. Krishna, why aren't you taking part?'

'Me?' Krishna laughed. 'Vrisha, I have too many wives!'

'Oh...' said Vrisha, remembering something else. 'Wasn't your father there, at the tournament? Karna told us that he died recently. I'm sorry...'

'Thank you, Vrisha, thank you. So, whom else do you recognise?'

'There's Ashwa, over there...' Vrisha pointed him out. 'He's grown since the tournament! He doesn't look as though he's competing, though.'

'It's interesting that he's here in spite of Drona's absence... But then I don't think he took part in his father's raid... Though it's not that which stops him competing: he's a brahmana, Vrisha. They are not usually expected to take part in these affairs. Brahmana men are expected to marry brahmana women. All the brahmanas here are just spectating... At least, I imagine so... There certainly are some strange-looking ones here today — look at those two over there, the one with the hunched back and that huge one with him — they are armed with bows and quivers. But of the kshatriyas, tell me, whom do you fancy to win?'

'I think it would be easier for me to guess who *isn't* going to win! Shakuni, for a start!'

'You know him? Of course, I expect he must go to Varanasi quite often?'

'Yes, he usually visits Charvaka every few months. He's a great mathematician, but I don't think he has the strength to string the bow!'

'He's stronger than you think, Vrisha. But you're probably right. Even if he managed to string the bow, his eyesight is not good enough for the next stage. I also doubt that the young man next to him will fare much better. Do you know him? That's Prince Uluka, King Shakuni's son. Yes... Many of the warriors here already have wives and children, and a few will be competing against their own sons and nephews. Soma-datta, for example — do you remember him?'

'Yes, he was at the tournament. He's from Balhika, isn't he? And is that his son, Bhuri? They look incredibly strong! If anyone could string the bow, they should!'

'Oh yes. And they have a very good chance. They are accurate as well as powerful.'

'Are they actually Bharatas, Krishna?'

'They are descended from King Shantanu's brother, so Soma and Bhuri are certainly Bharatas. You can think of the Balhika people as almost a clan of the Bharatas. Though they are decidedly more partial to King Dhrita than they ever were to Pandu. And they certainly don't seem to have been in mourning for the Pandavas...'

'There was another king at the tournament, wasn't there? I wonder if he's here?'

'You must mean Shalya, Madri's brother... King Shalya of the Madrakas... Where is he... Yes, look, see, over there...'

'Oh yes, that's him... He looks gloomy — oh, of course, the twins were his nephews... What about his chances?'

'I would not bet on him, Vrisha. Shalya is a very considerable warrior, make no mistake about that. He has a remarkably elegant style, quite as good as Drona's or Arjuna's. And you should see him on horseback. He has a way with horses. And in a fight he would be quite a proposition, especially if you can get him angry, which is not too difficult. He's a very proud man. He's one of these people who's most efficient when his blood is hot!' Krishna growled and flashed his eyes in mock anger. 'But — his aim is not quite natural enough for the problem he will have to face here today. If it was *style* that was being judged, then yes, he would be a favourite.'

'Why can't they take that into account?'

'A warrior's style?'

'Yes, why can't the winner be the warrior with the best style, the one who is most graceful? Why is it always strength and accuracy with these kshatriyas? Sorry, I know you're a kshatriya, too... But don't you think elegance has every right to compete with power?'

'Vrisha!' Krishna lowered his voice. 'Don't let Karna hear you say that!' He put his arm around Vrisha's shoulder. His eyes wrinkled in a smile. 'Vrisha, there are two kinds of competition in which men engage. There is the kind, as we are about to witness here, in which the circumstances of the world decide the winner, not the judgements of mere men. Today that golden fish out there will judge the winner, not us. And that object is quite blind to style. All it will notice is whether it is struck or not!

'But there is another kind of contest,' Krishna continued, 'in which the preferences of men are set up to judge. Only within such a game could you compete for style. Such contests do exist, Vrisha, but I myself don't care for them.'

'Why not?'

'Because the judges are not blind enough. They see too much, and are too easily distracted from their purpose. For the dangers are that the contestants will begin to play for the judges, and the judges will begin to pander to the contestants.'

'Why should the judges do that?'

'If you set up the eyes of men to judge over men, then, being men, the contestants will begin to exaggerate their movements to catch the eyes of the judges; and the judges will begin to exaggerate the vision of their judgement, to catch the eyes of each other. And then, before you know it, the simple substance of the contest is quite taken over by the decoration. Do you follow?'

'I think so... My parents once took me to a tournament of music in Anga where the flute players competed. I suppose that must be like you describe. You play the flute, don't you? Karna says you play very nicely.'

'I do, I have to say. But I never enter such contests, neither for the flute, nor for my dancing. I enjoy the spirit of the music, of the dance, but only the spirit. And yet it is not the spirit which is judged, not the feeling... No, such qualities are much too simple, much too natural, much too easy, to occupy the weighty arbitration of our judges. The judges want to see something a little more difficult. They want to see this simple nature improved by ingenuity, by invention. That's fine, at first. But the spirit of invention soon becomes the slave of contrivance. Beneath the chains of which... the soul is lost. Quite lost. The artifice turns artificial. No, Vrisha. You *could* set up judges to consider the style of our warriors. But I fear that then the simple elegance rewarded at the start would soon sprout flowery wings, to flutter against each other, and in the end fly out of all recognition! It's bad enough having here a *golden* fish, and *golden* arrows! Delightful as adornments. But where would it end? You would see warriors using the most ornate missiles, the most preposterous bows, the most spectacular costume — altogether, the most inappropriate manner to misappropriate the matter! Let the target be the judge today, Vrisha, please!'

'But the target's not meant to be the judge today! Draupadi might be more impressed by style than substance. I think she must be if she preferred Arjuna to my brother.'

Krishna laughed. 'I will not enter that debate! Not with Karna within earshot!'

'But seriously, what happens if the winner is someone she doesn't want?'

'She is not obliged to choose the winner, Vrisha. You are right, the contest is just an excuse to catch her eye. But then of course, there might be a winner who would not have *her*. Satyaki, for example, where is he?... There...'

'The small one? Is he strong enough?'

'As your friend Charvaka is fond of saying, there is more to strength than strength! Don't you know Satyaki? He is king of the Shinis, and a great friend of Drupada's.'

'But why wouldn't he want Draupadi?'

'Because he's such a friend of Drupada's. I believe he's even married to one of Drupada's former wives... Or is it the other way round? But he's like an uncle to Draupadi. No, he's entering just for the fun of it. And perhaps also to flatter her, as an uncle might. But if he were to win, neither of them would take offence at the other's rejection!'

'And you think he really stands a chance?'

'Oh yes. King Satyaki is one of the most underestimated of kshatriyas. Take it from me, that man is an ati-ratha. Among the present company there are probably only three, perhaps four warriors that could match him in battle. And no more than two who would have any chance of beating him.'

'Who?'

'Mind you,' continued Krishna, ignoring Vrisha's question, 'it is possible that he might not be able to string the bow. As you suggest, strength is not his strength. But if he can string the bow... Of course, he normally uses a much lighter bow. This may surprise you, Vrisha, but Satyaki and the Shinis have proved quite a match for King Soma and the Balhikas. Those two have had several skirmishes lately. But neither Soma nor his son Bhuri, fierce as they look, have been able to defeat Satyaki.'

'What have they been fighting about?'

'Land, Vrisha, land.'

'Do you think there might be a proper war between them?'

'May the gods forbid it. It would be a conflagration.'

'Why's that?'

'Because Soma and Bhuri would be able to count on the support of King Dhrita and the Grandsire! And if that weren't enough, well, just of the kings assembled here, let me see... Shakuni and the Gandharas, they would definitely be on the side of the Balhikas... And King Bhaga and the Vangas... See, over there...'

'He looks very impressive!'

'Indeed. King Bhaga-datta is very powerful. You know that he prefers to fight on an elephant than on a chariot. In fact he is training a most magnificent animal. What's his name?... Supratika, that's it. A magnificent animal. He is just reaching his full height. Yes, he must be about thirty years old. A little young for battle — but in twenty years time I doubt there will be an animal to touch him. It's not just his size. He has an exceptional temperament for a bull, even when he is in musth. I have never seen the like. Not that he will be able to help Bhaga today. He'll certainly string the bow, but I doubt he can shoot well enough.'

'Who else would be on Soma's side? If there was a war between Soma and Satyaki?'

'Well, let us see... Yes, those three over there. That's King Krita-varman, of the Bhojas. Next to him is King Shruta-yudha of the Kalingas. And the other one is King Jaya-dratha of the Sindhus.'

'And they would all side with Soma? Surely Satyaki wouldn't stand a chance against all those!'

'It would be difficult, but I think he would stand a chance. That's why it would be such a conflagration. Remember that Satyaki would be able to count on

Drupada's support. And the Panchalas are very powerful. In fact, it's interesting that Drona's attack didn't spark a major conflict between Drupada and the Bharatas. But Satyaki would get other support as well. I suspect that King Shalya, for example, though he has in the past been an ally of both Dhrita and Soma, he might now choose to fight with Satyaki against Dhrita — remember that he is uncle to the Pandava twins. I'm sure he must at least partly blame Dhrita for what happened...'

'Are there any others that would support Satyaki?'

'Yes... Over there, King Indra-varman of the Malavas... He's another one for preferring elephants to chariots. He has a fine young animal called Ashwa-tthaman, of all things!'

'Was it named after Drona's son?'

'Oh no, it's just coincidence. If you believe in coincidence. Next to Indra-varman is a great friend of his who would also side with Satyaki and the Shinis: King Kunti-bhoja. He is poor Pritha's stepfather. My aunt Pritha must have been killed in the fire — *if* the Pandavas really were caught in it. Who else? Let's see... Ah! King Cheki-tana of the Vrishnis. He was a great friend of King Pandu, and I think he rather resents Dhrita. So I'm sure he would want to be fighting against Dhrita. And I suppose the same goes for King Virata of Matsya. He'd also want to oppose Dhrita...'

Krishna pointed out a worried-looking warrior from a group of four or five rather morose kshatriyas.

'The man next to Virata is called Kichaka. He is Virata's brother-in-law, and is effectively in charge of Virata's army. And his cattle, by all accounts. They have much cattle, the Matsyas, but Virata, perhaps because of his greedy general, will not share them out among his people. Next to Kichaka is Virata's brother, Shatanika... Yes... And those two behind Kichaka are Virata's sons, Uttara and Shankha. They don't get along with Kichaka. In fact, even though he is their uncle, they only tolerate him because they need him to defend the Matsyas against King Shusharman of Trigarta. He's that other one, right next to them — you can tell he's trying hard to control his contempt! The Trigartas and the Matsyas have been quarrelling for years.'

'Does that mean that Shusharman would fight on the side of Soma and Dhrita, against Virata — if Virata joined Satyaki's side?'

'Exactly!' Krishna beamed at him, his gold tooth glinting as he smiled.

'Krishna, who is that huge one near us, near Dur... He's nearly as big as Bhima was!'

'Ah, now that is King Jara-sandha. He's king of Magadha. That's his son with him, Prince Jaya-tsena.'

'So *that's* Jara-sandha! I've certainly heard of him, Krishna!'

'Of course! Not a nice man to have as a neighbour!'

'I've never been through his kingdom, but it's south-west of Anga... I think it's probably only because of our links with Hastinapura that he hasn't tried to conquer Anga.'

'I'm sure you're right, Vrisha. Yes, Jara-sandha is everybody's enemy! Did you know that he drove my people out from Mathura? Yes, in a war between Satyaki and Soma, he'd probably stay out of it, and then attack the weakened survivors! Anga has been lucky. He's always fighting his neighbours. He's a remarkable wrestler, you know. Reputed to be one of the finest in the land. And he's a great believer in single combat to subjugate his enemy! As you can imagine, he always stipulates wrestling as his preferred means to victory. Yes, a great wrestler, in spite — so I'm told — of having a weak back —'

'Look!' Vrisha lowered his voice. 'Next to Jara-sandha!' Vrisha nudged his brothers, and they also stared.

The man who had caught their attention was wearing an unusually flowing headcloth, which tended to obscure his eyes. Every few moments, however, he would jerk his head slightly, revealing for an instant the unusual shape of his head. It was doubtful whether he could look at an object with both eyes at the same time: his huge brow was angled, each eye looking out from the side of his head in a different direction. The lower part of his face was hidden by a bristly beard.

'He is *horrible*! He has eyes like a rabbit! Who is he, Krishna?'

'That, young man, is the king of the Chedis.' For a moment the brightness left Krishna's voice. 'His name is Shishu-pala.'

'Do you know him? Have you met him?'

'Yes I have,' replied Krishna. 'His mother is a sister of Queen Pritha. He is a cousin of mine.'

'Oh! I'm sorry...' Vrisha covered his mouth with his hand.

'No, no... Don't apologise in case you have offended me, Vrisha, for you have not. Shishu hates me, and hates all my side of the family. As a matter of fact, he is not a nice man. He is one of Jara-sandha's few friends. He and Jara tried to set fire to Dwaraka, just after we had taken refuge there. I believe, though I do not know for certain, that he is now King Jara-sandha's executioner.'

'Why does he hate you?'

'He was not born looking like that, Vrisha. He... When he was younger his parents asked me to cure him. As you see, I could not — not completely. For that, I think, he hates me. The other day he very nearly attacked me, right in front of King Drupada and the others. Fortunately he was restrained, for he is a very dangerous man. They say that he can kill a man with one blow of his forehead.'

'What happened?'

'He is evil, but he is no fool. I had my discus on me. Fortunately Jara-sandha managed to calm him.'

'Is he going to compete today?'

'Oh, no. He cannot judge distance.'

Vrisha found that he could not help staring at Shishu-pala. He forced himself to look away. As he did so his eye was drawn by a figure dressed entirely in red.

'Krishna... Who is that? He is not a warrior, is he? He looks a bit fat for a fighter...'

'He is a rishi,' replied Krishna. 'His name is Durvasa.'

'But why is he wearing red? Everything on him's red!'

'Oh, Durvasa always wears red.'

'Why?'

'Why? Why indeed... He wears his cloth but as the fashion of his faith.'

'What faith is *red*?'

'It's not the colour, Vrisha, but the constancy.'

'Is he very devout, then?'

'Not at all. I think the only thing constant about his faith is the colour of his cloth!'

Vrisha laughed.

'But what's he doing here?'

'He has been here in his capacity as rishi for the past fifteen days, presiding over the festivities. I believe it's the first time Karna has met him. Yes, Durvasa was most interested in your brother...'

'Krishna,' Vrisha asked after a pause, 'how do you come to know all these people? I mean, you've known them for ages, it's not just the last fortnight that you've met them, is it?'

'I've been here and there, you know. As a matter of fact, Vrisha, I think the first time I saw most of these — the older ones, at any rate — was when I was a child, at King Pandu's Rajasuya.'

'Rajasuya? What's that?'

'The Rajasuya is a great ceremony. Perhaps the greatest of all. It is held to celebrate the King of Kings. All the kings in the surrounding lands recognised Pandu as their King of Kings.'

'Had he beaten them all in battle?'

'Not exactly! Pandu was still very young at his Rajasuya. Hardly older than you, I dare say. But the Grandsire was his general. Bhishma was then in his prime. No one would challenge *him*!'

'Krishna, what side would you be on — if the Shinis fought the Balhikas?'

'Ah, look!' cried Krishna, taking advantage of a good excuse for evading the question. 'Draupadi's brother is lighting the ceremonial fire! It can't be long now... By the way, did Karna tell you?... No, he probably wouldn't have known it was Prince Drishta... This brave young prince was injured by your brother when the Kurus attacked Kampilya. Drupada had scrambled onto his son's chariot, and Drishta was trying to defend his father against Karna. He will be a great ratha, mark my words, Vrisha. Yes, I expect Drishta to become one of the greatest warriors in the land. And, for that matter, so will his —'

'Oh, yes! I remember Karna telling me... So that's who it was? I remember Karna saying that he had to dislocate his arm or his shoulder, or something, because he was fighting so well. But there was another warrior on that chariot, as well as Drupada and Drishta. It must have been this other one who injured Karna —'

•

'Palmira! We'll never remember all these names and details!'

'That's all right, boys. When you meet these people again there won't be any danger you'll embarrass yourselves — they're not going to find out you've forgotten who they are.'

•

'Sssh!' Krishna raised his hand. 'We'd better be quiet, Drishta is going to announce the challenge!'

The young prince walked slowly away from the brazier he had just set alight. It was placed close to Draupadi's vacant seat. The smoke from the scented wood began to fill the air with its heavy perfume.

Drishta stopped beside a tall pole right in the centre of the amphitheatre. Leaning against the pole was the huge bow which the now silent warriors had been holding in their imagination. Just before he started his prepared speech, he could not resist glancing briefly at his friends in the crowd, giving them a broad grin. Then he composed himself.

'I, Prince Drishta-dyumna, brother of Princess Draupadi, and son of King Drupada of Panchala, invite all the warriors assembled here seeking the hand in marriage of the princess, to consider carefully their task.

'You see before you, suspended at the top of this pole, a golden fish. That fish is no larger than the hand of Princess Draupadi.

'Below the fish, by exactly the height of the princess, and above the ground by exactly three times the height of the princess, you see a solid gold wheel, with the pole through its centre. As you can observe, the pole serves as the axle around which the wheel will freely revolve.'

Prince Drishta moved into the shade directly beneath the wheel.

'The diameter of this gold circle' — as he said this Drishta paced across the shadow which the wheel, like a parasol in the midday sun, cast around the base of the pole — 'is exactly the distance from fingertip to fingertip when Princess Draupadi holds her arms outstretched.

'Near the edge of the wheel you see a small hole, the width of Princess Draupadi's wrist.

'You see down here, against the pole, a metal bow; it is so unrelenting as to require the very greatest persuasion successfully to string.' He stooped in the shadow to pick up the coiled string, and draped it about the bow. Hanging near the base of the pole was a quiver containing five extremely slender golden arrows.

'Your task, if you wish to obtain the right to be considered by the princess, is to strike the golden fish with all five of these golden arrows, through the hole in the wheel.

'You may step forward to the challenge in any order. But from the moment you touch the bow, this weight will be hoisted up and released.' He pointed to a heavy weight held on a chain, dangling by the side of the pole. The chain drove a gear which turned the wheel.

'As the weight descends it will drive the wheel, faster and faster. You have to strike the fish with all five arrows before the weight falls back below this mark.' He indicated the mark on the pole.

The warriors shifted uneasily in their seats.

'Who will go first, Krishna?' whispered Vrisha.

'I don't know. It's a difficult problem. If you wait, someone else may win the princess before your turn. Yet if you go too soon, you will not be able to learn from the mistakes of those who go before you. I think that most of the warriors here will take too long to string the bow — if they can string it at all. So by the time they are ready to shoot, the weight will have fallen below the mark.'

'Even if it hasn't, surely, the wheel will be turning so quickly it will be almost impossible to aim through the hole!'

'Yes... Vrisha, I think you're absolutely right. Yes, it's going to be quite a problem — Ah! Here she is...'

All eyes turned now to Princess Draupadi. The fire seemed to spit and crackle with greater energy against the sudden hush. The princess was led in by her veiled sister, Shikhandi, to her place beside King Drupada.

In Draupadi's hand was a garland of white flowers. When she was seated, she let this garland rest upon her lap.

◊

Krishna was quite right. Very few warriors were able to string the bow. Some, like Uttara, Shruta and Jaya-tsena, were actually thrown to the ground by the tension in the weapon as they tried unsuccessfully to string it.

Shakuni bravely attempted to improve on the effort of his son, Uluka, who had gone just before him; but like his son, he failed to string the bow.

Krita did manage to string the bow. But he retired without shooting an arrow.

'What happened to him?' Vrisha asked Krishna.

'He must have pulled a muscle, trying to be too quick, perhaps... I believe he's carrying a shoulder injury at the moment, so he did very well to string it at all.'

Bhaga was another of those who managed to string the bow, and with little apparent difficulty. But as Krishna had predicted, his aim was just not good enough: his first arrow failed to pass through the hole in the revolving wheel. Dur and Duh, the only Kuru brothers to string the bow, fared no better with their aim.

Jara not only strung the bow, he also shot his first arrow through the moving hole. Unfortunately the arrow made contact with the sides of the hole as it sped through: it missed the fish, to the relief of the waiting warriors.

Shalya did even better: he hit the fish with his first two arrows. But by then the wheel was spinning too fast for him. He seemed to time his third shot well, but as in Jara's case the arrow was swept off target as it passed through the hole.

Both Soma and his son Bhuri had everyone holding their breath. Soma went before his son, explaining to him that youth had more time to obtain a wife elsewhere. They both hit the fish three times. Afterwards Bhuri joked to the spectators that he had not wanted to shame his father in public by outdoing him.

At last there were only two warriors left to go, Karna and Satyaki.

Karna, in deference to his rival's seniority, offered him the choice of going first.

'Shiva!' chuckled Satyaki, evidently well aware of Karna's reputation. 'If I don't go before you I won't get to go at all!'

Satyaki struggled for several seconds before he succeeded in stringing the bow. By then few would have thought he stood a chance, as the wheel was already spinning so fast. But he grasped all five arrows in his right hand, two between his second and third fingers, the other three between his remaining digits. All five arrows went through the hole. One was deflected away from the fish. Everyone applauded his attempt.

Karna examined the wheel above him very carefully. As the sun was now making a slight angle with the vertical, he had to decide on the best spot from which to avoid the glare through the hole.

He advanced slowly towards the bow, and took a deep breath. He picked up the bowstring and strung the bow almost before Drishta had time to hoist the weight off its mark. Like Satyaki, he grasped all five arrows in his hand, and took aim, drawing the bowstring so far back that the bow formed a semicircle. The arrows would have to travel very fast indeed if they were to stay undeflected as they flew through the hole. At that moment there was hardly a warrior watching whose heart did not sink in resignation.

But before Karna had found the precise moment to release the arrows, a voice was heard by everyone above the hiss of the fire.

'I will not accept the son of a suta for my husband...'

Karna's lungs, held full, collapsed in a chortle. But the bow was still straining in his arms.

'You heard what she said!' cried King Shalya from his seat. 'Put down the bow, you son of a suta!'

Karna lowered the huge weapon, with the arrows still drawn back on the string. He released the tension gradually until the bowstring was straight, then dropped the arrows into their quiver; he unclasped the bowstring.

Drishta came forward, unable to look Karna in the eye as he received the bow. Karna turned to look at Draupadi. She, too, averted her eyes.

There was a rising murmur from the contestants and spectators as Karna returned to his seat. But before they could fully digest what had happened, their attention was suddenly overtaken.

'Krishna! What's that brahmana doing?'

'I wonder... He's carrying a quiver and bow... Though how he can shoot at all with such a stoop... I do believe he's going to try...'

The brahmana in question was dressed in deerskins and bark. What little there was showing of his face, between the straggling hair and matted beard, was ingrained with grime. The white headcloth which flapped across his hair and his brahmana's sash were the only clean articles he was wearing.

His broad back straightened slightly as he addressed the princess in a hoarse and breathless voice.

'Princess Draupadi... I am not a suta, but a brahmana... Even so, I fear I am not worthy of your attention... Forgive me for my impudence if I ask you to give me leave to attempt the task which has defeated all... the kshatriyas assembled here. Princess Draupadi, may I take up that unwilling bow?'

The crowd strained to catch Draupadi's reply.

'If you can string that bow,' she said, 'you may also shoot the arrows.'

The hunched figure put down his own bow and limped slowly round the pole, pressing the spare folds of his headcloth against his face, apparently deep in thought.

As he examined the wheel, the emotions of the watching brahmanas snapped and crackled with the flames.

'If he fails, he'll make us look ridiculous!'

'We should stop him, before he makes a fool of us!'

'Let him make a fool of himself!'

'But look how broad his back is —'

'And how crooked!'

'How will he be able to aim into the sky, bent like that?'

'Perhaps he's a friend of Karna's. Maybe he's trying to ridicule the princess for refusing a suta?'

'She refused a fine-looking man. Why should she allow this dirty beggar to compete?'

'She's getting her own back for his impudence — can't you see — she obviously doesn't think he has a chance of even stringing the bow. His insult will rebound on him!'

'It's *we* who insult *him*! Don't judge him too hastily. Why shouldn't a brahmana take part? We brahmanas have our own powers.'

'Oh yes! Can you shoot five arrows through that hole?'

'Don't be ridiculous! You should never disregard a brahmana. You should never suppose a brahmana is not capable of achieving anything a kshatriya can do.'

'That's right — what about Parashu-rama? What kshatriya has ever defeated him? Not even the Grandsire! Isn't the great Drona-charya a brahmana? And what about Kripa? Who knows? This person before us may be just such a one—'

'That's it! It could be Drona, in disguise! He does resemble Drona! He's come to insult the princess and her father!'

The subject of their attention had now picked up the bowstring. He looked once more at the wheel. He nodded to Drishta, indicating that he was about to grasp the bow. Drishta hoisted the weight. The man strung the bow, grasped all five arrows in his hand, placed them on the string, straightened his back, drew the bow into a half-circle, and shot all five arrows through the spinning hole.

Most of the brahmanas shouted and cheered, stamping their feet and hugging each other. One or two of them were embarrassed.

'Look — you see, now he has made a fool of *us*!'

'But will she accept him?'

'All five arrows hit the fish — she has to, surely?'

This thought quickly silenced everyone watching, as the significance of the brahmana's feat took over from its brilliance.

'Princess Draupadi...' The brahmana had not bothered to revert into his twisted stoop as he addressed the princess. 'Will you accept me for a husband?'

'If my father permits me, I will be your wife.'

All faces turned to King Drupada.

'My permission is granted!'

Draupadi placed the garland of white flowers around her husband's neck.

Now it was the turn of the kshatriyas to protest.

'How can he give his daughter to a brahmana?'

'The swayamwara is for kshatriyas!'

'It's an insult to us! What is he doing, giving his daughter away to a filthy beggar?'

A number of kshatriyas were now literally up in arms: they were advancing menacingly towards King Drupada.

The king quickly gathered his guard and moved rapidly to take cover in a clump of trees and saplings at the edge of the amphitheatre. In the panic which broke out, the princess, with her sister and her servants, took refuge behind her father and the guards.

A dishevelled brahmana of enormous size joined Draupadi's new husband as they turned, with Drishta and Drupada, to face the taunts of the approaching warriors.

When Karna saw Dur jump down and join the other warriors he put his head in his hands. Near him Krishna and Bala were deep in conversation.

The huge brahmana who had just joined Drupada suddenly grabbed a sapling, uprooted it, and hurled it at the angry kshatriyas. Like a sudden cloudburst, a shower of arrows fell on both sides. Drishta and Draupadi's husband drove back the kshatriyas with a volley of arrows. Dur, who was struck in the leg, shouted to Karna for help. Karna looked up to observe the proceedings. Dur shouted again.

As Karna wearily strapped on his quivers he advised his brothers to take cover. And when he picked up a bow, it was Krishna's turn to put his head in his hands. Krishna's brother managed to remain unaffected by the events, though he did raise an eyebrow when the huge brahmana picked up King Shalya, as though he were another sapling, and threw him into the air. Bala then stretched his legs to leave, expecting Krishna to follow him.

When Karna joined in the affray to protect Dur against Drupada's force, the other kshatriyas took advantage of the respite to withdraw.

'Look at that, Bala!' cried Krishna. 'Look at that! They didn't lift a finger when Draupadi refused him...'

'And now they leave the suta to finish the dirty work they started... Which they started when she accepted a brahmana! Come on, Krishna, these people are all entirely mad, we are of no use here.'

As Dur limped to the side of the amphitheatre it became clear that there were now only two people discharging arrows: Karna, and Draupadi's husband. Karna's smile flickered as their arrows met.

When Karna ran out of arrows, the brahmana graciously paused to allow new quivers to be brought on. As he strapped these on, Karna addressed his opponent.

'You show great skill and courage, brahmana... Are you perhaps the great Drona-charya in disguise?... Perhaps you are Parashu-rama himself?'

'I am none of these... I am a simple man, who by the grace of his teacher has acquired knowledge of the power of Brahma.'

'In that case, great brahmana, if you permit me, I will retire from the fight. For, being only a suta, I have not been privileged to learn the use of the brahmastras... I cannot vanquish you. Even the great Prince Arjuna would have found it hard to conquer you. Acknowledging your superior power, I beg your leave to withdraw.'

'A warrior following dharma should never attack one who is defenceless, nor one who has lost his weapons or the ability to fight; nor should he attack one who flees showing no aggression, nor one who retires from the fight...'

Karna bowed at his opponent's words; and as he walked back to join Dur, Krishna came forward and in a gentle voice addressed the disarray of warriors.

'Rathas! Hear me, please! This princess, Draupadi, has chosen her husband. Her husband, moreover, succeeded fairly where all of you failed. You must respect Princess Draupadi's swayamwara. And you must respect this valiant and all-conquering warrior, her new husband. If you do not, you will bring eternal discredit on your names.'

As the kshatriyas dispersed, Draupadi and her husband disappeared.

◊

'Karna, what came over you? Why did you let that brahmana go?'

'Dur, I got you and your brothers out of that mess, now don't complain!'

'I don't understand you! If you had defeated him, you could have made off with Draupadi! It was a swayamwara, not a party! It's quite normal for the greatest warrior to carry off the bride by his superior show of arms. How do you think Bhishma won those three girls on behalf of Shantanu's sons?'

'Three? I thought it was just two? Ambika and Ambalika.'

'And Amba.'

'Three... I didn't know that, Dur. Three? Not bad for a man who's been heard to confess that he has never looked upon a naked woman!'

'There you are! And *you* haven't made an oath of celibacy! Why didn't you go after her? I don't understand you! Or Draupadi, for that matter! What possessed her to choose that brahmana? Do you think he exercised some special brahmastra over her?'

'Dur, don't be absurd, please — that was Arjuna! And don't tell me you didn't even recognise Bhima?'

◊

While the Kurus, along with the other kshatriyas, were packing their things ready to leave Panchala, Krishna rode out alone into the forest outside Kampilya.

Soon after nightfall he caught up with his quarry: Arjuna, Bhima and Draupadi. They had made camp for the night. Draupadi had gone to sleep, but the two Pandavas were still up. Arjuna recognised Krishna immediately by the light of their fire.

'Krishna! Krishna, how did you know? How did you find us?'

'Arjuna, you really shouldn't expect fire to be able to disguise itself in smoke!'

'Did anyone else realise?'

'Really, cousin, what a silly question — I agree that the ceremonial fire must have been burning the essence of stupidity, but... Bhima, are you feeling all right?'

'Yes, Krishna... I'm... tired.'

'Tired? You look ill to me...'

'He's very hungry, poor Bhima,' explained Arjuna.

'Yes,' agreed Bhima. 'I'm very hungry, that must be it.'

'Ah!' exclaimed Krishna. 'What a good brahmana he's become! Lowly fed and highly taught! So, Bhima, it's hunger that gnaws your five souls, is it?'

'Yes,' sighed Bhima. 'Perhaps if I try to sleep, now... If you'll excuse me, Krishna, I'll speak with you tomorrow... It's been a very eventful day... Arjuna, I'll sleep over on that side of Draupadi, shall I? In case hyenas come prowling...'

'Wouldn't you like us to find something for you to eat?' suggested Krishna. But Bhima shook his head and settled himself down to sleep beside Draupadi.

'He'll make himself ill if he doesn't eat,' whispered Arjuna.

'You think so? I rather think that mind shall pine, though the body banquet...'

After Bhima had fallen asleep, Arjuna and Krishna talked late into the night.

21 The kingdom divides

'What will they all think of us, Krishna!'

'You're well, cousin, that's the main thing. You know what they say, 'tis better to be well than well esteemed...'

'You know, Krishna, I feel a bit sorry for Karna.'

'Do I notice that the flames have burned away some of your hatred?'

'I didn't hate him... I don't know... But I think Yudhi's right, Dur would never have gone through with that plot if Karna had been in Hastinapura at the time.'

'So what happened? Whose were the bodies they found?'

'Ah! Well... Vidura had warned us of the plot, and that Purochanna was working for Dur. Almost the minute we arrived we started digging a tunnel, right under the moat. Vidura secretly sent us some men to help us. They lived with us all the time, but Purochanna never knew!

'We also received word from Vidura that if Dur heard of our escape he might try again... So we decided we should make it look as though we'd all perished, and live for a while disguised as brahmanas.

'The twins had the idea of getting some dead bodies, five young men and an older woman, and putting our jewels and rings on them to be discovered in the ashes. The bodies would get so badly burnt it would be almost impossible to identify us any other way. Yudhi was very unhappy about using other people's bodies in this way. So then the twins suggested just getting someone — Vidura could have easily organised it — getting someone to *say* they'd identified our bodies. Because once that was accepted, it would become a fact. But Yudhi liked that idea even less. He finds it very difficult to enter into any deception at all. He preferred the bodies, because then at least if people came to the wrong conclusions, it was their fault! But he didn't let us put any of our jewels or clothes on them! You know, he found it hard even to disguise himself as a brahmana! Until we told him he was just wearing deerskins — we let him off wearing the sash. Then, if people came to the wrong conclusion, it was their fault. That's one reason he didn't come with me and Bhima to the swayamwara. He would have felt uncomfortable trying to deceive you all. Not that he'd have succeeded, by the look of things... Anyway, he and the twins stayed behind with Pritha... The twins, as you'll probably see, don't make very convincing brahmanas. Or rather, they're just too recognisable, even though they're not exactly alike. It's their eyes, I think. They've had to almost cover their faces with their headcloths!'

'And I suppose you didn't want Draupadi to see them before she decided to accept you!'

'Of course!'

'So... you collected six bodies? I won't ask how, but I presume Yudhi didn't strangle them in their sleep?'

Arjuna's jaw dropped. 'Don't joke about that to Yudhi. I can't tell you how hard it was getting hold of them — and storing them. It was horrible! Nakula did his best to preserve them until we needed them — you don't think all six died conveniently the night before our escape!'

'And then you escaped through the tunnel... So, was it you that started the fire?'

'Yes. It caught Purochanna by surprise. Do you know, Yudhi even wanted us to warn him!'

'And then you set off disguised as brahmanas?'

'Yes. Vidura's men destroyed the entrance to the tunnel in the house itself, before they came through, so no one realised we'd gone. Do you know, it was my twentieth birthday two days after the fire! My worst birthday, I can tell you.

'For a while we didn't have any weapons. We were supposed to be brahmanas... I've never been so hungry in all my life... We had to beg for food. We even began to quarrel over food. So Pritha made us promise to share everything we found, or that we could get by begging. The tiniest portion of rice, we had to bring back before we could eat it... The dirtiest rag of clothing, we had to bring back for Pritha to decide whose it should be. Poor Bhima, he was desperate! You know what an appetite he has. In the end Pritha decided to split our food in half: one half for Bhima, and one half for the rest of us!

'Eventually we settled with the family of a very kind brahmana in Ekachakra. Do you know that town? It's lucky that we've all had to learn some of the sacred texts off by heart. Also, Nakula knows quite a bit about healing, so he was able to tend the sick in exchange for charity.

'Well, one day we received word from Vidura about Draupadi's swayamwara, suggesting that I go and compete... Yudhi said that I and Bhima should go to it. We didn't tell Pritha — she thinks we've been away collecting alms... The rest you know!'

'And what are your plans now?'

'We'll pick up the others in Ekachakra, and return to Kampilya. We can come out into the open now: with Drupada and the Panchalas as our allies, we'll be safe from the power the Kurus wield in Hastinapura.'

'Why didn't you leave Draupadi in Kampilya, then?'

'To be honest, with all those kshatriyas around — you know what swayamwaras are supposed to be like, Krishna! And with *you* around! I would have been mad!'

'Well, cousin, I see that being a brahmana has made you into a rather wiser kshatriya...'

At the crack of dawn they all set off to bring the good news to Ekachakra.

•

'Palmira, before we forget, what's an ati-ratha?'

'Really, Henry, couldn't you guess? You interrupt me just for that? Rathas, as you probably gather, are warriors who have distinguished themselves in battle. Then there are maha-rathas, who are even more distinguished than rathas. Then there are ati-rathas, who are even more distinguished than maha-rathas. May I continue now?'

'Not really, Palmira...'

'You didn't think we'd interrupt for anything as obvious as that, did you?'

'What we really want to know is, did King Drupada, and the princess, did they know all along about Arjuna and the Pandavas not really being killed in the fire?'

'Was the princess expecting Arjuna to turn up, Palmira?'

'Well... I'm not sure I can answer that.'

'What d'you mean? *Either* she knew that Arjuna was alive after the fire, *or* she didn't...'

'It's got to be one or the other, Palmira!'

'Mmm...' Palmira narrowed her eyes slightly as she looked at the two boys. 'Well... That does rather remind me of the time the Hodja overheard a couple of neighbours talking. Sssh! You asked for it, boys...

'"If God wills it," said one of his neighbours, "it will not rain tomorrow, so I can plough my field."

'"If God wills it," said the other, "it will rain tomorrow, and I will take the opportunity to finish my weaving."

'That evening the Hodja's wife asked him what he would be doing on the following day. The Hodja replied:

'"If it doesn't rain tomorrow, I will plough my field. If it does rain tomorrow, I will take the opportunity to work at my loom indoors."

'"Hodja! You should say *if God wills it*, like a good Muslim!"

'"Why? *Either* it will rain tomorrow, *or* it won't rain tomorrow. What could be more certain? It's got to be one or the other. I can't say, *if God wills it, it will either rain or not rain tomorrow*, can I? It would be an insult to God's intelligence! In either case I have decided what I'm going to do!"

'Well, next morning the sun was shining very brightly, so the Hodja set off to plough his field.

'On the way he came across some soldiers who were trying to get to such-and-such a village. When they asked the Hodja the way, he impatiently told them he didn't know — he was in a hurry to get to work. The soldiers then threatened to beat him up if he didn't take them to this village. So off he went with them.

'But the village was a very long way off. On the way it started to rain; and by the time they arrived the Hodja was absolutely covered in mud and drenched to the skin — he wasn't very suitably dressed, you see.

'It was after midnight before he finally got home. He knocked loudly on the door for his wife to let him in.

'"Who is it? Who is it?" called his wife. By then she was very worried.

'"It's me! It's me!... *If God wills it!*"'

'But Palmira, it was only the Hodja's plans that didn't work out. It still either rained or didn't rain, didn't it?'

'Yes, Palmira, don't change the subject! Either Draupadi knew that Arjuna was alive, or she didn't know! Which was it?'

'But Henry, perhaps she didn't know one way or the other.'

'Palmira!'

'Now, boys, remember that my story didn't really happen. So in fact it's true *neither* that Draupadi knew, *nor* that she didn't know. So clearly she did not know one way or the other!'

'Palmira!'

'Look, you know what we mean! Was she expecting him to turn up or not?'

'Well...' Palmira picked up a bowl of discarded olive stones from the table, and held it in her lap. 'Perhaps I just don't know the answer —'

'You've got to know! You're making up the story. You've *got* to know.'

'Really? Are you telling me that I've also *got* to know how many hairs she has on her head? Or what is the total surface area of her skin?'

'But...'

'No, but you could make up a number, couldn't you, just for us?'

'Yes, what difference would it make, Palmira? No one could check!'

'By the same token, Henry, how could anyone possibly check whether Draupadi *did* know all along that Arjuna would turn up? They'd only have my word for it. Haven't I always told you never to trust the word of someone who can't be proven wrong?'

'Don't worry, Palmira, we won't trust you! So you can tell us. Did she or didn't she?'

Palmira chuckled to herself. Then she got up, and went inside with the bowl of olive stones.

The two boys, who had been leaning on the marble table top, took their weight off their elbows. They peered through the balusters to see what Palmira was going to bring out; and pursed their lips in disappointment when they saw her carrying only the same bowl. She had refilled it with olives.

When she had settled herself against her cushion, she picked up two of the olives.

'Henry, suppose you ask me for some olives...'

'All right,' agreed the first Henry. 'Can I have some olives?'

'You want these olives? Good. I then give you these olives. Yes?' She gave them both to the first Henry.

'Then you say — please Palmira, will you take the stones out for me? So I obligingly take back the olives... and... take the stones out for you... thus... Yes? Then I give you back the two olives. But you just stare at them. Please, Palmira, you say now, will you chew them for me? So I take them back. I put the first olive in my mouth, thus, and... chew it... for you. Now, the question is...'

She spat out onto the ground what had become of the first olive, and held out the second olive in her hand.

'...Do you want to eat this olive or don't you?'

•

When they arrived at Ekachakra the two Pandavas took Krishna and Draupadi to the small house where they were staying. Inside, Pritha was already very anxious as a result of the long absence of Arjuna and Bhima.

Yudhi and the twins were trying to reassure her as they shared out the charity they had collected that day.

'You stay here,' Arjuna said to Krishna and Draupadi. 'I'll go in with Bhima and surprise her — she's got absolutely no idea we've been to your swayamwara, Draupadi!'

The two princes went inside.

'Mother!' called Arjuna.

'Arjuna... Bhima... Where have you been? Bhima! You look upset, are you all right? Arjuna, look at your brother, what is the matter with him? Arjuna, have you two had a quarrel?'

'No, mother! I've won a wonderful prize! Would you like to step outside to inspect it?'

The twins rushed out of the door, followed by Yudhi. But Pritha stayed inside with the other two.

'Arjuna!' cried Pritha. 'You know you must share your prize with your brothers —'

'But mother!...'

'No buts, Arjuna. So that's why your brother is so upset! Look at him, poor Bhima! You see, the sparkle is already returning to his eye... Arjuna, you wanted to keep the prize all to yourself. I can see it in your brother's eyes. Arjuna, you promised me that you would share everything equally with your brothers — except if it is food, when you must give half to Bhima. He can't help being so large, he needs to eat more than you do. Arjuna! Don't look at me like that!'

'It's not food, mother,' said Bhima, now looking rather more animated.

'Well, Arjuna, if it's not food,' — she moved towards the door — 'you must still divide it equally amongst all five of you. You promised me! There's an end to it...'

She stepped out into the light.

'Krishna! Krishna! What are you doing here?'

Pritha embraced her nephew warmly. A few paces away Draupadi was talking to the twins. A little nearer stood Yudhi, looking uncomfortable.

'Krishna, tell me, where is this prize which Arjuna... Who is that young woman? Arjuna!' Pritha turned back to her son, who had sheepishly followed her through the doorway.

'Mother... that is Princess Draupadi...'

Draupadi turned away from the twins to face Arjuna and Pritha.

'She is King Drupada's daughter,' continued Arjuna. 'I won her at her swayamwara.'

Pritha stared at Draupadi for a few seconds. Then Pritha approached her and, without saying a word, embraced her.

Pritha turned back towards Krishna, who, unusually for him, averted his eyes. She looked at Arjuna, who seemed about to say something; then at the twins, who did not notice her glance; and finally at Yudhi, who was still staring at Draupadi. Bhima had followed Arjuna out, but he now appeared to be engrossed by the stonework of the house.

'Arjuna, Krishna, come with me! Bhima, boys, you wait out here with... Draupadi. Excuse me a moment, my dear,' she said to her daughter-in-law.

Pritha led her son and nephew inside again.

'Arjuna... Who was at this swayamwara?'

'Oh, everybody, mother, everybody — I beat them all!'

'Even... Even Karna? Was he there?'

'Yes, mother, but he didn't really take much part, not exactly... Really, mother, why are you so afraid of Karna? You're as bad as Yudhi! Aren't you pleased with my prize? You sound as though I did *wrong* to win her?'

'Arjuna, you did not *win* Draupadi as a prize at her swayamwara. And she is not your *prize*. *She* chose *you*. At least, I presume she did — you did not carry her off by force, did you?'

'No, mother.'

'However, since you insist that she is your prize... and since you share everything with your brothers... then you had better share her with your brothers.'

Arjuna stared at Krishna in amazement. Pritha now turned to her nephew.

'What do you think?'

Krishna looked round, as if to gaze at the Pandavas outside. Then, with a grave expression, he spoke to Arjuna.

'Cousin... You know... it may be for the best... if Princess Draupadi were to make an alliance, shall we say, with all five of you... If she is willing. It may be for the best. Do you not think so, Aunt Pritha? Arjuna... if you wish to remain with your brothers... Yes? If you do not wish to arouse... jealousy among them... If that were the case, it may well be for the best... But Aunt Pritha, naturally, you must ask Draupadi... Cousin, think a little... why don't you fetch Draupadi in?'

Arjuna, in a daze, went out and came back in again with Draupadi.

'Arjuna,' said Pritha gently to her son, 'wait outside with your brothers.'

After Pritha had spoken for a while with Draupadi, explaining her anxieties to the princess, Krishna suggested that perhaps the most sensible arrangement, if of course she were willing, would be for her to spend an equal amount of time, perhaps a month or so — they could decide later — with each of the Pandava princes in turn; and that during this period her privacy with her partner should be respected absolutely by the others. Naturally, she might prefer to start with Arjuna.

Draupadi was quite understanding; and accepted the proposal agreeably. Four of the princes, who had been waiting outside in some confusion all this time, were equally agreeable to the proposal. And even Arjuna's spirits began to revive when Draupadi chose to spend her first two months with him.

King Drupada was a little surprised that his daughter had obtained more husbands than she had bargained for. But observing that she was happy with the arrangement, and after a long talk also with Pritha and Krishna, King Drupada graciously welcomed all five princes as his sons-in-law.

It was not long before everyone in the land got to hear of the sumptuous wedding feast held to celebrate the alliance between the Pandava princes and the Panchala kingdom.

◊

Back in Hastinapura, Dur was very worried about this powerful union.

'Karna, they're sure to wage war on us now! They're bound to see us as a threat. They'll surely want to reclaim Hastinapura. After all, they still see themselves as the rightful heirs to the Bharata kingdom. And now, with the help of the Panchalas, they might think they're strong enough to attack us. Karna! What's the matter with you these days?'

Karna ignored Dur's last question.

'Dur... You're a fool. While you were trying to eliminate their threat with a cheap trick — which anyone could see through — Vidura and the Grandsire have cleverly seized the opportunity to strengthen the position of their favourites. You have been outmanoeuvred. Before, the Pandavas weren't a military threat to you; they were rivals to your inheritance, I agree; but you should have been able to sort that out with your father. Now they're also a military threat.'

'Rubbish! We could easily defeat the Panchalas, even with Arjuna leading them!'

Karna laughed. 'Then what are you so anxious about, Dur? Perhaps you're frightened that if the Panchalas fight, then the Shinis will fight with them? I expect you'd like to face Satyaki on the battlefield, as well as Arjuna? And, of course, it's not just Satyaki. What about Krishna? He may be an old friend of the Bharatas, but he's also the Pandavas' cousin. Who knows what force he can muster? Dur, if you hadn't stupidly tried to take their lives you wouldn't now fear their revenge.'

'We must kill them, Karna. That's the only answer. Somehow, we must poison them, or... or make them jealous of each other — that's it! Sow dissension among them!'

'Don't be ridiculous! There's more dissension in your one body than there is in the five Pandavas! Even though the twins are Madri's sons, Pritha is obviously very shrewd — talking of which... you mustn't forget Madri's brother, Shalya... Yes, who have we got so far lined up against you? The Pandava princes; Drupada, Drishta and the Panchalas; Satyaki and the Shinis; Krishna and the Yadavas; Shalya and the Madrakas. Wonderful.'

'That's why subterfuge is the only way, Karna!'

'Listen, Dur... and please listen carefully, because though you ask a lot of me, you seldom actually listen to what I say. If you want to eliminate the threat of the Pandavas taking over your kingdom — that's your father's kingdom, may I remind you — there's only one way in which you'll stand a chance: in a straight fight on the battlefield. *If* that's what you want — to remove their threat — then there's no other way. Do you think you can sow dissension among five brothers who took the same bride to *avoid* dissension? Do you think you can poison them, or corrupt them? Not only have they friends like Vidura, Bhishma, Kripa, Krishna — but, don't forget, Dur, they themselves are *very* far from stupid! Even Bhima is quite clever in his own way. Frankly, Dur, they would never have embarked on a plot as stupid as yours, even if Yudhi had let them stoop so low. Which he would not. I'm sorry, Dur, I don't want to make you out to be a complete idiot... But as Charvaka would say, there's more to being stupid than being stupid. The plain fact is that no one is going to outwit the Pandavas, certainly not you. So *if* you were to want to conquer them, I'm afraid it would have to be by force of arms.'

'But would we defeat them? Who could we count on?'

'Well, the Grandsire — even Drona — would have to fight for you. It's their code of honour to support King Dhrita and the Bharata kingdom. Whoever King Dhrita decided to wage war on, or whoever you persuaded Dhrita to fight — or whoever waged war on him — Bhishma, Kripa and the others would have to fight them alongside you in defence of Dhrita's crown. While your father's alive, of course.

'Then... again, provided your father's still on the throne... you'll also be able to count on Shakuni and the Gandharas; you'll have Soma, Bhuri and the Balhikas. Jaya-dratha will fight with the Bharatas, won't he? And probably Bhaga and Shruta as well. That's the Sindhus, the Vangas and the Kalingas.'

'You really think we could defeat them on the battlefield?'

'If you were to fight soon, there's a chance perhaps that Krishna would not fight with them against King Dhrita's forces. I don't think you would have so much trouble, then. With Krishna against you as well, it would be much harder. Still — you should be able to kill the Pandavas in open battle. *If* that's what you want.'

'Why do you keep saying *if?*'

'Dur, please! Why d'you think!'

The gloom began to settle over Dur's countenance.

'Dur, listen... Whatever you feel or think about it, you really should speak to your father.'

◊

Dur found Vidura talking to King Dhrita and Sanjaya.

'Hello, Dur,' said Vidura, 'I was just telling your father what a good thing it is that the Pandavas have made this match, especially after the hard times they have endured recently. I hope they will now want to return to Hastinapura. Yes, this alliance is a great advantage for us all — for there are six kinds of advancement: there is one's own advancement, of course; but then there is also the advancement of one's friends; of one's friends' friends; the weakening of one's enemies; the weakening of—'

'Yes, Vidura, yes,' agreed Dhrita hastily. 'I am so pleased for them, after thinking for so long they were dead... Dur, you wish to speak to me?'

'Yes, father.'

Vidura left them. Sanjaya as always stayed by the side of the blind king.

'How *can* you be pleased, father?'

'I know what you are thinking, Dur. I, too, am worried. But what can we do? And I can't let Vidura know my disquiet at their union with Panchala — though I was relieved when I learnt they were alive and well.'

'Father, we will be destroyed by the Pandavas if they are allowed to become strong.'

'But Dur, why have you always quarrelled with them?'

'Why did you make them your heirs, father? I, and my brothers — *we* are your heirs.'

'Dur, Dur, I don't want to discuss that again. In any case, I am still alive. Yudhi is not king. But in the mean time they have every right to enjoy the hospitality of Hastinapura.'

'Who was it persuaded you to make Yudhi heir? Vidura? Bhishma? You didn't think to ask me, did you?'

'You were too young, Dur...'

'Well, I'm not too young now.'

Dur paced up and down in front of his father. Sanjaya discreetly avoided the prince's glare. The king did not reply until his son was still again.

'Listen, Dur, I will call together a council with Bhishma, Vidura and Drona... Kripa is away visiting the Pandavas at the moment — you can talk then if you want.'

◊

'Karna, I need you at this council meeting.'

'I doubt it, Dur. You know that Bhishma always seems uncomfortable in my presence now — to say nothing of Drona's attitude. I think you'd do better without me there.'

'No, I need an ally. My father just agrees with them, when they're around. And then he agrees with me when I contradict them afterwards!'

'Why not take your uncle Shakuni along?'

'Come on, Karna, you know what Shakuni's like. He'll start arguing in ten directions at once, and tie everything into knots. Or he might even end up agreeing with them!'

So Karna was persuaded to go along with Dur to the meeting.

Dur expressed to the elders his concern at the growing strength of the Pandava princes.

'I understand your position, Dur,' said Bhishma. 'But you should not antagonise them. At the moment they are being wrongly denied an equal share in the Bharata kingdom.'

'How is that?' asked Dur. 'Is my father not alive here before you? And as for the Pandavas being heirs — or Yudhi, which is the same thing — why should Yudhi be heir to *my* father's throne, when I am his eldest son?'

'It is natural,' answered Bhishma. 'Pandu, after all, held the crown of the Bharatas.'

'Yes, it is natural justice,' agreed Drona. 'In theory you would have been expected to inherit the whole kingdom, being King Dhrita's eldest son. But it is natural justice that Yudhi should be heir, since Yudhi is Pandu's eldest son.'

'But,' argued Dur, 'Pandu abdicated the throne to my father!'

'Yes,' said Drona, 'that is true. But only because Yudhi was then too young to take over from Pandu. Pandu always intended that the throne be passed eventually to the Pandava princes — as it would have done in due course had he not abdicated. So you see,' concluded Drona, 'it is not only the dictate of the law, as determined by your father, but also the inclination of natural justice, that Yudhi and the Pandavas receive the Bharata throne. We should welcome them back to Hastinapura with all due honour —'

'If I may say so,' interrupted Karna, who had been sitting quietly with Sanjaya next to King Dhrita, 'since your argument from natural justice rests on the succession from father to son... how can you deny the satisfaction of natural justice in the succession from Vyasa to his eldest son, Dhrita-rashtra, and to Dhrita's sons after him? Grandsire, is it not true that the good King Pandu passed the throne to his older brother in recognition of the natural *injustice* which had deprived Dhrita in the first place?... Or are you suggesting that the blind king before you now is as unfit to reign as he was unjustly thought to be then? Is it not true, Grandsire, that it was this injustice which the good king sought to rectify when he abdicated to Dhrita? That Pandu's purpose was not merely to give Dhrita temporary regency?...'

Bhishma did not have an immediate reply, so Karna continued.

'Moreover, the legality of the situation is that King Dhrita is king, not Yudhi; and that, while Dhrita lives, the Pandavas have none of the rights to which they may aspire on his death. Therefore, should they try to establish themselves in Hastinapura by force, by force they should be opposed. Neither King Dhrita nor his son Dur is obliged to extend any hospitality to them.'

Drona and Bhishma glowered at Karna.

Vidura took Bhishma to one side to try to diffuse the tension.

'I believe,' said Bhishma, walking away from Vidura towards the king, 'I believe there is a solution, King Dhrita. You should give the Pandavas half the kingdom; and then Yudhi can be king in his own right, and you can then make Dur the heir to your half of the kingdom.'

'Why should the Pandavas be given half of anything?' asked Karna. 'If they are rightful heirs, they will get everything in due course. If they are not, why should they get anything?'

'How can you say such a thing?' cried Drona. 'After they were all but burned to death by Dur's henchman Purochanna!'

Karna peered into Drona's face, seeking the brahmana's eyes.

'I'm afraid I don't know anything about that, Drona... I was in Anga at the time... As a matter of fact, I was recovering from wounds which I received in the city of Kampilya...'

'Talking of which,' said Dur, 'I couldn't help noticing that Prince Drishta—judging by the little speech he gave at his sister's swayamwara—seems to have forgotten that his father's kingdom is now merely *South* Panchala. I expect you'll be wanting to organise another expedition to remind him, Drona?'

Seeing Drona's discomfort, Vidura quickly changed the subject:

'King Dhrita, I think Bhishma's idea is very promising. It will be well worth the sacrifice to you. Remember, with man, as with the animals, there is in every conflict first the wagging of tails; then the bark; then the bark in reply; then the circumambulation; then the baring of teeth; then the roar; finally, the battle. You must not allow the situation to progress along this path. You keep Hastinapura for yourself and for your sons. Choose an area of land roughly equal to half your kingdom — which is of ample size, in any case — and give it to the Pandavas. This far-sighted means will surely end the antagonism that exists between these princes and your sons. For neither party will any longer feel deprived of a share in the Bharata kingdom. Dur will still be able to have Hastinapura, the ancestral seat of the Bharatas — and have it safe from the claims, peaceful or otherwise, of the Pandavas.'

After a little deliberation, King Dhrita decided that this was probably the best course to take. He assigned to the Pandavas a tract of land around the ancient ruined city of Khandavaprastha.

The city itself was now virtually uninhabited; for although the Yamuna river passed near to the city, poor irrigation had made the surrounding land barren.

When Vidura told the Pandavas of King Dhrita's offer, Arjuna and Bhima laughed at the idea.

'He's offering us a desert, and calling it half his kingdom!' cried Bhima.

But Yudhi and the twins thought more carefully about the proposal.

'It is true...' said Yudhi, after some consideration, 'it is infertile at the moment, but — with help — we can create irrigation channels from the Yamuna. I will ask Krishna's advice, but I think we should be able to irrigate quite a large area.

And we can rebuild the city.'

'Why go to all that trouble to accept a worthless *half* of what is entirely ours by right?' asked Arjuna.

'Why? Because what we would really be receiving — and what is worth much more than the land — is peace. If we accept this as our kingdom, the Kuru princes will be happy at Hastinapura, and will not bother us with their stupid conspiracies. We must accept the offer. Arjuna, don't you think Krishna will be able to provide help to rebuild the city?'

'Yes... I suppose so. Yes... And I suppose we could ask the Panchalas to help.'

'I've been once to Khandava,' said Nakula, 'soon after Drona's raid. It's not such a bad place. The river runs very close to the old city walls. We could certainly make something of it — we could divert a stream in and out of the city, and transport materials down the river itself.'

And so it was all arranged. The Pandava princes returned briefly to Hastinapura, with Draupadi and Pritha. They travelled with a growing retinue who, though originally Panchalas, were now calling themselves Pandavas, and were loyal to the princes and Draupadi.

From Hastinapura, after a ceremony to celebrate the creation of their kingdom, they travelled to Khandavaprastha.

As Yudhi had hoped, Krishna was more than willing to provide a workforce of Yadavas to help in the rebuilding of the city. Many of these were to stay on, swelling the ranks of the Pandava people.

But the new city needed a new name. Yudhi suggested that Arjuna should choose it, in recognition of the prowess with which he had secured his fortunate alliance, and the generosity with which he had shared it with his brothers. Arjuna named it after the god Indra. Thus Indraprastha became the new capital of the Pandava kingdom.

•

'It's getting dark, boys... I'm sorry, it was a bit long today... No questions, I see?'

'Well, obviously not, Palmira. Not if you're going to start spitting olives at us.'

'Excellent. I'm glad that worked. So, boys, see you tomorrow...'

•

Day Four: *The Two Cities*

22 Indraprastha

The conflagration in the house of lac was not the only skirmish with fire experienced by Arjuna during this period. For after leaving the house of lac, while Arjuna had been living as a brahmana, he had saved the life of Maya, a king from the mountains in the north.

King Maya, who was on a pilgrimage, had become trapped in a forest fire. He had fallen and injured himself while running from the advancing flames. Arjuna, who was gathering fruit nearby, heard his cries and reached him just in time. He carried Maya to the hermitage where the king was staying.

In gratitude Maya had offered Arjuna some sacred manuscripts which he carried with him on his pilgrimage. Arjuna then confessed that he was not really a brahmana, but one of the sons of King Pandu, and that it was not proper for him to accept these precious books. Maya agreed, declaring that his books were neither right nor fitting as a reward for such a noble kshatriya. Instead he promised Arjuna that should he ever visit his kingdom, he would present him with the great bow Gandiva, made of metal, indestructible, and with an enormous range.

This incident had almost slipped from Arjuna's mind by the time it was decided to rebuild Indraprastha. Then Krishna mentioned King Maya as a possible source of stone and marble for the new Pandava palace. Arjuna therefore decided to take up King Maya's offer, hoping to persuade the king to part with more than the great bow he had promised. Arjuna's hopes were richly rewarded. In a ceremony of great solemnity he received the bow, and also a beautiful conch with a mouthpiece of gold. During the ceremony Arjuna was obliged to vow that he would never let any other ratha use either the great bow or the conch; and that he would punish with death not only the theft of either of these treasures, but even the impugnment of his sole right to use them. Then, at the conclusion of the ritual, Maya offered him as much material as Indraprastha would require; not just for the palace, but for rebuilding the city itself.

By the time Arjuna had returned to Indraprastha, proudly carrying his new bow and conch, the first boatloads of stone had already arrived along the river. Not only had Maya sent his finest marble, he had also added jewels and precious metals with which to decorate the palace.

Krishna had advised the Pandavas to ask Charvaka to supervise the preparation of building materials; and particularly, to help with the large amounts of glass which the plans they had drawn up were going to require. The princes had hesitated. But Yudhi was curious to meet the rishi, in spite of his egregious reputation, and asked Krishna to invite him to Indraprastha.

Charvaka was delighted to help, and, with Vrisha to assist him, set up shop in Indraprastha. The rishi not only advised on the materials, but also tackled some of the engineering problems presented by the Pandavas' ambitious plans.

The quadrangles and cloisters of the palace contained pools fed by streams which flowed right into the building. Many rooms thus had channels of the clearest water running through them. One of the details which Charvaka encouraged the Pandavas to develop was the use of glass of crystal clarity in the construction of the borders of these pools. As a result it was in places almost impossible to tell where the crystal edges stopped and the water began.

Generally Charvaka got on well with Yudhi; and Arjuna and Nakula were also at ease with him and interested in his work. But Saha and Bhima were suspicious. Nevertheless even Bhima, who was involved closely with most of the construction, developed a working relationship with the rishi.

As for Krishna, he was quite familiar with the rishi: he had met him briefly as a child, but had got to know him when Charvaka spent some time in Dwaraka teaching Krishna's brother. Now that circumstances again threw them together, he and Charvaka resumed the debates which they used to have in Dwaraka. Usually after sunset, or sometimes in the late afternoon of a day of rest, but almost always against the sounds of the princes playing dice, they would discourse for hours. It was generally Saha and Nakula who occupied the dice table; and to Saha's annoyance, Nakula would often hold up the game to raise an objection against Krishna or Charvaka. Yudhi, though in his element neither with the dice nor in debate, was enchanted by these discussions; for both the ideas and the style of the two men tended to be sharply opposed, and the resulting arguments most animated. Arjuna too would sometimes stay to listen and ask questions, especially when the subject involved destiny or freedom; on these occasions the prince would come away feeling more exhausted than if he had been sparring physically; and later in the night the ideas would trespass upon his dreams.

◊

One afternoon Arjuna went to see Charvaka to try to clear up a question which had been troubling him. He found the rishi polishing a slab of marble which was lying flat on his bench. He was rather surprised to see Yudhi also in the workshop; and even more surprised to see that his brother appeared to be actually playing dice with Vrisha.

'You know what the twins are like,' explained Yudhi, slightly embarrassed. 'They are too impatient with me ever to explain anything. Vrisha is very kindly going through one or two things...'

'It's not that the twins are impatient,' suggested Arjuna to Charvaka. 'They find Yudhi's attitude exasperating!'

'I take it', said Charvaka, 'you haven't also come here to play dice?'

'No, sire... I have a problem...' Arjuna glanced at the other two.

'Would you like me to send them away? Well, if they become a nuisance, I will. Now, my boy, what's your problem?'

'It's... It's an argument that Nakula gave... It was a couple of days ago, sire, I don't know if you'll remember... Krishna answered the point... At least, he seemed to. But I can't remember what Krishna actually said. I usually agree with Krishna, sire — I like what he says — but I don't always understand it!'

'So you've come to *me* for enlightenment?'

'Yes, sire. I know I don't usually agree with what *you* say. But at least I can understand you!'

'I see. Go on...'

'Well, Nakula's argument I think went like this... Suppose that at some time in the future I end up killing Karna — I'm sorry about the example, it was Nakula who used it...'

'Yes, I think I remember. Go on...'

'So, suppose that in twenty years' time I kill Karna. If this really is what happens, then it must be true *now* that I kill Karna in twenty years' time. But if it's *already* true that I kill Karna, there's nothing that any of us can do to stop it! It's destined to happen...'

'Go on, my boy...'

'Well, don't you see? That was just an example. You could say the same of anything that turns out to happen. It's... all destined to happen, and there's nothing that can change it! So that means that nothing that I do can be done of my own free will, since it all *has* to happen!'

Charvaka raised an eyebrow. 'Yes,' he said, 'a dreadful argument! I agree that truth does indeed appear not to be confined by limits of time. Thus it seems quite sensible to say, since the time is now and the fact well attested, that it's true *now* that Parashu fought Bhishma twenty-five years ago. Moreover, it's just as true now as it was last week, and as it was then, so, why not also as it was even before then? In other words, if it's true for all time *after* the event, why not also *before* the event? Surely, the argument goes, it's just as true *now* that you do whatever you do in twenty years' time as it will be *then*, and as it will be in thirty years' time, or at *any* time... Therefore, nothing that will ever happen can happen otherwise. For that would make it false now, and at every time; and in fact it's true now, and at every time — if it's ever true. So even though we don't know whether it's true or false, whichever it is, it *has* to be... How I detest such games of language, my boy! Though, to be fair to Nakula, I think he was being more provocative than serious.'

'But what's wrong with it, sire?'

'That's what's been troubling you, eh? Well, my boy, you never get more out of a pot than you put into it. If, as a matter of fact, you do kill Karna in twenty years' time, don't expect to get any more from this fact than that, as a matter of fact, you kill Karna in twenty years' time. So there must be something wrong with the argument.'

'Yes, but what?'

'Who knows? Does it matter exactly what?'

'In any case, Arjuna,' interrupted Vrisha, 'it could be a lot worse. At least you have the consolation that it's you killing Karna rather than the other way round!'

'Vrisha, please!' protested Charvaka. The rishi looked at Arjuna and scratched his beard. 'Yes, my boy, I can see that it matters to you... Very well... Let's say that it's true that you kill Karna in twenty years' time, eh? Very unlikely,' added the rishi with a chuckle, 'but suppose it's true. Suppose then that I elaborate: it's *now* true that you kill Karna in twenty years' time. What is this *now* doing? Either it adds nothing at all to what is true, in which case you can ignore the addition completely; or it adds a little bit of nonsense; in which case you must also ignore it. You cannot make an argument grow from a piece of nonsense. Where is the active ingredient of the argument? There is none. Nothing more has been added to the pot —'

'But why does it add nonsense?'

'Because, my boy, if you were to test the truth of the elaboration — test, in other words, that it's *now* true that you kill Karna in twenty years' time, as opposed to *simply* true that you do so, the test would impose no requirements over and above those necessary to verify the simple unadorned claim. So the elaboration does not add anything sensible to the simple statement. After all, could I not also assert, with just as little additional sense, that it's delicately, smoothly, or thoughtfully true that you kill Karna in twenty years' time? Or, an even better example, that it's true in Hastinapura that you kill Karna in twenty years' time. If you add nonsense to sense, you may get less, but you certainly can't get more than sense.'

'Did you know,' interrupted Vrisha from the dice table, 'that elephants do a lot of crop raiding in Anga? Oh yes, they do...'

Arjuna's mouth fell open. Vrisha continued, undaunted.

'You might as well argue that it's true *in Indraprastha* that elephants do a lot crop raiding, on the grounds that it's true in Indraprastha that elephants do a lot of crop raiding in Anga.'

Arjuna winced with confusion.

'Vrisha!' scolded Charvaka, shaking his head in disapproval. 'Crossing through the mud of language will never give you a short path to understanding. And you risk getting stuck in it.'

'That's just how I feel, sire,' said Arjuna, grateful for the rishi's sympathy, ' — stuck in it.'

'Come over here, my boy...' Charvaka beckoned to Arjuna. 'Look at this...' He pointed to the marble block. 'Suppose you were a god, able to look at the world from outside of our time and place. Your god would have to be in his own time, I suppose. At any rate, you must imagine that he could see our world laid out like the surface of this marble. Suppose we are here in our time and place...' Charvaka put his finger on the marble. 'And that to the left of this event is our past, and to the right of this event lies our future. Eh? Now, this god is able to see all of this, and examine it in detail. And in much more revealing detail than we can. He could say — look, there's a little chain of circumstances where the later events all inevitably follow from the earlier... Here, on the other hand, is a different sort of event. Here shown in the marble is something that the great prince Arjuna chose, freely chose, to do... See, he could have done otherwise... We must suppose the god can tell such things just by examining the graining of the marble. Yes, the god declares, Arjuna did this freely, for it is clear in the marble that what happened before his choice did not determine it.

'Similarly,' continued Charvaka, 'the god would be able to point here and there around the marble, to all those things that were not part of an inevitable chain of causes — events which could well have been otherwise. Some for the better, some for the worse. If things had happened differently, a different pattern of the marbling would have resulted. The god might say... What a pity that Arjuna chose this... What a pity that Arjuna chose to fight Karna at this time and place... If he had chosen differently — which he could have — the marble would have turned out so much nicer. Well, there's your freedom, Arjuna — if you want it — even though it is set in marble for all time. For the god sees your life from beginning to end, from outside time, from neither before nor after. And still that doesn't make your actions any less free. For if they were to be determined, this would not be the case just because they follow the past — that they do is undeniable — but because of *how* they follow it.'

'Oh...' Arjuna smiled. 'Thank you, sire, thank you! I think I understand that!'

'Good. Because we mustn't have you throwing away your cherished gift of free will through a mere trick of language, eh? There are much better reasons for shedding your precious illusion!'

◊

When most of the heavy construction of the palace was complete, flowers and trees were planted in the quadrangles to bloom with a delicious fragrance. Among them roamed peacocks, carefully avoiding the panthers which dozed lazily at the end of golden chains. Sometimes even an elephant would sway gracefully through these bowers, rumbling softly beneath the tinkling of its bells, guiltily feeling the branches with its trunk, even succumbing on occasion to taste the forbidden leaves. Around and in the pools there were colourful waterfowl, swans, ducks and cranes; and in the limpid water brightly coloured fish and terrapin mingled with the lotuses.

The Pandava people who had built all this were encouraged by Yudhi to pause from their toil and browse with pride through their own handiwork. At night many of them stayed to sleep in the palace, and in many cases continued this habit even after their own homes were ready. They would waken to the comforting sound of breakfast being made in the kitchens. At this time of day Yudhi was always to be found here, assisting with the cooking, or washing the dishes which had been left to soak during the night; and when the food was brought into the hall, Yudhi would help to serve it out. Yudhi had never in his life been happier.

◊

The new city of Indraprastha was becoming rather famous, and many of the visitors it was now attracting chose to stay on and live there. As a result the number of brahmanas soon increased, a fact which Charvaka was quick to notice.

Charvaka's skill was no longer indispensable; and the rishi saved Yudhi the embarrassment of a confrontation with the brahmanas by announcing his departure.

'Are you going straight back to Varanasi?' asked Krishna.

'I am. If you're ever in the region, you or Bala, do come and see me.'

'Charvaka, have you thought of visiting Hastinapura?'

'You know I'm banished from there...'

'It may be different now. From what I hear Prince Dur-yodhana is now rather influential. With Dur and the Grandsire on your side, the brahmanas there may be moved to tolerate you... Kripa would protest, perhaps not as loudly as Vidura and Drona, but he could probably be induced to accept you there. Why don't you go there incognito, and ask Karna to sound things out with Dur. Is Karna there at the moment?'

'Yes, I think so.' The rishi stroked his beard. 'As a matter of fact, I haven't seen the boy for a while... Yes, I might well take your advice, Krishna.'

◊

'Charvaka!'

'Sssh! Someone might hear!'

'Oh yes, I forgot, the river is so full of ears at this time of year. I presume you have some request, since you're sitting on my stone. Would you like me to cut off some of my hair to protect your chin? Is that an attempt at disguise? I don't think I've ever seen you in a white cloak before. Almost as hooded as Lord Indra. In fact for a moment... Don't tell me that you dressed like this in Indraprastha? Have you brought Vrisha with you?'

'Yes, or rather, the other way round. Vrisha brought me to your stone. He's gone back to try to arrange somewhere for me to stay... It may not be prudent for me to stay at the palace...'

'So, what are you doing in Hastinapura?'

'I've come to visit you, my boy.'

'You mean, to scold me and remind me of my obligations!'

'It's certainly time you went to see Parashu.'

'And perhaps, sire, it's time you went to see King Dhrita.'

23 Charvaka moves

'I agree, it can only be a calculated insult on Dur's part. For we brahmanas would have to endure the contempt the rishi shows for the religion that first nurtured his ill-used powers. Charvaka's return to Hastinapura, if it were permitted, would surely mark the descent of the Bharata people into the age of Kali.' Kripa ran both hands slowly through his hair. 'I am therefore inclined to agree with you, Drona, that we must not allow it. Dur and his brothers have already sufficient disrespect for the dictates of religion as to place our authority as brahmanas, with the added voice of Charvaka, in considerable doubt.'

'And is he not also a sorcerer? How can they think of allowing a worshipper of Kali to practise freely in Hastinapura?'

But Kripa continued, hardly aware of Drona's question.

'We must consider also that in league with his pupil Karna he will be able to control Dur like a puppet. And if the son, then also the father; and if the father, then the whole Bharata kingdom will come under his influence.'

'But surely King Dhrita would not allow the rishi to remain against our advice?'

'That's the trouble, Drona. We can only *advise* the king. Vidura will certainly support us. But we cannot rely on Bhishma in this regard. Remember that Bhishma was against his banishment in the first place, despite the rishi's complete indifference to every article of religion, to every law of morality. I fear that with Bhishma and Dur at his ear, Dhrita will be deaf to our guidance.'

'I have never understood why the Grandsire did not sanction his execution as an apostate.'

•

'Palmira, what's an apostate?'

'An apostate is someone who abandons their religious beliefs. It comes from the Sanskrit *apa*, meaning *off* or *away*, and *stha*, meaning *stand*. But really, boys, please try not to interrupt when these people are speaking!'

•

'Indeed,' replied Kripa, 'it is surely a measure of the man's evil and corrupting influence that someone as correct and incorruptible as Bhishma should be so disposed towards him.'

◊

'They think I'm a devil because I don't believe in a god.' Charvaka constantly fidgeted with his stubble as he spoke. 'But then neither do I believe in devils!'

'You see, Shakuni,' said Bhishma, putting his arm round Charvaka, 'this mouse has even less faith than beard!'

Dur, Karna and Vrisha were also with them, on a balcony at the royal palace; the tension between Bhishma and Karna was noticeably eased by the presence of Charvaka.

'That's not entirely true,' said the rishi. 'I agree, I have little beard at present. But I do think therefore that in comparison I have rather more faith. After all, I believe with the utmost conviction that all such faith is illusory. Isn't it strange that men are even prepared to die for this illusion?'

'Not as strange as the readiness you have shown', replied Bhishma, 'to die for your own conviction!'

'I wonder...' ventured Shakuni, turning to Dur and Vrisha as though appealing to them. In fact, Shakuni's short-sightedness often led him to check his bearings as though he were actually addressing the people and objects around him. 'If Charvaka believes in nothing, he can hardly be said to die for it...'

'That reminds me,' said the rishi, 'do you know, I am no longer even sure of nothing! I used to think that I ought to feel absolutely certain of just one thing: that there wasn't nothing. I used to be sure that there was *something* in existence, as opposed to nothing. But recently I have become increasingly disturbed by the thought that, although I seem to know what *something* is like, I really have no idea at all what *nothing* is like. And that therefore I had no right to consider all this' — his arms waved in an attempt to embrace everything before him — 'as something rather than nothing, to conclude that it is like the one and not the other! You see, how can I be sure that all this' — again he waved his arms — 'isn't really just part of nothing! No... I fear that until men really come to understand *nothing*, they will indeed understand nothing.'

'But surely men will never understand nothing!' exclaimed Bhishma. 'For how can nothing be known? It's so empty that it cannot contain time and place, nor even a knower. Therefore it cannot be named, since there is nothing there even to be named!'

'Take care, you old boar,' warned Charvaka, 'take care lest we become obliged to banish you. For are we not told in the sacred texts that there is nothing which Brahma is not? That there is nothing which Brahma understands not? And yet you have just suggested that even Brahma cannot understand nothing: since by your argument even the supreme being could neither imagine nor name a condition in which he himself did not exist!'

'Another thing, Bhishma...' said Shakuni, looking round at each face as though checking that no one had recently appeared or disappeared. 'A point I am not in perfect agreement with... You say that nothing cannot be named, since it cannot be known... and so forth... Suppose you are right, and nothing does indeed elude ineffably all our attempts to name it; then I'm afraid, my dear, you cannot have succeeded in concluding that *nothing* cannot be named, since, by your own conclusion, you have failed successfully to speak about it. Thus if you are right, then consequently you are wrong. I am therefore more comfortable with the latter possibility, that you are wrong, and that nothing can indeed be named, and that therefore your claim is nothing but a defamatory falsehood in regard to its good name. More generally, my dear, I incline therefore to the view that there is nothing at all about which we are demonstrably unable to speak: since such a demonstration would demonstrably fail...'

Bhishma smiled, and appealed to Charvaka for support. But the rishi sided with Shakuni.

'Don't you know,' said Charvaka to Bhishma, 'Shakuni is even considering the use of a cipher to represent the *quantity* there is in nothing.'

'The number of nothing?' cried Bhishma.

'May I remind you, my dear,' said Shakuni, 'that what cannot be known directly may nevertheless be referred to obliquely. There are many numbers which cannot be known directly, since they cannot be represented by any combination of numerals, nor even by means of the four simple operations of arithmetic. Yet they can be referred to by less direct methods quite successfully. Compared to these, the cipher is a trifle! And I believe it would be most convenient to endow the cipher with all the rights and rules enjoyed by the other numbers that we count with —'

'Oh, I see!' exclaimed Vrisha. 'So this cipher is the number you'd get when any other number is combined with its opposite —'

'Opposite?' repeated Shakuni. 'What a delightful idea... A mirror made of nothing...'

'But that only makes me more certain that I cannot speak with certainty about nothing,' observed the rishi. 'For two opposites, each of which is something, would combine to form nothing. Why, then we could be part of nothing' — Charvaka's arms beat the air — 'even though we are something. Yes, I believe I am quite right to doubt that there is something rather than nothing.'

'How strange,' muttered Shakuni, almost to himself. Then he turned to Vrisha. 'Do you know, it rather reminds me of that one wish of yours, do you remember my dear, when I first met you? Yes... I'm not sure that we can allow nothing to exist, on its own... A mirror with nothing to reflect? For wouldn't a reflection of nothing be something? And therefore a reflection of that something would... From nothing would follow everything...'

'You see!' interposed Charvaka, looking around at the others as though Shakuni was his own performing animal, doing tricks for their amusement. 'Evidently there is a lot more to nothing than mere nothing — or perhaps in this case it would be better to say a lot *less* —'

'Best of all,' interrupted Karna impatiently, 'perhaps you should say nothing at all... Please, sire, can we not talk of something rather than nothing? What are you going to do? The brahmanas are accusing you of saying that worship is wrong, goodness is bad, that the gods don't exist, that they shouldn't pray —'

'I don't say that worship is wrong. Only that *I* would not worship any god who wants or requires worship. *Men* wish to be worshipped by other men, to assure their own importance. But no god worthy of *my* worship would have such an infantile desire. However, if the brahmanas wish to worship, I have no objection. I don't say that goodness is bad! True, I believe that *my* goodness and badness, such as they can be, must be judged according to my relationship with the world I see and touch, people, animals, plants, things; not by my relationship with gods, whom I know nothing of. The brahmanas, instead, prefer the latter method. If that is their preference, I have no objection.

'Nor do I say their gods don't exist,' continued the rishi. 'I say only that any god whom I could respect would also respect my disbelief in him. A god who held my faithlessness against me, who treated with contempt my sincere error, such a god would lie beneath my own contempt; and could only be conceived in the image of the weakest of men: men who need constantly to bathe in the unquestioning regard of their fellows. But if the brahmanas wish to believe that their gods despise me for my faithlessness, or will punish me, by all means let them believe so.'

'But sire,' said Vrisha, 'the brahmanas want to punish you themselves, on behalf of their gods.'

'My boy, I have no power over their beliefs, nor their desires, nor their actions. Nor do I wish to have such powers. I only have power, of a pitiful sort, over my own voice. Which I do not raise against them in anger, nor in exhortation, nor in entreaty. No one obliges them to hear my voice. If they wish to approach and listen, I let them. I do not shout in public where they cannot escape my words. Nor do I hide my thoughts from them if they come to listen. Yet they wish to punish me because they come to listen, and are disturbed by what they hear! If they do not wish to be disturbed, let them not come.'

'But sire,' persisted Vrisha, 'haven't you put your views in writing?'

'Yes. But I do not press the leaves into their hands. And if they do not wish to be disturbed by what they read, let them not read. I do not force them to.'

'But sire,' said Dur, 'don't you mock their prayers, their rituals —'

'That is not true. I do not mock anything about them. I merely assert my difference. It is they who find my difference insulting. Dur, I have never even claimed that they should not pray. I only say that *I* do not pray, and I say why I don't: I would not pray to any god who would unjustly prefer me above my fellows by answering *my* prayers. Why? Because I think that the granting of one prayer is most probably the denial of another's. When I am in deep forest, why should I pray for protection from the tiger? Why should any god prefer *me*, who also consumes and destroys material that lives, to the tiger? And deny the tiger's interests by protecting mine. Moreover, if a god should exist, he would know my prayers even before I did: before I even formed the thought, let alone clothed the thought in words. What possible reason, then, could I have to pray to a god who already knows my prayer, for whom my prayer could only serve to confirm my humility? Which he would have the measure of in any case, without my outward show. My prayer could only serve as a gift of veneration, which no god should need or want.'

'But Charvaka,' said Dur, 'aren't you being arrogant in refusing to humble yourself?'

'My boy, don't confuse a confidence which one has laboured to inflate, with a conviction one has been unable to deflate. It is true, I do not *feel* doubt. But I force myself to *think* it: for I know I may be wrong, and they may be right. Even if I was sure they were wrong, I would not seek to change them. There lies my humility, such as it is. If it were arrogant to disrespect a god who valued merely my servility, who cherished a devotion acquired without thought, without struggle, without choice, as an infant suckles milk... then it would be arrogant to use the very gift of reason such a god is credited with giving me. And remember, Dur, these very men who celebrate their servility before god, they seek at the same time to rule the spirits of their fellow men. There lies *their* arrogance. These men who would place themselves high above their fellows, make themselves low, in prayer, before their god. I would rather it was the other way round; but if they believe it's fine, let them be. I just explain my beliefs. I do not ask anything of the brahmanas. They ask of me, and mistake my replies for insults, my attempt to make clear for intent to corrupt.'

◊

'What particularly alarms me, Kripa... is the possibility that Dur may exploit Charvaka's powers for his own advantage against the Pandavas.'

'What precisely do you mean?'

'Is it not well-known that Charvaka can construct weapons with unnatural properties: bows which are indestructible, helmets which cannot be pierced except by arrows of his own invention, fire powders —'

'Yes, Drona, I understand. Fortified by Charvaka's military artifice, Dur would surely be tempted to consider an attack on Indraprastha.'

'I have an idea, Kripa... While he has been in Varanasi, Charvaka has not had access to the materials he needs to make these weapons. But just consider what may happen now. Dur, with his increasing means and influence, will surely find a way to supply him with materials in Varanasi — even build a new workshop for him there. Look what he contrived with the Pandavas' house of lac!'

'Yes, you may be right. Are you suggesting that...'

'It would be better to have Charvaka here in Hastinapura, where we can keep an eye on him. We must first of all protest vigorously to King Dhrita, on behalf of all the brahmanas...'

'Yes, I think I understand: we must insist that he remain banished... unless he were to recant his blasphemies in public. Preferring rather to die than to profess to what he does not believe, he would of course refuse even to contemplate such a retraction. However, he may yield to the extent of merely undertaking never again to undermine those eternal values, for the benefit of all those choosing to be guided by which, the brahmana caste strives constantly to observe and preserve.'

Drona nodded and cleared his throat before developing his proposal.

'Then, Kripa, when the Grandsire and Dur again urge Dhrita to allow him residence, we will insist that we are prepared to accept his presence here in Hastinapura on one further condition: his undertaking not to practise sorcery of any kind, not to conduct any of his unnatural experiments, not to manufacture any weapons or military materials...'

'Excellent. I suspect the rishi may be willing now to endure such restrictions. And I myself would be prepared, if that were the case, to trust his word. But in any case, as you suggest, Drona, we should be able here to keep an eye on him.'

◊

When Charvaka was summoned by King Dhrita to face an assembly of brahmanas, he was not willing to 'undertake never again to undermine' their religion and values.

'I cannot undertake to refrain from something which I may not even realise I am doing; or which others may not realise is being done to them. All I am prepared to promise is that I will not speak in public with the conscious intent of undermining your religion. Nor, if you wish, shall I speak at any Bharata assembly, on any subject at all, unless requested to do so.'

The brahmanas were not at all happy with this. But Kripa and Drona quickly moved on to the other conditions they were proposing.

'I have never practised sorcery of any kind,' replied Charvaka when they had finished. 'So I cannot sensibly undertake to stop it. While I am within the city boundaries, however, I am prepared to abandon those experiments, which you describe as unnatural, by which in fact I have striven to understand what is natural: to understand the natural laws which inanimate materials appear to obey; laws which may also, as I profoundly suspect to be the case, govern the most unnatural of men. I am in addition, while I am within the city boundaries, prepared to abstain from the manufacture of weapons and materials which may be used for military advantage.'

Again the brahmanas were unhappy with this response. But Kripa's authority won the day. And so Charvaka was officially allowed back to Hastinapura.

He returned briefly to Varanasi to close up his workshop. Then he took up his new residence.

Dur now had two wives, and he had recently completed a new palace, not only to establish his physical independence from the old court, but also to house his growing family and guests. Karna had preferred to stay on at the royal palace, despite pressure on King Dhrita to force Karna to follow his patron. Shakuni, on the other hand, had gone with Dur. Now Charvaka joined them in the new palace.

Bhishma would regularly visit Shakuni and Charvaka. But on the whole the Bharata elders stayed well clear of the rishi. And even when Charvaka wandered the streets of the city, the brahmanas took pains not to be seen near him.

Soon after Charvaka had settled in he went to see Karna to speak to him again about Parashu-rama.

'You may learn something from him, my boy. Don't you want to master the weapons you keep in your red sack?'

'You mean my pillow? By the way, you promised me some powder for the javelin... Anyway, Charvaka, I thought you said he only teaches brahmanas. You perhaps remember that I am a suta?'

'Ah! Of course, I forgot — it must be your great erudition, your daily devotions, your delicacy of sentiment, your refinements of expression. Evidently I have come to think of you as a brahmana... Idiot! As a matter of fact, it will do you good to pass as a brahmana. The pretence might rub some worthy qualities into you — it certainly seemed to improve the Pandavas, from what I saw.'

'In that case, sire —'

Karna was interrupted by a messenger.

'Please... make yourself comfortable...' Karna offered his visitor some food and drink, but these were politely declined.

'Lord Karna...' The messenger hesitated under Karna's impassive stare.

'Please, continue,' said Karna. 'What is it you wish to tell me?'

'Lord Karna, King of Anga... My master, King Jara-sandha of Magadha, wishes to render you a challenge of single combat, using the sword, or the mace, or, if you prefer, no weapon at all. Should you defeat him, you may take the town of Malini and with it the whole region of Champa, of which it is the capital. Should you lose, you will surrender to him the entire region of Anga.'

Karna smiled kindly.

'Tell King Jara-sandha that if I were to defeat him, I would not accept any gift of land, livestock or people. I have no desire for any of these. Therefore, there is no reason for me to fight him. If he can find a gift which I should desire, then let him issue his challenge again. Tell him also,' added Karna, 'tell him that Anga is no longer in my power to give.'

Karna motioned to the messenger to make himself comfortable, but he left immediately, without a word.

'Karna... be careful.' There was anxiety in Charvaka's voice. 'I have heard bad reports of Jara-sandha.'

'So have I, sire. He is a dangerous man.'

The conversation did not on that occasion return to the subject of Parashu-rama.

24 News from Anga

Before he returned to Dwaraka, Krishna had reassured Yudhi that Indraprastha would soon be prospering. In fact, the very first harvests around the rebuilt city exceeded Yudhi's hopes. The cattle, too, were thriving. Most of the livestock had been a gift from King Drupada. But to these herds had been added those acquired by Arjuna and Bhima during their period of raiding. Yudhi sent word to the original owners offering to return the animals; but in every case he received the reply that it would be an honour if King Yudhi-sthira of the Pandavas kept the cattle as a contribution to his new kingdom.

It would be difficult to imagine a ruler as well loved by his people as Yudhi. It is true that much of the credit for the success of the administration must go to his brothers: Arjuna was in charge of military matters; Saha had organised with Yudhi a system for drafting and applying the law; Bhima was overseeing the many engineering and building works still in progress; and Nakula had with Charvaka's help arranged medical facilities not just for the people of the city, but also for the livestock in the surrounding region. As a result, the risk to the region from shortages of food and supplies, from fire, from disease, and from flooding, were all greatly reduced.

But in all these projects the touch of Yudhi's wise and gentle hand was felt and recognised by nearly every citizen of Indraprastha; moreover, there was hardly a single person who did not feel that the king was as much in their service as they in his.

Yet, though Yudhi seemed happy, people would sometimes catch him looking longingly towards the forests north of Indraprastha; and they would then be tempted to take him by the arm and turn him back, lest he should leave the city never to be seen again. He was like the centre pole of a large tent, but one which always seemed on the point of collapsing, and which could only be kept upright if neighbours paused from their quarrels to strain together at the ropes.

When setting up the administration, Yudhi had been particularly concerned to control the excesses and corruption which he had seen everywhere among the kshatriyas at the expense of the poorer castes. The strict penalties which the kshatriyas had traditionally imposed for arrears of rent and debt were relaxed by him; and those for extortion were increased.

Similarly, he was well aware of the tendency for power to subvert the law at the expense of the weak. So Yudhi himself insisted on the principle that the greater the position of power, the more public and rigorous the trial of its abuse, and the more severe the penalties incurred.

'Saha, our laws are only going to prevent corruption if we take the bull by both horns: we must, holding one horn, assume that a person is innocent unless it is proven that he or she is guilty. But we must also hold the other horn, and assume that the system of justice is being abused, and that corruption of the law exists, unless it is proven otherwise. Otherwise we will not be able to keep the precious dew of dharma from evaporating.'

'But Yudhi, if you hold both these horns at once, you cannot move the beast. How can you work a system which you are assuming does not work right?'

'You can still use a boat which you suspect of leaking. Suppose that we are examining the case of a man accused of theft. There is some evidence against him, but we cannot prove his guilt. We let him go, innocent and free. If we have made a mistake, we have made a mistake in just this one case —'

'Not if he steals again.'

'Bear with me, Saha. Suppose, on the other hand, we are examining the case of an official who is accused of covering up crimes which he has investigated, or of making false allegations. There is some evidence against him, but we cannot prove his guilt. What if we let *him* also go free? In this case, if we have made a mistake and he is after all guilty, then our error may immediately spread beyond just this case: it may cause the miscarriage of justice in many others, even if our accused official were never to repeat his offence. And if he does offend again... You see the difference?'

Saha nodded uneasily.

'You want to assume that, as an individual, the official is innocent, and thus set him free if the evidence against him is inconclusive. But we must also consider him not as an individual, but as an instrument of justice. And as such he must be assumed to be guilty if there is good evidence against him, even if the evidence is inconclusive.'

'Are you saying that in such a position a man is to be assumed guilty unless he can prove his innocence?'

'In such a case, where there is good evidence against an instrument of justice, but this evidence turns out inconclusive, those indicted should be deprived of office: as instruments of justice they cannot be given the benefit of doubt, but must be assumed guilty. However, as individuals they are still assumed to be innocent, and since the case was not proven incur no further punishment than loss of office. If and only if their guilt is established should they in addition then be punished as individuals for their crime. It may seem unfair on those who are working as part of the machinery of law, Saha, but how else can the law protect itself from becoming the very worst instrument of injustice?'

'If you find a piece of wood which you suspect is weak,' continued Yudhi, 'and it is above the water-line of your boat, you can leave it until it breaks, only then need you replace it. If instead you suspect a piece of wood which lies below the water-line, you must replace it straight away — though it may still be good enough to use elsewhere above the water-line.'

◊

During Krishna's stay in Indraprastha his younger sister, Subhadra, came to visit. Just before Krishna left for Dwaraka, Subhadra married Arjuna.

Draupadi was jealous at first. Although she had grown very fond of all five brothers, it was Arjuna to whom she was most attached. Nevertheless, Subhadra soon became her friend. And Draupadi was with her co-wife when in due course Subhadra gave birth to Arjuna's son.

As often happened when a royal child was born, the parents wanted a rishi to be present at the child's naming ceremony. The boy was to be named Abhimanyu, meaning 'close to passion'. Arjuna naturally wanted Narada to hold the ceremony, since it was this great rishi who had presided over his own naming. So Narada was invited to visit Indraprastha.

After the ceremony the rishi had a few words in private with Subhadra. Arjuna was impatient to find out what Narada had said about little Abhi, but it was a while before Subhadra allowed Arjuna to see her.

'He is going to be a great hero like his father,' she said reluctantly, when pressed by Arjuna.

Narada remained for a while to marvel at the new city. He also had an important suggestion to put before the young king, but one which he knew would require some delicacy if he was to overcome Yudhi's probable resistance.

'Yudhi,' said the rishi, 'your palace is wonderful. The whole city renders me speechless in admiration... I am told that Charvaka and Krishna gave you a lot of help.'

'Yes, sire, we are very grateful to both of them. Charvaka was most amusing. I had not met him before. You know that he is like an uncle to Karna... Have you met Karna, the king of Anga? I think he still actually lives in Hastinapura —'

'Yes, I have met Karna... Yudhi, they all want to come to see your city — Bhishma, Vidura, Kripa, Drona. They send their regards and respects. I visited them in Hastinapura on the way here. Gandhari too, she would like to visit. I have conveyed her love to your mother. Yes, I think they are all secretly envious of Charvaka, for having been able to participate in this... new birth. But it's amazing that they have allowed him back there.'

'Is he in Hastinapura? I thought he had returned to Varanasi.'

'On the way, apparently, he decided to face the big city. Now the mouse is actually living there. He is not exactly welcomed, but his presence is tolerated.

Why he has chosen to return to live in Hastinapura I don't know — he is forbidden from engaging in his usual activities. By all accounts, when he is not discussing mathematics with King Shakuni, he is playing dice with him! So... have you plans to invite them all here?'

'I would like to, of course. But I'm afraid... afraid that it would look as though I'm showing off what we have achieved.'

'Yudhi, they love you, it will give them pleasure to see you prosper; it will fill them with pride —'

'Sire, the Kuru princes do not love me. I do not want to irritate them.'

'And are you going to deprive all the Bharatas of the glow of pride in your achievement, just because of Dur and his brothers? Think of what the Bharatas have done for you. Do they not deserve your hospitality?'

Yudhi was looking worried, and did not reply. Narada continued after a moment.

'I have been thinking... Yudhi, you know that your... your father, King Pandu, held the Rajasuya ceremony... That would be a very appropriate occasion for them to see Indraprastha!'

'No, I am not doing that, sire. *King of Kings*! Every minute of the day I question my right to rule *these* people, here in Indraprastha! I do not even want to be *their* king, let alone the King of Kings. You know, sire, I have been thinking that I should in any case only rule by the consent of the people. If so much as one citizen of Indraprastha were to prefer that I resign my power and retire to the forest, I ought to do so.'

'Yudhi, that is crazed. What if a madman says that you offend him?'

'He may be mad, but if I give him offence his displeasure is none the less for afflicting him without, perhaps, sound reason.'

'But Yudhi, will you not give the rest of your people greater displeasure by resigning for the sake of one dissenting voice?'

'Sire, dharma has no scales by which I may weigh the displeasure of one against the satisfaction of the many.'

'It is true, Yudhi, such things cannot be weighed. But they can be counted —'

'That is not the same, sire. Happiness and sadness need to be weighed, not counted.'

'Counting is better than nothing, Yudhi. Listen, just suppose that all your people, *all* of them, were to want you to hold the Rajasuya. How could you face the displeasure you will give them by refusing? What right have you to give them that displeasure?'

Narada later mentioned the idea to Yudhi's brothers, and they were all very keen on it. Together they persuaded Yudhi to issue a proclamation asking any citizen of Indraprastha who did not want the Rajasuya, to come forward with their objections. But no one came forward.

'You see,' said Narada, 'they all want you to hold the Rajasuya.'

'But it does not affect just them. What about the kings who by attending the ceremony will place themselves beneath me?'

'If they attend, it is because they want to. You will naturally have to issue an invitation to all the kings in the surrounding regions. If they are willing to attend your Rajasuya, then they are willing. What offence will you cause them?'

'And if they are not willing?'

'Well, there may be a minority who are not... at first.'

'Sire, if you permit me, I will ask Krishna. He will very likely know how these kings feel. But I do not want to have to send my people to their deaths just to subjugate kings who are unwilling.'

'I understand, Yudhi... Yes, that is an excellent idea, consult Krishna... He will certainly advise you how best to proceed.'

Narada left Indraprastha soon after messengers were dispatched to seek Krishna's advice. These returned from Dwaraka a week later, not with Krishna's advice, but with Krishna himself.

◊

'Are you sure? I cannot trust the advice of my brothers on this point. They are much too biased. Arjuna and Bhima will go into battle under any pretext.'

Arjuna and Bhima laughed uneasily.

'You are more objective,' continued Yudhi. 'But you do understand, Krishna — I do not want the Rajasuya for my benefit. I will consent to it only if you think more good will come of it than if I refuse.'

'Yudhi, your Rajasuya will benefit all the surrounding kingdoms: it will bring peace and stability to these regions.'

'But will all the kings be willing to accept me?'

'Not all. A minority, the troublemakers, will resist the idea. But your brothers here can take care of these with little if any bloodshed.'

'But why should I impose my will on these unwilling kings, even if there were no cost in blood?'

'Listen, Yudhi, your most serious problem will be King Jara-sandha of Magadha. He will certainly oppose you. His army is extremely strong. Moreover, he has a powerful ally in Shishu-pala.'

'No. I am not going to war simply so that I can become the King of Kings. Let's forget about it, Krishna, please.'

'Listen to me! Wait till I have finished, Yudhi. Let me tell you about Jara.'

Krishna turned away from Yudhi and sat down. He continued:

'Jara is a cruel and oppressive king. He has brought terror to his neighbours. And he is now seeking to expand his dominions. When I travelled through the eastern part of Panchala on my way here, I saw refugees fleeing from his army. Drupada himself is having to protect his eastern borders.

'Jara has already subdued many kings in the east, and he exacts terrible tributes from them. You treat your friends and neighbours as equals, Yudhi. You are widely known as the son of Dharma. Because of that, kings will humble themselves to you. Not because of your superior military might, but because they respect you.'

'Jara will not,' said Yudhi.

'Do you want to know what Jara does with the kings he defeats in battle? He imprisons them, and their generals, in his palace. His dungeons are full of kshatriyas he has captured in this way. He puts in place his own generals to collect the taxes from the peoples he has conquered. Then he sacrifices the captured kings to the god Rudra.'

'Krishna,' interrupted Arjuna, 'I will lead a force against Jara. If we succeed, we will free his prisoners.' Arjuna turned to Yudhi. 'Since we have the ability, brother, it's our duty to do this. If we don't, the world will condemn us for shirking our duty.'

'Wait a moment, Arjuna,' said Krishna, standing up again. 'You may be able to defeat Jara in battle — but you possibly may not. He has a very large and experienced army. Even with the help of Drupada and the Panchalas your army would be no larger than that of Jara and Shishu. More importantly, you would find them reluctant to engage you in open combat. They are masters of ambush.'

'But we can ask the Grandsire to help,' suggested Bhima. 'With Bhishma and the Kuru army it will be easy.'

'It would, Bhima, I agree, it would. And Bhishma himself would be willing. But the Kuru army is only under Bhishma's control if King Dhrita places it at his disposal. Do you think Dur will let Dhrita send his army to help you and Arjuna against Jara?'

'No, of course not, Krishna, let's forget it, please. Please, no more about the Rajasuya.'

'Yudhi, there is another way. Listen. King Jara-sandha is an extremely strong and proud man. The vanity he feels over his physical prowess is his weakness. If he is challenged to single combat — with bare hands, no weapons — he will always accept the challenge, particularly if to refuse would embarrass him in public. He has been challenged in the past on several occasions. Unfortunately, he is so powerful that he crushes everyone. He is unbeaten, a pestilence that hitherto has had no cure —'

'Krishna, please —'

'Cousin, I have not known you to be so impatient!' Krishna grasped Yudhi's arm and turned with a smile to Arjuna and Bhima. 'He *will* be the patient that should be the physician! Cousin,' Krishna continued, releasing Yudhi's arm, 'you perhaps recall that you have some brothers to dispense?'

'Yes... Are you...' Yudhi cast a sidelong glance at Bhima.

'Bhima has an excellent chance against Jara. A better chance than almost anyone I can think of. Bhima is certainly stronger than Jara, especially if the rumour is correct that Jara has a weak back. Not so skilful a wrestler; nor as experienced, but — well, my own brother, Bala, can give him some tips.'

Bhima's face lit up to speak, but he deferred to Yudhi.

'I will think about it, Krishna.'

'Don't think too long, Yudhi. Remember, there are good people languishing in Jara-sandha's jail. Besides, you do not own your brother.' Krishna grinned at Bhima. 'He may decide to come with me to Magadha!'

'Of course I do not own my brother, Krishna! Bhima can do what he wants. But as you know, one doesn't have to own someone for them to take one's wishes into consideration. As to what I wish... I will think about it, Krishna. It's not just Jara — it's the whole Rajasuya that I am uncomfortable about. But I will think about it... Will there be others whom we have to... persuade?'

'Yes, but as I say, that should not be a problem. Only evil kings will oppose you.'

'Will they be evil by definition, Krishna? Just because they oppose me?'

'No,' chuckled Krishna. 'Evil not by definition, but in virtue of opposing virtue. Have I not described Jara? Do you not trust me, Yudhi? Would you perhaps like a second opinion? Charvaka, perhaps?'

◊

At that very moment, in Hastinapura, Charvaka was sitting on the river bank with Karna.

'This is the only place I can ever find you, my boy. I never get to see you, these days. I think I saw more of you when I was living in Varanasi. And I see Vrisha more often than you, even though he is so busy in Anga — doing your work...'

Karna smiled. 'You complain you don't see me. And yet in a moment you'll be telling me to go away... I will go, sire, I will go... But there is trouble in Anga at the moment. I can't leave just yet. As soon as things become more settled, I promise... Charvaka, do you still think I should go as a brahmana? Why exactly does he only teach brahmanas?'

'It's not that so much, as that he won't teach kshatriyas... But I think Parashu is best left to speak for himself on that matter, my boy — indeed, as on most matters pertaining to him... I did used to argue with him about it, though. I think he was wrong, but his arguments are subtle. He's a strange man, the mongoose... Not an easy man to understand, let alone argue with. He has a beautiful speaking voice... Too melodious, in fact, for I can never remember his exact words. Who knows what his attitude is now, for it's such a long time since I last saw him... But yes, I think you should go as a brahmana...

'For one thing, my boy, it will mean it won't start the other brahmanas there talking... If you were to go as a suta, they might find it strange... You don't want to draw too much attention to yourself at first... And it would be more likely that Parashu will know immediately who you are: he may have heard of the suta with the golden mail who became king of Anga at the tournament... If he has already decided to kill that king of Anga, you would have no chance.'

'You think he would be able to kill me?'

'If he is sure immediately, yes. If you have a few days' start, for you to get to know him, that will give you more chance. But only a chance. You will have to be at your most vigilant, Karna. He would not use weapons to which you are accustomed. You would probably not see him strike.'

'Would he use his axe? I suppose if I blindfolded myself I might not see him strike.'

'It is not a joking matter, Karna. So you know about his axe? No, I'm not talking about that type of thing. Remember, a weapon does not need to be a weapon.'

'But is it true that he really fights with an axe?'

'In the old days, when he went into battle, usually against kshatriyas, of course, he often used his axe. He is supremely skilled with the bow, the sword, and the javelin. But he preferred not to use these unless he really had to. Why? You'll have to ask him yourself. But he used to say that it was because the axe served a purpose other than to convey death or injury.'

'Is that why Krishna's brother is supposed to use a plough?'

'I have heard that said of Bala, but I rather doubt it. He never mentioned it when I was in Dwaraka... Parashu, at any rate, in single combat, or when he needed to defend himself, would of course resort to the bow, or he would be long since dead.'

'And how do I... present myself, sire?'

'Ah yes... You must say that I sent you to him —'

'But won't he know then immediately? He must know that the famous suta was a pupil of Charvaka's?'

'Of course. But Charvaka has also taught brahmanas. Not so many, recently, I grant you. Remember this, Karna — he may suspect who you are, but until he knows for certain, he will not try to kill you. He will in any case put you under his scrutiny. You should of course assume some other name, in case he has already heard of you.'

'Should I take some token from you, some message?'

'No, there is no need. Tell him I sent you: that I sent you hoping he would take you on as a pupil. When you feel the time is right, show him the two weapons in the red sack. But don't show him the actual sack — take that with you, but keep it hidden. Well hidden. Now that you no longer have your mail or ear-rings, that red sack is all you have left to mark you as... the son of Surya. Keep it hidden. But when you think it is safe to tell him who you are, then tell him.'

'What if such a moment never arrives? What if I think it's too dangerous?'

'My boy, there is very little point you going to Mahendra unless you discuss with him who you really are. You must take that risk. It is a question of when, not if... I wouldn't be suggesting that you go unless I...'

Charvaka saw that Karna's attention was distracted, and turned to see someone running towards them.

'Vrisha!' Karna got to his feet. 'What are you doing here?'

His brother was out of breath.

'Karna... We are being attacked... Jara-sandha... His warriors have started raiding Anga... The villages in the south-west. He'd heard that Anga was no longer under the protection of Hastinapura. He wanted to take the new king of Anga captive. We told him that we were no longer ruled by a king... That the shudras owned all the land.'

'What did he do?'

'He didn't believe us. Not at first. I don't know. We tried to explain that power had been given to the shudras...'

'And?'

'He replied that power is never conferred on those who rule, that power can only be assumed by those who have the power. I tried to argue with him, but he said if it seems otherwise, it is because you only see what you are shown... that every master hides behind a servant who rules his slaves for him in their own language...'

'So you spoke with him?'

'Yes, and Vai did. But I'm afraid for Vai's safety. The last raid was quite small. I think Jara wanted to see the strength of our defences. I think he'll attack again. But the worst thing is that the kshatriyas are now holding Vai prisoner... to give to Jara if he attacks again —'

'The kshatriyas from Anga? What... they're going to say he is their ruler?'

'Yes. They've taken over now, more or less. They said that if they were going to have to fight Jara, they had to take command of Anga. But I don't think they'll fight him. I think Jara just wants some tribute in grain and cattle. And our ruler.'

'And the shudras let the kshatriyas take over?'

'Yes. A few didn't like it, but most were in favour...'

'Why are you so surprised?' said Charvaka to Karna. 'The hare that stays brown in the snow is caught by the eagle.'

'Sire, I must go. First to Anga... Then I'll pay a visit to King Jara-sandha. But after that, I promise you, I'll set off for Mahendra.'

'Do you intend to accept Jara's challenge to single combat?'

'Of course.'

The rishi gave Karna a worried look.

'I understand, Charvaka. I will try not to kill him.'

'And then you'll go to the mongoose?'

'Yes, sire. Come, Vrisha, we must leave early tomorrow. I need to prepare my things.'

'Karna...' Charvaka put his arm round him as he spoke. 'Please be patient with Parashu. He is a strange man. For someone who professes to think that life is just a game, he shows very little sense of humour. Humour him if he tries your patience, eh? Especially when you first meet him...'

That evening Karna and Vrisha dined with Sanjaya and his family. Next morning, when his chariot was almost ready, Karna fetched his red sack and carefully placed it at the back of his chariot.

◊

Some time after Karna left for Anga, King Dhrita received word from Yudhi asking if the king and his court would be willing in principle to attend Yudhi's Rajasuya.

Dhrita called a council with Dur, Bhishma, Kripa, Drona and Vidura.

'You see, father, he now wants to become King of Kings! He will even expect tribute from us.'

'No, Dur, it is clear from his message that he only expects a nominal contribution,' answered Dhrita, checking the fact with Sanjaya.

'And what does that mean? He does not want our money, just our subservience? We don't need to pay for his privilege, merely to grovel before him!'

'Dur,' explained Drona, 'it is quite normal at the Rajasuya for the attending kings to present a tribute as a token of their regard.'

'What about those who refuse to attend, is he going to conquer them?' asked Dur. 'Is he asking Jara-sandha along? Shishu-pala? Virata?'

'He says he hopes to subdue King Jara-sandha —'

'How?' interrupted Bhishma.

Kripa answered for Drona.

'Should he receive from his more amicable neighbours a response sufficiently favourable to warrant proceeding to the Rajasuya, he plans to send his brother Bhima to challenge Jara-sandha in single combat.'

Bhishma smiled pensively.

'What about the others?' he asked Kripa. 'There are a number of kings in the region who would need some persuasion.'

'Yudhi will send Arjuna and Bhima to visit them... with some assistance from the Panchalas. He does not envisage the need to make any demands on you, Bhishma. Not in that regard, at any rate.'

'Mmm... It's going to take them a few months, then. You're sure he is not asking us for help?'

'No, Bhishma, they intend to do all the necessary fighting themselves.'

'I think', said Bhishma, turning to King Dhrita, 'it would be courteous to offer Arjuna assistance. Even though he will probably refuse any help from us.'

'And are we going to surrender the supremacy of Hastinapura to Indraprastha?' protested Dur. 'Just like that?'

'What supremacy?' Bhishma turned impatiently on the young prince. 'King Dhrita has never held the Rajasuya. You are perhaps too young to remember, but the last Rajasuya was held by King Pandu. There has not been one since. King Dhrita,' he added in a softer voice, with a kindly glance which was lost on the blind king, 'do you intend to hold a Rajasuya, perhaps?'

'No, Bhishma, I certainly neither want nor merit the title.'

'King Dhrita,' repeated Drona, rather cautiously, 'would you have any objections to your nephew's Rajasuya?'

'None, Drona.'

'Father! How can you let your nephew —'

'Dur,' interrupted Bhishma, 'the land needs a Rajasuya. We need to consolidate peace. So do most of our neighbours. Are you suggesting that merely because you feel personally slighted we should deny the region all the benefits of stability?'

Dur held back his anger.

'Prince Dur-yodhana,' said Drona, more confidently now, and with a tone calculated to annoy, 'wait first until you are king before you dream of becoming King of Kings. Then, if you so wish, you can send a message to Yudhi inviting him to *your* Rajasuya. But for the present, as you see, your father is unwilling to assume the honour of that onerous position.' Drona turned to the king. 'King Dhrita, do I take it then that we can reply... thanking the Pandavas for their graciousness in first asking your permission, and... encouraging them to proceed with their plans, with our blessing and assistance, if required?'

The king's blindness saved him from his son's black look.

'Yes, Drona. I will reply to them in that vein.'

◊

The thought of Bhima and the twins gloating over him at Yudhi's Rajasuya plunged Dur into depression. Normally Karna's expression of disgust when he caught his friend in these moods was enough to make Dur put on the pretence of accepting the situation. And after a while the pretence would cease to become an effort. But there was no Karna to drag him out of his dark mood. Charvaka and Shakuni, when he sought them out for comfort, were too busy discussing the laws of Kali. Dur's brothers found it rather easy to enjoy themselves, and would quickly lose patience with their brother.

After a few listless days, Dur decided to try Charvaka and Shakuni again. He was also beginning to worry about Karna, wondering whether he should have gone with him to confront King Jara-sandha.

Dur found Charvaka and Shakuni playing dice.

'Charvaka, do you really think Karna will be all right?'

'Of course, my boy. Don't you worry about him. Why don't you come and join us in a game?'

Dur had never been very interested in this sport. The expression on his face did not indicate much enthusiasm.

'Come, my boy,' encouraged Charvaka, 'we'll teach you Shakuni's method: for more than ten years now your uncle has been using his excellent system of animals, but there are still players who'll have none of it... Many of them still think it's all in the hands of the gods!'

Dur could not hide a hint of curiosity amid the gloom of his countenance.

'What do you mean... animals?'

'Shakuni has developed a system for classifying the numbers, my boy. You know of course that in the royal game we aim to strike the prime numbers. For this purpose the most powerful number to throw from is the tiger; and then comes the lion, the leopard, the cheetah and the cat. For example, 16, 28 and 40 are tigers, are they not, Shakuni?'

'Indeed, my dear. And, of course, before every tiger there is a lion, so 15, 27 and 39 are lions.'

'So the next tiger, after 40, is 52?' suggested Dur.

'Ah! No, you miss the point, my dear boy. The next tiger is 58... By the way, Charvaka, did I mention to you a problem my sister set me? It's most interesting, but I haven't been able to resolve it. She posed to me the question: is there an endless number of tigers? That set me thinking... it is easy for me to prove that there is no end to the number of leopards, of cheetahs, and of cats — domestic cats, you understand... Remind me to show you the proofs. But, do you know, I just cannot begin to resolve the question in the case of the lions and tigers!'

'Shakuni, you will put your nephew off if you go on like this. Come, Dur, you can be my second. It will take your mind off other things. And I will certainly need assistance against your uncle.'

Dur ended up doing nothing but playing dice for the next fortnight.

It was in the middle of one of these games that Vaitanika was shown in to see them.

Dur jumped up with excitement.

'Vaitanika!' he cried. 'What happened?'

'Prince Dur-yodhana, Charvaka, sire...'

'This is King Shakuni,' explained the rishi. 'You may speak in front of him.'

'Karna asked me to tell you what happened —'

'Did he kill Jara?' asked Dur excitedly.

Charvaka gestured to Dur to be quiet.

'Sire, I was handed over as prisoner to King Jara-sandha... by our kshatriyas in Anga. Until recently I was a captive in his dungeon. In fact, I feared very much for my life. Then suddenly... I was set free... Karna didn't say very much about what happened, about the fight, I'm afraid, Dur.' Vaitanika had noticed the disappointment on Dur's face. 'The first I knew of it was when I was released from my chains and brought up into what must have been Jara's banqueting hall. It was full of people: kshatriyas and their wives and children... servants everywhere — but the centre of the floor was clear. They were all silent... they looked shocked. It was obvious that Jara and Karna had been wrestling. Both of them were dripping with sweat. Jara was sitting down on his throne. He looked in pain, he was holding his back... And Karna was standing before him. King Shishu-pala was standing there next to Jara, twitching his head at Karna. Just to look at Shishu-pala again filled me with terror — I had seen him shuffling round the dungeons. Who knows what goes on in that rat's head of his? He looks at you first with one eye, then he cocks his head to see you with the other one... Anyway, Karna took a quick look at me, I think he was just making sure I was in one piece. And then he spoke to Jara...'

'Well? What did Karna have to say, my boy?'

'He said that... He was speaking loudly, so that everyone in the hall could hear... He said:

'"On my way back from Mahendra I will visit you again, King Jara-sandha. If you have not released your prisoners, all of them, or if I hear that you or your kshatriyas have again been attacking your neighbours, I will challenge you again. Next time we fight, though, I shall kill you."

'And Jara replied: "And if I don't accept your offer of single combat? What if I have you put in my dungeons when you visit?"

'"I will come armed with my bow," answered Karna. "You will not be able to capture me," he said. "But if you decline to fight with me again, I will ask King Dhrita-rashtra and Lord Bhishma for permission to lead the Kuru army against you. Then not only will you die, but also every kshatriya in this great hall."

'Jara was silent for a few moments, and then he replied:

'"Lord Karna, in combat you are unfathomable. My mind cannot contain, nor my eyes see, what your body does. You do not dance, when you fight, for the admiring warriors and their wives. Your dance is only for the gods to see. We cannot behold your greatness." At this point he started to clap his hands together, looking from side to side at his subjects round the hall. And when the people saw this, they also clapped. But they looked terrified. Then Jara-sandha stopped, and there was a hush again.

'"Suta," said King Jara, "you are an honourable man. I am not." He smiled when he said this, and there was some laughter, nervous laughter, right round the hall — except for Shishu. I don't think he has proper control over the muscles on his face, he often has to wipe away his dribbling. Then, when the king became serious again, everybody fell silent.

'"I am not an honourable man, Karna, but I will make an exception for you. I will do as you ask. If I have failed to discharge your requests by the time you return, you may fight with me again. If I have pleased you by achieving them, I shall be honoured if you return the pleasure with the gift of friendship." Everyone applauded again at this point. Then Jara stood up, and said, "You may leave in peace with your slave." Then Karna went to pick up his shirt and coat, and a bundle he had with him. Jara indicated to me that I should join Karna, and I approached them. When Karna turned to go, Jara asked him, this time in quite a low voice, which only we could hear:

'"Lord Karna, it is said that you were born with golden armour. It is said that you gave this away. Is this true?"

'Karna nodded.

'"And have you also tried to give away your power?"

'Karna just stared at Jara, without moving.

'"Power is not transferable, Lord Karna. It may be lent or borrowed; it may be nurtured; it may be taken away; but, like water, once drunk it cannot be given away. And whereas water drains back to the lowest point, power flows to the highest, to those with the most. You are still Anga's ruler; though you hide, like many a master, behind the face of your own slave."

'I couldn't see Karna's face at this point: he was in front of me. But when he turned he had that smile of his. Then he bowed his farewell, picked up his bundle and... and then we left. He unharnessed one of the horses from his chariot, and sent me back on it. He set off for the mountains, for Mahendra. He asked me particularly to tell you, Charvaka, that he was on his way to see Parashu-rama.'

As Vaitanika finished speaking Dur looked over to Charvaka and Shakuni.

'How could he beat Jara? Jara is nearly the same weight as Bhima!'

'My boy, Karna can move faster than most people think. In fact, I sometimes wonder if he moves even faster than he thinks...'

'Surely that's not possible, my dear. By definition all voluntary movement, having some purpose in mind, must be preceded by a purpose in the mind, that is to say, some mental activity which we could describe as...'

'Come Vaitanika, you must be hungry,' said Dur, putting an arm around him. Leaving his uncle and the rishi to their various pursuits, he took Vaitanika away.

•

'Look, boys, do you mind if I finish here for today? The next bit is going to be quite hard for me. I need to think about it. We'll start at midday tomorrow — it may be quite long, I'm afraid. I will sacrifice my siesta.'

'Palmira, are you sure you're all right?'

'Off you go, boys! Yes... I'm afraid tomorrow is going to be rather serious. Absolutely no interrupting... Understood?'

•

Day Five: *The Mountain*

25 Mahendra

The sight of the steam which his tired horses were now snorting shook Karna from his reverie. He could see his own breath curling into the thinning air. It was not yet quite cold enough to put on his new bearskin coat, but the thought made him stop and get down off the chariot. He continued on foot, leading the two horses. At the last village he had left one of his horses on loan to a vaishya, in exchange for the bearskin. His host assured him he would soon need it.

The following day Karna again led his horses on foot; and as he tethered his exhausted animals for the night he decided at the next opportunity to exchange the chariot and horses for a mule. The tracks across the sparsely wooded slopes were not yet too treacherous for the horses, nor was their burden so heavy: they were exhausted from fear. They were unused to the tiger spoor which was beginning to mark their trail. In the open, when they could see downwind, the animals would follow Karna cautiously. But in the woods they strained fearfully, shivering constantly as Karna coaxed them forward.

Next day he recognised, from Charvaka's description, a little village set deep in a narrow valley. It was the last settlement he would meet before his final destination. On the other side of the translucent river which flowed down to the village, the foothills rolled upwards: a tired, dusty green, scarred with woodland and grey rock, but steep enough to obscure the mountain beyond.

While Karna was loading up the mule he had selected, the villagers stared at him and whispered. One of them examined a bow and a small javelin which Karna had strapped to the side of the mule.

'You are a brahmana?' the villager asked, directing his attention now to Karna's white sash and headcloth. Without waiting for a reply he touched Karna's headcloth. 'Like Mahendra,' he joked.

Another man pointed to Karna's bow.

'You should keep it strung and on your back.'

Karna smiled and held up one of the bowstrings he kept ready, tied to the quiver at his waist. But the villager shook his head.

'The tigers in these parts are very large. They are almost grey, not orange like the little cats you're used to. And there's not so much game at this time of the year. You should be careful... It is two days' climb to Mahendra. Listen to your mule. You have chosen well. Very well. This one has made the journey many times before. You're lucky it's down here today. It's well-known, this mule. It is a favourite of Rama himself. Is he expecting you? He usually sends a guide down when it's your first time... No matter, this is as good a guide as any...' He patted the mule. 'Yes, you are lucky to have got this far, with your horses in such a sweat. We will keep your chariot safely... until we see this mule again, with or without you! String up your bow!'

Karna thanked him for his advice. He strung his bow, perching it on his shoulder with a grateful smile, and forded the river, leading the mule. Then he set off up the winding track on the other side.

As soon as he was out of sight of the people below, Karna took off his bow, unstrung it, and strapped it up again to the side of the mule; he took up the javelin and, using it as a staff as he climbed, tapped the blunt end occasionally against the rocks.

The mule, though constantly alert, was very calm. On one occasion it suddenly froze. There must have been fresh tiger spoor near the track. Karna struck the butt of the javelin against a nearby rock. The ring of the metal echoed and re-echoed. Karna listened intently, not to the sound itself but to the silence into which it curled. The mule seemed to be reassured, for it started off by itself up the track.

Later on Karna himself stopped and tethered the mule. The thinner air had made him light-headed, and had begun to play tricks with his eyesight. He lay down on his back and closed his eyes, regulating his breathing as Charvaka had taught him. He opened his eyes and tried raising his head; but his vision still seemed less real than his hearing, so he laid his head back again. A little while later he tried again, and this time rose to continue his journey.

That night he slept soundly, covered in his bearskin. The following morning he set off quite slowly, now wearing the coat, and paced himself more carefully against the conjuring breeze.

During the course of the day he saw some deer, a wild boar, a bear, and heard the calls and cackles of monkeys; but no tigers. He did, however, come across a sight more startling for him than any tiger.

Karna and the mule were making their way across a gentle slope. It was covered in unusually smooth, short grass. A few small trees were scattered further down the slope to the left.

The mule stopped first, cocking its head to look up the rise of the slope to the right. An instant later Karna heard the faint sound which had alerted the mule. He saw, less than fifty paces away on his right, a man, completely naked, very thin, and quite old. He was urinating on the grass. A pigeon was perched on his shoulder. His hair and beard were long and knotted. With him also was a goat which had stopped nibbling at the grass to look down at Karna and the mule. On the grass near the goat were some more pigeons. The old man himself seemed unaware of Karna's presence.

When he stopped urinating the man flicked himself dry, and started to walk down the slope; not directly towards Karna, but heading about twenty paces in front of where Karna and the mule had stopped.

The goat and pigeons followed the old man. Karna and the mule watched in silence. Once or twice the man's glance crossed Karna's, but there was no flicker in the eyes, no sign of recognition, as though Karna and the mule were invisible. And yet he was surely not blind.

As he came nearer, Karna noticed that although his face was wrinkled and old, his hair and beard were still quite black. He carried no stick, no implement, no decoration, no clothing of any kind. His bare feet made no sound on the velvet grass and, as he walked, all four of his spidery limbs moved with a strange confidence, gracefully, his arms winding the air in time to his thin legs.

Karna stayed rooted to the spot as the little procession made its way down the slope on Karna's left, weaving in between the trees; he watched until he could no longer separate the tiny figures. Even then, it was the mule who started first, pulling him back on his journey.

◊

Early next day as the morning mist cleared, Karna emerged from a thick wood onto a narrow pass. The air, the trees, the sounds, had all been changing. The chattering of monkeys had ceased. Once through the pass he saw the country fall before him into a closed valley which was skirted on the right by the track. From its lowest point the ground rose up again like a dividing wave to form two crests, one just behind and to the left of the other. Through the gap between these two crowns, halfway up the steep slope of the huge, looming mountain beyond, he saw the place Charvaka had described.

The stone walls merged with the rocky outcrops from which they seemed to take root. Karna was just able to make out columns of rising smoke: fine dark lines drawn against the slate-grey mountain, fading to nothing below the white-clad summit. Karna's gaze fell back from the mountain peak to the square turrets and upper walls, dotted irregularly with windows. Below these, following the curving bed of rock, stretched a vast wall, uninterrupted save for a black rectangle at the bottom right-hand corner. From here, descending slowly towards the right, Karna's eyes carefully followed the thin white line of track until it was cut off by the crest in his foreground.

By the time Karna and his mule had become two tiny black spots on that white line, the shift of the moon was taking over from the sun; the last golden rays were drawing out the shadows from the rocky crags.

As the two travellers approached the dark rectangle, Karna saw that it was formed out of two huge carved gates. Set into one of the gates, just one panel of the larger carving, was a small door. It opened silently to receive them. The doorway was just wide enough to admit Karna's laden mule.

A grey figure took Karna's hand and pointed upwards into the darkness. When Karna failed to respond, the grasp tightened. Karna peered upwards, and now was able to make out the vaulted ceiling of the arch above him. The mule started up the steeply rising cobbles, and Karna followed.

As the mule led him up the tangled web of narrow passages, some vaulted over, others open high above to the darkening sky, Karna heard the hum of voices from within the walls. Some of the windows high above him betrayed the flicker of candles; but only the light of the moon filtered down to him, bathing the cobbles in a patchwork glow.

Occasionally the top half of a wooden doorway was open. From within came the smell, the heat, and the rustle of animals. At one doorway a cow stuck her head out to examine the passing mule.

The smells of cooking which Karna had been aware of below were now dispersed by the strengthening breeze, as he gradually climbed up towards the moonlight. Some of the alleys now emerged into little squares, from where he could glimpse the dark mountainside beyond the turrets.

Suddenly he was looking out over the valleys he had skirted. He strained his eyes to make out the two dark crests. He peered down over the wall, measuring in his mind the sudden drop, vertical until the gentler slope of the mountain took over from the stone and rock. The wind made waves in the fur of his coat, and he held on to his headcloth.

He was standing in a small square, cradled by rocks at the back, bordered with turrets at the sides. His arrival had startled some pigeons, asleep on the turrets, but their stir was now subsiding. Behind him the mule was drinking steadily from a trough. The spring water which fed the trough issued silently from the rocks, draining away through a grating set in the flagstones.

The water was ice-cold, uncomfortable for Karna to drink. When the mule had finished, Karna took shelter with the animal behind a turret.

He had only just fallen asleep, when a touch on his sleeve woke him. In the moonlight he saw a silver beard, crisp and short; though the eyes he looked into were cold and without expression, the hands which clasped tightly round his forearms warmed him like an embrace.

Without speaking, Parashu led the mule away and beckoned to Karna to follow him down.

Soon afterwards they were again immersed in the warren of alleyways. The rishi knocked at a door. It was opened by a young man holding a candle.

Parashu led the mule inside, where the floor was covered in straw. In a corner of the room stood two little troughs, one full of feed for the animal, the other with water.

The man pointed to some steps leading up, and Karna climbed into a loft above the mule. Along one wall was a strip of clean, fresh straw. In a little dish by the straw burned a candle. Beside the candle was a large, wide-rimmed bowl of clear water, and a smaller bowl of steaming rice. Across on the other side of the loft was a small window. The shutters were half-open, creaking softly in the breeze.

Karna quickly took off his bearskin and dropped it by the straw bed; he climbed back down to thank Parashu and the young man, but they had gone.

Karna unloaded the mule and carried his belongings up into the loft. He drank some water from the bowl. He stared at the window for a moment, and then went down below and felt the water in the trough. It was much colder. Returning to the loft, he took off the rest of his clothes and lay on the straw, supporting himself on one elbow as he ate from the bowl of rice. He pulled the bearskin around him. Beneath him, except for a patch under his calves and feet, the straw felt warm. Though he lost consciousness long before he had emptied the bowl, Karna did not sleep soundly that night.

26 The nuts

Karna woke early. A little light was coming in through the shutters. He tried to shake away the jumble of memories that had infused his dreams. He heard the mule slopping at the trough in the room below. He got up and opened the shutters. Then, at the little window, he finished off the left-over rice.

The sun had only just risen. The patches of sky visible between the roof tops above him were not yet blue. He heard a dog bark, and looked down to see it scampering out of sight. In the alley below, a woman was leading some goats down to be put out on the slopes. Across on the other side of the alley the shutters were still closed.

After washing, shaving, and clearing out the mule's straw, Karna put on a white dhoti and shirt, some strong sandals, and the white sash and headcloth he had lately adopted. He left the bearskin covering his red sack. With the mule he then made his way up to the square at the top, where Parashu had found him the night before. Karna would have preferred to leave the mule behind, but he was not sure he could have found the square unaided.

Parashu was there already, sitting on a ledge near the water trough, a hunched figure hooded in a light-blue cloak. The cloak seemed full of folds and pockets. When Karna approached him, Parashu drew back his hood and waved away the pigeons that had gathered around him. He appeared to be younger than Charvaka; but Karna knew he was a little older. There was neither friendship nor hostility in the rishi's eyes.

'Who are you?' he asked.

'If I knew that, rama, I wouldn't need to be here.'

'What is your name?' The tone of the rishi's voice was as impassive as his face.

Karna hesitated for a moment. There was much less breeze than the night before; the air was cool and dry; as it filled Karna's lungs it seemed to quench a thirst within him.

'My name is Karna.'

'Does it have a meaning?'

'I used to wear golden ear-rings. I was called Karna-veshtakika.'

'A brahmana with ears adorned?' The rishi's tone grew a little more in expression. 'What happened to them?'

'I gave them away, rama.'

'You gave them away... Very wise. Wearing gold next to the skin makes men more beautiful to the eye; so gold finds its value, becoming wealth.' Parashu now began to lilt his vowels fastidiously, as though they were sweet cells of nectar honeycombed within his consonants. 'And since wealth is the most beautiful skin to foolish men, they find themselves more becoming wearing wealth. Kshatriyas wear gold, Karna.'

Without rising, Parashu edged to where the spring water fell bleeding from the rocks, and trailed his hand idly in the stream.

'Rama, you were expecting me to arrive. How did you know?'

'Look over the valley. We can see all who come and go along the road.'

'But... the sun was already very low when I turned into the valley.'

'It took less than an hour to get fresh straw, water, and to cook your rice.'

'The water for the mule was cold, rama. My water had been warmed during the morning by the sun coming in through the window of the loft. My bedding too, I think.'

Parashu blinked.

'I see that the sun is a good friend of yours. You are quite correct. You were noticed crossing the tiger country. But I'm sure you did not come here to ask me how I knew that you were coming?'

'Rama, you know better than I do why I'm here.'

'That's probably true. Almost all the brahmanas who come to me do so because they wish to learn, through force or through wisdom, how better to control their fellow men.'

Karna thought for a moment before replying.

'I think I'm more interested in controlling force than in controlling men. As for wisdom, I think I've more use for knowledge.'

'Whether I can help you control force will depend on whether you have sufficient power. As for knowledge, that is a wise pursuit for a wise man but a folly for a fool. Which are you?'

'Wouldn't it be the worst of follies to say that I am wise?'

'That, Karna, is the answer of a fool who would appear wise, or of a wise man who would appear a fool. No. Worse would be to *think* that you are wise. And worst of all would be to think that what they *say* marks out the wise: to think the naked thoughts in those you take for wise match the cut of the fine words which clothe them...' Parashu raised his hand from the water, watching the drips fall back, and augmented his voice, almost as if to mock himself. '...To think that from unsullied springs their gracious actions flow, this is the height of folly, this is to misconstrue the mortal. Chart first the springs and eddies of your own dark fancies, by all means; but then anatomise the same red blood, the self-same veins and vanities, in the wiser-seeming vein of man. Make them out, but not of other stuff than you. To know yourself to be full of folly, yet not to credit others with due volume of that matter, that is the master of wise foolery.

Do you understand me, Karna?'

'Yes, rama.'

•

'Palmira! We didn't understand a word of that!'

Palmira smiled patiently, and her voice was soft as she scolded the twins.

'You are disgusting, uncivilised boys... How can you interrupt the great Parashu-rama in full flow?... Let me tell you a little story that Mevlana Djelaleddin Rumi was fond of recounting. Well, you shouldn't interrupt! The Mevlana tells the story of an Arab poet who visited a great Turkish king. This poet had composed some verses in honour of the king, but in Arabic. He did not realise that the king, unlike most of his courtiers, didn't know any Arabic.

'The king and his courtiers took their seats in court to listen to the poem. The poet began to recite his delightful verses.

'Out of respect for their king, and also because the courtiers were uneasy about the king's reception of this poet, they all remained silent, neither laughing at the humorous passages nor applauding the eloquence. But they were astonished to see that the king was nodding appreciatively at all the rhetorical flights; that he was smiling, even laughing aloud, at some of the comical episodes; that he looked amazed at some of the poet's more startling metaphors; and that his face became sad or anxious at the more disturbing images.

'Afterwards the courtiers could talk of nothing else.

'"Our king doesn't know a word of Arabic! How is it that he could understand this poem?"

'"Maybe he *does* know Arabic, but has kept it a secret... Woe betide us if we've said nasty things about him in Arabic, thinking he couldn't understand!"

'The courtiers were so worried at this possibility that they actually paid one of the king's attendants to find out if he did know any Arabic.

'"No, I have no knowledge at all of that language," the king told this servant.

'"But how is it you understood the poem, Your Majesty?"

'"I didn't understand the poem, I only understood the poet. I could see in the poet's face when he was praising me, when he was trying to make me laugh, when he was trying to impress me with his eloquence. I did not need to understand the *words* to understand what he was doing. I knew quite well what was going on..."

'So you see, boys,' continued Palmira, 'you don't need to understand what Parashu actually says. The important thing is to know what's going on. Do you see?'

'Yes, we see. But what's going on?'

'Shut up!' said the second Henry.

'But how can we tell what's going on if we can't even see Parashu's face?' persisted the first Henry.

'Don't take any notice of him, Palmira, he's in a mood today. Our mother was cross with him last night...'

'Very well, boys, I'll continue. Henry, all you have to do is to *imagine* Parashu's face. Then you'll know exactly what's going on...'

•

'Look over the valley, Karna. We can see all who come and go along the road —'

•

'We've had that bit, Palmira!'

'Really? Mmm... Oh yes... As Karna was saying: "Rama, you know better than I do why I'm here."'

'Palmira! We've passed that bit too!' The second Henry glared at his brother. 'Now look what you've done!'

'Oh dear, boys — we've done that bit too?... Have we... Have we got to the part where Karna is saved from a leaping tiger by a single arrow from the bow of a beautiful princess?'

'What!' The first Henry turned to his brother, whose face had now crumpled in silent exasperation. 'Oh!... Sorry, Palmira...' he apologised contritely. 'I promise I won't interrupt...'

•

'So, Karna, what kind of knowledge do you seek?'

'I want to learn about the use of certain weapons.'

'Last night I saw a bow and a javelin strapped to the mule. You already have the look of a ratha. You have the hands of one accustomed to the bowstring. Is there some other form of combat you wish to master?'

'I have two rather strange weapons, rama. May I show them to you? I have them below with my things.'

The rishi raised his eyebrows. 'Fetch them...'

Karna glanced at the mule, which was waiting patiently; but decided he would find his own way.

He reappeared after a while with his red sack. He laid it carefully down before Parashu, who was still sitting on the ledge. Karna took out the snake arrow, still in its leather sheath, the two parts of the javelin, and the leather pouch.

Parashu looked at them without expression. He picked up and examined the red sack. When he saw the little pillow inside he turned and for a moment stared at Karna. Then he put down the sack. But he did not touch the weapons.

'How did you get hold of these?' He pointed at the weapons. 'The rishi Charvaka?'

'Charvaka sent me to see you. But I didn't get the weapons from him... just the powder... I promised not to reveal who gave them to me.'

'So the mouse sent you here. Why?'

'He said you were the only one who could show me how to use these weapons.'

Parashu stared at Karna. 'Was there any other reason?'

'Yes. I was found as a baby on the river... in Anga. I had with me that red sack, my ear-rings, and some golden mail. No one has ever told me who my real parents were. Though,' Karna added with a smile, 'it has been suggested that Surya was my father.' Karna paused to study the rishi's expression, but it showed no change, and he continued.

'Charvaka never told me very much... My understanding was that if I chose I could... take the snake, he called it — which he never really explained, but which would gain something for me... at the risk of death. I never knew what it would gain... and I couldn't imagine what it would give me that I wanted... So I decided not to take the snake. I gave away my ear-rings and my mail —'

'To whom?'

'I cannot say... But apparently the matter didn't just end there. Charvaka thinks you may want me dead. So he sent me here for you to try to kill me, should you think that was appropriate.'

'For me to try to kill you?' Parashu stressed each word distinctly, and Karna noticed his eyes flash for an instant. Then the rishi smiled. 'That implies that I may not succeed. Is that what you think, or what the mouse thinks?'

'I don't know you, rama. But Charvaka... I know Charvaka. I don't think he would have sent me here if he thought I could not defend myself.'

'And he knows you well?'

'Yes, rama. I have been a pupil of his since I was a child.'

'He must have a high opinion of you.'

Karna smiled. 'I think he has an accurate opinion of me.'

'I'm surprised a pupil of the mouse appears so arrogant.'

'Isn't it better to appear arrogant for the sake of truth than to appear humble for the sake of approval?'

'It is also far better to look a fool than be one. But it is very easy to look a fool *and* be one. Indeed, there are those who wear their folly on their sleeve so as not to be accused of concealing it. Perhaps you clothe your arrogance in arrogance so that it will not be discovered hiding beneath humility?'

'Perhaps I do, rama.'

Parashu looked at Karna for a moment, studying him. 'And do I want to kill you?'

'Not yet, rama. I expect these things take a little time.'

'It usually does take a little time to prepare for death,' replied Parashu, returning no trace of Karna's humour. 'Why are you wearing a brahmana's cloth?' he added coldly.

'Charvaka thought it might help me to blend in with my surroundings.'

'So the lion of Surya puts on the tiger's stripes?' Parashu stood up. He took a few idle paces towards the mule, who came forwards to receive a pat from the rishi. 'And would you like to learn about your weapons first, or proceed straight to your execution?'

'I am more curious about life than about death.'

'You seem more curious about the means to end life than the end itself.'

'What can you expect from someone who has grown up under the shadow of death. A shadow cast by my good friend Surya.'

Parashu sat down again on the ledge. The pigeons began to converge on him, but he ignored them.

'And you expect me to welcome you, a complete stranger, and to prepare you for death? How can I believe you?'

Karna looked at the red sack.

'You could have stolen that,' observed Parashu. 'Have you no message, no letter from the mouse?'

'What could he have given me that I couldn't have stolen?'

'That no doubt I shall discover in due course.'

'While you make your mind up, rama, perhaps you could show me how to use the snake arrow?'

'I have to see how you walk before I show you how to run. Who taught you the bow?'

'Drona was my last teacher. I believe he was your pupil.'

'He was. Where was this? In Hastinapura? Tell me, Karna, have you seen the boar in action? Bhishma?'

'Yes.'

'How would you say he compares to Drona?'

'The Grandsire's aim is more natural than Drona's. He sees more. But his hands I don't think are quicker than Drona's, not now. Perhaps when he was younger...'

'Yes, when he was younger... What about yours, Karna? How well do you see?'

'I seem to be able to see what I need to... And my hands are quick enough.'

Parashu stood up. 'I asked only about your eyes. First comes the mind, then the eyes, then the hands. Come here...'

As Karna approached the rishi, Parashu took out a bag from a pocket of his cloak. The bag contained nuts. He counted out five of them. Facing Karna, he bared his right arm to the elbow. He raised this arm to shoulder height, palm downwards, and pointed it at Karna.

'Place these nuts on my arm. Space them evenly between my knuckles and my elbow.'

Karna took the five nuts and put them in position.

'Have you seen this little trick before?'

'No. What are you going to do?'

Parashu held his left arm out of the way behind his back, and lowered his right arm very slowly until the nuts were about to slip. Then he flicked them all up into the air. As they fell he caught each one in his right hand.

'Could you do that?' he asked Karna.

'I'm not sure. Perhaps.'

'I want you to try it. Try it with six nuts. I've never yet seen anyone who could do it with six.'

Parashu picked another nut from the bag in his pocket. Karna bared his right arm and held it up flat. The rishi moved over to Karna's right-hand side and spaced the six nuts on his outstretched arm.

Karna lowered his arm gradually.

'Wait there... You say your eyes are good enough...' Parashu supported Karna's arm as he spoke. He stared hard into Karna's eyes. 'But first comes the mind... Even the best of eyes have to look in the right direction...'

Parashu released his hold and moved away.

Karna's arm was still outstretched, but the nuts had disappeared.

'Where have they gone?' the rishi asked.

Karna relaxed his arm. 'Four are in your left hand, rama, the other two are in your right hand.'

Parashu opened up his fists. Four nuts were on his left palm, but his right hand was empty. The rishi chuckled.

'You know, Karna, it used to annoy the mouse when I did things like that.'

'I have heard him say that those who start off playing with magic can end up forgetting that it's only a game.'

'Yes... I too have heard him say that. In a way he is right, for toying with the credulity of men is no game —' Parashu broke off suddenly. The mule snorted, sensing him straighten. The rishi stared at Karna.

'You knew those two nuts weren't in my hand,' he exclaimed. 'Why did you lie to me?'

'I only return your own deception, rama. Why is mine worse than yours?'

The rishi stared at him in silence.

'Would you like to see me do it with six?' asked Karna.

Parashu smiled. 'No, I'm not interested in whether you can do it with five or with six. Yes... Your eyes can see outwards well enough. But we must examine what your sight will show when it is turned inwards.'

Karna closed his eyes. 'What do you wish to know, rama?'

The rishi chuckled. 'I'm not interested in what you have to *say*.' As he spoke now he modulated his voice and exaggerated his expression. 'With words we disguise ourselves as gods; it is through actions that we are revealed; as animals, though all the wiser for knowing it. *Man* is merely a polite conceit for those who prefer the simple comfort of the word to the tangled truth it clothes. Come...'

Parashu started to move towards the way down from the square, and he beckoned to Karna to follow him. Karna quickly put his weapons back into the red sack, and went to fetch the mule.

'No... Leave the mule behind, Karna. And there is no need to tether him, he knows his way around here better than we do. Yes... of all animals it is only man, striving in vain to trace his divine paternity, who falls prey to his animal vanity...'

27 The headcloth and the sash

Parashu waited by the door to Karna's lodging while Karna replaced the sack up in his loft, beneath his bearskin. A few steps below the doorway another alley led upwards to the rocks above Mahendra. Parashu took this turn and Karna followed. The alley was so narrow that when they came upon a brahmana leading his cow up, they could not overtake. The brahmana turned to greet the rishi, and apologised for holding him up.

The alley opened out onto a crossroads, behind which loomed the rocks. As well as the little alley, another track, wide enough for a cart, led down into Mahendra. From the crossroads the track continued slowly up to the left, the west side of the grey mountain. Karna saw this slope dissolve into greener foothills rolling away in the distance.

Another way led off the crossroads to the right. It was a steeper, narrower path, giving access to the east side of the mountain. Parashu set off along this way. Karna looked up and saw the groove of the path circle up to his right. He followed the rishi.

Parashu remained silent as they climbed up briskly. There was very little wind, and the sun was now hot enough to break them into sweat. Along the way Karna noticed a few cows roaming free on the slopes below the path. He guessed that these were more of the sacred homa cows, the responsibility of the brahmanas.

Soon after the valley of Mahendra had disappeared from view behind them, the path began to circle down towards the north side of the mountain. However, before Karna was able to get a clear view of the northern valley, a rocky scarp began to rise steeply on his left.

Parashu left the path, clambering up the scarp with great agility, picking out the holds in the rock like the notes of a familiar tune. Karna followed, carefully placing his hands and feet where the rishi had gone.

Suddenly the rock face ended. Climbing over the edge they found themselves upon its roof. The surface was flat and even, like a frozen stream. A huge tooth of rock was splintered off from the mountain ahead of them, protecting this stone table from what would otherwise have been a sheer drop to the right. The smooth ledge continued to flow between this tooth and the mountain slope on the left. Karna saw that about fifty paces past the tooth the table came to a sudden edge, beyond which there was only sky. The marvellous stillness of the air surprised him.

Parashu came up to him and untied Karna's headcloth.

'Look ahead of you. Tell me when you think your eyes have grasped what lies before you.'

A few seconds later Karna nodded to the rishi. Parashu then tied the headcloth around Karna's face to form a blindfold. He was careful to leave his ears well exposed. The rishi pulled Karna gently forward, away from the edge over which they had just emerged. He spoke softly:

'Karna, I will ask you to walk in front of me, between the splinter of mountain on the right, and the slope on the left... until you come to the edge beyond. Once you have started walking, you must not remove your blindfold until I permit it. Nor should you cease to walk. If you stray too near the mountain or the splinter I will warn you. I will stop you before you fall over the edge. You must trust me. Remember, do not remove your cloth; and once you have begun to move, do not stop.'

While he waited for the rishi's command, Karna pushed all the air carefully out of his lungs, and inhaled slowly.

'Start walking now,' instructed Parashu.

Karna proceeded, slowly but steadily. He could hear the rishi following close behind.

As Karna came abreast of the huge tooth of rock, he felt its shadow, and veered slightly away to his left.

'Karna, why have you turned? Go back to the right a fraction.'

Karna obeyed, and continued steadily in a straight line. As he walked he concentrated on the picture in his mind. He imagined the perspective slowly changing as he approached the edge. He listened hard to the dull shuffle of the rishi's feet, and deliberately brushed his own against the stone to generate more echo. He knew that he was nearly there. He felt a faint ripple in the air.

Then his memories began to jostle and rise, escaping like bubbles from the deep to rouse him... the image of Bhishma standing in line with the tree at the Academy; Charvaka's grey head nodding down at him from the clutter of his workshop; Draupadi's face on the balcony at Kampilya; his own blood as Duh-shasana screamed nearby; he felt the golden mail peeling from his back... his ears, light without their ear-rings... He was standing still. He felt Parashu's breath behind him.

'Why have you stopped? You are in no danger yet of falling. You are still many paces from the edge.'

Karna did not reply.

'Do you not trust me, Karna?'

Still Karna did not reply.

'You do not trust me?' repeated Parashu.

'Of course I don't trust you.'

'What if I get in front of you, and take you by the hand. Will you follow me?'

'No. Why should I trust you blindly while I still have eyes to see for myself?'

'There are things which cannot be seen.'

'If they cannot be seen, rama, you cannot see them either.'

'Do you not believe there may be things which I can see that you cannot?'

'If that were the case I would still have to see that your vision was superior. I will not trust you blindly.'

'Do you really think I would let you fall to your death?'

'I don't know, rama. I would have first to learn to read you before I gave you my trust.'

'And at my age I am not easy to read, for my characters have faded. But if you really do not trust me, what are you doing here? Have you not considered that I might push you over the edge?'

'Of course.'

'Then why do you take a risk trusting that I will not?'

'I am taking no risk, rama. In fact, I should tell you that you are taking the risk. For though I need you alive, if you tried to push me over the edge, I'm not sure I could save you as well as myself.'

'You are very confident, Karna...'

'Either I'm more confident than you are, rama, or, since you haven't already made your move, I have nothing to fear from you. Therefore I have nothing to fear.'

Parashu pulled off Karna's blindfold and hurled it over the edge. They were standing just two paces from the vertical drop. Karna took one step forward and watched the white headcloth flap down like a dead bird to the green valley below. In the centre of the valley a city lay encrusted round a winding river.

'That is the kingdom of Maya,' said Parashu, stepping forward to join Karna at the edge. As Karna looked down the rishi studied his face.

'That is where the stone for Indraprastha comes from,' said Karna. 'You have heard of Indraprastha?'

'Of course. You see the quarries and the mines eating into the hills around the valley? Prince Arjuna came to visit Maya. You must know him. He was also taught by Drona in Hastinapura.'

'Yes, I know Arjuna. Have you met him, rama?'

'No. But I have heard of him. People say he is the most consummate archer that has ever lived...' The rishi waited for Karna to respond. But Karna was gazing silently across the valley.

'There were still two paces left,' continued Parashu. 'If you had continued to walk, it is possible that I might have warned you, or even pulled you back.'

Karna smiled, but did not reply or even turn his head.

'Now you will never know whether I was going to let you fall to your death... You will never know if you could have trusted me... Yes... Charvaka was never very interested in such questions either. Though for someone who professed such little concern for unanswerable questions, he seemed to ask rather a lot of them...'

They were still standing on the edge of the precipice.

'Will you take your sash off now...' Parashu instructed. 'I would like you to blindfold me with it.'

Karna did as he was asked.

'Now, turn me around so that I face the edge we climbed up over.'

Again Karna did as he was asked, pointing the rishi back. The rock splinter was now on their left, and the main slope on the right.

'You may follow me if you wish, Karna. But you must on no account speak to me or touch me. Do you understand? Do not under any circumstances disturb me.'

The blindfolded rishi immediately set off, walking so fast that Karna had to strain to keep up. As Parashu passed through the gap between the splinter and the slope, he seemed to accelerate. And as they approached the edge, it seemed to Karna that the rishi was about to break into a run. Karna grabbed hold of Parashu's cloak and pulled him back, just in time.

The rishi undid the sash and threw it down the scarp.

'That is twice that you have disobeyed me,' said Parashu in mock anger. 'Don't make a habit of it, Karna, or I will be able to control you as easily as if you always did my bidding.'

'Rama, tell me the truth... Were you ready to die, or would you have known when to stop?'

'You want the truth?' Parashu chuckled. 'The truth is just the name men give to what remains when their confusion ends...'

'You were almost running, rama,' persisted Karna, ignoring the rishi's remark. 'It was as though your eyes were wide open. Did you really know where the edge was?'

'Oh yes. Though I would find it hard to prove it to your doubting eye, while you won't stand to see me move so apt to die... The truth is, Karna, that I would have been able to do it only because I was thus apt to die: some things are only in your grasp when your hands are freed from holding on to life's last gasp... But I think that perhaps you already know this?'

'As they say, rama, there are times when you can only reach your morrow by being ready to surrender your today.'

'Do you think that it is possible to choose the moment of one's death?'

'They say the Grandsire can.'

Parashu laughed. 'He can certainly choose the moment for others! I am only alive now because he chose not to kill me.'

Karna was staring down over the scarp, his gaze resting vacantly on the path back to Mahendra. He turned to the rishi.

'Perhaps you also chose not to kill him?'

'There are those who think that. They are wrong. I tried to kill him; and I came nearer to it than he to killing me...'

Parashu got down over the edge of the scarp and started threading his way towards the path below. Karna followed.

For a while they returned in silence. Then, soon after the valley of Mahendra came in view, Karna asked the rishi if he would like to examine his skill with the bow.

'I am not yet interested in your handwriting, Karna. When I have finished with your thoughts, then I will look at what you write... Tomorrow we will go down to the tiger country. I think you are ready to die, Karna. But I believe you still think you will be giving your life away for nothing. And you don't wish to give your life away for nothing.'

'In my walk of life that's considered too cheap, rama.'

The rishi laughed. 'I think you should be more generous, and offer me your life for nothing. For in your walk of life, Karna, nothing interferes so much with success as the fear of achieving it. And when success is the preservation of your life, then you will only achieve it when you do not fear to lose it.'

'I don't fear death, rama.'

'No. But you have the idea that it is worth something. That it should be exchanged for something, and not nothing. You fear a cheap death, Karna. Yet the value is only in the eye of the vendor. When you are not afraid to die for nothing, then will you not be afraid. Then you will understand that nothing in this life is worth more than nothing, nor less than something.'

'Rama, a man can practise facing death. But how can he safely practise not wanting to cling on to life. How does a ratha know when to cling to life and when to leave it?'

'That is the art, Karna. That is the art. When do you ride your horse, when do you dismount to lead it? The journey is full of contradiction. No pupil of Charvaka's can fail to know this...'

'When I was still very young, rama, Charvaka showed me a boat he had made, a boat with sails. Most of the other sailing boats could only move with the wind behind them. But Charvaka had put a wooden fin underneath his boat, so that the wind would not so easily push the boat sideways in the water. His boat sailed fastest when it was almost against the wind. He would say that sometimes you must sail against the gust of your desires in order to achieve them. And that if you did not learn to do this, you would be blown along with all the other boats.'

They had now curved back around the mountain side. Mahendra was perched beneath them.

'Good... So, you will come with me tomorrow to the tiger country?'

'Certainly, rama.'

'Even though it may be your last day?'

'Whenever my last hour comes, rama, whether it is tomorrow or when I am an old man, all I will have in my possession at the time will be one brief moment, one brief moment laden with memories. If I hold that moment dearly enough, even if it is tomorrow, I will be able to give all the rest up cheaply. That moment will then weigh just as much as if it were an old man's. But rama, it won't be as easy for me as it would be for you.'

'Why not?'

'You're an old man already.'

28 Tiger country

'I think I can control my reaction to pain quite well already.'

'Which sort of pain, Karna? There is the pain which drives the body without thought to move and to cry out. We do not need to think or know to feel this pain. But then there is the pain that hangs within our thoughts. This is the kind of pain that tears apart our very being, yet has no teeth; that scratches our eyes till they drown with tears, yet has no claws; that drains our heart of joy, yet leaves our blood undrawn. This pain too can drive the body to move and to cry out. But we cannot push it aside so easily, for it is closer to us than our body, and harder to distinguish: it hangs within our mind to blur and fester. It may be fear; it may be envy; it may be anger; it may be unfulfilled desire. Do you understand me?'

'The first sort of pain is harder to bear but easier to escape,' replied Karna. 'The second sort is easier to bear but harder to escape.'

Karna and Parashu were walking along the track which skirted the valley of Mahendra, the same white line that Karna and the mule had traced in the opposite direction to reach the mountain.

Although it was still early in the morning, Karna was hot inside his bearskin. The rishi was using a huge axe as a staff. He held it just below the blade, which was almost level with his head. At each step he tapped the ground with the end of the wooden handle. Karna had no weapons upon him, not even a knife; all he carried was a water bladder.

'Tell me then how you escape the first sort of pain,' asked Parashu.

'When I was very young, I would just distract my mind from pain in my body. But Charvaka taught me two ways, which amount to the same thing in the end... One way was to step back, to look at the pain, to look at all my senses, as though they were happening to somebody else. The other way was to drain the pain of meaning, as though I were draining the objects in my vision of all meaning... so that there are only patches of colour, and no Parashu-rama, no axe, no mountain side...'

'So the mouse taught you the yogas.'

'He never called them that. And I prefer to follow his example. Charvaka has made me wary of names, rama.'

'Yes... He used to think that names became encrusted with more than is entitled... So, Karna, suppose you were in yoga now, as we walk, what would happen if I were to bring my axe down upon you?'

'While I was not in yoga, as you call it, I would see the axe approach me, and move back. In fact, rama, I would move back long before you even raised your axe, because I would already see you move. You can try it if you like, there would be no risk this time. There is no precipice. I would just disarm you.'

'No, Karna, I am not yet interested in how well you avoid the infliction of pain, but in how well you escape its affliction... What if you were already in yoga when I raised my axe?'

'I would no longer be in the same place as you. As the axe came down, I wouldn't see an axe. There would be an image which grew larger in my vision, but not an axe that approached me. The picture changes, but doesn't touch me.'

'And what would happen when the axe did catch your flesh?'

'It is the same with all the senses. They become just images. I would feel something, but I wouldn't know it was an axe, nor even that it had anything to do with what was happening in my vision. The colours, sounds and feelings would all be disconnected. The cords which tie them, and which tie my mind to them, have been cut loose. The pains try to pull this way and that, but like horses which have been cut loose from my chariot: I watch them go this way and that, unmoved.'

They had rounded the first of the two crests which stood guard over the valley of Mahendra.

'Tell me, Karna, why do we ever feel pain? Why do we *suffer* pain? Why do pains bite us more than sounds and images?'

'I can only tell you what Charvaka thinks.'

'Can you not think for yourself?'

'I can. But not always better. And though Charvaka's answer does not satisfy me, I can think of nothing better.'

'Tell me then what Charvaka thinks.'

'Why? You surely know already what he thinks. Why don't you tell me, instead?'

'Karna, you surely know already how much I like the sound of my own voice. But much as I like it, it will still be here tomorrow. Who knows if yours will? Let me hear your voice while you still have it.'

'Charvaka says that if pains were like the parts of a picture, then by the time a child had learnt to read the whole, he would be dead. If a child had to weigh two pains in his mind, using thought, before he could decide which one he could afford to ignore, then he'd be injured — it would be too late to avoid the danger. But because the child *suffers* the two pains, he doesn't need to calculate which one he should attend to... he doesn't need to *examine* the two pains to determine their respective weight...'

'Of course not. Pains come with their weight already written in the hurt. Your child attends to them faster than thought, because pain moves him without thought. If pains were not suffered, we would have to learn to read them. By which time we would be injured. And it is the same with pleasures. They are *enjoyed*, so they move the body without thought. If they were not, we would have to learn to read them. And where is the pleasure in that?'

Parashu pointed to the water bladder, and Karna passed it to him. The rishi took one gulp, and returned it.

'As we grow out of infancy,' continued the rishi, 'we learn to put thought in the way of pain and pleasure. We learn to control our reactions to pain and pleasure. Is that the difference between men and animals?'

'No, rama. Animals also can be prudent. A cat trapped up a tree by a dog will control its hunger. Even young animals learn to still their cries of anguish rather than alert their foe.'

'So even animals can control their desires?'

'I didn't say that, rama. In animals, as in man, one desire can ride over another, pulling it more strongly. The fear in the prudent cat is stronger than its hunger, so it will not move. The fear in a prudent man, that he will starve tomorrow, is stronger than his hunger, so he puts aside some rice...'

'And though we *say* that the man is controlling his desire,' declared the rishi, 'this is a structure of speech which does not bear any load. It is not a controlling of desire on the part of the man, though we flatter ourselves with the illusion. It is the control of one desire by a stronger. Yes... even infants soon learn prudence, when their desires begin to fight each other. But then what is the difference between the child and the man?'

'The desires of a child are not as... abstract as those a grown man may be capable of?'

'I'm not sure that's the right way to put it, Karna. I would say that the child's desire has not yet grasped such abstract means of satisfaction, such subtle intermediaries, as his elders find to fill their own still childish dreams. For you must know that the old are old only in the disguises of action, not in the youthful springs from which their actions flow... Tell me, Karna, do desires always control each other prudently?'

'No, rama. The shame of a man afraid may be stronger than his desire to cry out; so that he is not moved to shout for help. The fear of what others think may quite imprudently overcome his instinct, and cost him his life.'

Karna looked back over his shoulder to catch a glimpse of Mahendra between the two crests. Parashu slowed his pace and studied his companion.

'Karna, are *you* afraid?'

'No, rama,' he replied with a smile. 'Though perhaps that is imprudent of me.'

'Pity... Still, every man has his tiger. Perhaps we shall find it...'

The sun was now high in the sky, and Karna was sweating heavily under his coat. He was also feeling hungry; he had been given nothing to eat in the morning before leaving Mahendra.

'So, Karna, in the exercise of prudence a man does not really rise above desire. Surely, only in the exercise of yoga does a man escape desire. For in yoga it is not one desire controlling another, it is the severing of the cords between the man and his desires.'

Karna made no comment, and they walked on in silence until Parashu prompted his companion.

'Does a man escape desire through yoga? Tell me what you think, Karna.'

'Rama, I thought you said you were not interested in what I say, but in what I do. What I was doing was not speaking, and you should make do with what I do.'

'I am also interested in what I can make you do. Tell me what you think, Karna.'

'I can tell you what the brahmanas think, rama... They think that only through yoga does a man transcend desire. But Charvaka doesn't believe it's possible even through yoga. Though he also thinks that even if the brahmanas were right, even so, while we play our part in life we have to respect how men are accustomed to speak about each other. And they are accustomed to say that a prudent man who saves his grain is controlling his desire. And that works for men, in life. Only when we step outside of life, to observe, and not take part, only then, seen from without, prudence is not what it seems from within. Very little is what it seems. But when we rejoin the world, we have to join it, and forget what it looked like from outside.'

'Naturally,' said the rishi. 'If you turn the world on its head while you stay upright, everything will look strange from beneath. But when you turn yourself to join it again, everything is soon familiar, and the strangeness only half-remembered... Not that we can even succeed in stepping outside life, not even when we cut the cord in yoga. We try, but it's as though we tried to step outside of our own skins. While we live, we cannot. We may move to a different place, but there is nowhere we can step that is not still inside the world. Even in yoga... It seems, when you are in yoga, and your eyes are open, that you can watch your images as if you watched a troop of shadows performing, masks with no actors behind them. But there is no seat, no auditorium, nowhere from which to watch. And when you close your eyes, it is not darkness descending upon your stage. It is beyond that: the images just cease. When you reopen your eyes, there they are again, images jostling and charging your thoughts, yet nowhere near or far from them... You do not watch those images, Karna, you are too close to watch them. They are already part of you. Your thoughts may be about them; but these thoughts do not themselves have eyes, nor is there beyond them in your mind an eye to be your *I*. There is something, yes, but not an eye; for eyes watch without being touched; but this is touched without watching.'

'But I *seem* to watch — when I detach myself from my senses, when I cut the cord in yoga... I seem to step back and watch.'

'Yes. It seems as though you move back. But there is no movement. All that happens is that the images from your senses lose their significance. When your thoughts are unyoked from your senses, your senses are still there, happening, but now there is no thought of them. So they lose their significance. Did the mouse not train you to listen to a familiar word being spoken repeatedly, until it just became a sound?'

'Yes. I had to learn not to understand the sound as a word. He did that with written signs as well. I had to stare at them until they became meaningless. I always complained to him: first you teach me how to read, then you teach me how to not read.'

'When you seem to step back from your senses, you are unyoking their meaning. They no longer make the usual ripple in your thoughts. Just as the familiar word of Charvaka's exercise melts into a mere sound that is voiced, so that very sound, in yoga, melts into noise, and flows into one voice of the world.'

Parashu had quickened his pace as the track steepened downhill through a wood. High above them monkeys were now chattering and scampering through the treetops.

'Karna, do you understand what you must do tonight?'

'I think so, rama. I must cut each cord that ties me to my senses. I must cut each cord that binds me to my needs. Then, if the tiger comes, its smell will move me no more than the smell of air. Its claws, its teeth, will brush my mind with the softest breeze, even as my limbs are torn apart. While my body turns like a chariot wheel, my mind will stay as still as the centre bearing of the wheel, as still as the eye of a storm; until it loses sight, and slips gently into death.'

'But do you understand what will be your greatest danger?'

'I think so, rama. As I sever my desires, the bearing of the wheel becomes ever smaller. If I shave the last cord too thin, there will be nothing left at the centre of the wheel. The stillness will vanish to a point. If the last cord is severed, I will not need to live; and I will die, even if the tiger does not come to take me.'

'And be careful, Karna. If you unyoke that last cord, I will not be able to rouse you. If the tiger's claw is like the brush of a butterfly, how will my hand disturb your peace? You will starve. You may even stop breathing. What must you do?'

'I must leave the last cord till the last moment. At the centre of the wheel, I must still want to be. Until the tiger comes.'

'And how will you know when the tiger comes. How will you know when to sever your last desire?'

'I will leave my hearing open; if I read from this that the tiger comes close, then I will sink into the deep yoga, and stop wanting; only then will I stop reading its rustle or growl. After that it will mean no more to me than silence. Until that point, I will not be deaf.'

'Good. That will be the hardest part. When you are in the deepest yoga, you are stable, though departed. But if you're not quite there, and there is too much of life in you, your fears may return to rouse you. Then, fearing your fears, to escape them you may sink too deeply and too soon. Do you understand? You must find the balance.'

'Yes, rama.'

'So do not go into deep yoga too soon. Do not panic while panic still has meaning to you, and cease to live before you need to. I once lost a pupil like this. The tiger walked up to him slowly, just out of curiosity, and nudged his shoulder with its paw. My boy went too soon. The tiger left him without a scratch, but I could not rouse him.'

'Do not fear for me, rama. And I must thank you... It's very kind of you to take such trouble, not only to arrange my death, but to teach me how to die. Perhaps this is what is meant by the kshatriya death...'

'There is a proper way to live, and a proper way to die. Karna, you understand that I do not ask my pupils to wait for the tiger unless they have studied for some years. It is only because I see that the mouse has taught you that I am sending you this way. Even so... it may not be wise...'

'On the contrary, rama. It is very prudent of you — how else could you kill me? In any case, as Charvaka says, it's not wise to be wise all the time.'

'As it is sometimes prudent to abandon prudence...'

'In deep yoga there is no prudence, rama. The future is all the same to you.'

'And yet we enter yoga from the world, in which there is prudence. In which there is purpose. Once in yoga, there is no purpose left, and no purpose felt. But to enter it, you must have some reason. So, tell me, Karna. Is it wise for you to enter yoga? Is it prudent? What is your purpose in abandoning all purpose?'

'Rama, I will do it for no other reason than to do something for no reason.'

Parashu looked up to check the position of the sun, which was now past its hottest point. He remained silent for a while as they walked.

The forest was dispersing into clumps of sloping woodland, nestling among the hills. In the patches of open country the sounds of the monkeys receded, and were replaced by the traffic of birds. On the rocky spurs they could see sturdy mountain goats staring back at them, climbing two steps nearer safety as they passed. Deer, catching their scent, darted nervously for shelter onto higher ground or amongst trees, setting the birds to flight. Parashu watched carefully as they walked. He took in the movements of the animals, and of Karna. He was surprised by Karna's alertness: he noticed that Karna had already distinguished the disturbance they themselves had caused, from the ripple of the tiger that was tracking them. But he did not mention this to Karna.

'Nothing, Karna, is its own reason. Unless you make it so, nothing, not even yoga, is an end in itself. For a man whose aim is to starve to death, it is prudent not to eat. And if his aim is wise, his means are as wise as they are apt. Yoga may be a means to many ends; to death; to life; to anything between the two. And there are those who do make it an end in itself. I have not the wisdom to judge if it is wise for them to aim thus. But for these there is only one yoga, one which is so deep that it sits at the top of the mountain, needing nothing, offering no resistance to the yoke of the world. Yet even among the yogas that come near to this, there are many different kinds. There is only one point at the top of the mountain; but just below it there is already a small circle of many points.

'A man may cut off as many or as few of his desires as he chooses — and I say *chooses*, Karna, in the glib parlance of the world. Moreover, a man may have many different reasons for doing so. Yesterday, when I walked blindfold, I was in yoga, but with one and only one desire remaining: to walk within one pace of the edge. I narrowed all my senses to that single end. The desire to live did not take part to spoil my concentration. Nor did the reason why I entered yoga, which was to show you what I could achieve by it. But once I entered yoga I did not even feel your presence. I put myself entirely beneath the yoke of the action. You must have been taught to use such yogas when you are handling your bow. If it is wise to hit your target, then it is wise to enter yoga when it will help you strike. The art of yoga is to feel which desires to surrender, and which to surrender to.'

Parashu continued to observe his companion carefully. Every so often Karna was turning to peer in the direction of the tiger, which was now padding its way in full sight of them along the slope below.

'Yoga has many uses,' went on the rishi. 'Generally those who use it are trying to achieve happiness, if not for themselves, then for others. Tell me, Karna, how is happiness achieved?'

The tiger growled as it marked out its territory beneath them. Karna was looking down in its direction, but his gaze seemed to pass through it, as though he were more concerned with the trees and bushes behind the animal. As he replied to the rishi's question, his manner was distracted, his attention obviously elsewhere.

'There are two ways of achieving happiness. By the satisfaction or by the elimination of desire. Unhappiness is caused by the failure to satisfy a present desire, and I include the desire to avoid pain or distress —'

'Karna,' interrupted the rishi, amused at the mechanical tone of his companion's voice. 'How then may yoga be used to achieve happiness?'

Karna replied, still in the same tone.

'Yoga may assist you to achieve your present desire, or it may assist you to remove that desire, should you desire the latter course...'

'Why are you distracted? Are you afraid of the tiger?'

'Of the tiger... What tiger? I see no tiger, rama. There is a greyish-orange patch in my vision with dark stripes; there is also an occasional growl. But these are like clouds in the sky, rama, I neither read them nor fear them... No, there is something else following us. I don't know what. But it concerns me, for I haven't yet cut off even a fraction of my concerns. My yoga is still near the bottom of the mountain.'

Parashu smiled. 'And if I tell you that you do not need to be concerned with anything else that may be following us, will you cut off that concern also?'

'If you command me to, rama, I will obey you.'

'Why do you trust me now?'

'It is nothing to do with trust, rama. If I were in the world, I would still not trust you. But I am beginning to step outside of it. There is no trust or distrust now. I have placed myself under your yoke, for better or for worse. And outside of this world there is no better and no worse.'

Parashu stopped. They both took a drink from the water bladder. Below them the tiger had also stopped.

The rishi glanced at the afternoon sun and estimated the length of his shadow. 'Darkness falls fastest where tigers are feared worst...' he muttered to himself. Then he set off again.

'Tell me, Karna... Inside the world, what is better and what is worse?'

'The brahmanas,' replied Karna, 'generally maintain that what is best is that which causes the least suffering to others.'

'Many indeed will argue that the prevention of suffering is the highest good; but all too few will suffer to lower themselves in pursuit of this. The pain they see around them is never their fault. They blame some grotesque monument to evil which they erect in order to revile, in whose shadow their own dark omissions stand unnoted. But even the best of men, Karna, even one who is prepared to endure suffering to prevent it in others... even he cannot see all that he needs.'

'What is best may not be for the best, says Charvaka.'

'Ah yes...' The rishi's eyes glazed over as he unleashed his voice for the birds to hear. 'The fruit of many a glorious action has poisoned its intention, while many a dull stroke has reaped a splendid harvest. We are too impatient, both in the act and in the judgement. The hasty hero's deeds may wither like autumnal leaves, though he outsing the patient sower of ripe seeds; whose silent years, unseen, by men unsung, in time to come become our ears.'

'But in the end these also are consumed.'

'Of course. Without seeing the end, we cannot begin; yet life drives us blindly on to make us think we see. And seeing thus far, some choose to leave the blind dance, and climb the mountain of yoga. But it takes a very great ambition to climb the whole mountain, only to discard itself at the summit. There are even those, despising this ambition, who will stay close in sight of the peak, who will refuse to satisfy the wish to reach it. Others, who also laugh at this desire for self-mastery, believe that it no more deserves indulging than those slavish needs it locks up in subjection. Tell me, Karna, do you know the rishi Durvasa?'

'I have met him, yes.'

'That red fox often mocks those whose desire for self-mastery is gluttonous, by abandoning himself to honest gluttony. For there are many who practise austerity of the flesh only to wallow in an opulence of the spirit. A man's soul is warmed and fed by the admiring looks of others. For some, the fulfilment of desire does not outweigh the pleasure of applauded sacrifice. But Durvasa's yoga allows him to control both his desire for admiration and his fear of ridicule. They say that only Pritha, the mother of the Pandavas, was able to endure his company for any length of time. For which, they say, he rewarded her with the rare gift of union with the gods.'

In the distance Karna saw the track cut through a familiar velvet slope of grass. He could just make out some goats which were grazing peacefully upon it.

'Yes,' continued Parashu, 'there are many yogas... Did Charvaka not speak to you about his own?'

'No... He rarely uses the word, and in any case, he seldom talks about himself directly... I know that sometimes he was in yoga, while to a stranger he appeared inside the world... He can appear to be angry, excited...'

'And yet inside he is watching the world from outside. Yes... I too have seen him angry with me, when inside he is no more angry than with the rain for wetting his head. He will go through the outward play, because he knows it is the only way he can engage with you. To encourage you he may congratulate you, comparing you flatteringly to others, while inside he judges you no more deserving of praise for your merit over other men, than a large rock for its size over a pebble. To improve you he may criticise your faults, even admonish you with passion, while underneath he blames you for them no more than he would a pebble for not being a rock. Yes, when he chooses, the mouse is able from within the world of men to live outside it.'

'But he can *feel* all these emotions when he is out of yoga...'

'Of course. And even in this yoga he still has many desires... Though he has other yogas with much less... We used to practise together sometimes, because of the danger of falling out of the world altogether. He could take his yoga down very gradually. Not like Drona, who was in danger of going down too deep. Charvaka could go down as deep as it is possible to go, and still return. There was almost no desire left in him. He had no complaint with the world. There was almost no change in the world which he would have preferred to any other. There was almost no need for him to breathe, since he had no complaint with a world in which he did not breathe. I believe I could have cut his limbs off one by one, and he would not have responded. But still I was able to bring him back. There was a small grain of desire left in him. He would say, while there is life, there is desire. And yet with Drona, I could never let him get as deep as this, or he would never have returned.'

'Rama, what about when Charvaka was tortured. He never speaks to me about it. But from the little he has said, it doesn't sound to me as though he was in this deep yoga.'

'No, you are right. He certainly still had desire.'

'Do you mean that it was a desire to conquer his fear that made him resist the pain?'

'No. That is perhaps what a kshatriya might have done. They are well-trained in such shallow yogas. But if the mouse had really wished to pursue heroic self-control, he would have recanted. He would have appeared a weak and cowardly fool. The physical pain he could ignore like passing clouds. Of death itself he thought no more than of the shadows which his sandals cast beneath him. So what greater challenge for him than to recant, to bear the heat of such a brand when he could brave the fire he would have seemed to fear?'

Parashu was walking on Karna's right, where the track was slightly lower. Karna appeared to be deep in thought, staring to his left up the slope, at the goats they had caught up with. He turned to the rishi as if to speak, but then changed his mind, and returned his gaze towards the goats. The animals were edging cautiously up the slope as the two men approached. To the right of the track the smooth grass slope was interspersed with trees.

'Tell me, Karna, why do you think the mouse did not recant? There was no one else involved who would have suffered. They did not ask him to incriminate anyone else... What was to be gained by such stubbornness?... The barbed eyes of scorn he could have outstared as if they were mocking faces painted on a palm leaf, whose expressions leap with life off the page, and yet have no contempt behind them. He could have sounded the words his torturers desired, as if he were humouring a parrot with a pretty phrase. If he had wished, the mouse could have made the world and its opinion melt away. So why didn't he recant?'

'Rama, he would not abandon truth.'

'Truth? Charvaka is prepared to lie as well as any man.'

'He never explained to me, rama. But I don't think he would abandon truth. Lying is not the same as abandoning truth.'

'No... I think you are right, Karna. He did not want to leave truth itself undefended. The mouse is prepared to forsake and deceive men, but not to forsake truth itself. Especially not when he was asked to forsake truths of nature. To the petty facts of men he can be quite inconstant; but never to the facts of nature. He is Kali's slave, after all...'

'Isn't it also possible that he wanted to influence those who tortured him?'

'That is true also. Yes, the mouse has a strange dharma. One moment he can ignore all the people in the world; at other times he tries to engage with them, to change them. Yes, the mouse has a strange dharma...' Parashu chuckled softly to himself. 'And the desire for dharma is only one desire among many, is it not? The desire for truth just another... What is so good about them?'

Without interrupting his step, Karna turned to catch the rishi's eyes. Parashu seemed to look right through him. Further up the slope to Karna's left, the goats also stared down. He heard the flap of pigeons behind him, and turned sharply to see them alight on a tree. Karna saw, far beneath them, where the grass levelled out at the bottom of the valley, two tigers. They were lying on their sides. Near them, with its rump eaten away, was the body of a large deer.

'Karna, some water please...'

Karna returned his attention to the rishi, and passed him the bladder.

'So, rama, do you think Charvaka was a fool, not to recant?'

'The line between folly and wisdom is drawn up by fools. But if the mouse is a fool, he is a most delightful fool.' Parashu took a sip of water and wiped his mouth. 'Most men wish to bathe in the regard of other men...' He returned the bladder to Karna. 'Some men wish to bathe in the regard of their gods. It is only a very few who act for their own approval. The mouse is one of these. But tell me, Karna, what is so good about desiring the admiration of one's future self? Is it better to strive to please oneself than to please others?'

'Rama, that sounds the sort of question best left to a brahmana. Or even better, a rishi.'

Parashu chuckled. 'I try not to step onto such battlefields of folly, where men struggle to enlarge themselves, yet fancy that they plead for causes larger than themselves.'

Ahead of them the track became obscured, as the trees which interrupted the grass began to clump together, heralding the denser wood beyond. The sun was reaching the end of its journey, and the shadows were growing around them. Karna looked back fleetingly at the tigers. One of them flicked its tail, raised its head, and yawned.

'You are preoccupied, Karna. Yet you are afraid neither of me nor of the tigers.'

'Almost at this point, rama, on my way to Mahendra, I came across a naked old man —'

The rishi interrupted Karna with a guffaw.

'You are worried about *him*?' Parashu arched his eyebrows. 'Once upon a time,' continued Parashu, 'many years ago, there lived a most accomplished, handsome and dignified young boy. His father was a great rishi, Parashara. His mother was the wise and beautiful Satyavati. When his mother later fell in love with the illustrious King Shantanu, intending to marry the king, this young boy grew troubled and depressed. He became jealous of another young man, Bhishma, not much older than himself, who was Shantanu's son by the king's first wife. Bhishma was thus the heir to the Bharata throne. Our boy, the rishi's son, feared that Bhishma, becoming his stepbrother, would grow to hate him as a possible rival, and perhaps have him killed. He went to see his father the rishi for advice.

'"My son, I see you covet the Bharata throne. I see you are already jealous of the sons which your mother is likely to have by her future husband, King Shantanu."

'"Yes, father."

'"Listen to me. If you do as I say, you will be offered the Bharata kingdom."

'"Tell me what I must do, father."

'"It will not be easy, son. But I wager you that if you follow the course I recommend, you will have the kingdom in your grasp."

'"What must I do, father?"

'"For fifteen years, my son, you must pretend to be mad. If you succeed, then in the sixteenth year you will be offered the kingdom."

'The boy told his father that he had no idea how to appear mad.

'"Father, how can I study madness when madness defies study? How can I learn to behave like one who cannot learn to behave?"

'"It is really very easy, son. You see, there are thought to be two kinds of madness. In the first kind, the mad person does not share the same world as other people. And in the second, he does not share the same desires as other people. It is not easy to create a whole world of your own, son, so I advise you instead to choose the second sort. It has the added advantage, while being equally distinctive, of not really being madness at all. For it is really remarkably common — people just learn to hide it very well: they learn what desires they are *supposed* to have, and they take it from there. The madness is only when you stop hiding it. Now, the easiest way to achieve the desired effect, in this case, is just not to hide it. Just abandon all your fears — for it is fear which makes us hide. Then, my son, in no time at all, people will think you are quite mad!"

'The boy soon learned to abandon his fear of other people, and even his fear of the future. He ceased to care about his clothes and his appearance. He would wander around naked in public. He would urinate and defecate where he stood. He would take people's food and belongings without asking. Often people would drive him away from their villages, and he would live in the wild among the animals.

'It is a strange thing that this boy — he was a young man by this time — was such a great storyteller in those days. He would stand up anywhere, in a village square, in a small alley, and start a story, talking to himself; and people would gather round to listen. Occasionally people would come across him by chance in the middle of a country road, telling himself a story, or talking to birds or animals.

'Charvaka and I would often go to listen to him. The two of us, and just a very few others, were even able to talk to him: we suspected the truth of his condition, but kept it a secret. He even talked to Bhishma. By that time, of course, Bhishma had already, and for other reasons, vowed away his right to the Bharata kingdom; but Bhishma still felt concerned, fearing that his father's marriage to Satyavati, and the birth of their two sons, had deranged his young stepbrother.

'By the time the fifteenth year was up, Parashara had died, and no one knew where his son could be found. Bhishma searched for him far and wide, and eventually traced him. By which time both King Shantanu and Satyavati's two sons by the king had all three died. Bhishma offered his stepbrother the Bharata throne.

'"Lord Bhishma," his stepbrother replied, "even kings have fears. I am freer than any king."

'"At least come and live with us at the Bharata court — you have lived alone for so many years!"

'"Lord Bhishma, when I am alone I am no more alone than when I am drunk with the illusion of company. Even now, as I talk with you, I am alone with my illusion. If, somewhere, there really is a Bhishma, who is sharing my dream, no matter. I cannot, in any case, touch his soul. I can only see his mask in my dream."

'That seems to have been the last time anything intelligible was heard to issue from his lips. He may listen to you, though it may not appear that he is doing so; and he may respond with action — he has even stayed with me in Mahendra. But he will not speak. At any rate, as you see, he refused Bhishma's offer. Though he was prevailed upon to couple with Amba's sisters, Ambika and Ambalika. I am told that he did not break his silence even then. It was thus that he fathered King Dhrita-rashtra and the late King Pandu.'

'So that old man was Vyasa...'

'Old? He is younger than I am, Karna.'

'He looked at me, but I don't think he saw me.'

'Oh, he did. It was Vyasa who warned me you were coming. He sent me a pigeon. Even in the old days, when he was pretending to be mad, even then he was often surrounded by pigeons. People even thought his madness was caused by eating the flesh of doves.'

'Has he lived all these years on the mountain slopes?'

'Vyasa comes and goes. From outside the world of men he lives within it. His yoga is as remarkable as Charvaka's. He has been all over the mountain. Well, Karna, the sun is sinking. It is time to find a quiet place where you can climb your mountain. Remember, do not venture too near the top, unless you hear the tiger's hunger.'

Parashu led Karna off the track into a clump. The rishi found a comfortable spot, beneath a gnarled old tree. Karna noticed claw marks on the trunk and lower branches, and smelt the scent of tiger clinging to the wood.

'Drink your fill of water, then take off your clothes and sit down here at the bottom of the tree. You may rest your back against the trunk if you wish, though it is better if you hold your back up yourself.'

After he had drunk from the water bladder, Karna placed it by the tree with his bearskin coat. He took off his shirt.

'Your dhoti too,' advised the rishi. 'Otherwise you may wet it.'

'That would be most unpleasant for the tiger,' said Karna. He removed his dhoti, cleared away the twigs, and sat down naked on the ground. He crossed his legs neatly.

'Rama, who is Amba?'

'Not now, Karna.'

Parashu knelt down beside him. The rays of the setting sun glanced through the leaves and branches in a silent shower, lighting up Karna's chest.

'Karna...' The rishi noticed Karna's chest. 'How did you get those scars?'

Five very faint scars were just visible, three on Karna's chest, two on his left arm.

'You received these all at one time,' observed Parashu. 'Your opponent was a very fine ratha indeed, to pierce your defences with five such well placed arrows. Either that, or you are a very poor ratha indeed.'

'At the time I was distracted, rama.'

Parashu hissed. 'Well, do not be distracted tonight, Karna.' The rishi waited for Karna to settle. Then he crouched beside Karna, and put his hand gently on Karna's arm, holding it there. He spoke in a gentle whisper.

'Close your eyes now. It will get very cold outside you, Karna. Do not worry if your body begins to shake. Your mind will stay still. It will ignore your trembling body as it will ignore the shivering leaves above you. Though the world may fall about your head and crush your body, you will not yet rise from yoga. Though you may sit here for days, without food or drink, you will not yet rise from yoga. Though you may starve to death, you will not yet rise from yoga. Only if you hear your name whispered in your ear, only then will you rise from yoga. Your name is Karna.'

Gradually every smell, every sound, every breath of air on his skin, every curve and corner of his body, melted all into one stream, to ripple outside him like a river lapping against the smooth pebble of his soul.

When the rishi eventually withdrew his hand and left him, Karna was aware only of a shadow which dissolved into the stream and disappeared into nothing.

•

'Palmira, it's obvious he isn't going to die!'

'Oh yes?'

'You've only been going a few days.'

'You said the story would take a lot more than a week.'

'Ah, yes, but after Karna dies I go back and tell the story of how he came to be born.'

'What?'

'I don't think so, Palmira.'

'Don't say that — she'll kill him just to spite us!'

The boys had been sitting opposite Palmira; but while they were speaking they had sidled round and rearranged their cushions against the west wall.

'Yes... I might just do that,' said Palmira. 'In fact, that's a rather promising idea. It was getting a little tedious, wasn't it. A nice clean end, bones licked white by tigers... Yes, that would certainly put an end to those interminable conversations with Parashu-rama. And then we could move on to the really exciting part about Surya leaving a copy of himself to shine in the sky, while he descends from the heavens... Eh?'

'We found the conversations rather interesting, Palmira,' said the second Henry politely. 'Didn't we, Henry?'

'Yes, they were very interesting...'

For a moment there was an awkward silence as Palmira stared at them.

'Oh, Palmira, you know your friend Vyasa, not the one in the story... Did he have good yoga?'

'Much too good, I'm afraid, Henry. Unfortunately he shared the view of Socrates, that to need nothing is divine, and that the less a man needs, the closer he approaches to divinity. But then, of course, Socrates also had good yoga.'

'Socrates? But he was a Greek.'

'So?'

'Yoga's not a Greek word.'

'Neither is the Sanskrit for speech. Nevertheless Socrates was able to speak.'

'Yes, but...'

'Remember, boys, beneath the different skins of language we are all as similar as we are different under the same skin.'

'What?'

'Yes, rama.'

'Oh — yes, rama!'

The boys saw the amusement on Palmira's face begin to darken.

'If you think this is the way to curb the hunger of the tigers —'

'Palmira! I know who Vyasa reminds me of, the Vyasa in the story — that other Greek man...'

'You know... the one who lived like a dog...'

'You mean Diogenes?'

'That's it. He was... he was a... something...'

'You mean he had an epithet? Diogenes the cynic.'

'Didn't he live in a kennel?'

'A barrel. He lived in a large earthenware jar. You know that he was a friend of Socrates, before he moved into his jar. Yes, he seemed unimpressed by the customs and niceties of normal society. In spite of his reputed rudeness, he was able to survive very well by begging.'

'Didn't he meet Alexander the Great?'

'Yes, he did. But I must have told you about that before?'

'No, Palmira.'

'Definitely not. How did he come to meet Alexander?'

'Are you sure I haven't told you before? This won't help to revive Karna, you know... Well... This was after he had moved from his jar... In fact, I believe he was sold as a slave to someone in Corinth. His new master was evidently impressed by the fact that Diogenes did not seem to be enslaved by the desires and fears which govern most people. In any case, he could never have beaten or starved Diogenes into submission, so there was nothing much else he could do with his slave: he appointed him as tutor to his children, and made him a free man again. It was there in Corinth that Alexander visited him.'

'Why should Alexander want to visit him?'

'The powers of self-control that Diogenes possessed, his courage and outspokenness had become very well known throughout the Hellenic world. So, one sunny day, when Alexander was passing through Corinth, he decided to visit him.

'"I am the most powerful man living in this world," said the mighty Alexander as he stood, his head as usual leaning wryly to his left, before Diogenes. "If there is any way in which I can oblige you, anything which is humanly possible for me to grant you, I will do it for you!"

'"Alexander," replied Diogenes, "you could perhaps oblige me by not standing in my light."

'Alexander immediately moved aside, letting the sun shine on the face of Diogenes. After a moment's thought, Alexander said:

'"If I were not Alexander, I should wish to be Diogenes!"'

'Why should Alexander want to be Diogenes?' asked the first Henry.

'Because Alexander understood what Diogenes had meant. You see, Alexander had always been dominated by an insatiable need to overshadow all those who were around him. As he himself had implied, there were more people under his power than under any other person living. But Diogenes knew that the most difficult thing for Alexander to accomplish was to humble himself before Diogenes, not to eclipse him as he did all other men. So, if Alexander were not Alexander, so powerful that he could achieve happiness by fulfilling all his desires, he would rather be Diogenes, so powerful that he could achieve happiness by conquering all desire.'

'But Palmira, it doesn't sound as though Diogenes *had* conquered all of his desires.'

'No,' agreed the second Henry, 'he seemed to want to impress Alexander. And us. I mean, look how famous he's become because of it. Didn't Alexander think of that?'

'I don't know, Henry. At the time it looks as though Alexander chose to overlook that interpretation. Perhaps he was just relieved that Diogenes hadn't asked for the command of the entire Greek army...'

'Palmira, I don't think your Vyasa would have even noticed Alexander blocking his light, let alone spoken to him.'

'Probably not, Henry. And so we wouldn't have heard of him...'

'Palmira, what exactly is a cynic?'

'Well, originally it came from a Greek word meaning dog-like. But now a cynic has come to mean someone who, when he has any doubt, denies the rest of humanity the benefit of it.'

'Yes, rama.'

'Yes, rama!'

'I think, boys, it's time to see what's left of Karna's bones.'

'But Palmira, we —'

'Shut up, boys! You don't deserve the benefit of anything.'

Palmira picked a date from a bowl on her table. She chewed it slowly. She took the stone out of her mouth, and gave it an extra lick to pick it clean.

'Ah, yes!... Just like Karna's bones...'

•

29 The field of the brahmanas

Something briefly disturbed. A bubble of time swelled up out of nothing, and then burst, ceasing.

'It *is* you...'

The stream fluttered and splashed.

'Karna...'

The idle flickering of fish turned suddenly into a monstrous shoal, an outline, curves, corners...

'Karna!'

The sound glided off the touch on his neck. He opened his eyes.

'*Draupadi!*'

'No, it's not Draupadi... Sorry.'

Karna stared at the face. Now that he saw that it was not Draupadi, he could no longer see Draupadi in the face; nor any longer did he want to see Draupadi there.

'Where am I?'

The eyes stared straight back into his. The hand was still touching his neck.

'Why, you are in heaven, of course.'

'In heaven?'

'Yes. You are dead. You were eaten by a tiger. Don't you remember?'

Karna kept staring into the eyes. They warmed. They smiled. They glowed. The eyes suddenly looked down at Karna's body.

Karna followed them.

'But... I have my body still. I seem to have... desire again. Do they not say that in heaven there are no desires?'

'Well, in that case perhaps you're not quite in heaven yet. Anyway... oh yes... I see that you have quite fully risen from your yoga.'

Karna noticed an acrid smell, and as his eyes began to take in his surroundings, he caught sight of the striped tail behind her.

'A tiger!'

'Very good, very good! Well... now that you have somewhat extended the body *and* the mind, perhaps you should try to stretch the legs. But gently, very gently.'

With her help he began slowly to uncross his legs.

'I'm surprised the tiger did not wake you, Karna.'

'It did not call my name.' Karna peered round her, at the dead tiger. He noticed her quiver of arrows.

'Why did you shoot it?' he asked. 'Am I worth more than this tiger?'

'Not in the eyes of Surya, perhaps. But I'm not Surya.'

'Who are you?'

'I am Princess Shikhandini. But —'

'Did Parashu-rama ask you to shoot the tiger?'

Her eyes rounded very slightly.

'Of course. You didn't think he would walk all that way and back just to lose a pupil, did you?'

'I'm not sure that I quite count yet as a pupil... So, he sacrificed this poor animal for my education?'

'He gave me careful instructions to wait till the last possible moment, in case the tiger did not find you sufficiently appetising. If I thought the tiger was about to spring at you, or tear you, or otherwise damage your divine body, I was instructed to kill it. You should be more grateful, Karna. It was extremely boring staying up all night and half the day just in case a tiger came near you. Several times I nearly set off back to Mahendra. I could have made some excuse about the manner of your death. However... it's not so easy for me to lie to Parashu. I also am his pupil.'

Seeing Karna look round by the tree, she reached over and passed him the water bladder. The water was warm and rather stale.

'Poor animal,' he said, after putting down the bladder. 'If I had known it would be sacrificed —'

'What about the elephants at Kampilya, then? And the soldiers and the guards who died?'

'Who *are* you?'

'I've already told you my name, but you seemed more interested in this tiger. What about those poor soldiers that were killed, yours and ours, when you attacked us?'

'They were people, they had more choice. The tiger —'

'Karna, we see choice where and when we choose to.'

Karna looked down at his legs and tried to straighten them along the ground.

'I'm sorry I interrupted you, Shikhandini... Are you —'

'Yes, I'm Draupadi's sister. Most people call me Shikhandi. I am the daughter of King Drupada.' She passed her hand over the faint scars on his chest and arm. 'First you, and then that prancing fool Arjuna and his brothers...' She sighed, measuring the space between the scars with her fingers. 'Just think, if I had aimed more ruthlessly, I wouldn't have had to bother staying up all last night. Pity that you didn't all kill each other the next time you visited my city, at my idiot sister's swayamwara! I wasn't sure it was you until I came close just now. There are not many people called Karna, but...'

She helped Karna get to his feet.

277

'Shikhandi, how is it that Parashu —'

'Because I could not ask Parashu about you. Not without telling him too much about the Karna *I* had come across. The suta. The suta who shed his golden armour. You were in the guise of a brahmana, so I didn't want to give you away... Parashu doesn't appear to have heard of you.'

'I think it's just appearance, Shikhandi. He certainly knows now. But thank you... How is it that he teaches you?'

Shikhandi grinned. 'You mean because I'm a kshatriya, or because I am a woman?'

Karna did not reply, but bent down slowly to stretch the back of his thighs.

'He teaches this kshatriya,' said Shikhandi, 'because she is a woman. I let him do what he likes with my body in exchange for some refinements to my archery.'

Karna's face softened into a smile. 'You are lying, Shikhandi.'

'What makes you think I'm lying? Do you think I should not do such things? Do you wish that I didn't?'

'I was taught by a rishi from an early age to try to distinguish what I wish from what I see. I merely see that you are lying.'

Karna limped slowly to pick up his dhoti from beside the tree.

'I suppose you're right,' admitted Shikhandi. 'I was lying. Well, half-lying. It's perfectly true that I let him do what he likes with my body...' She glanced at Karna's face. 'But all he seems to like doing with it is sending it away to stay up all night and peer in the dark at naked young men sitting under trees. In exchange, he does indeed improve my skills with the bow... There is one other thing which I have promised to do for him, which apparently only a woman can do — oh dear!' she exclaimed painfully, at the sight of Karna struggling with his dhoti. 'Excuse me while I slip into yoga...' She took a deep breath. 'You know, Karna, I was not even permitted to speak to you... except to rouse you... from yoga.'

'What is it you are doing now, then?'

'I'm not permitted to obey rama *all* the time.'

Karna picked up his shirt. 'Is this all part of Parashu's plan to develop my education?'

She did not reply. Karna put his coat on. 'Do we go back now?'

Again she did not reply, but collected her bow, which she had placed on the ground near the dead tiger, and withdrew the single arrow which had killed the beast. She wiped it clean and returned it to her quiver.

◊

For a long time they walked in silence. Karna needed to drink frequently from the water bladder, and he stopped occasionally to pick nuts and berries from the trees and bushes.

'Shikhandi, you said there was something else... Something else you promised to do for Parashu...'

'Oh yes... A hermit called Amba came to see me in Kampilya. She'd heard of my skill with the bow. She said that if I mentioned to Parashu-rama a promise which he had previously made to her, he would take me on as a pupil. She explained that Parashu had once undertaken a task on her behalf, which he had been unable to carry out. But that I may be able to... that the fact that I was a woman might help me to succeed where Parashu had failed.'

'And you agreed, without knowing what it was you had to do?'

'No. I said I might agree to do it if she told me what it was. But she wouldn't tell me. So, when I arrived here, I explained to Parashu that I would be prepared to consider this... task, whatever it is. But of course I couldn't promise to do something of which I did not yet know the name or nature. When the time is right, apparently, he will tell me. And then I can choose to do it or not.'

'And you choose to think you'll have a choice, then? Where is Amba now?'

'She died soon after I agreed to go to Mahendra. Do you know anything about her, Karna?'

'Very little. I have heard her name mentioned. She is, was, the sister of Ambika and Ambalika.'

'Who are they?'

'They were the mothers of King Pandu and King Dhrita. They were widowed — Shantanu's son had been their husband, but he'd died leaving them childless. Vyasa is the father of their sons. Have you seen Vyasa?'

'No, never, but it's rumoured that he lives near here.'

'Yes, he does — I've seen him... Shikhandi, have you also waited for the tiger?'

'Of course. Like you, I didn't realise that someone would be protecting me. In my case it was Parashu himself. I'm obviously more important than you. You didn't know, did you?'

'I knew that someone was following us. It had occurred to me that whoever it was might try to kill me, should no tiger be up to the task.'

'Would you have just let yourself be killed?'

'I'm not sure, Shikhandi. I didn't start out with the intention of letting myself be killed. And I tried to stay alert enough so that I would notice a human approaching —'

'Ah, that must be why you didn't detect my divine presence —'

'— as well as a tiger,' he added, ignoring her interruption. 'But I had stopped thinking about life or death. I don't think it was just the yoga... Somehow, I felt in no danger.'

'Karna... Why are you here?'

'For the same reason as you are.'

'No, Karna. I'm not pretending to be a brahmana in order to... to what? You don't need to improve your skill with the bow. Though I have to say that your yoga still leaves something to be desired.'

'How do you know? About my skill with the bow?'

'I've seen you! You're already faster and more accurate even than Parashu. Though I don't think he can have any idea...'

'Perhaps I'm only faster and more accurate than you've seen Parashu to be.'

'That's possible, but I doubt it. Remember, I've seen you fully extended...' She suppressed a giggle. 'I watched you very, very closely when you were cornered. I haven't seen anything like that before or since. It really was the most pathetic exhibition. It wasn't as though my sister needed the flattery, you know. You don't seem worried that I might tell Parashu?'

'About my distraction or about my skill? No, I'm not worried, either way... I'm sorry that I didn't notice you properly, Shikhandi... You must have watched me very well to miss my heart and lungs.'

'I couldn't kill you, Karna. In spite of the number of our guards I thought you'd killed —'

'But I tried *not* to kill them —'

'I know that now. I'm amazed at how few died, though many are still not fully recovered, even now. But at the time I didn't know. What I did know was that you'd spared my father and my brother... when with just two arrows you could have killed them and been the hero of your side. You know the Pandavas must have set a trap for you.'

'Not the Pandavas. Yudhi would never... It must have been Drona's idea.'

A little while later, Shikhandi repeated her question.

'Karna, why are you here? You don't need to improve your skill.'

'Perhaps I don't need to, but I'm sure I can. But you're right, there is something else... I'm sorry Shikhandi, it's something I can't tell you about.'

'Like your armour?'

'That's a mystery even to me. I don't know where that armour came from.'

'Didn't your parents tell you? They didn't know? One thing is certain, Karna...'

'What's that?'

'The rumour can't be true... that you're the son of a god, as the Pandava princes are supposed to be.'

'Why not?'

'Well, if you were the son of a god, you would expect him to have endowed you with qualities if not more divine at least more distinctive than mere armour... At the very least he would have made you beautiful, or intelligent, or provided you with some charm or sense of humour. I mean, what kind of a face was that you pulled at my sister at the swayamwara? Is it surprising that she turned you down? But you know, you shouldn't take her remark about you being a suta too much to heart... She would have refused you even if you'd been a kshatriya. Even, for that matter, if you'd been grinning away like you are now.'

'She would still have refused me?'

'Of course. I told her that I would kill her if she chose you. What could she do, I'm her older sister —'

'You're lying again.'

'Oh, what a clever man you are, Karna, you see right through me.'

Karna cast a sidelong glance at her. But her face grew serious.

'Karna, why did you let him get off like that?'

'You mean...'

'Yes, my wonderful brother-in-law, Arjuna. The great and glorious son of Indra.'

'What makes you —'

'Come on, Karna! I may have been required to wear a ridiculous veil, but I was permitted to open my eyes occasionally beneath it. Even my father, who was extremely busy at the time, remarked to me afterwards how you seemed to be playing with Arjuna. Remember that he and my brother also had a good look at you when you attacked Kampilya.'

'I couldn't disarm Arjuna in front of his new wife. She obviously didn't want me... I don't find pleasure where I give none.'

'Oh, Karna! I had no idea you were so romantic!' She giggled, putting her arm around his hips and squeezing him. 'But no wonder you find so little pleasure in life!'

Karna's pace faltered.

'Karna, please, where is your yoga?'

Karna sucked in a sharp breath, and his face returned to normal.

'What remarkable control you have!' she exclaimed. 'You know,' she continued, 'it would have served them both right if you *had* blown away Arjuna's bow and stormed off with my idiot sister. All three of you would have got what you deserved!'

For a while they walked in silence. Then Karna turned to her.

'Is there really a rumour that I am the son of a god?'

'Of course. When people cannot believe that a mere suta can be a hero, they turn him into a god. Don't you know the legend of Princess Kurangi? No? She fell in love with and married a chandala who heroically saved her from an elephant in musth. And of course, her saviour turned out all along to have been really the son of the god Agni. She would not have had the poor taste to want a real chandala! But Karna, everybody knows that gods don't sweat...' She ran her finger over the perspiration on Karna's brow. 'And the feet of a god don't touch the ground...' She pointed down to Karna's feet. 'And the clothes of a god never become soiled...' She flicked some dirt off Karna's bearskin. 'Just think,' she added, 'if you were a god and I married you, I would never have to clean your clothes!'

◊

By the time they got back to the narrow alleys of Mahendra it was late into the night. Karna was not sure he would be able to find his lodging in the dark, but Shikhandi seemed to know the way quite well. Karna was so tired he could hardly light his tinder for a candle. He greeted his friend the mule, for whom someone had changed the straw and replenished the water. Shikhandi kissed him lightly on the cheek and left. He slowly climbed up the steps to the loft. There was a bowl of cold rice and vegetables waiting there beside some water. When he had finished both food and water, he fell soundly asleep.

Next morning the cloaked figure of Parashu was waiting for Karna in the little square at the top. He rose to pat the mule, who had come up with Karna.

'I was hoping to have got rid of you, Karna. It seems my other pupil got the better of the tiger.'

'Have you only two pupils here, rama?'

'No, there are several brahmanas I am teaching here at present. You will meet them soon. How was it, Karna?'

'It was a terrible experience... I thought I would never make it. The tiger part was easy enough, though.'

'I see, so it was coming back with Shikhandi which tested your resources. Karna, you will not need your coat today. Nor do we need you...' The rishi slapped the mule on its haunches, and it went off by itself, no doubt to find a pleasant spot to spend the day. 'I think it's time I saw you use your bow. Fetch it, and meet me up by the rocks where the paths divide.'

Karna left his coat in the loft, picked up his bow, his gloves and two quivers, and climbed up to the crossroads above Mahendra.

This time, instead of taking the path leading round over the valley of Maya, they took the wider track going left towards the west of the mountain.

They passed several farmers leading their animals to the steep grazing. Some areas of the slopes were densely terraced, and Karna noticed the irrigation channels and the culverts which trapped and distributed rain water. Other parts of the slope were interspersed with trees and rocks, among which grazed cattle, sheep and goats. The track began to lead down gradually, and the slopes billowed and levelled into saddles which were flat enough to be ploughed. From some of these the trees had been completely cleared.

They overtook two brahmanas travelling in the same direction, who greeted Parashu warmly. And they saw several sacred homa cows. These were roaming free, to travel and graze where they wished.

Then Karna saw ahead of them a mule and cart being led off the main track by a brahmana. The cart was laden with bows, quivers and other instruments of combat. Parashu and Karna followed the cart over a ditch into a sheltered field. It was very large, and dotted regularly with trees, almost like an orchard, though the trees were much more widely spaced. A number of brahmanas were already practising. Shikhandi was there too.

Some of the brahmanas interrupted their activities when they saw the blue cloak of the rishi. Some looked with interest or suspicion at the rishi's companion, who wore neither a cloth around his head, nor a sash around his waist to match his white shirt and dhoti. But many of the brahmanas ignored the new arrivals completely, and carried on with their work.

Parashu led Karna to one of the carts laden with equipment, and instructed his newest pupil to arrange various targets which he would have to shoot at.

When they were all set up, Parashu watched Karna work first with single arrows, then with two arrows at a time. Next the rishi threw up targets for Karna to hit in flight. After watching Karna shoot repeatedly with ease two simultaneous arrows, Parashu waved to him to stop.

'What is the largest number of arrows you are comfortable with on the bowstring?'

'Four,' Karna replied. Some of the brahmanas nearby heard this, and turned from what they were doing to watch. Shikhandi joined them.

'For both height and distance?'

'Yes, rama... and spacing.'

'And spacing?' repeated the rishi. 'Come with me.'

Parashu led Karna to a far corner of the field. Some wooden stakes were embedded there in the ground; they formed a regular grid of twelve rows, nine to each row. The stakes in the front row were driven so far into the ground that their tips were only just showing. Each row stood taller than the one in front of it, the back row standing well over the height of a man.

Parashu asked Karna to stand thirty paces from the front row of this raked grid. He and another brahmana attached four painted cork rings to the tops of four of the stakes; they were chosen, it seemed, at random: two of the targets were to the left, one of these low in the front, the other in a middle row; a third target was in the centre, and the fourth ring was at the back, high on the right. The rishi had to be lifted up by another brahmana to fix this last target.

By this time all the brahmanas had stopped what they were doing and had wandered over. Shikhandi watched intently, fiddling with a cork ring in her hand.

Karna carefully placed four arrows on his bowstring. But as he began to draw the bow, Shikhandi walked briskly across to the stakes and attached the ring she was carrying to the stake furthest to the right in the second row.

'Karna,' she exclaimed, 'don't waste the rishi's time!' She looked across to Parashu and said in a quieter voice, but still quite audible to the assembled company: 'You, Parashu, are an idiot. Can't you see this boy has a problem?'

A smile flickered on the rishi's lips.

'Surely, it's not possible to do it with five?' shouted one of the brahmanas.

'Even rama can't do it with five!' cried another.

Parashu shook his head.

'I know of no one who can do it with five when all three dimensions are allowed to vary. I certainly cannot.'

Karna's face was expressionless as he regrouped five arrows onto his string, drew back the bow and released all five.

The astonished brahmanas applauded. Parashu stood silently gazing at the rings; he shook his head as Karna walked over to the targets and retrieved his arrows. Shikhandi went off to resume her practice.

'Princess Shikhandini!' cried Parashu. She turned back and approached the rishi with an innocent smile.

'Shikhandi, how did you know he could do this?'

'I didn't know for certain. But I could see from thirty paces that he was being modest. Don't you see, he didn't want to show up an old fool like you...'

Karna had joined them, and was waiting, still with a blank expression on his face.

'I think', continued Shikhandi, looking round at him, 'we must teach him to show off with better grace than this. Karna,' addressing him now in a slightly sterner tone, 'haven't you been taught to smile when you're in yoga? It's the polite thing to do when there are other people around. It stops us feeling uncomfortable. *Other people.* You know what they are?'

As she returned to her practice, she added, digging Karna in the ribs with the horn of her bow, 'Arrogance and Modesty fuse very ill as fellows-in-flesh.'

Parashu stood for a long while, with his eyes almost closed, thinking. Then he took off his cloak, strapped on two quivers, and picked two wooden bows. At the sight of the rishi removing his cloak, the brahmanas, who had dispersed, began to gather round again. Parashu perched the spare bow over his left shoulder, and tucked two bowstrings into the white sash at his waist.

'Karna, fill up your quivers, and pick up a spare bow — you may need it.'

Karna did as he was told.

'Now,' said the rishi, 'I want you to try to disarm me. By all means break my bowstring or my bow, or cut off my quivers. But I ask you to avoid injuring me. Similarly, I will avoid piercing your flesh.'

Parashu offered Karna a face guard, but he declined to use it, following the rishi's example. The audience began to settle on the ground.

'I must ask you one other thing,' added the rishi. 'You must extend yourself fully. I cannot help you unless you try your utmost. Do you understand me?'

'Yes, rama.' Karna made ready a spare bowstring in each of his quivers.

'You must not play with me, Karna.'

'I will be absolutely ruthless, rama.' Karna looked over at the princess and the brahmanas and smiled at them, widening his cheeks especially for Shikhandi.

'Shikhandi, start us off, will you,' said Parashu.

Within a few seconds of her shout, Karna had lost one of his two quivers and his bowstring was broken. But both of Parashu's quivers and their contents were scattered on the ground with the remains of half his bow. By the time the rishi had let the other half of his bow drop uselessly from his grasp, Karna had restrung his, and was ready, aiming with four more arrows.

While the audience applauded, Parashu stood deep in thought amidst the remains of his weapons. Shikhandi went over to the rishi and put her arm round his shoulders.

'There, there, never mind, rama. At least you managed to get one of his quivers.'

After a few moments Parashu walked slowly over to Karna and led him away from the excited brahmanas. He sat down on the ground, and Karna joined him.

'Karna,' began the rishi, 'your action is not elegant — it is if anything more like Bhishma's than Drona's. It *was* Drona who taught you?'

'Yes. Though I had been taught by a kshatriya in Varanasi before Drona. And I taught myself a lot.'

'But Drona went through the four stages with you?'

'Yes. We were taught to keep our bows relaxed and unstrung. The first action is stringing the bow, *a-tan*; the second action is fetching the arrows from the quiver to the string, *prati-dha*. Then there is the bending of the bow, *a-yam*.

Finally, releasing the arrow, *as*. Of course, when the bow is already strung, we have just three.'

'And he taught you at first to shoot as fast as you can say the words?'

'Yes. But most of us soon left the words behind, so that we could shoot as fast as thought, not as slow as language. Why do you ask me all this, rama? Every boy — every kshatriya boy, knows all this.'

'I ask you because you shoot so fast that I cannot discern in your action any trace of the stages. I thought perhaps that you had been taught in another way.'

'No, I don't think so, rama. It's just that language is so slow compared to thought.'

'Yes... Indeed... That is why animals are so fast... Unencumbered by language... they are not weighed down by words... The monkey, as it darts from tree to tree, choosing branches like lightning, thinks much faster than language. But you are right, of course, we also do this. Shakuni — perhaps you know him — when he is playing a game of dice at speed, he leaves language far behind. Similarly, the ratha must move and think faster than words. What is it Charvaka says?'

'Many think only to speak. Few think.'

'Ah, yes... Yes... And, indeed, does not an infant already need to think to learn to speak? Of course, we only watch ourselves think when we have the luxury of time... when, since we have the time, we think slowly enough to dress our thoughts in language, fitting them for others, making them pretty and presentable. But even as we dress the thoughts in language, we leave language far behind. For we cannot also dress the dresser. And as you are listening to me now, understanding my words, you also leave language far behind, for you cannot also undress the servant who undresses... Does not the mouse say something else on this?'

'We think more than we think —'

'— and we speak much less! Ah yes... Men are too proud of their languages. They stare at them in wonder, as though language were their master, not their servant. By putting his own creations on a pedestal, man exalts also himself... But as I was saying, Karna, your action goes beyond what I can see, and therefore beyond what I can speak of... However... Your stance is perhaps a little acute for your needs. You could afford to stand a little more square on to your opponent. You would present a larger target, it is true, but on the other hand you would be more mobile. But I must wait to see you against three or four of us. Your eyes and hands are the best I have seen. Bhishma, the old boar, comes — I should say, came — close. He of course fetches from his quiver across his body.'

'Is that not a disadvantage?'

'There is a disadvantage against a single opponent, certainly. But facing three or four spread around you, it means that his body moves more as he crosses for his arrows. Your body, on the other hand, is almost stationary while you are shooting. You would present a narrow target to one or two of your opponents, but a large stationary one to the rest.' The rishi paused, and then continued, shaking his head. 'But even in our prime, neither Bhishma nor I were as fast as you. Though I was, and still am, very accurate. At any rate, perhaps you can work on your stance. And there may be one or two other things you can improve. What are you like in the dark?'

'I would like to improve that, rama. I would like to improve my hearing.'

'Good, good. And of course, it is not only in the dark that one cannot see... I wonder... Perhaps your eyes and hands are so good you may be relying on them too much. Let me see...'

The rishi looked into Karna's remaining quiver; it was half-empty; his other quiver was still lying where it had fallen. Parashu counted Karna's remaining arrows, and then rose to his feet.

'Take up your bow again but do not refill your quiver.'

Parashu picked up a quiver for himself and counted in the same number of arrows as were left in Karna's. He selected another two bows.

'Try to disarm me as before.' Parashu waved to Shikhandi to come to start them off again. Again the brahmanas gathered round excitedly, noticing the single quivers.

This time Karna did not have his bowstring cut. Nor did he lose his quiver. He was hardly touched, in fact. Parashu, on the other hand, lost his quiver, and his first bow was broken as before. He did have one arrow left in his hand, though; and as he slowly took the second bow off his shoulder, Karna could only stand there with a smile, for he had run out of arrows entirely.

The brahmanas all applauded; but Shikhandi glared coldly at Karna.

'You see, Karna,' said the rishi, carefully placing his last arrow onto his bowstring, 'sometimes speed only hastens your appointment with death. You see how a man's strength can become his weakness; how my weakness, by luring you to exploit it, became my strength.'

The rishi lowered his bow and approached Karna.

'You are relying too much on your speed. You are not using your arrows as efficiently as you should be, given your great accuracy. You are still shooting at what you see in the world, and not at what you see in your mind.'

The rishi picked up a fresh quiver. He led Karna by the arm right away from the brahmanas, towards the back of the field, where the ground began to rise up as it merged with the background slope of the mountain side. He stopped by the gnarled and pitted trunk of a dead tree, looked around on the ground, and picked up a stone which fitted neatly into his palm.

'The cobra', said Parashu, squeezing the stone in his hand, 'always strikes in the dark, however light it is. Its head is like an arrow — like most arrows, at any rate; for, once it has started on its strike, it cannot change its course, even if the target moves. That is why the mongoose usually avoids being struck; it is quick to see the snake launch its head, and knows the snake cannot turn to follow as he moves aside. But if the cobra could only guess to where the mongoose will try to dodge, it could aim its strike there. But the cobra cannot read the mongoose. It is the mongoose who reads the cobra. Do you understand me, Karna?'

'Yes, rama.'

'Has not Charvaka told you, the world is there to be read, not merely to be shot at?'

'Probably, rama.'

'You must learn to read movement from both sight and sound. But first you must read your own movement. Let me show you a little trick. Perhaps Drona has shown this to you — though he was never very good at it. He may have improved over the years.'

Parashu dropped the stone he had been playing with and emptied his quiver; he picked five arrows and placed just one of them on his bowstring. The other four he left waiting in his quiver.

'I'm using fresh wooden arrows, that split easily.'

He stood fifteen paces from the dead tree. 'Take my sash and blindfold me, Karna.'

When Karna had applied the blindfold, Parashu shot the first arrow into the tree. He then shot successive arrows from his quiver, each one splitting the previous arrow. The rishi took off his blindfold and looked at his pupil.

'I have never tried that, rama.'

'A maha-ratha should know the consequences of his actions. From the position of his limbs, he should know where his arrows will go. A mere ratha will concentrate on his target, will aim at something outside his body, outside his mind. The maha-ratha can aim within himself, at a condition of his body; he can fix his mind on the means, not on the end. Do you think that you can do this, Karna?'

'I think I should be able to. I can do it with my eyes open, and, after all, the target isn't moving...'

'Try it. Remember, choose young, fresh arrows — wait a moment...' Parashu called Shikhandi over. She ran across to them.

'Great rama,' she exclaimed unctuously, 'your desire is my imperative...'

The rishi took her aside for a moment and spoke softly, out of Karna's hearing.

'Shikhandi, I am not reading Karna well today. I would like you to tell me afterwards if he misses on purpose... Do you understand?'

'Yes,' she giggled, 'and if he doesn't miss, would you like to know if that also is deliberate?'

Karna repeated Parashu's trick perfectly.

'You have never done that before?' asked the rishi.

'No, rama, not with a blindfold.'

'You have a strange and rare skill, Karna.'

'Rama, I doubt I could do it at thirty paces. I will practise at longer distances.'

'You must also practise while turning. Choose three widely spaced targets, and try to split your arrows on each one — all without taking your blindfold off... Not now!'

'I will make sure he does it later, rama,' said Shikhandi. The rishi's lips curled slightly in amusement.

'Thank you, princess. Your generosity to the brahmana caste will surely be rewarded in a later life.' He turned to Karna. 'But you not only have to read your own movements, you have also to read the movements of other people, of other things.'

The rishi looked for the stone which he had dropped earlier. When he found it he threw it up in a slow arc, watching it all the way until it hit the ground.

'Karna, I want you to throw that stone as I have just done. I will stand here with my eyes closed. You must give me three shouts: *Open... Close... Shoot.* On the first shout I will open my eyes, and I will take in the movement — not just the stone, but the future of the stone. On the second shout I will close my eyes, and follow the stone only in my mind. On the third shout, with my eyes still closed, I will release my arrow.'

Karna threw the stone up several times, sometimes throwing it high, sometimes over a distance; sometimes he would leave Parashu waiting with his eyes closed until the stone had almost touched the ground. The rishi missed on only two occasions.

Parashu noticed the excitement in Karna's eyes.

'Can you do this, Karna?'

'I don't think so, rama... But it's so obvious, so simple... Yet I've never thought of trying it. Why didn't Drona show us?'

'Because Drona was never very good at it. Try it now.'

Parashu threw the stone several times for Karna, while Shikhandi sat and watched. Karna was almost as surprised as the rishi that he could hit the stone, every time.

While Parashu stood rooted to the spot, Karna sat down beside Shikhandi.

'It's so obvious. I can understand the stone... It's in my mind... How can I have not realised before? I've been trying to shoot my targets where they are, before they have time to move... not where they will be.'

'I don't think that's true, Karna,' said Shikhandi, speaking quite softly so that Parashu could not hear. 'You've probably just not realised at the time what you've been doing. I think you anticipate your opponent's movement without even realising you're doing it. In fact, I'm sure of it. These gurus are very good at teaching you to notice what you can already do. And noticing it for the first time, you think you've only just been taught the skill. Karna...' She lowered her voice almost to a whisper. 'Just now, when you fought Parashu the second time, with half quivers, did you lose on purpose?'

'I think he was right,' said Karna. 'I did use too many arrows the first time. The principle was correct, Shikhandi. Speed has its cost. I admit that I realised why he made me use a light quiver.' He saw the anger in her eyes. 'You're angry because I didn't try? Because I didn't extend myself to my utmost? Shikhandi, I did. I did what I was asked to do: I was trying my utmost. And I succeeded. I was trying to deceive him. Previously, I've failed. Today I think I succeeded. Even he should be pleased at my improvement.'

Parashu approached them.

'Perhaps in a week, after you have practised with Shikhandi, then I will examine you again. I want to show you something else now which you will probably need to work on. Go to the cart and fetch some light practice arrows. Also, you will see something there which looks like a pair of tongs, with bronze semicircles at the tips. Bring that too.'

While Karna went to the cart, Parashu spoke to Shikhandi.

'Shikhandi... I can't make him out today...'

'I think he's trying to make you feel useful, almighty and all-seeing rama.'

'Sssh, please, be serious with me for a moment. Do you really think that?'

'No, rama. Not entirely. I think he really has learnt something today. Or rather, he really thinks that he's learnt something today.'

'You have met him before, have you not? Before Mahendra?'

'Yes, all-seeing rama.'

'But you do not wish to tell me about it?'

'No, rama.'

'And... I see that you...'

'Yes, rama, I do,' she interrupted with a smile.

'But...'

'I will, rama,' she said with a sigh. 'I will. But not for very long,' she added, her smile becoming more mischievous.

'Isn't your yoga good enough, Shikhandi?'

'Oh yes, it is. I just hope it won't be good enough for very long, that's all...'

Karna returned with two quivers of practice arrows, and the tongs.

'Ah!' exclaimed the rishi. 'I will need you to wear your gloves, Shikhandi —'

'Your needs expressed, O master, I go, your slave, expressly!'

She left in search of her gloves.

'Now, Karna, can you shoot by sound alone?'

'Yes, but not very well.'

'Who taught you? Drona?'

'No, I taught myself.'

'There is a particular difficulty with sounds, Karna... Close your eyes.'

The rishi clapped his hands.

'What did you hear?'

'A clap, rama.'

'How many claps?'

Karna understood, and smiled.

'You heard one clap,' continued the rishi, 'and yet I have two hands. It is not so easy to count by sound, is it? Listen again.'

The rishi clapped his hands a second time.

'Could you hear the sound of each hand clapping, Karna?'

'No, rama.'

'I will teach you. That is, I will try to teach you. Not everyone has the ear for it. But if your ears are half as good as your eyes... Ah! Here is the princess with her gloves on. Karna, blindfold me again with my sash.'

The rishi, blindfolded, stood ten paces from Shikhandi. He held his bow and an arrow in readiness.

Shikhandi adjusted her lizard-skin gloves, and clapped her hands once, just in front of her breasts. She did not fold the hands into each other, but clapped them as mirror images, into a vertical position. She held her hands there, together, as though assuming a position in a dance.

'Once again, please, Shikhandi,' asked the rishi.

She clapped her hands again in exactly the same way, holding them together absolutely still.

'Karna, which hand would you like me to strike?'

'Her right hand, rama.'

Parashu released the arrow, and the wood struck the edge of Shikhandi's right glove, just below the fingers.

Parashu repeated the feat several times, on each occasion Karna choosing the hand.

'One moment, rama,' said Karna. He went over to Shikhandi and whispered to her. This time she held her left hand pointing flat, palm up, towards her right breast. She brought her right hand down to clap on top of it, the fingers of her upper hand pointing towards her left breast. In this horizontal position she held them absolutely still.

When Karna now asked the rishi to strike her right hand, he duly hit the edge of her uppermost hand.

Karna stood silently for a few moments in appreciation. Then he indicated various positions for Shikhandi to hold her hands. But each time the rishi struck the hand Karna requested.

'I cannot believe how that is possible, rama.'

'Do you want to try, Karna?'

'I know I cannot even begin to do it,' laughed Karna.

'All you have to do is to learn to hear the sound of one hand clapping. You can start by practising with the tongs.'

At the two ends of the tongs were two curved bronze clappers. These were not in fact perfect half-circles: for when the tongs closed, the clappers came together to form an ellipse; the tong handles were at right angles to the longer axis of the ellipse, and the tong ends were attached at the two vertices of the ellipse.

'You must learn to shoot through the centre of the ring, blindfolded, just from the sound of the two halves coming together. You will need to use arrows with modest flight feathers, or they will not go through the aperture; and then, the harder part, you must learn to hit each clapper separately, whatever the position of the tongs.'

'I will try, rama.'

'Shikhandi will teach you. Her hearing is better even than mine. She can even tell how fast an arrow is, and where it is directed, by the pitch and tone of the bowstring that releases it!'

'Great rama, you exaggerate.'

◊

Over the next few days Karna practised diligently with the tongs, going through many different exercises blindfolded. But though he was able easily to send an arrow through the centre of the bronze ellipse, he was not at first able to perceive its orientation.

Karna also decided to try wearing two sets of quivers, one pair on each side, so that he could choose whether or not to draw across his body. He fought for many hours, using practice arrows, against three or four of the brahmanas at a time; but he felt frustrated by his lack of fluency when fetching across the body.

'Karna,' suggested Shikhandi, 'leave off your usual quivers, just wear the pair on your left, so you're always fetching across. And try it in single combat first. I think you're being too ambitious, you're beginning to repeat your fumbles instead of eliminating them. Try it against me.'

So he began to practise in this manner against Shikhandi. At first his clumsy fetching meant that she was much too good for him; but gradually he caught up with her.

'When you can beat me regularly, Karna, then I may allow you to put your right-hand quivers back on. And then I hope *I* will begin to improve. I need rather better competition than this!'

Karna found that at close range Shikhandi gave as good a test as anyone. But in one respect, her anticipation of Karna, she was superior even to Arjuna. As a result, Karna began to take more trouble disguising and varying his shots, and to rely less on his sheer speed.

◊

'You are beginning to look more and more like the old boar, with those crossed quivers of yours,' said the rishi, after watching him fight against Shikhandi. 'You have never seen him fight, have you, Shikhandi?'

'I've never even set eyes on him. Why is it you call him the boar?'

'Yes,' added Karna, 'and why are you the mongoose, and Charvaka the mouse? Charvaka never had the patience to tell me.'

'Ah... That is a delicate issue. We were all younger, of course... But the animal names came because of what brought us together. Yes, it wasn't even like what happened in the story, in the tale of the banyan tree... Except for the fact that in that tale the animals were also brought together, even though they did not at first trust each other... So, somehow, we started to use the names of the animals in that story... You know the one, surely... No? Charvaka has never told it to you, Karna?'

'No, rama.'

'Tell us, O great and accomplished guru!'

30 The banyan tree

'In the middle of a forest there stood a large banyan tree. It gave a most delightful shade. Its upper branches were the favourite haunt of a certain dove, and also of an owl, the first being especially partial to spiders, the second having a particular fondness for rodents.

'A very wise and intelligent mouse lived in a hole at the foot of the tree.

'The lower branches of the tree were the preferred hunting ground of a cat, who devoured daily a considerable number of smaller birds incautiously alighting there; and who would have been more than happy to dine also on the mouse, or indeed on the dove, had he the opportunity.

'The tree entertained four other regular visitors: a spider, who devoted his own great intelligence to avoid being eaten by the birds and the mouse; a mongoose, who further added to the perils of the poor mouse, but who gave no great comfort to the spider; a fox, who was a rather unpredictable personage, but who could be relied upon to persecute the mouse and the mongoose, and who made hungry eyes at the birds; finally, there was a man, a chandala, who inspired fear in the hearts of the cat, the mongoose and the fox.

'The chandala had lately moved to the forest and built in it a hut in which he resided. Every evening, after sunset, he spread his traps and nets, which were made of a very fine but tough twine. Frequently he placed a small snare in the vicinity of the banyan tree, to the great inconvenience of the mongoose and the cat, who were both of a size and disposition to be trapped. Less often he would leave a larger trap, to the great annoyance of the fox.

'So far, however, the animals had had the measure of the man. Then one evening, in a moment of little heed, the cat was caught in one of the chandala's traps. It lay there, tangled in the netting, meditating on its fate.

'Soon the fox appeared.

'"O excellent fox, with your coat so red, can you not release me from this net? I can hardly turn my head."

'"You know as well as I do, foolish cat, that my teeth, like yours, are far too large to make an impression on this insidious fabric." The fox demonstrated, biting at the net; and sure enough, the twine merely got caught up in the gaps between his teeth.

'The fox stayed to watch for a while, laughing and preening its red coat; and then went on its way.

'Later that evening the mouse emerged, and began to rove courageously in the area around the great tree. During his meanderings the mouse came across the meat with which the chandala had baited the trap; and then he noticed the cat himself. Much of the meat had been spilled around the cat at the moment of capture; the mouse stepped with impunity all over the helplessly entangled cat in order to consume this feast.

'But while he was eating, the mouse failed to notice one of his terrible enemies arrive: the restless mongoose, with fierce coppery eyes.

'The mongoose sat on his haunches, licking the corners of his mouth, anticipating a suitable moment when he would be able to spring and catch his prey.

'The mouse suddenly became aware of this new enemy, and, almost at the same instant, of the owl, who was sitting in the branches of the tree; where it was waiting for the opportunity to swoop down on the appetising rodent.

'Beneath the mouse the cat's eyes shone at him with a fierce light.

'The mouse thought carefully. What should I do? If I were to climb off the cat onto the ground, the mongoose will surely get me. And if I stay up here exposed, above the body of this cat, the owl will certainly swoop down before long and pick me off. I could snuggle down by the cat, but though he cannot escape, he may be able to crush me — he may even eat me to ward off the pangs of hunger as he waits for the dawn of his own doom, when the hunter will return to claim him. However, a person of our intelligence should not lose their faculties in panic. It seems to me that the safest refuge is with my enemy the cat. For though he is my habitual persecutor, he is in distress, and thus perhaps susceptible to a reasoned discussion which may turn to my advantage. They say that it is better to have a rational person for an enemy than a hothead for a friend.

'"Cat, are you still alive, down there? I am addressing you in the spirit of friendship and mutual convenience. If you undertake not to kill me, I will rescue you. The mongoose and the owl are both waiting for me — I can see that wretched owl eyeing me up this second from his branch. O noble cat, I am very frightened. But without my help, you are lost yourself, since you cannot, immobilised as you are, sever the bonds which imprison you. Provided that you abstain from devouring me, I will cut your net and free you. For my small teeth can come to grips with it. We have both dwelt as enemies for many years beneath this banyan. Now is the time to trust each other. Let us join forces. I will help set you free; but you must shelter me."

'The cat eyed the mouse gently, and replied to him in a sweet and sincere tone:

'"O excellent mouse, with your coat so grey, I am delighted with your proposal. You have brought hope to my dismay. By all means put into operation whatever you consider may have beneficial consequences. Let there be between us a compact without any delay. I will do whatever you deem necessary and opportune for our affairs to proceed to an agreeable conclusion, O wise and intelligent mouse."

"'This is my plan, noble cat. I will hide under your great body. But you must not crush me or otherwise cause me injury or death. On the contrary, your body must protect me from the mongoose and the owl. While I am thus sheltered, I will cut through the strings which tie you."

"'There is no time to waste then, gentle mouse, come down here with all your haste!"

'The mouse climbed down and nestled close to the cat. The mongoose and the owl both scowled in anger and amazement. Then the mouse began to cut through the twine — but slowly, very slowly, waiting till the proper time to finish the work. The mongoose and the owl soon left, seeing that their hopes were dashed. But the cat grew impatient.

"'Please hurry, pleasant mouse; you make me worry: how is it that you are taking such a time over your task? Are you no longer interested, now that your danger is past? Please cut these strings with all speed so that I may again enjoy the appetising taste of freedom!"

"'Wait quietly," said the mouse. "You must trust me. You can see that after all I am still here. I have not deserted you for the shelter of my hole, though well I might, had I been fickle and inconstant. But you must understand, O cat, that should I release you right now, it would do little to favour my condition, for I would have to stand here under the shadow of your fearful liberty. No, wait patiently for the proper time. I will wait for the hunter to return. As he approaches, then will I cut the last of your fetters. For at that instant we shall both be afraid, and, given liberty, your prior concern will be to secure safety by scrambling up the tree. I will then enter my hole quickly, without fear of you."

"'But I rescued you from your danger with considerable speed, and allowed you without hindrance to climb under me and feed. Now you are slow in discharging your side of the compact. You should hurry, my good mouse, if you want your behaviour to be correct and consistent with dharma. If you are dwelling on the times in the past when I have chased you and frightened you, put that all behind you: I crave your forgiveness."

'The mouse, who was very intelligent and had a thorough knowledge of all the sacred and the learned texts, replied as follows:

"'By remaining here with you I have demonstrated plainly that my behaviour is not directed purely to the furtherance of my own interests. But you have done nothing which suggests any concern for my interests —"

"'How can I, since I'm plainly not at liberty to do so. Free me. Then you'll see how tenderly I treat you. Remember, gentle mouse, I have already discharged my part of our agreement, albeit from within my cruel confinement."

'The mouse replied as follows:

'"The sort of friendship in which there is fear should only be maintained with the utmost caution by the fearful. Our relationship lacks the symmetry you are impatient for my actions to reflect. Look, I have cut through all the strings save one; and I will cut that one too, with great urgency and precision, when the time is right. Then will our agreement be acquitted. Be patient, and be comforted."

'The night passed very slowly for the cat. When at last morning came, the chandala approached the scene. His appearance was terrifying. His hair was straggly, his hips were huge, his mouth stretched avidly from ear to ear; and he was heavily armed with a multiplicity of weapons. The cat trembled as helplessly he watched the man approach.

'"O mouse! O mouse! Please consider the very ripeness of this instant for the fulfilment of your covenant!"

'The little mouse quickly severed the last string. The cat scrambled up the huge banyan just in time, while the mouse darted into his hole. The hunter arrived, took up his ruined net, and quickly left the scene in anger and disgust. Unnoticed by all, the spider crawled about its business.

'From the branches of the banyan the cat called down to the mouse in his hole:

'"Without attempting to further our conversation, your mind seems now bent only on evasion! I hope you do not suspect me of any intent to oppose your best interests, little mouse. I have swallowed all such inclinations! My only desire is for your good."

'The mouse did not reply. The cat continued:

'"I am most grateful to you, gentle mouse. You have done me a great and exemplary service. During the long hours of the night my trust in you wavered. But you have inspired me with your wisdom and veracity. Why do you not now venture out to approach me at this time, when friends should celebrate the sweet and succulent success of their relationship."

'Still the mouse did not reply.

'"Remember, gentle mouse, it is said that he who forgets his friends never can find them in time of need. All my relatives will honour you and toast your health, dear friend. I swear by my life that you will have nothing to fear from me or my relations."

'From the safety of his hole the mouse replied.

'"I have attended to your pleasant words, kind cat. But just as friends can assume the guise of enemies, so may enemies appear also as friends. What you say to me now has no serious meaning that I can trust. For it is only what you would say if you were merely serving the interest of your appetites. This is now the time of day when you feed. If not you, then your spouse and children will cheerfully consume me. Since it is not in your interest now to refrain from eating me, and since it is in your interest to deceive me for the sake of an easy meal, the balance of probability must lie towards your lying."

'"O mouse, do not take me for what I am not! Accept my keen affections!"

'While they were talking, the spider began crawling up the tree to where was perched the dove. Both of these had taken a great interest in the night's events. The dove, who had been often troubled by the cat, was rather disappointed by the outcome. The spider, who was frequently disturbed by the mouse, was also rather dissatisfied by the turn of events. While the spider continued his brave journey, the mouse continued:

'"Wise cat, listen to what I have to say. When friendship arises because of a temporary convergence of interests, the very motive for friendship may prove to be the enemy of friendship: selfishness. Self-interest is very powerful, fierce cat. As an enemy can turn into a friend, so when the occasion requires it, can a friend turn into an enemy. The very reasoning that discovers friendship in old enemies can turn up enmity in friends. What selfishness can create, selfishness can destroy.

'"By nature you are my enemy," continued the mouse. "Through circumstance you became my friend. But the circumstance has left us like a cloud leaving the sky. There cannot now be a friendly union when we are related so unequally. But, if you really think I have done you a service, then oblige me with your friendship when I need it again: when I may carelessly stray close to your claws. Then, if you wish, you may show your gratitude."'

'"But friendship is not something which can be removed like a coat when the passing cloud reveals the heat of the sun! I do not wish merely to show gratitude!" pleaded the cat. "I feel affection for you, gentle mouse."

'While the cat was speaking, the spider had managed to crawl right up to the dove. Seeing the spider, the dove was reminded that it had not eaten at all during the night, so consumed had it been with the unfolding events. The dove was just about to devour the spider with a single peck, when it noticed the spider's face: the spider was smiling fearlessly at its enemy. "What is the meaning of this?" wondered the dove, as it looked in astonishment at the spider. Then a thought suddenly occurred to it, and the dove flew off in great haste, leaving the spider unharmed. A little while later it returned to the banyan tree, but now in the company of the owl and the mongoose.

'The mongoose called to the mouse, who was still discoursing with the cat from the safety of its hole.

'"O paragon of mice," began the mongoose, "consider what I have to propose to you and the cat. The traps of this fierce hunter are an overriding source of concern to both myself and your old enemy, the cat. I was just now about to introduce this wise bird, the dove, into my jaws, when it risked its life to explain to me the substance and sense of your discussion. I confess that I feel no affection for you whatsoever, gentle mouse, except in regard to your edibility. However, it would serve my self-interest if you would agree to free me from the hunter's traps in exchange for my agreement not to eat you. Rise up now to the surface of the ground, where I will inhibit the cat from any activity injurious to you. Then we can formalise our agreement, in which I am sure my rival, the cat, will be only too happy to partake."

"'What about the owl?" asked the mouse. "What is to stop the owl from swooping down to feast on me? What advantage does my safe passage confer on the owl?"

"'I have undertaken to find alternative food sources for the owl," said the mongoose. "Just as I have undertaken not to attack the dove, in recognition of his wise and timely proposition."

"'O wise and gentle mouse," interjected the cat, "I too will help to supplement the owl's requirements if you would only help us against the hunter, as the learned mongoose has outlined. But in my case, dear mouse, affection joins sincerely with self-interest to promote our friendship."

"'Very well," said the mouse, "but on one condition. You must all promise not to harass or chase the gentle dove, who has brought us together."

"'O most sensitive mouse," proclaimed the dove, "it is not entirely through my own despatches that this agreement has so gloriously been gained. My idea was inspired by the spider, who bravely planted the thought in my mind. Wise mouse, I intend to abstain from dining on the spider, and I beg you to join with me in this, should you also be tempted to ingest him."

"'Your loyalty inspires me, O dove," cried the mouse, who emerged from his hole unmolested by his natural enemies, the cat, the mongoose and the owl.

'And thus it was,' said Parashu, 'that the spider, the dove, the owl, the mongoose, the cat and the mouse lived in peace and amity, to their mutual advantage. And soon the fox was recruited as a willing party to these arrangements. In time, self-interest gave way to affection, and affection to love. Except in the case of the owl, whose desire to devour the mouse I suspect still lies dormant. Come to think of it, the dove, too, has always entertained an unreasonable suspicion of the mouse... but then life is never quite like a story...

'As for the chandala,' concluded the rishi, 'he eventually stopped coming to the tree, and was forced to set his traps elsewhere. But by then the love between our friends survived the passing danger which had joined them.'

'But rama,' asked Karna, 'what of the boar? What of the Grandsire?'

'Ah, well, Bhishma was in fact the cat. But the name just could not stick — it is not easy to associate Bhishma with the feline species. Particularly when he loses his temper. You're surprised? Yes, he very rarely loses his temper now, but in his youth... he would literally charge at you, like a boar... So we took to calling him the boar.'

'And the others?' asked Shikhandi.

'Surely you two can work them out between you...'

◊

After some weeks Karna had mastered all the exercises which Parashu and Shikhandi had set him. He could overpower either of them with just a few arrows drawn across his body from a quiver on his left. And with quivers on both sides he could easily take both of them on at once. But though he was now a match for Parashu when it came to shooting by ear, he was still not up to Shikhandi's level with this technique. So in order to improve it he was up early every morning to practise with the rishi or Shikhandi, usually in some secluded spot, away from the distracting noises of the training field.

One morning, after a spell working blindfold with Shikhandi, they took a break to exercise their touch on the bowstring. For this they used chalked arrows, which were made of very light wood, and with extremely sharp tips. The tips were dipped in white chalk dust before shooting.

Karna and Shikhandi stood fifteen paces apart, naked down to the waist, each with a bowl of chalk by them on the ground. They took turns to shoot at each other's bare back. So precise was their control that they would leave only a white chalk mark on the skin, without drawing blood or even leaving a graze.

Karna was just strapping on a new quiver ready to shoot at his partner, when she turned round to face him.

'This is not hard enough for you, Karna. Do you want to try something softer?'

The seriousness of her expression was now quite familiar to Karna; he concealed all trace of amusement when she raised her hands to point at her nipples.

Karna obligingly took two arrows from his quiver, dipped them in his bowl of chalk, placed them on his bowstring, and released them. As they fell, brushing her nipples with the lightest of glances, she caught one in each hand.

'Oh, Karna, you have such a wonderful touch!'

Karna remained impassive as he drew out two more arrows; he raised his eyebrows to enquire whether she wished him to repeat the exercise.

When it was Shikhandi's turn, after directing a few arrows as usual against his back, she stopped to complain.

'Karna, your back is too easy for me. It's not fair. You had my breasts. I also need something harder. Could you take off your dhoti, please?'

Karna made no reply; he stood there with his back to her, motionless. She went up to him, put her hand on one of his buttocks, and peered around him to catch his eye.

'Come on, Karna. I just want another peep. None of the brahmanas will let me see theirs.'

'It must be their reluctance to show themselves to a kshatriya.'

'But you have no such reservations, have you, my little calf? And if you have, all the more reason to stretch them.'

Karna remained silent.

'Besides,' she laughed, 'I am in such need of the challenge. So very small a target at this distance would be a great achievement for me...'

She had just started to undo his dhoti when they heard approaching the dull pace of the rishi's axe.

'Pack the mule, Karna,' called out Parashu. His voice was weaker than usual and a little short of breath, as he had been fasting for some days. 'It is time you learnt to use Vijaya.' After delivering this short message, the rishi turned and left them.

•

'I'm afraid the next bit's going to be rather dull, boys. For your infantile tastes, anyway. So you'd better brace yourselves for a long and difficult haul.'

'Oh, won't there be...any...'

'No, nothing will happen at all. No more tigers, no more princesses, no fighting, nothing.'

'But we didn't *really* have much in the way of tigers, I mean —'

'Palmira, it's not that we're complaining...'

'So you think you want more tigers, eh? You should be grateful I don't bore you with one of Aesop's fables. Yes. And you are very lucky I don't give you the Hodja's opinions on tigers as well...'

•

31 The worm in the cave

The mule was laden with the provisions and bags for the journey, and also with Vijaya, a huge and beautifully made bow belonging to the rishi. Next to this bow Karna had fixed his own red sack. When he saw this the rishi scowled, but he did not say anything.

'Rama, why do we have to travel so far, just so that I can learn how to use this metal bow?'

'I want some time alone with you,' was all the rishi had to reply.

Beyond the training area of the brahmanas the track began to climb up again, winding between the foothills which buttressed the west side of the mountain.

Parashu, wearing his blue cloak, walked steadily in front, pacing with his axe. Behind him followed the mule; and then Karna, with a bow perched over his bearskin.

The rishi was still quite weak from his fast; he conserved his breath as they climbed, so that the two hardly talked. Nor did they exchange many words when at dusk they decided to stop for the night in the shelter of a cave.

The floor of the cave was covered with pebbles and small fragments of bone and flint. Among these were embedded some much larger stones and boulders. The air inside the cave was stale, and even colder than outside.

The mule was reluctant to enter the cave. Once persuaded inside, it refused to lie down. Without taking its eyes from the entrance it backed slowly into the depths of the cavern until the fading light showed only its peering eyes and twitching nostrils.

Karna tried to clear a small area next to a boulder; he sat down cross-legged and leaned against it, still huddled in his coat. Parashu curled up on his side with his back to Karna, and laid his head in Karna's lap. Karna cradled the rishi's head in one hand, and with his other hand tucked the spare folds of his bearskin around the rishi's neck and shoulders. There was now scarcely any light coming from the entrance to the cave on Karna's left; to his right he could no longer see the mule at all, but he could hear that it was still awake. In this position the two men fell asleep.

Karna was woken in the middle of the night by the appearance of the moon; it was creeping across the edge of the cave mouth nearest to Karna. Parashu's head still rested peacefully in Karna's hands, undisturbed by the rays of light. Karna gazed up at the moon.

He heard the mule shake its ears. Then, near his thigh, next to the rishi's shoulders, Karna felt a slight movement.

He looked down from the moon into the darkness by his side; as his eyes adjusted again to the gloom he saw what appeared to be a worm. It was as long as his hand, nearly as thick as a finger. Slowly it climbed up the bearskin; it stopped over his thigh.

As the moonlight grew stronger Karna discerned tiny legs and bristles on the creature. He could see its jaws burrowing into the bearskin. Karna looked back at the moon.

When the animal reached the skin of his thigh, Karna felt the little bristles, as sharp as needles, while it searched for a choice spot. Having settled on a point of entry, the animal then bored methodically into Karna's leg.

Eventually so much blood had soaked into Parashu's cloak that the wetness about his neck began to seep into his dream; the rishi woke with a start.

Parashu groped around for the source of the blood. Then, without attempting to speak to Karna, the rishi uncovered the bleeding thigh and saw the tail end of the worm still exposed. He tried to pull the worm out, pricking his fingers on the bristles, but it straightened its bristles and clung firm inside Karna's flesh.

'Leave it, rama. After a while I will lose consciousness from the bleeding. And then I will die. It may not be as noble as the kshatriya death, whatever that is; but I hope it will suffice. If there are any ritual mantras which you need to perform, to finalise the execution of your sentence, by all means proceed with them. Otherwise, you may consider now whether to speak to me. For I imagine that whatever silence binds you, it binds you only before the living. Surely you are permitted to talk to the dead. Perhaps you could therefore find the kindness to consider me as dead already; and to explain to me, as I die, why it is I have to die...'

The rishi stared through the moonbeams. He was motionless, except for his breathing, which the walls of the cave picked up out of the silence and rendered audible.

Parashu turned his head slightly. He peered down at the floor of the cave. He picked up two stones. Placing one beneath the exposed tail of the worm, he brought the other down to crush against it. This time, when he pulled, the worm did not resist; Parashu was able to extract it. He crushed the animal's head between the stones, and threw it out of the cave. He crawled over to Karna's quiver and picked out a bowstring. To stem the bleeding he tied it tightly round Karna's thigh above the wound.

The rishi glared at Karna.

'Why didn't you pull the thing off?'

'I didn't want to disturb your sleep, rama.'

'Bah! Only a kshatriya would do such a stupid thing!'

'I thought it was quite clever. But then I'm a suta...'

'You thought you could read me so well?' Parashu's eyes shone angrily in the moonlight. 'So it was all a device to release you from the kshatriya death?'

'Of course.' Karna smiled at the anger in the rishi's face. 'As a matter of fact, I planned it all many centuries in advance. In a previous incarnation I was the unfortunate and innocent victim of an evil demon called Alarka. In order to advance my course as Karna in this life, I cursed this demon, causing him to be reincarnated as a worm, to live in this dark cave for centuries; in readiness for this fateful moment when we two should come by, to release him from his lowly state, to release me from mine...'

Parashu laughed. He undid his sash and wiped his own bloody fingers on it.

'I'm sorry, Karna. Please forgive me. My brain is grown weak from fasting. Perhaps I am still half-asleep. Please forgive my anger...'

By the time the bleeding had settled, Karna could see almost the whole orb of the moon hanging outside the entrance of the cave. For a while neither of them had spoken, though Parashu had inspected Karna's injury. Then the rishi broke the silence.

'Karna... I cannot release you. Only if you take the snake, and survive, only then are you released from the kshatriya death. But I will promise you this, Karna: I shall not pursue your death. I shall not try to kill you. Nor shall I try to cause your death. You can tell that to the mouse, when you return. He will be pleased...'

He relaxed slightly the tension on the bowstring around Karna's thigh. Parashu had used his sash to bandage over the wound itself.

'You played a dangerous game, Karna.'

'But danger is relative to desire, is it not, rama?'

'Remember that the man without desire does not move upon this earth. Your danger is to deceive yourself that you have no desire.'

'Well, at least I won't now need to deceive you. I'm sorry, rama, about my little deceptions — you know I let you beat me, when I ran out of arrows... And I had no intention of succumbing to any tiger...'

Parashu laughed. 'Karna, deception drives the world around. Men busy themselves laying one lie over another, until in the end they lie themselves right out. Our very history is the history of deception; of force, by the mind; of the mind, by words; of words, by truth itself. But yours, Karna, were easy, honest deceptions, of the kind which can be picked out clean like an arrowhead, leaving the wound to heal. The worse deception of all is sincerity itself. It is a raft which floating in a sea without a coast is flattered into thinking itself land. Like the air, it seems not to distract the end in view; and like the air, it passes undetected till a storm reveals its streams and currents. Most of all beware of this deception, which in the world is called by men being honest;

which is a sickness that afflicts the healthy; but like health, is a disease from which we die.'

The moon was now floating clear of the cave's edge. The mule, still standing, stirred behind the two men and snorted softly in the silver beams.

'If what you are saying is right,' replied Karna, 'you infect yourself with your own health; for you speak as though you were outside the world; aren't you trying to step out of your own skin?'

The rishi's eyes glistened in the moonlight.

'Perhaps you're right. I try to step outside the world, when outside is still a place within it. I try to point outside this world...'

'You're trying to point not just beyond this cave, not even beyond the moon, but beyond anything you can show me.'

'But at least you understand what I am *trying* to say.'

Karna chuckled. 'I know what children are trying to do when they run to escape from their shadows. But they only break free from them when it falls dark, and then they cannot witness their great escape.'

'But in the light of Surya, we may still, like children, dream of such escape...'

'Rama... Is it true, then... That without my ear-rings you can't tell me why?... How I came to be on the river?'

Before replying, Parashu glanced at the mule. Perhaps because now almost all the cave floor was lit up by the moon, the animal had at last decided to lie down.

'Yes... The ear-rings are necessary. You would have to be actually wearing them for me to speak to you on these matters. But in your case, Karna, I would not consider the ear-rings alone to be sufficient: I would only be prepared to tell you if you agreed to take the snake. Bear in mind that it is usual, when a man under kshatriya death declines to take the snake, for the sentence to be pursued in some other manner. It is an allowance I am prepared to make, because of your strange circumstances, that I will not act further to prosecute your sentence. But I'm sorry, Karna, beyond this I can tell you nothing more than you know already.'

'So if I had come here with my ear-rings, you wouldn't tell me anything until I agreed to risk my life for something I didn't know about?'

'That is so... Yours is an unusual case. Usually a person under kshatriya death is offered the ear-rings and the snake together... They know why they are under sentence. That was not possible in your case... But, as I say, I am prepared to make allowance...'

'And what if I had come here with the ear-rings, and agreed to take the snake; but then had broken my agreement — having learnt what it was about, say I had decided not to risk my life?'

'From then on, your life would be at risk from me. I would be bound to compel you. Failing that, to kill you.'

Karna's head fell slightly as he thought for a moment. Then he looked up again.

'And you have known about me for some time, haven't you?'

'Oh yes. It was the dove who first told me about you.'

'The dove? Vyasa?'

'No! Doves may perch on Vyasa's shoulders, but he is not the dove. Narada is the dove.'

'Narada... Yes, perhaps I remember Charvaka calling him that... When was this? When did Narada tell you?'

'Many, many years ago he told me of a boy called Karna, carrying the earrings. He said that the mouse had taken on this... this son of Surya as a pupil.'

'And why have you consented to teach me? I am not a brahmana. Charvaka told me you only taught brahmanas.'

'It's a long time since I last saw the mouse. I have changed.'

'But you must have taught kshatriyas at some point. You taught Bhishma, didn't you?'

'Of course. But it was due to Bhishma that I stopped teaching kshatriyas. However devout Bhishma has been, however true to his vows — and believe me, I know now how resolutely he has bound himself to them — he behaved like a kshatriya. For the kshatriya believes that property acquired by superior force is rightfully acquired. Even worse, Karna, the kshatriya believes that what he does acquire by force becomes his property, to be treated as such, be it livestock, servants or women.'

'The Grandsire? He has never struck me as one to think that way...'

'The boar has mellowed since his youth. Even so, you are right, he is one of the less odious examples of that castely way of thought. But it was not so much his example, which turned me, as one of his conquests. You asked me, that day in the tiger country, who was Amba. You know that she was acquired, along with her sisters, by the boar's superior force. She came to me, to plead her cause. It was she who first made me think, who first made me stop to look at what I was doing with my skill. And when I saw, I resolved never again to teach kshatriyas. It was my teaching that had given power to Bhishma, permitting him to vanquish Amba's father and all the other suitors — almost single-handed. It was my own skill that he was using, Karna. I did not wish my gift to be abused in this manner.'

'Is that why you fought Bhishma? Because of Amba?'

'Yes, it was because of Amba. But it wasn't just because of his use of force. No. Unfortunately, it was more difficult than that... In the end I listened to

Amba's plea... The mongoose fought the boar. And it was only because of the mouse that I saved my hide and got away with just a hiding. Poor Bhishma suffered more than I did: the mouse gave the boar such tusks that he gored himself.'

'You said that Bhishma could have killed you.'

'And he would have had to, without Charvaka's help. For as you know, the stronger you are, the less need you have to kill your opponent... As it was, I failed Amba...'

'And yet, you are fond of the Grandsire, aren't you?'

'I love him like a brother.'

'But you have a greater love for dharma?'

Parashu took a breath, as if about to correct Karna, but let his shoulders slowly settle. Then he said, almost to himself, 'When you pick up a weapon, you drop dharma.'

'Is that why you prefer that farm implement?' Karna nodded at the axe. 'At least you don't use a plough, like Bala-rama...'

The rishi smiled. He leaned over to pick up his axe, and laid the smooth wood of the handle across his lap. His smile faded as he spoke.

'There is another reason, Karna, why I prefer not to have to kill men with a bow. With a bow you kill a man by doing nothing. The bow is not a mere implement. The effort goes all into drawing the string, which absorbs your strength without even a wince; your effort has already been spent before the instant of administering death; at which moment you feel only lightness, leaving the arrow now to do your work. When you use an axe and feel the heaviness of the strike, then you do not think so lightly about the ending of life. I have never liked to hide behind my bowstring.'

'What about the brahmanas whom you teach the bow? Are they too good to allow such light means to overtake their heavy end?'

For a moment the creases on the rishi's face deepened.

'As I say, Karna, I have changed. I no longer make such a distinction between those who have been schooled as brahmanas and those who are trained as kshatriyas. But perhaps I did once upon a time confuse manners, which can be taught, with goodness, which must be learnt.'

Karna smiled. 'Did you prefer that brahmanas should politely farm their fellow men, where the kshatriyas before had hunted them?'

Parashu did not reply. Karna turned his head away from the rishi; as he did so he caught the shining eyes of the mule watching quietly from the floor of the cave.

'May I tell you a story of Charvaka's?' continued Karna. His eyes rested on the mule as he spoke.

'A group of creatures living in one part of the jungle decided one day that the law of the jungle was not for them.

'"The lion eats my relatives whenever he wishes," complained a little lamb.

'"And the leopard eats members of my pack whenever he can," added the wolf.

'"But you and your pack devour my family at will," exclaimed the deer.

'"We must have law and order," suggested the monkey.

'"But how are you going to make the lion and the leopard, and all the other creatures with sharp teeth and claws, restrain their ravages?" asked the goat.

'The monkey thought for a while, and then replied:

'"I will explain to them that if they continue with their lawlessness, they will be punished by the gods, who will bring death and disease to destroy them."

'They put the monkey's plan into action, and it seems that they succeeded in their aim. For one day, after their new system had been working for quite a while, another little lamb, who lived in a distant and lawless part of the jungle, came to visit his cousin to see how these new laws worked.

'He stayed as a guest in his cousin's house, and was royally fed and entertained by his uncle and aunt.

'"This seems so much better than our dreadful part of the jungle," said the visitor.

'"Oh yes, everything is very peaceful and well-ordered here," said the old ram, his uncle.

'Just then there was a knock at the door, and a monkey, looking very dignified in a white sash and headcloth, was ushered in. Using very courteous and precise tones the monkey spoke to the old ram:

'"My esteemed and excellent old ram, it is now your turn. I would be most grateful if you would accompany me."

'The old ram took his leave of his wife and children, and left with the monkey.

'"Where is he going?" asked the young visitor.

'"It is his turn to be eaten by the lion," replied his cousin.

'"But..."

'"This way at least we sheep get enough peace and quiet to raise a family. My turn won't come until I am grown older, and have a wife and children."'

As Karna stopped speaking, Parashu uncrossed his legs and shifted his weight. He put back the axe against a boulder. The blade flashed in the moonlight.

'Is it any wonder', said the rishi, 'that the brahmanas hate Charvaka? It is true, Karna, the power of the brahmanas is growing strong. And they have become skilled with the most powerful weapon of all, the tongue... I have heard that in Hastinapura only the boar can still stand up to them. Perhaps Yudhisthira can steady them in Indraprastha? But you are right. In earlier years, I was more foolish...' The rishi spoke a little louder now, letting his voice resonate against the walls of the cave. 'When we are young we do not see the world's injustices with an impartial eye. It is only favoured causes which weigh upon the scales of youth to trip them lightly into action. Then it seemed to me the world could change as easily as I seemed to change myself. The persuasion of the arrow and the bow deflected all my senses from the violence of the mind and tongue. My anger needed an easy object to pursue, which I found in the pursuits of the kshatriya. And like most men, I first drew my line across the grey, only afterwards to shade the parted regions into black and white.'

'How is it that people so often find such bright answers to such clouded questions?'

'But it's so easy, Karna. We draw the line where it gives the most comfort to the mind, or is the most opportune to ambition; afterwards we tell ourselves it is a track of logic which is traced, and not the parting counterpoise of our desires. For when it suits our appetite for order, we fit the world to black and white. But when it suits the order of our appetites, we feed upon its colour. By the stark light of black and white, men plan and praise the path they point; by obscuring it in colour, they gloss over its rambling cost.'

'So now, rama, in your grey age, you don't find the brahmana sash so pure and white?'

'To the brahmana, violence must never be a source of profit. But peace, which is their end, does not just end with peace.'

'As Charvaka says, there is more to peace than quiet. Those who urge peace, but ignore the injustices which fuel the fight, are seeking only their own peace of mind. They pour cold water in the cauldron, and leave the fire to burn beneath, out of sight. Without justice, peace will always crumble into violence. Until men gain what is theirs by right, the fire will always smoulder.'

'Agh!...' The rishi let out a deep guffaw; its echoes around the cave alarmed the mule, who started up onto its feet with a little whinny. As the rishi's smile faded, the strange shadows on his face turned his lips into a monstrous frown.

'Karna... there are no rights! Whatever it is that we can gain for cheer and solace in this world, that we must contrive from nature, or persuade her servant, man, to grant. And in this struggle, *right* and *wrong* are just the counters to keep score; they have no power of purchase. As for *justice*, this is nothing but a leaking shelter which man builds against the elements inside himself; builds most unfairly, upon the backs of fellow men and creatures. For the line around the guilty, around the incompetent, around the unfortunate, the line upon which justice is reserved just for the deserving, is a line unjustly drawn by those fortunate to be judged competent to serve thus.'

Parashu reached again for his axe. As he spoke now he caught on the blade the reflection of the moon, which was edging towards the far jaw of the cave mouth.

'Once, many years ago, I was discussing the topic of justice with the mouse. I was saying how easy and obvious it was to create justice. He took me by the hand and said: "Come, I'll show you just how easy it is."

'He chose two plants growing in the earth — two young shoots — and carefully dug them out, roots and all. He placed them on the scales of a balance. He added soil to one side until the scales balanced perfectly.

'"You think the scales of justice are as easy to operate as this? Now, take up your axe." I had this same axe with me even then. He took me away from the scales.

'"I want you", he said, "to balance your axe upright on its handle. Justice requires that everything is in perfect balance. It was so easy with the scales, wasn't it? Try adjusting the position of your axe now, until its desire to fall is in such perfect balance that it cannot choose in which direction to tumble."

'I thought he was joking, Karna, but he really made me try and try again. Like you, he had little respect for his elders. I managed only to make it stay upright for a few seconds.

'"All right," I agreed, "sometimes justice is hard to obtain. But it was easy with the scales. You see," I added, being clever, "if you have the right mechanism in place, justice is quite possible."

'Then he took me back to the scales. We had not been away from them for very long. Less than an hour. They had now tipped slightly: they were no longer balanced!

'"How is that possible?" I asked. "Nothing has been added or removed from either pan."

'"It surprises you, eh?" he said. "The wise man, with great care, can weigh the laws of Kali. Many fools do not wish to go to this trouble, but prefer instead to use the scales in their own imagination."

'"But in the end," I argued, "the mind has to weigh everything. I believe my eyes only because I trust you. How is it possible that they no longer balance, Charvaka?"

'"You do not have to trust me," he said, at first ignoring my question. "You can weigh nature without me, and she will behave with you just as she does with me. You see, Parashu, in her blindness, Kali is both just and unjust. Only when you cannot appeal to her, when you cannot construct a balance, only then should you attempt to predict the verdict of Kali in your mind. You see," he said, now answering my question, "while you were busy failing to stand your axe on its end, these two plants have been breathing and growing! Injustice is in the very air we breathe. And everything breathes, Parashu. Never forget that everything breathes," he said, "for one day the air may tire of being ignored, and run out of breath."'

Parashu paused, and turned his axe slowly in the rays of moonlight. The mule snorted and pricked up its ears. Parashu stretched his arm towards the animal, as if to indicate that he could not reach to pat it. Then he continued.

'The mouse knows more about nature than anyone I know. She — of course, he calls her Kali — she is the only one he is prepared to worship. Because she is impervious to his worship, blind to the guiles and prayers of her creatures, as deaf to the honeyed charm of Krishna as to the dumb writhings of your worm. Both are subject equally to her laws. The mouse would say that the man is fortunate indeed who is able to weigh the laws of Kali without having to suffer from their weight. And he has suffered. First they call him a sorcerer; then, when he shows them that there is no magic in his arm, and that he is as much nature's puppet as they are, then they accuse him of interfering with nature's natural course. As if a puppet could interfere with the puppeteer!'

Parashu passed his finger slowly along the edge of the axe blade. Karna held his chin in his hands, looking vacantly down at the cave floor.

'No, Karna,' continued Parashu, returning to his earlier theme, 'by imposing order on an unwilling world, justice breeds against itself. Unless a world has neither rule nor difference, you will find that injustice plagues it from birth to death. From your birth to your death, Karna. For you were born with golden ear-rings, golden armour; and though you tried to give them away, they will return to haunt you and to weigh you down.'

Karna looked up at the moon. It was now just touching the cave's farther jaw.

'Are you thinking of Vijaya?' asked Parashu.

'Vijaya?'

'Yes — the hare in the moon, not the bow. The little hare in the old story, the hare whose threats moved the mighty elephants away from his land, when he pretended he was an emissary of the moon... Tell me, Karna... Where did you first meet Shikhandi?'

'It was at Kampilya, rama.'

'Ah yes, her sister's swayamwara —'

'No. The royal women were kept apart from us during those festivities. No, it was before that, during Drona's raid. That's when she first saw me.'

'Drona's raid?'

'Didn't you hear about that?'

'No, Karna. I hear a lot, but not everything. Not that you have to hear each syllable to understand the sentence. But do not talk to me of Drona. Not while I am open to the world. He arouses my anger. He therefore weakens me. Anger is the seed fed by the sap that rises. Watered, as you say, by the streams of injustice. Yes...' The rishi raised his voice slightly to draw the echo from the stone. 'In the gentle nursery of peace the seeds of war are planted. In peace they're nurtured, fed and plotted, till ripe they blossom into blood-red flower. And though the scattered petals may fade and disappear, their seed again is husbanded with tearful care, to plant the red end of another day.'

'Why does it seem so difficult to stop the flower in the bud? Why does it so often end with unsheathed weapons?'

'Because no strife ever starts without them being unsheathed. The plant grows almost imperceptibly, as on Charvaka's scales. And the line at which the buds of war emerge, the line which points at those first to draw the wound of war, that line is drawn itself into the bloody ground of war. Who can say whether the bite starts with the tongue or the tooth?'

'You think the tongue is a weapon, like the tooth? But the tooth is designed for cutting flesh, for drawing blood. That is its function. The function of the tongue is not to injure?'

'What is injury, Karna? It is, or causes, pain. Anything which can hurt, can deliver injury. The fact that certain forms of pain do not bleed outwardly serves only to give to others the illusion that there is no injury. And thereby just intensifies the victim's pain.'

'But such an injury does not cause death... It doesn't impair the body. Words don't touch the body, they don't move the body, literally, not in that way...'

'The poisoned meat left on the ground as bait does not itself move, does it? It stays still, it does not of itself fly down the tiger's throat. So therefore, do you argue that it's not the meat that kills the tiger? Do you say it is the tiger's hunger which kills it, and not the trapper?'

Karna hesitated. 'But words are not the objects of desire, like the tiger's bait.'

'So? Like the smell of the meat, they light a path down which desires will roll the body. Do you think the object of the tiger's hunger is the smell of meat? No, it wants the meat itself. And yet does not the signal, smell, kill just as surely as the meat? No, Karna, words move the body no less than do the senses, no less than the pain of bloody injury.'

Karna looked down pensively.

'By appealing to men's fear,' continued Parashu, 'both the sword and the tongue can repel men. By appealing to their interests, they both may draw men forwards. A single tongue may confound the babble of a crowd.'

'Perhaps...' conceded Karna, 'in the case of rough persuasion. But when the tongue is used instead to move by argument, by appealing to truth, to reason, then it is no weapon. It has weight, yes. But surely, rama, not the force of arms?'

The rishi sighed, turning his axe blade over slowly, playing softly with its sparkle. He turned to look behind his shoulder, to where the cave jaw was now biting into the bright orb of the moon. The mule was still standing, twitching its ears as the rishi modulated his voice.

'Every sentence uttered has its unspoken wish in shadow. Those, be they gods or men, who want for nothing, do not wish to speak. Likewise every sentence heard is swallowed in the shadow of desire. Those who want for nothing do not need to listen. The weight of your argument is only relative to the designs of the listener. Force of reason, sharpness of point, do not themselves persuade any more than fire of itself will ignite. An unwilling ear is no more turned by the tongue than a stone is by a flame. Yet just one spark from that flame, applied to tinder, will light it in a flash. Of course, there are some honeyed tongues whose voice will turn the most unlending ears. They spark a wish that rages through the hearer's mind, conducting all his other wants to chant their soft suggestion. Such gods and gurus have a sweet distracting power which soon goes sour. And yet the musty milk still savours sweet to those whom they have taught to swallow taste with trust and discourse with a bleat. Tongues such as these command with love as sure as others with the sword.' Parashu raised his eyebrows. 'You must have met Krishna?'

'Oh yes.'

'He is such a one. He does not tell you the meaning of life. But he leaves you feeling that you have heard it.'

'I'm quite fond of Krishna.'

'Let me warn you, Karna, it is always wise to know where he is standing.'

'But, rama, one can listen to the worth of a speaker's words, not to the power of their presence. Truth and reason can be judged and proved. They don't draw blood like a weapon...'

The shadows on the rishi's face turned his frown into a ghostly smile. He licked his finger and, as he spoke now, passed it slowly again over the cutting edge of his axe.

'The truth, the very reasonableness of what is uttered by the tongue, is like sharpness, like the sharpness of a blade which may be used both to trim wood or to draw blood. The blade is no more weapon, no less soft utensil, than the tongue. Unused it is as harmless as the quiet tongue.'

'But when truth needs proving between men, it doesn't need to strike or injure like a blade.'

'There are three ways in which the sharpness of the blade may be tested; and three ways, too, for truth. The first is where men go by appearance, and merely run their fingers along the edge, admiring its keenness.' The rishi raised his voice a fraction. 'In this first way, the sharpness of the blade is put to test only in the mind, as it is gently handled, passed and turned to draw the fickle comment of the eye. There may emerge a victor in this game, a winning blade, but who knows what sharpness lies hidden in the sweet grooming of its phrase? There may appear to be an argument, but if we look in detail, there is nothing but a dance: there are no blows, edge strikes not edge nor flesh amid the pretty clatter. Tell me, Karna, if you and Prince Arjuna were the two blades put this way to test, who would win the judgement of the day? From all accounts, you.'

'No! Arjuna, surely. He is much prettier to watch than I am.'

'It is not the beauty but the sharpness of the blade which is presumed to be judged... And in this respect, from what I've heard, it was you who made the greater impression at his tournament...'

Now only half the moon was left to give the cave light. Parashu put down the axe.

'Let us come to our second way, Karna, where the test seems more objective. Here the blade is put to some more deadly use, judged not in appearance but effect. Yet even now the sharpness of the blade, its truth, is lost from view amid the bloody clash of argument. True, the blade must have *some* sharpness, some force of bite. But is it the merit of the blade that makes the final cut? No. For if its strike is point-directed, if its timing sings the tune, a blunt blade thus well wielded easily conquers sharp-edged truth. Or, should a blade be over-honed ahead of time, too sharp for its blunt task, its fine edge when put to action may yet crack or stick abstractly. Or should a blade not have the hunger for the bite, its sharp teeth will never close to win its fight. No, the proof of the edge lies not in the hands of men, where skill of stroke or need of mind out-throat the ring of truth-edged tongue. Tell me, Karna, if you and Prince Arjuna were the two blades put to test this way, who would win the contest of the day? From all accounts, Arjuna.'

'Arjuna? My skill of stroke is greater than Arjuna's.'

'What use is your skill if you do not have the need of mind to use it? I don't doubt your hands and eyes are quicker, or your aim more deadly. But have you the hunger for your victory? Have you the desire to kill him? No. Your argument respects too much its reason, regards too highly truth, to be concerned with the mere conquest of persuasion. To live, one must be rational. To want to live, irrational. That, Karna, is your curse.'

The trace of a smile played on Karna's lips.

'But surely, rama, it's possible for men to try two blades more clearly against each other, like two weights across a balance. We can test them, not in the trial of conflict, but against materials. I agree that men neither need nor can rely on truth and reason to win their arguments; and neither need nor can rely on the sharpness of the sword — or ratha — to win their fights. But we can test truth not against other men, but against nature, against which sharpness is the only means to cut.'

'Ah! Surya's tiger is a true child of Charvaka's... That, Karna, is the third way. And perhaps it may be possible for men to follow this way. Though, even if they could, there would always be sharper blades to come in time to cut more finely, to part materials where the old blades left a clumsy mark.

'Yes,' continued the rishi, 'this third way may be possible. And if men observe its rules, and treat each blade with equal weight, they may indeed determine a blade's sharpness in some measure of cold truth. Truth may then be approached, detached from the twisting fire of argument. But only if man's aim is to uncover it. If it is some other aim that drives men on, for which truth is but a means, their evenness of hand may not survive the passions of pursuit.'

The rishi paused to glance at the mule, which was shuffling to catch the last quarter of the moon.

'And look around you, Karna. Men are very little interested in which blade is the sharper, but in which blade is the best. Where best is always judged against the end in view, against the object of the appetite. For men are less interested in truth, in the cold trials of metal against nature, nature against metal, than in the trials of their own mettle, through which *they* mean to make their mark; in which it is the man himself, not truth, which is on trial. Even now, it is not the truth of what I say that drives me on, but my desire to move you. What little desire I have for truth was sated on this question long ago: it is not for my enlightenment that I play this little game with you. Yet Karna, do not rush to think that of itself my dark desire must therefore blunt my tongue!'

'But rama, the pursuit of truth need not always be tainted with the promise of ulterior use. There are men, as you know, who don't seek knowledge for their own advantage; men who will themselves endure the trials of nature for the sake of truth.'

'There are? How many do you know, in whom the pursuit of knowledge is not moved by its utility? Charvaka? Who knows what moves the mouse! But for the great majority, knowledge is only a means, of little naked interest. Indeed, for many it's a source of great discomfort, which they engage with only when they absolutely must; preferring for the most part the neat world of their own dreams to the confusion truth discovers. Many, it seems, would rather grasp a blunt blade by its soft and pretty handle than a sharp one with no covering to ease the careful pain of skilful use. Does not the mouse himself say... most people would rather die with their dreams intact than live a moment without them at the mercy of reality.'

Karna smiled in silence.

'That's why they don't like the mouse,' went on the rishi. 'He asks them to detach the world they want from the world they find... to sift what is like to happen from what they'd like to happen. And they don't like what the mouse shows them. "Either there is something wrong with the world, or there is something wrong with this rishi," they say. And, in a way, they're right when they conclude the latter. For from within the world is there not something wrong with a mouse who hesitates over the worm he has to eat? Or with a spider who declines to spin his web? But when they need Charvaka's knowledge, then they use it; preferring to call it magic; by which means they can choose not to believe him when it better suits.

'No, Karna, most people's interest in truth is moved only by their interests; determined only by the advantages it brings to them in skirmishes of limb or tongue, against each other, or against the world they have to eat. And in that struggle it tends to drop altogether out of view. For, like a cork ball in a children's game, it is thrown and kicked about but as a means to victory; and all too often when the game turns to a real dispute, then eyes begin to wander off the ball; and finally it sits forgotten on the sidelines while the play continues to unfold beyond itself.'

Parashu paused, and with a quick glance back at the last sliver of the moon, he began to undress Karna's bandage. As he examined the wound, and began to reapply the sash, Karna picked up the axe and fidgeted with it.

'Of course,' continued the rishi, 'in many arguments, truth, even in the first place, is nowhere to be seen. The action has no ball at all. The play may have no victory and no defeat. There are many such engagements between men, in which the words and phrases have no sharpened edges to be measured against the cold trial of nature; being like the notes exchanged between musicians, which entwine together in a rapt discourse.'

'Perhaps truth has little place in contests between men,' conceded Karna. 'But beating Kali is no game. Only truth can tame her. Charvaka thinks the day may come when men find more to gain by taming Kali than by taming each other.'

'That may be so. There may come a time when men come to realise that truth, not faith, is their only instrument against Kali. Even so, if truth ever appears to be the object of pursuit, it will still only appeal because it spreads a useful mask behind which men may chase more earthly needs.'

Karna smiled. 'Do you think men ever drop their mask?'

'That depends on where I stand to watch them. Within the world, among them, I have to agree with reasonable men, that here a man is doing what he appears to do, while there a man's unmasked to show that he is not. This is what unmasking is, within the world. But if I watch men from outside the world, then I have to say that the most misleading mask of all is the true face. For within the world men do not question what the true face hides. And that's because what the true face hides, the true face hardly knows is there. How could it? When every slightest movement which a man begins to make, whether of limb or of body, whether of face or of tongue... when every slightest one is driven from the shadows in his heart... How can this true face see the world, move in the world, trace and chase the jostling eddies of the world; and still unwind, at the same time, the hidden strings that pull its mind?'

Now they were silent for a while. Both men looked up out of the cave. The moon had not long left them, but already a faint glow from the mouth of the cave held a hint of the sun. The mule had settled itself down on the floor of the cave and fallen fast asleep. Parashu took out a bag of nuts from his pocket, and put them in front of Karna. Suddenly a strange sound, like the cackle of a monkey, turned Karna's head back to the entrance of the cave. But the mantle of silence returned. Parashu pushed the bag further towards Karna, who took a few nuts and began to eat. Then the rishi crawled over to their provisions, and brought back their water bladder. Karna drank slowly from it.

'So, Karna, tell me about Prince Arjuna. You do not have such a high opinion of his skills?'

'I have not said that, rama. No, of those I have engaged with, his skill is second to none. I think he has been held back by Drona. Yes, Arjuna would benefit from your influence. I think his weakness at the moment is that he doesn't just want to be the best, he wants to be seen to be the best.'

Parashu chuckled. 'And yet it can be a dangerous thing to remove that weakness altogether... You cannot eat your egg uncracked. After all, it's contradiction that drives the world around.'

'I thought you said it was deception?' said Karna, looking out at the dim light from the world outside. Then he turned to look the rishi in the eye. A smile passed between them.

'Tell me, Karna, what are your ambitions, now? Beyond your devotion to the art of the bow.'

'Ambitions? I'm not sure what you mean, rama. I have no great dreams... I suppose I try to follow dharma...'

'In the world, Karna, a man is said to be ambitious not in proportion to his dreams, but to the extent he is prepared to make them real. Who knows but that we all in silence dream alike the worst superlatives who voice more modest comparatives, and act the most mediocre positives. All food for your precious dharma. For where is the virtue in pure virtue, got without the struggle with our dreams?'

Karna smiled, but did not reply.

'I was told that you were made king of Anga, after the tournament.'

'There is no king in Anga now,' replied Karna.

'What? You gave that away too? So you do not wish to follow the kingly path of the kshatriya?'

'No, rama.'

'Good... Yes, I suppose your most immediate ambition must be to walk again on that leg of yours. How is it? Do you think you can walk?'

'Shall I try?'

'Please.'

Parashu helped Karna slowly to his feet.

'Here, take my axe. A blunt blade in argument, but a good crutch for walking. Try it. I must wake up the poor mule...'

•

'Henry, don't you think you should wake up the mule? And do try to keep quiet while I'm telling the story... Cackling like that! You risk disturbing my characters...'

'It didn't seem to disturb Henry... But you won't be cross with him, will you, Palmira?'

'Cross? What do you think? How would you like it if I fell asleep while you were telling the story?'

'Yes... But you're not cross with *me*, are you? He's only being more honest, isn't he? He's just showing his true face, after all. I could be just wearing a mask...'

'Ah! Hello, Henry... Have you had a nice rest?'

'Ugh? Oh! Oh, Palmira, are they out of that awful cave yet?'

'Remember it's not fair to be cross with him and not with me, Palmira!'

'I think you'll find,' said Palmira, ignoring this plea, '*if* you can bear to make the effort to keep your eyelids apart a little longer — I think you'll find that they are well out of the cave by now.'

'Oh! Have I missed anything, Palmira?'

'*Missed*? Don't think I'm going to repeat myself, Henry. You'll have to ask your brother. I'm sure he'll explain everything clearly and concisely. I will examine you tomorrow... And if you fall asleep again I'll stop altogether. Now, if you don't mind, I would like to get through a little more tonight. Though I don't know why I bother. I might as well be telling it to a monkey and a mule...'

•

32 The snake

'It took me an entire day to get accustomed to Vijaya,' said Parashu, shaking his head. 'The sun has barely left the horizon and you already seem to understand this bow...'

'I think so, rama. But my arms will have to strengthen if I am to use all its power. You can hear how loose I'm setting the bowstring.'

A gently rising slope stretched out before them. A fire earlier in the year had left on it only the blackened corpses of once splendid pines. The rishi had been collecting their used arrows from among these scorched trees. Karna stood leaning on the huge bow to take some of the weight off his injured leg. On the way up from the cave he had borrowed Parashu's axe for the purpose.

'You will need the power of Vijaya to shoot the snake. The snake must spin as well as travel. It consumes the strength of an ordinary bow, even one of metal. But this is a very special bow.'

'I don't understand, rama... I thought you said I shouldn't shoot the snake without my ear-rings? Not that I could ever imagine what the ear-rings had to do with the arrow... But it's certainly a special bow, that I can see. Do you think Charvaka will be able to make another like it?'

'He won't need to. Vijaya is now yours.'

'You are giving it to me? Why?'

But for the time being Parashu ignored this question. 'Tighten the string this time,' he instructed. 'I want to watch your grip as Vijaya begins to sing.'

With the bow in full throat, Karna began to vary his range. It took him a while to regain his accuracy. Soon his arms began to tremble.

'Have a rest,' advised the rishi. 'It will take you some months before you can play all day with Vijaya. Fetch me the javelin and the pouch.'

Karna's red sack was lying on the ground beside his bearskin and the rest of the baggage. When he hobbled over to the sack the mule approached and nuzzled him. The animal watched, flaring its nostrils as Karna removed the two parts of the javelin and the little pouch.

'When you need to use this weapon you must pour the powder into the point.' Leaving Karna to hold on to the main shaft of the javelin, Parashu turned the hollow forward section to show the bore. This ran along its length up to where the cylinder began to taper to its solid point.

'When all the powder is inside, use the shaft to pack it — but very, very gently.' Parashu demonstrated how the long narrow rod at the tip of the shaft was an exact fit into the bore of the forward section.

'When the javelin strikes its target, then — providing the target is sufficiently solid — the dust inside catches fire. The fire makes air, and this air pushes the point beyond all resistance. It will then pierce anything. Even that armour you gave away... I know of no living being which could survive its impact... How the powder burns, I don't know — the mouse always insisted that burning is like breathing, that fire needs air...'

'I think the powder contains its own air, rama. I've heard him call it powdered air.'

'Ah, yes... The mouse knows a thing or two about air. Yes... it certainly creates enough air, this stuff. Not sweet air, for us to breathe, but foul and bitter air, which in confinement is even stronger than metal.'

'And what do I do to practise finding the aim and range of the thing... Do I fill it with sand or salt?'

'Exactly.'

'Well, that's easy enough. I need hardly have come all the way to Mahendra to find that out. But Charvaka doesn't like me using his fire powders and liquids, even now. He thinks they're more trouble than they're worth.'

'Yes, Karna, they are very dangerous — you cannot be too careful. But I presume the mouse has taught you how to handle them.'

'Yes, I managed to persuade him to show me eventually. Rama, can I use the javelin again, once I have used it with the powder?'

'No, it gets blown out of shape. So choose your moment well, if at all... Now, Karna, let's go and get your snake.'

When Karna had replaced the javelin and the pouch, he brought out of the sack the leather sheath containing the snake arrow. He handed it to Parashu.

'How is your leg, Karna? Can we sit down? Sit up here...'

The rishi helped Karna down to rest against their baggage, and then joined him.

'You have no fever?' asked the rishi. 'Good...' He gently drew the arrow, still wrapped in its silk covering, out of the sheath.

'Charvaka told me that it was very delicate, that I should avoid exposing it to the air. Is it yours, rama? He wasn't sure — he thought perhaps it wasn't.'

'He was a little right and a little wrong. It is mine. But it is not the true snake. The mouse was right: the true snake is extremely delicate; indeed, it can only be used once, perhaps twice; its surface is so sensitive. But this is the false snake. It is deaf, Karna. It is intended to be used only for practice, so that when the time comes to shoot the true snake, the correct technique has been mastered. The true snake, so they say, can listen to the gods.'

'But I was told when I was given this arrow that it was a powerful weapon, that it could be used many times; but that it could be used only once with its special mantra.'

Parashu chuckled. 'I am sure that whoever stole this arrow thought it was the true snake. Fortunately for him it was not, or he would be dead. If he had tried to shoot the true snake, it would have hovered for an instant in the air and returned immediately to kill him. Your ear-rings may have protected you, Karna. Without them you must never try to shoot the true snake.'

'Why? How do the ear-rings work?'

'Since you are not wearing your ear-rings I am not permitted to say. Even now, I am going to tell you more than I find comfortable. This snake, the false one, is of very little value as a weapon — it can easily be shot out of the sky. But I will show you how to use it, in case one day you find your ear-rings. Then you will be able to shoot the true snake, which, as I will explain, is a formidable weapon.'

'Have you still got the true snake?'

'Oh yes. But I will give it to you. Provided that you promise to look after it rather better than your ear-rings and your mail. The true snake is in Mahendra. I will give it to you before you leave. It is kept in a sheath just like this one, indeed, it is almost indistinguishable from this arrow. But it is wrapped in a white cloth, while this one as you see is wrapped in blue. I will teach you how to use this snake as though it were the real one: to handle it with the same care as you would the true snake. Then, if the time comes for you to use it, it will be second nature to you.'

The arrow, sitting on its cloth, was balanced on Parashu's left palm. The cloth was still folded over it.

'Always grasp the snake by the heads. Never touch any other part of it with your hands, if you can possibly help it. The grease off your skin may disturb its flight.'

He uncovered the arrow. The slightly raised heads glared at each other over his palm.

'Have you ever come across a metal so light, and yet so sharp? The true snake is made of the same metal. Remember, the slightest scratch anywhere on it, especially over the sharpened outside edges, can change the arrow's flight. Do not pass your finger over these contours.' The rishi pointed to the two loops of the snake's body.

'Once the true snake has bitten into flesh or struck anything substantial, it begins to lose the precision of its surface — it loses its powers. If you ever come to use the true snake, you will notice on its body more markings and undulations than on this one.'

Parashu covered the arrow up in its cloth, returned it to its sheath, and rose to his feet. He put the sheath in his quiver and picked up Vijaya. He set his eyes on a tree trunk which emerged slightly higher than its charred neighbours.

He took a baffler arrow from his quiver and shot it into the top of this trunk. The large, bright feathers waved back gently in the soft breeze above the dead forest. Then he perched Vijaya on his shoulder and picked up the leather sheath from his quiver.

'Watch carefully.'

With his left hand he withdrew the weapon from the sheath and placed the arrow sitting on its cloth in his right palm. With his left hand he retrieved Vijaya from his shoulder. Then, pressing his right thumb and fingers to hold the loops of the arrow through the cloth, he turned the arrow into a vertical position. He brought the two snake heads towards Vijaya's bowstring, and rotated his right hand so that the two tiny jaws could bite upon the string. When he was satisfied that it was firmly engaged, he wound the weapon several times around the heads at its centre, coiling up the middle of the bowstring, straining the bow into a curve.

'Don't wind the snake too many times at first. It's dangerous, it may not uncoil in time.'

Still supporting the clinging snake with his right hand, the rishi turned Vijaya into a horizontal position, raising it to eye level. The arrow in his right hand was now just above the plane of the bow. With the thumb and spare fingers of his right hand he flicked the silk free of the arrow, letting the cloth float to the ground. His right hand now grasped the two heads of the snake directly. He pulled the arrow further back towards him, drawing the bow into an even tighter arc.

'Notice that it is impossible in this position to make a precise aim. In a moment I will release the arrow. Watch how I dip the bow very slightly to allow the arrow to spin free above my left hand. Do not worry about gaining forward speed. You will never be able to draw the bow fully in this position. Your object in any case is not to impart speed, but spin. To achieve this you will need most of all to release the arrow clearly and evenly so that it balances in the air.'

He released the arrow. It spun free, floating into the air. It glided almost like a bird, dipping and rising slightly in the breeze. It approached its bright target in a slow, rising arc; but it missed the baffler feathers by a substantial wingspan; it continued on its path, but then it seemed to stall; still spinning, it began to float back along its outward trajectory. It came to rest along the ground near the mule, which had scampered away at its approach.

'It will only return if you send it up at a good angle. You will be lucky to get any closer to a stationary target.'

'Even with the true snake?'

'Oh yes. If anything, it is less accurate. The true snake will ride up and down in the air even more. It seems to have a mind of its own, and is even less predictable.'

'But at that speed even a child could shoot it down. Why is it so powerful?'

'Because it makes a child of anyone who tries. The true snake is designed to be shot down, Karna. Or rather, to be shot at. It rides the currents of air with a most exquisite sense. Should an arrow come heading towards the true snake, then before it is an arm's length away, the snake will have felt the air being pushed apart by this intruder. It will ride over the oncoming attack. It will thus ride over any weapon which is directed at it.'

'Is there any way you can show me?'

'No, you will have to take it on trust. And not just because you don't have your ear-rings. Even with your ear-rings to protect you, there are two reasons why you are only ever likely to witness it once. The first is that releasing the true snake even once, as I say, will almost certainly extinguish its power. So if your lack of trust drove you to test it, you would render useless what you test. The second reason is that shooting the true snake down is the most dangerous thing to attempt. For not only would it ride over your arrows, it would change course! It would begin to hover down along the line of the intruding arrow. That is why you hardly need to aim the true snake. As soon as your opponent starts to shoot it down, the true snake finds its course from the missiles sent to disturb its path. You understand me? No, Karna, you will just have to take it on trust.'

'But, rama, at the speed at which the snake was moving, wouldn't it be possible to get out of its way quite easily?'

'As I have just described, when an object moves towards it, the snake is disturbed by the forward ripple in the air, rides the object, and then changes course to fall along the path the object came on. But when an object moves away from it, the ripple draws the snake towards the fugitive, in his line of motion. When you move, you move the air around you. If you move away from the snake, it will be drawn towards you by the movement of the air around you. It will follow you! The more desperately you try to avoid it, the more violently you disturb the air, and the swifter it will ride down to strike.'

'But rama, in a crowd... How could I pick out a target in a crowd? In the heat of battle, I could hardly know where the snake would come to rest.'

'That is right. The air is too confused, too turbulent. As you say, the snake would be even more unpredictable than usual. But from above the canopy of horses and foot soldiers, it will pick out a single chariot fighter who tries to shoot it down. If he stays on the chariot, the snake will turn into his body, whichever way he bends to dodge it. Even if he tries to leap from the chariot at the last moment, the snake will swerve on the wave of air to cut him down. It will find its own target. But unlike an ordinary arrow, you can neither control nor predict its journey. Once it leaves your bow, the snake has its own destiny.'

The rishi went over to pick up the snake arrow.

'Rama, who else knows about it? I have never heard of this type of weapon before.'

'Very few know about it, Karna. Those few are mostly the rishis, and sworn to secrecy. Even in the old days it was seldom ever used as a weapon in battle. For if its properties became widely known it could no longer entice opponents to their death. In recent times, as you see, it has been designed again, as an instrument to execute upon a person the kshatriya sentence of death. Nevertheless, it remains a most formidable weapon. And now that its powers have been forgotten, it may work again in combat. Of course, you will need the ear-rings.'

'Why are you giving it to me? Why are you giving me Vijaya?'

'Perhaps one day you may regain your ear-rings. I would be failing in my duty if I did not give you the choice to take the snake. It would then be yours to use as a weapon, should you so wish. It is no use to me. So, if you promise not to let it go, you can take it. As for Vijaya, it is not just for the snake that I give you this bow. Perhaps you know that Prince Arjuna now has Maya's great bow, Gandiva. If you ever have to fight Arjuna, you may need Vijaya. Indeed, you may also need the snake...'

'Arjuna will have to improve for that to come about, rama. At present I'm quite able to beat him with ordinary weapons; I don't even need to kill him.'

'But as you must have heard the mouse say, there is more to being able than just being able; as there is more to beating than just beating. Your eyes see too much for your own good, Karna. There may come a time when you can use the blindness of the snake.'

'What about the mantra? What has that to do with it?'

The rishi chuckled. 'Who told you about the mantras? The person who gave you the snake?'

'Yes. He said I should ask you to teach me the mantra.'

'And what did the mouse have to say about that?'

'I didn't mention the mantra to Charvaka. You know that he doesn't believe in mantras.'

'And has he ever said anything to you that might suggest that *I* believe in them?'

'I think he once told me that you found them... useful...'

'Is your arm rested? I think it's time you learnt to float the snake,' said the rishi, putting out his hand to help Karna rise.

At first Parashu would not let Karna wind the arrow by more than two or three turns. Soon the rishi was confident that Karna could control the bow in the horizontal position, and would not snag the arrow as it flew off. Then he allowed his pupil to wind the snake another turn. Gradually Karna became more comfortable with this technique.

'There are two strategies with the snake, Karna. One is to float it directly at your opponent, in the hope that he will attempt to shoot it down. For this you must produce some reasonably credible aim, to entice your opponent into trying to parry it. The other trick is send the snake climbing, as I did on my first shot at the tree. Your opponent may ignore the outward climb. But when it comes back down at him from behind, if it is in line with him, he is more likely to be frightened into fighting it. You should practice both types of flight.'

◊

It was now the middle of the day, and the sun beat strongly down on them. The sweat glistened on Karna's face.

'Are you sure you have no fever?' Parashu asked him. 'In any case, your arm is tired. You must rest and have something to eat and drink.'

Parashu watched his pupil wrap the snake arrow in its cloth and return it to its sheath. Then he helped Karna to seat himself. The rishi brought out some lentil cakes and fruit. Karna was very thirsty, drinking frequently from the water bladder.

'Rama... Are you going to tell me about the mantra? I don't even understand what mantras are...'

'I'm not sure that I do, Karna. At least, perhaps I do, but I'm not sure that I understand them in the way that other brahmanas do. There are many different sorts of mantras. Tell me what you think...'

'I don't know. I've once or twice seen brahmanas using mantras. To try to frighten kshatriyas.'

'Did they frighten you?'

'No, rama.'

'You have noticed, perhaps that before men fight each other, before they quarrel, they signal the powers they are about to unleash. Usually they do not even realise that they do it. It is often just this warning which will end the dispute, without any further struggle.'

'The dog will bare his teeth and growl.'

'Most of us, even in the play-fighting of practice, bare our teeth as part of the combat, without realising that we do it; as though it were necessary to bark before biting. And, indeed, the bark is often the better part of the bite. You, however, neither bark nor growl. Did you know that?'

'I don't do it — not do it — deliberately, rama.'

'That is one reason why you look inelegant, almost unbalanced. We expect you to post your intent, mould your mouth, at least smoulder in your eye.'

'I don't dance like a cobra before striking.'

'You do not even spread your hood. But the dance has a double strike, has it not?'

'It strikes terror into the heart of the monkey, and courage into the heart of the snake?'

'It is just so with the mantra.'

'But how can a man be so easily deceived?'

'Deceived? Do you mean the one who uses the mantra, or the one to whom it is directed?'

'Both, rama.'

The rishi looked in silence for a while at the leather sheath, which was lying in the sun beside the red sack. He reached over and replaced the sheath inside the sack.

'A man's mind has many layers, Karna. The deepest layers are most like the mind of an infant, for whom anything is possible: the young child has not yet learnt what is impossible; and that is as it should be, as it needs to be, since a child cannot know in advance into what sort of world he is being thrown. Indeed, as mankind itself ages, the boundaries between what is and what is not possible change their shape.

'And there is another boundary which in the young child is soft and shadowy: that between other people's interests and his all-pressing needs. That is also as it needs to be: only he can map the boundaries between himself and others.

'But as the child grows, his earlier mind remains beneath the new layers, like the first rings of a tree. The deepest layers may still harbour thoughts which the outer layers deny. The deeper layers may still nurture desires of which the later layers may grow to disapprove.'

The rishi paused to swallow some tamarind.

'If you try to penetrate the bark, and discover the tree, the outer ring of the mind will not usually let you through. For usually, when a man speaks, listens, observes, decides, acts... the outer layer will mediate. It will hide the inner layers, even from himself. But there are ways to see the child in the man before the man has time to hide it. It is hard enough for a man, while he is awake, to glimpse it himself. The easiest way is when he is caught unawares, and suddenly has to decide, suddenly has to interpret, suddenly has to fill in from his mind a gap which the world throws at him. Thus, when someone speaks, and you do not quite hear the words, the mind races to supply the missing meaning. In those first moments, your mind rushes through from the inner layers outwards; until, if it has time, the outer layer corrects the wishful childish meaning which the first flash misconstrued. If it has time. But if it is not given time, the mind may have to move the body before the outer layer has a chance to press its wiser guidance. Then you will get a glimpse of the child in the man. But it has to happen very fast, before an eye can blink, or the outer layer will be reached before the body needs to act.'

Parashu took a sip of water.

'The art of using mantras — at least, insofar as I understand and use them — is this timing. So that you can make your opponent act before his mind is ready. If you overload his senses, he will not have time to consider them properly before he needs to act. Then you can unbalance him, and speak or listen to the child.'

'Rama... When a man sleeps... Is it not the outer layer that sleeps. And the inner layers that dream?'

'I think so. For there are some who can use the mantras, much better than I can, to talk to the dreaming mind, even to shape the dreaming mind, while the man appears awake. A mantra that strikes well may reduce even a wise man to a child. And there are times when it is wise to be a child. Some of the most effective mantras do not drain the heart of the victim, but charge the heart of the striker. Such mantras may be silent. They may be spoken in the quiet of the mind; or they may be images imagined; or sometimes just pure thought. I think this is how these work, by speaking to the striker; so that, like a child, he believes his power is doubled. The snake mantras seem to work like this. It is almost as if a man is able to borrow the elation of his victory to give him the very strength to reach it. The vision of the end seems to enable the means. The mind is tricked into thinking it is doing something else, the better to do what it doesn't know it's doing.'

'What do you mean?'

'Stand up, Karna...' The rishi got up with him. 'Now, give me your arm.'

Karna gave the rishi his left arm, while with his right hand he supported himself on the axe.

Parashu bared Karna's forearm up to the elbow, and pointed to an area of skin a little below the elbow. 'Karna, I want you to move this region of skin up and down.'

Karna could not. 'I don't even know how to begin!' Then his jaw dropped, as he guessed the trick. He wiggled his little finger.

'Ah, not quite,' said the rishi. 'For that piece of skin to move it has to be your first finger. Yes, that's it.'

The rishi raised Karna's arm until it was horizontal, pointing out in front of him, his left palm down.

'We can take it a step further. I am going to force up your forearm so that your arm becomes bent at the elbow. You must try to stop me.'

Karna tried to stiffen his arm, but he could not prevent the rishi from bending it up.

'Relax.' Parashu straightened Karna's arm again.

'This time, Karna, point your fingers out and imagine that arrows are flying out from each of them.'

Now the rishi was unable to bend Karna's arm.

'And you think a mantra can do this to a man's heart?'

'Some mantras do seem to have this effect, Karna. The mantras of the snake are like this.'

'So there is no magic in them?'

The rishi laughed. 'You should know what the mouse says about magic!'

'Yes... It is Kali's forbidden fruit, man's impossible dream. But rama, many men think that there is magic in the mantras — that a mantra works by invoking powers of magic, or of the gods...'

'Of course. Most men who use them think just that.'

'Are they all fools?'

'Karna, was it not foolish to imagine arrows flying from your fingers?'

Karna smiled.

'So, Karna, the mouse has taught you that it is foolish to believe in magic?'

'Yes. But he also says that fools often do very well on their folly.'

'Before you start imagining forbidden fruit, get to know the fruit which Kali does permit. Perhaps you have also heard the mouse say that?'

'Yes, rama.'

'But no, there is no magic in *my* mantras. But who knows what powers other people can conjure!'

The rishi sat down, and Karna joined him.

'Rama... You said the snake mantras... How many are there?'

'There are many mantras which legend ties to the snake arrow. But there are two that I believe may be useful for someone who is going to take the snake... For someone, perhaps. But hardly you. I don't know why you want to know about them, Karna. You see too much to use the mantras... Were you ever a child? I don't understand why you ask about them.'

'What do you mean? I'm curious, rama. And what did you mean earlier, I see too much for my own good?'

Parashu glanced at the mule. It was grazing quietly near them.

'Karna... Listen... You are travelling alone along a mountain track. You meet an old brahmana. You do him a great favour. Perhaps you save his life, or the life of his homa cow... He gives you a boon in return. "Son of Surya," he says, "Son of Surya, I give you as a boon a most exquisite choice. Whichever of the two paths you choose to take, that you shall fulfil."

'"What is this choice, O devout brahmana?" you ask.

'"I must warn you, noble hero, before you choose, that you will only be able to follow one of the two paths I offer you. Not both. Will you listen to what I have to offer?"'

Parashu paused, waiting for Karna to reply.

'I'm not sure that I would,' answered Karna. 'I might turn down his offer.'

'But just now you said you were curious. Will you listen to the brahmana?'

'I'm listening...'

'"Son of Surya,' continues this brahmana, "do you wish to become the greatest ratha who has ever lived? Or do you wish to become known and remembered, in the eyes of the world, as the greatest ratha who has ever lived?"

'One or the other?'

'One or the other,' repeated Parashu.

'And you want to know how I would choose?'

'Which would you choose?'

'I don't know, rama. You are asking me to predict my choice, not now to choose. At the moment of choice the strings may pull in a different way, tighter here, looser there. The balance may be changed. I'm not sure that I can predict how I will choose any better than you can predict how I will choose. The point of prediction, now, is not the point of decision, which lies in the future.'

'But you are at a point of decision now also. A different decision, but still a decision. You have to decide which prediction to give me.'

Karna smiled. He glanced towards the sun.

'Suppose I were to choose to be the greatest ratha. Suppose I did not wish my skill to exist only in the imagination of others, behind the eyes of men, in the world within their skulls. What would you say to that, rama?'

'How can I predict what I will reply when you have not yet chosen. The point of prediction is not the point of reply. I expect you can predict, quite as well as I can, what I would say.'

'You would say... If I chose to become the greatest ratha, you would say... "That is not possible, Karna, that path is false. You may perhaps become the most skilled with the bow; but not the greatest ratha. For the worth which a ratha achieves is based on his distinction; and distinction requires the eyes of men to pass their fickle judgement. You cannot at the same time live outside the world of men, where there are no rathas, and inside, where rathas are made in the eyes of men. You, Karna, would aspire beyond the eyes of men, above the eyes of men, to play before eyes existing only in your mind, before the judgement of your own private audience."'

Karna looked at the rishi.

'Wouldn't you say something like that, rama? You would ask, perhaps, "Is the son of Surya blessed with the gift to choose a higher audience than mere mortals? Then he is cursed to live outside the ranks of the rathas. Is he a fish that would choose to live in the air?"'

'And Karna would reply,' answered Parashu, 'that there are fish that fly.'

'But you would say that they are not in the air alive for long.' Now Karna imitated the rishi's voice. '"In the end, they return to the sea, in which they are forced to live. Fish may glimpse the water from the air, but the view is no better there than from the sea, for it is still only a fish that sees. Men do not acquire the eyes of gods just by standing for a moment on the mountain."'

The mule had stopped grazing; it was holding its head up, very still, watching the two men.

Parashu smiled. 'Go on, Karna, you're doing quite well...'

'"You asked me how to use the snake. I answered you, Karna. You ask me now also for the mantra. What good is a sting that can command the sea, to a fish who would sail in air alone? What use is a mantra meant to move a wave through all the waters of the ocean, to one who would rather sway a secret sky?"'

As Karna drank some water, Parashu softly clapped his hands.

'Don't you think that rather answers your question?'

'No, rama! I'm still curious about these mantras.'

But Parashu had begun collecting their things.

'We must return, Karna.'

'Are we staying in the cave again tonight?'

'No. I think it will be better if you keep walking. Your thigh needs attention. When we return I will bandage it properly with brine and herbs. You rest here while I get ready.'

Karna dozed briefly in the afternoon sun while the rishi retrieved their arrows. When he had finished strapping their baggage to the mule, he woke Karna.

Karna got up in a slight daze and picked up the rishi's axe. They set off with the mule leading the way. For a while they walked in silence. The air was much cooler now, and Karna stopped to put on his coat.

'Let me tell you a story,' began the rishi as they set off again. 'It's about Ghritachi, Drona's mother. I doubt it's true, of course; but it is sometimes told... This was when she was a very young woman, long before she met Bharadwaja, Drona's father.

'Ghritachi was returning to her village from the fields one day when she came across an old man of quite repellent appearance. As soon as this decrepit individual saw her, he beckoned to her to approach him. Ghritachi was, you may have heard, a woman to drive men wild. She was also very kind-hearted and brave. She came near to the old man, thinking that he might be lost or in need of help. For he was trembling, and looked to be starving.

'As she approached she saw his tangled locks encrusted with dirt, mud caked on his legs, and was overpowered by the stench of stale urine and faeces.

'"I thank you for your courage," said the old man, "and, indeed, your generosity, in allowing me to gaze on you from such a short distance."

'"What do you want?" asked Ghritachi, rather tersely, growing suspicious at the twitching folds of his disgusting dhoti.

'"Please forgive my profound impertinence, please know that I understand how unpleasant it must be, for all your senses, to stand so close to one as hideous as I —"

'"Please tell me what you need quickly then! If I can help you I will, if not let me continue on my way."

'From beneath the straggling locks his good eye squinted at her in desperation:

'"I am deeply sorry for having troubled you. Think no more of me, I beg you. Go your way."

'He tried to wave her on, revealing a ravaged, rotting stump where his hand should have been. Ghritachi shrank back in disgust, covering her mouth and nose. The grime-filled folds of his cheeks were moist with tears as he turned and shuffled away. He limped slowly and steadily, without looking back.

'"Wait!" cried Ghritachi. She caught up with him. "Please tell me if there is something I can do to help you."

'"It is enough that I have been fortunate to see your face and form. The very thought that a creature like me might crave your beauty must fill you with unspeakable revulsion. I hardly dare admit my admiration. I thank you again for listening to me."

'Again he turned to leave her.

'"Under Surya," replied Ghritachi, "we are all of us equally beautiful and equally repulsive. Look," she said, pointing at the flies which were trying to settle on the old man's face, "see, they find you much more attractive than me — my beauty means nothing to them — Oh! I'm sorry, I did not mean it that way... I understand that their attentions are quite unwelcome to you."

'"As mine are to you. But gratefully I accept your better meaning, most wonderful of women. Thank you for the kindness of your thought. You cannot imagine — I hardly dare confide in you — the thrill that your body awakens in me. Countless years have past since any woman was so bold as to stand so close to my stinking and diseased body. You are a dream beyond my asking. Go in peace away from me. The memory of this moment is all that I ask of you."

'As he turned again to leave her, his legs trembling, tears came to Ghritachi's eyes.

'"Wait!" she cried. Again she caught up with him.

'"Wait..." She looked around. There was no one else in sight. "I am truly sorry that this is all that I can bring myself to give to you. I am truly sorry that I am not stronger, more courageous, more generous to a fellow creature..." She drew aside the silk which covered her breasts; holding a very deep breath she stretched out her arm to place one hand carefully on his ear, turning his head gently to gaze on her; and, still keeping him at arm's length, and without allowing her tear-filled eyes to look down, she brought her other hand to press him through his dhoti.

'Suddenly, as if she had been struck by lightning, Ghritachi was thrown to the ground. Before her, standing in the most luxurious purple robes, garlanded with sweet-smelling flowers, with gold bracelets and ear-rings adorning his tight skin, was the most beautiful man she had ever set eyes upon.

'"Oh, Ghritachi!" he cried, his cheeks still moist, "your kindness overwhelms the wretchedest imprecation of a most evil, jealous queen. If you will accept the poor accursed wretch before you, I place myself humbly at your slightest command. My name, most desirable of women, is Rupaka." He knelt down at her feet.

'Ghritachi was speechless.

'"For years," continued the enchanting young man, "I have travelled the land in search of someone who could help to lift my most accursed state. Hearing of you, Ghritachi, of your courage, of your voluptuousness, and of the strength of your dharma, I placed myself in your path, at your mercy."

'Ghritachi was still in a daze.

'"If it is not an impertinence too rude from one so indebted, Ghritachi, I beg that you answer me: do you wish to accept my humble service?"

'With a tremulous voice Ghritachi replied:

'"I ask for the service of no man or woman. Your company, Rupaka, should you wish to linger with me a while, would be as welcome to me as my touch was to your former state."

'"I must warn you, Ghritachi, that my curse is only partly lifted. I am still weighed down by a condition most unfortunate, though in your company it lightens to the most infinite delight. Will you hear me, or do you wish to proceed along your way?"

'Ghritachi, confused, indicated to the kneeling figure to rise, and to speak on. As he rose, some acquaintances of the young woman, returning to the village from the fields, came into view. She saw them look aghast when their eyes fell upon her companion, their hands rising to cover their disgusted faces; one or two jeered and laughed at her as they hurried past. Ghritachi stared at the young man in consternation.

"'You see, Ghritachi, in your eyes I am a dream of beauty. To them I remain the same nightmare of stinking horror which you first saw. Even to my eyes, I am still as I was: when I look at this limb, Ghritachi," — he put out his copper-skinned arm circled with a gold bracelet just below his elbow, with gold rings on all his fingers — "there is no hand. It is a decayed, rotting stump. If I were not steeped in it, I could smell what you cannot. Only in your eyes does my beauty exist. If, most wonderful of women, if you wish to prolong our friendship, you must choose."

"'Choose? Choose what?'"

"'Do you wish me to appear sublime to you in your private pleasures, but hideous in public to your shocked and sniggering friends? Or, do you wish me to appear to the world at large in my most radiant form, your most desirable and splendid consort; while taking, in your eyes, the shape which you have lately seen, grotesque and nauseating?'"

'Ghritachi again was speechless.

"'You may have me in either form. But you must choose one or the other, Ghritachi.'"

"'One or the other?' she repeated, her voice hardly sounding in her throat.

"'If you do not pronounce and seal your choice with a kiss upon my lips, to the world I will stagger away, wretched as ever; we would probably never see each other again; but you would leave me rich in the most secret treasure of our meeting.'"

'Tears rolled quietly down Ghritachi's cheeks, and her head was bowed. Then she looked into his eyes.

"'Rupaka...how would you appear to yourself?'"

"'I would see myself as others would around me, Ghritachi. If you chose me to appear beautiful to others, then in public the weight of admiration would make me see a beauty I can now only imagine is reflected in your eye. With you, in private, I would see myself as you would then see me, as I still see myself now, withered and horrible. But if you chose me to appear beautiful to you, and vile to others, then in public the burden of disgust would deform me in my own eyes; while the secret intimacy of your rapture would infect my own eye with a heavenly contagion. The choice is yours, Ghritachi.'"

'She turned away from him, to avoid the distraction of his loveliness.

"'I approached you, Rupaka, to help you. Not to help myself. Should I not give to you, and to the world, the gift of your beauty? Would you not then be the most fortunate of men. And yet," her voice grew more distant, "if he truly does desire me beyond others, then perhaps the most unfortunate, being hideous to the one he wishes to delight. But if I chose to drink his beauty privately, condemning him to the disgust of the world abroad, would that not be too selfish of me? And

333

might I not be gaining vantage of his ugliness to other women, to keep him safely for myself? The derision of the world does not affect me. But him? Would our private pleasures outweigh the cruel torture he would still endure?"'

Parashu paused to glance at his companion.

'Now, Karna, if you were Ghritachi, how would you choose?'

Karna limped onwards, breathing slowly. A few seconds passed before he replied.

'If I were Ghritachi I would say that the choice is not mine to make. The man, Rupaka, he must decide which fate he most wants her to pronounce on him. Ghritachi should then seal his choice with her kiss. And so would I, in a manner of speaking, should your old brahmana ask me to choose: to be, or to be known to be. If I were offered the choice, I should accept whichever gift he chose for me. Let him decide.'

'Good. Let him decide. Let the snake decide. That is the first mantra.'

•

'Palmira! What happened to Ghritachi and Rupaka?'

'I'm afraid you'll just have to ask Parashu-rama. I don't know the end of the story.'

'Of course you do! You got it from our grandfather!'

'What? From old Henry? No, I didn't even get that story from Vyasa. I made it up myself. Why, have you really heard it before?'

'He didn't tell us *exactly* the same story, Palmira, but it was very like it.'

'Really... I don't remember anything like that — I heard several of his stories.'

'It had Sir Gromer Somer Joure in it. Don't you remember? Sir Gromer Somer Joure and Sir Gawain, and...' Henry looked at his brother for assistance.

'And Lady Ragnell.'

'I've heard of Sir Gawain, certainly. But I don't recall the other two... So what was this story, then?'

'You'll just have to ask old Henry, won't you.'

'But it sounds as though you remember it quite well?'

'Er...'

'Not too well, Palmira. I'm sure grandfather would have told it better. We're not very good at telling stories.'

'I don't know, I think you tell stories very nicely. And your dear departed grandfather is hardly in a position to tell me anything now, is he?'

'Well, you keep suggesting *we* go and ask Parashu-rama...'

'He's a bit departed, isn't he, Palmira?'

'Very well, boys... But you promise me you'll tell me about Gromer Somer Joure? But if it's a similar story, surely you know the ending anyway?'

'Perhaps, but we'd like to check to see if it really is the same.'

'I'm afraid, boys, there's hardly anything left to tell of it... You see, Ghritachi did more or less as Karna suggested:

'"Rupaka," she said, "it is not for me to decide how you wish to be. Tell me what you desire, and I will choose it for you, and seal it with a thousand kisses."

'Rupaka, fell down on his knees and kissed her feet, the tears pouring in ecstasy from his cheeks:

'"Oh, Ghritachi! Ghritachi! Your answer has lifted that dreadful curse from me for ever! Now you and everyone will see me as you see me now!"

'And when Ghritachi returned to the village with her new friend, the people who had passed her on the road stared wide-eyed and open-mouthed. There!'

'What happened after that, Palmira?'

'Why, they lived happily ever after, of course.'

'But... we thought she was Drona's mother —'

'Oh yes, sorry, of course, no... I remember, now you mention it... Yes, Rupaka lived very happily with her for seven blissful years, and then... he died. There. Now it's your turn, tell me about Gromer Somer Joure.'

The first Henry took a deep breath. 'This Sir Gromer Somer Joure...'

•

...He lived in a terrible dark castle in the middle of a lake, and he challenged King Arthur to fight him across this drawbridge. But it was magic, because King Arthur's horse, when it charged, it just froze, and he just couldn't get it to go any further.

Sir Gromer Somer Joure gave this terrible laugh from his belly — he was absolutely huge and horrible — and he went up to King Arthur on his horse and was about to lance him, but King Arthur was still frozen.

'Oh, spare me!' cried out King Arthur.

'I will spare you, you stupid cowardly king, on one condition. In one year's time you must come to me here with the answer to this riddle. What is it that women most desire in this world?' That was the riddle.

Anyway, King Arthur gave his word that he'd be back in a year, and he went about trying to find the answer. Oh yes, that's right, if he didn't have the answer when he went back in a year, Sir Gromer Joure would kill him on that bridge. If he did have the right answer, he could go free.

So King Arthur went around asking everybody, and filled up lots of scrolls and parchments with the answers he got, and when the year was about up he packed them all up and got on his horse to go back to Sir Gromer Somer Joure. This was when Sir Gawain turned up on his horse and said that he better go with King Arthur just in case.

So they went along to the terrible castle, but near to it they came across an awful sight. It was a woman on a horse. She was so ugly, much uglier than Sir Gromer Somer Joure. It might have been his sister, only she was too horrible even for that. She was loathly, and had huge slobbery cheeks, and black teeth nearly falling out, and was so big and fat that the horse could hardly carry her. Anyway, she said in this croaky voice:

'I know what you are here for, King Arthur. You're carrying all your answers for Sir Gromer Somer Joure's riddle, aren't you? Let me see them, because *I* know the answer he's looking for!'

So she read all King Arthur's answers, and said:

'You haven't got the right answer anywhere here. I'll tell it you on one condition.'

'What is your condition, good lady?' said King Arthur.

'I'll whisper the answer in your ear, on condition that you promise me that one of your brave knights will marry me!'

Well, King Arthur nearly fainted when she said she'd whisper in his ear, and he went pale as milk. He didn't know what to say, but Sir Gawain said:

'Good lady, if you save the life of my noble king by giving him the answer, I promise to marry you.'

When she heard this she wobbled on her horse like a huge fat toad, and croaked with joy, and got her horse to just about stumble next to King Arthur's so she could whisper the answer in his ear.

Anyway, King Arthur and Sir Gawain left her waiting there — oh yes, she was called Lady Ragnell, wasn't she — and they went off to see Sir Gromer Somer Joure. King Arthur first let him read all the answers he had written down, to give him some suspense, and then Sir Gromer gave this terrible laugh from his belly and got his sword out ready to kill him.

'Wait!' shouted King Arthur.

Then he told him the answer the Lady Ragnell had whispered.

Then Sir Gromer growled in rage, but he let King Arthur go free like he'd promised.

Anyway, they collected Lady Ragnell and she went back with them so that she could be married to Sir Gawain at King Arthur's court. And when they got married everyone watching was silent. They were all thinking, poor old Sir Gawain! And after the wedding, Sir Gawain and his new wife got into their bedroom. And Sir Gawain was pale as milk and shaking.

'Kissss me, darling hussssband, kissss me here on my hungry lipssss!' she said in her croaky voice. She made her lips all slobbery and ready.

Sir Gawain approached her with wavering knees, took a deep breath and gave her a kiss, a bit like your Ghritachi, only I think that's all he had to do. Anyway, he turned round and almost fainted. Suddenly he heard this beautiful, lovely voice:

'Oh, Sir Gawain! Oh, Sir Gawain! You have lifted Sir Gromer Somer Joure's evil curse. Look!'

And when he turned round Sir Gawain saw the most beautiful woman he'd ever seen. He was about to go and kiss her again when she said:

'Wait! The curse is not absolutely lifted. You've got to choose whether you want me to look beautiful like this during the night time when I'm in bed with you, and be ugly like I was during the day when I'm out and about, or would you rather I was ugly at night time when I was in bed with you and lovely like I am now during the day?'

And Sir Gawain said that she could choose. And then the curse was completely lifted and she was beautiful all the time.

•

'So, Henry, what was the answer to Sir Gromer's riddle?'

'Oh, it was —'

'We can't exactly remember, Palmira...'

'Oh yes, that's right, we can't exactly remember!'

Palmira smiled.

'Anyway, Palmira, you should know, you're a woman.'

'I'm only one woman, Henry. No one can speak for everyone. And I have no idea what this Sir Gromer thinks, do I? So... I see, so *that's* your game, is it?'

'Anyway, I thought you liked riddles.'

'I'll tell you what, Henry, if you give me the answer to the riddle I'm prepared to tell you a Hodja story which is similar to that...'

'No! Hadn't you better get on with Karna getting his mantra? It's getting a bit late, you know.'

Palmira sat smiling for a few moments. 'I wonder why old Henry never told me that one?' she said to herself.

Then she continued her story.

•

'So, rama, what's the second mantra?'

'I'm afraid I can't tell it to you.'

'It's secret?'

'Not exactly, no. But I cannot speak it.'

'Can you write it? Can it not be pronounced?'

'No, it's nothing like that...'

'It's a thought that can't be put into words?'

'No, it is not one of those, if they exist. No, it can be put into words. But I will not utter it. There are some thoughts, Karna, which choke on the breath of their own utterance. It is one of these.'

'Does anyone else know it?'

'Yes. As far as I know, only Vyasa and Narada...'

'But in any case, Vyasa doesn't speak, does he?'

'Even if he did, he would not utter this mantra. Nor would Narada...'

Parashu fell silent as they passed the entrance to the cave which had sheltered them the night before.

'Rama, can you tell me nothing about this second mantra?'

'It is supposed to be very powerful. It was Vyasa who first revealed it to me. Narada was with us at the time, in Mahendra. Vyasa was examining the snake arrow, the false snake. He was feeling the two little jaws of the snake. That is why we called it the snake mantra. In those days he still spoke, occasionally. He said: "Parashu, I have just had a thought... I want to tell it to you... but if I utter it, it will be consumed..." I looked into the spider's eyes, and caught the mantra. Narada also received it. It was Narada who marvelled at its power.'

'So it's just you three who know it?'

'Yes... Other people know of it, the fox, for example, and Drona. But they don't know the mantra itself.'

'How can you possibly know that?'

The rishi smiled. 'When you understand the mantra, Karna, I will see it in your eyes.'

•

'You could at least give us a hint, Palmira!'

'Sssh! Boys... I'm telling you absolutely *nothing*!'

•

33 The brahmana's cow

When they were back in Mahendra, Parashu made Karna rest his leg. It soon healed, and he was able to resume his work. Shikhandi was away, visiting King Maya; by the time she returned only a small scar remained on Karna's thigh. But she noticed it, and was rather amused that neither Karna nor Parashu wanted to talk about it.

'What *did* you to get up to, Karna? Did he try to bite you?'

Karna shook his head.

'Right, Karna, well, I think I'll go and have a chat with Anutseka. I'll get much more gossip from him.'

'Anutseka? Who's Anutseka?'

'Who? You don't know? Well, well, that shows, doesn't it. Didn't Parashu tell you his name? Goodness! You probably know the name of a dozen bits and pieces that you entrust to Anutseka. Like your new bow, Vijaya — yes, yes, I've heard, all the brahmanas are very jealous. And I'm furious... And you probably know each of your arrows by name. Yet you don't even think about the name of the poor slave who carries this little pantheon up and down the mountain for you. Anutseka is your mule, Karna, in comparison to you, a veritable orator!'

'I missed you, Shikhandi. But I need to be alone just now, for a few more days.'

'Oh! Well, thank goodness for that. For a moment there I thought that like Rupaka to Ghritachi, you were going to ask me for a kiss...'

◊

Karna regularly went up around the east side of Mahendra, near to where the rishi had made him walk blindfold. He would practise there with Vijaya, alone, except for the occasional homa cow.

He worked with the snake and with ordinary arrows. He also trained with the javelin, packing salt into the hollow forward section.

One day he was practising with Vijaya just after a heavy fall of rain. The bow was as tightly strung as it would go, so that he could get the greatest possible range from it. Some distance from where he was standing were three homa cows, peacefully feeding.

When he felt that he had found the measure of the bowstring, he worked on his mobility with the new bow, twisting and turning as he shot at his chosen targets.

Unfortunately, just as he was releasing an arrow from Vijaya, his foot became completely stuck in a patch of mud he had not seen. The wayward arrow struck the head of one of the cows, killing it instantly, and panicking the others.

He made a note of the markings on the dead cow, and immediately returned to Mahendra. He was soon able to find out who was its owner, and explained to the distressed brahmana the manner of his cow's death. The brahmana was severe with him.

'To kill the homa cow of a brahmana is a sin exceeded only by brahmanacide itself. The death of my cow cannot go unnoticed by the gods.'

'What do you mean?'

'It is your destiny, Karna, to have your own head struck in battle, as my cow's head was struck.'

'But my foot got stuck in the mud —'

'When the hour of your death approaches, the muddy earth will swallow up the wheels of your chariot. You will be stuck, unable to move. With a single arrow, your enemy will then strike you.'

'But it was an accident... You punish this accident with my death?'

'Accident? What is an accident, Karna? If you shoot arrows on a muddy mountain slope inhabited by creatures, with a bow as powerful as Vijaya, which you evidently are not fit to hold... is it an *accident* that you kill? If that is an accident, it is also an accident that you have come here to inform me. I know you bore no malice or intent against my animal. That does not absolve you. I, after all, bear no malice towards you.'

'You curse me with death and yet you bear me no malice?'

'It is not I who will punish you. I am merely predicting the manner of your death. It is no more a curse for killing my cow than a reward for your honesty in coming to tell me. I am just telling you your future. You are cursed, but not with my curse. Rama is right. You are cursed to live with one foot outside the world of the ratha. You are indeed just half a ratha.'

'If you didn't predict that I would kill your cow, how can you know what will happen to *me*? Your curse, your prediction, whatever you wish to call it — it doesn't frighten me. If you wish to punish me, ask me to fulfil some penance, ask for some sacrifice or labour on my part — which I will willingly do for you. But do not curse me, for I do not feel it as a punishment.'

'You *shall*, Karna! You obviously do not understand the power of the gods.'

'That's certainly true. I don't.'

The brahmana tried to clear the anger from his face and smiled at Karna.

'Perhaps it is hard... being a suta — oh yes, we know. Here, as you see, we do not treat you differently just because you are a suta... But perhaps it has been hard for you, a suta, trying to live the life of a ratha?'

340

'People never seem to be able to forget that I'm a suta. If it isn't kshatriyas, or brahmanas like you, it's sutas themselves. But though they can't forget, I can't remember. I never knew what being a suta was supposed to be. Don't worry yourself on that account.'

Karna's curse, as it became known, and his response to it, were soon the talk of the brahmanas.

◊

'Karna, I'm sorry the brahmanas have reacted in this way.'

'I too am sorry, rama. For that, and for my carelessness. Would you like Vijaya back? Perhaps you could give it to the brahmana whose cow I killed? I don't think he thinks a mere half-ratha deserves such a bow.'

The rishi smiled. 'Yes, I think they may have got hold of the wrong half of your stick. But no, Karna, Vijaya is yours. In any case, they are now offended more by the arrogance with which they consider you accepted your fate, than by the loss of the cow.'

They were sitting in the little square at the top of Mahendra, both of them side by side on the ledge near the water trough. The rishi was absently throwing grain to the pigeons pecking around their feet. Karna was passing his hand through the icy water of the spring.

'Well, Karna, I think you have all that I can teach you. Except perhaps the second mantra, and that is of little importance...'

'Oh, rama... Thank you for the snake — the true snake. I noticed that you put it in my sack. I won't give it away...'

'Good... You are travelling back the same way, aren't you? I'm sorry you will have to put up with Shikhandi, and grateful that you are so kindly providing her protection for the journey...' The rishi tried to stifle his guffaw. 'I have asked her to give my regards to her father in Kampilya. Can you remind her for me? He is a good man. Have you met her brother, Drishta? I haven't, but he is supposed to be a fine young ratha.'

'Yes. He was very friendly to me during the swayamwara, especially considering the circumstances of our first encounter. He kept very quiet about Shikhandi, though. Yes, I like him, he's very good-natured.'

'And will you of course give my regards to the mouse and the boar, when you return to Hastinapura.'

'Yes, rama. Well, to Charvaka, certainly. The Grandsire doesn't take so kindly to me these days, but I will convey your regards in any case.'

Later that morning Karna tidied the straw of his bed for the last time. He climbed slowly down from the loft. The mule, waiting in the alley outside with Shikhandi, was already laden with their belongings.

The sun was not yet high enough to strike the cobbles as they wound their way down to the huge gates at the base of Mahendra. When they stepped through the doorway in the gate, they found Parashu waiting for them on the outside, leaning against the carved panels.

Shikhandi embraced the rishi.

'Tell them to send Anutseka back as soon as they can,' said Parashu. Then he gave the mule a firm pat on the haunch, and they were off.

◊

'Pigeons or goats?'

'Preferably together.'

'Do you think it's the goats that keep all this grass so short and clean?... Any other animals you want me to find for you? What's so interesting about pigeons and goats? I certainly didn't see any of either when I was last down here. Look, there's a tiger... Not interested in tigers any more?'

'I think it may be interested in us.'

'And I suppose you want me to go and shoo it away while you hold the mule? I think it's your turn, my little calf. I've done enough tiger watching on your behalf. Oh! Goodness —'

'That's what I was looking for!'

'Well! You'd think he was an elephant in musth! Either that, or the tiger was pretending to be a rabbit! How did he do it?... Look... Is he blind? Who is he, Karna? It's... It's not Vyasa, is it?'

'Yes, that's Vyasa. And he's not blind. He can see very well. I wonder why the tigers are so frightened of him?'

'It must be those fierce pigeons on him. Oh! That's fun. I like him, Karna.'

'Yes, he did that the last time I saw him.'

'I must say this is very good of you, Karna. You certainly know how to entertain your girlfriends —'

'Sssh!'

The old man had now made himself comfortable sitting cross-legged under a tree. The pigeons had hopped off him and were quietly pecking in between the shoots of grass. Karna left Shikhandi holding the mule and walked over to him. He knelt down in front of him, put his hands gently round the thin, limp arms, and squeezed warmly. Vyasa's eyes suddenly lost their glaze, and as they did so the two men broke into a smile.

Vyasa raised one of his arms free of Karna's grip, and put his hand around Karna's left ear. He squeezed the ear gently, gripping it for several seconds. Then he let go. Karna leaned forward and kissed him on the forehead. When he looked again into the old man's eyes, they had recovered their glaze; and the arms had gone limp again.

Karna returned to Shikhandi, and the mule started off.

'Thank you, Shikhandi.' Karna grinned at her, but she could see on his face that it was going to be a while before he would talk; so she went up to join the mule.

Karna walked silently behind them.

◊

When eventually they arrived at the village where Karna had left his chariot and horses, they were greeted with some surprise.

'What happened to your white sash?' the villagers said to Karna.

They saw Vijaya perched on his shoulder.

'That is the great rama's bow! He *gave* you his bow?'

They hardly believed Karna's assurances; but they could believe even less that he had been able to steal the bow or kill the rishi. Shikhandi calmed their fears, but the villagers could not completely abandon their suspicions.

While the mule drank steadily from a trough, Karna relieved the animal of their baggage, transferring it to his chariot.

The sound of the river flowing through the narrow valley merged with the murmurs from the watching villagers. The mule interrupted its drink to receive a pat from Karna and a hug from Shikhandi.

With water still dripping from its mouth, and its nostrils twitching slightly, the mule watched the two horses plunge their necks forward as they started the chariot off on its long journey.

•

'Look, Palmira, if we tell you the answer to Sir Gromer Somer Joure's riddle, will you tell us what that mantra is?'

'Don't be ridiculous, Henry. I'll work out the answer to your riddle — you work out the mantra.'

'That's not fair, Palmira!'

'And why not?'

'You're grown up...'

'Remember, we're only children! We've got... we've got pressing needs —'

'All-pressing needs! Mind you, Palmira, I reckon that being grown up is just being able to hide that you're not grown up.'

'That must be what rama meant with all those rings, isn't it? On the trees?'

'Rubbish, boys. Being grown up is being less fearful of showing one's maturity... Ah! That reminds me... Just before you go — and I'm sorry it's so late — being grown up reminds me of a Hodja story —'

'Oh Palmira!!'

'Yes, just a little Hodja story, and then you can run off home.'

Palmira waited for them to settle down again. She peered up through the trellis above her. The stars were beginning to show against the darkening sky. The wind had started to die down soon after sunset; but it was still strong enough to sustain a constant murmur as it played against the pillars round Palmira's yard, rustling up the vine leaves.

'The Hodja and his young son', she began, 'once went to a nearby town to try to arrange some music lessons for the boy. On such journeys the Hodja usually went on his donkey, but out of respect for Anutseka the mule, who has worked very hard for us, and for really very little reward, I think on this particular occasion it's only appropriate that they travelled with a mule. A very nice mule, a bit like Anutseka, only I think this one was a she, not a he.

'It was a very hot day, with the sun shining brightly, hardly a cloud in the sky. We see, approaching, the Hodja himself, guiding the mule; his son was humming quietly to himself on her back. I think the boy must have been really quite musical, otherwise the Hodja would probably have been satisfied with a teacher from their own town.

'Very soon, after a bend in the road, they met an old man travelling in the opposite direction.

'"Look at that boy," grumbled the old man. "In perfect health, riding on the mule while his father has to walk. Young people today are so thoughtless, so inconsiderate! To say nothing of their lack of respect for their elders! And a learned man with a turban, at that! What disrespect!"

'As soon as the old man was out of sight, the Hodja's son stopped the mule.

'"Now, my son," said the Hodja, "you really shouldn't pay too much attention to what other people tell you. Don't get down just because of what some old fool says to you. Stand up for yourself! Make up your own mind!"

'The son dismounted.

'"Boy! What do you think you're doing?"

'"I'm standing up for myself. I've made up my mind, father, you get on the mule."

'The Hodja glared down at him.

'Just then an acquaintance of theirs came into view and overtook them on his donkey.

'"Oh yes, you two arguing again as usual, then?"

'"Oh no... no," said the Hodja, climbing up quickly onto the mule.

'They continued on their way in silence. The Hodja's son had stopped humming, and the Hodja himself had something of a frown on his face.

'Very soon they saw two young women travelling towards them.

'"Just look at that," murmured one of the women, in a voice just loud enough for the Hodja and his son to hear. "What a selfish man, taking it easy on his mule while his poor little son has to walk. Parents these days just have no idea, do they? These learned men, all they really know is how to tie a turban!"

'The instant they had disappeared from view, the Hodja stopped the mule.

'"Right, boy, you're coming up here as well. I don't see why I should take the blame for your stubborn foolishness!"

'So the two of them balanced unsteadily on the animal's back.

'After a little while the road began to rise up a hill, and the mule began to wheeze and cough. Just at this point they met an old lady coming down the hill with her three grandchildren and a dog.

'"Grandma! Look at that poor mule, it's going to fall down and die any minute."

'"You're absolutely right, children," she cried, "those cruel people must think animals have no feelings. What will the world come to if people show such lack of thought for their fellow creatures! They just presume whatever it suits them in order to justify this cruelty! It's a wonder that man is not ashamed to wear his turban!"

'The Hodja urged the mule to hurry up, hoping to get away from them as quickly as possible. Then he dismounted.

'"Come on, we'd best get down, son."

'As his son got down, the Hodja stared angrily at the mule:

'"I suppose we should have asked *you* for *your* opinion in the first place, eh?"

'So they continued, both on foot, leading the mule behind them.

'Shortly after they were over the brow of the hill they met three youths walking noisily along, singing and joking.

'"Aaargh-ha-ha! Is your turban too heavy for your mule, sir?"

'"Hooaargh! They'll be carrying that mule next!"

'"Wha-hey, old boy, don't you think you ought to take your sandals off as well — they'll get worn out with all that walking!"

'When they were gone, the Hodja and his son stopped and looked at each other.

'"We can't *carry* her, father!"

'The Hodja thought for a while. Then he took his turban off. He used it to bandage one of the legs of the mule.

'The rest of their journey to the town passed quite peacefully, and they received no more complaints from any fellow travellers. When they arrived at the town, they soon made all the necessary arrangements for the young boy's music lessons.

'On the way back they both walked, and kept the bandage on the mule.

'"This is obviously the best way to travel, my son."

'Very soon, however, they met the first old man they had encountered, who was now on his way back.

'"Ah! I see you've injured your mule! Young boy, let that be a lesson to you to respect your elders! All because of you, your poor father has had to use his turban to bandage the animal!"

'Then they came across the two women.

'"Ah! you've injured your mule! Let that be a lesson to you to look after your son properly! In your case, sir, your turban is clearly better employed as a bandage than as a sign of learning!"

'Then they came across the old lady with her grandchildren and the dog.

'"Ah, look, children, they took our advice and are walking back! Perhaps losing his turban made him think at last! Better late than never, I suppose!"

'Then they came across the three boisterous youths.

'One of them, almost choking himself with laughter, had to sit down in the middle of the road, pointing helplessly first at the Hodja's bare head, then at the mule's leg. The other two youths were in much the same condition; and since the road was too narrow at this point to get by, the poor Hodja and his son had to wait a while, trying to gain some inspiration from the quiet dignity of their mule.

'"Aarrgh-ha-haaargh! I didn't know... aaargh! I didn't know that's where mules are s'posed to wear their turbans!"'

•

Day Six: *The Rajasuya*

34 The invitation

'Draupadi is sure that she saw Karna in Kampilya — he must have returned from Mahendra.'

'Yes, she told me. I suppose he must have been on his way to Anga.' Arjuna turned his eyes to the ground as he said this, anticipating Yudhi's reaction.

'Oh!... There are times when I could strangle Bhima!... Like a ravenous fish, to satisfy his hunger he will rise to almost any piece of meat. And if there is a hidden hook he always seems to wriggle off, leaving us — leaving me — caught right upon it!'

'I don't think wolf-belly would like to be compared to a fish!' replied Arjuna, trying to make light of it.

'You are almost as bad, Arjuna. Did I not tell you all *not* to ask for any tribute? You were to *invite*, not subjugate!'

'But it is customary to pay tribute for the Rajasuya. We were *offered* the gifts, brother.'

'You are like little boys! You are like little boys who have been plucking all the unripe fruit from the neighbours' trees. You will not only fail to gratify your hunger, you will also spoil the seeds of your future contentment. If you *have* to satisfy your desires, at least pluck your fruit in season: then you will enjoy the fruit of the seed as well as the sweetness of the fruit. The tree may offer you its fruit. But you must judge its ripeness.'

'Yudhi, forgive me, but we didn't have to pluck unripe fruit. The tree holds on to that. This fruit fell. What we received was offered to us just as the tree releases what is ready —'

'Just as the lizard offers its tail, Arjuna!'

Arjuna raised his arms in exasperation. '*You* ask so little tax from your shudras and vaishyas... How else can we pay for the Rajasuya? Don't you realise the cost? Be practical, Yudhi!'

'As a bee collects honey, without destroying the flowers, so should a ruler tax his subjects, without injury. Do you think I do not know the cost of this wretched Rajasuya? I understand the cost rather better than you do, I fear. You remember what Charvaka said about such things: there is more to the cost than the price. Why should the Rajasuya be paid for by those who will not benefit from it? If you want it, Arjuna, you pay for it.'

'Yudhi...' Arjuna decided to change the subject. 'Did Draupadi tell you what Karna was doing in Kampilya?'

'No, she didn't. Why?'

'It's not the most direct route from Mahendra to Anga, is it? Besides, she was reticent. I think she knows something we don't... Didn't you get that impression?'

'No. I didn't question her about it. Listen, Arjuna, when you go to Hastinapura, to *invite* them, please, please do not accept any gift. You know how it would anger Dur. Do you not realise what will happen if Karna, who has every right to be furious, blows his anger on Dur's flame? What if Karna challenges Bhima? Arjuna! Listen to me. You think you have charmed lives, don't you? You think Karna can't harm Bhima? He defeated Jara, before Bhima —'

'But he did not kill him, brother.'

'And you think that's a sign of *weakness*? You and Krishna have both admitted that Bhima had to kill Jara — to save his own skin. And because of that, I don't hold your brother any more responsible than you or Krishna over Jara's death... It's his second act of killing that shames us all...'

Arjuna frowned, and looked down at his toes. 'All right, I will be at my most courteous. I will refuse any gift.' He looked up at his brother. 'You're right about Bhima. I also was ashamed... I think he did it partly for me — in revenge for the tournament. You know how much he hates Karna.'

'And you don't?'

'I used to, yes.' Arjuna thought for a moment. 'I don't think I do now. I feel sorry for him. If anything, I feel sorry for him.' Arjuna paused, and then changed the subject. 'Yudhi, why didn't *you* invite them — when you went over with Bhima?'

'*That* visit to Hastinapura was for one purpose and one purpose only. *Think*, brother. It would have appeared to add insult to apology...'

◊

'I only know what Vrisha told me just before he went back to Anga.'

Charvaka took Dur by the arm, trying to calm him, and guided him towards a stool. But Dur remained standing.

'It seems,' continued Charvaka, 'that Bhima killed him when he refused to pay any tribute. After that no one else in Anga offered any resistance — the kshatriyas there didn't shoot a single arrow! Bhima went off with cattle, goats and some grain. He took them all back to Indraprastha, together with the cattle from Magadha.'

'Was Arjuna still with him, sire?'

'No, no. Krishna and Arjuna left Magadha straight after the fight with Jara. Krishna, as you probably know, came here to give us the news about Jara. I imagine Arjuna must have returned to Indraprastha... But you were not here the night Krishna stayed, were you? Bhima must have taken Jara's cattle on his own initiative. And it must have been his idea also to enter Anga. Neither Krishna nor Arjuna had anything to do with it.'

'So Yudhi wouldn't have known either... And what d'you think Karna will do? Do you think he's heard? He must have. To think, *he* was going to visit Jara-sandha on his return from Mahendra. You've heard of course that he's due back any moment? How long has it been since we last saw him? Apparently he's been in Kampilya, of all places!... Sire, what did Yudhi do with the cattle? Is he keeping it?'

'I don't know, my boy, try not to work yourself up! I do know something which he made Bhima do. This will please you. You will never guess.' This time Dur took the seat which the rishi offered. 'Sanjaya told me. All the lower castes here know about it, but this is not something you will hear from the lips of a brahmana or a kshatriya. Though I suppose I count as a brahmana. You know of course that Vaitanika's family is still living here in Hastinapura?'

'Yes. I must visit his parents.'

'You are not the only one with that idea: Yudhi and Bhima came to Hastinapura — or rather, Yudhi brought Bhima here — on an unofficial visit. Apparently, they were both dressed modestly, in black... It did not occur to me when I first heard this, but of course, they must both have known Vaitanika quite well. I have a feeling that Yudhi was rather fond of him; though the others probably hated him — after the tournament. Yes, Yudhi and Bhima visited Vaitanika's family. Can you imagine it?'

Dur's expression brightened. 'What happened?'

'Yudhi made his brother pay homage to Vaitanika's parents. Poor Yudhi! It will only increase Bhima's anger. How can one punish someone like him? Humiliation only winds up his anger like a spring, to be unleashed on some future occasion.'

Dur was silent for a few moments. Then he looked up at the rishi, tentatively.

'The Grandsire and the others seem very reticent about what happened in Magadha. When I ask them what Krishna told them, they just say that it was you he spoke to, that I should ask you, sire. Why did Krishna not tell them about it?'

'He was in a hurry, my boy; he needed to see me, so it just turned out that I was the one he gave the news to. You want to know what happened, eh?'

'Yes, sire, if you're inclined to tell me.'

'Certainly, I'll tell you.' Charvaka paused to stroke his beard. 'You know that they went disguised as brahmanas, the three of them? Jara was always respectful towards brahmanas. But they didn't enter the city by the main gate. I don't know how they got in, Krishna didn't say.'

'Why the tricks? After all, Karna went there openly?'

'I suspect that Krishna didn't want to give Shishu-pala time to arrange their murder. You know that Shishu detests Krishna. I don't think Jara-sandha himself has ever been very bothered by Krishna. No, I think his persecution of Krishna was very much at Shishu's instigation. Jara was a little suspicious of them, of these three strange brahmanas, but he treated them respectfully, inviting them to dine with him in the great hall.

'Soon after they had started to eat Shishu hobbled in, and recognised Krishna almost instantly. They could see him shaking with excitement as he pointed Krishna out to Jara. When they finished eating, Jara summoned them to approach his throne, and addressed them:

'"Who are you, dressed as brahmanas, yet bearing the marks of the bowstring on your hands? The energy of a brahmana dwells in his tongue, not in his arm. In his speech, not in his actions. Why did you not enter my city through the great southern gate?'

'Krishna then replied:

'"King Jara-sandha, if you wish to see in us the energy of the kshatriya, gladly we will satisfy you. The main gate is used to enter the abode of a friend. The back way is reserved for enemies."

'"What injury have I done you?" replied Jara. "Why do you regard me as an enemy?"

'Krishna looked around the hall before replying. He told me that he raised his voice deliberately so that everyone should hear:

'"King Jara-sandha, you have wrongfully dragged into this city many warriors whom you offer in sacrifice to your god Rudra. It is for this offence that we regard you as an enemy. I myself have a more ancient quarrel with you. But it is not that which brings me here. It is the human sacrifice which offends us, and offends Dharma. We have come here, at the behest of a great king, to kill you. I am Krishna, son of Vasu-deva. My two friends are brothers of this great king, and sons of King Pandu: Prince Arjuna and Prince Bhima-sena. We challenge you, King Jara-sandha. Either release all the warriors you hold captive, or die under our arm."

'To Krishna's great surprise Shishu-pala started cackling, and there was a rumble of laughter right around the hall. Krishna was quite alarmed by this. Then King Jara-sandha rose up from his throne and replied:

'"If one of you is brave enough to engage me without weapons, I am ready to fight him."

'Now everyone fell silent. Krishna replied:

'"Which one of us are you brave enough to fight, King Jara-sandha?"

'It was so quiet that Krishna said he could feel Jara thinking. Shishu started to shake, but he did not say anything. Then Jara announced his decision.

'"I have heard of the great strength of Prince Bhima-sena. If I am to be conquered — and it seems to be in season — it is better to be conquered by the best. Let it be Bhima."

'There was a commotion of excitement around the hall, during which Shishu did his best to change Jara's mind. But Jara was not having it:

'"If I choose to fight Krishna, people will say I am a coward."

'"But he killed Kamsa!" cried Shishu. "Krishna killed your own son-in-law."

'"It is true, Krishna and his friends did remove my son-in-law from the throne of Mathura. For which Krishna has already received his punishment: did he not flee like a coward from Mathura? So, let him live a little longer in his shame. For even now as a coward he stands, safely under Bhima's shade, knowing that I would not waste my arm on him. No, Shishu... I will fight Bhima. But, if I defeat him, then, if you wish, *you* may fight Krishna."

'The following evening they wrestled.

'Bhima was just too powerful for Jara to subdue. And Jara was too agile and tough for Bhima to trap. After a while they both became exhausted, so they decided to continue the fight the next night. In this manner they proceeded for several days!

'On many occasions Jara appeared to have a good hold on Bhima, but this Pandava has such strength of limb that there was nothing for Jara to do but watch him shift his weight until he could explode out of his grasp.

'Bhima, for his part, was often able to lift Jara clear of the ground, and throw the king. But Jara fell so expertly that he seemed to bounce away before Bhima could hold him down...'

Charvaka interrupted his account, for at that moment Sanjaya appeared hesitantly at the entrance to the rishi's workshop.

'Ah! Sanjaya, come in! I was just telling Dur about the fight between Bhima and Jara. Come in!'

'I won't stay, Charvaka. I just came in to tell you that Karna's back. He's just arrived from Kampilya. And Vrisha's here as well — he's come from Anga. I expect they will be along any moment, sire. I thought I should tell you, since I was passing...'

'Did he say anything about?...' Dur's question trailed off, but Sanjaya understood.

'Not to me. Anyway, you'll be able to ask him yourself,' answered Sanjaya. Then he left them.

'Well...' Charvaka muttered to himself for a moment, and then continued with his account. 'Where was I? Ah, yes... In the end Krishna advised Bhima on a special tactic to overcome the king.'

'Sorry to interrupt, sire, but... should I broach the subject with Karna, or will you?'

'It seems to me that you will, my boy. May I continue?... The following evening, towards the end of the time allotted to the fighting, Bhima was able to grab hold of both the king's ankles. Before Jara could kick himself free, Bhima started to turn, whirling around and around until Jara was well clear of the ground. Bhima was turning so fast that Jara could not bend his body to reach him with his arms. The blood rushing to his head caused Jara to have a fit, and he was probably dead before Bhima let go of him.

'So...' Charvaka paused for a moment. 'So, that was the end of King Jara-sandha. And when Krishna then told Jara's son, Jaya-tsena, about the Rajasuya, Jaya immediately offered his allegiance to Yudhi.' The rishi paused while Dur swore under his breath. Then he resumed his account.

'Yes... Even Shishu offered his allegiance to Yudhi — he was quick to do so, since Krishna had to restrain Bhima from immediately challenging Shishu. Jaya-tsena, as a sign of friendship, invited Bhima to stay with him for a while as his guest, and Krishna and Arjuna left him there. Evidently Jaya-tsena must have offered Bhima the cattle to take away as a gift for the Pandavas. But Krishna swore that it must have been Bhima's idea to enter Anga.'

'And had Jara —'

Dur was interrupted by the sight of Karna coming in. Karna smiled at them. He went first to Charvaka, embracing him, then to Dur.

'You know about... about Vaitanika?' Dur asked him. 'Bhima has gone too far this time. Do you wish to challenge him, or shall I?'

'No, Dur,' Karna replied. The rishi, stroking his beard, took a seat and looked at his pupil.

'Let Yudhi punish him,' said Karna.

'Yudhi? You're not even angry, Karna! What's the matter with you? Vaitanika was *your* friend! *I* am more angry than you!'

'For my part, Dur, I might as well be angry with the wind... Isn't Bhima, after all, the son of Vayu?'

Dur was at a loss for a reply.

'As for your anger,' continued Karna, 'the brahmanas say that there is only one cure for it, and that is to fill the mind instead with kindness.' Karna paused for a moment to enjoy the effect on Dur. 'Sadly,' he continued, 'those caught in the gripe of anger have no stomach for this medicine!'

'Don't talk rubbish!' cried Dur, recovering his tongue. 'I can assure you that if I was this minute standing over a prostrate Bhima, listening to his pleas for mercy, my anger would be very well cured!'

'The anger would have drained out of *you*, Dur, certainly; but it would have all poured into Bhima. What sort of a cure is it when the disease leaves you, but only to infect others?'

'Let Bhima suffer from it! Once he is suffering from the infusion of my anger, then you can go and advise *him*. Yes, let *him* have the benefit of your excellent cure!'

'Boys, boys...' interrupted Charvaka, rising from his seat. 'I have to say, Dur, that Karna does have a small point: for while the disease remains in the world, it may return to reinfect you. Or if not you, then your children.'

'But Karna doesn't even seem to be at all *sad* about Vaitanika,' appealed Dur, 'let alone angry!'

'And why should I *seem* sad?'

'Didn't he mean anything to you?'

Karna glanced briefly at Charvaka. Then he took Dur by the arm.

'Listen, Dur... I will visit Vai's family today. Vrisha is with them at the moment, in fact. If they wish me to challenge Bhima, I will challenge Bhima. But if they do not, I will not. I don't think they will want Vai's death avenged by Bhima's. I don't think even Vai would have wanted that. And Dur, rest assured, so as not to disconcert his family, I will do my best to *seem* sad.'

As Karna was speaking, Sanjaya entered once again.

'What is it this time?' asked Charvaka. 'You came to warn me of Karna's visit — why didn't you warn me of yours? I was hoping for a quiet afternoon!'

'There are two men outside who want to see Dur,' said Sanjaya with a mischievous smile.

'Who are they?' asked Dur.

'Well...' Sanjaya jutted out his lower jaw. 'I think they're from Indraprastha... messengers, I expect. One calls himself Arjuna, and —'

'*What*?'

'This is terrible,' complained Charvaka. 'Can't you go away, all of you?'

'Sire,' asked Dur, 'may I speak with them here?'

'I believe they also want to speak to you, Charvaka,' pointed out Sanjaya. 'Shall I ask them in?'

'Bring them in, Sanjaya, bring them in...'

Sanjaya led in Arjuna and Nakula.

'We were told we should find you here, Prince Dur-yodhana,' said Arjuna, rather formally. 'Greetings, Karna... and you, sire...' He bowed his head towards Charvaka. 'Prince Dur-yodhana, we have just been to see King Dhrita-rashtra, and also Lord Bhishma. We have come to invite you all to the Rajasuya of King Yudhi-sthira, which will be held on the new moon after next. But you are most welcome to stay with us for the full sixteen days before the ceremony.

'Karna,' continued Arjuna, diffusing the embarrassment of Dur's silence, 'we greatly regret and apologise for the rash actions of Prince Bhima-sena in Anga. We did not think you would be here in Hastinapura — I thought you may have gone straight to Anga — but I'm sure that if Yudhi had known you'd be here, he would have charged me specifically to visit you with an apology... You have been in Mahendra?'

'Yes, Arjuna,' said Karna. 'And if I am included in your invitation, I look forward to seeing your great city.'

For a moment Arjuna and Nakula seemed taken aback by Karna's good humour.

'Of course you are included,' said Arjuna, recovering himself, 'and you, sire.'

'Thank you,' said Charvaka. 'But I think it may be wiser for me not to attend —'

'Sire, Yudhi insisted that we invite you specifically — apart from anything else, we owe you a great debt of gratitude.'

'You are most kind, Arjuna, but... Please tell Yudhi that I will be there in spirit, that my absence should not be taken by him as a sign of disapproval. Please be sure to tell him that I am concerned not to disturb the brahmanas — both yours and those who will be attending, from here and other places... I'm sure you understand, Arjuna.'

'Yes, sire.'

Arjuna and Nakula bowed to them, and left, accompanied by Sanjaya.

Dur sat down in gloomy silence.

Karna turned to Charvaka. 'In Kampilya I heard of Jara's death... Do you happen to know if, while I was away, he had released his captives? Vrisha wasn't sure.'

'Yes, Jara had let them all go... Krishna found that his dungeons were quite empty. The jailers spoke of their release, and of the restoration of much of the livestock. Jara had kept his promise to you.'

◊

'Charvaka! Stop trying to change the subject!'

'But Shakuni, please! You know that I think it's pointless talking about infinity. Even less can be said about it than about nothing! Yes... in that respect they're curiously similar... Anyway, why didn't you go when I was there?'

'Yes, I know I should have. But you were so busy, I would hardly have had time to talk to you properly... But I really am looking forward to seeing it, particularly the palace... By the way, when I return, do you think you can have a go at the eye-pieces you suggested? I can't see clearly much further than a dice table, my dear! I hope my eyesight will do justice to your designs... Yes, I'm very excited, Charvaka... By the way, I told Uluka to pick me up from here — I'm travelling in his chariot.'

'Do try not to quarrel with him,' said Charvaka, reaching out for a dice to start his throw.

'Yes... How is it that you never seem to quarrel with Karna? He is practically your son, after all. And Vrisha, too.'

'I'm sure that I *do* quarrel with Karna. The trouble is, with him, it's so hard to know that one is quarrelling. He so rarely shows his anger. It's not as though the poor boy doesn't feel it. And it's not as though he's never stubborn or contrary. On the contrary... As for Vrisha, however exasperating he gets, how can you possibly get angry with him?' Charvaka paused to position a betting counter. 'But there is a difference, I think, between your son and these two. I shouldn't be surprised if your son respects and admires many of his own friends more than you. But look at Vrisha — even though he seems to have so many friends, he has never forgotten what I have given him. Your Uluka is probably hardly aware of what you've done for him. Whereas Vrisha could hardly be more aware: remember how determined he was to come to Varanasi? To learn, to be taught... He was a marvel! And also Karna, though in a very different way. So... they seem to respect me. But it seems to be different with real offspring. It will take time for Uluka to detach himself enough from you to appreciate you...'

'By that time he'll probably have got himself killed...' Shakuni paused to point at the dice table. 'Why don't you ride Kali on that *4*?'

'Am I not on a pig? Oh dear, Shakuni — I miscounted! Now, if it was Uluka you were playing, and he had failed to keep his tally, you would be extremely short with him!'

'Don't miscount your luck as well, Charvaka!'

'So, there's a ladder on that *4*, is there? There must be, if you say so... Oh, yes...' Charvaka placed some betting counters and tapped twice.

'Are you going for a kill already? Most premature.'

'It's hardly a promising position, is it — you're always recommending the value of having a few clear *1*s to climb on, and there aren't any... Got you! Not a great line, I admit... You start...'

They cleared the dice table and placed their starting bets.

'And remember', said Charvaka, 'how much more patient you are with Dur than with your son. You will try to keep his spirits up, won't you? I'm sure the two weeks will pass slowly and unpleasantly for him. You know how upset he has been ever since the Rajasuya was first mentioned. And Karna is sometimes a little impatient with him.'

'Why don't you come, then? Dur has great respect for you. You will calm him.'

'No, that's out of the question, Shakuni... Ah! Vrisha...'

Shakuni and Charvaka put down their counters when they saw Vrisha enter.

'Vrisha!' exclaimed Shakuni. 'Have you got a ride to Indraprastha, my dear? Why don't you come with me and Uluka?'

'I'm not going, Shakuni.'

'You're not going?'

'I hate ceremonies. And anyway, don't forget that they're not letting sutas in — apart from my brother.'

'Are you sure you wouldn't be admitted?' wondered Charvaka. 'I hear that Yudhi has insisted on allowing women into the hall.'

'Yes, but I'm not exactly a kshatriya queen, am I! And anyway, he's only letting them in for the actual ceremony on the last day. And at a separate table. I say he — it's his brothers, not Yudhi. Yudhi wanted to admit everybody, but his brothers wouldn't have it. I heard that Yudhi even wanted to let his citizens not have to wear their coloured sashes and headcloths, not just during the ceremony, not ever! But his brothers wouldn't have it.'

'But what about seeing Indraprastha?' suggested Shakuni. 'Oh, of course, you practically built it with Charvaka, didn't you! Well, you'll be able to keep this poor rishi company, with all of us away... Have you any nice questions for him?'

'Please, Shakuni,' exclaimed Charvaka, 'don't get him started.'

'I do have one question, sire — when are you going to visit Vai's parents? Why don't you come with me to see them?'

'Yes, I should. I shall. Vrisha, do you think they really didn't want Karna to challenge Bhima? Perhaps they were being polite, not wanting to put such a burden on him...'

'On Bhima or on Karna! No, sire, they meant it — at least, I *think* so. Especially after Yudhi brought Bhima to them. They didn't actually tell me, but I think that Yudhi must have offered, or got Bhima to offer himself, for punishment. But I think they'd appreciate a visit from you.'

'I'll go with you, Vrisha. Perhaps later this morning, once I've got rid of Shakuni. And provided you have no more awkward questions for me today.'

'Take no notice of this rishi, my dear!' exhorted Shakuni. 'Just make sure you keep asking him for the meaning of life. Don't settle for anything less!'

'The meaning of life?' repeated Vrisha. 'I can't even get clear from him the meaning of *anything*! In fact, I don't know why I bother to talk to Charvaka about anything, since he can't even tell me what I'm talking *about*!'

Shakuni raised his eyebrows. 'What are you talking about, my dear?'

'Just that!' exclaimed Vrisha.

'It's his old trouble,' sighed Charvaka. 'Do you know that this boy once came in and suggested to Karna that he was merely shooting at sensations in his mind! I don't think you've ever quite got over that, have you, Vrisha?'

'Sire, it's you that hasn't ever quite got it over to me! Which isn't surprising, I suppose, since you say yourself you don't really know what we talk about.'

'That's not exactly true, my boy. I know at least what we *don't* talk about: we don't talk about what you *think* we talk about.'

'That's not exactly true either, sire! I accept that we don't talk about what I *used* to think we talked about. But that doesn't help me understand what it is we *do* talk about —'

'Vrisha, my dear,' interrupted Shakuni. 'You have lost me... I still don't understand what you're talking about. What precisely is your position?'

'Well,' explained Vrisha, 'when I was a young boy, as Charvaka says, I was struck by the fact that when we look at the world, even while we are talking about it to each other, we each have our own perception of it — and of each other! And, I agree, I was tempted to think in those days that what I talked about, when I seemed to be describing the world, was really only my own sensations. Because, after all, that was all that came before my mind, as it were.'

'I see,' said Shakuni. 'So, if I may take an example, you thought that *red* described something about your sensation, rather than the colour of a flower which exists for all to see outside your mind?'

'Exactly. That's what I used to think. Now I realise that must be nonsense. Red is a colour. It's an attribute of something another person may point to, pick up, and so on. It's not an attribute of my sensation. Even though it's because my sensations have such attributes that I can make sense of the world — including other people. A friend of mine in Varanasi had two quite different sensations of colour, depending on which eye he was looking with. He could identify red things perfectly well, but red was definitely not the attribute of either of his sensations... No, I realise all that now.'

'No thanks to the rishi, I'm sure,' said Shakuni. He glanced at Charvaka, who was scratching his beard as he listened. 'I expect all he said,' Shakuni added, 'was that there's more to sense than meets the eye... He can be a most unhelpful rishi!'

'No, that's not quite fair,' conceded Vrisha. 'Charvaka did try to explain what he believed was going on... That when people look at the world, there's some sort of correspondence between their sensations and what's going on in the world; and therefore there's some correspondence between what's going on in the minds of the various people... And that it's this correspondence that allows us to do what we do and say what we say... that our sensations make it all possible, even though they aren't what's being talked about.'

'And is it the huge complexity of this process that worries you?' suggested Shakuni.

'What do you mean?' asked Vrisha.

'I'm thinking of the fact that when we use language — which seems to be the focus of your worry, my dear — different observers not only have their own perceptions of the world they are describing, which must correspond, but also they have their own perceptions of the very signs and sounds they use to communicate with each other; which again, must also correspond. Is that the problem?'

'No, no. That doesn't bother me, Shakuni. No, I realise that all of these perceptions have to engage with each other in a very complicated way... and that we're hardly aware of all this process going on, underneath us, as it were. Charvaka uses the example of moving one's limbs... That we're unaware of how all the muscles link to each other to make it possible... we learn how to do it all without thinking. And it seems to work all right.'

'Good,' said Shakuni. 'So what's the difficulty?'

'Well... It's not just about language, Shakuni... I don't think so... If Charvaka's right so far, and I'm sure he is, I mean, I can't see another way... But if he's right, then isn't it as though the world — the world outside our minds, I mean — were casting shadows onto our minds?... But then... Well...'

Vrisha approached the dice table and picked up two of the dice.

'We were in the middle of a game!' cried Shakuni.

'Oh, sorry!' Vrisha turned to Charvaka. 'Sorry, sire!'

'Well, go on,' urged Shakuni, 'now that you've saved the rishi from a bad position...'

'I can't express it very well,' went on Vrisha. 'But... if a thing casts a shadow on a wall, the thing casting the shadow need have very little resemblance to the shadow cast... Surely, I can't be talking about the things that are actually in the world... since I only have before me the shadows they project... What I mean is, we use all sorts of words to describe the world, and yet there may not be things out there which do *exactly* correspond to what we see and talk about. *Some* correspondence, yes, I suppose there must be... but how much? All right, there's *something* in the world which is making me have the images I'm having, as I look at these two dice...' Vrisha rolled them in his hand. 'And which makes me have the appropriate sensations as I touch... *them.* But how can I be talking about the things in the world, when there might not even be *two* things corresponding to these... It could be one thing casting two shadows... To say nothing of the shape! I mean, we *say* the dice are tetrahedrons. But what sort of shape might not project what we describe that way?'

Charvaka shook his head and sighed. 'What sort of shape? Why, a tetrahedron, of course! Those dice *are* tetrahedra!'

'My dear,' said Shakuni to Vrisha, 'you must be careful not to speak as though there is something really out there which, if only we could get beyond the shadows, we, or some superior beings, perhaps, could see in its true light. There are no such beings. There is no such point of view. There is no such light that comes from no one point to cast no shadow. Certainly, there can be different points of view, different beings, different observers. Different *kinds* of observer. I agree, if a change projected onto one observer was not perceptible to another, they could not talk to each other about that change. But they would also be talking about the world. Either they're talking *about* their sensations, which you agree is absurd. Or else they're talking about the things that project these sensations — the world. What else is there for them to talk about?'

Shakuni saw that Vrisha remained unconvinced, and continued.

'You must have heard the story of the three blind men who came across an elephant for the first time? They spoke about it in very strange terms indeed. But still they were talking about something in the world, outside each of their minds.'

'About one and the same thing you would recognise as an elephant,' added Charvaka.

'All right,' replied Vrisha, 'what about this, then: suppose I've discovered a special distillation of Madhuca fruit, which doesn't just intoxicate people with illusions — this cordial of mine specifically gives them excellent illusions of elephants. We give various people this cordial; and then we watch them; and we listen to them talking to each other, remarking on the size and strength of the elephant's trunk; and so on. They feel the air, as though there were really something there. But we can see there isn't anything there! In other words, none of the sensations these people are having are caused by the world outside of their minds. It's like a dream. Well, what are they all talking about? What is it that they see and touch and hear? Since in this case there is nothing but their own perceptions, what else can they be talking about? Surely, it must be just their perceptions? Perhaps not directly, or literally...'

'You mean, perhaps,' suggested Shakuni, 'that what they're talking about must be explained as some sort of construct, some abstraction, based on their perceptions... Yes, I see... And presumably you want to argue that if that is what's going on in your cultivated dream, then why not also in reality? Yes... Yes, that is an interesting point, my dear... Well, Charvaka, what *are* we talking about?'

'Ah!' cried Charvaka. 'Saved by Uluka!'

'Oh, dear,' protested Shakuni. 'Listen, you two, when I return, we must hear what the rishi has to say, yes?'

'Off you go, Shakuni. Enjoy yourself. Look after him, my boy,' Charvaka advised Uluka. 'Don't let him get lost or fall into any of those pools in the palace!'

35 The mist

'You really must make me one of those little eye-pieces you promised!' said Shakuni to Charvaka. The rishi had heard that Shakuni was back from Indraprastha, and had lost no time in calling round to ask him how things had gone.

'Twice I stepped into pools of water,' continued Shakuni, 'thinking they were glass! And several times I tried to walk into your crystal walls! My dear, I hope I did no damage. It really is no place for the short-sighted. Though I have to say that Dur, who has perfect vision, was also much deceived. Make yourself comfortable, my dear, sit yourself down. I'm expecting Bhishma and probably also Dur very shortly. Have you seen either of them since our return? Most of the others are still in Indraprastha. It seems that Bhishma and I are the only ones who have work to get on with — we both would have loved to stay for longer. Dur, unfortunately, could not wait to get out of there.'

'No, I haven't seen either of them yet. Yes... I suppose it must have seemed a palace of illusions —'

'Oh, Charvaka! Your mirrors! They were wonderful! The huge ones in the great hall, especially. I wish I could have seen them in focus, from the very centre of the hall... How perfect they appeared close up. Hardly a ripple in the glass.'

'The glass came from Maya. It was quite a problem fixing the sheets onto the boats. So... You enjoyed yourself, then? Did everyone behave themselves? The Kurus and the Pandavas sat down together peacefully?'

'Oh yes. But there was one incident that was rather disturbing... Very disturbing... A fellow called Shishu-pala insulted Krishna, in front of everybody.'

'Really?'

'Yes... Krishna killed him.'

'*What*? Krishna *killed* him? What do you mean? Did he challenge him to single combat?'

'Not exactly... No, he killed him there and then. You know how these young men overreact in public. You had better ask Bhishma or Dur — I was rather engrossed at the time by your mirrors... You should have seen the lamps and torches multiplied inside them! You know, while I was gazing at those mirrors I was struck by a way of looking at that problem we were discussing before I left, that problem concerning the infinite. I think this analogy might interest you, since you seem to prefer reflection to reality!'

'I do? What are you talking about? You know I avoid similes like the plague!'

'Hah! You must admit that you sometimes find the fine mist of metaphor more attractive than the matter.'

'With you, Shakuni, I so rarely follow the matter that I am forced to follow the mist. But how did it all start?'

'That reminds me — where's Vrisha? You were just about to show us the way through *our* mist, you remember?'

'Oh yes... He's gone to Anga for a few days. When he returns we can resume that discussion... How did it start, Shakuni?'

'Well, as you know, of course, your mirrors confront each other across the main hall in almost perfect parallel. Those around me were too distracted to study what my eyes, in truth, could only guess at from that distance — that the mirrors, and all that they contained, were reflected in each other repeatedly. And that made me think. You remember you claimed that it was pointless talking about infinity, that nothing could be said of it —'

'I have a great dislike of infinity, as you know. *Nothing* is one thing — I am prepared to accept your cipher, but your infinite... Shakuni... I meant how did this *quarrel* start?'

'Quarrel? Oh! Yes, I think it was something to do with Krishna being given the seat of honour. Ask Dur, my dear, he certainly would have noticed all that. You know he is rather sensitive about such things, so I'm sure he paid attention. I'm afraid I was hardly listening. But if I may return to the point, my dear: if your mirrors had been in absolutely perfect parallel — I mean *absolutely*, beyond the absolute of the world, into the absolute of mathematics — then there would of course be no end to the number of reflections. So, I imagined that with perfect vision — *perfect*, you understand, with unlimited acuity — with such eyesight I could gaze at infinity, literally. For would there not be an endless number of reflections laid out there before me? And would they not all be represented in the surface of the mirror?'

'One moment, Shakuni, *please* — did Karna stay on at Indraprastha?'

'No. He sends you his love, by the way. Yes, he needed to drive some livestock to Anga, for some reason or other... As I was about to say... although I may *hope* to gaze at infinity in the mirror, you will be pleased to learn that my hopes must always be dashed: since my own reflection must always eventually come in the way! Even with unlimited vision, my dear, imagine, with an eye capable of seeing endlessly, it would have to stop counting when obstructed by its own reflection! Now, there are two ways I can think of in which I might try to get around this, yes?'

'Wait a moment, Shakuni... If your eye can see endlessly, why do you need to do it with mirrors? Ah, I see... You would either see nothing at all, or eventually whatever you did see would thereby block your line of sight... which would bring your endless to an untimely end... And you are saying that even with the mirrors, where you get a nice gallery of images to count... images which do not block each other... even so, you say your eye would bring itself to an untimely end? Well, what if the mirrors are set at a slight angle? Then your reflection need not be in the way.'

'Good. But in this case I will see the reflections curve away in the arc of a great circle. Eventually they will have to meet the mirror's edge: another untimely end. So there would no longer be an endless count of reflections in the mirror itself.'

'Unless... there was no edge to the mirror. Ah, I see, but that defeats your object. You are trying to see something endless within something finite. If you have no edges, then your mirrors are endless to start with... Yes... And however small the angle by which the mirrors miss the parallel... Yes, your point will always be reached... What about this then: I can make a mirror which you may stand behind and still see through! Yes, on one side it reflects, but on the other it appears as transparent glass. Now, if one of your mirrors were made of such glass — a half-mirror — you could then set them parallel. And instead of standing between the reflecting surfaces, thus eventually blocking your own view, you could stand outside, behind the half-mirror! Yes, this time the reflection of your head, your eye, whatever, would not appear in the mirror: only the reflections of the empty mirrors in each other!'

'I've thought of that possibility too, my dear. How does your half-mirror work? Am I not right in thinking that, with the half-mirror, the reflecting dust you put on its surface is less thickly spread — so that it stops some of the image, sending it back in a reflection, while letting the rest through? Where there is no piece of dust in the way, then you can see. But after a certain number of reflections, the images in the mirror will be smaller than your specks of reflecting dust! Again, they will be obscured to the cheating eye behind them!'

'Surely, Shakuni, this all goes to show that the senses cannot capture infinity. Beyond a certain number what difference would it make to us, even to a perfect eye? And if it makes no difference to sense, it makes no sense. It's not worth thinking about. And it might as well not exist, since it would make no difference to us even if it did.'

'Ah! Rishi of little faith! Surely, my dear, what did not exist would not elude capture so ostentatiously! I believe its elusiveness is so exact, that we can capture it by the tail! For even that which cannot be found among the numbers, which could not be counted by the senses, creates its own trail among them. And we must follow this trail wherever it leads. Yes... the more I think about it, the more I am inclined to think that, if we allow a number to what is left when we take all the numbers away — the cipher — then we must admit a number for what there is when all the numbers are returned. Surprisingly, these two strange numbers seem to have a lot in common. You remember one of the properties of the cipher which you yourself described —'

'That it has no parts?'

'Precisely. However we divide the cipher, we are left with the cipher. Well, it seems that however we divide the infinite, we are left still with the infinite. Just like the cipher, it seems that it cannot be built from smaller parts. At any rate, if it could, the parts would not be the numbers with which we are familiar. By the way, Charvaka, your mirrors set me thinking about something else, about the dice...'

Shakuni was interrupted by the appearance of Bhishma at the door of his chamber.

'What luck this man had!' Bhishma entered the room. 'And what a shame you weren't with us, my little mouse...' He patted the rishi affectionately on the back, and sat down beside him. 'Yes, Shakuni seemed to spend most of his time playing dice!'

'I take it your methods were successful, then?' Charvaka asked Shakuni. 'For undoubtedly, what this insensitive boar perceived as luck was in reality your skill. Did you beat them all?'

'Yes, yes, I believe I did, my dear. They just don't seem to understand the laws of chance as I do.'

'Shakuni, how can you say that!' exclaimed Bhishma. 'The dice escape all laws. Everybody knows that!'

'Really? They seem to drop downwards, when released, with subservient regularity.'

'You know what I mean!'

'Then how is it I won?'

'Your speed.'

'I am fast, Bhishma, yes. But so is Jaya-dratha. So is Soma. I beat them both. What good is speed without strategy. If I'm fast, it's because I know my numbers. But what would be the use of knowing all the ladders if I didn't know what to do with them? Who would fear you, fast as you are with the bow, if you could not aim? It wasn't my speed alone, it was my understanding of the laws of chance.'

'Doesn't the mouse understand your method? And yet you've won how much from him?'

'I think I owe Shakuni over a million jars of clarified butter,' admitted Charvaka. 'Yes, I understand his method, Bhishma — but my calculation is much too slow.'

'So,' Shakuni challenged Bhishma, 'how could I have achieved all this with unpredictable, lawless dice?'

'And in any case,' pointed out Charvaka, 'why should the gods wish to favour *this* man of all men?'

'Precisely,' added Shakuni. 'You would think the gods, in their supposed wisdom, would favour Yudhi. And yet Yudhi, if you recall, lost so badly to me that in the end his brothers stopped him playing!'

'Yes...' conceded Bhishma. 'Why the gods should favour a wicked old man like you I do not know. But they clearly do. Yes, you have more than a measure of luck. But that's all there is to it!'

Shakuni laughed. 'You have stumbled precisely on the point. Like much else, my dear, luck *can* be measured!'

'How can he say that?' muttered Bhishma, shaking his head. 'The dice obey no law... They are attached to nothing but disorder. That's why the game of dice is a game of chance.'

'You must learn to give chance a chance,' advised Charvaka.

'Bagh! The mouse always sides with you on these things —'

'Sides with me? And why is that, Bhishma? It's because he worships evidence and abhors preference. That's why he prefers my position on this matter. It is their very love of disorder that orders the dice, my dear. They obey the law of obedience to no law. That is why the game of dice is a game of reason.'

'The *dice* may have their reasons,' declared Bhishma; 'but of these, Shakuni, reason must remain in ignorance.'

'But Bhishma,' intervened Charvaka, 'there is more to reason than reason suspects.'

'But surely less than it hopes, my little mouse!'

Shakuni shook his head. 'If you disregard all laws as studiously as do the dice, then you obey a law, do you not? So, I don't let the dice surprise me. It's only when we know absolutely nothing that we are surprised by the unexpected. But we already know something about the dice: that they are unpredictable!'

Bhishma furrowed his brow in response. Shakuni continued.

'In any case, my dear, I'm not alone. I'm in good company. You will find now that the good dice players also believe that there are laws of chance; though perhaps they glimpse them through a thicker mist than I do.'

'Who?'

'Who? Well... Soma and Jaya-dratha are beginning to. Satyaki and Drupada both seem to understand the principles I use, and try to incorporate them. Though they haven't quite the speed to exploit them... And one or two of the younger boys. The Pandava prince, Nakula. He is very good. Oh, and Drupada's son, he's very promising too. What's his name?'

'Drishta.'

'Yes... And even my own son agrees with me on this! Then of course, there's my sister. Ask her.'

'But still you beat all of these quite easily.'

'But Bhishma, naturally. Their minds are too slow for this type of calculation. Even Nakula, who has some facility. Gandhari used to be quick, I have to say. But she has hardly played seriously since we were children. I think, my dear, before long you will find many more who understand my methods, even if they have not the skill to put them into practice.'

Bhishma turned to Charvaka. 'And you really think he's right?'

'Yes.'

'Tell me, Bhishma,' asked Shakuni, 'why is it that in our royal game we bet on whether the dice will strike a prime? Why do we bet on whether the dice will add up to a prime number? Why don't we play the common game, where they bet on evens and odds? Why, my dear?'

'Because, as everybody knows, the primes are believed to represent chance... They capture the essence of chance... They represent the unpredictable.'

'And why is that, my dear?'

'Because, as everybody knows, we don't know how the primes are distributed amongst the numbers.'

'Whereas,' explained Shakuni, 'we know very well how the even numbers are distributed.'

'Of course. But the primes are unpredictable. Why, the mouse himself once told me of a species of cicada, whose eggs only hatch every prime number of years... Eleven? Thirteen? I forget which, Charvaka — but it seems that this makes it harder for their predators to predict when the year is ripe for a feast!'

Shakuni raised his eyebrows sceptically.

'But my dear,' he insisted, 'if the dice really did obey no law, if we could predict *nothing* about the fall of the dice, then what possible difference could it make whether we bet on the striking of predictable evens or of unpredictable primes! Isn't it precisely because a good player can predict more easily the fall of evens, that we eschew the common game, preferring instead the greater challenge of the royal game?'

Again Bhishma looked to Charvaka for sympathy. But the rishi scratched his beard and smiled. Shakuni pressed home his advantage.

'And Bhishma, it's because the good players *feel* the laws of chance, even though they may not be able to articulate them, that there's a difference in their betting when they go from the common to the royal game. Yes? And why this difference? Because in the royal game they cannot calculate their betting as accurately. Prediction is more complicated; so it's more difficult for them to end in profit. Yes?'

'Because of the primes?'

'Well... As a matter of fact, I don't think that *is* the real problem. Because, after all, once you've memorised your primes, although calculation is more complex, it's still perfectly feasible.'

'In the royal game,' explained Charvaka, 'the very act and manner of the betting alters the odds.'

'Precisely. That's where the real problem lies, I believe. Nevertheless, the better players do *try* to predict, don't they? And how? Using the laws they feel... or observe through their dull half-mirrors!' Shakuni added, with a glance at the rishi.

Bhishma frowned.

'As I was saying to Charvaka,' continued Shakuni, 'while I was in Indraprastha those mirrors set me thinking —'

'Bhishma...' interrupted Charvaka. 'Can you tell me? I've been trying to get it out of this fool... What exactly happened between Krishna and Shishu-pala?'

Bhishma's frown deepened. Shakuni seized the moment.

'While I was looking at those mirrors, I began to think again about the problem of the cats and cheetahs... I realised that I could predict even the primes!'

'Now *that*,' cried Bhishma, 'is surely not possible! Even if you are right about predicting the *dice*... Everybody knows that the primes obey no law! Charvaka!' Bhishma appealed to the rishi.

'Yes, I have to agree with Bhishma. No one knows how the primes are in general distributed. You have admitted yourself, Shakuni, that you only know where they lie from memory; and then only the first few hundred. You have said yourself that it gets harder and harder to discover new primes... that beyond a certain number, even for you it's unknown territory. It's one thing to judge the odds of a dice striking a known prime; but it's another thing altogether to judge the odds of a number *being* prime.'

'Ah, my dear Charvaka, I do not need to tell *you* that there's always a certain constancy in inconstancy. I believe I have discovered how they are distributed!'

Charvaka glanced briefly at Bhishma and then stared at Shakuni. He scratched his beard. 'How can that be? We have both always supposed that the primes may only be recognised, but not predicted. Correct me if I go wrong... but when we consider all the various families of numbers, it's clear that we can predict their distributions from the various laws which establish their descent. Eh? The odds, the evens, the various multiples, squares, cubes... and so on.

But we know that the primes do not form such a family. In order to form a family of numbers, we need at least one parent, do we not? And the parent can be any number we like. Then we need a law of descent; such as multiplication by a parent, addition to a parent, whatever... Yet the primes are not descended from any parent, by any known law; even though they themselves may be used as parents to appear in their own laws, as we like, to generate their own families... Isn't that right? The primes can only be ancestors, not descendants. And it is only the descendants who obey the laws! But it is only in the case of the descendants that we can predict how they will be distributed amongst the numbers. Since the primes can't form a family — can't be descendants — we can never predict how and when they will appear.'

'My dear Charvaka, in that case primes belong to the family of numbers that cannot be descendants. The unpredictable is so only because it escapes the net with which you have learnt to capture the predictable. You must change your net!'

Now it was Charvaka's turn to frown. Shakuni continued.

'Nothing which mathematics may define or invent can escape completely from her net. Certainly, one mesh will not suffice for all her butterflies, my dear. But once you have found the right mesh...'

'But we can't catch the primes in any mesh!' declared Bhishma. 'They are Kali's numbers. She has given them freedom!'

'Every net has two sides. If your capricious quarry is not to be found *inside*, then it has to be found *outside*. So, make the inside more capacious, the outside less, and in the end caprice catches itself out! In avoiding all factors, the primes are influenced by a most interesting factor!'

'Surely, Shakuni, you haven't found a *pattern*?' Charvaka's eyes were wide open with excitement.

'Ah! It's not exact,' admitted Shakuni. 'It's not what we can properly call a pattern. You are relieved, I see... No, it is I confess only the mere contour of a pattern. And a rough contour at that. But it is there, I'm sure of it, like an outline seen through mist. It means that I could bet on finding a prime in quite unknown territory — far beyond the primes I have memorised — and still break even. More or less! Not that this is relevant to the dice, since our games never approach such unknown territory.'

'So with this law of yours, have you been able to solve Gandhari's question?'

'This is a problem my sister set me some time ago,' Shakuni explained to Bhishma. 'It concerns whether there is an endless supply of tigers.'

'I will never understand your animals,' said Bhishma, shaking his head. 'Give me a real tiger, and I know where I am!'

'Well...' Shakuni turned to Charvaka with an expression of regret. 'Unfortunately not. No. It was Gandhari's problem, particularly in regard to the smaller cats, that set me thinking, eventually to find this rough contour of the primes. But I fear that my results have been of no relevance to the question of the lions and tigers. Do you know, my dear, I'm not even sure that there *can* be an answer to that case.'

'Surely not,' protested Charvaka. 'Either there is an endless supply of tigers, or there is not, in which case there is a largest tiger! If the gods existed, they would know the answer! Shakuni, now you are being arrogant: just because you cannot answer it, you suppose there is no answer!'

'Listen to the mouse!' cried Bhishma. 'Have you ever heard him invoke the gods before? And to save an argument?'

Charvaka laughed. 'That's all they're good for,' he said, chuckling to himself.

'My dear, I hope you're right,' replied Shakuni. 'I hope it is only my arrogance. But who knows? Who knows what may be proven, and what may only be surmised... Ah! Is that Dur?' Shakuni looked round at the door to his chamber.

It was Dur. Shakuni rose to offer his nephew a seat.

'Greetings uncle... sire... Grandsire...' Dur turned to the rishi. 'Karna asked me to tell you, sire, he's gone to Anga.'

'So Shakuni tells me. Taking some livestock back, is that right?'

'Yes, sire. Yudhi returned it to him after the ceremony. But I expect you've heard all about the Rajasuya from my uncle and the Grandsire...'

'Not *absolutely* everything, my boy, no... But you look agitated, Dur... I'm going shortly, but perhaps I may visit you later? Then you can tell me all about it without these two interrupting, eh?'

36 The rat and the eagle

Soon after Charvaka left Shakuni's quarters, Dur also took his leave, for the uncle was not in a mood to pander to the nephew's feelings.

Later, Charvaka visited the prince, and was then able to pursue his enquiries.

'The cattle? Yes, sire... The day after the ceremony, Yudhi gave back most of the tributes his brothers had obtained. In fact, I myself itemised all the treasure and livestock. But you know, I think they kept Shishu-pala's. I think that's disgraceful! Anyway, Bhima had taken a lot of cattle from Anga. That's what Karna's taking back at the moment.'

'And why have you returned so soon? Your father is still in Indraprastha, isn't he?'

'Yes, yes, they're all there, except for my uncle and the Grandsire. I... I couldn't stand it any longer, sire. They hate me...'

'What do you mean, Dur? Surely they must have put enmity to one side?'

'They tried at first... before the ceremony. But even the day after, it began. First I fell into a pool, mistaking it for glass — in front of *all* of them. Nothing pleases them more than my discomfiture. You should have heard their laughter. It was the laughter of derision... hateful. And then another time I took my sandals off to walk through what I took to be a shallow pool —'

'The crystal floor?'

'Yes, of course, you helped to build it! I wish you'd warned me, sire. That palace is full of illusion. You should have heard Bhima's loathful bellows!'

•

'Palmira, didn't Solomon play a trick like that on the queen of Sheba? Didn't he make her walk on a funny glass floor that she mistook for a pool of water?'

'Who told you that?' asked Palmira, with some interest.

'I think it was our father, wasn't it?'

'There was a reason why he got her to do it,' said the second Henry, 'but I can't remember what it was...'

'Something about her feet, wasn't it?' his brother recollected.

'That's it! She was supposed to have hairy legs, wasn't she?'

'And he wanted to trick her so she'd lift up her robe to stop it getting wet, and then he'd see her legs.'

'Oh.' Palmira arched her eyebrows. 'I thought she was rumoured to have webbed feet. Is that what your father said, that she was supposed to have hairy legs?'

'I think so,' said the first Henry. 'Though you'd think he'd have noticed when they were having sex, wouldn't you?'

'It was probably before they did it,' suggested the second Henry.

'What makes you think they had sex?' asked Palmira, her curiosity aroused. 'I presume you're referring to the queen of Sheba and *Solomon*, not —'

'*Everybody* knows they did!' said the first Henry.

'Anyway, Palmira, didn't he have sex with *everybody*?'

'He was always doing it,' explained the first Henry. 'He had a thousand wives, didn't he?'

'Then why would he have wanted to have sex with Balkis as well?' asked Palmira.

'Was that her name? She was the most beautiful woman in the world —'

'That was *Cleopatra*!' interrupted the second Henry.

Palmira smiled. 'As a matter of fact, neither Cleopatra nor Balkis was particularly beautiful. They were both extremely talented, however. Balkis, in particular, was a very wise and intelligent woman. I think it was her wisdom that attracted Solomon to her.'

'If he was so interested in her wisdom, how come he wanted to see her legs, then? Eh?'

'He could've just talked to her if it was that.'

'Shut up, boys, you don't know what you're talking about.'

'Oh, and you do? You were there, were you?'

'Anyway, she admits they did it,' pointed out the second Henry to his brother.

'He could've asked her straight out, couldn't he, if he just wanted to know if her feet were... You mean like a goose?'

'Not exactly,' said Palmira. 'The rumour was that she had webbing between her toes. Geese don't really have *toes*, do they?'

'Still, it's a bit strange, there's never very much water where she lived, is there?'

'Anyway,' interrupted the second Henry before Palmira could respond, 'I thought Solomon was supposed to be able to control the jinn. Couldn't he have asked a jinnee to make himself invisible and find out *for* him?'

'There you are, Palmira — you see, he wanted to see her legs for himself!'

'Boys, please, this is getting rather silly. If you permit me, I will return to my story —'

'When are you going to tell us the story of the fisherman and the jinnee? You promised weeks ago... And whenever we ask you, you just say another time!'

'Another time... Now, boys, *if* you'll permit me —'

'Wait a moment, did she have webbed feet or not?'

'Listen,' said Palmira patiently, 'unless you have a *serious* question to ask me, I'll get on, if you don't mind.'

'I've got a serious question, Palmira...' the second Henry began. 'You know when they were talking about infinity... I thought you told us that there was no such number, that you could never get to infinity, however far you count. How come they think there is such a number?'

'I only told you that you could never *count* to infinity, even with all the time in the world. You could reach any ordinary number, however large, if you had the time. But infinity itself is not one of these numbers that you can count to. Or even come close to.'

'But even if you can't count to it, you should still be able to get nearer to it. What's the point of a number you can't even get *near* to?'

'Some numbers you can approach but never reach. As you know, you can get closer and closer to the root of two, but never actually reach it. Infinity is a number you can't even get closer to.'

'But then it can't be a number!'

'Why not, Henry? Who are we to say what's a number and what isn't? Boys... if you permit me, since you seem so interested in the queen of Sheba, I will try to catch two birds in one net. I'll tell you a little story about Solomon and Balkis. Yes? Good.

'Well...' continued Palmira, 'for some time King Solomon had been preoccupied with a rather difficult question: which are the more numerous, the days or the nights?

'Now, you probably know already, since you seem to know so much about Solomon, that the god of Solomon was supposed to have offered him a boon, a gift, and that King Solomon chose wisdom as his gift. His god was so pleased with Solomon's choice, as a matter of fact, that he gave him not only wisdom, but, amongst other things, the power to understand the language of the birds; and, as you say, to control the jinn.

'Wise and knowledgeable as he was, however, Solomon just could not resolve his problem about the days and nights, try as he might — and he tried very hard, by day and by night —'

'Palmira,' interrupted the first Henry, 'why on earth should Solomon be bothered with it? It doesn't sound very wise to go around thinking about that all day long, does it?'

His brother nodded in agreement.

'Well,' replied Palmira, 'yes... well... you see, he was rather stricken with the daughter of one of his ministers. Yes, I believe it was her legs which utterly engrossed him. At any rate, he repeatedly requested this minister for her... her hand in marriage. The minister was altogether too wise for Solomon, and advised his daughter to set Solomon the question about nights and days as a riddle. If Solomon answered it satisfactorily, he could have her hand in marriage — and her legs to boot.

'Now, if anybody could answer this riddle, thought Solomon, it would be one of the birds. For they could travel anywhere in the world, and they constantly overheard the most learned discourses among both men and jinn. So Solomon called to order an assembly of all the birds.

'All the birds arrived except for the owl and the lapwing. But Solomon was so impatient, so ardent was his desire for that pair of legs, that he couldn't wait for these two absentees; he put the conundrum to the birds who were present.

'"Of all of us, the owl is the wisest!" said the birds.

'"And the lapwing the most learned! You should wait, O King. We cannot illumine this intricate issue."

'Solomon was rather cross, and was on the point of leaving, when in flew the owl.

'"I'm sorry to be so tardy, King Solomon. I work by night and sleep by day, I'd shirk all flight and creep away to wait indoors until I'm bright; I'm late because it's much too light."

'"Well, *I* cannot wait until dark," said Solomon sternly. "I have an urgent matter to resolve."

'"Oh, very well. What is your problem, O King?"

'"Wise owl, I have been set a riddle by a certain young woman... Tell me, if you can, which are more numerous, the days or the nights?"

'"The answer is obvious, King Solomon: they are both equally numerous."

'"I don't doubt you, wise owl... but there must be more to it than that, or it wouldn't be a riddle, it would be too easy. What if she asks me for my reasoning... I understand that in questions of arithmetic it is not normally considered sufficient merely to enunciate an answer —"

'"Say that it follows from... from considerations of symmetry. That will surely satisfy her, O great and wise king."

'And when the king spoke to this young woman with the fascinating legs, sure enough, she asked him for his reasoning.

'"Er... by symmetry," replied King Solomon.

'But the young woman shifted her legs and stared at the king with a stony expression, just as her father had instructed.

'"What symmetry?" she asked.

'"Curse that owl," said Solomon, under his breath. He did some quick thinking, and ventured the following:

'"We are assuming, are we not, that the days and the nights go on forever, without end? That there is no last day and no last night? Well... if you put all the days into one pile, and all the nights into another pile, it's impossible to say that one of these two piles is bigger or smaller than the other... since they both go on forever!"

'Solomon was very pleased with himself. But the object of his desire had been well briefed by her father. She raised an objection which threw Solomon into some considerable confusion. Seeing the great king deep in thought, the minister's daughter slowly stretched her legs, arose, and politely terminated the audience, leaving poor Solomon in the greatest frustration.

'"Where is that owl? And that lapwing?" exclaimed the king angrily to the reassembled birds. Suddenly the owl flew in.

'"Where have you been?" shouted the king.

'"I work by night and sleep by day, an irksome plight that keeps me grey —"

'"Get on with it!"

'"I've been to fetch the lapwing," explained the owl apologetically. "I was beginning to have some doubts regarding the adequacy of the analysis I ventured, O King, and therefore sought the assistance of the most learned lapwing, who is... just now arriving..."

'And indeed just then the lapwing fluttered in, very much out of breath, to face the irate king.

'"O wise King! I think I may know of someone who may be able to help you. The queen of Sheba."

'"The queen of Sheba? Where is Sheba?"

'"Near Egypt, my gracious King. She is a most distinguished queen. Of whom it is rumoured, though I have been unable personally to confirm this, that she has webbed feet... or perhaps hairy legs; possibly even both conditions, concomitantly..."

'Solomon immediately urged the lapwing to tender his warmest invitation to this queen, soliciting her to enjoy his hospitality in Jerusalem.

'The queen of Sheba was evidently very intrigued by the lapwing's report of King Solomon, because she travelled the long journey to Jerusalem just to visit him.

'It was during her tour of King Solomon's extraordinary and sumptuous palace that the incident you boys remarked on took place, when she pulled up the hem of her robe to walk across a crystal floor.

'Later, when they were both in the luxury of Solomon's innermost apartments, their conversation, which had been light and insubstantial, took a more serious turn.

'"So, my most gracious Queen Balkis, how do you find my palace? Are not my treasures the rarest and most beautiful you have ever set eyes on?"

'"My most illustrious King Suleyman bin Dawood, I am flattered that you have been able to spare the time to receive me in such a manner. With a thousand wives, you must be a busy man."

'Reclining on his couch, breathing slowly, Solomon watched her through his long, black eyelashes.

'On her couch, Balkis was sitting upright and inscrutable. She continued:

'"However, I have not set eyes at all on that most precious of your treasures." A female servant entered with a tray of delicacies, which she placed between the two couches. "Nor can I," continued Balkis, "since it may be neither seen nor touched."

'Solomon gestured towards the delicacies, but Balkis ignored his invitation.

'"Your wisdom, O Suleyman, is legendary."

'"It... has its limitations. But you know that wisdom was the gift I chose from God."

'"In that case, quite clearly, you were wise already."

'"You are immeasurably kind... but..." King Solomon's eyelashes opened wide, and a smile tinged with sadness crossed his face. "I am clearly not wise enough. Queen Balkis, there is something I need to ask you?"

'"You *are* wise enough, great king. You are wise enough to ask me!"

'"I have been told that you may have the knowledge to be able to help me..."

'"What is your problem, mighty Suleyman?"

'"I need to know the answer to a riddle which has been troubling me... Which are the more numerous, Queen Balkis, the days or the nights?"

'"That is your riddle? Why do you need to know the answer?"

'"I... A young woman set me the riddle, Queen Balkis. She will accept me only if I am able to resolve this question to her satisfaction."

'"You desire her? Why?"

'The king hesitated for a moment, fidgeting on his couch. He had not expected such a direct question. "The truth is, I am fascinated by her legs, Queen Balkis."

'"Mmm... I have noticed that you have a certain curiosity regarding legs. You seem very open with me, Suleyman. Are you always this honest?"

'"Oh no, my dear Balkis. I am normally a very devious man. But since I don't know what the birds may have told you, it would be unwise for me to be dishonest with you."

'The queen smiled. "That is very frank of you. King Suleyman... Would you not prefer me just to turn the heart of this girl, so that the slightest stammer from you will prove satisfactory to her ears? Oh yes, I have the skill to do such things. Or would you really like me to clarify the riddle?"

'"Both, Queen Balkis."

'"Satisfaction too easily gained is too quickly forgotten. You seem to obtain your desires too easily for your own good, wise Suleyman. You may become too hard to satisfy. So, with your interests at heart, naturally, I will prolong your excitement. I will resolve your riddle only if you agree to forego the girl." Under her white robe Balkis slowly folded her feet up onto the couch, nestling them beneath her buttocks; but her body remained perfectly upright. "Alternatively, I will give you the girl; but remain silent on the riddle."

'Solomon sat up. He thought for a few moments, staring vacantly at her.

'"The riddle, please," he said at last.

'"The answer is obvious, Suleyman. The days and nights are equally numerous."

'"Why?"

'"It follows from considerations of symmetry."

'Solomon frowned. "What symmetry?" he asked.

'"We are assuming, are we not, that the days and nights go on forever, without end? That there is no last day and no last night? Well, if you put all the days into one pile, and all the nights into another pile, it is impossible to say that one of these two piles is bigger or smaller than the other, since they both go on forever."

'"But that is *exactly* what I said to her, Queen Balkis!"

'"It did not satisfy her?"

'"No, she raised this objection: 'King Solomon,' she said, 'surely you know that there are moonlight nights as well as black nights; and that there will always be moonlight nights as well as black nights? So, if we put all the days into one pile, and all the black nights into a second pile, then all the moonlight nights must go into a third pile. But since all three piles go on forever, it would appear, King Solomon, that there are more nights than days, since two of the piles contain nights!'"

'"But Suleyman, that is only appearance! If you now take the pile of moonlight nights and join it to the pile of black nights, so that the two piles merge into one — you see, this new pile is no bigger than the pile of days, is it?"

'"I thought of something like that, Balkis... but I did not take it up with her. You see, I found it rather worrying that the new pile, joined up, is no bigger than either of the two piles of nights that merged to form it. A thought struck me, Balkis, which I found particularly disturbing. If I took out all of the sabbaths from the pile of days, this new pile of sabbaths would be every bit as big as the pile of remaining days! There are therefore as many sabbaths as working days! That is most distressing."

'"Why? Don't tell me that you remain celibate on the sabbaths!"

"'No, it's not that," said Solomon, earnestly. "No, don't you see, Balkis, the part is equal to the whole!"

"'I should rather hope so, Suleyman, even on the sabbath!'"

"'Balkis, surely you see what disturbs me?'"

"'But of course, King Suleyman, it is almost too hard to swallow: if you add the moonlight nights, the black nights and the working days all together, this quantity does not exceed the number of the sabbaths. As you say, the part is every inch the whole! Add the parts together, and, sadly, there is no enlargement.'"

"'But...'"

"'You should at least be happy that, after all, you were right: the nights and days *are* equally numerous. You *have* become rather difficult to satisfy, haven't you?'"

Palmira paused, and looked up briefly towards the hills in the distance.

'But we must now leave Balkis and Solomon —'

'But Palmira, what about her legs?'

'For reasons best known to himself, Solomon was curious. We, however, are not. Sssh! Where was I?'

'No! Palmira, you can't leave it like that! Did he really not go after that minister's daughter?

'And what happened with him and Balkis?'

'Mmm...' Palmira pursed her lips. 'As a matter of fact, Balkis did an extremely generous thing. "Gracious king," she said, "to reward you for the wisdom of your choice, for preferring the answer to the riddle over and above the girl, I will absolve you of your promise. You may go to this girl and give her my answer. But, if you will be so kind, may I prolong my visit to await the outcome of your romance? My curiosity is, I have to say, somewhat aroused, great King."

'Solomon was extremely happy to extend his hospitality. Right, now, where was I? No, boys! Perhaps another time —'

'You promise?'

'Yes, I promise that *perhaps* another time I'll tell you what happened... By the way, boys, you won't... you won't tell your mother that I tell you stories like this, will you?'

'You mean, about infinity?'

Palmira smiled. 'You know what I mean. I sometimes think your mother is... suspicious of me. Why I don't know — she is otherwise very keen to promote your education. But seriously, boys, there's no need to make her more anxious than she is already.'

'We're not children any more, Palmira!'

'We are fourteen!'

'And don't worry, Palmira, we keep telling her that you prefer older men!'

'Palmira, why aren't you worried that we might tell father about your stories?'

'Your father knows me better than your mother does... In fact, he knows the world rather better, too... Good. Now, if you'll kindly permit me...'

•

'What was the ceremony itself like?' asked Charvaka.

'Well, that day *was* excellent, I have to admit — until the evening, of course. Yudhi excelled himself. He tried very hard. But, sire, really, he's under the control of his brothers. And of Krishna. But then that business in the evening with Shishu-pala... That was awful... It wasn't Yudhi's fault, of course — I'm not sure what he could have done, under the circumstances. You know, the morning after the banquet Yudhi summoned me and Bhishma, and told us that the treasure he'd accumulated was as much ours as his. He meant it, I'm sure. But they're just words, sire. His brothers would never let him part with anything if they could help it. Yudhi himself took care not to hold over me the honour he's received. But his brothers don't miss any opportunity to rub my face in their glory.'

'Perhaps you should change the expression on your face, then, my boy. Still, I gather that the princes didn't stop Yudhi from returning the tributes?'

'No, though Arjuna and the others weren't happy about it. I think Krishna persuaded them to let Yudhi have his way. Poor Yudhi did try, all the way through... You know that he delegated a lot of the organisation beforehand to my brothers and myself? Yes, Duh and the rest were involved in the catering, I helped with the tributes, recording them all —'

'Yudhi made you all work, eh?'

'Well, it didn't seem like work — we had all the assistance we could want. It was more that we were... consulted. And not just my brothers... Sanjaya, for instance, he was supposed to be in charge of the welfare of all the visiting kings and princes. But it only meant that he was consulted every now and then. No, he enjoyed himself — he even left my father sitting alone a couple of times. And my father certainly enjoyed himself. He would sit in the gardens listening to the animals — he's probably doing that this very moment. The sounds change in the evening, you see. My father loves listening to the sunset.'

'And what about Kripa and Drona, were they consulted?'

'Oh yes. Kripa... He was in charge of distributing alms to the poor. Bhishma and Drona supervised the ceremony itself. They made Krishna bathe the feet of all the brahmanas who were present... Satyaki held the sunshade for Yudhi at the ceremony... Vidura disbursed all the expenses. He was very pleased with himself — you know how proud he is of Yudhi. He's just as much my uncle, but he's never been the slightest bit interested in anything *I've* ever done — unless it bothered his beloved Yudhi. Yudhi was very sorry you weren't there, sire. Oh, and Narada asked after you.'

'The dove? Yes of course...'

'He was quite surprised that you've been allowed back into Hastinapura. I don't think he altogether approves of you, sire.'

'No... And was anyone else there — any other rishis?'

'No, sire.'

'Do you know if Vyasa was invited?'

'I don't know, sire. He certainly wasn't there.'

Charvaka put his hand up to his beard.

'How do you know that, my boy? Have you ever seen him?'

'No, sire, but I'm sure Narada was the only rishi there — I know Vyasa isn't exactly a rishi, but he would surely have sat with him at the banquet?'

Charvaka chuckled.

'Krishna was sitting next to Narada, sire. Krishna was given the seat of honour at the banquet. It was that which prompted Shishu's outburst.'

'Yes, I gathered that from Shakuni. But your uncle didn't actually tell me what happened —'

'But you know Shishu was killed?'

'That much I managed to learn. Little else I'm afraid. I would really be grateful —'

'Oh sire, how could Shakuni not tell you? Mind you, he *was* in a strange mood today, wasn't he? Yes, I'll tell you what happened, sire — what I can remember, anyway... Actually, I can remember most of it. It's the sort of thing that becomes engraved in your mind.' Dur winced at the recollection.

'Well... the sun had just set, and we all had to come in from the ceremony to eat, into the main hall of the palace. We'd taken our seats. Most of us, anyway — there were still a few coming in... We really were just about to eat. In fact we were all *very* hungry, because of course all day we'd had to fast — since the night before. Krishna had just been given the sign, as guest of honour, to begin *his* food. And we were all dying to dip our hands into the rice in front of us.

'There were lots of candles and lamps, and the smell of the burning butter was delicious! They were all scented, of course. And the smell of the food!... So, you can imagine how hungry we all were, waiting for the signal to begin — and then I saw Shishu get up and talk to Yudhi, who was still helping to guide the last few people to their places. We thought at first that Shishu's seat was perhaps uncomfortable... you know how deformed he is. I couldn't quite hear what he was saying, because of all the chattering, but it was soon clear that he was pointing towards Krishna. Then I saw the people at Shishu's table become silent — and then, suddenly, everyone was quiet.

'Yudhi was looking very uncomfortable, and Shishu was just glaring at Krishna, staring at him first with one eye, then the other, making his red headcloth shake like a cock's wattle — you know how he wears his headcloth long to cover his face. Yudhi walked quickly over to Krishna, and whispered something to him. But Krishna just carried on eating — he'd already been given permission to start, of course. Krishna didn't even look up. Narada, seated next to him, addressed Shishu in a soft voice, but we could all hear clearly — the acoustics in the hall were excellent. But of course, you know that. Yes, it almost seemed as though those mirrors were reflecting the sounds.

'"What is the problem, King Shishu-pala?" asked Narada.

'"There are many illustrious kings and princes gathered here..." Shishu began very quietly, and I remember that as he was speaking I could hear the chink of Krishna's rings as he picked up his silver goblet. "There are many venerable elders of the kshatriya caste, far exceeding Krishna in seniority of years. The Grandsire is present among us, undefeated in battle, unrivalled in fortitude. His authority and righteousness make dwarves of us all. Without Lord Bhishma, Hastinapura would be in ruins, Indraprastha but a dream in another world. Can Krishna even hope to rival his deeds in battle? King Dhrita-rashtra is also present, by whose gracious leave King Yudhi-sthira has been permitted to elevate his kingdom above his, and above all of ours. And yet these have to sit beneath the son of Vasu-deva?

'"There are with us today brahmanas of unsurpassed accomplishment and virtue..." Shishu was speaking a little louder now, but his voice was still quite even — you know how he begins to rasp and cough when he has to speak loudly. We were still as silent as death. And hungry! I remember I was wondering whether to try to put my hand secretly into the steaming rice on my table.

'"Who," asked Shishu, "seated here before me, would dare to place themselves above the venerated Kripa-charya? Who, seated here tonight, would claim precedence over the renowned Drona-charya?

'"Can Krishna match any of their accomplishments?" Shishu went on like this. "Is he a great teacher? In his knowledge of the scriptures, does he rival the most devout rishi of our time, the noble Narada, made to sit beneath this guest of honour?"

'Shishu paused and looked around at us. At this point there were a few who, judging by their faces, were in agreement with him!

'"Surely," continued Shishu, "surely it is not for his dancing or his flute that he is honoured above us all here tonight?" A few of us laughed at this. "Why, I ask you, King Yudhi-sthira, why is Krishna given the seat of honour, in precedence over all those deserving persons assembled here?"

'For the moment Yudhi was lost for words. While Shishu had been speaking, Krishna had wiped his plate clean, and we saw him hand it now to a servant. I think Krishna must have caught Bhima's eye, because Bhima got up quickly from his seat and went over to Krishna. Krishna whispered something in his ear, and Bhima rushed off with the servant to the kitchens. Shishu again addressed Yudhi directly:

'"King Yudhi-sthira, we have all paid tributes to you, and given you the honour of pronouncing you King of Kings. Not out of fear of you; nor from concern for our individual interests. We have bowed before you because we recognise your unsullied virtue, the purity of your motives, and your steadfast pursuit of dharma." You should have seen the expressions on some of the faces, especially the brahmanas, to hear Shishu, of all people, speak in this manner about virtue! "Why, then, do you insult us by placing Krishna above those more deserving of that honour? Is it for the help he gave you to build your marvellous city? If so, you should take care not, in honouring *him*, also to offend *us*. Is it because your brother, Prince Arjuna, is his brother-in-law? Is it because you are cousins? Is he not my cousin also? Are we not taught that such partiality is the very cousin of selfishness?" Again, you should have seen the disgust on some of the faces!

'"King Shishu-pala," replied Yudhi at last, "I am deeply sorry that you feel insulted. I am sorry also that I did not consult you, and all of you here, before determining to whom the honour should go —"

'The Grandsire got up at this point, signalling to Yudhi for permission to speak, which Yudhi immediately granted.

'"King Shishu-pala," said the Grandsire, "the fault is not Yudhi's. It is mine. Drona and I advised Yudhi to give the honour to Krishna. We did not think there would be any here who would object, particularly as many of those you have courteously mentioned would have declined the honour, and refused to place themselves above Lord Krishna."

'"You mean that Krishna was the only one vainglorious enough to accept?" retorted Shishu. "Is that a good qualification, friends?" He looked around at us, and just at that moment Bhima and the servant returned — Bhima to his seat, and the servant, who was carrying a plate of delicacies, to Krishna. He set down the plate before Krishna. I saw Krishna place a morsel in his mouth, and wipe his hand; then he waved to us all to begin; but we held back, hungry though we were. The Grandsire sat down, hoping, I think, that this time we could all begin to eat. But no, Shishu stood his ground.

'"This Krishna whom you honour," he continued, a little louder now, his voice beginning to break up, "this Krishna is a man who killed his own uncle, leaving King Jara-sandha's daughter a widow by this murder; a man who, when pursued in vengeance by Jara-sandha, fled like a coward. Not satisfied with the death of his uncle, Krishna then proceeds to plot the death of Jara-sandha himself. Not by his own cowardly hand — for what power could this Krishna have over that mighty king? — but disguised as a brahmana, after accepting Jara's hospitality, and protected by the brutish force of Prince Bhima-sena, who should be ashamed of the part he played in Krishna's game..."'

'I suppose Bhima must have needed some restraining at this point,' interrupted Charvaka.

'Indeed, sire, and not just Bhima! But instantly the Grandsire was up to wave Bhima down.'

'And what about Krishna?'

'Oh, he just carried on eating from his plate. And Shishu didn't waver, even though Bhima got within spitting distance of him before he and one or two others who had risen were persuaded to return to their seats. But now the Grandsire spoke again:

'"My friends... Lord Krishna has need of our defence, against this discourteous king, no more than an eagle against a rodent. But since our eagle is too gentle to humble this rat, grant me a moment, inopportune as it is, in which to enlighten you; after which we may compose ourselves for the lavish feast the King of Kings has set before us.

'"We all know," continued the Grandsire, "that the death of Kamsa, Krishna's uncle, was merely the deserved conclusion of his evil reign. For Kamsa was not content with usurping the throne of Mathura; his murderous intentions against his brother's family could have only one just end. And to attain this end Krishna, as we all know, worked bravely and openly. Then, as the eagle flies clear of the vengeful snake, Krishna wisely led his people out of range of Jara-sandha's strike. But when the eagle returned swooping to the serpent's lair, this clawless rat before you could only mewl his insults under cover of his guardian snake. Did not the eagle offer his own talons to fight King Jara-sandha? Did not our good King Shishu-pala do his best on that occasion to point the serpent at the eagle?"

'The Grandsire paused to look round at us. Shishu was breathing quite hard, his chest was heaving. But he didn't move from his spot. He just stood there. I think the Grandsire may have regretted being so hard on Shishu, because he softened his tone:

'"King Shishu-pala, of all people, you should be grateful to Lord Krishna. Most of us here know that it was he who cured you of your infirmities —"

'"*Cured me?*" Shishu shrieked. "Of my deformities?" We all just sat watching him there, heaving his great chest and grinding his jaws. He tried to steady his breathing, and after a couple of attempts he was able to speak again.

'"Shall I tell you how this... how this eagle you worship... *cured* me? Perhaps some of you know that I was born with an eye here?" He pointed to the ridge in the middle of his forehead. "I also —" he was almost laughing as he told us this — "I also had two arms. In addition to these!" He held his arms out like a scarecrow. "Yes, I was born with four arms. But only three eyes. My father, the king of the Chedis before me, and my mother, the queen, they could hardly bear to look upon me. My mother consulted all manner of rishis and gurus. No one could do anything for me. Then, one day, I was twelve at the time, my mother told me that she had found a young man who could help me. *Help me!* 'This young man is Vishnu incarnate,' she said. 'My son, he is no other than the god Vishnu, who will be able to make you whole.' *Whole!*" Shishu had to pause for a moment to control his shaking. "This young man was none other than my mother's nephew, my own cousin. I... I, too, I worshipped him... this beautiful god who would make me whole. He spoke so sweetly to me... They —" his eyes began to fill up with tears, and he started shaking again. "They intoxicated me with wine and fermented fruit, a fire was burning, and they held me down while Krishna cut off both my lower arms and burnt me to stop the bleeding. My eye..." He could not finish, but just stood there covering his face with his headcloth.'

'And Krishna?' enquired Charvaka.

'Krishna had stopped eating. I tell you, sire, before that moment I don't think I've ever seen Krishna's face without a smile on it. Shishu spoke again, this time to the Grandsire, who'd sat down.

'"So you presume to enlighten us, Lord Bhishma? Perhaps you also wish to enlighten us on how you captured Amba for your own brother? Do not presume to lecture me, you barren fool!"

'I tell you, sire, we held our breath. But the Grandsire didn't rise to this. He stayed seated. And Shishu carried on:

'"You worship this eagle, don't you?" he said to us, pointing at Krishna. "You fools. Have you not heard of that great eagle who always spoke tirelessly on morality, who spoke endlessly on the practice of virtue, and the avoidance of sin? Oh yes, the other birds would bring him gifts and sustenance; they left their eggs with him for protection while they went in search of food. But the great eagle would eat one of their eggs each day. Eventually one wise bird saw that the eggs were decreasing. In the end the eagle was discovered, and destroyed. Oh yes! Beware of this great one who dazzles you as he flaps his wings full of virtue, only to prey on you with talons of desire! This is no eagle before you — this is a vulture, feeding off the rotten parts of your foolish brains!"

'Kripa and Drona both stood up when they heard this. I couldn't catch Kripa's words in the uproar, but Drona pacified Kripa, and addressed Shishu calmly, when the noise fell.

'"King Shishu-pala, it is your brain which has become rotten, not ours. It is well known that evil cannot stand to look upon goodness. Indeed, your evil nature cannot stand to see goodness honoured. And yet, King Shishu-pala, it is *you* who should be honoured — through death at Krishna's hand, to mingle thus with the soul of Vishnu. For it is also well known that the spirit of Vishnu runs through Krishna's veins, and that it is the voice of Vishnu which speaks with Krishna's tongue!"

'"Blind fools!" shouted Shishu. "Vishnu does not need a man through whom to address us! Vishnu could speak, if he so wished, straight into our minds! What help can a god require of a mere man? Do you not realise that Vishnu himself would have the power to make me see his own divinity? Instead, I see there only the posturings of vile imposture!"

'As Shishu pointed accusingly at Krishna, we all stared. But Krishna just resumed his eating, slowly picking out the food from the plate, licking his fingers gracefully. Narada now took the floor, and as he did so the others sat down again.

'"It is true that Vishnu could instil respect in you, if he so wished," said Narada. "Without speaking a single word through mortal mouth, Vishnu could inspire in you respect for Krishna, and belief in his divinity. But do you not see, King Shishu-pala, that it is to test your faith that Vishnu restrains his power? Do you not understand, King Shishu-pala, that unless belief is born in an act of faith, there is in it no virtue?"

'"In that case, sire," answered Shishu, "virtue parts company with wisdom!"

'Drona and Kripa were up on their feet instantly, but Narada waved them down.

'"Faith, King Shishu-pala, is beyond wisdom."

'"In that case, sire, let Vishnu give me the strength to leap beyond wisdom." He shuffled around a bit, as if to demonstrate that, like an elephant, he could not jump. He was dribbling slightly, which I'm told he always did when he got excited. "You see, sire, I am fortunate to have received no such gift — in my weakness I remain grounded, a wise man with no virtue among fools of every faith! Oh yes! Faith and folly are close cousins. For a faith that has no weakness is a folly! If I may use the words of a rishi who is here not in the flesh, but in reflection only —" he spread his arms out towards the mirrors — "that which you can defend against any assault, is not worth defending at all.'"

'Mmm...' mumbled Charvaka, 'I wonder how he got hold of that? I think it was rather a happy decision of mine *not* to attend that occasion! Sorry... please continue, my boy.'

'Shishu was now in full cry, sire, his throat was crackling with every word:

'"Believe, then, if you will! Deceive yourselves if you must! If Vishnu can throw his voice into that... that vulture in peacock's feathers, then he can throw his voice at *me*! Why does he need to test my faith? Or does the ventriloquist wish to play a trick on his own puppet?"

'"Do not tempt the punishment of Vishnu!" shouted Drona.

'"Why should I be punished? Because I do not praise him to the sky as you do? Because I criticise him? Do you not know that praise merely raises the body aloft? It is through criticism that the spirit grows to reach new heights. But I am wasting my words. Krishna is not interested in reaching new heights. He is only interested in reaching your hearts! Yes, I am wasting my words. You judge me evil. Therefore, you will not give my words a hearing." His voice grew quieter, falling to a mumble which was barely audible to us. "Let Vishnu punish me then, if he will. No doubt some accident will befall me. Oh yes! If an accident befalls the wicked, it's a punishment. But if it happens to befall the good, then it's just to test their faith."

'The wind seemed to have blown out of Shishu at this point, sire, and Yudhi, quickly taking the opportunity, went up and spoke gently to him.

'"Shishu, all of us here are ready to honour Krishna. If you wish to dissent from us, and cannot accept this, by all means do so. No one here will punish you. But if you will not eat with us now, in peace, then you must leave us."

'"All of us?" cried Shishu. "Have you *asked* us all?"

'"Look around you, Shishu. You are the only one here who objects."

'That was a delicate moment, sire. I think that if Shishu hadn't been so unpleasant about it — and if we weren't all so hungry — a few of us might have supported him. But we all avoided his gaze as he lurched around.

'"Look at you!" he cried, waving his arms despairingly at us. "Look at you! Intoxicated by the inspiration of your own faith!... Go on, then, feed your hunger! Your hunger for a god among you — that is all you need!" Then he turned to address Krishna:

'"*You!* If you insist for long enough that you are a god, you see, you are sure to find fools who will believe you, just in case you are!" Then he shuffled around to face the door, and took a few paces, jerking his head at us and cackling as he went. "He who allows himself to be turned into a god, in the end comes to believe in his own lie! And the more he believes in his own lie, the more his followers follow it!"

'We just sat there in silence, waiting for him to leave. After a few more paces, though, he happened to pass where Karna was sitting, and, seeing him, Shishu stopped and turned to us again:

'"You hungry kings are looking for a god? Here is among you a suta whose deeds attest to his very divinity. But does he place himself at your head, craving your adoration? No, he sits here with you. When we all left our weapons outside this hall, who among you did not marvel at that great bow of his, Vijaya?" Yudhi had forbidden any weapons to be brought into the hall, and it's true, many of us did remark on Karna's bow. "What kind of suta could obtain the great bow of Parashu-rama?" Shishu went on. "Unarmed as he is now, this man defeated the mighty Jara-sandha, and in less time than it took Prince Bhima-sena to grease his arms! Not only did he defeat Jara without harming a hair on his body, he also turned Jara's spirit to his will. Why does this suta not stand shining at your head?" He stared around at us. "Who among you knows the divine secret of his birth?"

'Sire, there was a deathly silence. All eyes turned on Karna. Don't ask me what Karna was thinking. It was just then that we heard a quiet voice from the other end of the hall.

'"King Shishu-pala —"

'"Ah! Is that the voice of Vishnu I hear at last?" mocked Shishu. "Does the fair face of Vishnu sink at last to smile upon *my* hideous countenance? If such great beauty, painted large upon a city wall, can make mean lands flourish for the price of a little praise, what trick might it not turn upon *me*!"

'Our eyes now turned to Krishna, who had stopped eating, and was wiping his hands, still looking quite unconcerned.

'"King Shishu-pala," he repeated, "my beauty, though but painted, needs not the mean flourish of your praise... Today you have overstepped your bounds —"

'"Oh! I have offended the great Lord Vishnu-Krishna?" Shishu was dribbling with excitement again. "Well, let us see if the voice of Vishnu has also the arm of Vishnu! Let him strike me down dead from where he sits. Then I will believe most devoutly in his divinity!" He croaked with laughter at his own jest. "I give him my full permission. Let him hasten my departure from this life, and let no blame be attached to his divine gesture!" Shishu started to cackle and cough with laughter, and then he managed to get down on his knees.

'"Mighty Krishna, my life is yours, take it, I pray you! I will be greatly honoured, through death by your hand, to mingle with the soul of Vishnu!" He bowed his head until his forehead touched the ground, still trembling in silent laughter.

'"King Shishu-pala," began Krishna again, in a very gentle voice. "Before I answer your prayer, let me say a few words, without interruption, if I may. Perhaps you will be so gracious?"

'Shishu looked up from the ground, and then raised himself so that he was kneeling upright. Krishna now continued, in a voice so soft we could hardly hear:

'"Soon after the birth of her baby boy, the queen of the Chedis, one of my father's sisters, was on the point of abandoning the child. The boy was born, as you have been told, with three eyes, and with four arms. But my aunt had a dream, in which she was urged to look after the boy. It was revealed to her, in this dream, that her son would one day lose his two extra arms, and also his third eye; and that he would take his rightful place as king of the Chedis. But in the dream she also learnt that her son would one day be killed by the very man who took away his deformity."

'Shishu was hunched on the floor, chuckling quietly and hissing to himself. But Krishna continued, undaunted.

'"The king and queen for years were unable to find anyone who could rid their son of his deformity. I was a very young man when I first set eyes upon my cousin, who was kept hidden away from the world. Before I agreed to try to help him, the queen told me of her dream. But she expressed to me her wish that I should help her son, even if, at some later date, I was indeed to be the instrument of his death. She begged me, however —" here Krishna raised his voice above the noises coming from Shishu — "she begged me not to enter into any dispute with my cousin, to avoid all conflict with him, if at all within my power; and to forgive my cousin if he should ever offend me."

'"I assured my aunt that even if he were to offend me a hundred times, a hundred times should I forgive my cousin Shishu-pala. That I should strive to avoid all quarrel with him, however he provoked me; and that if he made demands of me, then where I possibly could, I should comply."

'Shishu was obviously so overcome with anger now that he could make no sound at all: we thought that he would choke, or have a fit. He tried to raise himself from the floor, to kneel again. And as he struggled there, I saw Krishna start to pick again at the little food that remained on his plate, as though nothing had happened! He wiped his mouth and hands with a cloth, and watched Shishu for a moment. Then he spoke softly again:

'"Perhaps Shishu thinks that this dream of his mother's is my own invention? For he finds false that which displeases, liars those who oppose him. But he perhaps remembers the others whom his mother begged for help? To all of us, his destiny was known, though till this moment he has been spared all knowledge of his fate. No longer need he struggle to patch ignorance with wit."

'Shishu had managed to get up now, but he was still unable to speak.

'"Many of you here tonight know", continued Krishna, "that this cousin of mine has never lost an opportunity to insult me. Perhaps he blames me, and not the sins of a past life, for the pain he has suffered, even for the transmutation of his body. But if we could see his soul now, his body would look beautiful in comparison. How can *he* put fair face upon so foul a truth, and what the worst is, make the best to be! For the sins he has committed in this life have disfigured his soul to a point beyond forgiveness."

'Krishna signalled to a servant to bring him a clean cloth, and as he began to wipe his plate clean, he spoke again, now in a louder, much sterner voice:

'"*I* also need forgiveness. I also beg forgiveness. For I should not have spared him. Better that I should have broken my promise, than have allowed to live Jara-sandha's executioner, the torturer of who knows how many brave and virtuous warriors: good men, who would have been with us here today but for this one man, whom nature worst endowed yet gave the more; whose mother's sacred prayer I did barrenly cherish. Even after Jara-sandha's death, even then I spared him, by restraining Bhima-sena. *I* also need forgiveness."

'Krishna's voice softened:

'"Here you see that this poor wretch before you is a victim of his own torture. It will be merciful now to deny him mercy in this life. With his, and your permission, I shall release his tormented spirit, and let us pray that at my hand he will find peace in his next life; or even escape at last the wheel of life, to join with Vishnu forever."

'There was not a sound... Not a sound! We were all staring at Shishu, who was standing there, rooted to the spot, as if in a dream.

'"King Shishu-pala, your time is come. In accordance with your wishes, I shall remain seated. You say that Vishnu does not need my voice to persuade you. Nor do I need Vishnu's arm to release you."

'All I remember next is Shishu's head flying off, sire, and the noise of cracking wood from the back of the hall, behind the spot where Shishu had been standing... and the cloth, which had been in Krishna's hands, floating to the ground, almost at the same time as Shishu's body folded... Afterwards Karna explained to me, though even now I can hardly believe it, that Krishna had been eating his food off his own discus!'

Dur paused while Charvaka drew a deep breath.

'So...' continued Dur, 'Shishu's body was removed... The mess was tidied up — one or two people at the back had been spattered with blood... The food that had gone cold was removed, hot food brought in... Finally, with little enthusiasm, we started to eat. There was a lot of bad feeling about the whole thing, as you can imagine, sire. The worst of it was that afterwards, over the next few days, Bhima and the twins walked around as though they were at Vishnu's right hand. It was awful. Yudhi was very upset. I don't think he's got over it, even now. He gave Shishu full funeral rites... Kripa made the speech —'

'Oh? What did the owl have to say?'

'Oh, that I can't remember! I can never remember what Kripa says. Something about Shishu being drawn helplessly to Vishnu like a moth to a flame... That we should not grieve for his soul, which had at last escaped from the cycle of births and was now one with Vishnu... That sort of thing, sire.'

'And what did Karna think of it all?'

'Karna? He wouldn't talk about it, sire. He just smiled his usual smile. But I think he was affected by it... He spent a long time sitting silently with an old beggar who had set up near the palace.'

'A beggar?'

'I think Yudhi also tried to speak to him — there are surprisingly few beggars in Indraprastha. Yudhi likes to give them hospitality inside. But I don't think he got anywhere with this one. Poor Yudhi, though it cast a shadow on him, Shishu's death seemed to light up his brothers. It was the day after that when I had my most embarrassing accident — when I fell in the pool. Did I tell you that Bhima ordered his servants to bring me a dry set of clothes, and a pair of sandals? The sandals were inlaid with gold thread, and the clothes were so much finer than the clothes I had been wearing. I just know Bhima wanted to rub it in. And when I stupidly took the new sandals off — I told you that I mistook that glass for a pool of water — Bhima shouted, for everyone to hear: "Look at Prince Dur-yodhana — he's so pleased with his new sandals he doesn't want to scratch them on the glass!" I wouldn't mind their prosperity, sire, if they didn't use every opportunity to rub my nose in it.'

'My boy, if you had a less sensitive nose they would soon leave it alone.'

'I tell you, sire, I'm not the only one. I think the Pandavas — and Krishna — made as many enemies as friends.'

•

Palmira looked up through the balusters of her south wall, at the hills beyond. The boys saw her eyes narrow, and immediately turned to follow her gaze. They saw the crawling dots which had drawn her attention.

'That must be the first consignment of ore... Boys, you know what to do... In case I forget to tell you later, will you remember to go over tomorrow and tell Mulciber? Oh, and there's the charcoal, too...'

'Does that mean that we'll have to stop the story?'

'There's no need to sound so pleased, Henry. I think it would probably be a good idea, though. I'm more fed up with it than you are. I didn't know what I was letting myself in for!'

'Palmira! You can't stop now!'

'We meant, do you have to stop for *now*, for today!'

'And you'll be going away — what happens if you don't finish it in time?'

'In that case time will finish it... Well, all right, I suppose we could just interrupt it. Perhaps I could carry on when I get back.'

'We'll work for you in the mornings, as usual, and then you can carry on with the story in the afternoons. After your siesta.'

'I'm not sure that would be a good idea, boys. I get a bit tired when I'm working the ore.'

'But that was the arrangement, Palmira! You can't expect us to help you for nothing!'

'How much longer will the story take?'

'Oh... it might take another week, I'm afraid, at this rate.'

'Anyway, Palmira, it'll stop you trying to work too late, if you tell us the story — you'd get even more tired if you worked late, wouldn't you?'

'Remember we'll be helping Mulciber clear up at the end of the day, too.'

'And you don't need to do as much of the story each day, Palmira... That wouldn't make it too bad, would it?'

'I suppose so... But it would drag on for longer... We'll see how it goes. I suppose I have time for a bit more now, before they arrive. Yes, all right.'

•

37 The web

'I fear for him, sire. I'm sure he's sleeping badly... And he finds little joy in anything. He doesn't even seem to take any pleasure in his work. I really worry that he might suddenly go, without telling anyone — I've heard him muttering with envy about that beggar! And you know he's always talking of giving up the throne, and living in the forest.'

'A beggar, did you say?'

Arjuna was taking this opportunity to speak to Narada about his brother, before the rishi left Indraprastha.

'Yes, sire, a beggar... a beggar who was here for the Rajasuya.'

'That's worrying. But perhaps he *should* go to the forest — to discover that it offers no escape. For as everybody knows, the man who cannot be contented with little is seldom contented with much; so the man who is not contented with much is even less likely to be contented with little. Yudhi would return from the forest having discovered that this throne, which sits heavily upon *him*, he carries deep within his heart. It is not a golden chair from which he can arise and walk lightly away.'

'Can't you talk to him, sire, before you go?'

Narada sighed. 'Arjuna... perhaps you remember that I was one of the first to suggest the Rajasuya... when your son Abhi was born. I think that Yudhi... It is not the time for me to speak with him.'

'*Someone* needs to talk some sense into him. Perhaps Krishna, then?' Arjuna saw the rishi furrow his brow. 'No, perhaps it's not the right time for Krishna to speak to him either...'

'Has he said anything to you?'

'Yudhi? No. He was certainly shaken by it. But he's not said a word against Krishna. Still, you're right, I think the memory is still too fresh in his mind.'

Narada thought for a moment. 'Arjuna... ask his uncle. Vidura is still here... he may be able to get through to him.'

Vidura had also noticed Yudhi's sadness. But he had been reluctant to question his nephew. He felt that it was better to leave it to Yudhi to air his troubles, should he feel inclined to.

But when first Narada left, then Krishna, then the remaining guests were getting ready to leave, and still there was no sign of happiness on Yudhi's face, Vidura decided to have a word with his nephew.

'Thank you for asking, uncle. I am sleeping well, now. But I had a dream soon after the day of the Rajasuya ceremony, which did disturb me. Since then, it is when I am awake that I am troubled. May I tell you about this dream? There was... Just before the Rajasuya, I noticed a beggar in one of the streets near the palace.'

'That is only natural, Yudhi. They come expecting generous alms from visiting princes. Like fishermen, they follow the fish to a feast.'

'Yes, I know, uncle. No... the reason I noticed this beggar was because Karna was sitting with him — both of them in silence. I think they were in yoga.'

'Karna is a very strange man, Yudhi. You should not dwell on his behaviour.'

'On the contrary, uncle, I have never found Karna's behaviour strange. And I often think about him. Frightening, sometimes... but not strange. Remember, I was virtually brought up with him.'

'Was Karna in your dream?'

'No, just the beggar. The dream was very simple, uncle. I dreamt that I was in my bed, in the palace, and that this beggar came through the door into my room — I woke up in the middle of the night, and saw him at the door, in his loincloth, slowly coming into the room on his thin legs. He stopped before he reached my bed, and stared at me, I don't know for how long. His face seemed sad. Then he turned and walked out as slowly as he had entered. As he moved he seemed to be trying to balance himself with his hands, as though the air would give him some support —'

'Yudhi, did you *dream* that he entered your room, that you woke up — or was he really there?'

Yudhi shrugged his shoulders. 'I don't know. I... I assumed that that was part of my dream... But the dream continued... He was in my room again, talking to me now, by my bed. But when I woke up, at a certain point in the conversation, I really did wake up, I'm sure of that. He wasn't there. I had definitely been dreaming.'

'Can you remember what he said?'

'Yes... It was a strange conversation, uncle...

'"Why do you not follow your dharma, son of Dharma?"

'I did not reply.

'"You asked others to help you decide."

'I didn't deny this. I think I just nodded to him.

'"You follow false dharma."

'"Why?" I asked.

'"To follow true dharma you must be truly alone. When you are swayed by those whom you respect, or by those you fear, then you enter false dharma."

'"No!' I cried. "That's not why I asked what they wanted. I needed to know whether my Rajasuya would offend them, or distress them..."

'"What did they reply?"

'"The majority seemed to be quite happy with it..."'

'"The majority shelter under that majority not for guidance towards truth, but for companionship in error."'

'"No," I replied. "*You* are trying to sway *me* now... Why should I listen to you? I *know* I did not fear them... I respected them, yes, but I did not lean on *their* dharma for support. I needed to know whether I would cause offence."'

'"Sometimes you cannot avoid offence. Sometimes you must not avoid offence... to men of unsound judgement."'

'"What do you mean, unsound?" I asked him. "Why were they unsound in their judgement?"'

'"Because they were in favour of your Rajasuya."'

'"How else could I find out if it was right to hold it? I had to ask them..."'

'"How did they know it was right? Did *they* enquire of those whom the Rajasuya might offend?"'

'"No... I don't know," I had to admit.'

'"*You don't know*... Your hall could be full of Jara-sandhas. Your hall could be full of Shishu-palas. You would respect their decision?"'

'"Of course... They deserve as much respect as I do... I would have to respect their decision... I have to respect everyone I ask."'

'"What about those whom you cannot ask, but whom you may most hurt?"'

'The beggar seemed to disappear — he was leaning against something, a pillar, perhaps, and then he seemed to wither away, to dissolve into the air... and then I felt I was again at the centre of all those kings, in the banquet hall... Except that now I was a fly... we were all insects, caught in a web... The spider was somewhere outside the hall, outside the palace... That was when I woke up. I was definitely alone, uncle... The next day I searched for him. But he must have left Indraprastha. There were no beggars to be seen.'

Yudhi wiped the sweat from the back of his neck.

Vidura looked at him for a moment.

'Yudhi... there is no need to feel guilty about the Rajasuya... Remember, it is said that to live properly one must offer gifts to gods, to guests, to servants, to parents, but also, Yudhi, to oneself.'

'But Vidura, I know very well how much this gift to myself must have hurt others.'

'Hurt others?'

'Of course. Do you think I don't know how upset Dur and his brothers were?'

'Dur and his brothers? Dur is avaricious, Yudhi. He is selfish, he is greedy. He thinks of nothing but satisfying his own desires and ambitions. His royal ambitions. Let him stay hungry. It will do him good. He must learn to control himself, and to accept the world.'

'He *ought* to, uncle, yes. I agree. He ought to. But *will* he? Before I enter the cage of a hungry tiger, do I say to myself, he *ought* to learn to weigh my desire for life against his desire for meat? Or do I ask myself, *will* he?'

Vidura was silent.

'Did you not see how upset he was? Please, uncle, when you get back to Hastinapura, try to calm him. Tell him that I understand his feelings. I don't think you know him as well as I do. You should have seen him when we were children, when he tried to poison Bhima. Everything around him was like salt on a raw wound. Worse, for salt at least helps the wound to heal. Our prosperity only aggravates him. If only he knew how it also aggravates me! If only there was something I could give him... a balm for his wounds...'

'Nothing that you can give him will soothe him, Yudhi. In truth, you could no more relieve him with balm than you could quench a fire with butter.'

'But I have done wrong, uncle. I have done something wrong. I should never have listened to Narada, or to Krishna, or to my brothers...'

◊

When Yudhi's guests returned to Hastinapura their effusive praise of the Pandavas plunged Dur into further depression. With Karna still away in Anga, Dur was able to confide only in Shakuni and Charvaka. And though they did listen to him, their patience at times was clearly stretched.

'Uncle, I'm *tormented* with envy... Why can't I be like other men? Other men don't seem to have their enjoyment of the simplest pleasures ruined by envy... Ruined at the thought of the greater happiness of others... The poorest, most miserable beggar isn't as wretched as I am! The thought of Arjuna, Bhima, the twins, basking before those adoring eyes... I can't even enjoy a simple strawberry without thinking of Bhima, eating under the gaze of his friends and admirers... enjoying himself without limit, without hindrance... I can't even take any pleasure in looking out at the view from my tower! I might as well be blind! I can't run my eye along the rolling hills... I can't lie on soft ground beneath a warm sun... I can't breathe in the beauty of a moonlight night... I can't do *anything* without thinking of the joy of the Pandavas... of their palace, of Indraprastha... It's like a stench which clings to me, which I can't escape! The keener the pleasure I ought to feel, the keener the pain when I find that it eludes me! I can't see my wives without thinking of the women who ache for Arjuna and the twins! I'm surrounded by all I could want. But like a man with a cold in his throat, I can't taste anything! Like a blind man, I can't shiver in awe at the moon... Like a eunuch, I no longer tingle with pleasure at a woman's touch. I'm only relieved from this pain when the clouds drive all joy from the day for others! When the sun no longer inflames *their* happiness to scorch *my* soul! Yes... My only relief is this brief clouding... of a pain which only death can extinguish...'

Charvaka discreetly nudged Shakuni; for Dur was evidently expecting some response.

'What about your duties, Dur?' enquired Shakuni, taking up his turn with the dice. 'Don't you find any satisfaction in the administration of justice, in the —'

'Uncle! Haven't you seen how the people *love* Yudhi? Haven't you seen them bring their disputes before him in Indraprastha? They seem to melt out of shame at the mere sight of him! It takes hardly a word of guidance for them to double their efforts to make Indraprastha a place that Yudhi can be proud of! The most *I* can expect is for people to hide their laziness, out of fear! Look at Yudhi's friends, his allies — they would die for him! He would be invincible in battle. Who would want to fight against him? Who would want to fight for *me*?'

'My dear, don't work yourself up like this. Certainly, it's true, the Pandavas are enjoying the fruits of their industry. But you know, it's not true that you have no friends or allies. You have your brothers —'

'*Brothers*? Of what worth is a man whom only his brothers are willing to defend? Besides, my brothers are the most good-for-nothing collection a man could hope to die with!'

'Dur, let me tell you this: I myself would fight for you — providing this good rishi can make glass for my eyes to see through, which he has been promising me for some time —'

'I'm sorry, uncle... And I truly thank you...'

'And my dear, though it's true that you would very little deserve their efforts on your behalf, may I point out that Bhishma, Kripa, even Drona, would fight for you.'

'Grudgingly!'

'Of course, grudgingly!' intervened Charvaka. 'A man so slightly attached to the joys of life can't expect any great weight of enthusiasm to help him preserve it!'

'They wouldn't do it out of love, would they?' persisted Dur, ignoring Charvaka's comment. 'I know you would, uncle, I know that, but...'

'What about Karna, then?' suggested Charvaka. 'He would certainly do it out of love. Though what on earth he should find about you to esteem quite escapes me. But he does seem fond of you, my boy.'

'Yes...' Dur's face brightened. 'Yes, Karna is my one and only consolation... That's true... Yes, I've only to think of Karna, and my spirits lighten!'

'There you are, my dear.'

'And he'll soon be back,' added Charvaka. 'Vrisha says within the week.'

'But uncle, do you think we could defeat the Pandavas in battle?'

397

'Don't be absurd!' There was now a distinct note of impatience in Shakuni's tone. 'What reason is there to fight them?'

'I'm afraid your nephew would like to humiliate them,' explained Charvaka. 'But my boy,' he warned Dur, 'bear in mind that the more civilised a people, the harder and more dangerous it is to try to humiliate them with force.'

'If they attacked you,' said Shakuni, 'why, certainly, that would be another matter. But not even Karna would lead your troops against the Pandavas for no other reason than to determine your comparative strengths!'

'In any case, my boy,' added Charvaka, 'you would find no pleasure in victory. For as everybody knows, the man who cannot be contented with little is seldom contented with much; so the man who cannot be contented with much is even less likely to be contented with more.'

'Precisely,' said Shakuni. 'Now, my dear, the rishi and I have work to get on with...'

Dur took the hint and left them, but in scarcely higher spirits than when he had arrived.

'Where *is* Vrisha?' exclaimed Shakuni.

'Give him a chance,' protested Charvaka. 'He only got back yesterday!'

'You did say here and not your place? The sun will be down soon. Oh, that reminds me... There was a brahmana from Maya at the Rajasuya. Arjuna and Nakula introduced me to him... a very learned man... He has calculated when the sun will next be in yoga... I must check his calculation — according to him it should coincide with the next Shiva but one. Apparently the other brahmanas aren't at all pleased!'

'I'm not surprised — at a Shiva festival! I shouldn't be surprised if they choose to ignore such a prediction altogether.'

'Yes, I think you're right — it's extraordinary what they can ignore when they put their mind to it. This man from Maya, though he was quite open-minded compared to some, he still refused to believe the earth is a sphere! How he has done the calculations, I don't know. I must check them. And when the moon goes into yoga, he refused to accept it's the shadow of the earth!'

'By the way, Shakuni... I've been thinking...'

Charvaka was holding a dice in his hand. He put it down and searched inside his pocket for a heavy coin. He held it in his palm, raising and lowering his hand to feel the coin's full weight against his skin. Then he put the coin down on the dice table.

'You agree with me that the earth exerts a pull upon all bodies — like the sun and the moon on each other and on the earth... And that this is why objects fall, indeed, why they have what we know as weight... But I've been thinking... It *seems* that I can't perceive this pull of the earth on objects other than myself... I can only *infer* its existence, through motion, through the weighing balance, and so on... Whereas it seems that I myself can feel it, as my weight... Vrisha!'

'Is that Vrisha? My dear, come in!'

'Sorry I'm late...' Vrisha sat down on a stool beside the dice table. 'But sire, when you're just *looking* at an object, obviously you can only infer that the earth is pulling it down... But what if you hold the object. Surely, you feel the pull on it then?'

'Ah!' exclaimed Shakuni. 'I see what you mean, Charvaka! Let me answer him... What I think the rishi will argue is this: if you were to hold this dice or that coin in your hand, Vrisha, you would feel a downward force, yes?'

'Exactly,' replied Vrisha. 'That's the coin's weight — the pull of the earth on the coin, isn't it?'

'Well, my dear, to be exact, no! You feel a downward force, yes. But what you feel is a force exerted by the coin upon your *hand*. That is not the same as the force of the earth upon the *coin*. It cannot be the same force, Charvaka will tell you, because, for one thing, the first force is acting upon the surface of your hand; while the second force is acting upon the metal of the coin! No, you infer the second force, acting on the coin, from the first, acting on your hand.'

Vrisha grinned. He looked at Charvaka. 'I expect that now you're going to tell me, sire, that I don't even feel the pull of the earth on *me*!'

'I'm afraid that may also be the case,' said Charvaka. 'You see, perhaps all that we ever *feel* is not the downward pull of the earth upon us, but the upward force from whatever it is that is preventing us from falling lower — the force of the stool upon your buttocks, my boy... Or of the ground upon your feet...'

Vrisha stood up and sat down again. 'Sire, if you're right, then suppose I jumped... or was falling freely without anything to stop me... then I oughtn't to feel any force on me, either down or up?' Vrisha closed his eyes. 'I think you're wrong... Perhaps I could try an experiment, and jump down from Dur's tower — I could shout the answer to you an instant before I hit the ground!'

'Yes, but I'm not even sure that experiment would clarify it,' Charvaka pointed out, 'because of the resistance of the air upon you, forcing you up...'

'Perhaps we should leave that experiment for another day,' suggested Shakuni. 'Though I'm inclined rather to agree with Vrisha, that he would feel the force from the earth... But Charvaka, you were going to tell Vrisha and me what it is we talk about!'

'Yes...' said the rishi, with a frown. 'Though you know how I hate talking about language...'

'Come on, my dear,' insisted Shakuni, 'you promised...'

'Anyway, sire,' observed Vrisha, 'you're the one whose always saying there's more to language than just language!'

'Precisely,' concurred Shakuni. 'We're just as much talking here about what we think of as *things*.'

Charvaka took a deep breath.

'Well... my belief is that, in the end, when all's said and done, all we can say is... that the things we see are the things we see... and that we talk about what we talk about. And that we have to leave it at that.'

Vrisha appealed to Shakuni.

'You see why I'm confused?'

'I do indeed, my dear. If I remember rightly, you were inclined, on the one hand, to the very natural view that the things we see and talk about are in the world outside of our minds. Yes? But on the other hand, you were prevented from embracing this view straightforwardly, by considering examples such as that of your Madhuca cordial... An example which I believe tempted you to an alternative view, that we only ever see and talk about, let us say, fabrications of perception... Yes? Well, Charvaka, I'm surprised at your singularly unhelpful statement. I would have bet on you taking the first of these views. I would have thought you would say simply that there is no question but that the things we talk about, and see, are in the world outside our minds.'

'I don't believe it's as simple as that,' replied Charvaka. 'The difficulty is that you are asking me to say something, from one view, standing in one place, as it were, which you want to apply to all views. In fact, I think the answer has to depend on where you are standing...'

Shakuni nodded pensively.

'In one sense,' continued Charvaka, 'the answer is simple: Yes, of course. What we see and talk about of course is really there, outside of us. While I am in the world of men, speaking the common language, of course I refer to what is really there outside my mind. For that is the agreed truth; so much agreed that it defines the very meaning of what we say. That is how the difference between illusion and reality is agreed upon. But in another sense, if we step back, if we disengage — or try to disengage — from the natural language of the world, then I can concede to Vrisha that talking about the world may not be quite as simple as it seemed.'

'Yes, sire, you know I have no problem with the common way of speaking. But we've stepped back now! And from where I stand now, it's not just that our common talk isn't as simple as it seemed — from where I stand now, it just *can't* be about the world! However much I'd like it to be, and however much I normally intend it to be.'

'And is this because of the problem of illusions?' asked Shakuni.

'Yes. I've been thinking, Shakuni, about that example... I can make the example even more difficult to ignore... I know it's far-fetched, but it's the principle of the thing... Suppose that with this special cordial, you could not only get people to have illusions, but you could feed it to a child, to a baby, so that it grew up in a world of its own, thinking there were things around it that weren't really there, thinking that there were people around it who weren't really there. It could even learn a language. And all the while, from our point of view, the child would be moving and talking and gesturing and pointing to the empty air! Do you see what I mean, Shakuni?'

'Oh yes. And of course, you know that Charvaka believes that all our sensations and perceptions are occurring in a person's brain. So he would have to concede the principle that these events in the brain might be manipulated, not in the normal way, by the usual impact of the world, but directly. In principle, of course... Yes... in which case the world of such a person would be no more real than the virtual image of an object in a mirror. And yet to them it would seem as real as ours. Such a person would believe they were seeing, listening, talking, as we do now... Yet from our view there would be nothing there for their language to refer to, nothing there for their hands to point to. And of course, within their experience they would also have what *they* took to be illusions, dreams, which they would wake up from... There would be truth and falsehood, as taught by their virtual companions... and so on... I think for the sake of the principle we can readily overlook the details of how we could sustain such a person's life with food and drink!'

'And, Shakuni, would you admit,' asked Vrisha, 'that if such a person, in their illusion, picked up a bow and shot an arrow at a target, we could hardly say that they shot at a target in the world?' Vrisha turned, grinning, to Charvaka. 'They couldn't possibly be aiming at something in the world!'

'Naturally,' agreed Shakuni. 'From our point of view, such a person could not be aiming at something outside of their mind...'

'But then,' maintained Vrisha, 'what exactly *is* such a person talking about? What *are* they seeing. And what's the difference between their case and ours? To us everything seems just like it seems to them. So why should we be talking about different sorts of things, which are really out there?'

'But my dear, suppose I gave you an account of how a certain friend of mine visited a certain place, and had various adventures... And suppose that after I have finished my account, I tell you that it was just an invention, just a story. You wouldn't ask... but who *was* the person in my story? Where *was* the place he visited? Yet if the story was true, then, quite simply, there *would* be an actual person corresponding to the appropriate phrase or name I used. There would be a real place in the world corresponding to the place I described. And so on. What makes one account true and another false depends on whether we can link up the words and phrases to the world. Well, similarly, what makes an experience real or illusory depends on whether we can link up the objects seen, the objects talked about, with the world.'

'I don't think it's as simple as that,' interjected Charvaka, shaking his head with a sigh.

'Poor rishi!' said Shakuni to Vrisha. 'He finds us most trying!' Then Shakuni noticed Vrisha's pensive expression. 'Oh dear! Not only have I fallen foul of Charvaka, I did not even resolve your question!' Shakuni turned to the rishi. 'Well? Why isn't it as simple as that?'

'I agree, Shakuni,' began Charvaka, 'that there is no need to ask, of a character in a story, who they really are. Or rather, if you ask who such-and-such was, I simply tell you, he was a character in a story. Or, if we were talking about a dream of mine, he was a person in my dream. There is nothing more to say. And, moreover, if we try to say any more about what exactly we are talking about, in a story, to unwind or analyse what exactly we are referring to, we will not succeed: for nothing says it better than the natural language. Nothing gives you greater understanding of who and what these things are than for me to tell you that they are characters in a story, things appearing in a dream, or whatever. But you see, this all goes to show how very easily language works without there having to be anything in the world to correspond to the phrases used. There is a regrettable tendency to think that, when we use words to say all the things we say, these words must, if we speak the truth, connect up in a simple direct way to the world which we are talking about. You may think, perhaps, that the difference between a story and an account of something which actually happens, is that in the latter case we can *point* to the things referred to. Certainly, this sometimes is the case, or appears to be the case...'

Charvaka picked up a dice from the table and dropped it.

'Suppose I say,' he continued, 'that... *Charvaka picked up the Kali dice, but dropped it almost immediately...* There seem to be two things in the world which are involved here, Charvaka, and the Kali dice. And happily enough, there are two words in the statement, or two phrases, at any rate, which seem to connect very conveniently with the world. A third one, *it*, here also refers to the Kali dice. And it seems very comforting to say that I was talking about these two things.

'But the truth is, I believe, that even when we speak the truth, we can do so very well without such a facile correspondence between words and things. After all, even in the sentence I just now employed to talk about the Kali dice, what bit of the world did the word *up* connect with? I know what you're thinking: you saw my hand move upwards. All right, what about *almost*? I suppose you're trying to think of a small gap in time? Very well, then, what about *but*? These words are contributing their work towards the sentence as a whole, but not by connecting simply to the world. All right, you say, these words or phrases may not be bearing the weight of linking the sentence to the ground. That's fine, not every wall or pillar serves that function in a building. But surely, you will say, there must be *some* part of the building that carries the weight to the ground. *Charvaka. Dice.*

'Well..' he continued, 'my belief is this: although the simpler examples of our language appear to support this naive picture, when we look more carefully we are forced to accept, first of all, that there may not be a simple correspondence between things in the world and the weight-bearing phrases that we seem to lean on. And secondly, that in much of our talk we are hard put to pick out any weight-bearing phrases *at all*! Nevertheless, the talking works very well, with the speaker engaging and moving the listener, but without ever seeming to touch the ground!'

'That is clearly what seems to happen when I tell a story,' said Shakuni, nodding, 'unless my listener is moved to fall asleep. Where indeed do I touch the ground? And yet you understand me perfectly well... Even though in such a case I agree, it is absurd to worry what precisely I am talking *about*—'

'There is more to being than being,' interjected Charvaka. 'Or perhaps, I should say, less...'

'But could you give me another example of this, where you say something *true*?'

'Certainly. After all, a true account is just a different kind of story, one to which people respond in a different way.'

'But sire,' objected Vrisha, 'how can a statement be true, be actually about the world, if it isn't because of how the words connect to the world?'

'Because what makes it true may not be the simple connection tying any of the words with objects you can point to — even though the sentence as a whole is true because of the condition of the world. Let me give you an example, where fact takes on something of the character of fiction, while yet remaining fact. Eh? Look...'

Charvaka cleared the dice table; and then picked up two dice; he placed them next to each other in the middle of the grid. On one of the dice the yellow vertex pointed upwards; on the other dice it was the black point uppermost.

'If I told you that on the table there was one dice adjacent to another, would you say this was true or false?'

'True,' said Vrisha.

'And if I told you that on the table there was one dice with its yellow point up next to another with its black point up?'

'True.'

'And if I told you that there was a dice showing *3* next to a dice showing *4*?'

'True.'

'And if I told you that I was riding Kali on a *3*? True or false?'

'I'm not sure, sire. The *4*'s obviously riding Kali, because it's on your betting row, not on the dice row... But I'm not sure it would make sense to say it was true unless you were actually in the middle of a game.'

'Very well, to save time I won't set it up, but imagine that you came into the room and we were in the middle of a game, and there were other dice and bets around these two on the grid... And I told you that *I was riding Kali on a 3*. Would you say true or false?'

'Yes, sire. True.'

'Can you show me what bits of the world my words would tie up to? Not *say*, of course, that's cheating — *show*. Eh? You could point to me, and say that *I* connects to this rishi... And you could point to the dice... But, my boy, let me make it just a little harder: you say that at present, given the actual circumstances in this room, my statement is either false or not quite sensible. It's not true, at any rate, eh? Well, can you show me exactly what bits of the world would have to be in place for my words to tie with, in order that the statement was true? In other words, could you point your finger at exactly that which made the statement true in one condition of the world, not true in another?'

'No, sire. Not very easily, anyway...'

'And yet my statement, if it was true, would be true in virtue of some condition of the world, wouldn't it?'

'Yes.'

'Very well, my boy, let me take the whole thing one stage further. Let's suppose that Shakuni and I had succeeded in constructing a machine that could play dice. Just a mechanical device with wheels and cogs, but let's suppose it gave a tolerable game. Perhaps it wasn't quite up to beating Shakuni; but it could easily beat Yudhi, for example. Eh? Now, let's suppose we reach a certain point in a game between our mechanical player and Yudhi. At this precise moment the mechanical player taps twice. Well, at this point, we could describe very accurately how all the various cogs and wheels moved, resulting in the double tap. Accordingly, I could detail precisely what happened; I could then ask you if my description was true or false; you could check, and if I was right, you would say, yes, that's true. It would be a fact, eh? Well, someone else at that moment, overlooking the game — Shakuni, perhaps — might say, *Oh, our player is aiming for a kill on the limit!* Now, my boy, would that be true or false?'

'Well, it might be — if the limit was the only prime available—'

'Of course, let's assume that... Well?'

'Yes, it would be true, I suppose.'

'And would that not be another way of describing the same fact? The fact of which I gave you a precise mechanical description?'

'I suppose so, sire. I'm not sure. Perhaps.'

'At least, would you not say that one and the same condition of the world made both these statements, the one detailed and direct, the other brief and oblique, true? It would have been one and the same world which I and Shakuni were, in our different ways, describing. Would it not?'

'Yes, sire.'

'But would you have been able to point your finger at anything corresponding to the word *kill*? Could you point your finger at the *limit*?'

'No, sire... No.'

'And yet, to repeat, both statements, mine and Shakuni's, would be made true by the condition of one and the same world. Eh? Yet, in spite of that, you couldn't draw neat lines from the words in the one statement to the words in the other. You would in fact be hard-pressed to draw any lines at all. Why? Because Shakuni's sentence connects up as a whole, and in a very subtle way, to the same world my sentence describes, not simply in virtue of the correspondence of its component phrases.'

Vrisha grinned. 'I'm sure there's a rat in there somewhere!'

'And what exactly was that about?' Charvaka contested. 'What is this *rat*? Where exactly is this *there*? All right,' he added, seeing the expression on Vrisha's face, 'even if I don't use the phrase figuratively — though I don't see why I should make things any easier for you — if I tell you that... *the rat is a pestilential animal...* You understand me perfectly well, as I understood you. What I say does its work... But what are the *precise* bits of the world I am talking about? No *one* rat, certainly. No particular number of rats, in fact...'

'Yes, sire... but... at least with your detailed description, of your mechanical dice player, at least with that we can tie the phrases to the world, can't we?'

'Ah!' cried Shakuni. He beamed at Charvaka. 'I think I know what you're going to say, my dear... Let me answer him!' Shakuni turned to Vrisha. 'You remember that I set Charvaka on this track by maintaining that when I *really* see something, there is something there in the world corresponding to the components of my perception, which would not be there if my experience was just an illusion. And, rather similarly, that when I make a true statement, there is something there in the world corresponding to certain phrases in what I put together... The point I believe Charvaka now wishes to make is this... Yes, Vrisha, *we*, given the senses we have, are able to provide a mechanical description of the world, in terms appropriate to our senses, in which the parts of speech are neatly tied to the ground. But for another kind of being, another kind of observer, for another form of life, with the senses they have, even Charvaka's description may not stand easily on the ground of their perceptions. For such a being it might be as difficult to tie Charvaka's description to what they could point, as it was for you to tie *kill* and *limit* to the ground. And yet such a being may be observing one and the same world as ours, one and the same event. How foolish of me! I should have realised when I gave you the example of the three blind men and the elephant! Yes... And, Vrisha, just as you accept that one and the same condition of the world made true both Charvaka's description and mine, so might this different form of life recognise that the condition of one and the same world *he* saw, also made Charvaka's detailed description true. And without necessarily being able to point to what Charvaka's words connected with.' Shakuni appealed to the rishi. 'Isn't that your point, my dear?'

'It is... But of course, we must remember that the words and things go together, at least in the natural language of our respective forms of life. There may be no one *thing* which such a being could see, by means of his natural senses, which corresponded to a thing I saw. Even though we were observing one and the same world — even though one and the same world made both our experiences real and not illusory, even though one and the same world made both our statements true. And of course, our two languages would be different in a much more profound way than any two languages of man...'

Charvaka looked at Vrisha.

'You mean,' said Vrisha, 'this being might not be able to say — see — what we were talking about?'

'Exactly. But he might be able to tie what he saw to what our language *did*. To how we moved each other with it.'

'But...' Vrisha picked up a dice. 'But doesn't that support my point... That this is perhaps *not* a dice?'

'You must be careful where you're standing, my boy. If you're standing in the world of men, there is only one possible answer: of course that is a dice: a single, tetrahedral dice, and nothing but a dice. Our common language is expressly designed so that what I have just said is perfectly true. It is designed expressly so that anyone denying that fact is uttering a blatant falsehood! We cannot, within our daily round, stretch the common language beyond its natural range.'

'Yes, but we can stand in a different place —'

'You think you can jump out of your skin and not be a man, and get inside the skin of another kind of being? You can *imagine* — or rather, you can *try* to imagine — standing in a different place, from which the common language is not quite as natural as it might seem. You want to stand where reality, which you breathe in and out like air, assumes a strange guise; where you cannot take it for granted. But if we venture under water, to try to get beneath the whole thing, to see our world from below, well, yes, you certainly can't take the air for granted, then; but neither can you breathe, or talk... You want to swallow your egg without cracking it, my boy. You want to stand under water, breathe in this new medium, and at the same time describe it to us...'

Vrisha smiled, and shook his head.

'Charvaka,' appealed Shakuni, 'can't you give him an example?'

'It's very difficult, Shakuni. You want me from within this, our view, to show another view... I will try...'

Charvaka scratched his beard and frowned.

'Very well...' he began. 'I have heard that in some of the wet forests there are tiny spiders that live, almost like ants, on a single giant web, a web that can be as tall as a tree. These spiders live all their lives upon this web, and know of nothing else. When something lands or gets caught in their web, they sense it very precisely from the vibrations of the thread, how big it is, where it is, and so on. Now, let's imagine, then, that there existed spiders rather like these, but which were very clever, which could talk to each other. Let's imagine also — and you'll have to indulge me here — that they were blind, and that somehow they could never touch anything directly except perhaps through their mouths, to feed... That, in other words, their main sense was from the quivering of the web... Their world would be no less real than ours, for being sensed in a different light. Well, when they talked, what would they be talking *about*? What would they, as it were, *see*? Suppose a pink feather landed on the web. They would make no sense of its colour. There are ways in which we could describe the feather which they could not point to. Not, at any rate, with their natural sense. If a fly landed on the web, it would be in contact only at certain points, like the feather. Whereas it would make sense for *us* to describe the height of the fly's body, above the web, or the texture of its wings... what sense could the spiders make of these? Similarly, could we point to what they sensed, to what they described in their language? And yet one and the same world would be seen by us and seen by them. One and the same world would render our statements true or false, and their statements true or false. Moreover, and this is my point, Vrisha... however much more powerful or varied are our senses, we could not say better what they talk about than in *their* language.

'As you stand to them,' continued Charvaka, 'gazing at their lives playing out upon this web, so some being might stand to us. And however much more powerful or varied were this being's senses, he could not say better what *we* talk about than in *our* language.'

'But supposing this being's senses are better, sire, why can't he say what we talk about, but using his language?'

'My dear,' replied Shakuni, for the rishi, 'we don't need such far-fetched examples to see that. Even when observers differ comparatively slightly, a similar problem may arise. After all, your sight is superior, in a sense, to that of people who are completely colour-blind — who are so colour-blind that, *you* say, they can only see shades of grey. That's the nearest you can get, from within your view, to imagining their view! The point is, of course, they are not seeing different shades of *grey*. Nor are they seeing different shades of *green* — how could we know it isn't green rather than grey that they see? In short, they are not seeing different shades of any one tint *you* can describe. Grey cannot be grey when you know no other colour. When there is no other word for a colour. Black, white and grey belong to your experience, and these terms belong to your language. You could only express properly what they see in *their* language. Colour-blind people may try to use our words for colour, but it is an approximation of convenience. We may use our words to describe what a colour-blind person sees, but again, it is an approximation of convenience.'

'Remember, my boy,' added Charvaka, 'the colour-blind people and you are looking at one and the same world. What they see is as *real* as what you see. Their descriptions, as far as they go, are as true as yours, as far as yours go. And yet you cannot point to the colour they describe; nor can they point to yours.'

'If we can't point to the same thing,' said Vrisha, 'how can we be seeing the same thing? Oh, I think I see what you mean... It's the same world, but not the same thing?'

'If you can both point and speak in agreement with each other,' stressed the rishi, 'then it is the same thing. If you cannot, all you can say is that it's the same world making your disparate descriptions true.'

'But sire, surely... If it's the same world... then mustn't there be some way in which I can point to something the spiders, or whatever, can point to...'

'That's an interesting point, my dear,' said Shakuni. 'May I answer him, Charvaka? Our natural language goes hand in hand with our natural senses. Yes? It may be possible, by augmenting our senses artificially, by means of instruments, to point to the world, to describe the world, in a subtle and oblique way. And by that means, to communicate, and signify, if not precisely *point*, in agreement with another kind of being. I don't know if such people exist, but suppose we meet men who can tell what direction they are moving in, absolutely, without having to take their bearings from the world about them. They just sense where west is, for example. Yes? Well, by using one of Charvaka's special iron needles, nursed with lodestone, which point in an absolute direction, you can also point to the west, and find some measure of agreement by this means. Without which your understanding of these terms, used by these people to indicate absolute direction, would be quite limited... In such a way you could, in a sense, extend your natural perception, extend your natural language. And how precisely such an unnatural language might turn out can only be discovered by examining the world. Do you not agree, Charvaka?'

'Yes... But I believe one should resist the temptation of thinking that, if we could extend our language in this way, we would be getting closer to the real world than in our natural language. Just as there is no place to stand, no set of senses, which alone show you things as they *really* are, so there is no language which refers, unlike other languages, to things as they *really* are. However much we might extend language in this way, it could still not jump out of its skin, and get closer to reality than we already are.' Charvaka picked up an ivory betting counter. 'However we might describe this thing in such an extended language, what we would say would not be *more* truthful than my natural statement that this betting counter is made of ivory. It might say different things about it, but these would not be more true!'

Charvaka replaced the counter; but then Shakuni immediately picked it up.

'When I put this down on the table in a game, my dear,' he said to Vrisha, 'it may be worth quite a lot, yes? But if I put it under one of the feet of the table, to level the surface, it's worth something rather different, no? Which is its true worth? Which is its true use? Perhaps you think that it's *natural* use is as a counter. But then again, it was once part of an elephant's tusk...'

Vrisha smiled. 'I'm afraid you've lost me there, Shakuni...' Vrisha turned now to Charvaka. His smile broadened to a grin. 'I'm still not happy about whether we need reality at all, sire...'

'What do you mean?' asked Charvaka.

'You seem to have avoided my original problem, sire! You remember in the example — where a person was living under a complete illusion, seeing and talking to other people who were just illusions in his mind? To such a person life would seem just as it does to me, to us... Surely, then, what is significant is what's going on in their *mind*. What is *really* in the world seems to drop out of consideration. I mean, it's all very well for Shakuni to say that it's whether or not there *are* things happening outside his mind that make the difference between reality and illusion. But the fact is, how could I ever distinguish between a world in which there really was something, a reality, outside my mind, from one which was a specially arranged... fiction?'

'My boy, what is reality if it isn't a specially arranged fiction? Your sword is all blade and no handle. You have demonstrated eloquently that there is no difference between reality and specially arranged fiction. For what cannot in principle be distinguished, is one and the same!'

Vrisha turned to appeal to Shakuni.

'I'm afraid I am powerless to dispute that, my dear.'

'It's not a question of disputing it!' complained Vrisha with a laugh. 'What does it *mean*?'

'All right,' said Charvaka soothingly. 'Let's go through it step by step, eh? Let's try and agree on what we can say sensibly about your earlier example. Clearly, a person can discover that they were under an illusion. You can wake up from a dream. Or indeed, a person may wake up, as it were, from one of these Madhuca intoxications, to discover that all their experience had been an illusion... Now, the question is, what is real and what is not? Eh? When we say that the cordial drinker's experience was not real, but an illusion, we must take care to note where we must be standing, what is our view, eh? And our view must be this: we are with the watchers, those who are watching this person gesturing to the empty air —'

'Ah! Of course!' exclaimed Shakuni. 'From this view, the cordial drinker has a virtual image. But from another view again, the watchers themselves may also be judged to have a virtual image. And so on, and so on!'

'Please be quiet, Shakuni. Don't confuse the boy. Step by step, I said. Now, Vrisha... As I said, from the point of view of the watchers, the cordial drinker's experience is an illusion. The watchers will take as fact the deception of those they are watching. But by the same token, namely, that from within any one view, *total* illusion is indistinguishable from reality, what the watchers take to be reality may, to their own watchers, also be judged an illusion. Eh? And of course, this tale points in both directions. For our intoxicated cordial drinker may, in his experience, with his virtual friends, come upon someone talking and pointing into thin air... From within the cordial drinker's view, this person would be experiencing an illusion. And the moral of this tale, my boy, is this: the fact that from one view a person's experience will be judged to be manufactured, fabricated, is just a fact within that view. From another view again, the experience of the first view may be seen to be contrived. In other words, my boy, there is no place from which you can get an absolute view. My belief is that you cannot say, *absolutely*, this experience *is* a fabrication. You can only say: from a certain point of view, the experience is a fabrication. But from another point of view, it may be judged differently; for one very simple reason: namely, that what is judged as *real*, within a certain view, can only be defined against what is judged, *within* that view, as *illusion*. Not against what is observed from some other view. Not against some higher absolute. Reality and meaning are judged from *inside*, not from outside. Reality is defined within a view, in contrast to illusion; truth in contrast to falsehood; object in contrast to image; certainty against uncertainty; the possible against the impossible; the objective against the subjective...'

'But sire... Doesn't that have the consequence that... Surely you're not saying that when I have a convincing dream, it is *real*!'

'I'm afraid that logic drives me mercilessly to the following conclusion: from within your dream, while it is happening, if it is convincing — that's to say, if your experience within your dream is organised so that there appears to you a clear distinction between illusion and reality — then that experience, *within that view*, is as real as anything can be. Ask yourself this, my boy: when do you judge the dream to be just a dream? It is when you wake up. In other words, when your view changes, when it ceases to be that within the dream, and becomes outside it: remembering, watching or considering the dream, from outside it. Naturally, from within the view of your waking state, your dream was an illusion. But from within your dream, if it was convincing, it was as real as real. When you wake up it seems as though you are standing in a neutral space, comparing one experience, the dream, with another, reality. But you are not in a neutral space. You are now in what you judge to be reality. From where the dream was an illusion. You are always confined to a view, my boy. In other words, your world is always real, unless you change your view, and discover that it was just a dream.'

'My dear,' said Shakuni, seeing the smile of disbelief on Vrisha's face, 'I'm afraid I have to agree with the rishi. There is no way to distinguish a good illusion from reality, except by waking.'

'What about a bad one?' asked Vrisha.

'It is bad,' explained Charvaka, 'when within it you do not have a sense of the difference between illusion and reality; between truth and error, between the regular and the irregular. In a convincing story, what is true within the story is clearly differentiated from what is false. Remember, for some people even all this' — Charvaka spread his arms — 'does not seem to separate clearly fact from fiction! For us it does. We are lucky, my boy. But why should not reality admit of degree?'

Vrisha smiled wistfully and took a deep breath. 'So where does all this leave my question?'

'What question, my boy?'

Vrisha picked up one of the dice.

'Ah!' exclaimed Charvaka. 'Don't tell me you're still wondering... You're not still asking, is what we see and refer to as *that dice* just a subtle construct of your related perceptions? Or is it really a thing, out there in the world outside of your mind?'

'Exactly, sire! Which is it. One or the other?'

'My boy, haven't you learnt to leave well alone! It's neither, and it's both. Remember, what cannot in principle be distinguished, is one and the same. How could you possibly, while standing in one place — as you must — distinguish between the two? I tell you once again: the things we talk about are, in truth, the things we talk about! What else can they be? Suppose you tried to analyse *that dice in your hand* as a construct of your perceptions of sight, of touch... and presumably, also, of the perceptions of others... through your perceptions of them! After all, you need to ensure it isn't just an illusion you alone are having! Well, how would you know your analysis was right? Only if it meant that when you actually saw and held the dice, you saw and held the dice! What better way of putting it can there possibly be, than just that? Moreover, you spent your childhood learning to perform that complicated analysis with all the ease of your natural language. Your poor brain has already done the work once over! Don't now ask it to start again at the wrong end! You're trying to climb out of your language, when in fact you can no more do that than climb out of your own skin.'

Charvaka pointed at the dice in Vrisha's hand.

'Even if you managed to analyse in some complex way precisely what that entity is, you would be communicating the results of your arduous enquiry, when it's over, in language. Well, you can do *that* already. And I know of no better way... My boy, *that's a dice!*...'

•

The sounds of the mule train arriving interrupted Palmira.

Sorry I dragged that out, boys. I didn't expect them to take this long,' she explained. 'Perhaps they had to stop along the way...'

She got up and went out through the passage overgrown with prickly pears, at the north-east corner of her yard. The two boys heard the shouts of the driver stop; and a moment later the rumble of the hooves died down. They could hear the mules snorting and coughing.

The boys got up and also left the yard, one to get the feed ready, the other to fill the buckets they had left earlier by the cisterns.

When all the sacks were unloaded and the mules were feeding, Palmira and the boys returned to the yard with the mule driver, a Berber. He and the twins knew enough Arabic between them to communicate. The mules and the driver were going to spend the night there before returning the next day to the hills.

Palmira had brought out some food for the driver, and he was now busy eating.

'How many more to come?' the first Henry asked Palmira.

'Just two. I hope they're both in tomorrow. I really want all the ore in before dark tomorrow.'

'You'll have enough for an army! Who's it for?'

'Tunis, of course.'

'I know, but after that —'

'It's a bit strange,' interrupted the second Henry, 'you making weapons when you say you dislike using them so much.'

'They need them to defend themselves,' answered Palmira.

'But I thought you said there weren't going to be any more crusades?'

'Sicily and Naples are still across the sea. But I don't think it's the Christians that are worrying them in Tunis. They're more worried by the Muslims further along the coast. And even further east — not just the Memluks. And I've heard the Ottomans have started moving.'

'But there's been nothing recently?'

'That's probably because of the plague, Henry. But it won't go on for ever. By all accounts it's past its peak.'

The mule driver, who had rather bolted his food, thanked Palmira and went to settle the mules for the night ahead.

'Isn't he staying for the story?'

'There isn't going to be any more today, you'll be pleased to know. In any case, Henry, you know Berbers don't much like stories until after sundown.'

'Why's that?' asked the first Henry.

'Maybe it's because they don't want to get them confused with reality!' suggested his brother.

'I don't know...' said Palmira. 'But I expect later I might tell him a story or two, but not until you two have gone.'

'I bet you that in Tunis they'll be sold to Sicily,' said the first Henry.

'But aren't the Genoans always buying things there?'

'I don't really know where the swords will end up,' admitted Palmira. 'Some will probably go to Sardinia, as well. But I won't just be making swords, you know. There will be knives, scalpels, and I'm going to try one or two instrument parts, for the Genoans.'

'There you are, admit it, you do like making weapons. You don't *need* to make swords at all.'

'And if you did need to, you'd sell them at a decent price. You ought to be rich from selling those swords!'

'Rich? You know that one day the Hodja bought a large quantity of eggs at the market, and he immediately set up his own stall, selling the eggs at a loss.

'"Hodja!" the people said to him. "Why are you selling those eggs at a loss? You should be selling them at a profit!"

'"Do you think it would profit me," he replied, "to become known as a profiteer?"'

'That only proves, Palmira, that you make your swords because you like making them!'

'I suppose you're right... It gives me power!' Palmira chuckled to herself. 'Power over men!' she added, flashing her eyes. 'To my knowledge there isn't anybody else making Indian steel, certainly not of this quality, west of Baghdad. As for my steel that doesn't breathe —'

'Did Vyasa show you how to do that as well?'

'Yes, though we managed to improve on his method.'

'Are you making any of that this time?'

'Oh yes, for the small stuff, the knives and scalpels... What's going on?'

The boys were grinning at her.

'You're an idiot, Palmira, you know that?'

Palmira's eyes widened in surprise. 'What are you talking about?'

'Why did you say you made those swords?' prompted the first Henry.

'*Gromer Somer Joure,*' whispered his brother at Palmira.

'Oh! Ahah! Thank you boys, you are most generous. That's very kind of you. What is it that women most desire in this world? Power over men! Is that the answer?'

'Well, I think the proper answer was to *rule* over men.'

'That's what old Henry said, anyway.'

'I see — not only do we want power, we want to exercise it as well, eh?'

'But Palmira, I thought women just married important men when they wanted that. Grandmother was always saying she'd made a mistake with old Henry!'

'Because he wouldn't do what she wanted?' asked Palmira. 'Or because he had no power himself? Anyway, I'm too selfish even for that, boys. I don't like to mix power and love. Not that kind of power... not that kind of love... But boys, I think old Henry was wrong. Though I have to say it's not unlike a man, even a nice man like old Henry, to mistake our desire to enjoy freedom for a desire to impose rule. I don't think I do want the power to rule over men, I just want the power to stop them ruling over me.'

'You could give us a hint now about that mantra, couldn't you?'

'Yes, Palmira, you could be a bit generous, like us.'

'But I've already told you more than you boys deserve.'

'What? You said absolutely nothing! You said so yourself!'

'Well, that's more than you boys deserve, which is saying something. There, you see, I've been doubly generous, which is twice as generous as I should be... Believe me, the less said about that mantra the better. Now —'

'Are your blades really the best?'

'Flattery, eh! Henry, that depends on whether you want to test the truth or the sharpness of the blade! Have I ever told you about that famous Chinese blade? No? This was told to me by a Rabbi I met in Alexandria. He told me that somewhere in China there is a blade so sharp that it can never become blunt.'

'Why not?'

'Because it's so sharp that the blade, the very edge, never actually touches what it cuts.'

'How's that possible?'

'The blade is so narrow at the edge, that it fits into the spaces inside the material it is cutting! Only the sides, like a wedge, touch the material, separating it out.'

'I don't believe that!' said the first Henry.

'I wonder what would have happened if Dido had used it?' said his brother. 'Or even one of Palmira's blades. Carthage would have come right out to here — she could have made the strips of hide so thin that she could have cut millions off the one hide!'

'An interesting thought, Henry. Well, not anywhere near here. But certainly, if she had used one of my knives — had they existed then — Carthage could have started out twice as large. That reminds me. Can you fetch me a new leather apron I ordered, on your way here tomorrow? What else did I want you to do?'

'Tell Mulciber...'

'Oh yes, and that reminds me —'

'Oh, Palmira,' interrupted the first Henry, 'you know how Mulciber doesn't like you calling the Hodja *Hodja*... Why don't you call him *Djuha*, like everybody else?'

'Because my favourite Hodja stories were told to me by a Turk. I know some of the stories are similar to the Djuha stories, but the Hodja was quite a different person. After all, some of the stories in Sicily about Giufa are like the Djuha stories — but these are young lads, not at all like the Hodja Nasreddin...'

'Do you think you'll cross the sea again, when the plague is over?'

'Perhaps. Who knows?'

'Who was that handsome Italian you were going to send one of your daggers as a present?'

'Boccaccio.'

'Didn't you say he was going to write a book about you?'

'Boccaccio? No, certainly not. It's true, he thinks that one day he may write a book about some of the women he has known. But I made him promise that he'd never write a word about me!'

'Oh, why not, Palmira?'

'Never you mind — off with you, now. Oh, wait... Since I'll probably be going away soon, we'd better abandon all work tomorrow and devote ourselves entirely to this wretched story... We'll make an exception and start it early in the morning. So, no work for you tomorrow. Not that kind of work, anyway...'

•

Day Seven: *The Dice*

38 The vine and the strawberry

Duh and Chitra both gestured to Karna, as if to say there was nothing they could do for their brother. Without bothering to interrupt Dur's train of thought, Duh rose quietly, touched Dur lightly on the shoulder, and left; his footsteps, as he climbed down the steps of the tower, quickly receded. Chitra raised his eyebrows at Karna and followed, leaving Karna alone with Dur.

The stone walls of the little room, in which Dur was spending more and more of his time, absorbed what was left of the fading light; but they were unable to stifle the drone of his voice, seeming instead to extend it as a dull echo, warding off the brooding silence.

'Dur!' interrupted Karna, all of a sudden. 'Please, be civilised! All you can think of is war. Don't you know that the more civilised the people, the easier it is to humiliate them *without* the use of force?'

Karna had been quiet for so long that Dur was taken by surprise. He looked at Karna blankly, expecting him to repeat what he had just said. But as Karna waited in silence, Dur's mind caught up with the echo of Karna's words.

'Without the use of force?'

'Yes. If you want to beat Indraprastha so much, why don't you find some other way to beat them. Why not beat them at dice, perhaps?'

'Are you serious, Karna?'

'Of course not, Dur. *I* am not serious. *You* are serious!'

Dur did not give Karna's suggestion much thought that evening. In the morning, however, he was knocking at Shakuni's door before his uncle had finished washing.

'Are you *serious*, Dur?' But Shakuni did not need a reply. 'My dear nephew, this is the first time in a while I have seen you up before... before noon...'

Shakuni paused with his mouth agape, seeing that Dur was too impatient to listen to such niceties. He closed his mouth into a frown, then patted his beard.

'Pass me that towel, my dear...' Shakuni finished drying his beard, and started fiddling with his hair, straightening out over his ears what little there was of it.

'You want me to play your cousin? Why don't you play him yourself, Dur...' Shakuni gave a little grunt at the thought and continued. 'There are a number of problems... I don't wish to disappoint, my dear.'

'But uncle, it's so obvious!'

'Nothing is obvious! Nothing. Or do you think that it will be as easy as it was for Pushkara to beat his brother Nala? You know the old tale? In the first place, my dear, you will have to persuade Yudhi to agree to play you... me. In the story, Nala apparently succumbed to temptation because he forgot to wash his feet before prayers! Yudhi may not be so careless. Secondly, my dear, I do not need to tell you that your father would also have to agree. And you can be sure that the brahmanas will abhor the idea. They will all know what you are up to. Oh yes, my dear nephew. Then there is the small matter of persuading Yudhi to bet substantially! It is true, he can be quite a reckless player, remarkable when you think of his character. But then, of course, he does not take the game seriously. Indeed, he treats the game as little more than a game, and as our friend the rishi is fond of saying... Dur, are you listening? It is unlikely that Yudhi will behave like a child when he is no longer engaged in child's play. Where are we up to? Five? Then, having persuaded him to play like a madman, you require additionally that he must lose. Six. These six all add up, my dear. In fact it is worse than that, Dur, they don't add up: your difficulties multiply.'

'But uncle, I'm sure Yudhi will accept. We don't have to say straight away that he will be playing *you*. It will be three or four days of dicing. And I'm sure I can persuade my father. If anyone can make the Pandavas look fools, you can, uncle!'

'My dear, if I were so foolishly optimistic, I would be the one who loses! And don't forget, Nakula is a fine player. Yudhi is certain to be guided by his advice.' Shakuni saw Dur's face begin to fall. 'Look, my dear, if you can get your father to agree, then, perhaps, I might be willing to take a part in such an occasion, in some capacity or other... But...'

Dur embraced his uncle and left him. He went straight to his father, who himself had only just finished his ablutions.

'Dur, how is it that you want for nothing, and yet always you want?'

Sensing his son's impatience, the king raised his hand to silence him. Sanjaya supplied Dhrita with a cloth. The king slowly wiped himself about the face. 'Why is it that you are never contented? Why do you always carry envy in your heart? Will you never learn? It is a man who is content *without* envy who is the envy of other men.'

'Father, do not hide behind your blindness. Do not pretend to me that you don't see —'

'You are the one without sight, my son! Be careful, Dur, you go too far!'

Sanjaya removed the cloth from Dhrita's trembling hand and himself pressed it against the king's forehead. Dhrita's breathing eased slightly, and he regained his composure.

'Father, tell me, do you *really* think that discontent is a sin? Is it sinful to want to excel over one's fellows? Is it wrong for a warrior to wish to outdo other warriors? Is it right to let humiliation go unchallenged?'

'When have they humiliated you? Do not start that again. That is all long ago, Dur. You are no longer a child—'

'At the Rajasuya, and you know very well what I'm talking about. You turn a blind eye when it suits you, father. See no offence, take no offence. You know how they treated me: like a poor man from the country who has never seen a house of stone!'

'A small bowl is no less full than a large bowl, and a good deal easier to fill. Your vessel leaks with envy; it can never be filled. Mend yourself, my son. Enjoy what you have. How many times have I told you that even he who clings for his life to the vine can still enjoy the—'

'Let me tell it to *you*, for once! Yes, father, *you* are climbing down the vine, the tiger is waiting with open jaws on the ledge above *you*. Listen to it, father! You have forced me to listen enough times. Suddenly you notice also the tiger waiting for you on the ground below. The mice are slowly gnawing at the vine. There's no escape. But, ah, yes, here is a strawberry growing amid the vine, just next to your lips! You can reach it. Wonderful! Enjoy the strawberry! How many times have I been told to enjoy the strawberry? It is within your reach. But the hunger is all gone. Your taste has gone quite numb. Even if you were to put the strawberry in your mouth, you would not feel it. It may be my fate to be eaten by the tiger below. There may be nothing I can do about that. So, therefore, I may as well enjoy what pleasure I can find in this world. What could be more reasonable? But the fact that it is reasonable does not allow me to enjoy the strawberry. For if it is my fate to fall to the tiger, it is also my fate to be miserable about it. And is it not also reasonable for me to try to change my fate? Are you saying that if I see another vine on which I can escape, I should not try to reach it, but should remain content with my strawberry? Tell me what is reasonable, father, since you seem to know so much about it. If it was left to reason, why do we cling on to the vine at all. There is no *reason* for living. There is only a hunger for life. Give me medicine I can swallow, father. Not a strawberry!'

King Dhrita waited for his son to stop his pacing before replying.

'The Pandavas are not tigers, Dur. They are your own cousins, the sons of Pandu. Their happiness should be your happiness. Their vessel is joined to yours.'

'You know very well that unless blood is bound with friendship the ties of kinship mean nothing. What blood binds me to Karna? None. And yet I love him more than I love my own brothers. Father, it's not just that their bowl is

larger. That wouldn't be so hard for me to bear. It's that they *want* me to envy
them. Do you understand? What hurts me is that they enjoy my pain. They want
me to know that their bowl is larger, and to suffer for knowing it. It makes my
bowl seem quite empty... More empty even than empty, for are not the bowls of
the munis quite empty, and yet they are content. I have lost my taste altogether.'

Dhrita's eyelids trembled slightly as Sanjaya combed out the knots in his
hair. A sadness entered his voice, a sadness that was harder for Dur to bear than
his father's anger.

'Poor child, you are like a cat who has fought and been defeated once too
often; they too lose the taste for life. The fire goes out of them. You still have
a spark remaining, my son. I sometimes think I lost all my fire years ago, after
my brother died.'

'It was very different with you and Pandu, father. He felt your pain, as you
felt his. But I think perhaps he was the only one who felt your pain. Don't
think I don't understand how you've suffered. They treat you like a statue, to
be bowed to and prayed before. And when they need your assent, they tell you
just enough so that you have to agree with their decisions; then they ignore you
until the next time they need to make the statue nod. You have spent your life
sitting quietly on a vine, feeding on strawberries. Do you think I don't know
how much it hurt you to... to hear the Pandavas take the Rajasuya? Everybody
knows that Hastinapura is the most powerful kingdom in the land. But since the
king is blind, he cannot possibly want to be the King of Kings!'

Dhrita touched Sanjaya's robe with the back of his hand. Sanjaya stepped
back a few paces.

'My son... How do you think you will get your taste back?'

'I would rather die in battle against them than live in the shadow of their
gloating pride. I just want to see them lose for once, father. That is all. I just
want to see their kshatriya pride dented. If it cannot be on the battlefield, let it
be on the dice table.'

'And you think that will make you content?'

'Yes, father, it will make me very happy.'

'For how long, Dur? For how long?'

'For longer than a meal contents your stomach, father; which is not forever;
in the spite of which I see that you continue to eat.'

'A meal does not cost so dear, my son. Still... I will speak to them.'

◊

Bhishma had some enthusiasm for the idea; but he was soon made to think
again by Drona and Kripa, who were both very short with Dhrita. Drona, in

particular, was quick to brand the idea as one of Dur's malicious schemes. He made it clear that he thought Dur would never be able to get the better of the Pandavas, however he tried to compete with them.

But when they pressed Dhrita to refuse Dur's request, the king hesitated. Then they asked Vidura to speak alone with the king; and to return, if possible, with some assurances.

'But you will be there too, Vidura,' said the king, trying to reassure his brother. 'So will Drona, Bhishma — all of you will be there. It will not just be my sons and Shakuni. It will be an occasion for festivity. What harm can come from a game of dice, brother?'

'Harm? You know the story of King Nala? If that is what Dur and Shakuni are up to, they are as foolish as they are grasping. Life never turns out the same as legend. Nala may have succumbed to the magic of Kali, but do they really think the Pandavas will? Dhrita, you must tell Dur that his proposal is out of the question. Your son must accept his fate and be satisfied with what he has. You must curb his ambitions, or they will be the end of us all.'

◊

'Out of the question? Was the Rajasuya out of the question? You see, father, *I* must be satisfied with what I already have, while the Pandavas may be satisfied with what they should *like* to have! Were not the Pandavas also dissatisfied? Is not dissatisfaction the root of all prosperity? Vidura and the others didn't tell them to accept their lot, did they? No, they welcomed the Rajasuya. They're not opposed to ambition. I could at least respect them if *that* was the reason for their opposition. But no, they are opposed to *my* ambitions. The truth is, father, that ambition is endorsed by those who share its dream, and criticised by those who fear it. How can you listen to Vidura now? If it were up to him I would never have lived a week. And all because of some stupid omen. He just didn't want you to have any sons, did he? He has always been uncle to the Pandavas, not to me, not to my brothers. If it were up to him, the Pandavas would have your throne as well as Indraprastha. Why do you listen to him at all?'

Dur looked to Sanjaya for support, but Sanjaya remained discreetly silent.

'Father, do *you* think my ambition is sinful?'

'It is not a question of sin, Dur. I do not say it is sinful. I am not sure that I have ever known what sin is, my son. I leave that to the brahmanas. What I do question, Dur, is whether it is wise. Whether it is prudent. Hostility against those who are strong is seldom to be recommended.'

'But it is a dice match, father! At dice they are nowhere as strong as us. Saha and Nakula are supposed to be very good. But we have Shakuni. In any case, it is only a dice match. There will be no hostility, no violence. I do not intend to steal anything from them.'

Dhrita raised his hands, but Dur continued.

'If they lose at dice and wish to resort to violence, then *they* will be sinning, not me. And if they wish to attack us, they will be the foolish ones, not me. No, if they lose, they will just have to accept their lot and eat their strawberry. Vidura will then have to direct his advice to *them*.'

'And if *you* lose?'

'How can we lose?'

'*If* you lose?'

'At least I will have tried. But you know that Shakuni is invincible.'

'There is no one whom the fall of the dice cannot destroy, if fate decrees it.'

'Only if they make themselves vulnerable to it, father. Shakuni knows better than to stake more than is wise.'

Dhrita was silent.

'Father, do I have permission or not? Why do you have to ask them, anyway? It's your decision, not theirs. *You* are king, not they.'

'You accuse them of treating me like a statue. Is that not how *you* treat me? When have you ever taken heed of my advice?'

'Father, do I have your permission or not? If not, I will muster my forces. I have no wish to live any longer the laughing stock of the Pandavas.'

'Do what you will, Dur. Have your dice match. I can only pray that we will not all end up paying for your folly.'

◊

'You gave him permission!'

Dhrita could only guess at the expression on Vidura's face.

'What power does he have over you, Dhrita?'

'He is my son. Or have you forgotten that, brother?'

'There are five circumstances in which the seeds of doom may prosper to overwhelm a kingdom: a devastation of natural disaster; a corruption of the court; a depletion of resources; a misjudgement of policy; finally, there is attachment to the seven vices, to which, in your case, Dhrita, I add an eighth: the excessive attachment to family. You should not allow evil to come from partiality to your son. A man should curb this instinct if he can see evil consequences arising through the preferral of his family. You must forget he is your son.'

'I have curbed my instincts quite enough, Vidura, I thank you. But *you*? When have you been impartial?'

The anger in the king's voice took Sanjaya by surprise, his hand moving to Dhrita's shoulder. The king turned his head sharply, almost as though he had forgotten Sanjaya's presence. The king lowered his voice, but only to reveal in it a greater coldness.

'You have always favoured the Pandavas.'

For a moment Vidura hesitated, looking uncomfortably at Sanjaya.

'Not through partiality to kin, but to merit,' Vidura replied. 'Dur is also my nephew. And yet I wish that your son had never been born.'

'Merit? So when you advised me to have Dur killed, before the end of his first day of life, he was already evil, was he? While Yudhi was already showing his merit in the womb? Was Dharma already discernible in his son? And you accuse *me* of being partial, brother? If you had tried harder to understand Dur... If—'

'I did try, Dhrita. I did. It is too late for that. Do you not see the danger now?'

'Of course I see the danger. But fate is against me. I feel it in my bones. What is the point of putting on a show of resistance?'

'Your image of fate is affecting your reason, Dhrita. We are all blind to fate. Only the future holds her face. Our fate is not decided until *we* decide it, brother. The face of the future is only shaped in the last moment of the present...'

'What has blindness got to do with it, Vidura?'

'I see that not only are you blind, you are deaf as well. Why don't you listen to what I'm saying? We are *all* blind to her face, brother. In trying to make out the shape of the future, we are *all* as blind men. With clumsy fingers we try to discover a face drawn in the sand; a face redrawn in the very act of discovery. No, Dhrita, you must not give her a twisted mouth just because you cannot make the effort to draw her straight. Or do you think that because you are blind to the present, you have a sight of the future?'

'If you were blind, as I am, perhaps you would be distracted less by the show of the world. Perhaps you would then see that you are but a grain of sand caught with all the others, a mere speck on that face. Blindness has given me other senses, Vidura. I can see the rain clouds gathering. And when the rain clouds gather, the rains fall. And when the rains fall, do what we will, we cannot avert the flood. Do you wish me to bolt my door when my house will be washed away? It is useless to resist, Vidura. But perhaps you are more concerned with figuring large in the show of the present? Perhaps you prefer not to see yourself as a small smudge upon the face of the future? It is too late now. It is better to greet the future gracefully, whether she smiles on us or frowns.'

'Don't be a fool, Dhrita! It is always too late if you are never going to act! You cannot let it happen without a struggle!'

'Brother, let me hear you say that when you are caught in the quicksand. True, there is a time to struggle. I admit that it's my fault as much as anyone's for not striving harder. But that time is now past.'

'Be it on your own head, Dhrita.'

'That is kind, Vidura. For once to give me the head of a king! Perhaps then you yourself will be so kind as to go to Indraprastha to issue the invitation?'

39 Yudhi accepts

Saha and Nakula, who were both keen dice players, advanced immediately on Vidura. The other three Pandavas were unmoved, and clearly suspicious.

'Who's going to be there, uncle?' asked Saha.

'I think he's inviting all the neighbouring kings.'

'What about Shakuni?' Nakula asked. 'Will he be playing?'

Vidura turned to Yudhi, as though Yudhi had made the enquiry. 'Yes, King Shakuni will certainly be playing... So will King Drupada, King Satyaki... and many others, we hope... All the best dice players will be invited. But King Dhrita-rashtra especially invites you —'

'But isn't it Dur's idea?' suggested Bhima, accusingly.

'Yes... Yes, Dur is building a gambling hall especially for the games. He and King Dhrita invite you particularly, as guests of honour, in recognition of the hospitality you showed us all at the Rajasuya.'

The four princes turned expectantly to their elder brother. But Yudhi was silent.

'If it's Dur's idea,' persisted Bhima, 'I don't like it.'

'Perhaps Dur is hoping that Shakuni will humiliate us at the dice table,' suggested Arjuna.

'I've had suspicions about Shakuni,' declared Bhima, 'ever since the fire... I've often wondered if he wasn't behind the house of lac...'

The initial enthusiasm of the twins was now dampened.

'Yes...' said Saha thoughtfully. 'It's possible that Dur is hoping to take some glory back from Indraprastha to Hastinapura.'

'He may even be hoping,' added Nakula, 'to see the King of Kings humbled by Shakuni.'

'You must not accept, Yudhi,' urged Arjuna in alarm.

'Why not, brother?' asked Yudhi.

'Why?' interjected Saha. 'Everybody knows that you're an awful player! That's why!'

'If Dur wanted to humiliate us,' said Yudhi, 'surely, he would challenge the one who is considered to be our best player, not our worst. He would challenge Nakula, not me. Or, if he wanted to rub it in, why does he not hold a tournament, and have Karna challenge Arjuna to feats of archery —'

'*What?*' cried Bhima in amazement. 'What are you saying? It would be Karna who would be humiliated! And Karna knows it — otherwise they would have already tried that, you can be sure!'

'In any case,' said Nakula, 'though Shakuni would certainly beat me, I'm not sure that he could make me look so bad as to humiliate me. On the other hand, Yudhi, with respect, you can be reckless. It would not look good for a King of Kings to play like a child in front of such an assembly.'

'Yes, I think that must be what they're after,' said Saha. 'For the King of Kings to lose at a game of dice, especially if he loses badly, and in front of everyone — I think they must hope it would make him appear unworthy of the title. That's what Dur must be hoping for.'

'I may seem like an awful player to you...' replied Yudhi. 'But remember that the game of dice is not decided by the players; it is settled by those who control their destinies.'

Bhima, seeing the others frown, was quick to defend Yudhi.

'You can't judge a player seriously when the stakes aren't serious. When has Yudhi ever played a serious game of dice? The gods don't grant their favours on trivial occasions!'

'If I am destined to win a match,' declared Yudhi, 'whether it is with one of you, with Satyaki, with Dur, Shakuni, whomsoever — if it is my destiny to win it, I will win it. If it is my destiny to lose it, I will lose it. It must be one way or the other. But' — Yudhi raised his hands to acknowledge Nakula's protest — 'but if it is true that Dur wishes to humiliate me, he shall not succeed. For, if I lose, I will lose graciously; and, losing graciously, not permitting the anger of defeat to rise, then the victory will be ours, not his; and then it will not be the Pandavas but Dur himself who will be humiliated; and it will be Dur, not I, who has his ambitions thwarted.'

'That is well spoken!' said Bhima.

Vidura, who had been listening anxiously, seemed to breathe more easily. He reached out both his arms to clasp Yudhi's hand; and he seemed reluctant to let go, as though in the act of separation he would be transported back to Hastinapura.

'But Yudhi,' warned Nakula, 'Shakuni is a very tricky player. If you do have to play him, you must be careful.'

'If a man has his feet on the ground, he falls without injury. What have I to lose? You say that everyone considers me an awful player. What have I to lose, when I have no reputation to preserve, no illusions to be shattered?'

'Nevertheless, don't underestimate Shakuni.'

'I have heard about his abilities, Nakula, and I think I may have even played against him. I have certainly seen him in action. Yes, I know that he is supposed to be able to recognise a prime as easily as I can tell an odd number... that he can count the number of fruit on a tree in an instant... But don't you see, that is the great illusion, the great dream of the gambler, to think that his powers can touch the dice. In the end, Destiny does with us what she will. Her divine calculations are over before Shakuni's have even begun.'

For a few moments there was an uneasy silence. Then Saha spoke.

'He doesn't just play with the dice, brother.'

Yudhi turned to him with a puzzled look.

'You know that some people think he cheats,' explained Saha. 'Some even think he uses... magic.'

'Well,' replied Yudhi, 'he will not be able to cheat Destiny, nor even could his magic conquer her.'

'Nevertheless,' advised Arjuna, 'perhaps it would, all things considered... perhaps it would be better to turn down the invitation. Don't you think so, uncle?'

'Arjuna...' answered Yudhi, before Vidura could reply. 'It is unthinkable that I should decline their invitation. How could I have celebrated my Rajasuya if Hastinapura had been absent? How could I have held my Rajasuya if Dur and Dhrita had declined *our* invitation? No. I must go. It is King Dhrita-rashtra of Hastinapura, my father's brother, who invites me. Is that not so, Vidura? And if I am challenged to the dice, I shall not refuse to play.' As Yudhi looked round at his brothers now, a note of censure entered his voice. 'Even the humblest kshatriya will not refuse a challenge at dice. How can I accept the title of the Rajasuya, the title you were all so keen to gain, so reluctant to pay for — how can I pretend to be a King of Kings — if I am not seen to equal even the most humble of kshatriyas?'

◊

After Vidura had returned to Hastinapura with Yudhi's acceptance, Saha and Nakula continued to express their anxieties. Arjuna was more reticent, and tended to stay out of their discussions; he was as concerned as the twins, but rather more confident that Yudhi knew what he was doing. As for Bhima, his faith in Yudhi was even greater, and he was quite prepared to defend him.

'*I* have no fear of Shakuni!'

'Your lack of fear, Bhima, is not an argument...' observed Nakula, trying to contain his frustration.

'Even Nakula would hesitate to play Shakuni,' added Saha.

Nakula nodded in agreement. 'At least will you practise with me, Yudhi?' But when Yudhi turned away from this offer, Nakula threw up his arms in exasperation.

'Why should he practise with you?' challenged Bhima. 'He's told you before, it's a game of chance. If fortune favours him, he'll win. If not, he'll lose — whatever he does, however much he may practise. Even Shakuni has to bow down before the hand of Destiny.'

'But it is said that the dice escape even Destiny,' replied Saha. Nakula frowned at him and clenched his lower jaw over his upper teeth, as if to restrain himself from speaking.

'Then perhaps it is said by a fool,' suggested Yudhi, also with a trace of impatience.

'I was only repeating what is said, brother. Don't blame me for trying to help you.'

'Saha, if the dice do escape even Destiny,' argued Yudhi, 'then they would in that case surely escape also my own more modest influence; and that even of King Shakuni. In which case, why should I practise to control what is beyond the control of Destiny herself? On the other hand, if the dice are indeed touched by the gods, then, once again, they escape both my fingers and Shakuni's. In which case again, why should I practise to control what is beyond my control?'

'Yudhi, you fear Karna, don't you?' said Nakula. 'If you had the misfortune to have to fight Karna, wouldn't you bother to practise? Just a little? Or would you go into battle on foot, without a single arrow, telling us to rest assured, that if the gods wish it, Karna's own arrows will turn back to pierce him!'

'If the gods are on our side,' suggested Bhima, filling in Yudhi's silence, 'then they wouldn't need our help. It is fear for our lives which deprives us of reason and makes us practise...'

'Something is depriving *you* of reason, that's certain,' muttered Nakula.

'It is fear which makes us try to raise ourselves above Destiny,' Bhima tried to explain, 'to practise, to scheme, to try to cheat Destiny by arming ourselves uselessly against her.'

'I think that what's depriving you of reason,' asserted Saha, 'is your strange idea of Destiny. Surely, Destiny achieves her will through *our* wills, through our ambitions, our desires, through our fears, our prudence... our wisdom. Have you forgotten what we were taught as children by the brahmanas? The future isn't engraved in stone. It's figured in the sands of time, to change through *our* will, through *our* action. Listen to me, Bhima... To give up the need to act, as though the future were already fixed in stone, is to deny Destiny the very instrument by which she is fulfilled, by which we become her very own engravers.'

Bhima looked uncomfortably at Yudhi.

'Bhima,' pressed Nakula, 'suppose you went into battle against Karna — without a single arrow. In that case, I can assure you, strong as you are, you would have been destined all along to be killed by him! Or do you really think the gods would reward your faith in them by causing his arrows to turn back?'

'If it had been so decided by the gods, that I should win... yes.'

'Then why did you take so much trouble to learn to use the bow and the mace? Why, if you could instead rely on the gods to assist your weapons and to thwart your enemy?'

'Because...' Bhima paused, hoping for support from Yudhi and Arjuna, 'because the gods don't like to show themselves off in such a manner. They prefer to influence us by more subtle means...'

'Oh, I see!' exclaimed Nakula sarcastically. 'You mean that Karna's chariot would get stuck in some mud, causing him to slip and fall upon his sword? Or his driver would accidentally strangle himself on the reins? Or his —'

'Nakula!' interrupted Arjuna. 'You know as well as I do that the influence of the gods is subtle. You remember what Krishna says, that the gods play with us in such a way that we hardly know it. The gods contrive appearances to rhyme with our reason, not to jar it! That's why none of us would wish to force the hand of Destiny into the open, by going out unarmed into a fight. That's exactly what Krishna warns us against, forcing the gods to show themselves.'

'Then give that advice to Yudhi,' rejoined Nakula. 'Not to me!'

Saha touched Nakula on the arm to calm him, and then turned to Arjuna. 'You are right, Arjuna, of course,' he said soothingly. 'None of us would want to force the gods to... to trip Karna, for all to see, upon the seam of Destiny's design. But don't you see? Neither Nakula nor I could beat Shakuni *without* such a miraculous trip of Destiny. Let alone Yudhi!'

Arjuna and Bhima looked to their elder brother to respond. With a little sigh, Yudhi took up the challenge.

'What Bhima and Arjuna are trying to get you to understand, Saha, is that gambling is not the same thing as fighting. Nowhere are the gods more delicate and mischievous than when we try to hazard the future they have shaped for us. Fighting requires skill; and so Destiny herself requires her favoured combatants to strive, to practise, to exert their efforts fully in demonstrations of that skill. Otherwise, as Arjuna rightly says, the world would play a harsh tune with our expectation. But the dice cannot be aimed like arrows. And what we cannot aim, we must not presume to direct.' Yudhi raised his hand to register once again Nakula's objection. 'I know, Nakula, I know you think it is a game of skill. But your skill with the dice is like an empty ritual, born of your desire to throw the dice like spears. You would do better to pray to the gods, brother, for it is easy for them to turn the dice, while it is floating in the air, without showing any trace of their hand. You should be humble enough to throw the dice blindly, brother. If it were a game of skill then the skilful would generally win. But as we all know, brother, anyone can win, and anyone can lose.'

'Believe me,' said Saha, 'Shakuni generally wins. So either he is very skilful, or he cheats. And if he cheats, he is so skilful a cheat that you should be worried about his skill.'

'Surely he could not cheat in front of everybody?' exclaimed Yudhi. 'In front of the brahmanas?'

'You yourself have just said,' rejoined Saha, 'how very easy it is to turn the dice without showing the touch!'

'He would not need to cheat,' said Nakula, shaking his head. 'He would crush you without needing to cheat, Yudhi. He does not, as you seem to think, presume to *direct* the dice, either by hand or by sleight of hand. Only to *predict* them.'

'Then,' replied Yudhi, 'he is trying to predict the unpredictable, which is impossible.'

'Can you then explain to us how it is that he wins so often?' invited Nakula.

'Because his opponents are frightened of him,' suggested Arjuna. 'They are intimidated. They retire too soon. Wouldn't most warriors lose to Karna, even before a single arrow has been loosed? Even if they dared to engage him, they would surrender or withdraw after the first onslaught. It is because I do not fear him, and stand my ground, that he cannot defeat me. Remember what Krishna says: nothing makes victory harder than the fear of defeat. It's good that Yudhi is not afraid. Fear is Shakuni's weapon!'

'Arjuna is right,' said Yudhi. 'I fear only the gods. And Karna,' he added quite seriously, not intending to make the others chuckle. 'But I do not fear Shakuni. The gods control the dice, not Shakuni. So if they wish me to win, then I will win. How can men presume to predict them! You, Nakula, surprise me. Do you not yourself often ridicule the fanciful conjectures of groundless augury?'

'It *is* possible to predict the dice —'

'You wish to think that, brother. But the dice obey no human laws. The dice are blind to the affairs and the desires of men. They have no memory, they have no family. They listen neither to me, nor to Shakuni. You may think you can conspire to whisper to them... like a child who thinks he has befriended a caged leopard by bringing to it meat. No. The dice are even less predictable than the leopard; even harder to propitiate. How can you search for a pattern in something which follows no pattern?'

'Yudhi,' persisted Nakula, 'even you must see that in some positions it's more likely than others for the dice to strike a prime!'

'More likely? It is either impossible or certain. That is all I dare presume to say, brother. And, perhaps, that *I* know of no reason why it should be the one rather than the other. How can I say that it is more *likely*, how can I indeed say *anything* more, without knowing the whim of Destiny? After the dice has fallen, yes, then I can say that it was certain; or impossible. But before the dice is still, what can I say?'

Both Saha and Nakula shook their heads in disbelief.

'When one result is certain,' persisted Yudhi, 'how can I say that another result is even possible? I have often heard those who play the shudra game say that an even score is as likely as an odd score. How can they say that, when the score is certain, and known only to the gods.'

'Even if it were known for certain only to the gods,' said Nakula, patiently, 'that does not stop us from watching and learning how the gods are playing it... The hunter, after all, may watch the leopard. From watching, we learn.'

'And what do you learn, brother?'

'That the gods — if they have anything to do with it — don't seem to favour odds more than evens, nor evens more than odds. So, we say, these are equally likely.'

'That only means that *you* can find no reason why Destiny should favour one rather than the other,' insisted Yudhi. 'Even the fall of a single nut, thrown by the lowliest child, even this concerns the gods if it serves to change the world. Just because you cannot find a reason why the dice should prefer to fall even rather than odd, you presume there is none. Remember this, brother: what you find most unlikely becomes absolutely certain, what you find most likely, quite impossible, should Destiny determine thus. One twist of the dice can overturn Shakuni's finest calculations.'

As Nakula turned away in resignation, Yudhi continued.

'Without an arrow I cannot strike Karna, even if he is in range. Without strength of arm, skill, and a sure eye, I could not strike Karna even with a hundred arrows. That is why, if Destiny had required me to strike Karna in battle, she would have required me to arm and to prepare myself; for which purpose she would have furnished me with fear, with ambition...' Yudhi paused, gesturing with his hand to fill out the rest of his meaning. 'But if I am in range of a prime score, brother, then, while I have the strength to raise my arm and to release the dice, I am able to fulfil whatever role Destiny has prepared me for. However unlikely you or Shakuni might reckon that I strike the prime. And, if I am able to serve as their instrument, then, with neither fear nor ambition, I am content to let the gods decide my role.'

40 The dice table

The brahmanas in Hastinapura were so incensed at the idea of Charvaka supervising the building of the gambling hall that Dur was forced to relent on this point, and accept a design of their choice. But Dur also tried to persuade the brahmanas that their sensibilities need not prevent Charvaka from being in charge at least of making the dice; on the grounds that dice were not instruments of war but of sport; and that their ban only applied to Charvaka's involvement in martial activities. A few thousand of the gold dice used in the royal game would be needed during the contests. Dur argued that only Charvaka had the skill to make such a large number in the time available.

Some of the brahmanas saw this as an opportunity to abandon the proceedings, but the majority believed this would create too much tension between them and their royal patrons; they eventually agreed to let Charvaka make the dice, provided that he stayed well away once the visitors arrived.

◊

After the excitement of working in Indraprastha, Charvaka had lately been feeling a growing discomfort with the constraints on his activities in Hastinapura. And though his task now was modest, it was new to him. He had worked extensively with gold, and gold alloys, but never before to make dice. Perhaps more important for him was the fact that he was now able to demand the provision of a workshop; a demand to which the brahmanas were forced to accede.

Some of the materials he needed for the task ahead had to be brought in from outside the city. Vrisha undertook to organise this supply; and this duty had the added advantage of keeping him away from the distractions of the workshop; which was just as well, since Shakuni's presence was bad enough.

Charvaka had set about his task with enthusiasm; soon his team of workers was producing nearly a hundred dice each day. Their biggest problem, especially during the early stages, was indeed Shakuni; he insisted on visiting the rishi's workshop nearly every afternoon.

Charvaka had been asked to make the dice slightly larger than was usual, so that they could be more easily seen by the audience. Shakuni claimed, with some justification, that he needed to practise with these larger dice; but his constant stream of complaints as he fumbled with them did not make him welcome. Then, as his handling improved, he found time to make himself a nuisance in other ways. He had arguments with Charvaka about the colours they should use, and even the table design; but the rishi threatened to ban him from the workshop altogether if he persisted with this interference.

One day Charvaka had another visitor: Sanjaya. The shudras and sutas interrupted their work to greet him; as the royal chariot driver, he was of course well known to them. Sanjaya approached the table at which Charvaka was sitting. Sanjaya picked up one of the gold dice and rolled it in his palm.

'This isn't at all like the nut.' Sanjaya pulled up a stool as he spoke, and joined the rishi.

'Yes,' said Charvaka, 'the vibhitaka nuts are much less regular. You would be very lucky to find an unbiased nut. But since, for all their bias, it's almost impossible to predict how they will fall, there is no good reason why the nuts shouldn't be used for the royal game also — except that they would be too common for these kshatriyas. The important thing, of course, is that the nut can only land in four ways. That's why these dice are tetrahedra. You know, I have never before had occasion to make a tetrahedron. I have made cubes and spheres before, but not this. Isn't it a wonderful shape?'

Sanjaya tried to roll the dice on the rishi's table.

'It doesn't roll very well, Charvaka.'

'Of course, it doesn't roll like the nuts! They go all over the place — they are not true tetrahedra. No, this will hardly roll. Shakuni explained to me why.' Charvaka slid the dice along the table back to Sanjaya. 'Yes, Shakuni was able to show me that the heart of its weight lies at a point just a quarter of the way up from its base.'

'Which base?'

'*Which* base? *Each* base!' Charvaka flipped the dice over to demonstrate.

'Remarkable, Charvaka. In a cube it's half the way up from the base, isn't it?'

'Exactly. The cube is much less stable. The tetrahedron is like a cat.'

Again Charvaka demonstrated, this time raising the dice slightly above the level of the table, and dropping it point downwards. In hardly more than its own height, the dice flipped over to land flat.

'You see how hard it is to make it land on its point!' Charvaka picked up the dice again, and this time threw it spinning onto the table. 'Yes... it must be thrown. It turns through the air... but will hardly roll when it hits the surface. Of course, it's only on special occasions that the royal game is played with gold dice. It may cause some of them problems if they are not used to handling them. Mind you, I think it's harder to pick up the nuts. You are familiar with the royal game?'

'No, Charvaka. In fact, I've only played just a little even of the simple game. But never the royal game. That's what I've come to you about.'

'Ah! Will you have the task of keeping King Dhrita abreast of the games?'

'Yes, that's it. I would be very grateful if you would explain the rules to me.'

'You don't know the rules? But why then doesn't Gandhari do it?'

'She would lose patience after one game! No, I have to do it. I did ask King Shakuni to explain the rules, but I'm afraid he did little to reduce my ignorance. I didn't understand the question of the Kali dice at all.'

'But it's really exactly as in the simple game, Sanjaya —'

'I'm afraid I've never played the simple game using the Kali dice rules. I've only ever played the *very* simple game, Charvaka.'

'Mmm... Yes, there are so many versions of the game — of the royal game too, I have to say.'

'I see that the colours seem to be the same. Do they mean the same?'

'Oh yes. The black point is the *4*, the yellow point is *3*, red is *2* and white is *1*. Just as in the simple game, no? I did have an argument with Shakuni about it — he wanted the *4* to be left natural gold... for some obscure reason. Ridiculous!'

'But we often leave the *4* blank on the nuts. I suppose their colour is dark enough, we don't need the black point. Perhaps he's more used to the nuts?'

'He certainly leaves the *4* point unmarked when he does use the nuts. But I think he had some other reason. You know, I'm a little worried that the colour will come off the points. I would rather have inlaid the vertices with gem stones — like teeth, you understand. But it would have taken too long. And Shakuni would have complained that the different weights at the vertices would destroy the integrity of the dice. Not that he couldn't have worked round that. He might have liked the extra challenge —'

'When you say like teeth, do you mean that you could do it with teeth also?'

'Yes, of course. A very similar process. I have often done broken teeth.'

'You can do that?'

'Why yes, Sanjaya, of course.'

'Well, well.' Sanjaya chuckled to himself. 'Well, well, what a little liar!'

'What are you talking about?'

'Not you, sire. No — Karna!'

'Karna?'

'Oh yes. He said you wouldn't be able to do it.'

'What do you mean? When did he say that?'

'When?... Oh, a long time ago, Charvaka. A very long time ago. He never told you, obviously. One can see why.' Again Sanjaya chuckled to himself. 'What a fool that boy can be.' Sanjaya saw the curiosity on Charvaka's face, and explained. 'He was very young — he hadn't been with me for more than a year. Perhaps two. We were eating, my family and Karna, and the boy screamed —'

'Karna? Karna *screamed* ?'

'Oh yes.'

'*Out loud* ?'

'Of course he screamed out loud! How else could he scream, Charvaka? He had broken his tooth. A pip or a stone, something like that. Clearly he had bitten whatever it was right into the eye of the tooth, and the boy screamed.'

'I have never heard him scream, Sanjaya.' Charvaka was visibly shocked.

'Well, yes... I suppose I can believe that. But on this occasion I assure you he did scream. We were all quite startled. When I saw what the problem was I asked him if he shouldn't go back to you to have it mended. I thought it likely that you could do something with the tooth —'

'Of course I could have!'

'Yes, that's what I thought. But Karna insisted that you had no experience of teeth, that you certainly couldn't mend teeth... First he asked me to forget about it. He tried to carry on with his damaged tooth. He didn't scream again, but you could see him wince. After a couple of days I offered to examine it again, and this time he asked me if I could suggest something. I had another look — it was awkward, at the back —'

'Did you seal it?'

'I tried to, but the poor lad was sweating and shaking beneath me. He didn't utter a sound, but... No, I pulled it out for him. He thanked me, and off he went!'

'Do you think...'

'With respect, sire, you are a brahmana. More, you are a rishi. More, you are — you were — his guru. In those days he thought the world belonged to the brahmanas and kshatriyas. He would not scream in front of you.'

'Do you think he was afraid he would break down in front of me, if I tried to mend his tooth?'

'You know what teeth are like, Charvaka. I have known warriors who would rather have their teeth pulled out than mended. Oh yes, I think he was afraid, most certainly. Of course, *now* he wouldn't scream for anyone.'

'You think he knows better? You think he has discovered that it's not a brahmana's world?'

They both laughed.

'Rishis, brahmanas, kshatriyas... they come and they go,' said Sanjaya, still smiling. 'Even the gods... No, sire, every one with any sense knows that it's a rich man's world! It always has been and it always will be. But if you don't mind — I have work to do. I cannot sit here gossiping all day. The dice!'

'Very well, very well. Just one more thing, Sanjaya... Don't tell me that you have also heard Karna sing?'

Again they burst out laughing.

'So,' began Charvaka, after he had recovered his composure, 'you have played a version of the simple game. Do you start with an odd?'

'Yes. But first we place our starting bets. That's another thing, Charvaka, I have never even played dice on a proper table. I've either played along the ground, or on a plain surface. But I have seen the kshatriyas playing on tables with very neat rows for the dice and the counters.'

'Naturally. If you are using the Kali dice, then each bet must be carefully positioned. Come, help me fetch a table.'

In a corner of the workshop there were some large wooden boards leaning against the wall.

'These are just the table tops, Sanjaya. They wouldn't let me make the tables complete! They permitted me only to make the playing surface.'

Charvaka turned one of the boards round. The playing side was plated with a gold sheet; this was etched over part of its surface with a grid of small squares. The gold was neatly folded over the edges of the board.

The grid was in the shape of a long rectangular strip, perhaps sixty squares by fifteen. Over a small area near one edge of the grid the gold surface had a window cut out of it to expose the wood beneath. The edges of the gold that bordered this exposed part were raised and unfinished.

'They are going to have to fit gold legs to these. Then they can say that I did not make the dice tables! Just like the dice hall! Have you seen it? It's nearly ready, I hear. It's rather difficult for me, advising them through Dur! That area,' said Charvaka, noticing that Sanjaya was looking at the exposed wood, 'is where the dice are thrown. It would be too noisy throwing them onto the gold. It's called the paddock. As you can see, I have still to tidy the paddock fence, eh! To keep in the dice.'

Charvaka cleared a space on his work bench, and then they lowered the board onto it.

'You are lucky, Sanjaya. I have seen tables where the grid was triangular — where the dice would nestle exactly into each triangle. Those grids are hard to follow.'

Charvaka shuffled off leaving Sanjaya to examine the grid. He returned with two boxes, one full of the gold dice; the other with small round ivory pieces. All of these circular counters were marked with a single dot at their centre; but some in addition had concentric circles around the dot. Sanjaya was obviously puzzled by them.

'You know of course they used to stake gems and small valuables on the table,' said Charvaka. 'In recent times the fashion seems to have been to use counters to stand in their place. Many of the kshatriyas dislike this practice. The brahmanas rather like it, though: they are embarrassed to be seen handling real wealth!'

'Hah! You mean they are embarrassed for their poverty to be seen! We just bet with sweets, cardamoms, whatever we can get. Even rice grains sometimes! What are the rings for?'

'They indicate how much the counter is worth. Those with just the dot and no circle, they count for one; with one circle around the dot, they're worth two —'

'Two circles are worth three, three circles four?'

'No — not for this tournament, at any rate. This has been a matter of some dispute, Sanjaya. The customary way is, indeed, as you suggest. But for this tournament they will almost certainly use Shakuni's numbering. You see, some years ago Shakuni proposed a new method of interpreting the markings. But the brahmanas have always been very reluctant to abandon the traditional numbering. They insist that the tetrahedral shape of the dice makes the traditional method more appropriate. Shakuni, on the other hand insists that his system of numbering serves much better the convenience of the game. And I have to say that I think he is absolutely right — and most of the players do now as well.'

'So what is Shakuni's way?'

'The dot without circles is worth one; with one circle it's a two-bet, the same as in the traditional system; but then two circles is a four-bet; three circles is an eight-bet; and so on. We have them up to six circles round the dot — that's worth seven in the traditional system, but sixty-four in Shakuni's; but I'm sure that if Shakuni's system is adopted, they'll use only the pieces up to thirty-two, that's with five circles.'

'That sounds most *in*convenient, Charvaka! I don't see what the traditional way has to do with the shape of the dice, but it seems much easier to me!'

'Believe me, Sanjaya, it's much more convenient to play with Shakuni's system.'

'Is that where the line of dice goes?' Sanjaya pointed to the row of squares running along the length of the grid at its centre; this row was marked out by thicker lines. 'How many?'

'There are fifty-nine squares along the dice row, including the starting square.' Charvaka pointed to a square at one end of the dice row; it was inlaid with a red stone.

'Why do you need?...'

'These betting rows? Yes, there are seven betting rows on either side of the dice row. Six, really, because the last one, the seventh, is the camp.' Charvaka moved across to the other side of the table, so that the two men faced each other across the long dice row. 'Yes, these are large boards, fifty-nine dice columns by fifteen rows. Well, you will learn about the betting rows in due course, Sanjaya.

As a matter of fact, we seldom use more than three or four of the rows. The first betting rows I expect you know about.'

'I place my bets along my side of the dice row?' Sanjaya pointed to the row of squares just below the dice row along the centre.

'Exactly. We call that your first betting row. And this,' — Charvaka pointed to the row just above the dice row, on his own side of the table — 'this is my first betting row. My second betting row is next to the first, and so on. The area including the back row of the grid, in this case the seventh, and the edge of the table is called the camp, and it is out of play.'

Sanjaya passed his hand along the smooth surface between his edge of the table and the grid. 'So this is my camp?'

'Yes, it's mainly used for captured bets. As I say, it does strictly include the seventh row itself, but some players prefer to leave that row empty and use just the smooth edge, so as not to get the counters confused with the play... But for the moment you must ignore all but the first rows. You will be placing your bets along your first row, I will place my bets along my first row; and, of course, each square in my betting row, as you can imagine, holds my bet for the dice to be placed above it — *above* as seen from my side of the table, you understand... Likewise for you. So, Sanjaya, when we start, we first place our starting bets on the squares above and below the starting square. I place mine on my side...'

As he spoke, Charvaka placed an ivory counter on his side of the jewelled starting square, signalling to Sanjaya to place his bet.

'...And now you must place yours. I don't know how you are used to starting in the simple game, but our starting bets must be the smallest possible, so we use counters worth one. Good. Now, in the simple game you usually wager that your first dice is an odd number, don't you? And after that you can choose to bet for either odd or even, yes? Go on, you have the first attack, throw your first dice.'

Sanjaya's dice landed on the wooden area but it bounced over the gold lip and out onto the playing surface. 'It must stay on the wood. I must mend my paddock fences! Throw again.' This time it remained within the landing area, with the yellow point uppermost. 'A *3*, which of course is odd. So, in the simple game you could now continue your turn.'

'And I could now go for either odd or even.'

'Exactly. Every time you score what you aim for, you can continue your turn, eh? Well, in the royal game, which you must play now, Sanjaya, you can also continue your turn, because *3* is a prime! You see, instead of going for an odd at the start, you must go for a prime. Now you can choose whether to go for another prime, or for a common number. And, just like in the simple game, if you score what you go for, you may continue your turn. Go on.'

'I think I'll go for a common number.'

'Fine. In that case you just throw your next dice. When you are aiming for a prime, you signify this by tapping your dice against the table.'

'Oh yes, we do that in the simple game when we want to go for an odd — well, we slap the ground when there is no gold table available! And the betting for my next dice, do I put it here?' Sanjaya put his finger on the square in the second column next to his first bet.

'In the royal game you are only allowed to bet when you are aiming for a prime. Since you said you were now going for a common, you can't bet on this dice. But yes, if you were going for a prime, that's where you would place your bet.'

Sanjaya threw his second dice. It landed with the red point uppermost.

'A 2,' said Charvaka. 'Yellow and red make 5, which, being a prime, means that you have missed. For my turn, now, I will go for a prime, and therefore I tap my dice.'

'What about the kills — do you go for a kill as in the simple game?'

'Of course. But one is not allowed to go for a kill until there are at least three dice already placed on the table. I believe that in the simple game you can kill immediately, even after the first dice, is that so?'

'Yes, we slap the ground twice for a kill on two odds in succession, that's with an open palm; but for a kill of two evens in succession we strike the ground with fist closed. And then if I get my two odds, or my two evens, I kill my opponent and win that glaha. We call each round a glaha.'

'As do we. And the bets?' asked Charvaka.

'Well, if my opponent retires before I get a chance to kill, then he has to pay me, depending on whether he's retired out of turn or not.'

'Yes, that's like the royal game. If your opponent retires during his own turn, then he need only pay up to the value of your betting line at the time; which does mean that he has to pay up the difference, if his line is smaller; but it also allows him to retain part of his line, if he has staked more than you. Now, if he retires during *your* turn, then he has to pay a further penalty for retiring out of turn: he is obliged to surrender *all* of his betting line, he cannot retain any of it, even if it's much more than yours —'

'But if his line is less than mine, in this case he must still pay up the difference? Yes, that's what happens when we retire in the simple game. So, can I retire at any time?'

'Not quite. There is one time when you absolutely cannot retire: that's during the period between the dice landing, and the placing of it. Even if it's your own turn, you cannot retire at this point, but you have to go through with your turn and place the dice somewhere. And if your opponent has the dice, you must wait until he has placed it. Once it is in position, even though it may not be your turn, you may retire.'

'And the kill? In the simple game, if I make my kill then it's as if he's retired out of turn: if he's staked less than me on his betting line, then he has to pay up the difference. If he has the same or more, he still loses his whole betting line. Is it like that in the royal game?'

'Exactly. Except of course that the kill is made differently. But the bets go more or less as you describe.'

'So how is the kill made?'

'Patience, Sanjaya. I believe it's my turn, is it not? We're on 5. Now, I am going to aim for a prime, which entitles me to bet.' Charvaka tapped the table once with his dice, and placed a single ivory counter on his betting row, in the vacant column reserved for his next dice. 'Of course, I'm not obliged to bet, you understand. One is only obliged to bet at the start, or under certain circumstances when one is going for a kill.'

'Ah! Is it... If my betting line is smaller than yours, I have to place down enough to equal yours before I can go for a kill?'

'Exactly. You have to be prepared to pay a little for the privilege of going for a kill...' Charvaka shook his fist with the dice inside it.

'Charvaka, one moment. Could you have bet more just now? I seem to remember that we are not allowed to bet just any amount, not in the simple game... What's the rule?'

'You are right, I would not be allowed to bet more than one at this stage —'

'I remember — because you only had a one already on your betting line. Is that right? You mustn't exceed the total of your betting line in any one bet?'

'Correct. That is why it is obligatory to bet on the first dice: otherwise we wouldn't be able to place any more than nothing on a subsequent bet! Out of nothing, nothing grows, but out of one... Shakuni would disagree, I fear...'

'So after you have placed a bet worth one, you can place another one; after that you could place at most two, then at most four, eight, and so on. Ah! That's why Shakuni wants the betting counters to come in these numbers!'

Charvaka had thrown his dice while Sanjaya was speaking.

'Another red. Good, I am now on 7. Quite a nice prime. You notice there are now three dice in the dice row, so I can go for a kill. To kill, in the royal game, I have to go for a prime, but I must tap twice. So really, killing is simpler than in the simple game, where you have to go for two odds or two evens in succession. Well, Sanjaya, I'm tapping twice for a kill. And I will now place a bet of two on the betting square for my next dice.'

'Charvaka, if I were to retire now, since I'm out of turn, it's exactly as though you'd killed me, isn't it? So I would have to give you my single bet and an extra three to make up the value of your line.'

'Exactly. But at least you lose a little now rather than a lot later!'

'Well, it's not my property I'm playing with... I think I'll stay in there.'

'You're right, Sanjaya, we should be playing for real stakes. Shall we say a single piece is worth one jar of clarified butter?'

'No, Charvaka, if you don't mind — I don't gamble.'

'Are you sure, Sanjaya? You know that a game is not worth playing unless it's more than just a game.'

'Sire, please remember I am not here to play any sort of game — I have to be able to make sense of it to King Dhrita.'

'My apologies. That is quite another game, is it not! How is the poor man, by the way?'

'Well, he is much restored by Dur's good humour.'

'Yes, I've noticed that Dur is looking much happier.'

'Karna says that he's never known him in a better mood.'

'Oh, Karna has been speaking to you, has he? I didn't think anyone enjoyed that privilege at present.'

'It was I who spoke to him, Charvaka. It was in connection with... I felt I should... about Vai's family.'

'Are they still upset with Karna?'

'Of course they are. They didn't expect to be asked like that. I mean, if Karna came to you and said, if you wish me to challenge him, I will — would you ask someone else to fight your fight? It should have been Karna's fight without him having to ask them.'

'Perhaps the boy thought that they might genuinely not wish Vai's death avenged in that manner. That seemed to be Vrisha's opinion, too.'

'I know that, sire. But he could have found that out more appropriately, couldn't he? I mean, when Karna is standing in front of you, looking you straight in the eye, who's going to tell him what they might wish in private. He could have asked *me* to find out what it was they would have preferred.'

'And did you tell him this, Sanjaya?'

'Yes... I did.'

'What did he say?'

'I got what I deserved, I suppose. He said it was too late now. He asked me why I hadn't spoken to him at the time. That *was* my fault. I should have spoken to him then. Or to you, sire. I don't know why I waited. I'm cross with him, but I'm also angry with myself. I know what he's like, I should have spoken to him earlier.'

'Sanjaya, perhaps it's for the best. I wouldn't like to have seen Bhima die for it. We seem unable to receive injury without proceeding to multiply it. Bhima's death would have spread the poison of Vai's death, not eased it. Don't you think that was in Karna's mind as well? Don't you think that was a way out, for him. Eh? You find that surprising? Come, this is fruitless, let me try to kill *you* instead, eh?'

Charvaka threw his dice. 'White! 1 and 7 makes 8, which is no prime at all. You are still alive, Sanjaya, and it is your turn.'

'I think I will go for a kill. I tap twice. So, because I'm going for a kill, I must bet, because my betting line is only one and yours has four. So I will bet three to equal your line.'

'There is a slight problem —'

'Oh yes! I can see — since I have only one bet down, I can only add one at this stage to my betting line. Does that mean I'm not able to go for a kill?'

'Well, it depends, Sanjaya. Some people adhere to the strict rule, and they have to build up their line gradually in order to kill. You would thus be restricted to bet just one now; and then, assuming that you got your prime, you could then place two, equalling my four, and so aim for a kill at that stage. What is generally done nowadays, especially in the full Kali game, is that the defending player is given the discretion to allow his opponent to try for a kill. So in this situation, since you request to kill me, I can give you permission to place a bet of three. Such a bet is known as a bad bet, because it's technically illegal.'

'Why should you want to let me go for a kill now?'

'Ah! As you will see when I show you how the Kali dice work, it's sometimes desirable to let one's opponent develop a stack of counters on one betting square. Because if you fail to kill me, I might be able to capture your bet. Indeed, you sometimes see quite huge stacks all on the one square — or in the one column. It makes playing the Kali dice more exciting. On this occasion you will be pleased to know that I give you my permission: place your bet and go for a kill.'

Sanjaya stacked two ivory counters, a one and a two, on his next betting square. 'Could I make a bet of more than three?'

'No. You should never exceed your opponent's line with a bad bet. Why, there would be no limit to what you could jump to! With a good bet, yes, you can always exceed your opponent's line, as I did when I tried to kill you just now. A good bet has always been earned. But never on a bad bet, not even if your opponent would like you to! The referee would not permit it. Of course in a private game... You see, in the royal game you are delicately tied to your opponent. You have to struggle sometimes to catch up with his betting, or to fly off. But I believe this is also the case in the simple game when that is played with the Kali dice.'

'I wouldn't know, Charvaka. The Kali dice are a mystery to me. Could you —'

'Wait, Sanjaya. Let's finish this glaha, please. We are on 8. You need a *3* to kill me. Throw your dice.'

'Yellow! I have my *3*. So I take your four counters, is that right? And retain my four. Can we have another glaha? How many do they play?'

'That will vary, probably depending on the limits. Perhaps ten, twenty, thirty. Whose turn is it to start?'

'Yours.'

Sanjaya started to clear the table.

'Ah, now, we must do this properly.' Charvaka found an empty box and placed it by the paddock. 'You see, they have this absurd custom — the cause of all my problems — they don't like to use the same dice twice in a game. So you start each glaha with new dice. That means they will have one bowl with fresh dice — can you believe it? And another bowl for the used dice. So, after each glaha, we put away the dice in this box. You know, on each day of the games they will require bowls of virgin dice! If they knew we were corrupting them here with our dirty hands!'

'What about the counters?'

'Oh no, there is no problem with them. *They* do not have to be preserved for the feathery touch of the gods!'

They cleared the table and placed their starting bets.

'You mentioned the limits, Charvaka. I have usually played the simple game to a limit of just 21.'

'Ah, yes. Yes, the royal game is also usually played to a limit — for this tournament I don't know, but it will probably be either 13, 23 or 43, who knows? Perhaps 53 or even more. I have even seen brahmanas play to 108 — this is not a prime, but it is an important number for them, which for this purpose they make an honorary prime... Of course, I have seen Shakuni play to ridiculous limits, and even with no limit at all. What rules are you used to, on the limits? You lose your betting line if you go over?'

'Yes. And if I strike the limit it's like a kill.'

'Well, it's a little more complicated in the royal game, because it depends on what you aimed for. Essentially, and quite naturally, you stand to win more if you strike the limit — which is always a prime — when you're actually aiming for a prime. So... Imagine you're within reach of the limit, say, on 20, playing to a limit of 23. Eh? Now if you aim for a common, it goes like this: if you *strike* the limit, your opponent pays you exactly the value of your betting line, no more, no less. If he's short, he must pay up the difference, and if he's staked more than you, he can retain the difference.'

'Oh, so it's as if he'd retired on his turn?'

'Exactly, Sanjaya, exactly. Now you'll see what happens if you *exceed* the limit, instead of striking it. You're on 20, and still aiming for a common, eh? And you throw a *4*, so you *exceed* the limit of 23. Well, in this case you lose precisely the value of your opponent's betting line, no more, no less. If you're lighter than your opponent, you pay up the difference, and if you have more, you can retain the difference. So it's as though *you* have retired on your turn, eh? Now, if on the other hand you were all the time aiming for a prime near the limit —'

'I can guess, Charvaka — if you go for a prime near the limit, you stand to win more, but also to lose more.'

'Naturally. You're on 20, you tap the dice aiming for a prime, and you get a *3*. So you strike the limit. Then it's as though you have killed your opponent, or as though he has been made to retire *out* of turn: he has to surrender *all* his line, retaining none of it, even if it is worth more than yours; and if he is light, he must pay up the difference between his line and yours. But if you aim for a prime and get a *4*, going over the limit, then you must surrender your entire line, retaining none of it, and pay up any difference if you're lighter. So it's as though *you* have retired out of turn.'

'I see... I think so... Let me just try and get my mind round it... If I'm going for a common near the limit, whoever loses has to pay as though he were retiring *on* his turn... And if I'm going for a prime near the limit, whoever loses has to pay as though he were retiring *out* of turn. So... there's no point going for a kill on the limit?'

'It depends, Sanjaya. If there's another prime available to strike before the limit, yes, there is a point. Certainly, in our example, sitting on 20 with a limit of 23, there's no point going for a kill, because there's no other prime in sight. You only need to tap once for the prime, and you will automatically achieve a kill if you strike the limit. Of course, there is a difference from the ordinary kill, a very important difference: if you strike the limit, while aiming for a prime, you get the result of a kill without having to equal your opponent's line. You understand?'

'Oh, I see... I could have only my single starting bet, and still get the equivalent of a kill — without having to raise my betting to equal my opponent's line... Yes, I see...'

'Well, shall we play to a limit? Say, 13?'

'Very well — you go, Charvaka.'

Charvaka threw his first dice. The red vertex came up.

'You don't need to knock the dice on your first go?'

'No, since you *have* to aim for a prime at the start: you've already placed a starting bet, you see. Well, I've thrown a *2*. I will bet another counter...' Charvaka tapped his next dice against the table, placed his bet, and threw the dice. 'A *1* makes a total of 3. I get my prime.' He tapped again, placing a bet of two against the next dice. 'So, now I need either a *2* or a *4* to give me a prime. Excellent, another *2*.' He placed the dice in position. 'That makes 5. I will be extravagant and place a four-bet on this next dice,' he said, tapping the dice as he spoke. But he threw a *4*. 'Oh well, it's now your attack, Sanjaya.'

'So we're on 9. Just 4 away from the limit. You have... eight in your betting line, so since I only have one, I need to place a bet of seven if I want to go for a kill. A bad bet — may I place a bad bet?'

'No! Why risk losing all your bets, when you have a good chance of getting my betting line cheap? You see, when one is playing for a limit it's easier to win your opponent's betting line cheaply. When there's no limit you can only acquire wealth by going for a kill, or inducing your opponent to retire — either way, you need an impressive betting row.'

'I will take your advice. I will go for a prime. But I won't bet — I don't have to bet, do I? So, if I land on 13, the glaha is over, and I get your line. Is that right?'

Sanjaya tapped and threw his dice. 'Only *1*! So, we're on 10. What are you going to do?'

'Mmm... Well, if I'm going to go for a prime at all, I might as well go for a kill: if I just go for a prime without going for a kill, and get a *1*, although I get my prime, 11, it would be risky for me to carry on — I might be forced over the limit. Of course, if I were to get a *3* instead of a *1*, I would land on 13 and kill you anyway, even if I had tapped only once. But it seems better to go for a kill in the first place, that way I finish the glaha on either a *1* or a *3*, without the risk of having to exceed the limit. So, I'll try to kill you, Sanjaya, and I will be reckless, since we're not really playing for material — though, of course we can hardly therefore call it being reckless — I think I will bet another eight. There we are. Now, let's see... A *3*! My glaha! I take your single bet and you have to pay the difference, fifteen.'

Charvaka cleared the table, putting the used dice into their box. Sanjaya counted out his debt.

'What I fail to understand, Charvaka, is that if I was meant to lose, why do I have to lose in such a difficult way! I could have just bet you the sixteen on the throw of a single dice. This dice game makes you work very hard for the same result.'

Charvaka chuckled. 'Life makes you work very hard to achieve death, does it not? Perhaps you should stop breathing now, Sanjaya, eh? But I believe you wanted to see the Kali dice in action? A little more work, I'm afraid. Are you ready?'

'I'm ready. But seriously, Charvaka, you don't really believe it makes any difference, do you?'

'What?'

'Trying to anticipate the dice. I have met one or two who think like that, even in the simple game. We laugh at the efforts they go to in order to lose!'

'Mmm... I see that you are not a believer. Or, rather, that you *think* you are not a believer. Don't worry, I will not try to convince you. But make sure Shakuni doesn't hear you talk that way! So, the Kali dice... They say that they were invented by the kshatriyas, who found the pure and subtle game of the brahmanas too dull for their brutal tastes. It is possible to place a Kali dice only when you throw a *4*. If, during the course of your turn, you throw a *4*, you can of course place it as normal on the next vacant square of the dice row, adding as normal to the total of the dice row. But you can do something else with a *4*: you can place it as a Kali dice, not on the dice row, but on your opponent's *betting* row, so that it rides just like a bet on one of the dice already thrown. Then, instead of adding 4 to the dice row, it multiplies by 4 the dice on which it rides. Let me show you. Place your starting bet. I will start. And let's not bother with a limit for the moment.'

•

'Palmira, wouldn't it be easier to just tell *us* the rules?'

'You know those little wooden pyramids you've got inside, are they anything to do with it?'

'That's right, Henry —'

'I always thought those were models of the Egyptian ones,' said the other Henry.

'The Egyptian pyramids have rectangular bases. At least, the ones I've seen all have. My dice are tetrahedra, and so have triangular bases.'

'Is it a real game? Did you used to play it with Vyasa?'

'Oh yes.'

'Couldn't we get them out so we can follow it better? Have you got the betting things as well?'

'Very well. Yes... there are some wooden betting counters in a box somewhere near them. Share them equally and you should have the right numbers for Shakuni's system. Use his system. And you... you better use a chess board. We did have a much longer board, but I think I used that for something else. One will be enough for the moment, but you might need to put two or three chess boards together, later.'

The twins went inside and soon emerged carrying their equipment. They set up the starting bets and Palmira continued.

•

Charvaka threw a *3*, placing it on the starting square between the two starting bets.

'I won't do any betting for the moment, but I will tap for another prime,' he said, and threw again.

'Another *3*. The total's 6, a common, so your turn.'

Sanjaya threw without tapping, aiming for a common number, but getting a *1*, thus bringing the total to 7.

'My turn,' said Charvaka, throwing immediately, without tapping. 'Another *3*! When are we going to get a *4*? I'm on 10 now. I will go for a prime.' He tapped and threw his dice, getting a *1*. 'Now look, Sanjaya, although this *1* will do for me, putting me on 11, let's imagine I had thrown a *4* instead, or we'll be here for ever. So I'll turn this *1* round into a *4*. Now, if I place it on the next square of the dice row, that would make a total of 14, which is not prime. Instead I can use it as a Kali dice by placing it here.'

Charvaka placed the *4* on Sanjaya's betting row, just beneath the third dice in the row.

Column number	1	2	3	4	5	6	7	8	9	10
Charvaka's camp (Seventh row)										
Third row										
Second row										
First betting row	ⓞ1									
Dice row	/3\	/3\	/1\	/3\						
First betting row	ⓞ1		/4\ ←							
Second row										
Third row										
Sanjaya's camp (Seventh row)										
Dice aim and total	p3	p6	c7	c10	(p13)					

p: *aiming for prime*   c: *aiming for common*
Underline: *Sanjaya's turn*   Brackets: *total using Kali dice*

449

'Now, Sanjaya, 4 times 1 is 4, so the *1* in the third column of the dice row has increased its value to 4. The dice row total now makes 13. So I get my prime. I could also have got a prime by making the Kali dice ride on any of the *3*s. That would make the *3* increase in score to 12, which would have made the dice row total 19.'

'What if we were playing to a limit of 13?'

'Then naturally I couldn't use the 19. But I could still use the 13.'

'What happens if there are bets on my betting line where you would put your Kali dice? Do you put it on your betting line, instead?'

'No. No, the Kali always goes on your opponent's side. If there is a bet on the square I need — this is the nice part, Sanjaya — I take the bet! I capture it. Right off the grid, into my camp, to keep, whether or not I win that particular glaha!'

'All the counters? I mean, if they are stacked up on the square you want?'

'All. In fact, all of the bets in that betting column. Because you will see that sometimes it is customary to place the bets not on the first betting row but on the second or third. All of those go if the Kali dice rides in that column. But...' Charvaka paused to clear the table. 'I can only take your bet with a Kali if I score a prime with it. Now remember this, Sanjaya, because most beginners are confused by it: it doesn't matter a bit what I aim for. If I am able to *score* a prime, I can take your bet. If I am only able to score a common number with the Kali, I can't capture your bet if it is on the square I need. I can't even *use* the Kali on that square. Not to score a common.'

'So... you can aim for a common number, but still take my bet — if your Kali dice scores a prime by landing on the bet?'

'Exactly. The only thing is, of course, I cannot continue my go — since I don't score what I'm aiming for. And remember, even if I *aim* for a prime, that doesn't allow me to take your bet if I only score a common from that square: in fact, I am only allowed to score a common by riding a dice that has no bet against it. Both our betting squares must be empty. Such a dice, with no bets above or below it, is called a clear dice. One can only score a common by riding a clear dice.'

'Charvaka, I am very confused.'

'Naturally. It's all the fault of the kshatriyas! Let's have a go.'

They placed their starting bets.

'No limit again, eh?' suggested Charvaka.

'Fine. You start.'

Charvaka threw a *2*. He tapped, placed another bet of one, and threw again, this time a *1*. He tapped again, bet two, and threw another *2*.

	1	2	3	4	5	6	7	8	9	10
Ch										
	Ⓞ1	Ⓞ1	Ⓞ2							
	△2	△1	△2							
	Ⓞ1									
Sa										
	p2	p3	p5							

'Let's see, I'm on 5. I'll go for a common number.'

He threw a *4*. 'Excellent. Now I will use this as a Kali dice: I will place it on the square where your starting bet is; and slide your bet over to my camp.' Charvaka removed Sanjaya's bet. 'My score is now 11, a prime, of course. So now it's your turn, since I aimed for a common. Ah! Wait a minute, there's something else I haven't told you. Yes, sorry. When you have your bet captured, as in this case, it's up to your opponent, up to me, to dictate whether you have to replace the bet immediately or not.'

'Where would I put it?'

'Below my Kali dice: on the same betting column as before, but the square beneath it in your second betting row.' Charvaka pointed the square out.

'And do you want me to replace my captured bet?'

'As a matter of fact, yes. If your opponent asks you to do so, you are obliged to replace it, or else retire from the glaha. He may also forbid you to replace it, if he should wish. In this situation here, strictly speaking, if I forbade you to replace it, you would not be able to start up your betting again with a good bet: you have no counters left in your betting row, and out of nothing, nothing grows, remember? In practice, though, when players find themselves with an empty betting line, they're permitted to start off their betting again at the next opportunity, with a unit bet. In any case, I'll ask you to replace it, eh?'

'Very well, sire.' Sanjaya replaced his captured bet.

	1	2	3	4	5	6	7	8	9	10
Ch	⓪₁									
	①₁	①₁	②₂							
	△₂	△₁	△₂							
	△₄	←								
	①₁									
Sa										
	p2	p3	p5	(c11)						

'So, I'm on 11,' said Sanjaya. 'I don't think I will bet on my next throw, Charvaka, but I want to aim for a prime.' Sanjaya tapped his dice and threw a *2*. '13. Mmm... I'll go for a common this time.' He threw a *4*. '13 and 4, that's 17, which is prime. Can I use it as a Kali?'

'Yes... but not in this case if you want to continue your turn, Sanjaya. You see, there is only one clear dice on which you would be allowed to score a common, that's in the fourth column, the last dice in the row. Unfortunately, since it's a 2, your new total would be 19, which of course is prime — so you wouldn't score a common there in any case. No, you can't use the Kali to make a common. If the *1* was clear in the second column, you could have ridden it to make 16, and carried on your turn. But as you see I have a bet against that dice. Probably your best move is to take my two-bet in the third column with your Kali, and finish your turn on 19.'

'Very well.' Sanjaya slid Charvaka's counter to his camp, replacing it with his *4*.

'Do you want me to replace my bet?' asked Charvaka.

'Oh, I forgot about that. Why not? Yes.'

Charvaka put a new two-bet just above the Kali dice which Sanjaya had just positioned.

'Right, it's my turn. We're on 19. I'll go for a common.' Charvaka threw a *3*. 'What a shame. Sanjaya, do you mind if I cheat again and turn it into a *4*? It will be more instructive. Good. Now, you notice that 19 and 4 makes 23, which is prime, so if I play straight and place the *4* at the end of the row, I would have to stop my turn — I'm aiming for a common, remember. Yes? Now, how could I use the *4* as a Kali?'

Sanjaya thought for a moment. 'Charvaka, are you allowed to ride a dice which is already being ridden by a Kali?'

'Yes indeed, Sanjaya. You just multiply it by 4 again. Suppose I were to place my *4* underneath the *4* in the starting column, which itself is riding the *2*, that would make them worth 4 times 8, 32. So my new score would be 32 add 1 add 8 add 2, that's 43, a prime. I would stop my turn, but at least I would capture another of your bets. But, after all that, I don't think I'll do it, Sanjaya. Instead I will ride the last *2*, bringing my new score to 25, a common. This way I continue my turn.'

Charvaka positioned his Kali dice.

'Now, 25, let's see, I will go for a kill, and bet four.' Charvaka tapped twice and placed the four-bet in position. He threw a *2*. '27! You still live, Sanjaya.'

	1	2	3	4	5	6	7	8	9	10
Ch	①									
			②							
	①	①	△4̲ ←		④					
	△2	△1	△2	△2̲	△2					
	△4 ←			△4 ◄						
	①									
Sa			②							
	p2	p3	p5	(c11) p13̲	(c̲1̲9̲)̲ (c25) pp 27					

p: *aiming for prime*   c: *aiming for common*
Underline: *Sanjaya's turn*   Brackets: *total using Kali dice*
pp: *aiming for kill*

'You are on a lion,' continued Charvaka. 'You could try for a kill...' But Sanjaya was not persuaded. 'There are two primes coming up, Sanjaya. I think you should go for a kill here. I will let you place a bad bet.'

'I can't afford to. It would cost me another seven bets — I have to equal your betting line, don't I? Besides, if I'm not destined to score a prime, I won't, no matter how many primes are coming up. I'll go for a common.'

Charvaka chuckled to himself. Sanjaya threw a *1*.

'Now you're on 28! A tiger. You *must* go for a kill, Sanjaya. Put down your seven bets — you'll get them back when you kill me.'

'What's this about the lion and tiger?'

'Oh, that's just part of Shakuni's system. Several good players are using it now. Just wait till you see them in action, Sanjaya, that will convert you.'

'I'll go for a prime,' said Sanjaya, unimpressed, 'but not for a kill.'

His dice was a *3*.

'There you are, you see, you would have killed me on 31, Sanjaya! What did I tell you?'

Sanjaya threw again, without tapping.

'A *4*! Can I take your bet of four, sire?'

'Certainly. You will be riding a *2*, so your new score would be 37, a most excellent prime. However, you will stop your turn. Is that what you want to do.'

'I think so.' Sanjaya captured Charvaka's four-bet, sliding it over to his camp.

'Now, Charvaka, I would like to retire from this glaha. May I?'

'Of course. But you are out of turn — since you didn't aim for a prime your turn has ended, the attack has passed to me. So, if you insist on retiring now you must pay up to my line, that's four. Plus the one I captured means you have lost five. You have captured six and lost five, so over all you gain only one. I cannot accuse you of avarice at the table, Sanjaya. You realise, by the way, that if you had not asked me to replace my two-bet in column three, you would be richer on retiring? So, you think you understand the game now?'

'Well, a little... I haven't got some of the details straight, about how much to pay up... I would like to play a few more glahas, if I may, if you have the time. Not now... I think I've taken in all that I can sustain for the time being. In a few days?'

'Certainly, Sanjaya. The settling up does take some time to master, and the Kali dice, so it's quite natural to find it confusing. But don't worry, the main thing is to get the bones of the game first, eh? I have to say, though... there is one other important complication, I'm afraid —'

'These kshatriyas again?'

'Naturally. They have managed to convert a quiet and leisurely game of chance into a test of speed and dexterity.'

'I suppose they play it fast?'

'Well, Sanjaya, I have seen dice rows grow almost as fast as the words are coming out of my mouth.'

'I imagine Shakuni must be particularly fast.'

'Surprisingly so, really, quite surprising. I'm not talking about the speed of his calculation, which goes without saying. But his speed of reaction. Remarkable, when you look at him. You see, Sanjaya, you are allowed to *block* the Kali dice — if you are fast enough.'

'Block them?'

'With betting counters. Can you bear to play one more little glaha? I will show you.'

Charvaka cleared the table. They placed their starting bets.

Sanjaya started, throwing *1*. He tapped for a prime but didn't bet, rolling the dice gently into the paddock.

'A *3*,' said Charvaka, as soon as Sanjaya's dice became still. 'With your *1* that makes 4, so my turn...' The rishi waited for Sanjaya to place his dice in position, and then picked a dice for himself from the box. Charvaka tapped for a prime, placing a single bet. 'The blocking works like this: once I have thrown, and the black point of the dice points up for a *4* — the dice does not have to be absolutely still, you understand — you, my opponent, may block *any* column. All you have to do is to place a single bet on a square in that column — usually on your second betting row, but they're not strict about the rows, only the columns. But you must touch the column before my Kali dice touches the square it wishes to occupy. If you succeed I cannot ride my Kali dice in the column which you have blocked. So, if you have a bet already on the first row, threatened by my Kali, and you touch down first in that column, then your bet is saved. And if you have no bet there, you still succeed in blocking that position: I can't occupy a position you have blocked. However, as soon as I touch down with the dice — no matter which column, so long as it is a lawful position — you can make no further blocks.'

'Does it make any difference what you're aiming for?'

'None, nor does it matter what I would score from the square I desire. If you touch first, then I am blocked — but only for that turn, of course. In the next turn I could capture both the original bet and the blocking bet, if the opportunity arises!'

'What happens if my square on the second row is already occupied — by a bet, or by a Kali dice?'

'Then you block beneath it, on the third row. Eh? And so on.'

'How many blocks can I make? I mean, if you're slow, could I put counters along my whole row?'

'Yes, if you thought it was worth it. You can block as many as you have time for. But you can only block with unit counters — you cannot use the higher values for blocking. In practice they seldom manage to block more than two columns, one with each hand. You see, you are not permitted to hold the counters ready just in case in your hand. You have to pick them up from your camp, where you try to have them waiting by the appropriate column at the edge of the grid. So if the attacker is very quick with the Kali, the defender does not get a chance to block — or may not be able to calculate quickly enough *where* to block. The defender does have the advantage, though.'

'How?'

'Well, look at the paddock. It's a much longer journey to pick up the dice and take it over to the square you need, than to place the blocking counters: your hand can wait by the columns you want to protect, whereas I have to pick up the dice from the paddock.'

'Isn't it unfair on one of the players — having the paddock always on their left, or right, depending on which side of the table they're sitting?'

'That's what I used to think. But no, they don't seem to mind. They throw the dice before a match to choose which side of the table to play on, and accept it as their luck. Most of them have learnt to play equally well on either side. Each way seems to have its advantages and disadvantages. In any case, Sanjaya, you will find that sometimes the attacker deliberately waits, and allows the defender to block. Now, let us return to the game; we're on 4.

'I will go for a prime,' continued Charvaka, tapping his dice. 'And I think I will cheat a little and throw a *4*.' Charvaka threw the dice and turned the black point up. 'You see that my turn finishes if I play it straight at the end of the dice row, to make 8. But I could place it as a Kali, either on your starting bet, capturing it — I would be riding the *1*, taking my score to 7 — or, instead, I can ride the *3*, to score 13. But you can block both those positions, *forcing* me to play the *4* straight, and giving you the turn on 8. Go on, then, block those two!'

'All this trouble for nothing! These kshatriyas love to complicate their lives, don't they? What a luxury! And when the fall of a single dice would suffice! Very well, then.' Sanjaya placed his two blocking counters on the first and second columns of his second betting row.

'Good. So, I will play my *4* straight. Your turn, Sanjaya.'

Sanjaya tapped, but did not bet. He threw a *2* to bring the score to 10.

	1	2	3	4	5	6	7	8	9	10
Ch										
	Ⓘ		Ⓘ							
	△1̲	△3̲	△4̲	△2̲						
	Ⓘ									
	Ô	Ô								
Sa										
	p1̲	p4̲	p8	p10̲						

p: *aiming for prime*   c: *aiming for common*
Underline: *Sanjaya's turn*   Brackets: *total using Kali dice*
pp: *aiming for kill*   Ô: *blocking bet*

'Right,' said Charvaka, 'we're on 10. A tiger, but it's too soon to go for a kill. I will just go for a prime —'

'Charvaka, one moment. Where would you place a Kali dice on the first column, where my two bets are? Which would you capture?'

'Oh, both. I capture whatever is in the column. I would put the Kali dice as usual on your first betting row. There isn't any need, really, for the two bets to be spread out like that — or for your blocking bet in the second column to be on row two: it could just as well go on your first row. It's the custom, that's all. In fact, some players do stack up their bets to make the table neater. I suppose spreading them out does help when you need to see quickly how much your opponent has got in bets — if you lose count, which you shouldn't. Eh? So, I'm tapping for a prime, and I will place a two-bet. I am going to get a *4*, I warn you — if necessary I will cheat like last time. So remember, once the black point is up, you may block if you wish.'

Charvaka obtained a *4* without any intervention. He paused for a moment, allowing Sanjaya time to respond; but seeing Sanjaya reluctant to commit his resources, Charvaka placed his Kali dice on Sanjaya's starting bet.

'So I capture both your bets in the starting column.' Charvaka slid them over to his camp, where he stacked them neatly. 'The score is now on 13. Please replace your captured bets, Sanjaya. Yes, both of them — well, you can use a two-bet, that is simpler. Just under my Kali. Good.'

	1	2	3	4	5	6	7	8	9	10
Ch	② (=2 x ①)									
	①		①		②					
	⟁₁	⟁₃	⟁₄	⟁₂						
	⟁₄ ←									
	②	ⓞ̂								
Sa										
	p1	p4	p8	p10	(p13)					

'Now, I am going again for a prime, and I will bet four this time, my maximum permitted, since I have four down already. But look where I place the four-counter: there is already a two-bet by my next dice square. This often happens when one has just used a Kali. The custom is to place the subsequent bet on the next betting row, so I will place my four-bet just above the two-bet. Eh? Also, it shows that it's a good bet: otherwise you would have suddenly a stack of six.'

'Does that matter? To show which bets are good or bad?'

'Well, no, not here, you're quite right, it wouldn't make any difference to stack the bets up onto the first row — but, you know, there are many versions, even of the royal game, and in some versions it does matter, you see. Shakuni even plays a version where captured bets can be recaptured! Imagine that! Sometimes players will even agree to a change of rules in the middle of a match!'

'Charvaka, suppose you had placed some blocking bets in addition to your normal bets: would your limit go up as well?'

'Absolutely, Sanjaya. Indeed, that is very often why players block — to raise the amount they can subsequently bet! Yes, the whole of your betting side is reckoned up. So... I'm on 13, and I want a prime.'

The rishi threw a *1*, making 14. The attack passed to Sanjaya, who tapped, but again placed no bet.

'Please, Sanjaya, try to make it more realistic! Bet, once in a while, will you? Don't be mean with my counters!'

Sanjaya obligingly placed a single bet on his next betting square.

'You are permitted to bet up to three, you know!'

Sanjaya smiled and threw his dice, but without adding any more to his stake.

'Excellent!' said Charvaka, seeing Sanjaya's dice land on *4*. Charvaka quickly placed two blocking bets in the second and fifth columns. 'You see, Sanjaya, you can make a prime score by riding either a *1* or a *3*. If you had been quick you could have captured my six bets on the *1*! Now I have blocked the *1* and the *3*, so you must play your *4* straight, making 18. The attack returns to me.'

'But what about the starting *1*. Could I not still capture your starting bet?'

'Ah, but that is no longer a *1*, Sanjaya. It's ridden by a Kali, so it is now worth 4. Riding that again would not give you a prime, but a common.'

'Just as a matter of interest, if I had been able to make a prime from it, where would I have put my Kali?'

'Always on your opponent's side, so you would have put it on the square presently occupied by my starting bet, capturing it. The *1* would have been ridden from both sides, to be worth 16. But, as you see, your total would then be 26, so unfortunately you cannot use that possibility.'

Sanjaya placed his *4* at the end of the row.

	1	2	3	4	5	6	7	8	9	10
Ch	(2)									
		(1̂)			(1̂)					
					(4)					
	(1)		(1)		(2)					
	△1̲	△3̲	△4̲	△2̲	△1̲	△4̲				
	△4̲ ◄—					(1)				
	(2)	(1̂)								
Sa										
	p1	p4	p8	p10	(p13) p14	p18				

'Now we're on 18,' said Charvaka. 'I think I'll go for a common.'

Charvaka threw a *2*.

'That makes 20. And now for a prime. And I will bet... My betting line is at present worth ten — we don't of course count captures as part of the line; captures are off the board... Yes, I will bet a further ten.' Charvaka placed an eight-bet and a two-bet stacked together on his next betting square. 'Now, Sanjaya, I warn you again, I will get a *4*.'

Charvaka turned his next dice round into a *4*, and, taking his time, placed it as a Kali dice, riding the *3* in the second column.

'Notice that although I capture the bet in your second row, I still place the Kali directly beneath the *3*, on your first row.' Charvaka slid the counter into his camp.

	1	2	3	4	5	6	7	8	9	10
Ch	②	①								
		Ô			Ô					
					④					
	①		①		②			⑩		
	△1	△3	△4	△2	△1	△4	△2			
	△4	△4				①				
	②									
Sa										
	p1	p4	p8	p10	(p13) p14	p18	c20	(p29)		

'Count yourself lucky, Sanjaya. If we were playing one of Shakuni's favourite versions, you could recapture your captured bet by placing a Kali in its original column! But don't worry about that, I'm sure they won't be playing to that rule in an important match. Now, let me see, by riding the *3* my score has gone up to 29. Right, I'm going for a kill. And I will bet the maximum I am allowed, twenty.' Charvaka stacked a sixteen and a four into position. 'You know, Sanjaya, you really are lucky you aren't playing Shakuni. Another of his variations is to make all counters in the second row worth double their face value — and double that in the third row, and so on!'

'Is all this really necessary, Charvaka? I still don't really see why you can't bet me twenty, or thirty or whatever it is, on the fall of a *single* dice. I suppose if you wear ear-rings your bets treble their face value?'

Charvaka ignored him and threw his dice.

'Look, a real *4*! Excellent. Let me think... I'm on 29... Yes, I can make 41 by riding in the first column.'

Charvaka placed his Kali to capture Sanjaya's bet in the starting column.

	1	2	3	4	5	6	7	8	9	10
Ch	④	①								
		Ô			Ô					
					④			⑳		
	①		①		②			⑩		
	△1	△3	△4	△2	△1	△4	△2			
	△4	△4			①					
	△4									
Sa										
	p1	p4	p8	p10	(p13) p14	p18	c20	(p29) (pp41)		

463

'Do I have to replace the captured bet, Charvaka?'

'It makes no difference. Since I have killed you, you must pay up the difference in our betting sides. You have a single bet, I have forty. That's thirty-nine. Or, looking at it another way, you have lost forty, plus the five I captured earlier.'

'I think I've had enough for one day, sire.'

'Yes, poor Sanjaya. Just one more *tiny* little thing, or I might forget to tell you. You notice you had just the one bet left on your betting line? There is a very common variation, which they may well use during the games. If the *whole* of your betting line is eliminated at some point during the glaha — so if you only have one bet left in the line you are particularly vulnerable — in this variation, if your opponent requests it, you would have to pay up the value of your opponent's line, at the time your own is eliminated, in order to continue: you have to pay up as though you've been killed.'

'What difference would that make. I still lose a lot!'

'The difference is that it doesn't matter what I'm aiming for: I may be aiming for a common, but if I get a *4* and can capture your only bet on a prime, you have to pay up the whole of my betting row. If that becomes a possibility then it's sometimes better to retire.'

'I see... Yes, otherwise I could stay with just a single bet, hoping for cheap pickings.'

'Exactly. You see, Sanjaya, all these details have evolved for a reason — this rule makes a very small betting line vulnerable, and thus discourages mean players like yourself! Now, try to practise a little, Sanjaya. Play some games with yourself. Come back and ask me if you find any problems. I'm sorry I can't lend you these dice, but I'm sure you can find some.'

'I will, Charvaka. Thank you for your patience. Yes, there isn't much time, and I need to be able to follow things fairly well, especially if there are large bets being put down.'

'Is Dhrita still worried? That Dur will do something silly to try to humiliate the Pandavas?'

'I think so. But what can happen? The worst that can happen is that the Pandavas show that they are no match for Shakuni. But everybody knows that anyway.'

'True,' said Charvaka. 'But remember how much these kshatriyas indulge their sense of honour.'

'I've heard that Dur is planning to give pride of place to a match between Shakuni and Yudhi. I think he intends to make it the final match of the event... And I believe that Yudhi is not considered a good player. But I would have thought he also is the least likely of the Pandavas to feel humiliated.'

'Yes... Most people would say that Yudhi was little better than you are, Sanjaya. No disrespect to your skills, you understand... On the other hand, no one knows for certain. Yudhi has never really taken the game seriously. But in any case, it would be such a strange match. Yudhi is sure to lose it, and he is humble enough to know it — I think he is the most humble of us all. Yes, I rather agree, I don't think he will mind losing in the least. So what Dur can gain by having Shakuni defeat him I really don't understand. It's true, Yudhi can be reckless with the dice. He certainly was when I saw him playing in Indraprastha. But he will be coming here as King of Kings, not to play children's games.'

'Perhaps that's it, Charvaka. He is King of Kings. The King of Kings would not be expected to lose. It will not be Yudhi who is defeated, but his title.'

'You may be right, Sanjaya. Yes... particularly if he is bled dry. Losing is tolerable — even for the King of Kings. But to be bled dry, that is the ultimate humiliation at dice.'

'What do you mean? Oh — if your opponent wins all your material?'

'Exactly. If a player loses all his counters, especially if it only takes a few glahas, that is a humiliating defeat. And it is the aim of every player not merely to win, but to bleed his opponent dry.'

'And does that happen often?'

'In tournaments the players do not start out with very many counters, so some matches will surely end that way. Particularly if Shakuni is playing! If the King of Kings were to be bled dry... yes, for them it would seem unseemly.'

'How many counters are they given at the start?'

'That will depend on the dice limit on the glahas, and also on whether they use the brahmanas' numbering or Shakuni's. If they play the traditional system, then they will be given at the start either fifteen, twenty-one or twenty-eight counters each, depending on the dice limit. In the early rounds the dice limit will probably be 23; and they would each start probably with just the fifteen counters, to the value, in total, of thirty-five. Or possibly with twenty-one counters, to a value of fifty-six. On the other hand, playing to a limit of 73, they would probably start with twenty-eight counters each — with a value of eighty-four. This would use all seven values of the counters. This is, of course, using the brahmanas' system —'

'Well I hope they don't use it!'

'Yes. It is pretty, but so impractical. Still, what can you expect from brahmanas whose only work is to make work for themselves. Now, in Shakuni's system, which is much more logical and convenient, they would probably also start out with fifteen counters each, for short glahas. But the total would be worth thirty-two. And for longer glahas they would use thirty-one counters, worth eighty in total; or even — if they use each value of counter up to five circles and a dot — sixty-three counters, worth a hundred and ninety-two.'

'That's logical?' Sanjaya frowned. 'It must be *very* convenient.'

'It is perfectly logical, Sanjaya. Let me explain it —'

'No, sire, please! Another time. I must leave you to get on. Thanks again.'

'Not at all, Sanjaya, remember, I will have to thank *you*. You will have to tell *me* all about it, as well as Dhrita.'

'About what? Oh! You mean they won't they let you even watch?'

'No.'

'I don't know why you put up with it, Charvaka.'

'I probably won't for much longer. I have decided to leave Hastinapura as soon as this little affair is over.'

'Leave? Where to? Back to Varanasi?'

'No. Perhaps to Indraprastha, if they will have me. But you must not mention it, please. So, Sanjaya, if you need any teeth mending, now is the time to ask me.'

•

'Palmira, you haven't got your toothache again, have you?'

'Yes, Henry, as a matter of fact —'

'Oh, no! You can't just go breaking Karna's teeth just because *you've* got toothache!'

'Why not?'

'Palmira!'

'Anyway, boys, how do you know it wasn't the other way round?'

'What d'you mean?'

'How do you know that my toothache isn't the result of Karna's broken tooth? Eh? And don't lose those dice...' With her toe Palmira pushed a stray dice out from under the table.

'Palmira,' asked the first Henry, 'is it seven counters before fifteen, with Shakuni's way of doing the counters? You know, the counters they're each given to start with...'

'Ah! Yes, good. And what are they worth?'

Henry rearranged the counters in front of him on the marble. 'Twelve.'

'So what comes after a hundred and ninety-two?'

'Give us a chance! We know how many counters, it's the value we haven't got yet —'

'I think I've got the next one for the brahmanas' system — it's thirty-six counters isn't it? Worth a hundred and twenty.'

'Good... Now, if you will kindly let me get on...'

•

41 The dice hall

The dice tournament was to be spread over four days, but the contestants were already beginning to arrive in Hastinapura ten days before the games were due to start.

The Pandavas took up residence in the royal palace of King Dhrita-rashtra five days before the opening. At Yudhi's insistence they had travelled without any servants or attendants whatsoever; just six of them: the five brothers and Draupadi.

Only the twins had submitted their names to participate in the tournament. But Yudhi expected that he also would be called upon to play. For it was already common knowledge that Dur intended to honour Yudhi, as King of Kings, by inviting him to a match against the eventual victor of the tournament, whoever this turned out to be. This match, a prelude to the banquet which would bring the proceedings to a close, was to begin as the sun touched down on the fourth and final day.

Although Dur had been the driving force behind the construction of the gambling palace, most of the details had been left to the brahmanas. Dur certainly had wielded considerable influence; he was, after all, paying for it. But he could only suggest, not command.

Considering the relatively short time in which the palace had been built, and the large number of people with a hand in its design, it drew very little adverse comment; even from those who could rarely resist a chance to belittle anything associated with Dur.

And this was not just for fear of offending the others involved. Most of the brahmanas had seen Charvaka's work in Indraprastha, and were well aware that their efforts would inevitably invite comparison with his, particularly as they had outlawed any direct contribution from the rishi.

The consequence was that their gambling hall had avoided all the ornate decorations and ostentatious encrustments which Charvaka and his supporters would have ridiculed; while at the same time using very sparingly the glass, the mirrors, the many striking finishes and materials which set the tone of the palace in Indraprastha. In contrast, theirs was a simple building, whose character lay in its precise proportions and subtle control of light.

The main hall had a very high, flat ceiling; but for such a height its square cross section was surprisingly small, giving the impression of modest, almost intimate, scale; certainly nothing to compete with the mirrored hall in Yudhi's palace. The dozen rows of seats, finished simply in dark wood, were raked so sharply up around the four sides of the hall that only the light and the flow of air saved the space from being too close.

Most of the windows were arranged high up near the ceiling; and were accessible only from an upper gallery whose sole purpose was to allow control of the shuttering; this platform was too remote to afford a view of the play below. Some of the windows were set back into the thick walls, forcing the light to hover at the top of the chamber. Just below the level of the gallery, on three sides of the chamber, were a few small openings, designed more for draught than for sun. As a result, very little direct light filtered down during the heat of the day. Only in late afternoon could the sun's rays reach the lowest parts directly; for in the fourth wall, which caught the late sun, a carved wooden grille was set just above the topmost tier of seats; and this could scatter shadows right onto the floor. Later still, the shadows would begin to flicker as the torches were lit.

Thus at all times of the day the impression was of light without heat, perhaps more subtly achieved than with the mirrors used in Yudhi's palace. And, with the shutters fully open on the upper windows, a considerable draught would build up through the morning. Marble ducts, whose vents opened out between the rows of seats, allowed this air to circulate freely between the main hall and the smaller chambers arranged around it.

Some of these rooms, including the main entrance chamber, led directly into the hall through passages cut into the lower rows of seats. There were four of these, one in the centre of each side of the hall, with steps leading to the upper rows.

On the eve of the tournament the Pandava brothers, with Kripa to guide them, stepped for the first time through one of these entrances, emerging onto the plain marble floor of the silent hall. Even Bhima was moved. Set directly in front of each of the four entrances to form a square, making the space in which they stood seem even more confined, were the four gold tables, glowing softly in the diffuse light. Several stools were standing untidily around each table. All of these were of the same dark hue as the seating, but in contrast to the uninterrupted wood surrounding them, their legs were braced with gold. The Pandavas paced uneasily on the marble, carefully avoiding the stools, and quickly left.

The following day, when play was about to start in the middle of the morning, the silent hall was transformed, first by the colour and bustle of the audience, and then by the musicians. After the musicians left the floor, Vidura opened the tournament with a short speech followed by a long reading of the rules; without further ceremony the contestants for that session were introduced and the dignified lull gave way, as play commenced, to the shouts and exclamations of the players themselves. Against this, the noise and movement around the auditorium was quite unobtrusive: it was easy to descend for a closer look, to move around to view the opposite table, to consult with the many experts in the audience, or partake of the food and drink on offer; all without causing the slightest disturbance to the play below.

◊

On that day, as on the following three, there were two sessions of play: one in the morning, which broke up soon after midday; the other in late afternoon, finishing in the evening in time for the gathering to move to the royal palace for a sumptuous meal.

At both sessions of the first day all four tables were in action, requiring four adjudicators. Kripa, Drona, Ashwa and Vidura were given this honour, in Vidura's case a special tribute, as he was not a brahmana. For the morning session Vidura was appointed chief adjudicator, and therefore to him had fallen the largely ceremonial task of reading the rules. In the afternoon Kripa took this role.

The supervision of play at a table was no small task. Each player was permitted up to two seconds to assist him. This help could range from advice on strategy, where the tempo of play permitted it, to counting bets, supplying dice, counters and so forth. The adjudicator had to call infringements, settle disputes, and generally keep the players and their seconds in order. In addition, when bets where placed in a stack, so that the exact amount was not easily visible to the audience, the adjudicator would, if possible, signal the value of the stake.

Before the start of the tournament twenty contestants had entered the lists to play; or, rather, twenty had been admitted. Shikhandi had submitted her name, but she was excluded by the brahmanas, in spite of an appeal by Dur. It was with some difficulty that Shikhandi and Dur persuaded Drupada to remain in the lists after his daughter's disqualification.

The precise number of contestants gave rise to a rather complex plan of elimination. Of the twenty players, four were to be late starters, scheduled for the second day; the other sixteen starters would be reduced to eight after the first day. Of these surviving eight, four were to contest in each of the two sessions of the second day, occupying two of the tables in each session. The late starters were to play on a third table alongside them, two in each session of that day. Accordingly the fourth table was removed for the start of the second day, and the three tables rearranged in parallel. This did not provide ideal viewing for the central table, but it avoided having to squeeze the audience into three sides of the auditorium. Since there were now only three tables, only three adjudicators were required for the second day: Kripa, Drona and Ashwa. Ashwa was to open the first session, and his father, Drona, the second.

It was planned to use only two tables on the third day. The two survivors from the four late starters would fight it out in the morning session on one table, alongside two of the four remaining original contestants. In the late session, the two winners from the day's first session would compete alongside the last two original contestants. For this third day, Kripa and Drona were to adjudicate.

Then, on the morning of the final day, the two survivors from the previous evening would meet to decide the victor of the tournament. Drona was due to conduct this contest. The victor would then have the privilege of playing against the King of Kings in the very final session. Kripa was given the honour of taking this final game.

There had been much discussion before the start of the tournament concerning the precise rules of play, in particular, the betting and dice row limits. The latter issue proved the easier to resolve, the outcome being that on the opening day the limit on the dice row would be set, as a guideline, at 23; and that this would rise to 43, 73 and 103 on the three subsequent days. As with most of the rules, it was traditional for the two players to be allowed to alter details during the course of a game, by mutual consent; provided that the adjudicator also agreed. But low dice limits were not conducive to interesting matches. As a compromise, therefore, it was decided that the official limits set for a particular day could be changed by the players, but only upwards, and, of course, with their adjudicator's permission.

The question of the betting proved more difficult. The choice of numbering was the easiest part to resolve. When the brahmanas were reminded that even at Yudhi's festivities for the Rajasuya, Shakuni's numbering had been used, they yielded. The trickier part was deciding on the starting material and on the value of a unit bet. The starting amount was set, eventually, at eighty for the first two days; and at a hundred and ninety-two for the last two days. And the value of a unit counter was set at ten head of cattle.

It was also necessary to decide a limit on the duration of the contests, and this was achieved both by restricting the number of glahas played and by fixing a time limit. A water clock had been specially constructed for this purpose. The winner of a contest would be the player in possession of most material by the end of the allotted number of glahas, or the time limit, whichever was reached first. In the case of a player gaining all his opponent's counters, the contest would be decided in his favour before the allotted time. On the first day a maximum of forty glahas was fixed for each session. And on the subsequent days the limit was fixed at twenty glahas for all sessions, to accommodate the much longer glahas anticipated.

To avoid the need for contestants to transport their stakes with them, King Dhrita had agreed to enforce any exchanges of cattle which the contestants might fail to honour after their dispersal at the end of the tournament.

◊

The eight contestants for the opening session on the first day were Prince Vikarna, playing against King Shruta-yudha; Prince Bhuri-sravas against King Indra-varman; Prince Saha-deva against King Kunti-bhoja; and King Krita-varman against King Jaya-tsena.

Only two of Dur's brothers had entered the tournament, Vikarna and Chitra, and it was Chitra who seconded Vikarna to victory over Shruta.

Bhuri-sravas, seconded by his father, Soma-datta, was another of the morning's survivors, beating Indra-varman. Soma, who was a very well-respected player, had been drawn as one of the late starters; he was not due to play until the second day; and there was little for him to do by way of assistance on this first day. For Bhuri's game progressed rapidly in his favour. Indra was playing without assistance, not out of arrogance, but quite the opposite: he made it clear that he stood such little chance against his opponent that to employ a second would be a waste. But towards the close of this game there was considerable excitement when, as Indra-varman was running out of counters, Bhuri offered to stake all his winnings against Indra's pride and joy, an elephant on which he had travelled to Hastinapura.

It was Indra's turn. He was on 18, and would have had the opportunity of a kill on 19. However, not only was his betting line too low to equal Bhuri's with a good bet, he had not even enough counters left to place the bad bet he would have required. It was at this point that Soma suggested to his son that he allow Indra to place a rather unusual bad bet, by staking the elephant to make up for his lack of counters.

'*My* Ashwa-tthaman is worth considerably more than your entire betting line,' replied Indra. This raised a laugh from the audience: for curiously, the animal in question had exactly the same name as the game's adjudicator.

'In that case, King Indra-varman, my son will surely be prepared to hand over all our winnings so far' — Soma pointed to the pile of counters they had collected — 'if you succeed in your kill.'

'I'm sure *our* Ashwa will raise no objection if we agree on this stake,' added Bhuri, appealing to his adjudicator.

But in spite of the adjudicator's consent, Indra declined the offer, explaining with good humour to his opponents, both very large men, that it was hardly worth their while to win his animal; because his poor elephant would drop in value after having to endure their combined weight.

Instead, Indra tried to force his opponents over the limit of 23, in which case their betting line would have been his. But he ended up exceeding the limit himself; with the result that not only did he lose all his material, he ended up in debt to Bhuri. But this additional burden his opponents sportingly discharged. 'At least you have your Ashwa to return on,' observed Soma, with a note of regret.

For his game against Kunti-bhoja, Saha was assisted by Nakula; while Kunti employed Arjuna and Yudhi; they were virtually his grandsons, since Kunti was Queen Pritha's stepfather. But the sons of Pritha were quite unable to defend him against the sons of Madri.

The fourth game of the morning, between Krita-varman and Jaya-tsena, was perhaps the most evenly matched of the session. Jaya-tsena, possibly because he was the son of the notorious Jara-sandha, had some difficulty in finding a competent second. In the end Duh agreed to assist him, and this probably cost Jaya-tsena the few counters which decided this match, as Dur's brother had little knowledge of the game. Krita, who was not a strong player, was much better served by his second, Jaya-dratha.

Jaya-dratha was in action again in his own right during the second session, against Chitra; and Jaya confirmed his ability by the ease with which he disposed of his opponent.

Another impressive display in this session came from Drishta, who overcame Uluka in an excellent game. Many of the audience had hopes of seeing Shakuni at this match, helping Uluka; but Shakuni and his son got on particularly badly at the dice table; so Uluka was assisted by Dur. Drupada was not available to second his own son during this game, since he was also playing in that session, against Bhaga-datta. Instead, Drishta was assisted to victory by Satyaki, while Drupada overcame Bhaga-datta with the help of Shikhandi. Although there were murmurs of disapproval from Drona and Kripa, no outright objection emerged to her involvement.

When he was on the point of losing this game, Bhaga jokingly asked Drupada if he was interested in *his* elephant, Supratika, who was reputed to be an even finer animal than Indra-varman's Ashwa. But Drupada declined the offer, and proceeded to capture all Bhaga's material.

By far the shortest game of this first afternoon was between Nakula and Cheki-tana. It lasted only nine glahas, played at high speed. Nakula overwhelmed his opponent; and Saha, his second, had neither time nor need to contribute to the game. Nakula was applauded enthusiastically as he left the floor.

Several of those who had watched the twins in action on the first day took the opportunity in the evening to ask Shakuni if he was worried by the possibility of having to play either of them. Shakuni had certainly watched Nakula's game with great interest, from the first row of the auditorium. But he easily evaded these enquiries.

'You wish to know if I am worried? By the possibility of playing them? Well, my dear, I am prepared to stake my entire winnings from this tournament on the proposition that I will be drawn against either Nakula or Saha on either day three or day four. Watch me carefully when this happens, and then perhaps you will be able to determine whether I am worried now.'

Towards the end of the banquet, the draw was made for the second day's matches. Bhishma called for silence in order to announce the results, but he was soon interrupted.

'The late starters will play as follows —'he began.

'Late starters! You mean those who cheated early to start late!' joked Drupada.

'King Drupada,' continued Bhishma with a smile, 'I myself made the draws for the late starters... King Shakuni is to play King Shalya —'

'There you are!' shouted Bhaga-datta. 'Not only is Shakuni given a late start, now he has an easy ride!'

'So which of your horses is seconding you, Shalya?' cried Drupada.

'My stallions can outplay you any day, Drupada, even with your filly to distract them!'

'King Shakuni is to play King Shalya in the first session tomorrow...' continued Bhishma, ignoring these interruptions, and not bothering to raise his voice over the background merriment; for he realised that the implications of the draw would soon subdue the high spirits. '...And in the second session, King Satyaki will play King Soma-datta.' As Bhishma had expected, the audience were reduced to murmurs at the announcement of this pairing. 'The victors from our first day,' he continued, 'are drawn against each other as follows: in the morning, Prince Vikarna against Prince Bhuri-sravas, Prince Saha-deva against King Krita-varman. In the afternoon, Prince Nakula against Prince Drishta-dyumna, King Drupada against King Jaya-dratha.'

The contestants soon began to drift away to their quarters in order to prepare for the following day.

◊

'Remember that Drupada and Satyaki will both be busy. Neither of them will be seconding Drishta,' said Arjuna to Nakula.

'That's true, but did you follow his game with Uluka? I didn't see the beginning, naturally, but I was at the next table, and I *felt* him. He's become a great dice player, Arjuna, there's no doubt about it. The glahas I did see were conclusive.' Nakula was clearly concerned about his match with Drishta; he glanced anxiously at his four brothers; to Saha he added, 'You are lucky to draw Krita.'

'That's true,' agreed Saha. 'Yes, the afternoon's going to be heavy. It won't be easy for you against Drishta. And then Drupada with Shikhandi will give Jaya-dratha some opposition—'

'But didn't you see what Jaya did to Chitra in the afternoon?' asked Bhima. 'You saw he bled him dry. I don't think Drupada has a chance, even with Shikhandi.'

'And then what about Soma and Satyaki!' said Saha.

'That will be something!' agreed Arjuna. 'Yes, I'm looking forward to the afternoon!'

'They are still fighting, are they not?' asked Yudhi. 'Is it good land?'

'Oh yes,' said Saha. 'Enough for twenty thousand head of cattle!'

'Can Soma not give Satyaki even half of what he claims?'

Bhima and Arjuna laughed.

'He already has,' explained Nakula to Yudhi. 'And now Satyaki is asking for half of what remains. It could go on for ever, Yudhi.'

'It is land that old Balhika seized from Satyaki's father, is it not?'

'Yes, but that was long ago, Yudhi.'

'Long ago. Why will people always try to balance the present against the past, instead of with the future?'

There was no attempt to answer Yudhi's question, but Saha took the opportunity to be practical.

'Talking of the future, Yudhi, you should sit with one of us tomorrow, to get a feel for the play. You did very little in Kunti's game against me.'

But Yudhi ignored Saha's remark, and pursued his concern.

'Would it not be fairer if the past was wiped clean every generation? Many brahmanas believe that we should inherit neither the wealth nor the sins of our parents—'

'You mean Parashu-rama!' said Bhima. 'He's just envious of our wealth, Yudhi. He'd have liked to have been a kshatriya, to inherit wealth from *his* father.'

'Not just Parashu,' objected Yudhi. 'There are many others. Charvaka—'

'Charvaka!'

'Why not Charvaka? He is a brahmana, he is a rishi —'

'So why doesn't he practise what he believes?' said Bhima. 'Look what he passed on to Karna, or doesn't that count?'

'That's the point, brother. Karna was not *his* child. What he has given to Karna has been because of Karna's merit, not because Karna is of his family or even of his caste. Karna is lucky himself to have no past to bind him. What he has acquired he has earned. No, there is a certain justice in deriving neither advantage nor disadvantage from one's past; or from one's family, or birth.'

'No past?' said Nakula. 'No birth? You call the gold armour no past? How did Karna get into Drona's Academy, then? Have you not heard Kripa admit that it was because of Karna's armour?'

'We don't need to hear your views on that subject yet again,' said Arjuna, on the verge of anger as he spoke to Nakula. 'The gold mail is a mystery, and will remain a mystery. Drona, as you know, believes that it was a divine gift.'

'Ah!' cried Nakula. 'Hear that, Yudhi! Listen to Arjuna! The gods are allowed to pass on *their* wealth to their own children! Are you chiding men for trying to emulate the gods? What is good for the gods is not good enough for men, is it? The irony is, Yudhi, that only the gods could live up to your ideals! We men are not equal to equality!'

'Nakula,' said Arjuna, stiffly, 'you seem to forget our own origins. Isn't Yudhi entitled to aspire to being more than just an ordinary man?'

But as Nakula turned away in exasperation, Bhima brought the conversation back to the tournament.

'By the way,' he asked, 'you don't think that Drupada was serious, do you? It does seem that Shakuni is having rather an easy tournament. First a late starter, now Shalya.'

'You should have seen him watching you, Nakula,' said Arjuna, reaching out his arm to try to calm his brother. 'He was worried.'

'Worried!' Nakula laughed sarcastically. 'The only chance against Shakuni would have been today, with the limit on 23. He might, just might, have fallen victim to chance. Tomorrow it's already 43. That should give him all the room he needs.'

'So do you think Drupada was right?' asked Bhima.

'If Shakuni is prepared to cheat during the game, why should he not cheat before the game?' suggested Arjuna.

'Shakuni doesn't cheat, Arjuna, believe me!' cried Nakula.

'Believe you?' said Bhima. 'Why should we always have to believe you, brother? Other people think he cheats. Why should we not believe them?'

'Because if you ask them how he does it, they never seem able to give a satisfactory answer. They just don't like admitting his skill. Why, I don't know.

Well, I do know, yes: because they prefer to persist with the ridiculous idea that it's a game of chance, not of skill —'

'Oh, don't start that again!' cried Bhima.

'Didn't one of you say just now that Shakuni watched *me* play? Was it because the dice behave differently for me? Because I am luckier? If skill means so little, why do you say I have a good chance against Drishta tomorrow? An even better chance, because Shikhandi will be helping Drupada. Will I be luckier without Shikhandi there? You see, even you don't believe it is a game of chance.'

'Nakula, Nakula...' Yudhi put his arm around his brother. 'It is a game we play with ourselves, is it not? Like children pretending to be warriors, we like to think it is our skill, because it would be so dull if we really contributed nothing to the game. You know yourself that you can play as fast as lightning and still lose all your material!'

Nakula looked seriously at Yudhi for a moment. 'Sometimes I'm almost in danger of believing you,' he said, quietly. Then he broke into a smile. 'I'm sorry, brothers, I'm worried.'

'You're all either worried or miserable!' said Saha chuckling. 'Nakula is unhappy about his game tomorrow, Yudhi is Yudhi, Arjuna is missing Subhadra and little Abhi, who must be enjoying themselves at the seaside —'

'And little Abhi's uncle. I wish Krishna were here,' said Arjuna with a sigh. 'Occasions like this aren't the same without him.'

'At least Karna's not here,' Saha pointed out. 'Or at least, he doesn't seem to be. Have you seen him?... Occasions like this aren't the same without him, either!... So why is Bhima not the usual happy Bhima?'

'I'm not sure why, Saha. And it's strange that Karna's not here. But I'm always uneasy when Dur is *happy*. He must be planning something. You know that Shakuni has chosen him as his second?'

'Yes, I do,' said Saha. 'Dur won't have very much to do. Not tomorrow against Shalya, at any rate.'

'That's another thing,' said Nakula. 'I know that Uncle Shalya doesn't have a chance. But he would have asked one of us to second him if you weren't playing at the same time, Saha.'

'Then *you* second him, Nakula — he will need you much more in his game than I will against Krita. Excellent — I'll take Yudhi, you go with Shalya. You're right, Nakula. It would be humiliating for him, especially if he's bled dry. Even though he doesn't profess to be a dice player, you know how proud he is. Is that acceptable to you, Yudhi?'

Yudhi reluctantly agreed. 'That leaves Arjuna and Bhima with nothing to do,' he said, with a hesitant smile. 'Won't anyone require them?'

'Satyaki may need someone in the afternoon,' suggested Saha. 'Drishta is playing at the same time, so is Drupada. Yes, Satyaki will need someone against Soma. Who else is he friends with? Kunti and Indra, but they're not so —'

'They're even worse than Arjuna,' interrupted Nakula, dryly.

'Arjuna, you should at least offer your services to Satyaki,' said Saha.

'Why doesn't Bhima volunteer? He's better than me!'

Saha laughed. 'That's true, though it isn't saying much. You may be fractionally the better player, Bhima, but you wouldn't make quite as good a second, would you?'

Bhima laughed at the suggestion. 'We will both speak to Satyaki. There you are, Yudhi, it will not be our fault if we're enjoying ourselves in the auditorium tomorrow afternoon.'

42 Old wounds

Next morning, just before play was due to start, Arjuna and Bhima dutifully offered their services to Satyaki for his afternoon game. Satyaki was grateful, but hesitant.

'I have a feeling that Drupada may ask one of you to support him. If not, then certainly I will be glad of your help.'

The voice of Ashwa starting off the morning session ended this conversation, and Satyaki walked round the auditorium to join the crowd by Shakuni's table. Shalya and Nakula were starting off the attack against Shakuni and Dur. Arjuna stayed where he was, overlooking the table where Saha and Krita were now in play.

Soon he was joined by Drupada. Evidently there had been a change of plan for the afternoon, and Shikhandi would be seconding her brother, not her father.

'Nakula is formidable,' said Drupada, 'but my son has the vanity to presume some chance against your brother. Quite honestly, I have so little chance against Jaya-dratha, it's hardly worth taking Shikhandi away from Drishta... Otherwise,' he added with barely a smile, 'I would not be asking someone as weak as yourself to assist me.'

'Nakula and Saha won't be pleased. They don't altogether approve of your daughter, you know. *That* daughter!'

'Because she does not fall upon their thighs like most other young women? Well, are you on for me?'

'Yes, yes,' agreed Arjuna. 'You don't mind if my attention wanders during the game — it will hardly make a difference to you, will it?'

'Look at your brother now! No, not Saha! On Shakuni's table... See, Nakula is already furious with Shalya.'

'You're right... Dur is obviously enjoying it. Look at that! One thinks he is half-blind! How can he play so fast?'

'It's only beyond a certain distance that he loses sight. In any case, he sees the colours well enough — you know that he's just playing fast to make Shalya sweat. Shakuni probably has very little idea where he's *actually* placing the dice.'

'You're not serious, Drupada?'

'But look — Yudhi doesn't seem too happy.'

'No... Oh, by the way, do you know who will be our adjudicator this afternoon?'

'I know who it won't be,' said Drupada. 'It will not be Drona or his son.'

'I hope it's not Kripa — he's too fussy. Who are Drishta and Nakula having?'

'Neither Drona nor Ashwa.'

'That's not possible! There's only the three. Vidura isn't coming in for Drona, is he?'

'He will have to take the place either of Drona or of Ashwa.'

'Why? How do you know?'

'Arjuna, please!'

Arjuna's face darkened. 'Do you think they'll agree?'

'If they don't I'm not playing. Nor is Drishta.'

◊

Saha had some difficulty beating Krita, who played very steadily under Jaya-dratha's guidance. Nevertheless, Yudhi had very little to do and, as Drupada had observed, did not look comfortable. Neither did Soma, who was assisting his son against Vikarna. This was a very tough match which Vikarna narrowly won, mainly because of the number of infringements and inaccurate blocks which Kripa, the adjudicator, awarded against Bhuri. Throughout the match both Bhuri and Soma appeared very ill-at-ease.

Both these two matches and, to the surprise of some, Shakuni's, went the full twenty glahas. But only Shakuni succeeded in capturing all his opponent's material. It was clear to the more expert observers, though fortunately not to Shalya, that Shakuni had paced his game to avoid humiliating his opponent. In the final glahas Nakula gave up trying to advise his stubborn uncle, and settled down to watch Shakuni stalk his prey home.

As soon as play ended Drupada rejoined Arjuna; after a few words with his father-in-law, Arjuna stepped down among the tables to talk to his brothers about the afternoon session.

'Bhima and Kunti are seconding Satyaki,' he told the twins. 'I'm with Drupada —'

'*You*?' interrupted Nakula.

'Shikhandi is with Drishta, I'm afraid.'

'Mmm... So Drupada has given up against Jaya already?' Nakula turned to Saha. 'Pity you were playing, you should have seen Shakuni time his finish. The man is a complete master. He understands every element of the game. It was exquisite.'

Nakula tried to draw Saha over to look at Shakuni's table, where the dice from the last glaha had not been disturbed. But Saha was too drained to take much interest, and led his brothers out of the hall to eat and rest.

◊

Drona was the chief adjudicator for the afternoon session. After delivering the opening address, detailing the rules, and introducing the competitors and their seconds, he moved across to the table he was due to take, the central table, where Drupada and Jaya-dratha were waiting together with their seconds, Arjuna and Krita.

'King Jaya-dratha,' said Drupada courteously to his opponent, 'I fear that I cannot accept King Drona as my adjudicator.' Drupada's voice, though not unduly loud, was heard by enough people in the audience to silence the gathering. The other players interrupted their preparations.

'*King* Drona?' asked Jaya, looking in amusement, first at his adjudicator, then at his second, Krita.

'He is king of North Panchala,' explained Drupada. 'Didn't you know? And Prince Ashwa is therefore the heir to this half-kingdom.'

Kripa, who had left Nakula's table, whispered in Drupada's ear:

'You know very well that Drona has never set foot in Panchala since... He has never made any claim at all on your land.'

'You mean,' replied Drupada, for all to hear, 'that he half-killed my child just for the half-title?' With a gasp the audience stemmed its nervous laugh.

While Kripa consulted with Drona, Vidura made his way down from above.

'Is this true?' asked Krita. 'It is most unbecoming of a brahmana to fancy himself king.'

'Oh, brahmanas will do anything these days,' said Jaya, much amused by the turn of events.

Vidura rescued the three adjudicators by offering to take one of the matches. Kripa assigned him to Nakula's table, where Nakula and Saha greeted him with rather less enthusiasm than their opponents showed; for though the twins were fond of their uncle, they were evidently not convinced of Vidura's skill as an adjudicator. It was probable that Drishta and Shikhandi thought this might work to their advantage. Meanwhile Kripa himself took over Drupada's table, and Drona moved across to the rather crowded table where Soma and Satyaki were sitting, studiously avoiding each other's gaze. They each had two seconds, Shakuni and Bhuri on Soma's side, Kunti-bhoja and Bhima on Satyaki's.

'If Drona does not please my friend,' said Satyaki, seeing Drona approach, 'he will not please me either.'

Drona could not hide his mounting anger. Kripa tried to reason with Satyaki, but without success.

'Kripa, it's bad enough having to sit down peacefully at the same table as King Soma-datta,' said Satyaki.

'No one is forcing you,' retorted Soma.

Kunti-bhoja was too busy trying to calm Bhima to be able to influence Satyaki. On the other side Bhuri was as stony faced as his father, while Shakuni appeared altogether oblivious to the dispute.

'No one is forcing me?' repeated Satyaki. 'Naturally, King Soma-datta. Naturally, you do not entirely understand the subtleties that constrain one to civility. Force is the only language you recognise.'

Soma drew back his arms from the table as if about to rise from his stool. But the sight of Bhishma descending onto the marble floor stopped him. He lowered his hands carefully onto the cold surface of the table.

'Look at that!' cried Shikhandi from the other table. 'The Grandsire himself will adjudicate that match! He must surely expect that the language of force may have to be spoken!' Seeing the angry flash in Soma's eyes, she quickly added: 'Don't worry, Soma, I was only using the language of jest. The Grandsire may be a kshatriya, but we all know that he is as well versed as any brahmana, surpassing even the legendary Vishwa-mitra — after all, is he not free from the unclean touch of woman? What brahmana here could claim such a worthwhile devotion?'

Soma and Satyaki both stared at Bhishma, for a moment forgetting their quarrel. But Bhishma remained calm. It was Drona who reacted:

'It is only through the Grandsire's wish that we have permitted you to sit at the dice tables, Princess Shikhandini.'

'Ah, how generous of him. Perhaps he is at last feeling guilty about his treatment of women — of Amba, in particular?'

Drona glanced quickly at Bhishma, and went to speak to him, joined by Vidura.

'What I cannot understand,' continued Shikhandi, catching Drona straight in the eye as he turned his head back towards her, 'is why Drona, a brahmana, is allowed to play king, but I, a kshatriya, am forbidden to play dice?'

Bhishma put a restraining hand on Drona's arm.

'Why do you let her get away with this, Grandsire?' whispered Drona. 'These insults would be shocking enough in private.'

'Come, come, Drona,' whispered Bhishma, with a trace of amusement, 'what can be less shocking than the young trying to shock their elders?'

'That doesn't make it any less embarrassing, Grandsire. We must eject her.'

'Don't play into her hands, Drona. What is embarrassing is not *what* she says, but that she is so naive as to think that any words could embarrass the great Drona-charya, or myself. Let her stay. If she wishes to be removed from the tables, do not satisfy her.'

Without waiting for Drona's reaction, Bhishma turned his head, first at Drupada on his left, then at Satyaki on his right, spreading his great arms apart as if to draw the two kings like doves towards him. Satyaki and Drupada obediently rose from their stools and joined him.

The result of their little conference was that Drupada reassured Satyaki that he would not be offended if his friend were to accept Drona as adjudicator. As Drona duly returned to his position at Satyaki and Soma's table, Bhishma beckoned to Vidura to follow him to Nakula and Drishta's.

As Bhishma left the floor he passed along Drishta and Shikhandi's side of that table. At this moment the attention of the audience was on the adjudicators who had taken up their positions and were about to commence the play. Hardly anyone, apart from Yudhi, sitting quietly in the front row, noticed Bhishma's hand gently squeeze Shikhandi's shoulder as he passed behind her.

◊

The hostility between Soma and Satyaki led to some rash and heavy betting from both of them. Shakuni found it necessary more than once to place a restraining hand on Soma. But Kunti-bhoja and Bhima argued too much between themselves to exert any calming influence on Satyaki. Fortunes changed rapidly during the first few glahas of this match, leaving Satyaki substantially down by the tenth glaha. By the twelfth, however, Satyaki had managed to recover his early losses, and his nerve steadied.

At this stage Drupada and Jaya-dratha had played only seven glahas. Not only were they playing at a very leisurely pace, they also quite frequently interrupted their play to catch the action on the tables either side of them.

Nakula and Drishta were on their tenth glaha. They were both playing fast, but many of their glahas stretched to the limit of 43. Their betting had been cautious, and at this stage Nakula was marginally ahead. During this tenth glaha, however, Drishta tried a change of tactic, betting at every available throw to try to make a kill impossible for his opponent. But then Drishta repeatedly failed to kill Nakula, and ended the glaha going over the limit. The acquisition of Drishta's substantial betting line now gave Nakula a clear lead.

The next glaha between these two was interrupted when Saha suddenly complained to their adjudicator, Vidura, that Shikhandi was attempting to disturb Nakula.

'How is she disturbing you?' asked Vidura.

'She is looking at him provocatively,' explained Saha, speaking for his brother.

'Is this true?' asked Vidura, directly to Nakula.

'She stares at me,' conceded Nakula, who appeared to be more disturbed by his brother's intervention.

Drupada and Jaya-dratha looked with interest from their table.

'How could I possibly distract these divine twins, whose chivalrous fathers roam the very heavens... Look, Vidura, look up at this gracious company, rivalling the very gods with their beauty and wisdom.' As Shikhandi's eyes followed her sweeping arm around the faces above her, she noticed Karna sitting quietly up in the top tier. 'Do you see a single woman,' she continued, 'who can avert her eyes from either Nakula or Saha-deva?' She sighed. 'If these, the most beautiful women in the land, cannot distract the noble Nakula from his dice, how possibly could I, who am quite without the common charms of my sex? How could Nakula even notice me when his own wife, my sister, the peerless Draupadi, sits above us like... the crowning locution of a speech.'

A muffled cry was heard from the far table, as Shakuni, without lifting his gaze from his partner's dice row, muttered loudly in appreciation of Shikhandi.

Nakula, now clearly irritated, signalled to Drishta to resume the game, and turned impatiently to ask his brother, who was still looking angrily at Shikhandi, to prepare the betting counters for him. Soon afterwards Saha fumbled the counters, forcing Nakula to pause for an instant in the middle of a drive. This gave Drishta a moment in which to gather himself for the possible Kali. As luck would have it, Nakula's next dice was a *4*, and Drishta was able to block it just in time. Nakula's turn ended, since he had to play the dice straight and miss his prime. Drishta took up the attack. Shikhandi smiled beneficently at the twins.

Meanwhile, Satyaki and Soma had concluded their fourteenth glaha. Satyaki held the upper hand for the first time in the match. He was just about to start off the attack in the fifteenth when he put down the dice and invited Soma to raise the value of the unit counter, from ten to a hundred head of cattle.

'He cannot get my land using the language of force, so now he seeks to deprive me of my cattle through the language of the dice!' Soma turned to his second. 'Well, Shakuni, shall I go with him?'

'Certainly,' replied Shakuni, without a moment's hesitation. Drona agreed to the change of stake, and the game resumed.

With most of the excitement at the other two tables, few people had noticed that in his current glaha, his ninth, Drupada had suddenly started to bet so heavily that he had run out of counters. To Jaya's surprise, Drupada made no attempt to kill him, even though his betting line in this glaha far exceeded Jaya's. Instead, when it became Jaya's turn, Drupada invited Jaya to place a bad bet and go for a kill; Drupada's betting line, and the match, would be lost if the kill succeeded.

'Are you out of your mind, Drupada?' asked Arjuna in a whisper. Jaya and Krita also stared at Drupada in amazement. But Jaya gladly accepted the offer, and struck his prime, winning the match. The attention of the audience at this point was equally divided between the other two games, both at critical stages, and hardly noticed this strange conclusion. It was only when they saw Kripa escort the party away from the central table and up into the auditorium that they realised this match had ended.

After some changes of turn at the beginning of the glaha in progress in Nakula's game, Nakula was now holding the attack. The betting lines in this glaha were substantial, and both players were risking heavy losses. Nakula was driving smoothly, but on 35 he hesitated, distracted by the voice of Soma from the other table: for with the departure of Jaya and Drupada from the central table, the noise from the far table had sharpened into focus.

'You want a hundred head of cattle *and* the land to graze them? For a single counter?' Soma turned first to Bhuri, who shrugged his shoulders, then to Shakuni, who looked back at him as though surprised to be disturbed at such a time. The previous glaha had been short and fast, to Satyaki's advantage. Clearly, Satyaki was intent on pressing his edge home.

'Yes, my dear. Why not?' Shakuni beckoned to Drona to ratify the change of stake.

Nakula looked across from his table and raised an eyebrow.

'Listen to that, Drishta,' said Shikhandi, mischievously. 'Didn't I tell you that the old man's canter mounts a count on the young man's gallop?'

Drona seemed reluctant to accept the change of stakes, in spite of the fact that both players were willing.

'My dear Drona,' said Shakuni, reaching out to take his arm, 'rules exist to serve good play, not to command it.' Drona relented, and the new glaha commenced.

Meanwhile Nakula had resumed his attack, undeterred. Arjuna, who was now sitting in the first tier, shouted out encouragement; but his cries probably did not penetrate his brother's concentration. Nakula was soon on 40, just three away from the limit of 43. He paused at this point, spending what was for him an unusually long time to take stock of the table. It was almost certain that he would now be going for a kill, by trying to strike 41 or 43. But he appeared to be debating whether to increase his stake, thus increasing Drishta's loss should he achieve his kill; or to play safe and conserve his dwindling stock of counters.

'A man of your reputation, Prince Nakula,' said Shikhandi, 'I should not expect to falter just as the pot is about to boil!'

Nakula was able to ignore Shikhandi's interjection; Saha, mindful of his earlier fumble, was trying to.

'I think,' ventured Drishta, grinning at his sister, 'I think he's afraid that if he pours from his pot now, he will not have the steam to ride on!'

'You mean he is going to slip the saddle like a young boy on his first ride, and leave the filly to fend for herself?'

Both Nakula and Saha tried to avert their gaze from Shikhandi's probing eyes. 'You would think,' she continued, turning to her brother, 'that with his experience he should be able to keep the lid on his steam.'

Nakula appeared undecided; Saha nudged him impatiently.

'Why are you hesitating?' he whispered. 'You're on a tiger, there's a *1* near the end of the dice row, another at the beginning, *and* a third in the middle! What are you waiting for? Three ways of riding Kali, and far apart... Nakula!'

At the mention of riding, Nakula looked at his brother and frowned.

'A *4* you can ride for a kill,' continued Saha. 'A *3* will kill. A *1* will kill just as dead! A *2* will leave him under pressure. You never think twice about a position like this!' Saha waited for a response. But Nakula was still thinking. 'Drishta is fast, but you have three ways, remember!'

Nakula was passing the dice carefully between his fingers as his brother was speaking.

Shikhandi turned to her brother. 'Mmm...' she began, softly, but not so softly that the twins could not hear. 'Perhaps his beauty is the better part of his accomplishment?'

Drishta's grin widened, and his reply was rather louder: 'His steam is all in the nostrils, do you think?'

Nakula held out his left hand to receive from Saha the counters necessary to equal Drishta's line. As he placed the stack in position, he tapped twice for a kill. He closed his right fist tightly around the dice. As he released it into the paddock, his hand followed it like a hawk, ready to swoop it up again.

For an instant the black point showed for all to see. Then, as the tips of Nakula's fingers closed upon the *4*, Drishta's two hands started to move in opposite directions. He had to block the three points on the dice row where Nakula could ride a *1* to strike 43. Shikhandi had of course prepared by placing three single counters at the appropriate points, just off the edge of the grid, in Drishta's camp.

At that moment Satyaki let out a piercing cry. The gold tetrahedron slipped from between Nakula's fingers. By the time he had retrieved it, Drishta had been able to block the first two positions, nearest the paddock. The remaining *1* was furthest from Nakula's hand; when Nakula smacked his dice down beside it, Drishta's third counter was already occupying the column. Nakula did not bother even to appeal to Vidura. He knew he was beaten. He formally placed his dice at the end of the row, adding 4 to the 40. While Drishta acknowledged the applause of the audience, Shikhandi cleared the table, sliding the counters in Nakula's betting line towards her brother's camp.

Satyaki had lost his glaha, his match, and his cattle. And he now owed Soma nearly all the land whose return he had managed painfully to negotiate many years earlier.

Nakula's defeat came soon after Satyaki's. In the very next glaha, Nakula used up his last counter trying unsuccessfully to kill Drishta, and was himself killed during Drishta's subsequent attack.

◊

Saha was angrier about his brother's defeat than Nakula himself. Nakula put on an outer face of calm resignation, and his inner feelings soon followed. But the feasting did nothing to calm Saha. Saha retired early from the banquet, and was soon joined by Nakula and Yudhi.

'So, you're drawn against Vikarna tomorrow morning,' said Nakula to Saha. 'Saha!' he added, seeing the resentment still playing in his brother's eyes. 'Don't waste your anger on a past you can no longer touch. What are you going to do, have a quarrel with Drishta? Your own brother-in-law? You saw him apologise to me tonight.'

Yudhi nodded his approval.

'And he played well,' continued Nakula. 'Very well. You see, Yudhi... Do you still think it's a game of chance?'

'I'm afraid I still do, brother.'

'What about Shikhandi?' asked Saha, anxious to avoid this familiar speculation.

Nakula smiled. 'Shikhandi is Shikhandi. There are no rules in dice or war.'

'Of course there are rules! Vidura should have had her thrown out. I'm surprised the Grandsire didn't earlier.'

'You know what it reminded me of,' said Yudhi, 'seeing the Grandsire with Drona... You can be sure Drona was urging him to throw her out... It reminded me of the day he let Karna stay in the Academy. Do you remember, after the fight? The Grandsire stood there almost in a trance. But you were probably too young to remember.'

'No, we remember. It was after he'd made a fool of Karna,' said Saha. 'And today he let Shikhandi make a fool of him.'

Yudhi chose to ignore this. 'Did you notice Karna this afternoon?' he asked.

'No, was he there?'

'Oh yes, right at the top.'

'It's rather strange of him to appear like that halfway through the tournament — you'd think he would have been at the opening ceremony. He's Dur's friend, after all.'

'He is also Charvaka's friend,' observed Yudhi.

'Anyway, Yudhi,' said Saha, changing the subject, 'I want you seconding me with Nakula tomorrow morning.'

'Yes, Yudhi, you can't escape the dice.'

'What is the other game in the morning?' asked Yudhi.

'Soma against Shakuni,' replied Saha.

'Is it possible that Satyaki will bribe Shakuni to try to win his land back?' wondered Nakula.

'Drona shouldn't have let them change the stake like that,' said Saha.

'Why not?' said Yudhi. 'It is better than killing each other for it. I think it's a pity that Virata and Shusharman didn't enter the tournament, instead of staying at home to fight each other over their cattle.'

'Is that what they're doing?' asked Nakula. 'You don't think they just want to show their contempt for Dur by their absence?'

'No, I don't,' said Yudhi. 'I think it's Virata's general who is the problem. What is the man's name?'

As Yudhi pondered on this, Saha returned to practical matters.

'Yudhi, you may be needed in the afternoon also, against Shakuni.'

'Against *Shakuni*?'

'Of course,' said Nakula. 'Shakuni will beat Soma, Saha will probably beat Vikarna, unless he is foolishly distracted at a critical moment. So that means Shakuni will meet Saha in the afternoon, alongside the match between Jaya and Drishta.'

'Very well,' agreed Yudhi. 'Who are the adjudicators?'

'Kripa and Ashwa,' replied Saha. 'And in the morning, against Vikarna, I want *you* to keep count *and* — yes — and prepare the blocking counters. It should be all right, Yudhi, Vikarna isn't a fast player.'

'No, but you are,' said Yudhi, despairingly.

43 The Brahma cycle

As Nakula had predicted, in the morning Saha won his match against Vikarna, and Shakuni beat Soma. In the second session, to the surprise of some, Drishta managed to get the better of Jaya-dratha. But this game was played in an unusually cordial manner; although Shikhandi was again on Drishta's side, she made no attempt to disturb Jaya's concentration. Moreover, Jaya asked Drupada to second him alongside Krita, a compliment which Drupada happily accepted; and by accepting, returned: for there were those who thought that this flattery was purely a ruse to induce Drupada's presence to inhibit Shikhandi; a possibility emphatically denied by those who claimed to know either Jaya-dratha, Drupada or Shikhandi.

Saha found it difficult to suppress his frustration in his match with Shakuni. Nakula and Yudhi had to calm him on several occasions. Because of the great length of some of the glahas in this encounter, only sixteen were played during the time period, at the end of which Shakuni had a sufficient margin of victory to make a formal count of material quite unnecessary. Nevertheless, Saha insisted on a count, and then walked briskly from the hall without a word.

Yudhi, Arjuna and Nakula chided him later for his ungracious behaviour.

'Ungracious?' protested Saha. 'What about Shakuni? Turning his back like that... That was gracious?'

Nakula explained to Yudhi and Arjuna what Saha meant.

'You remember that Shakuni retired from two or three of his glahas when there was hardly a hand of dice in the row? That we call turning one's back. It's regarded as cowardly.'

'Yes, I noticed that,' said Yudhi. 'You should find that flattering, Saha. That he had to resort to such tactics against you.'

'I don't think that was what was going on, Yudhi,' said Nakula with a wry smile. 'He chose to do it. Shakuni didn't have to. I think he did it just to provoke Saha. But...' Nakula paused to glance at the unhappy loser. 'It's Saha's fault to have such a weakness for him to exploit.'

'At least he didn't get all your counters,' said Yudhi consolingly to Saha. 'And he did try, didn't he, Nakula?'

'Yes,' Nakula agreed. 'But if you had kept your head, Saha, you could have done better than just avoid being bled. You should have learnt from my mistake yesterday. If I had kept my head I would have beaten Drishta —'

'Do you know what Draupadi told me...' interrupted Arjuna.

'Oh, how is she?' asked Saha. 'I noticed she wasn't here today.'

'A little worse,' replied Arjuna. 'She will probably have to miss tomorrow as well... She said that Shikhandi told her that Drupada threw his game against Jaya just to put pressure on Nakula.'

'On me?' But even as he opened his mouth, Nakula understood. He laughed. 'Well, it certainly worked. Wait till I see him!'

'By the way, Saha,' said Arjuna, trying to lighten Saha's spirits, 'did you notice how excellently Dur backed up Shakuni?'

Saha laughed, for Shakuni had had virtually no need of assistance, not even to prepare the counters or to pick the dice from the dice bowl. He always liked to pick his own dice and position his own counters in readiness. Dur's task had been virtually confined to clearing up the used dice.

'Well, it's all gone a lot quicker than I expected,' continued Arjuna. 'What do you think about Drishta's chances tomorrow, then?' For, of course, the fourth and final day would now bring together Drishta and Shakuni to decide the victor.

'Not a chance, I'm afraid,' declared Saha. 'But we must try to give him some support. There's a problem, because Drona is down to take the game. Perhaps he and Kripa will swap — Kripa is down for Yudhi's game in the afternoon.' Saha turned to Yudhi. 'Well, brother, how are you feeling about tomorrow?'

'I am nervous.'

The others laughed.

'There's nothing to worry about,' said Saha, his sourness now gone. 'There's no indignity in losing to Shakuni — that's assuming that Shakuni beats Drishta. No one will be expecting miracles. Me and Nakula will both be with you, and with luck we'll prevent him from bleeding you dry. Get a good night's sleep, brother.'

◊

In order that Drona should not have to adjudicate over Drishta, Kripa was given the morning session of the final day, as well as the second session, between the victor and Yudhi.

As the hall began to fill up, the musicians entered and arranged themselves with their instruments along three sides of the square formed by the front row of seats. There were seven of these players: two groups of three were standing facing each other across the floor, with the single dice table occupying the centre between them. One of the two groups stood beside three large drums. The group opposite carried smaller drums. The seventh player was occupying the third side of the square on his own. He was sitting cross-legged, cradling a small drum in his lap. Facing him, in the front row, was the still empty seat of King Dhrita-rashtra.

During the previous days, King Dhrita had occasionally sat with Sanjaya near the top of the auditorium. He had tried his official seat in the front tier during the opening ceremony on the first day, but found the noise of the players even more confusing than the shouts from the audience. From the top of the auditorium Sanjaya had managed to give him a very general idea of the progress of the games, but the circumstances had not been conducive to Dhrita's understanding of the details. For one thing, Sanjaya from this distance was just too far away to have a proper grip on the games below. But now that there would only be one game in progress, and also because the occasion again demanded his official presence, Dhrita was expected to fill the seat reserved in his honour.

The first musician to play began by just touching with one finger the skin of his drum, an instrument so large that standing on the floor it was almost his height. At first the resonance was impossible to perceive. Gradually it was felt, but not heard, beneath the noise of the gathering audience.

At this point King Dhrita came out onto the floor, guided as always by Sanjaya, and made his way up into the first tier. When Dhrita was seated, Ashwa entered, carrying a pair of cymbals, and occupied the fourth side of the square of players, just below the king. Ashwa sat down cross-legged, like his counterpart opposite him, bringing the number of players to eight.

Suddenly, without any apparent signal, all the musicians sounded a single loud beat from their instruments; but they instantly choked the sound down almost to nothing.

Now, at last, the big drum was just audible. It had a steady, regular tone, proceeding almost uncomfortably fast for such a low sound; for it was much quicker than a heartbeat. Such was the skill of the player that he was able imperceptibly to raise the volume without stressing any single beat; each tone seemed to be the exact equal of its predecessor.

The player next to him, barely audible, was striking a slightly smaller drum, with correspondingly higher pitch. Again the pulse was entirely without accent, but it sounded less frequently, only on every second beat of the big drum.

The third drum of this group, slightly smaller again, was sounding on every third beat.

Opposite to Brahma, Vishnu and Shiva, the lesser drums were also in voice: these three higher pitched instruments, representing Indra, Dharma and Surya, were sounding on every five, seven and eleven beats of the huge Brahma drum.

Ashwa's cymbals were resting silently in his lap; but the single player sitting opposite him was now playing: his small drum had burst out in a high metallic tone above the others, seeming to weave in and out of them, playing right across the Brahma beat, compressing and expanding it.

Although the sound seemed to ripple unevenly like the surface of water, not one of the musicians was playing a rhythmic phrase. If one chose to listen to any single drum, cutting out all the others, all that remained was a simple, regular pulse, without accent, without decoration. And this was true even of the highest drum. Unlike the others, its pulse sometimes stopped, dropping out of sight altogether; but when it did sound, it was as regular as the beats around it. The difference was that its own pulse did not seem to fit that of the others. Sometimes four of its high beats were compressed onto just three of the Brahma beats; or stretched over five, or seven. It was like a dolphin riding the swell, diving out of sight, then resurfacing to leap the waves around it with an altered stride.

The drums grew louder and louder, until, exactly halfway through the Brahma cycle, Ashwa raised the cymbals from his lap and brought them almost together. But he did not allow them to touch. After this silent beat of the cymbals, the drums grew gradually quieter again, in a perfect mirror of the first half, dying down, as they had started, almost to nothing. Finally, at the completion of the Brahma cycle, all six of the standing drummers coincided for the first time since the opening stroke; and on this beat Ashwa's cymbals and the high drum joined them. The sea became a sheet of ice. Everything was suddenly still.

The musicians cleared the floor.

The players now entered with their seconds, and seated themselves around the table.

As usual the rules were proclaimed by the adjudicator while the players waited to start. Although incense was burned and torches lit during the recital of the rules, people were permitted to talk softly and continued to move around the auditorium.

The exposition of the rules was prepared in advance by the individual adjudicator, and varied greatly in style. It was generally very much longer and more detailed than strictly necessary, and in parts could be quite impenetrable to the untutored listener; but this ritual gave the audience time to settle themselves, and the contestants time to compose their thoughts.

As Kripa was speaking, Shakuni played idly with a handful of dice. Dur, his second, sat impassively with his own hands invisible beneath the table. Drishta made no attempt to conceal his nerves; his mobile face seemed to change from moment to moment, one instant looking tight with worry, the next breaking out with his infectious grin, as if confessing surprise at having come so far in the tournament. Next to him Shikhandi and Drupada were more dignified.

Occasionally, during Kripa's speech, Shakuni's eye accidentally caught Shikhandi's; and on each occasion Shakuni involuntarily bowed his head and raised his cheeks in a courteous smile. At one point a detail of Kripa's must have fired Shikhandi's imagination, for she leant over the table and whispered something to Shakuni, who was clearly much amused.

When the game got under way it was clear that Shakuni was in a supremely confident mood. So smoothly and quickly did he play the first few glahas that it seemed as though he knew exactly how each dice would fall.

Drishta was visibly demoralised, and there was little that Shikhandi or Drupada could do to lift him. The sixth glaha, however, was much longer and more interesting; but it too eventually fell to Shakuni, who inflicted serious losses on his opponent. As Dur collected up Drishta's betting line, cries of encouragement came for the young prince, from Saha and Bhima, who were seated with the other Pandavas in the first tier.

The next glaha, the seventh, was the first that Drishta won; and with it, a substantial line of bets. There was much rejoicing among the Pandavas and Panchalas.

'I see the gods can still surprise you, King Shakuni,' cried Saha, amid the applause.

'Drishta,' cried Bhima, 'remember it's the gods who decide the dice, not Shakuni!'

The next glaha was another substantial victory to Drishta; it put him slightly in the lead, and prompted further cries from the audience.

'Where is your magic now, Shakuni? Why don't you let Dur take over?'

'What has happened to your divine powers? Where is your second sight, Shakuni?'

'He should look through Charvaka's glass — that'll give him second sight!'

As Shakuni turned his head towards this vocal faction, Nakula and Yudhi restrained their brothers from adding to it. Although Shakuni's expression betrayed nothing, he may have been taken aback by these remarks, for he took some time before starting the next glaha.

With one exception Shakuni won the next five glahas. In the one which Drishta took, Shakuni retired early, clearly preferring to cut his losses than to persevere with what he judged to be an unpromising position.

When in the fourteenth glaha Shakuni again withdrew early, Saha, Bhima and Arjuna could not resist making their feelings known.

'Is this your magic, Shakuni? It looks like cowardice to us!'

'Why don't you play the next glaha facing away from the table?'

'At least it requires courage to cheat, King Shakuni. Can't you rise even to that?'

But Shakuni now appeared quite comfortable and replied to these taunts with some lightness and humour in his voice, hardly raising his head at all, appearing rather to address the company around the table:

'There are those who believe that I have magical powers. Or even that I use deception! Being fools, such men prefer to believe any fantasy in order to avoid confronting their own folly. They have not yet learnt even the meaning of deception. As for those who think my play lacks courage — being boys, such men are afraid to show their own boyish fear; they have not yet learnt even the meaning of courage.'

Without any further interruption, Shakuni took the next two glahas and the match. Drishta, who was left without counters, was more than courteous in defeat, apologising to Shakuni for the misdirected enthusiasm of some of his supporters. He and Shikhandi rose from their stools and, one on each side of Shakuni, guided their opponent towards Kripa.

To the applause of the assembled company, Shakuni was proclaimed the victor of the tournament.

44 Yudhi comes to the table

'Each player places a single bet to commence their respective betting lines, the position for these being in the first, or starting, column of the player's first row.

'The player's first row is that row which is immediately adjacent and parallel, on the player's side, to the central dice row. The player's second, third and subsequent rows — on this table reaching to the seventh row — are those immediately adjacent and parallel to the first row, counting away from the centre and towards the player's side, leaving — on this table — the seventh row nearest to the player's camp.

'The player's camp is that region between the edge of the grid, including the seventh row, and the edge of the table nearest the player.

'The first or starting column is that column — running, like all columns, perpendicular to the dice row and all other rows — which contains the squares along one of the two short edges of the grid, specifically, that edge which is closest to the dice paddock.'

Kripa tended to pause excessively between paragraphs, perhaps in an attempt to avoid clashing with the sounds of the other brahmanas around the floor; these were engaged in lighting the torches and incense, sprinkling sacred water on the ceremonial rice bowls, and other similar activities. For King Dhrita, sitting again in the front row along with most of the royal family, these pauses provided a useful opportunity to interrogate Sanjaya.

'Did Kripa say it was just the twins sitting with Yudhi?'

'Yes. And who else could give Yudhi such good advice? You know, sire, people say the final should have been between Nakula and Shakuni — that Nakula would have beaten Drishta, if it hadn't been for all that disturbance...'

'Why does Yudhi need two seconds?'

'I don't know. But Saha is almost as good as Nakula. By the way, sire, the young man assisting Shakuni is —'

'This is not a time for levity, Sanjaya. What are the limits for the match?'

'We don't know yet.'

Kripa continued:

'The starting column is therefore the leftmost column relative to one player, the rightmost relative to his opponent. The players have thrown a dice to determine who will take which side of the table. The victor of the tournament, King Shakuni, will have the paddock on his left. His opponent, Yudhi-sthira the King of Kings, will have the paddock on his right.

'The opening player throws the first dice and places it on the starting square, between the two starting bets.

'For this as in every throw the player may use only his nominated hand to throw, retrieve and handle the dice. On the present occasion both our illustrious players have nominated for this purpose their right hands. Either hand may touch and handle the betting counters.

'The player's seconds, in number of which he may have up to and including two, may handle the dice and counters with either hand, provided the handled objects are not in play and in position on the table, but, rather, are yet to be used. In exception to this, the player may cause his second or seconds to handle positioned dice or counters in, and only in, the act of removing them from the table at the end of a glaha; or after a capture or other equivalent transaction requiring the removal of material from the grid; at which point such dice or counters are deemed no longer to be in play. In any case, such activities on the part of the seconds are only permitted when play is idle; that is to say, in the period between the placing of a dice, at an appropriate position on the table, the dice having been previously transferred by the attacking player from the paddock, and the release of the next dice into the paddock.

'The attacking player is the player whose turn is in progress or about to commence. As soon as his turn ceases he becomes the defending player, and remains so until his opponent's turn ceases.

'An appropriate position is one to which neither the defending player nor the adjudicator raises an objection.

'The opening player, having positioned his first dice on the starting square, may continue with the attack provided that the number indicated by the dice either has no factors smaller than itself excepting 1, or is itself 1. Therefore the opening player has to cede the attack on throwing *4*.

'The numbers are signified by the colour of the upper vertex of the stationary dice, or, indeed, of the still moving dice, provided that it is stable and does not emerge from the paddock; according to the scheme in which white signifies 1; red, 2; yellow, 3; and black, 4.

'After the opening throw the player who holds the attack will with his nominated hand, at each subsequent turn of his attack, tap or knock the dice once, audibly, against the surface of the table, if and only if he is aiming, through the appropriate positioning of the dice after it has determined its number in the paddock, to achieve a prime total from the dice row.

'If and only if the player taps for a prime he may, during the remainder of the idle period, until he releases his dice, place a suitable bet at an appropriate position on the grid. But the player is not in this case obliged to bet.

'If the player omits to tap the dice, or if the tap was heard by neither the opposing player nor the adjudicator, it will be assumed that the player is aiming for a common rather than a prime total. In this case he is obliged not to bet.'

Kripa paused for a few moments while a bowl of spiced lentils was presented around the dice table. Yudhi rather nervously took the bowl from the brahmana who was attending and picked up a very small amount in his fingers, probably only out of courtesy; he passed the bowl to his left, to Saha, next to him. Saha also hardly ate; but Nakula, who was sitting at the far end of the table from the paddock, helped himself to a handful. He passed the lentils across the table to Dur, who was opposite him. Dur hardly touched them, holding them out to Shakuni on his left. Shakuni was sitting further from the paddock than Yudhi, and as a result was almost opposite to Saha. He had his head buried in his hands, and when he failed to respond to the bowl which Dur was presenting to him, Saha reached across and tapped his arm. Shakuni looked up at Saha, noticed the bowl which Dur was offering, and passed it straight across to Saha. Saha then offered the bowl back to him, and this time Shakuni scooped out a handful of the lentils, holding back his beard carefully as he licked them up from his hand.

'A suitable bet by the attacking player may be up to and including the total value of his betting line already in position on the table; or a single bet to restart his line should his line be entirely eliminated during play. In special circumstances, a bet exceeding these restrictions may be permitted when it is mutually agreed by the players and the adjudicator. The position appropriate for a bet is in the column awaiting the dice which is to be thrown; the bet is placed within that column, preferably, but not compulsorily, on the lowest available row, that is to say the nearest to the dice row.'

Yudhi, who was looking a little more relaxed now, accepted some soured milk, and then washed his hands in a bowl provided for the purpose. Shakuni also washed his hands, afterwards drying each finger carefully with a white cloth which a brahmana gave him.

'Having placed his bet, or not, as the case may be, the attacking player releases the dice into the paddock with his nominated hand. At the instant of release, the hand must not transgress the confines of the paddock. Only when the dice is stable, but without requiring it to be perfectly at rest, may a player allow his hand to pass over the paddock edge to grasp the dice.

'Unless the dice is a *4*, in which case the player may choose otherwise, the player will place the dice at the next vacant square of the dice row. The new total is formed by adding the number signified by this dice to the existing total. If the new total achieves the result to which the player aspired, be it common or prime, the player will continue the attack; and may do so directly, without pause, unless the adjudicator interrupts his play.

'The defending player may appeal to the adjudicator to interrupt the attack; but if no good reason is indicated, and the attacking player is judged to have played within all the bounds of legitimacy, the defending player will have to pay the attacker the sum of the attacker's betting line on the table at the time of the interruption.

'If there is a transgression during active play, the interruption of which by the adjudicator would disadvantage the innocent player, the adjudicator will normally elect to allow play to continue, until or unless the transgression places the innocent player at greater disadvantage than the interruption.

'When there are three or more dice in position on the dice line, including in this number any Kali dice which may be in place on the first or subsequent rows, the attacking player may, in addition to announcing that he is aspiring for a prime by tapping once, indicate that he is intending a kill, by tapping a second time. Both taps must again be audible to both opponent and adjudicator.

'Having announced in this way that he is attempting a kill, the attacking player may be obliged to bet: but only in the event that his betting line totals less than his opponent's; in which case the attacking player is required to place a bet whose value is, at least, the difference between the two lines; and, at most, the total of his own existing betting line. If the difference between the two betting lines is greater than the attacker's line, then the attacker will not normally be permitted to place the required bet, and, therefore, may not attempt the kill. The attacker may however appeal to his opponent; with his opponent's permission the attacker may place an illicit bet, greater than the value of his existing line, in order to equal the defender's line and thus attempt the kill.

'If the attacking player announces his intention to kill, but fails to achieve a prime with his next dice, then the glaha continues and the attack, as is usual when a player fails in his aim, passes to his opponent. If the attacking player succeeds with the kill by obtaining a new total which is prime, then the glaha terminates. The defending player who falls victim in this way to a kill is obliged to surrender his betting line; and in addition, if his betting line is less than that of his attacker, he is obliged to pay his opponent the difference.

'The glaha may also terminate as the result of two other events.

'First, either player may retire from the glaha, providing that at least three dice are in position on the grid, and that play is idle. If the attacking player retires, he is obliged to pay the exact value of the defender's line, no more and no less, whether it is greater or less than his. If the defending player retires he must pay the value of his entire line, whether it is greater or less than his opponent's; and in addition he must pay the deficit where his line is less than his attacker's.

'Secondly, if the game is being played to a mutually agreed limit, the glaha will terminate when that limit is reached or exceeded, as follows.'

Kripa paused to clear his throat.

Dhrita impatiently questioned Sanjaya.

'But what are the limits for *this* match?'

'I'm sure he'll tell us in a moment, sire.'

'In the case...' continued Kripa, oblivious to any restlessness in the audience, '...in the case that the attacking player cannot place his dice without exceeding the limit, the glaha terminates in favour of his opponent. If the attacker had been aspiring for a prime, then he is obliged to surrender his entire betting line and in addition, where his opponent's line is greater in value, the deficit. If the attacker had been aspiring for a common, then he must surrender the exact value of his opponent's line, no more and no less.

'In the case that the attacking player can and chooses to place his dice so as to achieve the limit exactly, the glaha terminates in his favour. If the attacker had been aspiring for a prime, then he receives his opponent's entire line, whether or not his own line is greater; and in the latter event, he receives the opponent's deficit in addition. If, however, the attacker had been aiming for a common, he receives exactly the value of his own line, no more and no less, whether or not his opponent's line is of greater value.

'If at any time during the attack the player obtains a *4*, he may elect not to place the dice at the next vacant point of the dice row; instead, but subject to certain restricting conditions, he may choose to place the *4* next to any of the dice earlier thrown and positioned along the row. When a *4* is used in such a manner it must be positioned on the defending player's first row, in the column pertaining to the dice to be adjoined. Such a *4* is known as a Kali dice. If there is already a Kali dice which has been previously positioned at a point in the defender's first row, the attacker may choose to adjoin this existing Kali dice with his current *4*, which will thus be placed in the defender's second row; or if this row is in occupation, the subsequent row; and so on.

'When a *4* is placed as a Kali dice in the defender's first row, the value of the dice it adjoins is multiplied by 4; and this new and increased value is used in determining the new total for the dice line. When a Kali dice is placed in the defender's second row, adjoining an existing Kali, the previously multiplied subtotal for that point is again multiplied by 4, and this new subtotal is then used in determining the new total for the whole line; and so on.

'I mentioned that the positioning of a Kali dice is subject to certain restricting conditions. These are as follows...'

'Why do we have all this again and again, Sanjaya? I am hardly clearer than when I heard it the other day.'

'You are lucky then that Kripa is so tired. If he had his usual zest, sire, you would be much more confused. It is a mercy to us that his faculties are so fatigued.'

'...First, in the case that, and only in the case that, the new total for the whole line, as a result of the placing of a Kali dice, is *prime*, then the attacking player may place the Kali *4* in his opponent's first, second or sequent rows, as required by their state of occupancy, to adjoin at *any* such position in the dice line, to occupy, therefore, any one of the comprised columns; provided, I repeat, the resulting total is prime. If on the square, or indeed on any square or squares within the implicated column which the attacker wishes with his Kali *4* to occupy, there is in place an existing betting counter or counters staked by the defender, and by existing I mean already in position when play was previously idle, then the attacker is empowered, by touching down in that column, but not necessarily making contact with any of these counters, to authorise the removal of this counter or counters; and in such way to cause his Kali *4* to supplant it or them. The counter or counters in this way captured are taken out of play to join the estate of the attacker.

'Secondly, in the case that the new total for the whole line, as a result of the placing of a Kali dice, is *common*, the attacker may place the Kali *4* in his opponent's first, second or sequent rows to adjoin only such positions, to occupy, therefore, only such columns, as have no existing betting counters pertaining to them from *either* player. Such permissible positions must therefore be entirely free of bets from either side of the dice row.

'In view of these two conditions it must be realised not only that it is impossible to capture bets by placing a Kali which generates a common total; but also that the possibility of capture depends only on the resulting total and not on the declared aim of the attacker. If a prime total enabling a capture is not the declared aim of the attacker, the capture is permitted but the attack passes to his opponent.

'There is a third restriction on the use of Kali dice. At the instant the dice settles in the paddock, play is no longer idle. As soon as but not before play becomes active, that is to say, from the moment the *4* is visible to both the defending player and the adjudicator, the defending player may place with either or both his hands a single betting counter, of unit value, in any and as many of the columns as he chooses, but only until active play ceases: that is to say, until the thrown dice, having been transferred by the attacker from the paddock, is made to touch down at an appropriate position on the table.

'The defending player must not be holding in his hand or otherwise touching a betting counter at the time the dice is released into the paddock: at the commencement, in other words, of active play. As soon as active play commences the defender may pick up a counter or counters in order to transfer them onto the grid; and these may have been previously placed at his convenience anywhere in his camp, though not therefore on the playing grid, during a period of idle play prior to the release of the dice into the paddock.

'If such a betting counter is transferred so as to touch down correctly in any part of a column during active play, that is to say, before the attacking player is able to make contact with either the table surface or any existing counter or counters within the column in which he wishes to place his dice, then the attacking player may not lodge the *4* as a Kali dice in the column thus blocked by the defender; though the attacker may do so in that column at a later time in a subsequent throw of the dice. The attacking player, being thus prevented from lodging the *4* as a Kali in the column of his first choice, may nevertheless lodge the *4* as a Kali in any other suitable column on which a blocking bet has not, within the current period of active play, been touched down.

'If there are no suitable columns to accommodate a *4* as a Kali dice, whether through the defender's blocking, or through inherent limitations of the position, then the attacker is obliged to place the *4* in the normal manner at the next vacant position of the dice row.

'Finally, there are some customary regulations which we have chosen to adopt as standard throughout the tournament, and which the illustrious players this afternoon will be encouraged to respect.

'Captured bets will form no part of the calculation of betting line totals, and are deemed therefore to play no further part in the glaha, with just this proviso: after a capture, the attacking player may request the defender to replace the captured bet with a counter or counters equivalent in value to the captured material, to be placed in the column previously occupied by the captured material; and this even if the capture coincides with the termination of the glaha, though in such circumstances the replaced material will be removed along with the betting line as the position is cleared from the grid. The defending player is obliged to comply with such a request. Such requests may be made only immediately after a capture, before the next period of active play, and any clear and pertinent gesture will be understood to constitute such a request. But the attacking player, after making his request known, may continue his play without pausing for the bet to be replaced.

'If a captured bet is the only material at that time in, or remaining in, the defender's betting line, then the attacking player may request the defender, who would otherwise be left with an empty line, to pay, in addition to the captured bet, the exact value of the attacker's line at that time. The defender is obliged to comply with such a request. If and while a player has an empty betting line, he may not claim any material from his opponent should the glaha terminate in his favour. He may, however, take and keep any captures made while in this condition.

'In any cases of dispute the adjudicator will determine the result to his best judgement, and, if necessary, restore the position of the grid to the most recent acceptable position.

'This match will consist of twenty glahas, each to be played to a limit agreed by both players and adjudicator. There will be no time limit on the match, which will therefore terminate either on completion of the twentieth glaha, the victor being in possession of greater material, or earlier, should one player acquire the entire estate of the other. The value of the unit counter will be determined by the players with the agreement of the adjudicator.

'At the commencement of the match, each of our illustrious players will be distributed with sixty-three betting counters in the following manner: thirty-two unit bets, sixteen two-bets, eight four-bets, four sixteen-bets, and one bet of thirty-two; in value totalling one hundred and ninety-two betting points.

'The rules of play, as we have endeavoured to permit throughout the tournament, may be altered with the mutual consent of the two players and the adjudicator.'

There now followed an interval during which Kripa discussed with Yudhi and Shakuni the length of the glahas and the value of the unit stake. As the players conferred, the audience speculated.

'He looks amicable enough,' said Satyaki to Drupada. These two were sitting in the second row, above Dhrita and Sanjaya. To the left of Sanjaya sat Queen Gandhari. Next to her was Queen Devi, Satyaki's first wife; and then Queen Sakhi, who was married to both Satyaki and Drupada. She had married Satyaki's friend after Drupada's first wife and the mother of his children, Queen Patni, had died giving birth to Drishta.

'He *looks* amicable,' accepted Drupada. 'But you never know with him. They should never have accused him of cheating.'

'But look how he's smiling at Saha. He is in good humour, Drupada.'

'All the same... Queen Gandhari...' Drupada called down to her. 'You know your brother better than we do, but he looks to me to be unusually edgy, no?'

'I'm more concerned about my son. You know how he feels about the Pandavas. I wish Pritha were here, King Drupada.'

'You think her presence would keep them all under control, Gandhari?' asked Drupada.

'Of course, not, Drupada... Since when can we mothers manage that? No, she helps me to forget my sons, not to control them...'

'Where is Pritha?' Satyaki asked Drupada.

'With Krishna,' he replied. 'Her grandson and Subhadra are there too.'

'With Krishna?' Satyaki lowered his voice. 'I thought he was supposed to be fighting... there was some talk of Shishu's old allies... You think...'

'I do. They would hardly be visiting him if he were involved in any serious fighting. No, I think he may still be a trifle reluctant to show his face — or his discus. Would he miss this for any other reason?'

At this moment Kripa addressed the audience again:

'The first glaha will be played to a limit of 23.' There was a murmur of disapproval from the audience at this low figure. 'The value of a unit counter will be one hundred head of cattle. King Shakuni will open the attack in the first glaha.'

Kripa took up his position at the paddock end of the table.

'Why so short?' Dhrita asked Sanjaya; but before Sanjaya was able to offer his own opinion, the question was intercepted by Satyaki, above them.

'It's natural, Dhrita, the longer the glahas, the greater the advantage to Shakuni. I am surprised that Shakuni has agreed to start at such a low level.' Satyaki turned and waved to catch the attention of Arjuna, who was sitting with Bhima next to Queen Sakhi in the first row. 'Your brother strikes a harder bargain than we thought!' he cried.

'If I know Yudhi,' replied Arjuna, 'he'll have suggested a limit of 73 to favour his opponent! I think you'll find that it's Saha who did the bargaining, Satyaki.'

'Where is the beautiful Draupadi?' Satyaki asked Arjuna. 'She was absent yesterday, was she not?'

'She hasn't been feeling well...'

At that moment Kripa formally announced the commencement of play.

'I have the great honour, as agonarch for this illustrious tournament, to start the play between our victor, King Shakuni of Gandhara, and the King of Kings, Yudhi-sthira of Indraprastha...'

Shakuni picked his first dice from the bowl of fresh dice kept by the paddock. With his left hand he placed his starting bet, and invited Yudhi to position his.

With both counters neatly in position, Shakuni squeezed his right fist and released the first dice into the paddock.

45 The lines are set

Shakuni placed his first dice on the starting square of the dice row, with its white point uppermost. He knocked his next dice against the table and placed another single bet in the next betting square. But his next dice was a *3*, so the attack went over to Yudhi.

Yudhi tapped and bet a single counter; he turned up a *1*, bringing the total to 5. He tapped twice, and placed a two-bet.

	1	2	3	4	5	6	7	8	9	10
Y										
	Ⓞ(1)		Ⓞ(1)	Ⓞ(2)						
	△(1)	△(3)	△(1)							
	Ⓞ(1)	Ⓞ(1)								
Sh										
	p1	p4	p5	pp						

Y: *Yudhi*

Sh: *Shakuni*

p: *aiming for prime*

c: *aiming for common*

Underline: *Shakuni's turn*

Brackets: *total using Kali dice*

pp: *aiming for kill*

Ô: *blocking bet*

'What's that?' asked Dhrita, hearing the ripple of surprise around the hall.

'Yudhi is going for a kill already, on 5,' said Sanjaya.

'Is there anything wrong with that?'

'I think it's just that it's so soon, sire.'

Meanwhile Saha was trying to restrain his brother, but Yudhi insisted on going for the kill: 'I can win four bets. That is four hundred head of cattle, Saha!'

'But the glaha is only just begun!' said Nakula. 'And you're on a leopard without claws, Yudhi! That's no better than a cheetah.'

In a whisper Yudhi spoke sternly to his brothers. 'Listen, the sooner I can get this glaha over with, the better. It may be a cheetah or any other animal you care to call it, but it can kill, and what is possible is possible.'

But Yudhi threw a *1*, placing it in position to make the total 6. The attack passed to his opponent.

Shakuni, without tapping, landed a *3*.

	1	2	3	4	5	6	7	8	9	10
Y										
	①1		①1	②2						
	△1	△3	△1	△1	△3					
	①1	①1								
Sh										
	p1	p4	p5	pp6	c9					

In a leisurely manner Shakuni picked his next dice and threw a *4*, again without tapping. As soon as Yudhi saw the black point, he grabbed a betting counter and placed it on the grid. Shakuni watched, holding the dice in mid-air above the grid. Yudhi placed two more counters by his existing bets, apparently trying to protect them from capture. There was laughter among the audience as Shakuni slowly placed his *4* at the end of the row, making 13.

	1	2	3	4	5	6	7	8	9	10
Y										
	Ô1		Ô1	Ô1						
	O1		O1	O2						
	△1	△3	△1	△1	△3	△4				
	O1	O1								
Sh										
	p1	p4	p5	pp 6	c9	c13				

'Yudhi!' cried Saha, despairingly. 'The 9 is a pig. How many times have I told you?'

Dhrita, catching Saha's words quite easily, questioned Sanjaya, who described Yudhi's placement of the counters.

'But sire,' Sanjaya confessed, 'I'm afraid I'm not sure about these names they use...' He turned round to Drupada and Satyaki for help.

'It's Shakuni's system that Saha is using, Dhrita,' explained Satyaki. 'He calls such numbers pigs because on them you cannot ride Kali to make a prime.'

'So it was pointless Yudhi blocking? Is that why they laughed?' asked Dhrita, anxiously.

'That is why they laugh,' confirmed Satyaki. 'But they laugh foolishly, for what Yudhi did was far from pointless. Though I'm not convinced he intended it.'

'I'm not sure, either,' added Drupada. 'You would expect him to have blocked the *3* in column five. Does Shakuni not like 18, Satyaki?'

'He doesn't, not with the limit at 23. Otherwise he certainly would have ridden Kali on that clear *3* to make 18. Look, Yudhi's trying to kill Shakuni again!'

Sure enough, Yudhi had tapped twice and stacked a one, a two and a four-bet on his next betting square; and seven was the maximum he was allowed to bet in this position. As he prepared to throw, holding the dice tightly in his hand, Nakula whispered to Saha.

'Let Yudhi be for the moment — I don't think we know our own brother. I think he may have been laying eggs, not blocking. You see that he's flying clear now.'

To a sigh from the audience, Yudhi threw a *1*, putting him on 14. The attack passed to Shakuni.

As Shakuni picked up his next dice, Saha prepared a counter for Yudhi to block with, whispering to him: 'Block your seven-bet if he gets a *4*.' But Shakuni threw a *2*, putting him on 16. He had not tapped, so it was still his turn.

'Guard that bet again!' whispered Saha to Yudhi. And as Saha warned his brother at the table, in the audience Satyaki explained to Sanjaya and Dhrita:

'Shakuni is on what he calls a tiger — the best place to attempt a kill — but he cannot equal Yudhi's line with a good bet, so he won't go for the kill.'

Shakuni tapped his next dice, but did not bother to bet. He landed another *2*, totalling 18; so, since Shakuni failed to strike a prime, the attack returned to Yudhi.

'I think I will try for a kill again,' Yudhi muttered. But as he considered whether to bet, Saha tried to dissuade him even from going for a prime; Yudhi ignored his advice. Saha turned to Nakula, but Nakula could not change Yudhi's mind either.

Yudhi tapped twice for a kill, but did not place any further bet. He threw a *2*, leaving Shakuni with the attack, on 20.

	1	2	3	4	5	6	7	8	9	10
Y										
	Ô			Ô	Ô					
	①			①	②		⑦			
	△1	△3	△1	△1	△3	△4	△1	△2	△2	△2
	①	①								
Sh										
	p1	p4	p5	pp 6	c9	c13	pp 14	c16	p18	pp 20

Shakuni tapped for a prime and got a *3*, landing exactly on the limit, to some restrained applause around the hall. Dur collected up Yudhi's betting line with a smile.

'That was a strange one,' said Satyaki to Drupada. 'Shakuni was playing so slowly, and as for Yudhi —'

'Do you think he intended to fly clear? It looked to me as though he was trying to block on a pig!'

'Who knows? Shakuni was lucky to win it, though. I wonder why he let Yudhi fly clear. He could have placed his *4* promptly and stayed in touch with Yudhi's betting.'

'Yes,' agreed Drupada, 'and I'm rather surprised he didn't ask Yudhi for permission to place a bad bet when he was on the tiger. He is always asking to place bad bets.'

'He's always offering them, too! Perhaps he just wants to get the feel of Yudhi's style.'

Drupada laughed. 'Style! Well, we'll soon see.'

It was now Yudhi's turn to open the attack in the second glaha. His first dice was a *1*. He placed another single bet and threw a *4*, knocking his dice as required. Then a two-bet, followed by a *3*. With the total now on 8, the attack passed to Shakuni, who threw without knocking.

	1	2	3	4	5	6	7	8	9	10
Y										
	⓪₁	⓪₁	⓪₂							
	△₁	△₄	△₃							
	⓪₁									
Sh										
	p1	p5	p8	c						

When Shakuni's dice turned up *4*, Yudhi quickly placed counters in the first and third columns. Shakuni, who had moved with deliberate slowness, held his *4* in the air, and invited Yudhi to protect his other bet in the second column. There was laughter from the more alert members of the audience, who realised that Shakuni could not capture in this column.

Yudhi declined the invitation, and Shakuni placed his dice at the end of the row, making a total of 12. Continuing the attack, Shakuni obtained a *1*, without tapping, and the attack returned to Yudhi. Yudhi promptly tapped twice for a kill, and placed a bet of six.

	1	2	3	4	5	6	7	8	9	10
Y										
	Ô(1)		Ô(1)							
	O(1)	O(1)	O(2)			O(6)				
	△(1)	△(4)	△(3)	△(4)	△(1)					
	O(1)									
Sh										
	p1	p5	p8	c12	c13	pp				

But again Yudhi failed to kill Shakuni: his next dice was a *2*, putting his opponent in on 15. Shakuni aimed for a common, but struck 17 with another *2*, giving Yudhi the dice again.

The hall was very quiet now that the glaha was so close to the limit. Yudhi went for another kill, putting counters down worth twelve, the maximum. As Yudhi passed the dice along his fingers, Shakuni took his hands away from the two blocking counters he had prepared in his camp.

'At least he's on a leopard this time!' whispered Satyaki down to Sanjaya. 'Last time he tried to kill on a cheetah!'

'What does that mean?' asked Dhrita, gruffly.

'Yudhi can ride Kali on either of the *2*s to get his kill,' explained Satyaki. 'Or he can strike 19 with *2*, also for the kill.'

Arjuna and Bhima, along the row from Sanjaya and Dhrita, both gasped in frustration as Yudhi achieved only a *1*.

	1	2	3	4	5	6	7	8	9	10
Y										
	Ô(1)		Ô(1)							
	(1)	(1)	(2)			(6)		(12)		
	/1\	/4\	/3\	/4\	/1\	/2\	/2\	/1\		
	(1)									
Sh										
	p1	p5	p8	c12	c13	pp15	c17	pp18		

As soon as Yudhi's right hand left the *1* which he had just positioned at the end of the row, and before Saha or Nakula could warn their brother, Shakuni threw his next dice into the paddock. The black vertex showed only for an instant before Shakuni retrieved it, flashing the dice into position, riding Kali on the *1* in the fifth column.

'Shiva!' cried Satyaki. 'He's on 21, and he didn't pause to knock — he still holds the attack, Dhrita.'

	1	2	3	4	5	6	7	8	9	10
Y										
	Ô1		Ô1							
	ⓞ1	ⓞ1	ⓞ2		△4	ⓞ6		ⓞ12		
	△1	△4	△3	△4	△1	△2	△2	△1		
	ⓞ1									
Sh										
	p1	p5	p8	c12	c13	pp 15	c17	pp 18	(c21)	

'If he had played the *4* straight, sire,' explained Sanjaya, 'he would now be on 22, which is also common. Which means he would have had to go again, but only one off the limit. He's better off on 21.'

'So he will now aim for a prime, hoping for *2*?' asked Dhrita.

'Yes, sire,' confirmed Sanjaya. 'As you so rightly imply, 21 add 2 is 23, a well-known and much respected prime. But if he only gets a *1*, it will be Yudhi left on 22.'

Shakuni knocked his dice against the table, but did not bet.

'A *2*!' cried Drupada. Bhima hissed loudly from the row below.

'Shiva! He is lucky again.'

'That's winnings of twenty-four he makes this time,' said Drupada, as Dur collected up Yudhi's line. 'What was it last time?'

'Fourteen,' said Satyaki. 'So Yudhi is down thirty-eight already. At this rate Shakuni will bleed him dry by the tenth — that's if he dares to do that to the King of Kings, in front of us all.'

Judging by the look on the twins' faces as Shakuni prepared for the third glaha, the prospect had also crossed their minds.

Shakuni opened the third glaha playing rather faster, picking up the new dice, tapping, placing his betting counters, releasing and positioning the dice all in one continuous movement. But his opening attack halted after three dice, *3*, *4* and *2*, leaving his betting line worth four, and putting Yudhi in on 9.

	1	2	3	4	5	6	7	8	9	10
Y										
	①									
	△3	△4	△2							
	①	①	②							
Sh										
	p3	p7	p9							

Yudhi could not equal his opponent's betting line, but Shakuni tempted him with the offer of a bad bet. Yudhi looked at the twins, and they shook their heads. He knocked just once, and bet the single counter he was allowed. Yudhi threw a *4*. Shakuni had what seemed like plenty of time to place a counter in the first column before Yudhi touched down at the end of the row, achieving his prime on 13.

'Shakuni was laying an egg,' explained Sanjaya to Dhrita. 'That means he was trying to keep ahead of Yudhi's betting line so that Yudhi can't try to kill him.'

'Then why did he offer him a bad bet just now, for that very purpose?'

Sanjaya did not have time to proffer an opinion on this, perhaps confused by the fact that Shakuni was again offering Yudhi a bad bet. Again Yudhi declined, placing a two-counter against his next throw and tapping his dice. As Yudhi prepared to release the dice, Saha whispered something in his ear.

Yudhi threw another *4*, quickly retrieving it from the paddock to attempt the capture of Shakuni's third column bet. But Shakuni was too fast for him. Shakuni's block forced Yudhi to place the *4* at the end of the row, but at least the prime had been secured with 17, so Yudhi's attack continued.

Now Yudhi was able to attempt a kill with a good bet: he tapped twice and bet four. Shakuni had a blocking counter ready in his camp, but he did not need it. Yudhi's dice was a *1*, giving Shakuni the attack on 18.

	1	2	3	4	5	6	7	8	9	10
Y										
	①			①	②	④				
	△3	△4	△2	△4	△4	△1				
	①	①	②							
	Ô1		Ô1							
Sh										
	p3	p7	p9	p13	p17	pp 18				

'Poor Yudhi!' cried Satyaki. 'That's another leopard he's tried and missed.'

'Satyaki,' reminded Drupada, 'against Shakuni the climbing cats hardly have claws.'

'You're right, it's so difficult to ride Kali against Shakuni—'

'Unless he wants you to.'

There was complete silence now as Shakuni took up his attack. He started to shake the dice in his fist. Saha and Nakula both looked anxious, wondering whether he was going to tap it down before throwing it. Shakuni released it into the paddock without first bringing it down to the table. In an instant Shakuni transferred the dice from the paddock to the end of the row, and in the same breath picked up the next dice, touching the table with it on the way to the paddock. By the time the newly placed *2*, at the end of the row, had registered on his opponents, Shakuni had swooped down into the paddock for his next dice, a *4*, and placed it to capture Yudhi's four-bet.

	1	2	3	4	5	6	7	8	9	10
Y										
	①①			①	②	⚠4 ←				
	△3	△4	△2	△4	△4	△1	△2			
	①	①	②							
	Ô1		Ô1							
Sh						④				
	p3	pZ	p9	p13	p17	pp18	c20	(p23)		

Yudhi was in some confusion as Shakuni gestured to the four-bet which he had just removed. Nakula picked up another four-counter and placed it in the sixth column, just above Shakuni's Kali. Dur now removed Yudhi's betting line.

Sanjaya looked to Satyaki for assistance.

'Shakuni was aiming for a prime when he struck the limit,' explained Satyaki, 'so Yudhi lost his entire line... Shakuni was asking Yudhi to replace the bet he captured. So Yudhi lost the captured four, the replaced four and the four along the betting row! That's twelve.'

'And if Shakuni hadn't tapped the dice, it would only have been... ten?'

'That's right: the captured four, plus the value of the killer's line, which was six.'

'Why didn't Shakuni bet some more on that last throw? He could have put down another six.'

'To save time. If he had placed a bet it would have given just enough time for Yudhi — or Nakula, more likely — to prepare a blocking bet against the possible Kali.'

'So now Yudhi is down by fifty. Three glahas in a row!'

'Yes... Shakuni was lucky again.'

'Lucky?'

'Yes,' interceded Drupada. 'He was lucky that Yudhi didn't take up his offer of a bad bet. Shakuni does that too often for comfort.'

Yudhi thought for a while before starting the fourth glaha. Saha and Nakula both tried to advise him, but he wished not to be disturbed, and they sat in silence beside him.

When eventually he opened the glaha, Yudhi was able to place three dice, *1, 2* and *1*, betting the maximum permitted each throw, tapping as required, before ceding the attack on 4. Shakuni's next throw was a *4*, having put up a single bet, but curiously he gave his opponent just enough time to touch down two blocking counters, and so was forced to take the dice to the end of the row, returning the attack on 8. Yudhi ventured a bet of six on his next dice, but knocked only once.

	1	2	3	4	5	6	7	8	9	10
Y										
	Ô(1)		Ô(1)							
	(1)	(1)	(2)		(6)					
	/1\	/2\	/1\	/4\						
	(1)			(1)						
Sh										
	p1	p3	p4	p8	p					

He landed a *4* and, with Shakuni making no attempt to block, made his first capture of the match: Shakuni's starting bet. On Saha's advice Yudhi did not ask Shakuni to replace the starting bet. But now Yudhi knocked twice, and bet twelve. As was customary in such positions where the previous dice had been used as a Kali, leaving the end of the dice row still vacant, the twelve-stack was placed in the row above the previous bet of six.

	1	2	3	4	5	6	7	8	9	10
Y	①(1)									
	Ⓞ(1̂)		Ⓞ(1̂)		⑫					
	Ⓞ(1)	Ⓞ(1)	Ⓞ(2)		⑥					
	△(1)	△(2)	△(1)	△(4)						
	△(4) ← ◯(1)									
Sh										
	p1	p3	p4	p8	(p11) pp					

'Yudhi's on to win double if he gets another *4*,' said Satyaki to Sanjaya and Dhrita. '*If* he gets a *4*, and *if* he is fast enough, which I doubt, he could capture Shakuni's only remaining counter. So Shakuni would have to pay up the value of Yudhi's line for being left with no line himself. And of course, having also been killed, he would have to pay up Yudhi's line for that too!'

Shakuni prepared a blocking bet.

'Shiva! He's missed again!'

Yudhi's *1* left Shakuni with the attack, on 12.

Shakuni now aimed for a common, getting it with a *3*; he bet one and threw another *3*, returning the attack on 18.

As Yudhi checked his betting line, Saha's frown deepened. Saha reluctantly passed Yudhi the two counters he asked for, a sixteen and an eight. Yudhi tapped twice and stacked them on his betting square.

	1	2	3	4	5	6	7	8	9	10
Y	①(1)									
	Ô(1)		Ô(1)		(12)					
	①(1)	①(1)	②(2)		⑥(6)			(24)		
	△1	△2	△1	△4	△1	△3	△3			
	△4	←		①(1)			①(1)			
Sh										
	p1	p3	p4	p8	(p11) pp12	c15	p18	pp		

Nakula covered his face as Yudhi prepared to throw.

'What is it he needs now, a *1*?' asked Dhrita.

'Yes, sire,' confirmed Sanjaya. 'But why is Nakula so displeased?' he asked, without addressing the question to anyone in particular, confident that an answer would be forthcoming.

'Because it is a rather... brave bet, shall we say,' explained Drupada. 'He risks leaving Shakuni on the 20, which is almost as good as a tiger. But that was strange play from Shakuni. Did you see him go for a prime on 15? When does he risk leaving his opponent with the tiger unless he's flying clear?'

'Leave on strong, you're not for long. Still,' mused Satyaki, 'if any one does, Shakuni knows when to break the rules! Perhaps he was protecting his line?'

Yudhi threw the dice into the paddock.

A huge cheer came from Bhima and Arjuna when they saw the white point of the dice, giving Yudhi his first glaha.

'How much does he win?' asked Dhrita.

'There's the single bet he captured...' began Sanjaya, 'and then there's the value of his line, that's forty-eight. Forty-nine, sire! That means he's back with a hundred and ninety-one. He's only down one from the start!'

'That'll teach Shakuni to take liberties with Yudhi,' said Bhima, quite loudly enough for Dur and Shakuni to hear.

'Only a fool treats the King of Kings like a fool!' cried Shalya, who was sitting across the floor on the opposite front row.

Saha and Nakula smiled at their supporters in the audience. Yudhi, on the other hand, looked more worried than ever.

But he succeeded again in the fifth glaha, winning another sixteen from Shakuni. Yudhi was now ahead, and the excitement of the audience was growing audibly, both in the clamour of their encouragement and in the depth of their silence.

In the sixth glaha Yudhi got off to a promising start, quickly increasing his betting line. But when this stood at sixteen, against Shakuni's single starting bet, Shakuni retired, thus losing another sixteen. And his decision to withdraw drew a number of jeers from the audience.

'Only a false champion turns his back!'

'Show your tail to the King of Kings and he'll catch you by it!'

'Where's your stomach, Shakuni? We don't wish to see your rump!'

Dur appeared calm in the face of these insults, indeed calmer than he had been at the start of the match; but Shakuni seemed to be affected by the taunts. At the start of the seventh glaha, before placing his starting bet, he spoke hesitantly to his opponent.

'Perhaps... perhaps the King of Kings would prefer a limit more suited to his status and his good fortune... The gods can scarcely do their work in a glaha of 23. Would you care to rise to 43, Yudhi?'

Before Yudhi could reply, Nakula leant across Saha and grabbed Yudhi's arm.

'*Don't!*' he whispered. 'He can halve you in just one glaha of 43!'

Yudhi stared at his brother for a moment, then at Shakuni. On Yudhi's face now there was no trace of his earlier anxiety.

'Certainly, King Shakuni. Let us rise to 43.' Yudhi looked at Kripa, who agreed, announcing the new limit.

'What do you think, Drupada, is he really losing, or is he letting Yudhi get the upper hand?' Satyaki spoke almost in a whisper, his eyes hardly leaving the dice table. 'Shakuni's had hardly any drives to speak of, nothing more than three or four dice, as far as I can remember. And he's not playing at anything like his usual speed. Perhaps Yudhi's strange play is forcing him to reflect more than usual? I can't believe that he's not up to something, Drupada.'

Drupada chuckled.

'But look at Dur, Drupada, look at Dur. No one can read Shakuni, but Dur, he is much too calm.'

'Mmm... Perhaps he is *too* calm.'

As if he had heard Satyaki, Shakuni started off the seventh glaha with a drive of seven dice: *3, 2, 4, 1, 4, 3, 1*. The first few were played out so fast that Yudhi scarcely had time to blink. With the fifth of these dice, Shakuni captured Yudhi's starting bet. Yudhi was left without a bet in his line, and was asked to pay the value of Shakuni's line at that point, four. Shakuni placed this payment in the fifth column of his camp. Shakuni also requested Yudhi to replace his starting bet.

Shakuni ceded the attack when he struck 23 with his seventh dice while aiming for a common. And Yudhi then secured a common with a *3*, taking the total to 26.

	1	2	3	4	5	6	7	8	9	10
Y										
	①1									
	△4 ←									
	△3	△2	△4	△1	△3	△1	△3			
	①1	①1			②2					
Sh	①1				④4					
	p3	p5	c9	c10	(p19) c22	c23	c26			

Yudhi seemed discouraged from going for a prime at this point, but Saha urged him to bet.

'If he captures your single bet you'll have to pay up again, Yudhi, remember? And you must try to stay in touch with him — you cannot try to kill him unless you stay in touch with his betting line.'

Yudhi was persuaded to bet, but of course he had to aim for a prime in order to do this. He obtained a *1*, and the attack returned to Shakuni on 27. Shakuni bet four and threw another *1*, leaving Yudhi with the attack on 28.

'Did you notice that?' whispered Satyaki to Sanjaya. 'Shakuni was able to risk leaving Yudhi on the tiger, since he's flying clear now.'

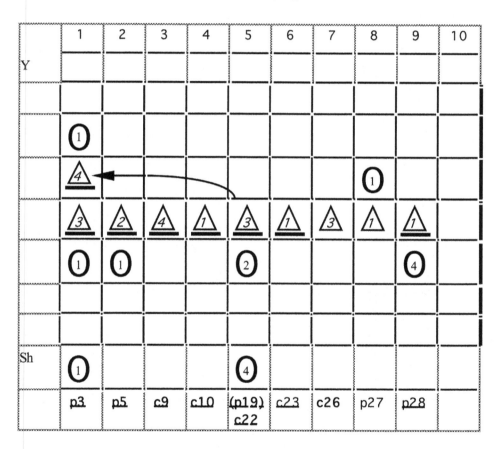

Nakula now advised Yudhi to ask Shakuni for permission to place a bad bet. But Shakuni refused, thus denying his opponent the opportunity of going for a kill at this point. Some factions in the audience expressed their displeasure with Shakuni over this. But Shakuni stood his ground, and Yudhi proceeded to stake a two-counter, the maximum he was allowed. He then threw a *2*, missing the primes and ceding the attack.

'Well, it's a good thing you didn't go for the kill,' consoled Saha.

'If I had gone for a kill,' said Yudhi, 'I might not have got the *2*.'

As Shakuni set down an eight-bet, Nakula hurriedly placed two blocking counters in Yudhi's camp. 'If he gets a *1*,' he whispered, 'get ready to block the *2*s — he likes to strike 37.'

Shakuni delivered his next three dice, a *1* followed by two *4*s, at lightning speed, even managing to place a sixteen-counter with his left hand as he was throwing the last dice. It was remarkable that Yudhi was able to react at all. For when he saw the first *4* follow the *1*, he managed to touch down one of his blocking counters to protect his two-bet in the tenth column, and almost succeeded with the other block. Unfortunately, Shakuni was not interested in the prime at this point — he had thrown this *4* without tapping — instead he touched down with the Kali riding the *3* in the seventh column. This took him to 40. And by the time this had registered with his opponents, he had put down his final bet and dice, capturing on the eighth column to strike the limit.

	1	2	3	4	5	6	7	8	9	10	11	12
Y												
	①									Ô		
	△4 ←						△4	◄4		②◄		
	▲3	▲2	▲4	▲1	▲3	▲1	▲3	▲1	▲1	▲2	▲1	
	①	①			②				④		⑧	
												⑯
Sh	①				④			①				
	p3	p5	c9	c10	(p19) c22	c23	c26	p27	p28	p30	p31	(c40) (p43)

'*That's* more like Shakuni!' cried Satyaki, amid the applause.

'How much did he win that time?' asked Dhrita.

'Two single captures, and four for Yudhi's empty line, plus the thirty-two for striking the limit, thirty-eight in all, my gracious King. Satyaki...' Sanjaya turned round to catch his attention. 'Why didn't he ask Yudhi to replace that last capture?'

'There's no point, Sanjaya, Yudhi still has to pay up to the value of Shakuni's line —'

'Of course — it would only matter if Yudhi's line was greater than Shakuni's. Oh, and Satyaki, that last sixteen counter of Shakuni's, why didn't he put it in the first row?'

'Shakuni is a fastidious player,' interceded Drupada. 'He was respecting the empty bet covering his first *4*. Shakuni is a great respecter of nothing, Sanjaya.'

Meanwhile, Saha was reminding Yudhi to try to stay in touch with Shakuni's betting.

'What could I do?' complained Yudhi. 'He didn't give me a chance.'

'The gods didn't give you a chance,' muttered Nakula, sarcastically.

In the next glaha, the eighth, Yudhi again got off to a bad start, even though he had the opening attack. Shakuni was able to control the glaha, and killed Yudhi on 29, gaining another sixteen. Yudhi was now down twenty-three from his starting level.

'Shakuni's playing faster now,' commented Satyaki. 'I don't think Yudhi can last much longer.'

'Speed isn't everything, Satyaki. The arrow has also to hit the target!'

'But you can see that the man is imposing his authority now, Drupada. His drives are getting longer, for one thing, so he *is* striking his target.'

As if to confirm Satyaki's assessment, Shakuni opened the ninth with a drive of six dice, played out at breathtaking speed: *1, 2, 4, 3, 1, 2*, and accumulating a betting line worth eight. He passed the attack to Yudhi on 13.

'You must bet,' whispered Saha, 'to protect your line — you only have the starting bet!'

'But that risks leaving Shakuni on the tiger,' warned Nakula.

'He must take the risk,' urged Saha.

Yudhi put a single bet on his next dice; this turned up *3*, which would return the attack to Shakuni. Yudhi placed it carefully at the end of the row.

	1	2	3	4	5	6	7	8	9	10
Y										
	(1)						(1)			
	△1	△2	△4	△3	△1	△2	△3			
	(1)	(1)	(2)		(4)					
Sh										
	p1	p3	pZ	c10	p11	c13	p16			

As soon as Yudhi's fingers retreated, Shakuni was in action again. He tapped, placed his bet, threw and retrieved, all in one continuous motion, obtaining and placing a Kali to capture Yudhi's starting bet. Without stopping to ask Yudhi to replace the bet, or placing any bets himself, Shakuni flashed out his next two dice, a *1* followed by a *4*. With this last dice Shakuni captured Yudhi's remaining bet, to strike 29. Shakuni did not ask his opponent to replace this capture either. But he did request a payment of sixteen for the elimination of Yudhi's line. Since Shakuni had aimed for a common, the attack now passed to Yudhi.

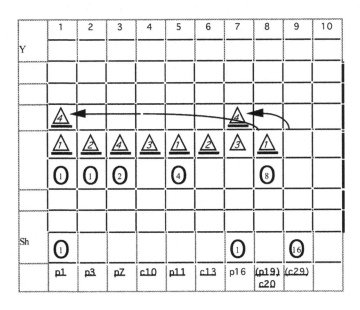

Under pressure to restart his betting line, Yudhi aimed for a prime; but his *1* immediately transferred the attack to his opponent. The seventh glaha, in which Shakuni launched a lethal climb from 30, was fresh in the minds of Nakula and Saha; but they were left helpless again, as Shakuni unleashed his next three dice, *2*, *2* and *4*, without pausing to bet. And yet again Yudhi was obliged to pay sixteen for the loss of his line.

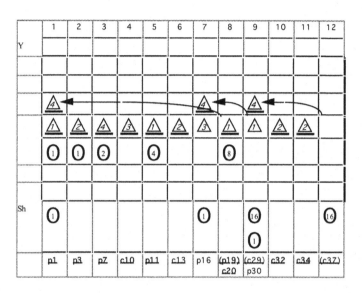

The applause for Shakuni was quick to die down, with the limit now so close. Shakuni had made the capture at the expense of losing the attack, but the pressure on Yudhi now to bet restricted his options. He placed a single bet, and obtained a *2*.

'What's Shakuni going to make of this, I wonder?' muttered Satyaki. 'It's always a tricky one, 39.'

'Nevertheless, he doesn't normally *stop* to think.'

'Better to lose the lion than leave the tiger. Yes, that's what he's doing!'

Shakuni was aiming for a common. His *2*, leaving Yudhi on 41, reduced the auditorium to silence.

Yudhi tapped his dice, but did not place a bet.

'He's going for a prime?' asked Dhrita.

'Yes,' confirmed Drupada. 'He has to — he wouldn't lose any less if he went for a common, since his line is smaller than Shakuni's. And he'd only win the single. He has to go for prime. It also means that if he gets a *1* Shakuni has to go in again.'

'A *3*! He's lost it!' cried Satyaki.

'He's lost it!' echoed Drupada.

'How much has he lost there?' asked Dhrita impatiently, disturbed by the noise of the audience.

'For missing the limit on a prime,' said Sanjaya, 'sixteen — that's Shakuni's line. Then there were the two lost lines, that's two sixteens; and the three captured singles. Fifty-one, I believe, sire. Would you like me to tell these people to be quiet?'

Dhrita ignored Sanjaya's last suggestion with a grunt. 'So what's the state now?'

'The state of play is that he's down seventy-four.'

'How many has he left?'

'I believe that one hundred and ninety-two minus seventy-four is usually found to be the exact equivalent of one hundred and eighteen, sire. Ah! Yudhi's starting off now.'

Yudhi opened the tenth glaha with a drive of five dice, *1, 4, 1, 2, 3*, his longest of the match so far, drawing encouraging applause. But he had been able to place only two bets.

	1	2	3	4	5	6	7	8	9	10
Y										
	⓪₁	⓪₁								
	△₁	△₄	△₁	△₂	△₃					
	⓪₁									
Sh										
	p1	p5	c6	c8	c11					

It was with some difficulty that the twins managed to persuade Yudhi not to go for a prime on the last three of these dice. When his attack was interrupted by the prime, Yudhi could not help casting a reproachful glance at his brothers.

Shakuni went for a common, but his *2* put him on 13, and the attack reverted to Yudhi.

Again the twins restrained Yudhi, and he obtained a *1* and *2* going for a common, to put him on 16, holding the attack.

At this point the twins let him bet. Yudhi wanted to go for a kill straight away, but his brothers urged him to be patient, and reluctantly he yielded to their advice, tapping just once to place the two-bet.

	1	2	3	4	5	6	7	8	9	10
Y										
	⓪₁	⓪₁							⓪₂	
	△₁	△₄	△₁	△₂	△₃	△₂	△₁	△₂		
	⓪₁									
Sh										
	p1	p5	c6	c8	c11	c13	c14	c16	p	

'You have three *1*s to ride on if you get a *4*,' Saha pointed out. 'Go for Shakuni's bet. He'll block that, but you should have time to touch down on one of the others.' As it turned out, Yudhi had the easy route to a prime, getting a *1* to put him on 17.

'Now you can go for a prime again,' whispered Nakula. 'You're only on a leopard, but there are enough *2*s to climb on, and, what's most important, Yudhi, you're flying clear. Play safe on the ground, take risks in the air: if you lose the attack he can't kill you.'

'Then I shall go for a kill —'

'No, Yudhi! No! You're in a strong position, don't waste it. Patience!'

Yudhi restrained himself. With a pair of *2*s, betting on both, Yudhi drove on to relinquish the attack on 21.

When Shakuni now asked to stake a bad bet, Yudhi seemed inclined to allow him to go for the kill; but the twins were firm again, and Shakuni was only permitted to bet one for a prime. He held the attack for the next four dice, *2, 1, 2, 3*, passing it back to Yudhi on 29.

	1	2	3	4	5	6	7	8	9	10	11	12	13	14	15
Y															
	⊙1	⊙1							⊙2	⊙4	⊙8				
	△1	△4	△1	△2	△3	△2	△1	△2	△1	△2	△2	△2	△1	△2	△3
	⊙1											⊙1			
Sh															
	p1	p5	c6	c8	c11	c13	c14	c16	p17	p19	p21	p23	c24	c26	c29

'Now is the time to go for a kill, brother,' said Nakula. He lowered his voice. 'Unfortunately this leopard has no claws — I don't think you're fast enough to ride Kali against Shakuni when there's only the one mount. So, if you do get a *4*, let him block the second column, you just play the dice straight. That will leave him on a pig.'

Yudhi tapped twice and bet sixteen. The kill came immediately with a *2*, to prolonged applause around the hall.

'That was well played by Yudhi,' said Satyaki. 'You see, Drupada, he is surviving.'

'Cautious, that's what he needs to be,' said Sanjaya, half-turning round to address his advice to anyone willing to listen. 'When Shakuni doesn't have the luck, he looks as vulnerable as anyone. And when he doesn't get the Kalis. Did you notice there were no Kalis, Satyaki? Only one *4* among the lot of them. Charvaka's goddess is deserting him!'

'Sanjaya,' said Drupada, 'I have played a variation against Shakuni where no Kalis are allowed at all. I was not left with any impression of his vulnerability.'

The next two glahas, to the surprise of almost everyone, and to the widespread approval of the audience, were also won by Yudhi. What is more, he converted the deficit of forty-two which he inherited at the end of the tenth, to a surplus of thirty-one.

'He threw away the last one, Satyaki. Going for a prime off a cheetah? And when his line was so low?' Drupada shook his head slowly in disbelief.

'He had to protect his starting bet. Yudhi put him under the same pressure he'd applied earlier. What else could he do?'

'What pressure? With his speed there was little danger of losing his line to Yudhi. Soma or Nakula, perhaps. But not Yudhi. I would like to know what he's playing at.'

'I will thank you not to mention Soma in this connection, Drupada. You give Yudhi too little credit. He is tightening up his game. I think Yudhi is unnerving him.'

Drupada laughed derisively. But the thirteenth glaha did little to confirm his view: Shakuni retired from an unfavourable position, losing another thirty-two. Yudhi was now sixty-three up from the start. The applause for him was mixed with cries of contempt at Shakuni's withdrawal.

'Afraid to stay in the fight, King Shakuni?'

'Better get back to 23, Shakuni!'

There was much laughter at this suggestion. Apparently stung by this, Shakuni invited Yudhi to extend the limit to 73.

As the twins anxiously whispered to Yudhi, the laughter died down.

'You see, Satyaki,' said Drupada, gravely, 'he is taking Yudhi for a ride.'

'Pah! Drupada... ' Satyaki paused to look carefully at his friend. 'You're serious, aren't you. You think he really wants to humiliate him?'

'His brothers. You cannot humiliate Yudhi.' Drupada paused. 'Look at Dur. You yourself said earlier how calm he was looking. Look at him now. You would think he was in yoga, if that were possible for him!'

At this moment Kripa raised his hand to the audience, requesting silence.

'I am quite happy to play to 103,' said Yudhi, calmly.

As the audience roared with delight, Nakula put his face in his hands.

46 The net tightens

'Remember, you must try to keep up with his line,' said Saha, speaking softly, so that their opponents across the table could not hear. 'If you let him fly clear he can bleed you dry in just one glaha. Do you realise that, Yudhi?'

'And what is wrong with that, brother? *Someone* has to win. Why should it not be Shakuni, if the gods are willing? If happiness comes into this world, what difference does it make if it is his or mine? The only difference is that his will be much greater. Why should I deprive him of his pleasure, when his loss would bring me so little?'

Saha turned in exasperation to Nakula, and then back to Yudhi.

'Are you telling me now that you want him to *win*, Yudhi?'

'No. As a matter of fact I am rather ashamed to admit that I wish to beat him — though the gods may punish my desire to win, by denying me victory. What I am saying is that if he does beat me I can console myself in the knowledge that I will have given the world more happiness than if I beat him.'

Nakula laughed under his breath, shaking his head with a wry smile.

'Well, Yudhi,' he said, darting his eyes at Shakuni, who was tidying his counters, 'be careful not to take too much *pride* in the happiness your loss would bring Shakuni; lest the gods punish your self-interested desire to please them, and force victory on *you*.'

The fourteenth glaha was so short that it drew laughter from many in the audience: Yudhi scored a very early kill, winning him eight more betting points.

'That's just what they're expecting, Saha, and what Dur wants,' whispered Nakula. 'It's demeaning for the King of Kings to go for early kills like that. And dangerous.'

'What can he do?' responded Saha. 'Are you suggesting he risks Shakuni flying away with it? And where's the danger? At least he's managing to stifle Shakuni. If the great champion can't escape from a corner like this, what is he?'

The same tactic worked again for Yudhi in the fifteenth, where he managed to kill Shakuni on 23, winning sixteen points. And again in the sixteenth glaha, where Yudhi went for another early kill, winning another eight points.

'How much is Yudhi up now, Sanjaya?'

'Ninety-five, sire, ninety-five!'

'Do you think Shakuni can recover?'

'I don't think he's been this much down in the whole tournament.' Sanjaya turned to the experts behind him.

'It is a large margin at this stage,' said Drupada. 'There are only four glahas left for Shakuni to do anything. But it is possible — for him. He still has nearly a hundred points left to play with.'

'But your son is beginning to look very anxious, Dhrita,' added Satyaki. 'The drives just haven't been happening for Shakuni.'

The seventeenth glaha was altogether different. Shakuni got off to a good start. He drove out at speed, establishing his betting line. His third dice, after a *2* and *1*, was a *4*; and though Yudhi touched down first with his blocking counter, Shakuni continued regardless: he proceeded to place his next dice, a *3*, for a common, knowing that Yudhi in his eagerness had picked up his blocking counter before the dice had settled. Kripa waved Yudhi's counter off the grid without interrupting Shakuni. Betting again, Shakuni rode Kali with his next dice on the fourth column. Here Shakuni paused, giving Nakula just enough time to take stock.

Shakuni then rattled off a pair of *3*s, pausing again. He picked up his next dice, preparing to throw it without knocking. Nakula whispered to Yudhi, moving counters into his camp.

	1	2	3	4	5	6	7	8	9	10
Y										
	①			△4➤						
	△2	△1	△4	△3	△3	△3				
	①	①	②		④					
Sh										
	p2	p3	pZ	c10	(p19) c22	c25	c			

The dice fell for *4*. As Shakuni swooped it out of the paddock towards Yudhi's starting bet, Yudhi had picked up a blocking counter, cleanly, this time, but was moving it towards the other end of the dice row, ignoring the danger to his bet. Shakuni's right hand flew past the starting bet, and by the time he had reached the end of the row, Yudhi had touched down in column six, against the clear *3*. Shakuni appeared to be so surprised by Yudhi's decision that he hesitated with the dice in the air, giving Yudhi time now to protect his starting bet. Finally Shakuni placed the *4* to ride Kali against his earlier Kali in column four.

For a moment the crowd held its breath. Then, as Shakuni bowed his head to his opponent, passing him a dice for his attack, the audience broke into applause.

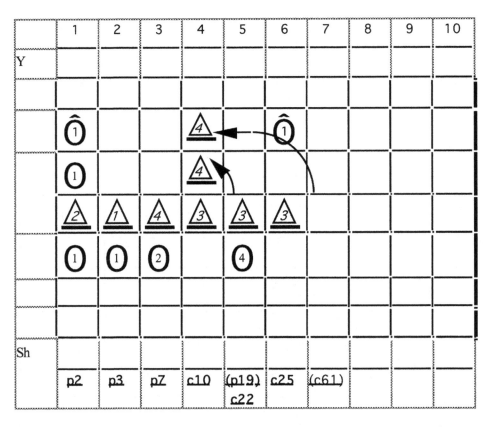

'I think he tried to bluff Yudhi, and failed,' suggested Satyaki. 'I think he wanted all along to ride Kali on the last *3* — that was the only way he could get a common to continue the attack. He hoped Yudhi would protect his starting bet. But Yudhi forced him onto a prime. Well, well, who would think Shakuni would be caught out like that?'

'He was doubling his bluff, you idiot,' said Drupada. 'He is happier to leave Yudhi on 61 than if he had captured the bet!'

'But he would have emptied Yudhi's line —'

'Rice grains, Satyaki, rice grains. Shakuni is after a big kill. Gandhari...' Drupada called over to Shakuni's sister. 'Don't you think Shakuni was bluffing?'

'Who knows?' she replied. '*I* could never tell. He's put Yudhi up on a common patch, though. And also, remember that my brother likes to have clear *1*s around to climb on; perhaps he's hoping Yudhi will provide him?'

'What did I tell you, Satyaki?'

'Pah! Fantasy...'

Just then Yudhi threw his next dice, without knocking. It was a *2*, putting him on 63. He looked at his betting line, and prepared to bet.

'It's only a cheetah!' whispered Saha. 'Why don't you retire, Yudhi... you can afford to retire early, Shakuni won't be able to catch you up!'

'You think that is the way for a King of Kings to win a dice match?' said Yudhi.

'That's just what they are tempting him to do, Saha,' interjected Nakula angrily. 'It may win him the match, but he will lose all respect! You're right, Yudhi... but don't bet just yet, go for the common.'

Yudhi threw his next dice without tapping. It was a *1*.

'That's better according to you, isn't it?' said Yudhi. '64 is a leopard, no? I'll bet —'

'Wait!' whispered Saha.

'Wait? Weren't you telling me to keep up with his betting line. How else can I get more counters on my line?'

'Yudhi,' interrupted Shakuni, softly, so that the front rows had to strain to catch his words. 'I see that not only are you gracious enough not to retire, you are also brave enough to go for a prime. The least I can do, since I would be at your mercy if you chose to retire in the remaining glahas, the least I can do is to offer you a bad bet. Place the five you need to equal my line, and go for a kill if you wish.'

'Wait, Yudhi, there's a tiger coming up! If you miss he'll probably get onto it!'

Yudhi ignored Nakula's advice, knocked twice, placed two betting counters down to make the five, and threw his dice. A burst of applause exploded round the auditorium as he made a *3* to strike 67 and win the glaha. When the audience realised that Yudhi was now up over a hundred on his starting level, they rose to give him an ovation.

'Shakuni's as calm as a cobra, Satyaki!'

'But so is Yudhi — look, he seems almost to be enjoying himself. Up by a hundred and three! And Dur is beginning to sweat, look at the shine on him!'

'Still, Shakuni is cool as a cobra,' repeated Drupada.

'Well, Drupada, I'm waiting for him to bite...'

The audience loudly encouraged Yudhi as he opened the attack at the start of the eighteenth. But when after two *1*s Yudhi's third dice was a *4*, the noise quickly evaporated. Like two cobras, Shakuni's hands moved to place his blocking counters.

	1	2	3	4	5	6	7	8	9	10
Y										
	①₁	①₁	②₂							
	△₁	△₁	△₄							
	①₁									
	Ô₁	Ô₁								
Sh										
	p1	p2	p6							

Shakuni now reeled his bets and dice out before his opponents could react. Kripa had to remind Yudhi to take his hands off the counters in his camp between the throws, otherwise he would not be able to permit any blocks he might attempt. When Shakuni relinquished the attack on his sixth throw he was already in a commanding position, having placed further bets of three, six, twelve and twenty. He had thrown *4, 4, 3, 1, 4, 1*. The first *4* he played straight, the other two to ride Kali, capturing on the second and third columns.

	1	2	3	4	5	6	7	8	9	10
Y										
	(1)	△4	△4							
	△1	△1	△4	△4	△3	△1	△1			
	(1)				(3)	(6)	(12)			
	(1)	(1)					(20)			
Sh		(1)	(2)							
	p1	p2	p6	c10	(p13) c16	p17	(p29) p30			

'Look at that, Drupada! Look at that!'

'Now do you believe me? The fangs are out, Satyaki!'

Sanjaya turned to his neighbours for assistance. 'Why didn't he place more down on that last bet? He could have put twenty-four.' But Satyaki and Drupada were too engrossed with the events at the table to reply. Shakuni was now offering Yudhi a chance to go for a kill by placing a bad bet.

'What's going on, Sanjaya?'

'One moment, please, sire...'

Yudhi was still considering Shakuni's offer.

'You might as well go for it, Yudhi,' advised Nakula.

'Either that or retire,' added Saha. 'If you want to stay in it you must bet in any case to protect your line,' added Saha.

Yudhi set down a stack of forty-three, after tapping twice.

'Is he going for a kill, Sanjaya?'

'Sssh... Yes, sire... Ah! He's missed it! He had to get a *1* to strike 31, but he got a *4*, and Shakuni blocked with a single counter at the end of the row... Why

did he do that? Why did Shakuni bother to block? Yudhi was on one of those...
a pig, wasn't he?'

'Yudhi couldn't have captured on 30, you're right,' said Satyaki. 'No,
Shakuni was laying an egg. You watch, in a moment he'll fly clear again.'

'Is it Shakuni to play, Sanjaya?'

'Yes, sire, he's on 34, and he's betting, you heard the one tap... Kripa is
signalling a bet of forty-four!... How is that possible? Shakuni only had eighty-
nine points at the beginning of this glaha? He's now got eighty-nine down on
the grid — forty-five and forty-four, and yet he's got three in his camp?'

'Don't forget he's captured three,' observed Drupada.

'Are you saying that Shakuni has only three counters left, Sanjaya?' asked
Dhrita.

'Yes, sire, sssh! Shakuni's thrown a *1*. Yudhi has the attack now, sire, he's
on 35. He's asking Shakuni if he can place another bad bet, sire, he wants to try
for a kill again. Shakuni is refusing!'

'Refusing?'

'Yes, Dhrita,' explained Satyaki. 'Yudhi's on a leopard. Shakuni won't give
an opponent the chance to kill from a leopard.'

'I've seen him offer on a leopard,' contradicted Drupada. 'But only when
he could block the Kali to take the claws off: in this position he hasn't enough
counters left to block all the mounts in the row! If Yudhi were to get a *4*, he
would have all the time in the world to kill Shakuni.'

'You're right!' said Satyaki, impressed with Drupada's reasoning.

'What's going on, Sanjaya?' interrupted Dhrita impatiently.

'Yudhi's betting another forty-four — that's the most he can do as a good
bet. He'd only need one more to go for the kill! So *that's* why Shakuni laid the
egg!'

'And you see now why Shakuni only placed twenty down that time?' said
Satyaki. 'I think you asked us earlier, Sanjaya — well, he knew he was running
low. Shakuni always tries to keep at least a couple of singles to block with.
That's also why he only bet forty-four on his last bet: he could have bet forty-
five, but that would have left him unable to block properly. Even as it is he's
cutting it *very* fine!'

'Watch this now!' interrupted Drupada. 'With a Kali next dice he can capture
Yudhi's bet...'

'What's that?' asked Dhrita, agitated.

'Shakuni's got the attack again, sire,' explained Sanjaya. 'He's on 38: Yudhi
has just got *3* from his last throw, leaving Shakuni in on 38. Shakuni's not
tapping —'

'*Shiva*!'

'Oh, dear! Look at that! This man's a cobra! Did you see Yudhi foul that last block, and Shakuni *still* made the capture! Dhrita, Shakuni's just captured Yudhi's last bet, the forty-four! Well, well, he's got counters to play with now!'

Shakuni's Kali had come at the end of a rapid sequence of four dice: *1*, *3*, *2*, and *4*.

The tension was now very evident on the faces of Saha and Nakula; but Yudhi was still quite serene as he prepared to throw his next dice. Without tapping, he landed a *2* to put himself on 55.

'It would be no disgrace to retire in this position, Yudhi,' urged Nakula.

'But he can still keep in touch with Shakuni's line,' Saha pointed out. 'Why give up? Shakuni is only just clear.'

Shakuni, seeing the indecision of his opponents, offered Yudhi a bad bet.

'He's crazy!' exclaimed Satyaki. 'He's flying clear by just one, and now he's giving Yudhi a chance to catch up, not to mention to *kill*!'

'I think he wants to lure Yudhi into leaving him the tiger,' suggested Drupada. 'Then he'll be in for the kill himself. I just hope Yudhi washed his feet before saying his prayers this morning. He seems to be following in Nala's footsteps.'

'Two taps? Is Yudhi taking the bad bet?' asked Dhrita.

'Yes, sire. He's putting down forty... yes, forty-five. Both their lines stand at eighty-nine now, sire!'

This time, when Yudhi missed the kill with a *3*, leaving his opponent on 58, Saha instantly placed some counters ready by the grid. As Saha whispered feverishly to Yudhi, Shakuni knocked his dice once and placed a stack of forty-three.

'Now Shakuni's got a line of a hundred and thirty-two, sire!' cried Sanjaya. 'He's only got four left off the grid, and he's not even going for the kill —'

The moment Yudhi saw the black vertex of Shakuni's next dice, he was ready, darting to protect his last stack at the end of the line. Since the dice row was now rather long, Shakuni did not seem to care for his chances of reaching there first: his hand had to travel all the distance from the paddock, whereas the blocking counter prepared in Yudhi's camp was already at that end of the row. Instead, Shakuni captured Yudhi's starting bet, reaching 61; and since he had aimed for a prime, Shakuni was able to continue his drive almost without a pause, to flash out two more dice, a *1* and another *4*. Now he touched down this last dice unopposed, making the big capture at the end of the row: the twins had not had time to position another counter for Yudhi to block with.

'Look at that, Sanjaya!' cried Drupada. 'Yudhi need hardly have gone to the trouble to block the first Kali! Shakuni has taken his original stack *and* the blocking counter!'

Yudhi smiled at Shakuni in appreciation. Shakuni acknowledged his opponent's gesture with a little nod.

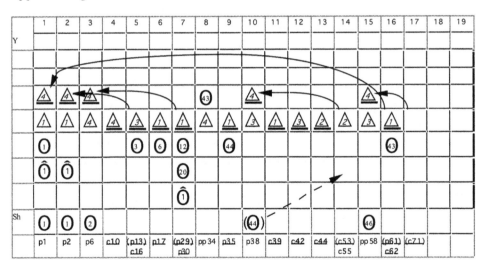

It was now Yudhi's turn, on 71. He immediately asked Shakuni if he could place another bad bet.

Nakula remonstrated with Yudhi. 'It's too expensive now. All your lead can disappear in one capture!'

'But he could finish the match with one dice,' Saha pointed out.

As it happened Shakuni denied his opponent's request. And Nakula succeeded in convincing his brothers that Yudhi should merely protect his vulnerable line with a single bet rather than place the maximum allowed. Accordingly Yudhi knocked just once, and placed a single counter. His *1* now gave Shakuni the attack again, on 72.

Shakuni tapped once and placed another large bet, forty-four; but his *2* skipped over the prime at 73 to return the attack to Yudhi on 74.

'How much has Shakuni got on his line now, Sanjaya?'

'His line is worth a hundred and seventy-six. Would you believe that, sire? He has only seven off the grid.'

'And Yudhi?'

'He's got forty-four on his line, and a hundred and fifty-seven off the grid.'

'Oh, so he still has quite a bit in reserve.'

'Oh yes, sire. His material at this moment is still greater than Shakuni's.'

In the mean time Yudhi had achieved a common with a *1*. Immediately Shakuni offered him a bad bet, to the consternation of the crowd.

'The man is mad!' exclaimed Satyaki.

'What?' asked Dhrita. 'What was that?'

'Not at all, Satyaki,' contradicted Drupada. 'The 75 is a cheetah. He is not mad, merely courageous.'

Saha and Nakula were arguing with each other, but Yudhi silenced them, and tapped twice for the kill.

'Sanjaya!'

'Sire, yes... yes, Yudhi is accepting Shakuni's offer to place the bad bet!'

'Anyone who earlier called Shakuni a coward,' continued Drupada, 'will be swallowing their tongue. He's playing a dangerous game. Gandhari!' Drupada caught the queen's attention. 'Your brother's courage is equal to his skill!'

'And what about Yudhi?' Sanjaya ventured. 'No one can accuse *him* of lacking courage!'

'What does he need?' asked Dhrita, urgently. 'Sanjaya, how much does Yudhi need to place?'

'But Yudhi has a lot less to lose, Sanjaya,' said Drupada, oblivious to Dhrita's frustration. 'Look at him, look at the smile on his face! I think Yudhi's the only one out there enjoying himself!'

Dhrita reached out and grabbed Sanjaya.

'Yes, sire... Do you realise, sire, he's putting down a stack of... *a hundred and thirty-two*, sire! He *has* to get a *4*. If he gets it Shakuni is finished!'

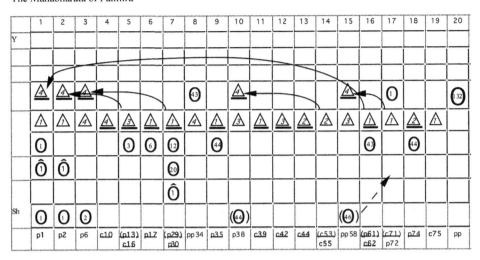

'I wouldn't put it past Yudhi to bleed Shakuni dry if he kills him,' said Satyaki. 'Shakuni would have seven points left, to last him two more glahas! He will either be bled or disgraced.'

At the table Nakula was warning Yudhi:

'If you miss, then watch it if he strikes 77 — he can capture your forty-three bet from there. If you get a *1* you will leave him on 76: a Kali then will allow him to capture your last bet. You *must* block that one, Yudhi!'

Satyaki had been explaining much the same to Sanjaya.

'How does he see so quickly where to put the Kali?' wondered Sanjaya. 'He must know all the ways by heart'

'Oh indeed, Sanjaya —'

'He doesn't need to commit them to memory...' interrupted Queen Gandhari. 'The early primes of course he does know by heart — not even the legendary Rituparna of Ayodha could *predict* the next prime: one can tell if a large number is even or odd as quickly as one can a small number. But it gets harder and harder to tell if a number is prime. Not even Rituparna had a short cut. So of course, the primes my brother does commit to memory. But that is all. Dhrita!' She turned briefly to her husband, who had begun to complain. 'Do calm yourself, Yudhi hasn't thrown the wretched dice yet!' She resumed her account to Satyaki and Drupada. 'I also thought, years ago when I often used to play my brother, that he was memorising the Kali possibilities for each number. Not according to him. I didn't believe him, so I proposed that we should play a game in which the *3* was the Kali, multiplying by 3, you understand —'

'That is a variation I have not played,' interrupted Drupada. 'Yes... so all the even numbers would be pigs, instead of all the multiples of three. I beg your pardon, Queen Gandhari — how did your little brother fare with this variation?'

'There was very little visible difference in his speed of play. He seemed just as sure-footed, as though he knew all these new climbs by heart.'

'Just think,' speculated Drupada, 'if *1* were the Kali... Why, all the common numbers would be pigs!'

'Yes,' said Gandhari, 'we played that variation as well, but it was —'

'*Aaagh*!'

'*Shiva*! A *1*! Only a *1*! Poor Yudhi!'

'It was only a cheetah, Satyaki. What do you expect? Look at this!...'

As Shakuni now flew into attack, on 76, Nakula quickly moved some counters in readiness. But in his eagerness Yudhi picked one of them too soon, and as Kripa waved him back, Shakuni struck again: after a *1* and *3*, Shakuni had thrown a *4*, making the capture with the Kali to strike 83. Shakuni had not aimed for a prime, so the attack returned to Yudhi.

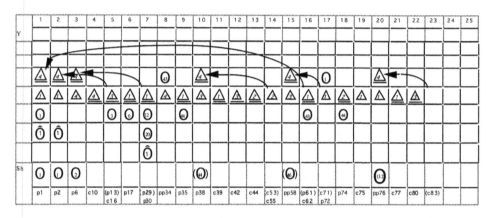

Nakula put his head in his hands, but Yudhi pressed on with his turn, without stopping to linger on his huge loss. He went for a common, and landed a *4* in the paddock.

'Quick!' cried Saha, 'his forty-four!'

Shakuni had picked up a blocking counter and appeared rather surprised to have so much time; he held it in mid-air, evidently waiting to see what Yudhi would do.

'That's what he wants you to do, Yudhi!' whispered Nakula. 'If you capture you lose the attack. You'll leave him with a common drive. Play it straight, Yudhi.'

When Shakuni saw Yudhi take the dice over to the end of the row, he lowered his blocking bet back into his camp. By playing the *4* straight, Yudhi retained the attack on 87.

'See there,' said Satyaki, 'Shakuni was definitely luring him to make the capture. He never was going to block! What's he doing now?' Satyaki leant forward to try to catch the voices at the table.

Yudhi was asking Shakuni if he could place a bad bet to try for the kill. Nakula raised his head in amazement, but said nothing. Saha, too, was struck dumb.

'Shiva!' whispered Satyaki. 'The 87 is only a cheetah!'

'My dear Yudhi,' said Shakuni, softly, 'I would be surprised if you had more than twenty-five points remaining at your disposal.'

Yudhi checked. 'You are right... I have exactly twenty-five. And how much would I need for the bad bet... Your line hasn't changed... I see, I would again have to place a hundred and thirty-two to equal you...'

There was not a sound from the audience.

'May I make a suggestion, King Yudhi-sthira?' asked Shakuni, now in a firmer tone, audible to the front rows of the auditorium. 'I see the disappointment on your face, and salute it as a sign of courage. It is not fitting that I should deny the King of Kings such an opportunity of despatching his opponent, when your energies are still in full flight. I will let you try to kill me. You may place just one of your remaining counters, but on the understanding that it represents something of an appropriate value.'

'Certainly,' said Yudhi, silencing his protesting brothers with a wave. 'I cannot refuse the generosity of your own courage, King Shakuni. What would you have in mind?'

As Shakuni hesitated, Dur made a suggestion.

'The full bet, Yudhi, would be over ten thousand head of cattle...'

'As much as that?' queried Yudhi.

'You have in your treasury,' continued Dur, 'a store of gold pieces — I remember your brothers showing them to me. I'm sure that this would be acceptable to King Shakuni, if you were to stake those on your kill.'

'Certainly. So I place just one counter...' Yudhi put it down on the twenty-fourth column of the grid, awaiting his next dice. 'This represents the chests of gold.' Yudhi looked up to make sure that Kripa understood and consented. Kripa hesitated, glancing quickly around the auditorium. Yudhi called him. 'My Lord Kripa?...'

Kripa's face showed clearly his resistance to this development. He signalled to Drona to step down, and conferred with him.

'They're not going to like it,' whispered Satyaki. 'It is stretching the rules, surely! Still, when it comes to rules... to the designs of men constructed, by the designs of men corrupted...'

'They can hardly claim it is against the rules,' observed Drupada, 'when they so readily allowed *your* change of stake, Satyaki. In any case, it is to the designs of brahmanas they are constructed, through the designs of kshatriyas corrupted... evidently, however,' he added with a little chuckle, 'at the expense of one particular kshatriya that I know.'

'Thank you for reminding me, Drupada. May I remind you of a brahmana who broke the rules at *your* expense? But all the more reason,' continued Satyaki, 'why I can't see Drona daring in your presence to enforce any rules.'

'In any case, what can they do?' muttered Drupada. 'How could they deny the King of Kings a chance of victory? I have to say, though, that this is a dangerous game for Shakuni, raising the stakes in this manner — if your example is anything to go by...'

Satyaki glared at Drupada.

'Look!' exclaimed Drupada. 'They've decided...'

Kripa, his face grave and drawn, gave his assent to the proposed stake.

'Well, Dhrita,' explained Drupada, 'nothing but a 2 will serve Yudhi...'

Yudhi promptly threw his dice. It fell for *3*.

By the time the audience, and Yudhi, could react, Shakuni had dashed out three more dice: *1, 1, 4*. With the last of these Shakuni captured Yudhi's most recent stake.

1	2	3	4	5	6	7	8	9	10	11	12	13	14	15	16	17	18	19	20	21	22	23	24	25	26	27
p1	p2	p6	c10	[p13) c16	p17	[p29) p30	pp34	p35	p38	c39	c42	c44	(c53) c55	pp58	(p61) c62	(c71) p72	p74	c75	pp76	c77	c80	(c83) c87	pp90	c91	c92	(c101)

'Sanjaya!'

'Sire, Shakuni has captured the... the gold. He is on 101. Is *that* a prime?... Yes. But he didn't tap, so Yudhi has the attack.'

'The limit is still 103, isn't it?'

'As far as I know, sire.'

'And it is Yudhi's turn?'

'Yes. *No!*'

'What?'

To everyone's amazement, Shakuni had just chosen that moment to retire from the glaha.

'I cannot believe this! Will Shiva tell us what the man is playing at?'

'Sanjaya,' asked Drupada, urgently, 'have you kept the account?'

'Yes. At least, until the retirement. What is it he has to pay up now?'

'Shakuni retired out of turn,' said Drupada. 'He loses his whole line! How much did he have in his line at the end, was it still a hundred and seventy-six?'

'Yes,' confirmed Sanjaya. 'He had a hundred and seventy-six on his line, which he now loses... but a hundred and thirty-nine available off the grid; plus the one counter which stood for the gold. So he will go into the next glaha with that.'

'And Yudhi had twenty-five — no, twenty-four off the grid. He retains what was on his line —'

'Forty-four,' reckoned Sanjaya.

'Shakuni left him forty-four on his line? That was generous.'

'So that's sixty-eight plus the hundred and seventy-six he wins off Shakuni. Two-four-four,' declared Sanjaya.

'Yudhi goes in with two hundred and forty-four? Thank you, Sanjaya. Well Satyaki, isn't that extraordinary?'

'Look at your poor sons-in-law, Drupada.' Satyaki was referring to Arjuna and Bhima, who were both sitting motionless, staring down at the dice table in disbelief.

'I'm not surprised, Satyaki. Have you seen the gold in Indraprastha? It is worth considerably more than Shakuni's line, I can tell you. Yes, maybe he's not gone mad. But it's a very dangerous game Shakuni's playing. Yudhi may stick in the cobra's throat.'

'You think so?' Satyaki pointed at the table. 'Look at Dur now! From the look on his face he's expecting Yudhi to go down like a new-born mouse! Remember, in spite of retiring, Shakuni gained fifty-one points out of that glaha! No! More — fifty ordinary points and one point representing Yudhi's gold! And that's in spite of throwing away his line!'

At that moment Yudhi raised his hand, quickly bringing the hall down to a simmer. But it was Kripa who spoke.

'For this nineteenth glaha King Shakuni is willing to return the gold of Indraprastha to the table.' Kripa pointed to the single counter in position at the start of Shakuni's betting row. 'For his part King Yudhi-sthira has agreed to match this starting bet by staking his sacred chariot and the eight pure-white horses which draw it.' Kripa indicated Yudhi's starting counter. 'At Prince Dur-yodhana's suggestion, and with King Yudhi-sthira's consent, the worth of any unit counter now brought onto the grid is revalued accordingly. Any unused counters will be valued at the original rate of a hundred head of cattle for every unit point.'

'What? No wonder the twins are looking like death!' whispered Satyaki.

'Shakuni opens,' announced Kripa.

'That chariot is solid gold!' whispered Sanjaya.

'Yudhi had better protect it well, then,' said Drupada.

Shakuni opened with the longest drive of the match. Apart from his starting bet, he placed no bets at all, though he did occasionally tap for a prime. His first two dice were a *2* and a *1*. His third dice was a *4*. But Yudhi, realising that it was not possible to make a Kali prime when the line stood at 3, resisted the temptation to block; which was fortunate for him, since if he had raised the counter he would have probably fouled the block which he needed against Shakuni's next dice, also a *4*. Yudhi's excellent block against this dice, to protect his starting bet, hardly interrupted his opponent's flow: Shakuni had aimed for a common, and achieved it riding Kali.

Shakuni's next two dice, *3* and *2*, put him on 15. Then, aiming again for a common, another *4* fell to him. Although as before it was impossible for Shakuni to capture at this point, Yudhi reacted at the sight of the black point. Shakuni could not achieve his common by placing the *4* at the end of the row; but there were too many clear columns for Yudhi to stop Shakuni riding Kali to keep his attack. Yudhi had only just replaced his blocking counter, in response to Kripa's gesture, when he grabbed it again for another excellent block against Shakuni's tenth dice, which was swooping down onto Yudhi's sacred chariot. But again Shakuni rode Kali for a common to continue his attack, hardly pausing for breath.

Two dice later Yudhi succumbed to his opponent's speed, losing both his chariot and the two blocking counters above it. Shakuni had thrown first a *3*, then a *4* to make the capture.

	1	2	3	4	5	6	7	8	9	10	11	12
Y												
	△4	△4			△4		△4					
	△2	△1	△4	△3	△2	△3	△1	△3				
	① [gold]											
Sh	③ [sacred chariot] [?] [?]											
	p2	p3	pZ	(c10) p13	c15	(c21) c24	c25	(c28) p31	(c37)			

Against the stunned silence could clearly be heard Bhima's voice:

'Where are these Kali dice coming from?'

'Who made these dice?' responded Shalya, from across the floor.

Drupada looked at Satyaki, bemused. 'The *4*s certainly seem to be coming now for Shakuni.'

'Sanjaya, what has Shakuni gained now?' asked Dhrita.

'They're sorting it out at the moment, sire. It's Yudhi's attack now, but they must settle what his blocking bets meant before they can continue with the glaha... Listen, we can hear...'

The discussion at the table was certainly audible to the lower rows.

'Our cousin is right,' Yudhi was saying, 'the blocking counters must have parity with the starting counters. What do you propose, Dur?'

'I remember seeing pearls decked with gold — one chest of them, I think.'

'Certainly. And the other counter?'

'Oh? Ah, yes, the other counter... You have a store of copper, iron and other common metals... in your treasury —'

'I see that your visit made a very accurate impression on you, cousin.' Yudhi glanced towards Arjuna and Bhima in the auditorium. 'Let my pearls and my store of metals stand on those two counters. Is that satisfactory, King Shakuni?'

'Perfectly satisfactory, of itself...' Shakuni hesitated for a moment. 'There is, I am somewhat reluctant to mention, the question of your line being voided.'

'Of course.' Yudhi turned to the twins. 'Why did you not remind me?' He looked down at the grid. 'So, you require three more counters —'

'No, no, my dear. You need only pay the value of my line. Just the one counter.'

Yudhi looked at Dur with expectation.

'You have... you have some elephants...'

Yudhi picked up a counter and passed it to Dur. 'My elephants.' Saha and Nakula watched in numbed silence.

'My dear, you will also need to replace your bet. I am quite sure, under the circumstances,' Shakuni glanced briefly at Dur, 'that a single counter will be quite acceptable to us.'

'A single counter...' Again Yudhi looked to Dur for inspiration.

'Your... cattle, Yudhi?'

'You mean *all* of them? Very well. Please, Saha,' — Yudhi turned to his brother — 'round up my cattle.'

For an instant Saha looked dazed, as though waking from a dream. Then, realising what Yudhi meant, he placed a counter on Yudhi's starting column, above the Kali dice.

'Well, King Shakuni,' continued Yudhi, 'I should like to go for a kill now, if I may. What would you regard as an appropriate stake?'

Shakuni and Dur conferred inaudibly.

'Sanjaya, what exactly has Shakuni acquired from this?' asked Dhrita.

'It's amazing,' observed Satyaki, drawing Sanjaya's attention away from Dhrita, 'how he always seems to be able to leave Yudhi on a cheetah! Anything less, and they wouldn't be tempted. Anything more, and it would be too dangerous for Shakuni.'

'But surely that means that one of these times his luck will run out!' suggested Sanjaya. 'It must be nearly empty as it is.'

'The dice have no memory, Sanjaya. Luck refreshes itself at every throw.'

'That can't be so, Satyaki,' objected Sanjaya. 'Why, if the dice had no memory, they would repeat themselves again and again like —'

'Sanjaya,' interrupted Dhrita, plaintively, 'what has he got now?'

'— like a blind doddering old man,' Sanjaya went on. 'I'll tell you in a moment, sire. I'm working it out —'

'I may be blind and somewhat older than you, Sanjaya, but I am not yet doddering —'

'No, but you do sometimes repeat yourself, with respect, sire, like a dice without memory, who forgets that the world has changed in between the throws, and lands again and again the same... But Satyaki, if the dice didn't have a memory,' continued Sanjaya, returning to the issue, 'why would the players insist on never throwing the same dice twice?'

'That insistence is pure stupidity,' interjected Drupada. 'It is just a custom of the brahmanas... But I think I see what you mean, Sanjaya... The dice do perhaps have a memory, but not regarding anything which might interest us. Butterflies perhaps have a memory for flowers, but if Satyaki and myself were to wager his remaining cattle — have you any? — on a bet as to which flower a butterfly would choose, it would flutter through its memories quite oblivious of our wager. Their aim to us seems aimless.'

'But even if the dice had less memory than a butterfly,' remarked Gandhari, who had been listening with interest, 'in their forgetfulness they would wander aimlessly into our net. If you know where to look, you will find them. Dhrita, you wanted to know the state of play?'

'Sanjaya will tell me, thank you, Gandhari, you need not trouble yourself, Sanjaya will see to it... *Sanjaya?*'

'I've completely forgotten, sire, my memory —'

'How can you jest at a time like this?' said Dhrita angrily.

'Off the grid,' reported Sanjaya, 'Shakuni has a hundred and thirty-nine ordinary points. He's also got, off the grid, four counters which represent Yudhi's sacred chariot, his pearls, his metals and his elephants. And he still has only the one counter on the grid, his starting bet, representing Yudhi's gold. I suppose you want to know what Yudhi has? Off the grid he's left with two hundred and thirty-nine in points. On the grid he has the one counter, representing his cattle — that was the replacement for the capture. Wait... he's putting more down...'

Kripa now explained the position:

'King Yudhi-sthira has been generously permitted by his opponent to attempt a kill. Moreover, King Shakuni has made an unprecedented offer, to replace some of the recently captured material onto the grid, thus graciously allowing Yudhi the chance of regaining it with his kill. To this end, Shakuni is bringing back onto his line a stack of three counters, representing the sacred chariot, the pearls and the metals; these are to be surrendered with his starting bet should Yudhi achieve the kill.'

Shakuni positioned his stack of three at the end of the betting row, beneath the vacant square awaiting Yudhi's next dice.

'Against these three counters,' continued Kripa, 'Yudhi is now to place three commensurate counters, making up his bet for the kill. This will bring Yudhi's line to four counters; in return for which Shakuni is prepared in the event of the kill to resign his four counters, that's to say, the gold, the sacred chariot, the pearls and the metals —'

'What about the elephants?' interrupted Saha.

'No, Saha, my line now contains only four counters,' Yudhi reminded him. 'I can expect only four counters back. Shakuni — or should I say, Dur — has chosen to retain my elephants.'

'The three new counters which have been set down by Yudhi against his next dice,' continued Kripa, 'represent material which will now be determined...'

'Prince Dur-yodhana,' began Yudhi, 'please tell me what I have just bet.'

'One counter could be your horses, perhaps?'

Yudhi nodded to Kripa so that he could record the valuation.

'Another could be your chariots.'

Yudhi nodded again to Kripa.

'The third could be...' Dur's voice faltered slightly. 'Arjuna and Bhima showed me their horses...'

'Arjuna and Bhima's horses?...' Yudhi glanced absently at the stack of three counters.

Arjuna and Bhima looked angrily down at Dur from their seat. After a moment's uneasy silence, Arjuna declared, but without taking his eyes off Dur, 'What is mine is yours, brother.' Bhima, not able to find his voice, nodded to Yudhi.

'King Yudhi-sthira,' said Kripa, 'in that case you may throw for a kill.'

Kripa resumed his position by the paddock.

'Sanjaya?' whispered Dhrita.

'Shakuni has a hundred and forty off the grid, one of which represents the elephants; on the grid his line consists of four counters: his starting bet, which is the gold he won in the previous glaha, and the three representing the sacred chariot, the pearls and the metals. Yudhi now has two hundred and thirty-six off the grid, and four in his line: his cattle — that was to replace his captured starting bet — and the three on his next dice: his horses, his chariots, and the horses of Arjuna and Bhima. So, if Yudhi kills him, he gets back everything except the elephants.'

'Why the elephants?'

'*I* don't know, sire!'

Satyaki leaned over and nudged Sanjaya.

'Oh, yes, sire, you remember that Yudhi is on 37. He needs a *4* to strike 41.'

'That's his only chance?'

'Yes, sire, a *4*.'

'And there have been enough of those recently,' added Satyaki.

Yudhi threw his dice. It was a *1*.

Bhima cried out, slamming his fist against his seat. Kripa held up his arms in an attempt to restore quiet.

Shakuni, ignoring the commotion, prepared his next attack, and Yudhi looked to Saha for more blocking counters.

'But what are you going to stake now, brother?' said Saha.

Dur urged his uncle to start his attack, but the audience were not yet quiet. Shakuni waited until Kripa was in position again, and then released his dice, without knocking, into the paddock. He obtained a *2*, placing it as quickly as if it had been a Kali, and then with no discernible pause he tapped his next dice, at the same time laying a counter with his left hand.

When Yudhi saw the black tip of the next dice, he went to block; but Nakula and Saha had perhaps lost their concentration; or, as likely, were numbed into inaction by the hidden weight of the ivory tokens; for there were no blocking counters prepared for him. Yudhi lost valuable time fetching a counter himself from Saha's pile.

Kripa pronounced with some regret that Yudhi's block hit the table after Shakuni's dice. Dur moved the captured counters into Shakuni's camp.

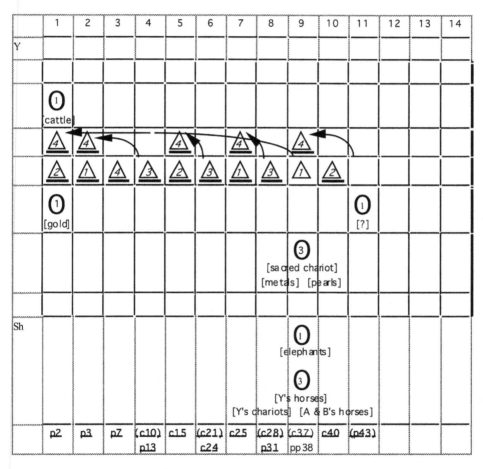

'By the way,' Shakuni muttered to Yudhi, pointing at his single counter on column eleven, 'that represents the elephants. I have put them back on the table.' He continued his attack with *3, 3* and *4*, ending his drive in another capture, on the starting column, again much too fast for Yudhi.

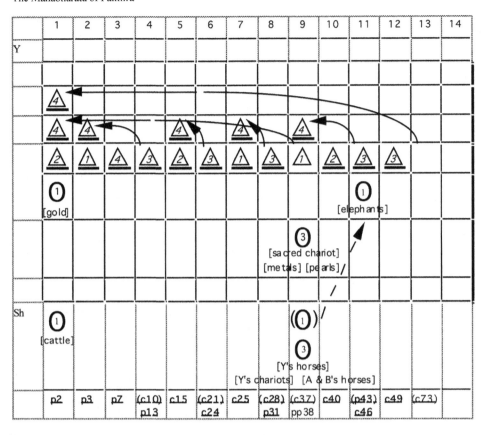

Saha held his head in his hands. Nakula looked at the grid vacantly. But Yudhi smiled courteously at his opponents:

'Do you wish me to replace my starting bet?'

Dur was eager to ask Yudhi to replace the more valuable stake of three in column nine; but Shakuni pointed out that as he had not indicated this to Yudhi at the time, Yudhi was obliged if requested only to replace the last capture from the starting column: the cattle. 'However, Dur, I do not intend to ask him to replace even that.'

'But what about the line?' complained Dur. 'You also eliminated his line, Shakuni!'

'Dur is right, King Shakuni. I owe you for the line. What can I give you for that? Have I anything else you want, Dur?'

'There is...' — Dur hesitated — '...the grazing land for your livestock...'

'You mean the land surrounding Indraprastha?' Yudhi silenced Saha's dazed protest. 'You require five points, Shakuni. Will the land cover this?'

'Amply, my dear.'

Yudhi passed the counters to Dur.

'Nakula...' Yudhi roused his second. 'What is the next prime, please? In case you have forgotten, brother, I'm on 73.'

'The next one is 79...' Nakula slowly closed his mouth as Yudhi prepared to throw the next dice, aiming for a common.

'Dhrita!' Satyaki caught the king's attention. 'Could you ask Sanjaya to bring us up to date, this is all very confusing.'

'Yudhi or Shakuni?' asked Sanjaya.

'Both, and make it quick!'

'Shakuni has five on the grid: the gold, the sacred chariot, the pearls and the metals. And the elephants. Off the grid he has a hundred and forty-eight points, of which four represent Yudhi's cattle, his horses, his chariots, Arjuna and Bhima's horses, and another five his grazing land. Yudhi has two hundred and thirty-one off the grid, and nothing on his line.'

'Sanjaya,' said Satyaki, 'you are a treasure.'

'Dhrita,' added Drupada dryly, 'don't let Dur put Sanjaya on the grid. We would be lost without him.'

'What will he do now?' asked Sanjaya.

'He must go for a common,' declared Satyaki. 'He's only on a cat. And not only that, he cannot capture any of Shakuni's material. Is that not so, Drupada?'

'That's correct. On 73 he could ride a *2* for a prime, or even a *2* once ridden. But as you see, none of Shakuni's counters are suitably placed. Yudhi must go for a common and try to get some sort of attack going — you see how Shakuni is able entirely to dictate the game.'

Sure enough, Yudhi released his dice for a common, getting a *4*. By the time he had placed the dice at the end of the row to make 77, Shakuni had moved three new counters onto his line.

'He's laying eggs,' whispered Satyaki.

'Rather substantial eggs,' added Drupada.

At the table Yudhi was waiting before continuing his attack.

'King Shakuni,' he said, 'your bets?...'

'Oh of course, my dear, my apologies. In the second column, near the gold, I have deployed, let's see... yes, Arjuna and Bhima's horses. Your own horses, Yudhi, are now accompanying them in column three. And in column five I have assembled... your chariots.'

'Very well. I am now on 77. May I go for a kill, King Shakuni? Will you permit me to place a bad bet — I may be able to find something to interest Prince Dur-yodhana.'

'Not on 77, Yudhi. I'm sorry, my dear, it's just too risky for me.'

Yudhi threw again, without knocking. 'A *1*. Is 78 more suitable, King Shakuni.'

'Indeed. 78 is a cheetah. By all means attempt the kill.'

Nakula and Saha straightened up on their stools.

'Shakuni can't keep getting away with it!' whispered Drupada.

'In any case, Yudhi *has* to bet,' observed Satyaki. 'Otherwise he'll win nothing even if he strikes the limit: he has nothing in his line. In theory he could make a capture, but in this position, against Shakuni, never.'

'I thought 78 was a pig...' said Sanjaya distractedly.

'It is,' said Satyaki. 'From it you cannot ride Kali for a prime. And because you can't climb Kali for a prime, you can never *capture* on a pig. But you may still be able to strike a prime from it by playing straight. Here with a *1*, no? So, some pigs are cheetahs.'

'Yes, even pigs can be cheetahs,' added Drupada. 'But they can never be lions. And of course, they can never be any of the three climbing cats. And did you know, Sanjaya, that not all pigs are multiples of three? No, there is one pig, which by the way happens to be a cheetah, which is not a multiple of three: 46. It is the only such pig that I know of. In fact it may be the only pig which is not divisible by three. I wonder if Shakuni knows... or Gandhari, perhaps...'

'Sanjaya!' called Dhrita in a hoarse whisper. 'He's tapped twice!'

'Yes, sire, he's going for the kill. He's putting down an... an *eight*?'

'King Shakuni,' said Yudhi, 'I am staking this eight-piece in order to recover all my losses, should I succeed with the kill... everything you have so far taken from me. Is that agreeable?'

'Eight?' said Dur anxiously. 'But we have eight in our line alone...'

'Eight will do perfectly, my dear,' assured Shakuni. 'Numbers mean no more than we charge them with, nephew. May I ask what...'

'The counter represents Indraprastha,' explained Yudhi. 'Its palaces, buildings, and the land on which it stands.' Yudhi looked at Dur. 'Is that satisfactory?'

Dur and Shakuni nodded in assent. Yudhi turned to Kripa for acknowledgement, and took Kripa's inertness for consent. Yudhi threw his dice.

'Look at that! Just when he doesn't need it, a *4*!'

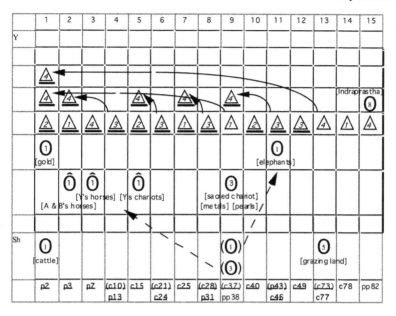

'How can he have such bad luck? Poor Yudhi! Shiva help him now!'

'But it isn't over yet,' reminded Sanjaya. 'They're getting near the limit now. Surely, he still has a chance!'

Kripa did not succeed in reducing the cries from the audience. Only the sight of Shakuni on the attack brought the clamour down briefly for a moment, but only to erupt once again: he threw *2*, *1*, and *4*, the last of these capturing Indraprastha.

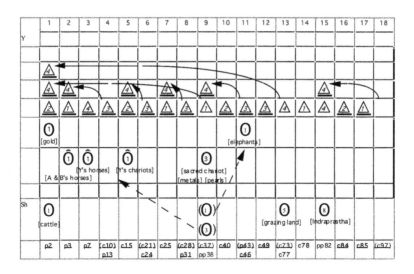

'Shiva! He's doing it again!'

'*Incredible!*'

'What?'

Shakuni, apparently quite oblivious to the commotion around the hall, had chosen this moment to retire from the glaha.

'Yes, sire, he's retired — and out of turn again! So he loses his line! Yudhi's getting back the gold, the sacred chariot, the pearls, the metals and the elephants. Oh, and his horses, his chariots, and Arjuna and Bhima's horses. And as well as these eight, he has two hundred and twenty-three in ordinary counters.' Sanjaya paused to check his accounts. 'Shakuni has a hundred and thirty-nine ordinary counters and in addition he still has one representing Yudhi's cattle, five representing the grazing land, and eight representing Indraprastha. I bet he wishes he'd tapped before throwing that final dice, then he could have retired while still on his turn: Yudhi would have been left with nothing! Well, of course, he'd still have all those counters! At least it doesn't look as though Shakuni is going to bleed him dry, sire!'

'Sanjaya,' muttered Dhrita, 'I will ask you kindly not to make light of Yudhi's terrible misfortune —'

'Ah! Sire, sssh! Kripa looks as though he...'

'For the twentieth and final glaha,' announced Kripa, 'King Shakuni has agreed to place as his starting stake the eight-bet representing Indraprastha. King Yudhi-sthira, for his part, has agreed to stake an eight-bet representing his gold, his sacred chariot, his pearls, metals, elephants, his horses, his chariots, and Arjuna and Bhima's horses.'

Kripa resumed his position at the paddock end of the table.

'King Yudhi-sthira will open the attack.'

47 The eye of Kali

After Yudhi had thrown his first dice, a *1*, Nakula advised Yudhi to protect his line by betting again. Nakula and Saha had swapped places for this glaha, so that Nakula was now on Yudhi's immediate left, with Saha at the farther end from the paddock, opposite to Dur.

'Yes, bet now, brother. At least for the moment, on 1,' Nakula added with resigned irony, 'the gods have ample opportunity to provide you with a prime.'

'But I have nothing left, Nakula. What else do I have?' Yudhi turned to Dur. 'I wish to place a bet, cousin, but I fear I may have nothing left to interest you.'

'At the moment we hold Indraprastha,' said Dur. 'And the surrounding land. Think where your people are to live, how they are to support themselves if they find themselves with neither dwelling nor land. Stake their allegiance to us, Yudhi. If you lose, at least they will still have their roofs over their heads.'

Yudhi considered for a moment. 'What value do you place on the people of Indraprastha?'

Dur looked to Shakuni.

'Put another eight down, my dear.'

'*Yudhi*!' The strangled cry came from the silence of the auditorium. It was Arjuna, who stared at his brother in horror. He continued, almost in a whisper: 'Are you going to give our people away into slavery?'

'They will not be treated as slaves, Yudhi,' came the prompt assurance from Dur. 'They will remain free to live in Indraprastha. I will not tax them for labour or for produce.'

For a moment Yudhi hesitated. Then he placed the eight-bet.

He threw another *1*, placed the dice, and then tapped once without betting. A moment later, as the dice settled in the paddock, Shakuni had two blocking counters in position. 'Two fifths of your land,' explained Shakuni, pointing at the pieces. Yudhi slowly placed his *4* at the end of the row for 6, finishing his turn.

Shakuni immediately launched his attack, but on this occasion it ended without capture after just two more dice, a *3* and a *2*, leaving Yudhi on 11.

Yudhi now tapped twice for a kill, but without any further betting; his line was still worth more than Shakuni's. Another *4* came up for Yudhi, but again Shakuni had his blocks in place before the audience had begun to react. 'Another two fifths of your land, my dear...'

As before, the *4* went at the end of the row; the attack passed to Shakuni, on 15.

	1	2	3	4	5	6	7	8	9	10
Y										
	[gold...]	[people of Indraprastha]								
	⑧	⑧								
	△1	△1	△4	△3	△2	△4				
	⑧									
	[Indraprastha]									
	Ô1	Ô1	Ô1		Ô1					
	[grazing 1]	[grazing 2]	[grazing 3]	[grazing 4]						
Sh										
	p1	p2	p6	c9	c11	pp15				

Nakula whispered urgently to Yudhi, as Shakuni started off at speed.

Aiming for a common, Shakuni made 16 with a *1*, and then achieved a prime with a *3* for 19. When his next dice, thrown again for a common, turned up *4*, Shakuni seized it rapidly. He appeared to head with it for Yudhi's starting bet. Yudhi instantly responded with a blocking bet, touching down just as Shakuni seemed to be dropping onto his opponent's eight-piece. Like a bird stalling in flight, the hovering dice moved on and landed in the fourth column, riding Kali on the clear *3* to achieve the common on 28.

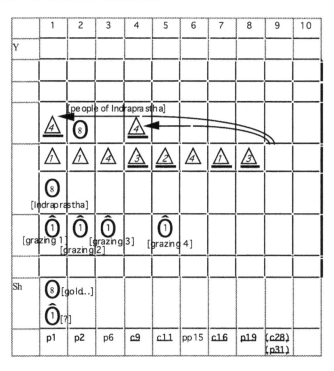

As Yudhi winced, realising that Shakuni could not in any case have made the capture, his opponent tapped and threw another *4*, this time capturing in earnest on the starting column. Yudhi had managed to scramble another blocking counter, but it was stranded in mid-air.

Nakula brought his hands up over his mouth and nose, and breathed slowly in. Bhima half-rose from his seat in the auditorium, and then sank down again.

Dur took Yudhi's captured blocking counter, now in Shakuni's camp, and held it up.

'I have no livestock remaining,' said Yudhi in response. 'I have no treasure left... My people are on the table... Take me as a slave, cousin. Undoubtedly I am not worth a full counter...' Yudhi managed a smile. 'But I have nothing else to give you.'

For a moment there was silence. Dur was still holding the counter up, as though his arm was frozen. Then Saha spoke.

'Take me instead. I cannot be free while my elder brother is in bonds. To enslave him is to enslave me. Dur, take me instead.'

Dur nodded, and lowered his arm, replacing the counter in Shakuni's camp. He whispered to his uncle. 'Aren't you going to ask him to replace?'

But Shakuni was away again. Without tapping for any of these dice, he dashed out 3, 1, and another pair of 4s. With the first of the 4s he played the same trick again, drawing out an unnecessary block from Yudhi as he headed this time for the second column, only to ride Kali for a common on the seventh; and then, with the second 4, actually making the capture.

'No, Bhima! No!'

'Where do these Kali dice come from,' cried Bhima, 'if not from Kali herself!'

Bhima had leapt out of his seat onto the floor. Arjuna followed after his brother and with some difficulty restrained him. As Dur gathered up the captured bets into Shakuni's camp, Kripa waved Bhima and Arjuna away to the edge of the floor.

'It certainly seems an unusually high number of 4s in this glaha,' said Drupada.

'And in the last one,' added Satyaki.

'And to get two pairs like that...'

'Do you think he's cheating?' asked Sanjaya.

'My brother has never cheated in his life!' declared Gandhari, who had overheard the conversation. 'Not even against me when we used to play as children, when for a while I was still beating him.'

'But Gandhari,' ventured Drupada, 'you must admit there have been an unusual number of 4s recently...'

'It is strange, King Drupada, I agree. But of course it happens from time to time. May I remind you that to throw any successive sequence of 4s is no less likely than throwing *any* specified sequence of the same length.'

'Could it be the will of the gods?' asked Dhrita.

Gandhari broke into a derisive laugh.

'It is the will of the gods that you are blind, husband! My brother neither needs, nor deserves, their help. It is Yudhi who needs and deserves their help!'

'So I deserve to be blind? I need to be blind?'

'Certainly, Dhrita. It is a deserving punishment for providing me with such sons as I have been cursed with; and a needful means by which you have been relieved of the sight of me in the getting of them...'

Gandhari turned away to look at the dealings down at the table.

'Sanjaya,' she continued, quite loudly enough for Dhrita to hear. 'Kindly inform my husband that Yudhi's affairs appear to have been decided in this manner: the single blocking bet which my brother has just captured, along with the people of Indraprastha... this turns out to be Nakula. And Arjuna and Bhima have offered themselves up in payment for the loss of Yudhi's betting line.'

Soon afterwards Kripa, in subdued tones, confirmed these details.

It was now Yudhi's attack, on 41. He asked his opponent for permission to go for a kill. But Shakuni refused, to the indignant cries of Yudhi's supporters.

Instead Yudhi aimed for a common, reaching 44 with a *3*. Again he asked Shakuni for permission to go for a kill. Again Shakuni refused.

Yudhi achieved another common with a *4* to make 48: he may have been tempted to go for a capture if one had been available, but there had been none. With a smile Dur started to offer Yudhi permission to kill on 48, but Shakuni struck his nephew sharply on the arm to stop him. The twins both glared at Dur.

Yudhi's next dice, aiming for a common, was a *1*, making 49.

'Is 53 the next prime, brother?' asked Yudhi.

'Yes,' replied Nakula. 'And you need something on your line, Yudhi. You might as well keep trying for a kill.'

'King Shakuni, may I go for a kill?'

Shakuni was deep in thought. He appeared quite impervious to the noise of the auditorium, even of those immediately around him. His eyes were tightly focused on the end of the dice row. Dur grew anxious, but he did not wish to disturb his uncle. At length, Shakuni roused himself.

'Very well, my dear. You may go for a kill. What do you intend to bet?'

'Myself... on the understanding that if I succeed, you return my brothers, the people of Indraprastha, and the land. You may keep all the rest.'

'No, Yudhi. You may have my line, as well as the captures you mention. Put down twelve points, which equals my line; if you kill me I will return your losses both on and off the grid.' Shakuni laid a restraining hand on his nephew's arm.

Yudhi tapped his dice twice, placed his twelve-stack, and threw the dice into the paddock.

Bhima and Arjuna groaned out loud when they saw its yellow tip.

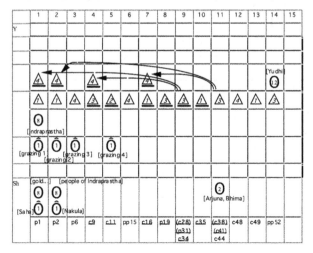

'Where are the *4*s for Yudhi!' cried Arjuna.

'These dice are not blind!' shouted Bhima. 'They see with the evil eye of Kali!'

Yudhi turned and signalled to his brothers to remain silent.

Shakuni prepared to attack.

'Listen brother,' whispered Nakula. 'He's on 52 now. He can capture you on his next dice, if it's a *4*. But his hand has to travel a long distance to reach your stack. You should be able to block first. Even Shakuni will not manage a capture like that at the start of a drive. If he fails to get a *4* straight off, he won't be able to capture you again until 58. You can be sure that he will be driving fast, but you'll know if he strikes 58 because he'll tap — he may even tap twice for a kill: 58 is a tiger. He will aim for a prime on the tiger. If you hear the tap and see the *4*, go for the block!'

'What shall I block with?'

'A counter, Yudhi, a counter! Worry about it later! And Yudhi, if he loses the attack, go straight away — if he has a weakness, it's defending against long drives: the next tiger after 58 is 70. You should go off on a common drive to 70, if you can make it — don't pause, just keep going...'

Shakuni rattled out four dice, *2*, *1*, *3* and *4*.'

'*Shiva!*' cried Satyaki. 'He's captured *Yudhi*!'

'He didn't even bother to go for a prime on that tiger!' Drupada shook his head in disbelief.

'Did you see that, Sanjaya! The *3* put him on 58 but he then went for a common!'

'He was expecting Yudhi to block,' said Drupada. 'Yudhi had a counter waiting there in his camp, ready to block in that column — Shakuni would never have beaten him to it, so far down the row. He may even have been wanting Yudhi to block. Did you see? He was heading to play that *4* straight to make his common — it was only when he saw that Yudhi had made no block, he actually went back down the row to take him! He doubled back! Did you see that?'

'Yes, I think you may be right, Drupada. And he would have had another chance to capture on 62 or 64; and then there's the next tiger...'

	1	2	3	4	5	6	7	8	9	10	11	12	13	14	15	16	17	18
Y																		
	△4	△4		△4			△4							△4				
	△1	△1	△4	△3	△2	△4	△1	△3	△3	△1	△3	△4	△1	△3	△2	△1	△3
	Ⓞ8 [Indraprastha]																	
	Ô1 [grazing 1]	Ô1 [grazing 2]	Ô1 [grazing 3]	Ô1 [grazing 4]														
Sh	Ⓞ8 [gold..]	Ⓞ8 [people of Indraprastha]								Ⓞ2 [Arjuna, Bhima]			Ⓞ12 [Yudhi]					
	Ô1 [Saha]	Ô1 [Nakula]																
	p1	p2	p6	c9	c11	pp15	c16	p19	(c28) (p31) c34	c35	(c38) (c41) c44	c48	c49	pp52	c54	c55	c58	(c67)

'This is the end,' said Drupada, sadly shaking his head. 'Poor Yudhi!'

'He's got plenty of counters left,' observed Sanjaya. 'At least he hasn't been bled dry. He didn't dare do that to the King of Kings, oh no!'

'*Sanjaya*! One more remark like that and by Shiva, we'll bleed you dry... What's this?' Satyaki strained to listen to Dur.

'Yudhi, it is your attack. Perhaps my uncle will permit you to place one last bet.'

Bhima and Arjuna, who were standing dejectedly at the edge of the floor, slowly raised their heads. Saha and Nakula stared at Dur, then at Yudhi.

'There is nothing else, surely, Prince Dur-yodhana, that you still desire of me. I believe I have given you all that is in my power to give, and more. You have my treasures, my land, my animals, my city, my people, my brothers, and myself. Is that not enough for you?'

'Do you not wish to have them returned?' asked Dur.

Yudhi raised his hands as though in despair; but his face was calm.

'Place another stack of twelve,' continued Dur, 'and go for a kill. If you achieve it, everything will be returned.' Dur motioned to Nakula to put the bet in place. Nakula passed Yudhi the counters. Yudhi put them hesitantly onto the grid. Against the silence of the hall the rasp of the counters was perfectly audible as they slid across the grid lines.

Shakuni turned to his second.

'What precisely is this bet, nephew?'

'It is Draupadi,' replied Dur.

The first sound to break the silence was a low, soft chuckle from the auditorium. Faces turned to see who it was. It was Karna, high in the upper tiers. He turned his head towards Shikhandi, who was sitting next to him.

'Where is your sister?' he asked. Against the silence his voice easily travelled down to the floor.

'She is ill,' cried Bhima, angrily.

'She is unwell,' said Arjuna, coldly staring up at Karna.

'It is perhaps better, then,' said Dur, 'that she is absent while she tries to restore the fortunes of the Pandavas.' He held out his hand indicating to Yudhi to prepare his dice.

But now, as Yudhi slowly stretched his hand out to the dice bowl, Shikhandi's voice arrested him.

'My sister does not belong to the Pandavas. How can she be placed upon the table?'

'If she does not belong to them,' cried Duh, 'who else does she belong to? Her father?'

It was her father who answered Duh:

'Neither my dead wife nor my daughters have ever belonged to me,' said Drupada. 'I cannot answer for Draupadi, whether she considers herself to be under Yudhi's command. However,' he added, 'I do not think my daughter would wish to decline the chance to save Yudhi and the Pandavas. Few of us here would. If you will accept me in her place, I will gladly put myself upon the table. Take *me*, Yudhi...'

As the audience applauded Drupada, Gandhari rose from her seat and reached up to press his hand.

Dur looked at Yudhi. 'When so many others would offer themselves, Yudhi, let Draupadi herself have the honour of coming to your aid.' Dur passed him a dice.

'Don't take that dice!' cried Bhima. 'Choose your own, Yudhi!'

Shakuni turned in the direction of Bhima. His eyes narrowed.

Yudhi reached into the dice bowl.

'Now perhaps we'll get a *4*!' muttered Arjuna.

But Yudhi changed his mind. He took his hand out empty, and reached towards Dur. He bowed his head slightly, and accepted the dice that Dur was offering. His brothers remained silent.

Yudhi tapped the dice twice upon the table. He took a deep breath, glancing briefly at Shakuni, who in turn bowed his head with a smile.

'Is it a *4* he needs, Sanjaya?'

'Yes, sire. For 71.'

Shakuni watched the brief dance of the dice on the wooden surface of the paddock, and then he himself reached calmly into the dice bowl, ignoring the uproar around him. He signalled to Yudhi to move the dice still sitting in the paddock, a *2*, onto the grid. Shakuni tapped his own dice twice, but Kripa, who was trying to restore silence, failed to hear it. Dur got up off his stool and went over to Kripa. Kripa beckoned to Drona for assistance with the audience, and himself returned to the paddock. Shakuni now repeated the double tap, and threw the dice. It was a *4*. Almost reluctantly he fetched it from the paddock, and placed it carefully at the end of the row. Then he rose from his stool, bowed to Yudhi, bowed to Kripa, and left the floor.

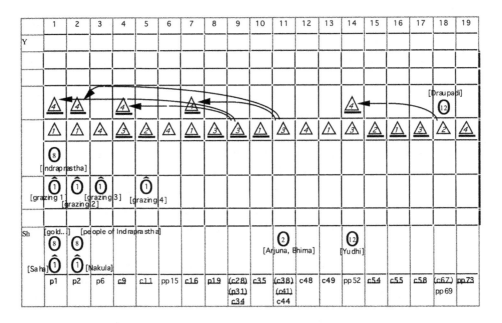

Dur summoned a messenger and whispered in his ear. The servant hurriedly left the hall.

48 Bhima's oath

Everything was much as it had been when the messenger had left. Saha and Nakula were still sitting there with Yudhi at the table. Bhima and Arjuna were still standing like statues at the edge of the floor. Kripa too was motionless by the table. And though no one in the audience had left the hall, a few, such as Drona, Vidura, Bhishma, Ashwa, Karna, as well as one or two of Dur's brothers, had come down from the auditorium and were gathered by the entrances.

At the sight of the messenger returning, the noise fell expectantly. The messenger approached Dur, who was waiting by his stool.

'She will not listen to me, Prince Dur-yodhana. She does not believe me.'

'You explained?'

'She became angry... The room was dark, Prince Dur. She sent me away.'

'Go and bring her by force,' muttered Duh. 'She is now our slave.'

Vidura, wincing at these words, began to pace slowly between Bhishma and Drona, and glanced anxiously at Yudhi. Seeing the reluctance of the servant, Duh took the task upon himself, and briskly left the hall, carefully avoiding Bhima and Arjuna on his way out.

Bhishma walked over to Bhima and put his hand on his shoulder. Kripa joined them, his head bowed. Vidura turned towards Dur.

'You have brought disgrace upon Hastinapura,' he said to Dur. 'Would that you and Shakuni had never been born!'

When Duh's purpose had been reported to Shikhandi, who was still up in the auditorium, she too descended to the floor, stopping her father on the way to send him back to his seat. She went straight to Dur.

'Dur, it is my sister's time of the month. She has been in great pain on this occasion. You cannot have her brought here to this —'

Shikhandi was interrupted by the muffled cries of her sister as she was dragged in by Duh, his hand over her mouth. Bhima started to charge towards Duh like a grunting boar, but Bhishma and Drona caught and held him. He broke free, but Shikhandi had already reached Duh and was now in Bhima's path. As Bhima swerved to avoid her, Bhishma and Drona caught up with him again.

'Release my sister, Duh-shasana!'

'She is our slave now, Princess Shikhandini...'

'Whatever you think she is, Duh, if you don't release her now from your grasp, I will detach with my bare hands what little manhood you have left.'

Shikhandi held her hands out to him like claws. Duh took his hand from Draupadi's mouth, still holding her tightly. Then he thought the better of it, and released his grasp. Shikhandi went to put her arms around her sister, but Draupadi pushed her angrily away.

'I must be dreaming!' gasped Draupadi. Her wild, staring eyes had dark shadows round them. She caught sight of Arjuna and Bhima, then turned to see Yudhi. 'What's happening? This cannot be true...'

Draupadi stood there wrapped in a white cloth; her legs were only partly covered; her feet were still wet: she had been stepping into a bath when Duh had surprised her.

She stared around her; then, becoming aware of her own appearance, she adjusted her cloth, knotting a loose fold to hide some spots of blood on it.

'Get away from me!' she screamed at Duh, who was still standing near her.

'Get away from her,' repeated Bhishma, quietly. Duh crept back towards the edge of the floor.

'You have been lost at dice...' explained Shikhandi.

'And that is reason for them to treat me worse than the lowliest bitch? With only my sister willing to defend me?'

'How could you stake her?' cried Bhima, his voice trembling. 'I could burn your hands off, Yudhi!'

'Sssh, Bhima...' whispered Arjuna, who had joined Drona and Bhishma. 'Even when a man has lost everything, he must strive to keep his dharma. We are now their slaves, Bhima. Don't you understand that? We have lost the right to challenge them.'

'Let him give away *himself*,' cried Bhima, 'but not others! Not *Draupadi* of all people!'

'How was I lost at dice? How can I be lost at dice? Father!' Draupadi caught sight of Drupada in the audience above her.

'Yudhi staked you at the table,' Drupada replied.

'*Me*?' Draupadi's eyes darted around the dice table as if to find some clue from it.

'He staked you all, and himself,' whispered Shikhandi. 'You, the twins, Arjuna and Bhima. You are all lost to Dur... to Shakuni —'

'But I was not even here...' she said, breaking into sobs.

'He had nothing else left,' said Shikhandi. 'You were his last hope... Father offered to stand in your stead...'

Draupadi looked at Yudhi, still sitting at the table. At first her eyes swelled with tears as he looked up. His face, though without expression, was calm. Draupadi's breathing steadied. She looked past Shikhandi at Bhishma and

Drona. She wiped away her tears and at the same time, without realising it, wiped dry her ankles against her calves.

'But he doesn't own me... nor his brothers...'

'They offered themselves, sister.'

'But I wasn't here, I wasn't here to offer myself! Who is the adjudicator?' Kripa turned towards her.

'Do you not agree, Kripa-charya, that I have not been won?'

'You were staked by Yudhi, as were his brothers. They were all captured by Shakuni's dice. You were lost when he made the kill.' Kripa forced himself to look Draupadi in the eye, but his gaze soon lowered.

'But my case is different... Grandsire?' She turned to Bhishma now. But he did not reply. 'Will someone not answer my question? How can I have been staked and lost. Is not my case different from the others? The others were here to put themselves forward. I was not...'

At first no one spoke. Then Dur's brother Vikarna rose from his seat near Shalya, opposite Dhrita.

'Draupadi's question must be answered. If no one else will give an opinion, I will: I for one do not believe Draupadi has been rightfully staked in her absence. But how is it that those wiser than myself cannot give her an answer?'

'The point you raise, Queen Draupadi,' said Bhishma, 'is not one that I can decide. I can only say this: it appears to me, judging by the laws of the dice game, that you have been staked and lost.'

'Grandsire! You cannot judge life by appealing to the laws of a mere game!' Draupadi stepped towards Bhishma and Drona, gently pushing them away from Bhima, who had now regained control of himself.

'Draupadi...' Bhishma beckoned to her, indicating that he wished to speak to her in greater privacy. She approached him.

'Draupadi,' he said softly to her, 'in every place, in every time, we have set up laws to be the servants of principle. Yet everywhere, and in every time, we see principle enslaved by our own creation; and everywhere, in every time, we seem obliged to behold, in desperation, those who exploit the imperfections of the law for their own unprincipled ends. It is because Dur knows that Yudhi values dharma so highly, because he knows that Yudhi will judge life by principles so high as to respect the laws of a low game, that Dur is able to hold judgement over Yudhi's life through the rules of a mere game. But now, if you insist on trying to escape the judgement, you risk losing your own dharma, by seeking to escape the rule of principle for your own ends.'

'That is my risk, Grandsire.' Draupadi turned away from him and confronted Kripa once again.

'Kripa-charya, Yudhi's brothers *offered* to stand. Can it be within the laws of the game that someone can put up a stake he has no right to? Why, Dur himself could put me up in my absence, on his side of the table!'

'No, because you are not Dur's wife!' cried Duh. 'You are Yudhi's wife. Of course he had a right to put you up!'

'I am not *owned* by Yudhi and his brothers, to be put up as a stake in my absence!' Draupadi appealed now to the auditorium. 'Duh has answered my question against me, but Vikarna has answered in my favour, even though as Dur's own brother he would benefit from the evil game which has just taken place. Has no one else the courage to speak?'

This time the uneasy silence was broken by Karna.

'It is not the courage to speak which we lack, Queen Draupadi, but the wisdom. But if you would prefer my folly to my silence, I will give you my opinion.'

'Frankly,' declared Shalya from his seat across the floor, 'I should have thought that Draupadi made it quite clear at her swayamwara what she thought of you and your opinions! And I have to say that I, for one, prefer your silence to your folly!'

'If Draupadi again prefers that I put down my bow,' replied Karna, 'then I will.' A trace of a smile played on his lips as he spoke. 'But if she permits, I will give you my opinion...'

Karna's expression, and the cold arrogance of his voice, visibly stung the Pandavas. Drona and Bhishma tightened their guiding hold on Bhima. Shikhandi moved away from her sister, to the side of the floor beneath King Dhrita's seat, close to where Kripa was standing. Draupadi herself did not speak.

'Well,' continued Karna, 'in my opinion, Draupadi, for the purposes of this game, you are indeed owned by Yudhi. For what is to own but to have power over?'

'Yudhi does not rule over me,' replied Draupadi, without attempting to disguise her contempt for Karna. 'He exercises neither power nor force upon me. Neither upon me, nor upon anyone.'

'But there is more to power than *power*, Draupadi. You complained just now that you were being treated like the lowliest dog. Well, a man may never cause a dog to do anything against its will, neither beating it nor shouting at it, giving it nothing but shelter, food and kindness. And yet we do not for that say that the man does not own the dog?' Karna ignored the reaction which his words brought down upon him, continuing unperturbed. 'Does not the man have power over the dog? Can he not without the use of force cause the dog to comply with his wishes? Why? Because the dog loves the man. And if a dog can love a man, cannot a brother? A wife? Are you telling us, Queen Draupadi, that had you been here you would not have offered to stand as stake, as Yudhi's brothers did? As your own father did when Yudhi had staked even himself upon the table? As the lowliest dog in Indraprastha would have done if he had understood Yudhi's misfortune? And yet you complained just now that you were being treated like the lowliest dog?'

The look of hatred on Draupadi's face seemed only to further Karna's amusement. Then, suddenly, her expression changed.

'Tell me, Lord Karna,' she asked unctuously, 'who was staked first? Which of us was put first upon the table?'

'First were the twins, I believe. Then Arjuna and Bhima. Then Yudhi himself.'

'So when did he stake *me*?'

'After he was himself lost. He had nothing else. You were his last hope, Draupadi. As you know, your own father offered to stand in your stead.'

'Was Yudhi on the table still, or captured?' Draupadi addressed this question now to Kripa.

'Yudhi had been captured,' replied Kripa gravely. 'He was already in Shakuni's camp.'

'After he himself was lost,' she said conclusively. 'Then I am not lost... I am *not* lost, I have not been won! You see, Lord Karna, if I had been here, as you so rightly have said, I would have offered myself along with Yudhi's brothers. If I had been here I would certainly have begged him to stake me before he put himself upon the table. But when Yudhi was himself lost, when he was captured, the glaha should have *stopped*!'

She turned again to Kripa.

'After that point, Shakuni was no longer playing against an opponent — for he owned his opponent, having already made the capture! After that moment,' she laughed, 'Shakuni and Dur were playing with themselves!'

Around the hall applause broke out for her. When it had died down, Draupadi looked scornfully at Karna, catching his eyes for an instant before turning her back on him.

But from the silence came Karna's voice again.

'You have made an excellent point, Queen Draupadi. I agree entirely with you. The glaha should have terminated with the capture of Yudhi.'

Draupadi resisted the temptation to face Karna, and turned towards Kripa.

'And I believe,' continued Karna, 'that it was hasty, ill-advised and most discourteous of Prince Duh-shasana to express the brutality of his behaviour against you; whether or not you belonged to anyone other than yourself.' As Karna paused, Duh shifted his weight uncomfortably. Draupadi's head wavered slightly, and she glanced at her sister, whose eyes were fixed apprehensively on Karna.

'On behalf of Prince Duh-shasana,' continued Karna, 'I apologise... Yes, I apologise, both for his behaviour, and for his presumptuous belief, which I confess I shared, that you would wish now at least to demonstrate, if not later to fulfil, your loyalty to your husbands... by joining them in servitude. As you know, Queen Draupadi, the wife of a slave, indeed, even the wife of the slightly more exalted suta, belongs to her husband's owner. So I must now conclude, given your passionate resistance to any claim upon you, that this assertion of your freedom will now extend, with full entitlement, to the choice, from among those less sadly fettered by their fate, of a new husband...'

Above the laughter which greeted this from Dur's brothers, rose the voice of Duh:

'Perhaps Draupadi may like to take one of the Kuru princes for a husband? Dur has the most excellent thighs, certainly but —'

'Command me, Yudhi, and I will kill these two Kurus now!' cried Bhima. Bhishma and Drona braced themselves to hold him, but on this occasion Yudhi's expression was enough to restrain his brother.

'Then may I be damned for all eternity,' cried Bhima, 'may I be damned for all eternity with all here present as my witnesses, if I do not break those thighs before I leave this life! You, Duh, you I will also send from this life to another. Let me hear you laugh again when I drink your blood! And remember, even though I am now your slave, Yudhi only has to give me leave, and you will leave this life. As for the King of Anga,' Bhima turned to face Karna, 'his mouth is better fitted to chew upon his ankle straps than to speak in the manner we have just heard.'

As Bhima finished speaking, Yudhi looked down vacantly at Karna's feet.

Draupadi now sensed the attention of the audience begin to turn expectantly towards her.

'I have no intention of being disloyal to the Pandavas,' she declared. 'I do not wish to claim freedom for myself while my husbands are enslaved. I only ask that I be staked in the proper manner, according to the laws of the game. I have not been given the proper chance to save Yudhi at the table. I should have been staked before he was, or not at all.'

Her words were received in silence. She looked for a response from Yudhi, but he was staring at the floor. His face was calm again, but he showed no sign of having heard Draupadi's words.

Bhishma spoke now, to Karna.

'You argued earlier against Draupadi. What do you say to this?'

'If Draupadi wishes to be launched again to try to carry the drowning Pandavas safely to shore, *I* have no objection. Let them play another glaha. As to whether it is lawful or not for Yudhi to receive another chance, I cannot say. Nor can I say if it is right. On this question I would accept Yudhi's own judgement.'

Some of the Kuru princes now began to look worried. But from Yudhi himself there came no answer. Bhishma asked him directly, walking slowly towards him as he spoke:

'King Yudhi-sthira, is it your opinion that you are entitled to stake Queen Draupadi again, in another glaha?'

But Yudhi was not aware of being spoken to. His eyes still seemed to be looking in the direction of Karna's feet.

'King Yudhi-sthira?' repeated Bhishma.

Now Kripa approached him. 'Yudhi, please,' he entreated softly, 'let this apricity of Karna's light your way... Accept his suggestion...'

This time Yudhi lifted his head, but only as if to seek someone out in the audience; however, not seeming to find what he was searching for, he lowered his head again, without acknowledging being spoken to.

Then Gandhari got up from her seat and leaned across Sanjaya to whisper to her husband. A moment later she sat down again. Slowly Dhrita stood up, leaning on Sanjaya. Bhishma and Kripa turned and saw the king rising behind them; they walked back to the edge of the floor.

'Queen Draupadi,' began Dhrita, his voice trembling slightly with emotion. 'Another glaha will be held, as you request. As it is now late, already evening, and we are all tired and hungry, it will take place tomorrow, in the morning.' Dhrita waited for the rustling and murmurs to stop. 'For the insult and humiliation you have received at the hands of my sons, you deserve much more than this. If there is anything else in my power to grant you, ask of me now, and I will do it.'

Draupadi waited for the applause to die down.

'King Dhrita-rashtra, I ask for no more than the freedom from bondage of the Pandava princes until this glaha is finished. At that time the gods may decide our fate.'

More applause followed this. Then, as Dhrita prepared to sit down, Sanjaya noticed Bhima about to address the king; Sanjaya nudged Dhrita, and the king straightened up again.

'Sire,' said Bhima. 'May I ask something?'

At these words the Kuru princes shuddered, anticipating some dreadful retribution. Dur, who had been sitting quietly since Draupadi's entrance, got up from his stool.

'You may ask, Bhima-sena,' said King Dhrita.

'May I ask that different dice be used?'

'Are you accusing my brother of cheating?' challenged Gandhari.

Bhima looked uncomfortable, but he withstood her glare. 'Did you not notice all those *4*s, Queen Gandhari? Remember that it was Charvaka who made these dice.'

'Bhima-sena,' she replied, 'I will ask you to remember that he was good enough for your palace at Indraprastha...'

'We know now why he helped us,' muttered Saha, fortunately too softly for Gandhari to hear. 'He was building for *your* sons, Gandhari, not for us!' Saha looked angrily at Dur.

'But Queen Gandhari,' continued Bhima, 'I have noticed that there are two sorts of dice. Look...' Bhima went to the table and carefully picked out a pair. He took them over to show Gandhari, who was still in the first tier of seats, near her husband. Saha and Nakula also examined some of the dice.

Gandhari looked at the two dice for a moment, and returned them to Bhima. 'Dur, fetch my brother!' She made her way down to the floor.

As she was descending, Bhima showed Arjuna the dice.

'You see, Arjuna, they are differently arranged.'

'But there may be all sorts of possible arrangements,' suggested Arjuna. 'What would that mean?'

'No,' said Bhima, 'there can only be two.'

'Bhima is right,' said Gandhari, who had now reached them. She took the dice again. 'These two dice are reflections of each other. There can only be two sorts of reflection... in this world, at least. Perhaps,' she added, 'if you were to ask my brother, he might tell you of worlds in which there could be more than two... But here,' she said, giving the dice back for Arjuna to inspect, 'here there are only these two reflections.'

As Kripa approached, Gandhari took back a dice from Arjuna's palm. 'You see, Kripa,' she explained, holding the dice up by the black vertex, 'in this one the white, red and yellow follow the sun. But on the other one' — Arjuna gave her the second dice — 'they go instead against the sun. Bhima, what exactly are you suggesting that Charvaka has done? Remember that my brother and Yudhi have both been taking from the same bowl.'

'He may have put something in the colour of one of the points, to make it heavier. He may have done it on just one of the two sorts of dice, so that Shakuni could throw a *4* when he needed one.'

'Lighter, Bhima.'

'Oh yes, I mean lighter. The black colouring could be lighter in one of the reflections. So... could we not weigh the two reflections?'

'We could,' said Gandhari, 'but it would not necessarily reveal what you want... Charvaka is quite clever enough to have made the other three points a little heavier to compensate, so that both reflections still weighed the same. Still, let us have a pair of scales.'

As the scales were being fetched, Dur returned with his uncle.

'Prince Bhima is accusing you of cheating,' explained Gandhari to her brother.

Shakuni's jaw dropped, and he bristled like a porcupine.

'He has pointed out to us,' continued Gandhari, 'that you have been using two sorts of dice. Look.' She handed Shakuni the pair of dice. 'He believes that one sort is conducive to the *4*. You perhaps noticed that there was an unusually high proportion of *4*s — particularly in the last glahas.'

Shakuni looked at Gandhari in amazement.

'They are reflections,' she explained.

'I can *see* that!' cried Shakuni, at the height of exasperation.

Just then the scales arrived. Gandhari placed the dice one in each pan, in front of her bewildered brother. They balanced perfectly.

'What an interesting experiment,' cried Shakuni sarcastically. 'Whose idea was that? Yours, Prince Bhima-sena? So you think the black vertex is lighter in one reflection?'

'Yes, that was the —'

'You can be sure,' cried Shakuni, glaring at his sister, 'that if Charvaka wanted to construct false dice, even though he knows he would only have to deceive a bunch of fools like yourselves, he would have made certain the false dice weighed the same as the true dice! I suppose you're going to scrape the colour off now and weigh that?'

'How do you explain the two sorts of dice, King Shakuni?' asked Arjuna.

'*How*?' Shakuni paused to regain his composure. 'Prince Arjuna, if you were painting a thousand dice, do you think you would paint them all the same way? Whoever applied the colour was quite rightly more concerned to give each vertex a different colour. The handedness is quite irrelevant. Quite clearly they have by chance made left-handed and right-handed dice. They have to be one or the other. Dice cannot be ambidextrous like yourself! You will probably find the reflections in equal proportion... Besides,' he added, 'I do not cheat at dice. Do you really think I *need* to cheat?'

Shakuni turned to Bhima.

'If you think I cheated, why don't you test the dice properly, instead of weighing them like a blind monkey? *Throw* them!' He shook his hand towards the table. 'Throw the pair... I don't know... sixty times each... Count the *4*s. If you are right, one reflection should give you many more *4*s than the other.' He grabbed Bhima by the arm and dragged him to the dice table. '*Do it!*' He pressed into Bhima's hand the pair of dice Gandhari had given him. 'Better still...' He took the dice out of Bhima's hand, and gave one each to Nakula and Saha. He beckoned to Arjuna. 'You count Saha's, Bhima can count Nakula's.'

Shakuni addressed the audience.

'If both these dice are equally true, they should not prefer one face to another, one vertex to another. So the wealth of falls should be divided equally, as among four...' Shakuni paused, turning to Yudhi. 'Those of you who believe that the dice are controlled by the gods will not expect the gods to show more favour to one vertex than another; so the gods will not allow one vertex to accumulate a disproportionate account.

'As you know,' he went on, 'we find, with true dice, that the vertices are distributed without favour, in such a way that we can never predict even a single throw. Whether you believe, as I do, that this is through the indifferent caprice of nature, or as Yudhi believes, that it is through the whim of the gods, one thing is clear: neither chance nor the gods would allow the division to be as exact as a father dividing his herd of cattle amongst his four children. For if the proportions were perfectly exact, it would allow us, mere men...' he paused to look at Yudhi, '...to predict precisely the fall of at least one dice.

'Because we are denied this exact knowledge,' he continued, 'the proportions will not be absolutely equal, but will approach this state rather as the outline of a portrait, which, with each dot of ink applied, approaches its contour more closely, never to attain it.

'So...' He gestured to the Pandavas to clear some space on the table. 'If one of these dice is false, and is made in such a way as to favour the black vertex — thus repelling the feathery touch of the gods — we should expect a disproportionately high number of 4s. Saha and Nakula, you will each throw your dice sixty times. If both these dice were perfectly true, impossibly true, they would each produce fifteen 4s. You, who accuse me of cheating, must name the number of fours below which you will accept that your dice is true enough, and does *not* favour the black point. Then, if one of these dice should exceed this amount, Yudhi can regain his losses instantly, and I will never again play the game of dice!

'I ask only this,' he added. 'Do not choose a number so low that even a true dice might readily achieve it without surprising you.'

The twins conferred briefly. Nakula replied:

'We will throw each of these two dice sixty times. If one of these dice shows a count of more than twenty 4s out of the sixty, then we will judge that dice to be false. If it is twenty or under, we will accept it as true.'

'More than twenty! With two dice!' Shakuni looked at Gandhari in alarm. 'If a single dice is perfectly true and fair, there's still a one in ten chance of such an extreme!'

'But only a one in twenty chance of a result as *high* as that,' Gandhari pointed out, frowning at her brother. 'Yes, more like a one in twenty chance of an innocent dice being found guilty...' She silenced her brother's protest, but appealed to the twins. 'That still could condemn my brother unjustly even if you were throwing just one dice...'

'If the gods show us that one of the dice is guilty,' said Bhima, 'we must not insult them by questioning their verdict. If both dice are honest, likewise, the gods will show us.'

Hearing this, Karna shook his head and chuckled. 'Bhima,' he remarked, 'what if Shakuni and his dice are dishonest, but the gods wish Yudhi and his brothers to be humbled, to live without wealth or servants under the command of others? You may let the dice decide your lives, if you will, but do not presume to interpret what they say!'

At the sound of Karna's voice Yudhi looked up.

'Lord Karna,' said Yudhi, 'I accept the will of the gods happily... Whether King Shakuni has cheated or not, my defeat, like everything, even the words I am now speaking, occurs only through the will of the gods... If King Shakuni has cheated, it is only through the will of the gods; and I would blame him, for what appears as his deceit, no more than I would accept praise for what to you in the past may have seemed to be my virtue.'

Yudhi turned to Shakuni.

'However,' he continued, 'I have to say that I am in no doubt that my opponent played correctly and honestly. My brothers believe otherwise, perhaps. But let the dice show what they will. Twenty out of sixty may seem a low number to King Shakuni, but it is high enough for the gods to hide behind. If neither of these two dice produces more than twenty 4s, then we will leave this hall and, as King Dhrita pronounced, return without any complaint to play tomorrow, using these same dice. If one of these dice reaches more than twenty on examination, then we shall return to play again tomorrow with our own dice. But I will not in this case accept King Shakuni's generous offer to return what I believe, through the will of the gods one way or the other, he fairly won from me today. The gods have taken once from me today... I will not insult them by asking them to contradict what has already been decided for us.'

When the applause for Yudhi had died down, Shakuni put a question to his opponent.

'Yudhi, my dear, what if both dice should yield more than twenty 4s?'

'If the gods wish to confuse us in such a manner, then we cannot hold you, King Shakuni, guilty of controlling the dice. If both the dice are guilty, then I am as complicit as you, for then all the dice are guilty, in which case we will decide as though both dice had been honest.'

Yudhi signalled to his brothers to start, and watched absorbed as the dice were repeatedly thrown into the paddock and gathered up again. Shakuni paced slowly around the table, casting an anxious eye at the tally.

Suddenly the clattering ceased.

'I have counted ten from this dice thrown by Nakula,' announced Bhima.

Arjuna looked surprised. 'There were eighteen 4s from Saha's.'

'Is that satisfactory, Yudhi,' said Shakuni, 'or would you like the experiment repeated? It may be just that chance has disguised my deception — or that the gods have seen fit to gild my guilt.'

Yudhi shook his head. 'No, King Shakuni, I am satisfied.'

For the second time that evening, Shakuni walked out of the hall, glaring fiercely at Gandhari as he passed her.

49 The gamble

'How can we hold our heads up after this humiliation? Even if we do win back our possessions?'

'Don't dwell on it, Bhima.'

'Don't dwell on it?'

Bhima was sitting on a cushion at a low table in the centre of the room. Arjuna was pacing up and down beside him. Nakula stood by an unshuttered window, looking out at the sunset; the view from the window was blinkered by the thick walls of the royal palace.

Yudhi was sitting quietly next to Saha in a corner of the dark room. Every few paces Arjuna would stop and glance uneasily at his elder brother.

'Here we are,' continued Bhima, 'like prisoners, ashamed of stepping outside this room. This is war, Arjuna. This is war!'

Nakula turned slowly away from the window. 'When the day comes for war, Bhima, you won't be standing around complaining.' Nakula finished with a little smile, to lighten his brother's mood, but Bhima ignored it.

'Nakula is right,' said Arjuna. 'Such decisions should not be made in anger. One should not act when blinded by anger.'

'Oh, so we should wait until *that* vision of stupidity guides us?' Bhima stretched his arm out to indicate Yudhi. 'That's what anger's for, Arjuna. To make us act.' Bhima shook his head, chuckling to himself, and got up. He joined Nakula at the window.

Nakula put his arm round Bhima's huge waist. 'Anger doesn't suit a slave!' said Nakula. 'You must practise a courtly and subservient manner...'

But Bhima pushed his brother's arm away.

'This isn't the time to tease me, brother. I'm going to see Draupadi.' Bhima started towards the door, but turned before reaching it. 'I may be angry, but I'm not blind.' He looked first at Nakula, then at Saha. 'How could you not see those dice?'

'There were other things on their mind, Bhima,' said Arjuna, 'and they were just too close to them. In any case, you saw that neither reflection appeared to give advantage to the *4*.' He added softly, 'Stay brother...'

For a moment they were silent. Bhima hovered by the door but did not leave.

'Well, Yudhi,' started Nakula, 'can you tell us at least what the gods have in store for us tomorrow? Since you won't tell us what happened to you *today*.'

'Either I will win, brother; or I will lose.' Yudhi spoke softly, but his voice was firm and confident. 'If it is meant to happen, I will restore our fortunes. If it is not, I will not.'

'Don't talk as if it's out of your hands, Yudhi!' said Arjuna. 'You can achieve anything you set your mind to, brother. Why do you always imagine others are writing your future for you?'

Yudhi seemed to ignore Arjuna's remark. 'If we do become slaves,' he said, 'then we must endure it gracefully and with dignity. Without accusation,' he glanced at Bhima, 'and without bitterness. There is always a better way and a worse way, whatever the misfortunes of the road —'

'Yudhi!' interrupted Nakula. 'Listen to Arjuna! With your attitude you might as well jump from the tower in Dur's palace. If you are meant to smash your skull, you will smash your skull, if you are meant to land softly on your feet, you will. So, brother, why don't you try that instead? Well? Why don't you go now, climb Dur's tower, and jump? At least you won't carry us with you!'

'I would not jump, Nakula, because I could not willingly do so. My fear would prevent me, just as surely as an elephant rope... We have been through all this before, brother... The gods have given me fear in order that I pull away from such a course. My fear is their instrument. Even you have said such things in the past. But I am not afraid of Shakuni. I am not afraid of the dice. I am happy and willing to let the gods decide.'

'If you don't try to act for yourself,' argued Saha, 'you will not be rewarded by the gods. They don't reward those who take the future lying down. You must help the gods to help you.'

'If they needed my help, they would make me help. Yes, the gods *could* cushion my fall if I jumped from Dur's tower. But they do not wish me to take advantage of their help. If the gods wished me to act for myself now, they would have given me fear, or desire.'

'But a baby would be happy to stroke the hair of a wolf, Yudhi! Without fear!'

'And indeed, Nakula, that might save its life.'

'Oh yes? You would be happy to send your child to be suckled by a she-wolf?'

'I am the child, Nakula, not the father. I cannot manufacture fear where there is none, desire where there is none.'

'What about *our* desires and our fears?' asked Saha.

'I am aware of them, Saha.'

'And in spite of that you staked us on the table?'

'That isn't fair, Saha,' said Nakula. 'We offered. We're as foolish as Yudhi. That's the truth of it, brothers. We're wrong to blame Yudhi for everything.'

Yudhi stood up and walked slowly towards the window.

'I have fallen — we have fallen. But our fall has been cushioned —'

'By Draupadi!' cried Bhima.

'So now you are ready to jump again?' asked Nakula.

'And to carry us with you?' added Saha.

'First you tell me not to take the future lying down. Now you tell me to lie down before I fall against the future?'

'Because you *throw* yourself down,' said Nakula in exasperation. 'You don't *climb* down. You think you can beat Shakuni by leaving the *dice* to do the work!'

With a puzzled expression Yudhi looked at each of his brothers in turn.

'I can't beat Shakuni at his own game,' he said. 'None of us can. Surely you know that. If you want me to beat him, this is the only way I can. To *try* — to help the gods — would be a waste of energy. I have done what I could. I could do no more.'

Nakula frowned, and turned again to the window. Then he sighed. 'In a way Yudhi is right, I'm afraid,' he said. 'Shakuni can't be beaten at his own game. But that doesn't mean, Yudhi, that you can beat him the way *you've* been playing!'

'Why not?' said Bhima. 'If Shakuni hadn't got all those 4s when it counted... Yudhi may be right... Perhaps it's Shakuni who's heading for the fall.'

'Why not?' echoed Nakula. 'Because if Yudhi is always trying to kill when there's only one prime available and three commons — surely you see, Yudhi! The dice is much more likely to strike one of the commons than the prime!'

'If the dice were blind, yes, Nakula —'

'But of course they're blind... at least, to the affairs of men... Whatever it is that they're affected by, they don't know they have been bet on! Or which number will bring success to which player!'

'The dice may not, Nakula, but the gods do. Brahma sees.'

'You think Brahma cares about one little throw of a dice?'

'Listen, Nakula... If a dice has been bet on, and with a sufficiently high stake, then the way the dice falls may indeed change the world. If on the other hand a dice carries no bet upon its back, then it will make very little difference to the world. The future could accommodate in this case any of its four vertices with indifference. But if the world has to become very different, depending on the throw of just a single dice, then the four vertices are not all equally possible: for it is only one world which is possible, and that is the one that exists already under Brahma's eye. And since only one future is possible, the one which already lies under Brahma's eye, then if that future can accommodate only one vertex of the dice, that vertex is certain. So, to us men it appears as though the gods have controlled the dice to bring about the future they have planned for us. But from Brahma's view, the past fits the future as much as the future fits the past.'

Nakula covered his face with his hands.

'Under Brahma's eye,' continued Yudhi, 'the past does not bring about the future. The future is not a blank for the past to grow into, like a growing tree which branches out depending on the sun, the wind, the rain. That is only how man sees it.'

Yudhi's brothers listened in silence.

'Nothing in this world is an accident of chance. If something appears so, it is because, try as we might to look back into its past for a reason why it should be as it is, we cannot find one. Even the most powerful eye imaginable may find there, in the past, no such reason. Why? Because the reason may not lie in the past, but in the future, which even the most powerful eye of man cannot see; but which lies still before the mind of Brahma as easily as the past. On the shore line where we always live, between the past and the future, we can only glimpse one half of Brahma's world. Yet, even in that half which we can see, we find dark shadows of the future into which we cannot peer... which we call Chance.'

For a while none of them spoke. Then Nakula approached Yudhi.

'And you think... You think that you are so important to this world that Brahma is not indifferent to your fate? That what happens to you... to us, is more significant to him than if you were a grain of sand, split in two by the point of the dice?'

Yudhi did not reply immediately. He walked slowly back to his cushion.

'That, Nakula,' he said, sitting down by Saha, 'that is my gamble. I am sorry that I have brought you... you and the people of Indraprastha, into it. At least if I lose,' he added, with a smile, 'you can see that I deserve to be humbled.'

Nakula's eyes glistened as he looked vacantly through the window.

'We were already in it,' said Arjuna, sitting down by Yudhi and putting his arm around him. 'And by our choice.'

'Whatever happens tomorrow,' said Saha, 'we are with you, Yudhi. Even Nakula. You know that.'

◊

When Shakuni had left the dice hall for the first time, at the end of the twentieth glaha, he had gone straight to Charvaka's workshop.

'Charvaka!' he had cried, almost before his foot was through the door. 'I cannot understand the number of 4s I got in the last glahas!'

'Surely... they didn't accuse you of cheating?'

'No, no—'

'Well? How did it go? Did you manage to beat him?'

Shakuni had then been obliged to give Charvaka an account of the game, and of Yudhi's losses. He had been just about to return to the subject of the 4s, when Dur found him, and took him away to face his accusers.

When Shakuni left the hall for the second time, he again rushed straight to Charvaka, and described the experiments to him.

'They first *weighed* two of the dice against each other?' asked the rishi.

'Yes! I told them it was useless — if you had made false dice you would have given them the same weight. But they put them on the pans, just the same.'

'How did they think I did it, then?'

'With the colour — by making the black point lighter. To think that I should *need* to control or predict the 4s to beat them!'

'Well, one day, I believe,' Charvaka speculated, 'we may know enough about the movements of objects, and be able to measure the weight and disposition of the dice *so* exactly, that it may be possible to predict every throw, and even how the slightest touch on the dice would influence its next fall.'

'Ha!' Shakuni chuckled. 'Even if you could do that, my dear rishi, and could measure the dice with unimpeded accuracy, why, you would need to measure the dice again after you first measured it — since, as you say, the slightest touch would change its future! I'm afraid, my dear, that only from outside the world, if such a thing were possible, from where our future could be seen in the present — as Brahma is supposed to see us — only from there could the future, even of so humble a thing as a dice, be known. While we remain trapped inside this world, our most potent knowledge would cast a shadow behind which we could not peer — and we would have to call that shadow Chance!'

Charvaka pursed his lips, and then frowned.

'You do not agree, my dear?' enquired Shakuni.

'I'm not sure... whether such a problem would affect our ability to predict *dice* — but that is not for us to judge upon. Only Kali can reveal that — when we have caught up with her! You will at least grant me that?'

'Oh, if it is not with dice it will be with something even more delicate; in time, Kali will prove me right. Can you fault the logic?'

'*I* cannot. But Kali may defy your logic. What is more logical than one dice and another dice making two dice?' As he said this, Charvaka took two coins from the pocket of his cloak. He put them both into the palm of one hand, and closed this hand into a fist. Then he opened it slowly to reveal just one coin. 'If she were so inclined,' he said, 'Kali could behave like this all the time, without my help. The last judgement you must always leave to Kali.'

Shakuni smiled. 'Yes... but those were coins... You said *dice*!'

Charvaka changed the subject.

'Those *4*s...' he said, 'was it just in the last few glahas?'

'Yes, remarkable. I cannot precisely remember the proportion —'

'And they... they helped you? Or —'

'Oh yes, my dear. Yudhi lost considerably more than he might have done. At least, it might have taken a little longer. He might have won back a thing or two, perhaps. He did have bad luck, though. He didn't kill me even once in those last few glahas — I had expected to have to return *something*...'

'And after they weighed the dice, they threw... just one pair, sixty times?'

'Yes. They got ten and eighteen *4*s respectively, with twenty as the margin, can you believe that? I was lucky! And *you* were lucky, my dear! As it was, your dice were declared true. So, they will use the same dice tomorrow — not literally, but the same batch, there are enough left in the bowl —'

'What do you mean?'

'Oh... Did I not say? Oh dear, I believe I may not have mentioned it: we are playing again tomorrow.'

'*Playing again*?'

'I'm sorry, my dear, I thought I had mentioned it — I didn't find out myself until Dur told me, when he came here to fetch me back —'

'But why?'

'Apparently, after I left, Draupadi complained that the last glaha was... irregular.'

'Irregular?'

'Yes —'

'And you are definitely playing again tomorrow?'

'Oh yes.'

'How many glahas?'

'Just the one, I believe.'

'And so... they will be using the dice... from the bottom of the bowl?'

Shakuni looked at Charvaka carefully. He looked at the rishi's beard, at his lips. Shakuni's eyebrows lowered.

'They agreed to use the same dice,' he explained, 'since that pair passed their examination...'

Shakuni looked into Charvaka's eyes, and, as he did so, his hands began to tremble. He lunged at Charvaka, but the rishi was too agile for him, and skipped back to take cover behind his bench.

'*Did Dur know*?' Shakuni's voice was not loud, but his jaws seemed almost to lock with rage.

'No, Dur had no idea.'

Shakuni waited, still trembling, on one side of Charvaka's bench, while the rishi stood his ground on the other.

'I put a tiny cube of wood in all of the dice,' explained Charvaka. 'Of course, I would rather have used a little piece of nothing instead, but that would have been too time-consuming. In most of them, I put the wood exactly in the centre. But in some of them I put it nearer to the vertex on which the black was to be applied. Still equidistant from the other three points, of course.'

'In one of the reflections, or in both?'

'No, no. The reflections were just an accident of chance. I left the dice ready for my painters with the *4* vertex pointing up, and instructed them to apply the black to the top vertex. When this dried, they gave the dice one flip each and applied the next colour. So the handedness was very much a matter of chance. The whole process was not utterly reliable, though: I noticed that one or two of the eccentric dice favoured a point other than black, where the men had flipped the dice by accident before applying the colour.'

Charvaka paused to gauge Shakuni's reaction. 'It was just a small proportion which were eccentric, Shakuni. *Much* less than half. And they only slightly favoured the *4*. Perhaps twenty-five or thirty out of sixty would have come up black.'

'Just for the last day's dice?' Shakuni's voice was calmer now, and he had stopped trembling.

'Yes. Just for the last afternoon, in fact. Just for Yudhi's game... I put the eccentric dice at the bottom of the bowl, and stirred them round just a little. That way they would mostly come into effect towards the end of your game.'

'*Aaagh!*' Shakuni slammed his fist down on the bench.

'Why are you so upset? No one discovered it. And it was perfectly fair — both you and Yudhi had access to the same dice. And aren't you always saying that the *4*s give advantage to the most skilful player? What is wrong with that? It makes the game more lively!'

Shakuni stared at the rishi, unable to speak.

'What about my armour, Shakuni? My weapons? Do they not favour the more skilful player? What about skill itself? How could any game between you and Yudhi *possibly* be fair? Is not your skill an outrageous advantage to you? Does that not make the game much more unjust than my eccentric dice?'

Shakuni was still speechless.

'The world does not treat people equally, Shakuni. It is only because we are all equally ignorant of how it will treat us, that we can take false comfort in the illusion of a just world. I must say, your reaction is *most* irrational, Shakuni. You surprise me.'

Shakuni took a deep breath to gain control of himself.

'If I wish to listen to such diversive rambling,' he said, 'I can consult my nephews. I do not expect it of you, Charvaka. I do not need to explain to *you* why I offer bad bets on a cheetah. Particularly, as you well know, cheetahs with the strike on *4*! Irrational! Do you think I would offer Yudhi a bad bet on a dice which is *likely* to strike *4*?'

'All I did was liven up the game. It was a little experiment...'

'At our expense!'

'It is always at the players' expense, Shakuni. Please! And not without a little risk to myself, may I add. It was a gamble for me too...' Charvaka knew from Shakuni's face that he understood what he meant, but he finished, nevertheless: 'If they... was it Bhima? If Bhima had picked a different pair to examine, I would have had to confess.'

'Would they have believed *my* innocence, Charvaka?'

'There is quite enough guilt in both of us, Shakuni. Do not try to hide inside a game to preserve your innocence. The grid has no edge. The board has no border within which the rules of war adjudicate your innocence... You know as well as I do that such rules are only there to allow the better of two evils to be called good. So that good may wrong under the name of right.'

Shakuni did not reply.

'You knew what Dur was up to. What he hoped for. Is it not enough that you are acknowledged the greatest player in the land?'

'They accused me of cheating, Charvaka, of magic, all of that nonsense... Aaagh!' Again he slammed his hands down on the bench. 'And now you...' He paused to recover himself. 'Now you have made me doubly guilty of the only innocence I had...'

'So because they had been accusing you, Shakuni, you grabbed for your pride like a little child? Destroying the Pandavas in the process? Giving Dur more than he ever dreamed of? Because of your *pride*? That is *innocence*?'

'The game isn't over, Charvaka... They are not yet destroyed... I certainly didn't expect Yudhi to lose so much.'

'You mean, my dear Shakuni, you never expected that your pride would spur you on so much? I'm quite sure you didn't dwell on the world outside the table until after the business at the table was over. Well, I *did* think about it, Shakuni. That is why I gave Yudhi what I stupidly thought was a little help. What do you think *I* feel like now?' Charvaka laughed at himself. '*Eh*? What do you think of *my* gamble, Shakuni? You were too good even for that... or too lucky. Oh yes, of course, the gods were on your side!'

Shakuni chuckled in spite of himself.

'Well, now you should be pleased with yourself,' continued Charvaka sarcastically. 'You even turned my weapon around. Poor Yudhi!'

Shakuni's shoulders sank, and he sat himself down on a stool by the rishi's bench. For a while he mulled over his thoughts in silence. Charvaka watched him closely. Then Shakuni rose slowly from the stool.

'Well, my dear,' he said, 'you are more unpredictable even than the dice. I sometimes wonder whether you have any principles at all... Beneath that layer of words you cover yourself with... Whether you are my friend or my enemy... It is only because you have warned me so often that you are nobody's friend that I cannot be angry with you.' He paused. Then, nodding his head slowly, he said, 'Tomorrow I think the dice had better be true. At least I know where I am when I am properly ignorant.' He smiled at Charvaka. 'Make sure the dice are true for tomorrow, will you, my dear? Please?'

◊

Before the meal that evening, Dur went to Karna's quarters in the royal palace.

'They think we cheated,' he said to Karna.

'It doesn't seem to bother Yudhi very much, whether you did or not.'

Dur could tell from Karna's voice that it was best not to pursue this issue with him. Karna was hungry, so they set out straight away for the banquet.

'Karna, I'm worried about tomorrow.'

'I'm not surprised, Dur.' Karna laughed softly.

'Karna! I need to set out terms to my father later on tonight. I need your help. Will you come with me to see him?'

'No. But I'll give you some advice, if it will help. Though I fear that it won't.'

'Say what you think, Karna.'

'It will be a merry feast tonight,' he said.

Dur frowned. They walked on for a while in silence. Then Karna spoke again.

'Jara-sandha said something to me...' Karna began. 'I think I understand it better now than at the time. I can't remember his exact words... He said that power cannot be given away. I'm worried, Dur, that if you succeed in your game, the Pandavas may lose their property but not their power.'

Dur grew more agitated as he listened.

'When power and wealth go together, or when they can flow into each other freely, things can be fairly steady... I think they call it peace... But if power and wealth are separated, or if the flow between them is obstructed, there is danger, especially to the hand that keeps them apart. Usually, of course, they go together, since power attracts wealth as surely as wealth seeks power. I can't help you much more than to say this, Dur: until today the Pandavas had great wealth *and* great power. If you remove their wealth, Dur, *if*, then you must make sure you don't leave them with their power intact to burn against you. If you can't do this, it's better that you should abandon your own wealth. You have known for too long what it's like to have great wealth and little power. If you can't satisfy your desires in this way, by achieving the power that eludes you, then it's better that you should abandon your own wealth altogether. You will be happier. And I'll still visit you...' Karna added with a smile, 'less often, perhaps...'

50 The two cities

'King Dhrita-rashtra, Queen Gandhari, Lord Bhishma and myself have given careful thought to the glaha now to be played before you all. The contestants, in particular, are requested to attend carefully.

'One glaha only will be played this morning, to a limit of 23. The two players will have at their disposal a number of counters, designated as follows.

'This counter...' — Kripa held up a two-stake to show the audience — '... denotes the person of Queen Draupadi. It is to be positioned by King Yudhi-sthira, if he agrees to these conditions, as his starting stake.' Kripa handed the counter to Nakula, who passed it to Saha, who gave it to Yudhi.

'Of these two counters...' — Kripa held up two more, both unit stakes — '... the first designates Indraprastha, its treasure and its people. And the second signifies the four Pandava princes. Together, these two counters represent the entire winnings made yesterday by King Shakuni, barring Yudhi himself and Queen Draupadi. And together, these two will constitute King Shakuni's opening stake, if he agrees to these conditions.' Kripa handed the counters to Dur, who passed them to Shakuni.

'This fourth counter represents the person of King Yudhi-sthira himself, who, at the bequest of King Dhrita-rashtra, along with Queen Draupadi, has his complete liberty returned, at least for the duration of this glaha. This counter is at Yudhi's disposal.' Kripa gave the counter, a two-stake, to Nakula.

'Prince Nakula and Prince Saha are also granted, at least for the duration of the glaha, the licence necessary to participate in the proceedings at the table, though formally they are at present bound over to King Shakuni. Prince Bhima-sena and Prince Arjuna, also bound over to King Shakuni, are likewise free from all personal constraint at least for the duration of this glaha.

'Of these two further counters, one represents the person of Prince Duryodhana, together with his entire estate; the other, the person of King Shakuni, together with his entire estate. They are at the disposal of King Shakuni.' Kripa passed them to Dur; they were both unit stakes.

'The value of the counters has been determined as follows. The two opposing opening stakes are considered to be of equal value, taking into account the regrettable treatment endured so nobly by Queen Draupadi; and also her merit, through which the Pandavas are held as by a rope hanging down into a precipice. With the two opening counters on Shakuni's side being taken each to have unit value, Queen Draupadi's counter is therefore double the value of the unit. The counter representing the person of King Yudhi-sthira is considered to be equal in value to Queen Draupadi's, bringing his material to four units. The counters representing King Shakuni and Prince Dur are deemed each to be of unit value, being one half the value of Queen Draupadi or the King of Kings. On this side also, therefore, the nominated material has a value of four units.

'No additional counters may be staked upon the grid unless each of these six hereinbefore designated counters is already on the grid. And no such additional counters may be placed upon the grid unless their designation and value is agreed by the players and myself *before* their appearance on the grid.'

Kripa paused now, and looked up at the audience.

'In the event of the capture either of King Yudhi-sthira, through the medium of his counter, or, similarly, of King Shakuni, the glaha shall terminate at that point, whether or not a kill is thereby achieved. In this event the betting lines at that time on the grid shall both pass to the surviving player, as though a kill were achieved.

'In the event that a counter, representing one of the persons hereinbefore named, remains among, or is added to, the possessions of the opposing player at the end of the glaha; that is to say, if King Yudhi-sthira at the conclusion of the glaha holds either or both of the counters representing King Shakuni and Prince Dur; or, if King Shakuni holds any or all of the counters representing the Pandava princes, King Yudhi himself, or Queen Draupadi herself; then the person or persons represented by these captured or otherwise gained counters, to whom I will refer hereinafter as the losers, shall be subject, not to servitude at the command of their opponents, hereinafter referred to as the winners, but instead to the following condition: they shall be committed to exile in the forests.

'The terms of exile shall be as follows. Twelve years must be spent by the losers in the forest, away from any village or place of habitation dwelled in by others. Furthermore, the losers shall be required to spend the whole of the thirteenth year in a village, town or city inhabited by others. If during the period of this year they are recognised or discovered, or otherwise made known to the winners, the losers shall be obliged to return to their exile in the forest for a further twelve years... to repeat the process.

'If the conditions of exile have been properly met, the losers shall, on the expiry of the thirteenth year, recover all the possessions from which they will have been separated. If the losers are the Pandavas, they shall recover Indraprastha and its treasures, regain the freedom of its people from subservience to Prince Dur-yodhana and King Shakuni, and regain their own freedom. If the losers are Prince Dur and King Shakuni, they shall recover their palaces and treasures, and the people who serve allegiance to them. Whosoever is the winner shall undertake to preserve intact the possessions of the losers, so that restitution may be made at the end of the thirteenth year.'

Kripa turned to the players at the table. 'Do both sides of the table undertake to abide by these conditions?'

The silence around the hall during Kripa's speech now began to fill with the murmur from the audience, slowly growing like a fire, hissing and crackling as it gathered strength.

Yudhi beckoned to Bhima and Arjuna, who were standing by near the dice table.

'This is *monstrous*!' whispered Saha.

'Remember,' said Yudhi to his brothers, 'it is only through the generosity of King Dhrita that you are not at this moment doomed to a life of servitude to Dur. These conditions, even if we lose, give us hope. Remember too that Shakuni and Dur had until now only their winnings to lose. If they agree to these conditions, they have much more to lose than they ever put on the table yesterday: they may be obliged to put themselves at stake. Their courage, if they agree to these conditions, deserves our respect.' Yudhi looked at each of his brothers in turn.

'My Lord Kripa,' said Yudhi, 'we agree to these conditions, provided that Queen Draupadi also accepts them.'

Kripa turned to Draupadi, who was sitting in the first tier next to Gandhari.

'I agree to them, Lord Kripa,' she replied.

'The Pandavas have agreed to abide by these conditions,' Kripa declared. He now turned to Shakuni and Dur.

'I agree,' said Dur, his voice drawn thin.

'King Shakuni?' asked Kripa expectantly.

Shakuni did not answer. He was deep in thought, looking down at his hands, both spread flat on the table. He raised one hand to his lips, resting his elbow lightly on the table edge. As Kripa approached him, Shakuni slowly lifted the fingers of his other hand off the table, without moving his wrist, so that they quivered like the probing tentacles of a snail. Kripa waited.

The silence was broken by Yudhi.

'I would be willing to absolve Shakuni from the condition of exile, should his counter fall into our possession.'

'No,' said Shakuni. 'I will agree to Kripa's proposals... I will abide by them — if... May I clarify a point, Lord Kripa? If I am condemned to the forest, may I receive company? Other than Dur, I mean... no offence, nephew, but you understand...' He turned to Dur and patted his arm. 'Or do I have to renounce *all* contact?'

'You may receive visitors during the period of twelve years,' replied Kripa. 'So long as you do not actively live in an established community, you may receive freely whosoever may wish to visit you, and the same would apply correspondingly to the Pandavas.'

Shakuni's shoulders fell in a sigh of relief. 'That is excellent. Excellent. In that case, you certainly have my agreement.'

'Then, if you permit me,' said Kripa, 'I will this morning dispense with any further reading of the usual rules of play, though these will naturally remain in application.'

There was no objection to this proposal from any quarter.

'Let play begin. Shakuni to open.'

Shakuni threw his first dice with little relish. It was a *1*. He threw again, in no hurry, knocking the dice for a prime. His *3* gave Yudhi the attack.

'You should bet on this,' whispered Saha, who was next to Yudhi at the table. 'You *must* protect your line. And remember that as soon as Shakuni places his two available counters on the grid, he won't be able to block — he *has* to declare the nature of any other counters first! That greatly weakens his sting!'

'But if I place myself on the grid to bet, I risk being captured, brother.'

'Yudhi,' whispered Nakula, 'if he captures Draupadi, who's also at risk, then he gets you as well — for eliminating your line. You must attack. With all your material on the table you'll force him on to the grid as well. And then he won't be able to block! With so few counters, Shakuni's game collapses. You must make him vulnerable, Yudhi.'

Yudhi knocked his dice, and placed his counter on the table. The dice fell for a *3*.

	1	2	3	4	5	6	7	8	9	10
Y										
	[Draupadi] ②		[Yudhi] ②							
	△	△3	△3							
	②									
	[Indraprastha & Pandava princes]									
Sh										
	p1	p4	p7							

'A common now, Yudhi!' urged Saha. 'You're in striking distance of two tigers, 10 or 16,' he explained. 'A *3* puts you on 10, and with a *4* — if you're quick — you can ride Kali on the clear *3* for 16.'

Yudhi threw a *4*, but Shakuni beat him to the second column, blocking with one of his two available counters. Yudhi was thus forced to place the *4* at the end of the row to make 11, finishing his attack.

'King Shakuni, can you remind me who that is?' asked Yudhi, indicating the blocking counter.

'That is my nephew. *I* am still safely off the grid.'

The silence of the audience was broken by some nervous laughter from Dur's brothers.

	1	2	3	4	5	6	7	8	9	10
Y										
	[Draupadi] (2)		[Yudhi] (2)							
	/1\	/3\	/3\	/4\						
	(2) [Indraprastha & Pandava princes]									
		(1) [Dur]								
Sh										
	p1	p4	p7	c11						

Shakuni gathered his next dice into his fist.

'There's nothing dangerous on for him this throw,' advised Saha. '14 is the first point from which he can capture.'

'And now he has only himself to block with, if he loses the attack,' added Nakula.

Without knocking, Shakuni threw his dice. It was a *2*, striking 13.

'Go for the tiger, Yudhi!' insisted Saha.

'Should I not try to kill him now, while I have the attack?'

'No, you must wait!' whispered Nakula. 'The 13 is only a cheetah. Go for a common now: 14 is a leopard, 15 a lion — not to mention the 16. If you go for the prime now, you risk leaving *him* on the tiger.'

Taking their advice, Yudhi threw without tapping his dice, getting a *1* to put him on 14.

	1	2	3	4	5	6	7	8	9	10
Y										
	[Draupadi] ②		[Yudhi] ②							
		△①	△③	△③	△④	△②	△①			
	②									
	[Indraprastha & Pandava princes]									
		Ô① [Dur]								
Sh										
	p1	p4	p7	c11	c13	c14				

'Go for a common again!' Saha's voice trembled with excitement. 'A *1* puts you on the lion, *2* gives you the tiger, and *4* — if you get a *4* you have him! You can capture either of his two counters! He can only block one of them!'

'And if you get a *4*, Yudhi,' added Nakula, 'just take your time. He'll try to defend *Dur*. I'm sure he will. Leaving you all the time in the world to win back us and Indraprastha!'

Yudhi shook the dice in his fist. As the dice settled on the black point, Shakuni instantly blocked the second column. Then he and Dur watched helplessly: to a huge cheer from the audience, Yudhi recaptured Indraprastha and the four Pandavas.

	1	2	3	4	5	6	7	8	9	10
Y	[Indraprastha & Pandava princes] ②									
	[Draupadi] ②		[Yudhi] ②							
	▲1	▲3	▲3	▲4	▲2	▲1				
	▲4 ←									
		Ô① [Dur]								
		Ô① [Shakuni]								
Sh										
	p1	p4	p7	c11	c13	c14	(c17)			

'I think I will retire now, brothers,' said Yudhi. 'The 17 is getting close to the limit...'

'No, Yudhi! *You'd* have to go into exile, and —'

'I would like to retire now, if I may,' said Yudhi to his opponents. 'My counter is worth your line, so if I pay you that then the other counters remain with us. Is that acceptable?'

'No, Yudhi,' said Dur. 'You would be retiring out of turn. Your attack is finished. Therefore you would have to surrender your *entire* line to us if you retire now. That means yourself *and* Draupadi. Is that not so, Kripa?'

Kripa confirmed Dur's assessment.

Yudhi appeared to be about to speak, but then seemed to freeze in mid-thought. Shakuni turned to talk to Dur; he stopped when he heard Yudhi's voice.

'I will not retire, then,' said Yudhi, softly. 'But in that case I must ask my opponents to replace the bet I have just captured.'

Dur bristled with indignation, and was about to appeal to Kripa when Shakuni replied.

'What would be a suitable stake, Yudhi?'

'Hastinapura,' said Yudhi.

'*Hastinapura*?' repeated Dur in astonishment.

'Yes.' Yudhi glanced at the front row where Dhrita was sitting. 'Perhaps you could ask King Dhrita-rashtra if he would be willing to place Hastinapura on the table. Nothing else is commensurate with the counter I have just captured. If you cannot fulfil this obligation, Prince Dur-yodhana, your partner will be obliged to retire from the glaha. Is that not the case, King Shakuni? You would have no material, so you would have to retire. In that case, if you retire, I would happily absolve you from having to produce the value of my line. Your line as it is would then suffice. Am I right in my interpretation? When a player has no more material, are they not obliged to retire?'

'You are perfectly correct, my dear. Come, Dur —'

'Father...'

'Running for protection again?' cried Bhima. 'To Karna for arrows, and now to your father to save you at the dice table!'

'It's *you* who's been protected by my father!' cried Dur. 'You were rightfully captured yesterday. It's because of my father's generosity to *you*, and his partiality to *you*, that you are able to be here now!'

'King Shakuni...' King Dhrita spoke without rising from his seat. 'Put Hastinapura on the table. If you lose, we will be privileged to pay homage to the King of Kings.'

Drupada, sitting above the king, clapped his hands. The rest of the audience were too stunned to notice his solitary applause.

Shakuni placed a two-bet on the first column of the grid.

'That is Hastinapura,' he explained, picking his next dice out of the bowl.

'Yudhi,' whispered Nakula, 'he can take the glaha riding the *2*, or he strikes 20 if...'

Nakula's voice trailed off as he glimpsed the black point of Shakuni's dice in the paddock. Perhaps Shakuni was not expecting his opponent to place anything further on the grid at this stage; perhaps it was just a heroic block by Yudhi, made slightly easier by the proximity of the two danger spots; the audience, certainly, did not stop to wonder as they erupted in tumultuous applause.

But though Shakuni had been forced to place the *4* at the end of the row, it was still his turn. Since he was on 21, a *3* or a *4* would now take him over the limit, resulting in a victory to Yudhi.

Shakuni did not dally over his next dice. He picked it up, tapped it, and threw it straight away into the paddock. The entire hall gave a gasp which broke up like a great wave falling upon rocks. Shakuni calmly placed the dice at the end of the row.

	1	2	3	4	5	6	7	8	9	10
Y	((2))									
				[Indraprastha] Ô(1)	Ô(1)	[Pandava princes]				
	[Draupadi] (2)		[Yudhi] (2)							
	△1	△3	△3	△4	△2	△1	△4	△1		
	△4 ←									
	(2)	Ô(1)								
	[Hastinapura]	[Dur]								
		Ô(1)								
		[Shakuni]								
Sh										
	p1	p4	p7	c11	c13	c14	(c17) c21	p22		

Yudhi stared hard at the grid, and turned to his brothers.

'I must get another *1*?'

'Yes, Yudhi,' said Nakula. 'A *1* and only a *1*, or we're all lost...'

Shakuni lifted his palms off the surface of the table, leaving his hand-prints written in sweat upon the gold.

'King Shakuni, Prince Dur-yodhana...' Yudhi addressed his opponents softly, but his voice was firm and steady. 'I see that as things stand my betting line appears to be worth more than yours. If I understand things right, this means that if I win you would still be in debt to me, since you do not appear to have the means on the table to pay the value of my line. However, I believe you were too modest in your estimation of Hastinapura. Allow me, if you will, to value this great city at four units, rather than the two on the table. In this manner our two lines will be equal in value. In return I ask two favours. If I lose, I ask that we may first visit Indraprastha one last time before going to the forests, so that I can explain to the people of that city what has happened.'

Dur nodded and opened his mouth to speak, but his words stuck in his throat.

The reply came from the auditorium. 'Your request is granted,' said King Dhrita.

'My other desire...' continued Yudhi, '...is that if I lose, I would spend my years more easily if I knew that the Grandsire... that Lord Bhishma would oversee from time to time the affairs of Indraprastha...' Yudhi looked at Dur, who nodded again.

'With Dur's permission,' said Bhishma, from the auditorium, 'I will do as you ask, Yudhi.'

'Thank you.' Yudhi picked up his dice and rolled it in his fist. He looked at his opponents, as though expecting them to speak. He turned to face the blind king. 'King Dhrita-rashtra, have *you* any request, should you lose Hastinapura?'

'No, Yudhi,' came the reply, without hesitation. 'We are in your hands.'

Yudhi knocked the dice once against the table top. 'You are more skilful than I am at this game,' he whispered to Nakula, with a smile. 'Would you like to throw this dice for me?'

'No, Yudhi. You throw it.'

Again Yudhi shook the dice in his fist. 'Then let Destiny make of us what it will.' He released the dice into the paddock.

•

'Well, boys, it's much later than I thought. We'd better end here for today... I expect you've had enough. I certainly have. Let's clear up the dice, shall we?...'

Palmira started to brush the dice off the chess boards which the boys had been using. They watched her with their mouths hanging wide open in astonishment.

'Tomorrow you'll have Mulciber,' she continued, lifting the chess boards off her table, 'so early to work, remember?...'

The boys looked at each other in disbelief. Then, suddenly, they put their hands together, as for a prayer, and bowed down to Palmira. Their heads almost touched the table top.

'Could Brahma please tell us what that last dice was?' pleaded the first Henry.

'I'll be back from Tunis before the end of the week.' She started gathering up the dice. 'Then... if Mulciber tells me you've been good... I might let you off the rest of the story —'

'This isn't funny, you know, Palmira. We've had to work very hard today.'

'And we didn't interrupt, did we? Well, hardly...'

'You can't go off and leave us not knowing... You *can't*!...'

'You do want us to help Mulciber, don't you?'

'Let me think...' considered Palmira. 'It was either a *1*, or a *2*, or —'

'*Palmira*!'

'I'm just not sure, boys —'

'What d'you mean, *you're not sure*?'

'I'll tell you what,' she said, her eyes widening innocently. 'Why don't *you* throw Yudhi's last dice for him. Yes, that *would* be a good idea.'

Their mouths fell open again.

'I mean, just imagine, boys: poor Yudhi wants to leave it to the gods, and he gets *me* instead! That's hardly fair, is it? We really should at least let the dice decide, instead of me. Yes! That way we *can* leave it to chance, eh? Now then, which one of you is it to be?'

'Palmira, you know very well already what the dice was.'

'We *know* you know, you can't fool us that easily!'

'I don't understand you, boys. You know I make up the story as I go along.'

'Palmira!'

'Anyway,' observed the second Henry, 'Yudhi himself said that nothing was an accident of chance. So you've got to know already. You didn't decide all those other dice by chance, did you? So why should you leave the last one to chance?'

'Come on Palmira, what *was* it?' pleaded the first Henry.

'What *was* it?' echoed his brother.

'I'm thinking, I'm thinking...' She raised her hands as if to keep them at bay.

'You're being very childish, you know, Palmira.'

'Really? Just because I don't answer your questions? You didn't answer *my* question, did you?'

'What question?'

'Why you were fighting...'

'*Fighting*? We haven't been fighting. When?'

'She means...' the second Henry reminded his brother, 'you know... That day before she started...'

'*That*? That *is* childish, Palmira. You should be ashamed of yourself!'

'You're absolutely right,' she agreed. 'Yes, I am being childish. Well, all right, I'll tell you. But the fact is, and this is really true, you know, I'm not *sure* what it was. Sssh! I really can't decide. Of course, I know for certain that the dice was either a *2*, a *3* or a *4*... I know that it *definitely* wasn't a *1*, of course — but I can't for the life of me decide which of the other three alternatives... Perhaps if I close my eyes... Mmm... it's very indeterminate, I'm afraid... Wait a moment! Ah, yes! He's throwing it, yes... Of *course*, the average, how simple! It's a *3*! Yes! Well, there we are...'

'A *3*?'

'You mean Yudhi lost?'

'Yudhi *lost*?'

'Well, I think so, boys... Wait a minute, I might have...'

'What d'you mean you *think* so?' asked the first Henry.

'Shut up!' cautioned his brother. 'She's told us once.'

'But she might change her mind? You could change your mind, couldn't you, Palmira?'

'I suppose so,' she said. 'All right. Very well then... Yudhi threw a *1*, but because he was so generous he gave everything back, made friends with Dur, and they all lived happily ever after —'

'*Palmira*!'

'Did he *really* lose?'

'Of course he lost, you idiots!'

'So he had to go to the forest?'

'Yes, boys. He most certainly did.'

The twins sat in silence for a while, looking up absently, through the wooden trellis, at the sky.

'Palmira... You know that Brahma cycle... Was it two thousand three hundred and ten beats that they played?'

'No.'

'No?'

'They played two thousand three hundred and eleven beats,' she corrected. 'Remember: the last beat...'

'Oh!'

Palmira cleared away the last of the dice.

'Right, you can take these boards in — we won't be needing them again, I can tell you. Come on! Tomorrow you must start work early...'

With their heads a little downcast, the boys took the chess boards back inside the house.

'Palmira, you know that thing about the future...' said the first Henry, as he stepped back into the terrace through the entrance in the north wall. 'Can the future really cause what happens in the past?'

'I thought...' said the second Henry, following his brother, 'I thought you were always saying that everything in the future is caused by the past, not the other way round at all.'

'I'm always saying that?'

'You seem to be. You're always nagging us to try to explain things by what causes them. Aren't you? And it's always something that's happened *before*. Even when something's got a purpose, you're always saying it only *seems* that the future's causing it.'

'I don't think it's possible, Palmira. How can something in the future get back to cause something in the past?'

'Mmm...' Palmira pursed her lips. 'Well... Perhaps you know that quite near where the Hodja had his house there lived two old men who were twins. Oh, you didn't know?' A stern look from Palmira prevented any further interruption. 'Oh yes. And they almost always did things together. Which was very lucky for their neighbours, because no one could tell them apart. At least if they were together, people didn't have the problem of finding out which one they'd seen... Anyway... One night the Hodja and his wife were sound asleep in bed. Under a nice warm quilt. It was winter, by the way. In the middle of the night, the Hodja's wife woke up to the sound of voices coming from outside the door of the house.

'"Hodja! Listen!" She woke up her husband. "Hodja, it sounds to me like those twins!"

'"It can't be. You can hear they're in the middle of an argument. Listen — it sounds as though they're fighting now! You know those twins *never* fight."

'"I tell you, Hodja, it's those twins. *And* they're fighting. Listen! You better go down and see what the problem is, it must be something very serious!"

'"But it's *freezing*..."

'"Don't make excuses!"

'"Can I take the quilt, then?"

'"Certainly not! Cover yourself in the carpet, if you must..."

'An ancient carpet covered the floor beside their bed. It had been handed down to the Hodja by his father, and by his father before him, and who knows before that... It was a wonderful carpet, though it was now a little ragged, slightly threadbare here and there, with an occasional patch...

'So the Hodja wrapped himself in it, and went down to the door.

'Sure enough, it was the twins. But the moment they caught sight of the Hodja, they snatched the carpet off his back and started tugging and pulling at it as though their very lives depended on it. Each of them tried to wrest it from the other's grasp. One of them managed to pull the carpet clear, and started to scuttle off down the street. The astonished Hodja watched the other one scurry off in pursuit into the darkness. Then he went back inside, shivering.

"'Well? What was that all about?" asked his wife.

"'You're right, it *was* the twins...'"

"'So what where they fighting about? What was the problem?"

"'It's very strange... very curious... It was our carpet... They were fighting over our carpet...'"

•

Main characters

Karna: adopted son of *Adhi* and *Radha*; Karna's brothers are *Sangra*, *Pra* and *Vrisha*.

The rishis:
Charvaka (the mouse), *Narada* (the dove), *Parashu* (the mongoose) and *Durvasa* (the fox).

Vyasa (the spider): stepson of *Shantanu*, the late King of the Bharata people.

The Pandava Princes:
Yudhi, *Bhima*, *Arjuna* (sons of Pritha); the twins *Saha* and *Nakula* (sons of Madri).

Princess Shikhandi: daughter of King Drupada, sister of Princess Draupadi and *Prince Drishta*.
Princess Draupadi: wife of the Pandava brothers, daughter of Drupada.

The Kuru Princes (sons of Gandhari):
Dur, *Duh*, *Vikarna*, *Chitra*, *Yuyutsu*, *Virimsa*, *Vivitsu*, *Kratha* and *Upanada*.

At Hastinapura, capital city of the Bharatas:
Kripa (the owl) and *Drona*: teachers of the arts of combat. Drona is father of *Ashwa*.
Vidura: son of Vyasa, half-brother to King Dhrita and King Pandu.
Vaitanika: Drona's servant.
Lord Bhishma (the boar; also known as the Grandsire): elder of the Bharatas, only surviving son of King Shantanu, and stepbrother to Vyasa. In his youth captured the three sisters, *Amba*, *Ambika* and *Ambalika*.
King Dhrita of the Bharatas: son of Vyasa by Ambika; half-brother to the late *King Pandu* (son of Vyasa by Ambalika), and half-brother to Vyasa's other son, Vidura.
Queen Gandhari: wife of Dhrita, mother of the Kuru brothers, and sister of King Shakuni.
Sanjaya: Dhrita's chariot driver.
Queen Pritha: stepdaughter of *King Kunti*, widow of Pandu, mother and stepmother to the Pandava brothers and co-wife of the late *Queen Madri*.

In neighbouring regions:

Lord Krishna of the Yadavas: younger brother of *Bala*, nephew of Pritha and cousin of the Pandavas. Krishna was also the uncle of *Abhi*, Arjuna's son with Krishna's sister *Subhadra*.

King Shakuni of the Gandharas: brother of Gandhari, uncle of the Kuru brothers. Father of *Prince Uluka*.

King Shalya of the Madrakas: Madri's brother, uncle of Saha and Nakula.

King Drupada of the Panchalas: father of Draupadi, Shikhandi and Drishta. Enemy of Drona.

King Satyaki of the Shinis: friend of Drupada and enemy of Soma.

King Soma of the Balhikas: nephew of Shantanu and father of *Prince Bhuri*.

King Virata of the Matsyas: Enemy of Shusharman; father of *Prince Uttara* and *Prince Shankha*.

King Shusharman of the Trigartas: in conflict with Virata over land and cattle.

King Shishu of the Chedis: son of a sister of Pritha's, cousin of Krishna; friend of King Jara.

King Jara of the Magadhas: hostile king who antagonised most of his neighbours; father of *Prince Jaya-tsena*.

King Bhaga of the Vangas and *King Indra of the Malavas*: renowned for their magnificent elephants.

King Krita of the Bhojas, King Shruta of the Kalingas and *King Jaya-dratha of the Sindhus*: allies of Soma.

Index of first mentions

Lightning Source UK Ltd.
Milton Keynes UK
UKOW05f1852230517

301868UK00007B/284/P

9 781911 412267